BADLANDS

BADLANDS

ELIZABETH FACKLER

A Tom Doherty Associates Book
New York

BADLANDS

This book is printed on acid-free paper.

A Forge Book
Published by Tom Doherty Associates, Inc.
175 Fifth Avenue
New York, N.Y. 10010

Forge® is a registered trademark of Tom Doherty Associates, Inc.

Library of Congress Cataloging-in-Publication Data

Fackler, Elizabeth.
    Badlands / by Elizabeth Fackler.—1st ed.
        p.   cm.
    "A Tom Doherty Associates book."
    ISBN 0-312-86230-X
    1. Strummar, Seth (Fictitious character)—Fiction.
    2. Outlaws—West (U.S.)—Fiction.   I. Title.
    PS3556.A28B34   1996
    813'.54—dc20   96-18275
                                                  CIP

First Edition: October 1996

Printed in the United States of America

0 9 8 7 6 5 4 3 2 1

To Michael

Autumn

★ 1883 ★

1

★

Crossing the yard toward the open door of Esperanza's casita, Seth could see her sleek black hair nearly touching the floor as she sat on a stool before her vanity. When he stopped on the threshold, she sensed him there and looked up.

"Seth," she said, her dark eyes laughing a naughty invitation. "Come in."

She seemed happy enough, which was more than he could say for himself as he sat on the edge of her bed and leaned back on his elbows, meeting her eyes.

At forty-four, she was ten years older than he and living on his charity. It was generous and stemmed from friendship, but carried no guarantees. She smiled warily. "Would you like a drink?"

"You keep whiskey in your room, Esperanza?"

"You left it here last time."

"I'm surprised Blue didn't drink it up."

Her smile vanished. "Does it bother you I sleep with him?"

Seth shook his head. "It bothers me that you're scaring Rico, though."

"Scaring her? I wouldn't."

"She's crying 'cause I'm going to town tonight. You got any idea why she might do that?"

Esperanza looked away from his cool gray eyes, across the yard to the light shining from Rico's bedroom, then turned back to Seth. "I don't control the cards," she said softly.

"You control what comes out of your mouth," he retorted, "and I'm tired of your gloomy predictions."

Slowly she crossed the room to kneel on the floor in front of him. "Don't be angry with me, Seth," she pleaded.

He just watched her.

"I won't read Rico's cards anymore, if that's what you want."

"That's what I want."

"Okay." She smiled. "Okay?"

"I don't know," he said. "I should burn the damn things."

"You wouldn't!" she whispered. "I brought them from México and they are very ancient."

"What good are they?"

"They predict the future."

"Bullshit."

Seeing a playfulness in his eyes that told her he was no longer angry, she laughed and leaned against his knee. "Ay, Seth. Why don't you come see me anymore, eh?"

"I'm here now."

She sighed, then asked mischievously, "How are you getting along with Rico?"

"We were doing fine before you told her I was gonna get killed in a saloon."

"It was in the cards, Seth."

"When it happens, you can all cry your eyes out. Until then, I don't want to hear about it. Is that plain enough?"

"But it's a warning. It's not a fact yet. You can prevent it."

"By staying home the rest of my life. That's what you and Rico want, ain't it?"

Demurely she dropped her lashes and said softly, "It would be wise."

"It would be hell," he said, angry again. "Get up."

She rose quickly and backed away from him.

Watching her closely, he asked, "You afraid of me?"

She shook her head. "I trust you with my life."

"Since that's the case, you think maybe my advice might be worth taking?"

"Not on this. You are wrong."

He stood up, so much taller that he towered above her. "What am I gonna do with you, Esperanza?"

"Shoot me?"

He nodded at her humor. "I might," he said, then turned and walked out.

The yard was dark, lit only by two fingers of light that didn't quite reach. In the casita behind him was a woman he'd taken on because her man threw her out, not through any fault of hers but because Seth had brought a younger woman to their home and she'd stolen Esperanza's man. In the house in front of him was a woman who held the place of his wife, a legality denied her because he had abandoned a wife back in Texas. Asleep in the house were their infant daughter and his seven-year-old son, the child of yet another woman. As he crossed the yard, Seth felt a fleeting inclination to kick himself free, as if the people dependent on him were shackles dragging at his stride.

He walked into the kitchen and saw Melinda sitting at the table over a cup of cocoa. He could see she'd been crying, and he silently sighed at yet another confrontation that sucked at his patience. But he didn't want to go back to Rico, who would resume their argument, so he sat down across from Melinda.

She sniffed. "Want some cocoa?"

He shook his head. She was a pretty woman, with dark sun-streaked hair and a delicate face just beginning to show signs of aging. At twenty-six she was half a decade older than Joaquín, Seth's partner, with whom she'd been living for two years now. As he watched her try to hide her tears, he wished he hadn't sat down. At least Rico was crying over something he could deal with. Melinda was crying over Joaquín, and Seth didn't want to edge so much as a knife blade into that situation.

"I'm sorry," she said, wiping her eyes with her fingertips. She sniffed again, then gave him a smile. "I feel like an idiot, Seth."

"Maybe you are."

She laughed. "I wish Joaquín was more like you."

He almost got up right then, suspecting what was coming. Instead he decided he might as well direct the conversation toward a constructive conclusion, so he asked with a fortitude he didn't feel, "How like me?"

She stared past him into the darkness outside. "I guess I worked in saloons too long."

He waited.

She gave him a teasing smile though her eyes were brimming with tears. "Remember when we were together?"

"Me and you?"

She nodded.

He frowned, unsuccessfully trying to recall her body among the hundreds of saloon girls he'd enjoyed over the years.

"I'm not tryin' to take anything away from Rico," she said. "I just keep rememberin' how you were."

"What do you remember?" he asked.

"You took what you wanted," she said.

"Yeah, that pretty well describes it."

"That's what I need," she whispered. "But Joaquín . . ."

"Cares about your feelings?" he bit off. "Doesn't want to hurt you? Treats you like a lady?"

"It's not my fault, Seth," she retorted, tossing her head defiantly.

"It ain't his."

"Maybe it is. Maybe he just needs to learn some new tricks." Seth kept quiet.

"I was waitin' for you here," she said. "I was hopin' you'd talk to him, teach him something, maybe."

"No," he said.

"It would be easy," she said. "Just take him into town and share a woman with him. Show him how it's done."

"How what's done?"

"You know," she said, holding his gaze.

"Take a belt to you, is that what you want?"

"Just a little spark, that's all, Seth."

"Maybe you oughta think about moving on."

She stared at him. "Are you throwin' me out?"

"That ain't my decision. It's Joaquín's."

"You're ruler of this roost. What you say goes."

He sighed, wishing he'd heard those words from Esperanza. "I ain't got nothing to do with Joaquín's bed. If you got problems, he's the one to solve 'em." He stood up, looking through the parlor at the closed bedroom door, then turned and walked back outside.

The stable was dark, no light coming from beneath Joaquín's door at the end of the aisle. Seth lit a lantern then backed his sorrel out of the stall and led it over to the rack of saddles, shouting down the distance, "Hey, Joaquín, want to ride into town?"

He was reaching under his horse's belly for the cinch when Joaquín came out. Neither of them said anything until they were away from the yard, trotting along the trail that wound toward the road into Tejoe. When Seth looked over, the kid gave him a bittersweet smile and said, "Melinda was crying."

"So was Rico," Seth said.

"Why?" Joaquín asked with concern.

"Esperanza predicted I'm gonna die in a saloon, so Rico wants me to stay home the rest of my life." When Joaquín didn't reply, Seth asked, "What about Melinda?"

The kid took a long time to answer. Finally he said, "She has been hurt by many men."

Seth looked across at his friend, who had once wanted to be a priest and still dressed all in black. "I was one of 'em, did you know that?"

Joaquín nodded, meeting his eyes. After a while the kid said, "Melinda will be all right."

Seth didn't believe it, but he meant to stay clear of the explosion he saw coming.

The Blue Rivers Saloon was crowded when they walked in the back door and climbed the stairs to a private room. Seth stopped on the threshold, assessing the woman on Blue's lap.

She was a succulent jewel of a female, her well-curved body encased in a gown of maroon brocade embroidered with a golden vine running rampant around her skirts. Leaping to her feet as the door opened, she stared at the men who had just come in, her laughter sounding forced.

Blue laughed, too, a much more pleasant sound. "Hey, Seth, Joaquín. I want you to meet my new manager, Lila Keats."

"Seth Strummar, no doubt," Lila said, coming forward and extending her hand.

Her green eyes nudged him with a memory he couldn't put a handle on except to think that Blue had just made a bad mistake. As with Joaquín and Melinda, however, Seth kept his opinion to himself and shook the soft hand that felt cool as a grave.

Lila turned toward his compadre, her smile deepening her dimples. "And Joaquín Ascarate. I would have known the two of you without an introduction."

Joaquín shook with her as quickly as Seth had, then met his eyes with a cautious amusement.

Blue said, "Sit down. You want a drink?"

"Yeah," Seth said, though he walked over to the window and

looked out. The entire block was saloons, their hitching rails crowded with horses illuminated in the yellow rectangles of light falling from the windows. Seeing his own shadow on the street, Seth stepped back and closed the shutters. When he turned around, Lila was watching him. Again, her green eyes nagged him with a memory he couldn't quite catch. "Why don't you sit down," he suggested.

"Thanks," she said, settling herself carefully in her tight skirt. With a taunting smirk she asked, "Aren't you going to inquire as to my qualifications to manage a saloon?"

"Should I?"

"Aren't you Blue's partner?"

"Silent partner. He makes all the decisions."

She laughed. "That's a relief. I thought I had two bosses to please."

Blue handed everyone a drink then raised his in a toast. "To Lila's success," he said.

"As long as it's helpful to yours," Seth muttered before downing his shot.

Lila laughed deep in her throat. "Since I get a percentage, it behooves me to do well."

Seth left his glass on the table and walked over to the window again, lifted a slat of the shutters and peered out.

Joaquín asked, "How long have you been in Tejoe, Miss Keats?"

"It's 'Mrs.' but you can call me Lila." She laughed again, and Seth thought she was so free with her laughter it had to be camouflage. "I just got here yesterday," she said.

"You were lucky," Joaquín said, "to find employment so quickly."

Blue chuckled. "I was sitting here at nine o'clock this morning feeling sorry for myself 'cause I'm always penned up inside this saloon, then the answer to my prayers came sashaying through the door and asked for a job."

"Nine o'clock," Joaquín mused. "So you must have come to the Blue Rivers first."

"That's right," Lila said, tension hardening her voice.

"Why?" Joaquín asked.

"Maybe it was the name," she answered. "It made me think of a fresh start, which is what I want."

Seth turned around and met her eyes. "Where're you from?"

"Wherever the wind blows."

"Where did it blow last?"

"Austin," she said in a tone entirely too intimate for his comfort. "I've seen Jeremiah."

Seth felt a cold slice of anger, the remnant of a rage he'd thought to expel by hanging the man who'd lynched Jeremiah. He'd discovered, however, that the rage lingered despite his vengeance, even though his kid brother had been dead for thirteen years.

"He's a fine boy," Lila said. "You should be proud."

"Who're you talking about?" Seth asked in a low voice.

"Your son." She laughed with self-deprecation. "You may wonder how a woman such as I would cross paths with a senator's grandson, but I saw him in the park along the river. I was walking with a gentleman friend who pointed out the child and his mother. And their bodyguard. They're accompanied by an armed protector everywhere they go. Did you know that?"

Seth shook his head, assimilating the news that his wife had named their son after his brother.

Lila smiled with barely hidden glee into his stony silence, then said softly, "I thought you'd like to know that they appear to be happy and healthy."

"Thanks," he said, not meaning it.

Turning to Joaquín she asked lightly, "You know her, don't you, Joaquín?"

He finished his drink and set the glass on the table, looking at Seth. "I'll be downstairs."

Seth smiled at his partner's wiliness in not answering her question. "See you later."

The noise of the spinning roulette wheel, men laughing and a few high-pitched squeals from the working girls flooded the room until the heavy door closed.

Seth poured himself another drink, then studied the woman over the rim of his glass as he sipped at the whiskey. Finally he said, "As a silent partner, I only make one demand on Blue's business: I get to try out all the new girls." He watched her face tighten with control. "That agreeable to you?"

"Yes," she whispered.

"Right now?"

She nodded.

He turned back to Blue. "There you are," Seth said. "She's a whore without virtue. Don't forget it." He set his glass down and smiled into her angry green eyes. "Don't take it personal. I got what I want at home."

Seth walked into the noise of the saloon, pulled the door shut and stood on the balcony a moment studying the scene below. Joaquín looked up, meeting his eyes across the congestion of tobacco smoke floating in the air. When Seth walked down to join his partner at the bar, the keep set another glass in front of them, and Seth poured himself a drink from Joaquín's bottle.

"What do you think?" Joaquín asked.

"She's trouble," Seth said, sipping the whiskey. He turned around with his back to the bar just as a man came through the front door. Their eyes locked, the newcomer's hot with hostility. Softly to Joaquín, Seth said, "Here's more."

Joaquín looked at the man who had just come in. His face was hidden behind a dark beard, and his clothes were covered with so much dust he looked as if he'd ridden a hundred miles in a hurry. He didn't head for the bar, though. He edged along the wall, watching Seth. Joaquín asked, "Who is he?"

"Don't know him," Seth said.

"He knows you."

"Looks like it," he said. Remembering all the times he'd faced a man's challenge in the past, Seth smiled in anticipation.

As the stranger continued to edge around the perimeter of the room, keeping a dozen crowded tables between them, the girls flitted across Seth's vision like brightly colored butterflies among the barely perceived field of dusty men. The stranger stopped at the end of an empty aisle and shouted across the din of noise, "You seen me."

The room fell silent in the catch of a breath. "Don't know you," Seth said in a normal voice that carried in the quiet.

"I know you, though." The man grinned through his thick beard. "You're my bonanza. Or will be soon as you're dead."

Men knocked chairs over scrambling away from the tables lining the aisle. "Maybe you'll be dead," Seth answered.

The man shook his head. "I'm still in business and been getting a lotta practice. You been living soft, retired as you are."

The upstairs door opened and Blue came out, his shuffling gait loud on the wood floor of the balcony. At the top of the stairs, he glanced at Seth and Joaquín, then demanded of the stranger, "What's going on?"

"None of yours," he answered without taking his eyes off Seth. "I'm collecting a bounty on a killer. Only one way t'do that and I aim t'do it."

"He ain't alone," Blue said.

"What's the matter, Strummar?" the stranger gibed. "You lose your nerve to face a man one on one?"

"Stay out of it, Blue," Seth said. "You too, Joaquín," he said in a softer voice, not taking his eyes off the stranger.

Joaquín stepped a scant distance away, feeling the chill of his partner's intention. Never having faced such a challenge, his mind spun through possible alternatives and consequences in a tumble of confusion which he knew could be lethal in such a situation, and he admired Seth's unified calm.

The stranger was no longer smiling. A magnetic intensity hovered in the air between him and Seth, seeming almost to hum with the escalating tension until the stranger reached for his gun. Seth's .44 appeared in his hand—Joaquín didn't see him draw it—and he fired once. The stranger grunted and staggered backward, dropping his gun as a stain of blood soaked through the front of his shirt. He stared at his gun on the floor, looking sick, then lost his balance and fell from the weight of a bullet in his heart. The room was silent, acrid with smoke from the barrel of Seth's gun. The stranger hadn't fired. Joaquín gave Seth a smile of congratulation, but he was scanning all the other faces watching him.

Seeing a cunning admiration behind a cruel indifference, Seth knew few of the men in the room would grieve for him any more than they did for the stranger. He raised his eyes to Blue at the top of the stairs. Lila stood beside him watching with an amused smile, and Seth felt an uncomfortable suspicion that the dead man was no stranger to her. He looked at the barkeep. "Sheriff's out of town, ain't he, Gus?"

Gus nodded.

"He knows where to find me," Seth said, holstering his gun. Then he smiled at Joaquín. "Let's go home."

Rico was awake when they returned from town. Lying in her dark bedroom listening to the hoofbeats of their horses in the soft dust of the yard, the creak of the corral gate, then the heavier moan of the stable door, she felt tears of relief that Esperanza's prediction had been wrong. After a few minutes she heard Seth approach the house, the silver jangle of his spurs accompanying his footsteps.

She listened to him enter through the kitchen, heard the crossbar laid in the latch, then his steps crossing the parlor and going into Lobo's room. He stayed there a long time, and she smiled, thinking of him looking down on his sleeping son. When she heard him go into Elena's room, however, her relief was swamped with a cold fear that he was saying goodbye to his children. Finally he opened her door and stood on the threshold. "Evenin'," he said.

She always marveled that he knew she was awake despite the dark. "Hello," she said, then listened as he crossed the room until she could see him standing silhouetted against the starlight outside the window. Sensing something wrong, she struggled to amend it. "I'm sorry, Seth," she apologized. "I shouldn't have carried on so."

He was quiet, surveying the yard for anything amiss. "I told you what to expect," he finally said without turning around. "Nothing's changed."

"I know. The longer we're together, the more I want you with me."

"Can't argue with that," he said, still staring out the window.

She often watched him study the yard before he came to bed, taking comfort from his strength between her and the darkness outside. Tonight, however, he did something she hadn't seen before: he pulled his gun and opened the cylinder, removed a spent shell, flicked it out the window and replaced it with one from his belt, then reholstered his gun. With accumulating dread she asked, "What happened in town tonight?"

Still not looking at her he said, "I killed a man."

Fear froze her heart. "So Esperanza was right."

"He died. I didn't."

"Who was it?" she whispered.

"A bounty hunter. I didn't catch his name."

"Then it was self-defense."

"He drew first," Seth agreed.

"So they won't hold it against you."

He shrugged. "Sheriff's out of town. We'll see what he has to say when he gets back."

"There were witnesses, weren't there?"

"Yeah," he said. Then, after a moment, "I shouldn't be here, Rico."

"Where?" she whimpered, afraid of his answer.

He turned around and faced her, though she still couldn't read his eyes in the dark. "What do you think the kids are gonna say to Lobo in school next week?"

"I'm sure he doesn't care," she answered. "Do you think they mean more to him than your love?"

"Sometimes I think they should." He closed the shutters, leaving the room in the ink of darkness.

She listened to him cross to the bedside, the rustle of the box of matches, then the hiss of the match as he struck it. In the flare of light, she nearly cried at the pain in his eyes.

"I ain't going to court," he said, lighting the candle and dropping the match to flicker out in the saucer. "I ain't surrendering my gun to any officer of the law for any reason. I'll die before I let 'em cage me, and the odds are good you and Lobo are gonna watch it happen."

"I don't believe that," she whispered.

"Which?"

"If we watch you die, it will be of old age in your bed."

"That ain't what you were saying this afternoon, is it?"

"I was wrong. I lost my courage for a while. We can see it through together, Seth. Without you, Lobo and Elena and I will be lost, to say nothing of Joaquín and Esperanza."

"That's a heavy load to carry, you know that?"

"Yes," she said.

He nodded, then unbuckled his gunbelt and hung it on his side of the headboard. She felt the weight as if the bed had tilted, though it hadn't. As she watched him sit down and tug off his boots, she restrained herself from touching his back.

He leaned his elbows on his knees and held his head. "Thing

that bothers me most is the indifference I saw in all those men. I was no more to them than that bounty hunter. They didn't care which one of us died."

"They don't know you, Seth."

"I've been living here for two years. I go into Blue's saloon nearly every damn night."

"And do what?" she asked carefully.

He snorted in recognition of her point. "Drink with Blue and Joaquín behind a closed door more often'n not."

"Exactly," she said softly. "All they know is your reputation and what you look like passing through. And whatever their children learn from Lobo, which can't be much since you've told him not to discuss his homelife at school. If they could see you being a father like them, trying to raise your family with decency, they would accept you as one of them. Maybe not the same, but close enough."

When he didn't answer, she said, "Tomorrow's Sunday. Maybe it would be a good time to join the community."

"You mean go to church?" he scoffed.

"What an excellent idea," she said with a laugh.

He looked at her and laughed, too. "It wasn't mine," he said.

"It would make you real to them instead of just someone living on the outskirts of town attracting certain unpleasant consequences."

"Attracting scum, is what you mean." He stood up and crossed to the washbowl, then poured water in the basin. As he pulled his shirt out and unbuttoned it, he faced her and asked, "You think they'll forgive me for shedding blood in their town?"

"If you'd prove to them you've changed, that you're not the man you were."

"You think if I show up in church, I'll sprout a halo for them to see?"

She smiled. "None of them have halos either, Seth."

He took his shirt off, crumpled it into a ball and threw it into the laundry basket in the corner, lifted handfuls of water to wash his face, then ran a wet cloth over his torso. The cloth, too, he threw into the basket. "I ain't been to church since I was a kid," he said.

"I've heard Mrs. Engle at the mercantile say good things about Reverend Holcroft," she said softly.

Seth emptied his pockets on the bureau, the coins clanking loudly, stepped out of his trousers and sat down naked to peel his socks off, then threw them all in the basket, blew out the candle and slid under the covers beside her.

Still he didn't touch her, and she waited in agony. He had killed men before but all that had been in his past and he rarely spoke of it. When he did it was to make a joke, as if his proclivity for homicide were nothing more than an amusing riddle. Now for the first time she realized it made him feel everyone he valued was threatened rather than protected by his presence, and she suddenly understood why he had always moved on after a killing, drifted to another place where he could build a new world he sustained on hope until it was shattered again with a bullet. She wanted to tell him this killing wasn't his fault, but she knew he would scoff at the notion; wanted to hold him close and love away his thoughts of leaving, but was afraid her touch now would be perceived as another demand he couldn't satisfy that would drive him away for good.

Across the dark space between them his voice was hollow. "Rico?"

"Yes," she whispered, turning on her side to face him.

"I heard news of my wife tonight."

"From who?" she asked, feeling another stab of dread.

"A woman working for Blue. Said she saw Johanna in Austin, and the kid, too. A boy named Jeremiah."

She held her breath, waiting.

"It's odd to think there's a new Jeremiah Strummar in the world." Abruptly he pulled her close and buried his face in the crook of her neck. "Jesus, Rico," he murmured, his breath warm on her skin, "I wish you were my wife. If there was only one thing in my past I could change, that would be it."

"It's enough to hear you say that," she answered.

He lay back with a sigh. "You think it'll be enough for the good people in church?"

"They only know what we tell them."

He chuckled. "Then we're married and I'll kill the man who says otherwise." He snorted with self-mockery. "I've made that joke and seen men dive for cover. Maybe I'll let the churchgoers think I'm unarmed. What do you think of that? Seth Strummar without a gun."

"You won't really go without one?" she asked with new worry.

He laughed again. "You think the do-gooders might kill me?"

"No," she said, "but anyone can go inside a church, Seth."

"I'll be proof of that," he said, ending their conversation with a kiss.

2

★

Homer Holcroft was forty-eight years old and had come to the Southwest for his health. When a series of debilitating lung infections forced his resignation as pastor of a modestly affluent parish in St. Louis, he came west seeking a comfortable hermitage in which to die. The hot, dry sun, however, cleared his lungs, and his hermitage turned out to be a thriving town without a Protestant church.

Holcroft decided to establish a place of worship in competition with the Roman Catholic diocese. To attract as many parishioners as possible, he chose to remain independent of the denominations which funded missions on the frontier, and he named his endeavor the Unified Christian Church of Tejoe. Using his own money he built a modest white edifice boasting a bell tower and enough pews to seat a hundred worshippers. Alongside the church he built a small adobe rectory, and he employed an old Mexican woman to care for him and the sanctuary. Tulia was Catholic and attended daily mass at Our Lady of Sorrows, but since there were no respectable Protestant women in need of employment, the reverend made do.

His parish consisted of the families of men employed in the local silver mines and the merchants who catered to their needs, as well as scattered ranchers who rarely made it into town for Sunday services. Except for the mine owners and the president of the Bank of Tejoe, none of the reverend's parishioners evidenced wealth. If their tithes were truly one-tenth of their incomes, he would be forced to conclude that his parish existed barely above subsistence.

Also pivotal in starting the first public school in Tejoe—though the school board was as poorly financed as his charity endeavors—Reverend Holcroft had reviewed the tax rolls many times searching for a citizen with hidden assets who might be induced to share what he had. There was only one whose record gave any hint of wealth. Unfortunately, it was unlikely he would join the church.

It was said he had a sizable balance in the Bank of Tejoe, was the financial backer of the most popular saloon in town, and lived on unmortgaged land without an income. He was reputed to be responsible for the support of six people besides himself, and gossip had it they mail-ordered their clothing from St. Louis and Chicago. His family came to town to buy groceries—always accompanied by a Mexican gunman who watched them with eagle eyes—and his seven-year-old son attended the public school. The teacher said that little Lobo was bright, and also, upon questioning, that he never talked of his homelife. If the subject of his father came into a conversation, the child fell silent. Miss Perkins had whispered that to the reverend, as if wary of saying the father's name.

Seth Strummar was the name, though few people said it out loud. Usually they referred to him as the outlaw. Reverend Holcroft had never heard of him before coming to the Southwest. After discovering the outlaw was living in his parish, the reverend did some research and learned that in the late sixties Seth Strummar and Ben Allister created havoc in Texas, robbing banks and terrifying citizens across the state. They escaped the law's retribution through eight years of pillage that finally ended when Allister was killed by his own wife. Strummar hanged the woman in vengeance, then disappeared. He was reported seen here and there, usually in connection with a killing, but the stories of his ultimate fate were varied and wild. It seemed only the people in Tejoe knew he was living five miles outside their town.

His presence was seen as a curse waiting fulfillment. Whenever his name came into a conversation, before the talkers were through they expressed their fear that a bounty hunter would find Strummar and then they'd have a killing in their town. If Strummar died the problem would be over, they would say, lowering their voices, but if his luck held and the hunter died, another would show up before too long.

The fateful event had finally transpired. Late on Saturday night Tulia knocked on Holcroft's bedroom door, jabbering in an hysterical Spanish that yanked him from sleep in alarm. Tying his robe as he hurried to open the door, he led the frightened woman into the kitchen and sat her down at the table, trying to calm her enough to speak in English so he could understand. She had been praying with friends at the wake of their father, she finally managed to say, when they were interrupted by the news and she'd hurried home to tell him.

"Tell me what?" he asked kindly, heating milk at the stove.

"He has brought death, as we knew always he would," she announced solemnly, her beady eyes sharp and black, her frizzy hair skewed out of its bun so it stuck up like a grizzled halo around her head. "It has come, the curse he carries."

"Who? What curse?" Holcroft asked, straining for patience. The woman was superstitious and excitable, and this wasn't the first time he had placated her fears.

"The outlaw," she whispered. "He has killed a man, just now, in the Blue Rivers Saloon."

Holcroft turned away and took the tin of cocoa from the cupboard, measured two spoonfuls into the simmering milk and stirred the mixture methodically while he tried to imagine the event Tulia was describing. He had never seen a gunfight and found it difficult to picture men coldly squaring off in deadly opposition. His mind full of questions he knew she couldn't answer, he splashed a shot of whiskey into the cups before filling them with hot chocolate.

"Now," he said, setting the cups on the table and taking the chair across from her, "tell me again what you heard."

"Just that, no more," she answered, greedily slurping the cocoa without letting it cool. "He is the devil walking among us," she said, her eyes glinting through the steam rising from the cup.

Holcroft smiled sadly. "He is only a man, Tulia."

"A man with the devil inside," she hissed. "He will kill this town, as he killed the bounty hunter tonight."

This new fact nestled into Holcroft's mind with a reassurance he couldn't credit to logic. "It's unfortunate, Tulia, but not as much as you seem to think. A bounty hunter, after all, is seeking someone's death, is he not?"

"Not his own!" she retorted fiercely.

"No," he answered with a smile. "And it's not an action we can condone, but we can't blame Mr. Strummar for defending himself."

"He is defending the wrongs he has done! I blame him for bringing his wrongs to our town so all of us must pay."

Holcroft sipped his cocoa, thinking of his sermon in the morning.

"He has doomed Tejoe," Tulia pronounced, setting her empty cup on the table.

Holcroft smiled gently. "No one is doomed living in the love of God."

"The love of God is for the heaven of eternity," she answered. "The outlaw has brought hell to us now, alive in our town."

Holcroft shook his head. "The act of one man cannot doom a pious community."

"Judas doomed the whole world," she argued. "He was only one man."

Holcroft smiled with indulgence. "Judas doomed only Jesus of Nazareth. Through His sacrifice, Jesus became Christ and His crucifixion redeemed the world."

"Who will redeem Tejoe?"

"The same Christ," he answered. "And all of His servants who unite against the coming of violence."

She shook her head. "The outlaw is stronger than all of us together."

"How can he be?" he asked with paternalistic patience.

"Because he has the evil eye of Satan inside him! You will see, Padre Holcroft. You are new to this country and don't know it as I do. The desert is the Devil's homeland; he rules here."

"Go to sleep," Holcroft said with compassion. "In the light of day you'll see that things aren't as bad as they seem in the dark of midnight."

"I will go to my room," she said, "but I will not sleep. I will pray for God's mercy."

He watched her trundle from the room, then Reverend Holcroft sat up late rewriting his sermon. He chose for his text Matthew 5:30: "And if thy right hand offend thee, cut it off and cast it from thee, for it is profitable that one of thy members should perish and not that thy whole body should be cast into hell." He felt dissatisfied with the message he was giving his congregation, but he hoped that in uniting against the outlaw they could achieve a strength of community he had found lacking among his widely scattered parish.

The autumn morning was bright and warm as he greeted the arriving worshippers. In his white robe, he stood on the steps of his white church, feeling humbled as he saw the effect of the killing in the faces passing before him. People were frightened that violence had disrupted the peace of their somnolent town, and they came craving leadership, many more than on any other Sunday since services had begun. Holcroft smiled and touched the people in greeting as he prayed that he not disappoint them and fail what he understood to be the true beauty of the church: the satisfying union of the congregation.

He left the doors open to catch the breeze, ascended to the pulpit, and faced the people with pride yet trepidation as he nodded at the pianist to begin the opening strains of the invocation. The people rose and began to sing: "Praise God from Whom all blessings flow."

Holcroft watched a buggy stop outside the door accompanied by a Mexican gunman dressed in black and riding a black horse. The weapon on his hip caught sunlight as he dismounted. He tied his reins to the back of the buggy, then went to the head of the team and held them.

"Praise Him, all creatures here below," the congregation sang as the outlaw's boots stepped into the dust. He wore a dark suit and no gun, his dark hat pulled low above his eyes as he turned to help his wife.

"Praise Him above the Heavenly Host," sang the congregation as Mrs. Strummar reached inside the buggy for a blanket-clad infant.

"Praise Father, Son, and Holy Ghost," the people sang as little Lobo jumped down with a grin.

The rustle of the congregation being seated covered the approach of the arriving family. Holcroft stood stunned, trying to force his mind to rearrange his sermon in light of this new development. The people saw him staring through the open door, and they turned to see what had caught his attention.

The outlaw stopped silhouetted in the door, his face still hidden by the brim of his dark hat. His right hand held the small hand of his son, whom most people had seen in school or around town. His left hand was on the waist of his wife, a pretty woman most people hadn't seen. Her blond hair was braided and wound at the nape of her neck beneath a pert bonnet that matched her dress, which was sky blue with a fashionably narrow skirt snug on her slender hips, and she held a baby wrapped in a yellow blanket against her breasts. The outlaw's eyes were pale, roving across the silent faces of the congregation. Letting go of his wife, he reached up and took off his hat, then nudged his son to do the same. Lobo complied, watching his father as the outlaw asked softly, "Is there room for us?"

Holcroft found his tongue. "There is room for everyone in the House of God," he said, searching the crowded pews for someplace to seat them.

Abneth Nickles leaned across his wife and whispered quickly to his oldest sons, then stood up. He was the outlaw's neighbor but had never garnered the courage to ride over and meet the man. "We'd be pleased if you'd share our pew, Mr. Strummar," he said as his three boys filed out to sit on the floor against the wall.

"Obliged," the outlaw said, guiding his wife forward with his hand on the small of her back. The two women, each holding a baby, sat beside each other, then the boy, then the outlaw on the aisle.

Reverend Holcroft watched the congregation drag its eyes away from the newcomers to face forward expectant of his wisdom. He looked down at his notes and knew they were wrong. His righteousness had been humbled by the very sinner he was prepared to castigate coming forward to worship God. Holcroft was not a simple man. He knew the outlaw had an ulterior motive for choosing this Sunday to attend, but Holcroft also guessed what that motive was, and he approved. Strummar wanted to be accepted as a citizen; citizens paid taxes and tithes and stipends to school boards. So Reverend Holcroft smiled at the outlaw, then opened his Bible.

"My text today comes from the Book of Job," he said solemnly. "Chapter three, verse twenty-six: 'I was not in safety, neither had I rest, neither was I quiet; yet trouble came.'"

He looked up and searched all the faces watching him for understanding. "What do those words tell us?" he asked rhetorically, wishing someone would answer him. "That life is a vale of tears no matter how virtuous we are? That we can do our best to build a decent God-fearing community, and the hand of Satan will always defeat us? Moses said, 'Look to it: evil is before you.' Did he mean it was preferred by God? 'Before you' can mean above you or in your line of vision. I think it is the latter. Evil is all around us, but no where in the scriptures does it say that evil will triumph."

He paused to meet the outlaw's eyes. "Yet it was alive last night, wasn't it? None of us can deny that in the noise and bustle of a typical Saturday night in the Blue Rivers Saloon, when the room was crowded with men gambling away their earnings and fallen doves wandering about in the hope of catching the spoils from the drunken men, the very cacophony of hell on earth—a human hell, ladies and gentlemen, one we built without any help from either God or Satan but with our own bare hands from the desires of our hearts—into that human world, the Devil walked. Who was the Devil in that room last night?"

He paused again, sweeping his gaze over all the men. Softly, he asked, "How many of you were there?" He smiled his forgiveness. "I understand from certain parishioners who operate businesses in competition with Mr. Rivers that his establishment takes more than a little of their trade." A murmur of chuckles followed his words. "It's a popular place, the Blue Rivers Saloon. Maybe it's the name." He stopped to smile at the outlaw again. "Sounds like new beginnings, doesn't it? Fresh starts? Making amends for wrongs done in the past and living clean again?" He looked at the women in the congregation. "There were three entities in that saloon last night: two actors and an audience. The audience did nothing. They watched. Whatever they felt about what was coming—and they all knew from the first instant of confrontation what was coming— they kept their opinions to themselves. You know why? They didn't want to attract attention. They didn't want either one of the actors to think they had taken sides. They were neutral. They had no effect. They were like a herd of mares waiting to see which stallion would rule." He looked at Mrs. Strummar. "Forgive me if I'm being too blunt." He looked at everyone else again as he softly said, "But I am talking about control, ladies and gentlemen. Control of evil."

He paused for effect, then let his voice ring out: " 'I was not in safety, neither had I rest, neither was I quiet; yet trouble came.' " He sighed deeply. "It's the 'yet' that's puzzling, isn't it. You expect that verse to end with God's reward, not with more trouble. Yet trouble came. Trouble always comes seeking destruction and death. The man who sought death last night in the Blue Rivers Saloon found it. The man who delivered it did not bring it, he met it. And this morning, ladies and gentlemen, he has brought his family to worship among us. As we bow our heads in prayer, let us remember Job's warning—I fought trouble, yet trouble came—and decide in the secrecy of our hearts whether Job would welcome into his sanctuary a man adept at meeting trouble."

He nodded at the pianist, and she began to play the quiet chords of "Nearer My God to Thee" as the ushers rose to pass the collection baskets. Locked on the minister, the outlaw's eyes were so pale and cool that Holcroft couldn't read anything in them. He knew he should look away but couldn't bring himself to break the gaze. Finally the outlaw broke it, looking down at the basket his wife held. He reached for his wallet and took out a hundred-dollar bill. It was United States currency, which Holcroft rarely saw in the territory, and his eyes picked out the amount hungrily. Handing the basket to the usher, the outlaw met Holcroft's gaze with a sardonic smile, and the minister laughed, making several people in the congregation look quickly back and forth between them.

"Next Saturday," Holcroft said, his voice booming happily, "the Ladies Auxiliary is holding our autumn picnic. We hope everyone will attend. On Wednesday . . ." his voice droned on with the announcements of the prayer meeting, the arrival of a new baby and an impending visit from relatives, his mind racing with an excitement he couldn't define except to know he felt pleased to have Seth

Strummar among his congregation. Holcroft closed his book and left the pulpit, expecting the opening chords of "Beulah Land," the hymn he and the pianist had chosen. Instead she began a melancholy melody that arrested everyone with its haunting sorrow.

The members of the congregation had risen to their feet and a few were preparing to leave, but all stopped as if turned to statues as they listened to Miss Gates play. She began to sing, her husky contralto filling the room with a spiritual Holcroft hadn't heard since leaving St. Louis.

"Sometimes I feel like a motherless child," Miss Gates sang as Holcroft walked down the aisle to the door, his hands folded within the voluminous sleeves of his white robe, his eyes on the floor, his thoughts far away in another time where sorrow was perpetual. "A long ways from home," she sang, "a long, long ways from home."

Slowly the people filed out. A few of the women were dabbing at their eyes with handkerchiefs, their husbands gruff and impatient. Buck Stubbins, owner of the Red Rooster Silver Mine, leaned close to mutter, "I know what you're tryin' to do, Rev, and I admire your ambition but you're playin' with fire, ya know that, don'cha?"

Holcroft met his eyes with determination. "All of life is playing with the fires of hell, Buck. I'm experienced and know my way."

Buck laughed softly. "I think ya done bit off more'n ya can chew and I expect ya to be spittin' it up 'fore winter's come."

"I hate to disappoint my parishioners but in this case I hope I do," Holcroft said gently.

Buck shook his head. "Try defendin' him after the next killin' and then tell me how optimistic ya feel." He slapped the minister affectionately on the back and walked down to his buggy where his wife and children were waiting.

Holcroft shifted his gaze to the Mexican who had come with Strummar. He was standing by the team, watching the crowd, his hand loose by his gun. Holcroft saw the stock of a rifle on the seat of the buggy, an extra weapon ready for use, and he raised his eyes to meet those of the Mexican's. Holcroft knew the gunman's name to be Joaquín Ascarate, that he had several killings in his past and was living at the Strummar ranch with a fallen dove from Tombstone. Holcroft had also heard that Ascarate had intended to be a priest before meeting the outlaw. Believing the story for the first time, Holcroft smiled into Ascarate's dark eyes, which spoke of a depth of kindness that didn't match his reputation.

Holcroft turned away and walked into the church to see Strummar and his family just standing up. The pianist continued to play softly though everyone else had left. Holcroft walked forward, extended his hand to the outlaw and introduced himself.

"Seth Strummar," the man said, and it sounded odd to hear the name spoken outright. "My wife and daughter," he said, "and my son."

Holcroft smiled at all of them. "I'm very pleased to see you among us this morning. I hope you'll favor us with your presence next Sunday."

"What're you gonna talk about?" Strummar asked with a playful light in his eyes.

"Perhaps the rewards of generosity," Holcroft said with a smile.

The outlaw laughed. "Well, I'll tell you," he said, turning around to give Miss Gates a smile, "I'd come back just for the music. That's a talented lady you got at your keyboard."

Miss Gates blushed. Holcroft saw Mrs. Strummar cast a worried scrutiny at her husband, who said, "You know Rico sings and plays a pretty guitar." He looked down at his wife. "It's a shame to let talent go to waste." She looked flustered at his words.

Holcroft said, "We'd be delighted, Mrs. Strummar, to have you sing for us. Perhaps you could get together with Miss Gates and choose a song you'd like to perform."

"I couldn't," she said, throwing her husband a puzzled frown.

"Well, you think about it," Holcroft said. "Is there any chance we'll see you at our picnic on Saturday?"

"No," the outlaw said. "But we'll be back next Sunday." He looked down at his son. "Won't we, Lobo?"

"Reckon," the boy said unhappily.

The outlaw shared a smile of friendship with the reverend, then guided his family down the aisle and out of the church.

3

★

Melinda and Esperanza sat at the kitchen table finishing off the breakfast coffee. Outside the open door, Joaquín's white dove cooed from the roof. "I hate that damn bird," Melinda said, draining her cup and studying the grounds left in the bottom.

Esperanza watched her warily.

"Can you read coffee grounds?" Melinda asked with a laugh. "Look at that pattern. Don't it resemble a hangman's noose?"

Esperanza stood up without looking at it, carried her own cup to the sink and washed it in the water left from the dishes.

Melinda laughed again, a harsh sound without joy. "You don't like me, do you?"

Esperanza looked over her shoulder as she placed the clean cup on the shelf. "I like you well enough."

"Seth doesn't, though, does he?"

"He's never said nothing to me about it," Esperanza answered. She carried the dishpan to the door and threw the dirty water out. When she banged the pan against the side of the house, the white dove flew away from the noise, then coasted to land on the top of a golden cottonwood. Esperanza considered the dove an emblem of love on the homestead, and Melinda's dislike of the bird was worrisome. When she went back inside, Melinda was pouring whiskey into her cup.

"That's Seth's whiskey," Esperanza said. "You think he'll be glad you drank it?"

"I ain't gonna drink it all! Seems like every time I turn around, somebody don't like something I'm doin'."

"You think that's our fault?" Esperanza asked.

Melinda looked at the large, dark woman who had been a beauty in her youth. Traces remained in the smoothness of her plump face, the flash of her black eyes and her equally black hair wound in a glistening bun on the nape of her neck. As if her words didn't carry a barb, Melinda asked, "Don'cha think it's funny Seth's had every woman on the place?"

Esperanza remained silent, wiping the stove with a wet rag that hissed with the heat.

"You think he didn't take us along," Melinda asked, " 'cause he didn't want to walk into church with his harem?"

"Did you want to go?" Esperanza answered, tossing the rag into the sink.

"Nah. Who'd want to go to church?" Melinda muttered, refilling her cup with whiskey.

"You gonna be drunk when they get back?" Esperanza asked.

"Maybe," she said with defiance. "Maybe I'll take all my clothes off and run around nekkid. What d'ya think of that?"

Esperanza smiled. "I think you will get a sunburn."

"Will I get a reaction from ol' Seth is the question," she said, sipping his whiskey.

"Is *that* what you want?"

"Yes," she said earnestly. "If I could do it without hurtin' Rico."

"What about Joaquín?"

Melinda smiled wickedly. "Think he'd fight for me?"

"With another man, perhaps. Not with Seth."

"He'd just hand me over and tell us to have a good time?" She laughed bitterly. "You're right. That's exactly what he'd do. How d'ya get away with it?"

"Away with what?"

"Sleepin' with Seth and not hurtin' Rico."

"Who says I sleep with him?"

"I've seen him go into your casita so late the coyotes are already in bed. You don't light the lamp and he don't come out again for a good hour, so it ain't hard to figure what you're doin'."

"You watch, do you?" Esperanza asked coldly.

Melinda sighed. "I don't mean to. It's jus' that I can't sleep so I'm awake a lot in the middle of the night. Don't be mad at me, Esperanza. Everyone else seems to be and I can't figure it out."

"It's because you're making Joaquín unhappy," she said softly.

"That's 'cause he's makin' me unhappy! Don't anyone care about that? I wanta stay here but Joaquín can't cut it and it's drivin' me crazy."

"What are you saying?" she whispered.

"You know what I'm sayin'," Melinda retorted.

"I don't believe he had a problem before you."

"Maybe it's not me. Maybe it's Seth. You know how Joaquín feels about him. He'd lie down in the mud and let Seth walk on him to keep his boots clean."

"You misunderstand," Esperanza murmured.

"I don't think so," Melinda said. "There's only one stud on this range, and it ain't Joaquín." She poured herself some more of Seth's whiskey.

"I agree," Esperanza said softly. "If it's a stud you want, Joaquín is not your man. But he is the only man here for you, so maybe it is time you weren't here."

"Thanks," Melinda muttered. "Your kindness is overwhelmin'." She drained her cup and refilled it. "I never could figure Seth choosin' weak little Rico. I wonder why he did."

"She is not weak," Esperanza argued.

"You'd think he'd want a woman to match his passion for bein' alive," Melinda said.

"You think you do?"

Melinda nodded, then spoke softly, staring into her cup. "When I first hooked up with Joaquín, I thought we could make it work. Everything was good at first, so good I thought even when Seth came back my love for Joaquín would carry me through. But that was a mistake 'cause it all fell to pieces soon as Seth rode into the yard. It wasn't 'cause of my love, though. It was 'cause of Joaquín's."

Esperanza didn't want to hear any more but she stood rigidly in place, listening to the woman's lament.

"It happened that first night Seth came home." Melinda paused for a sip of whiskey, then went on. "Joaquín was restless and wouldn't come to bed though I coaxed and pleaded. Then Seth came to the door and took him away. Just came and asked and Joaquín was out that door in less'n a minute. He was gone a long time, and even when he came back, he still wouldn't come to bed. He stood at the window and looked out at the dark 'til I fell asleep. When I woke up in the mornin' he was gone. And when I walked into the kitchen and asked Rico if she'd seen him, she said he and Seth and Lobo went ridin' and wouldn't be back 'til late. When they came back, Seth took Joaquín into town." Melinda emptied her cup. "He came home so drunk he was clumsy in bed, and I threw Seth's finesse in his face. Any other man would've slapped me. You know what Joaquín did? He took his blankets to the loft and he's slept there ever since."

"All this time?" Esperanza whispered.

Melinda nodded. "It's something, ain't it? Any other man would've kicked me out of his bed if he didn't want to share it with me. Not Joaquín, though." She laughed bitterly as she refilled her cup.

"Don't you think you've had enough?" Esperanza asked with worry. "You've drunk nearly half of it already."

"No," Melinda said. "I'm gonna be good'n snockered when they come home."

"Why?"

"Maybe so I can see if Joaquín'll defend me when Seth throws me out."

"Can't you wait 'til tomorrow when Lobo's in school?"

Melinda laughed, twisting in the chair to face her with a grin. "Don't you want Lobo to see his heroes in their true light? Ain't that what you're always sayin' about the cards, that they tell the truth and it's always better to know the truth?"

"I don't think you know it," Esperanza intoned. "But I know I don't want to see what you cause with your ignorance." She walked out of the house, across the bright, hot yard to her casita, feeling a strong foreboding of dread.

In the dim coolness of her room, she took her tarot cards from the cedar box over the mantle and sat at the table shuffling them, clearing her mind as she stared through the open door. Across the yard, the white dove landed gracefully on a saguaro. Esperanza took it for an auspicious omen and dealt the cards for Melinda.

Behind her was disappointment; covering her was a fiery woman with treachery in her heart; before her was Death; his aspect was the cup of abundance. Esperanza stared down at the cards for a long time, unhappy with the recurrence of Death every time she laid a cross for someone at the homestead. She gathered her cards and returned them to the mantle in their cedar box, then she stood at the door and felt the hot wind ruffle her dress, dreading what would happen when the family returned from church.

She heard them coming from beyond the mountain, and for a moment she doubted her inaction. It seemed there should be something she could do to prevent the catastrophe she saw coming. She was too late, however. The pair of matched chestnuts cantered into the yard pulling the buggy. Seth reined up in front of the door and stepped down to hand Rico out. Lobo leapt to the ground and ran ahead of them, and Rico called for him to change his clothes before playing outside. As she carried the baby into the house, Seth drove the buggy back toward the corral where Joaquín was just swinging off his horse.

Seth stepped down, then looked across the yard at Esperanza. He studied her warily a moment before turning to unharness the team. Asking herself what he would have her do, she decided it would be to get Lobo out of the way. Hurriedly she trudged across the yard, through the front door and into Lobo's room. He had shed his church clothes and was pulling on his dungarees. She smiled at his skinny arms and pale chest beneath the line of sunburn around his neck. "Where's your shirt?" she asked, picking his suit off the floor and shaking it out.

In her bedroom, Rico laid Elena in the cradle and sat down on the bed, letting herself fall back to stare at the ceiling. It was a marvel to her that they had comported themselves acceptably among the respectable people, that the preacher had actually asked her to sing in his church. It wasn't her talent she doubted. Rico had sung in public to high acclaim in her past. In fact, praise of her voice had been the topic of Seth's first conversation with her. That had happened in a Pinos Altos saloon where she was an entertainer fighting the lure of prostitution's wages. Though she'd managed to hold that line over the years, she and her friends were a far cry from respectable.

Rico was proud to be Seth's woman. Although she was denied the honor of being his wife, she considered herself fortunate to have the man she loved stay with her and their children. Seth was an outlaw, however, and despite her happiness, never in her wildest dreams had Rico hoped to be accepted on the proper side of town.

She giggled with pleasure remembering how everyone in church had stared at her and Seth walking in. All those wives who would have shunned her in Tombstone were admiring her now. She had seen it in their faces, how they pursed their lips as they took in the latest fashion of her frock and bonnet, their envious eyes acknowledging the power of the man at her side. Rico hugged herself, unable to believe it. Only last night Seth had come home with news of what seemed like doom. Only yesterday Esperanza had driven Rico to tears predicting his death. Now it was Sunday and she could still hear the church bell ringing, see the sun sparkling on the white church, the women's faces watching her without rancor.

In Rico's past, respectable women had been altogether another breed from the harlots who'd been her friends. She had known a few other girls like Melinda over her career in saloons: young and single, loose and lost in a world definitely not arranged for them, they latched on to each other like sisters, often sharing rooms where they ridiculed the men they had to please all night. Sometimes they even found love in each other's arms, but their intimacy was always brief. Invariably, a man came between them.

Melinda and Rico had been sharing a room in Tombstone when Seth walked into the saloon where Rico was singing and resumed the romance they'd started in Pinos Altos. When he left her again, she had been so devastated she'd tried to kill herself. It was Melinda who kept her alive, bandaged her wrists and gently chided her for ceding any man that much power, then spent her own money on food and lodging until Rico could fend for herself. After Rico gave up on Seth's return and married Henry Lessen, it was Melinda's friendship that helped her endure the hell her marriage became. It was even Melinda who convinced her to see Seth when he came back, then handed her into the wagon as Seth tied his horse on the back and she said goodbye to Tombstone and hello to being his woman.

Rico had felt pleased when Melinda liked Joaquín. Both she and Esperanza watched with concealed amusement as the experienced woman led the shy man through a mating dance delightful to witness. He was like a wild creature who needed to be coaxed to come near, so different from the men all three of the women were accustomed to, men who habitually barged in and took what they wanted. Joaquín seemed to doubt what Melinda was offering, or that it was really him she was offering it to, even whether he wanted it. When he finally decided he was reading her right, he still hesitated before giving in.

Rico understood. Joaquín was a thoughtful man who sought the deepest value in everything he did. He was also disciplined and didn't easily let loose of his passion. He lived deliberately, weighing every act, assessing every thought, honing himself in his quest for the truth though he was neither stuffy nor self-righteous. Delicate in his playfulness, his subtle humor often turned on the ambiguity of a word, and to Rico his company was like a cooling breeze across the desert. Yet Melinda had grown weary of his delicacy.

It started when Seth came back from Isleta with Blue Rivers. At first Rico thought it was Blue who had caught Melinda's eye. Certainly he was a more obvious choice for her than Joaquín. But as far as Rico could tell, Blue's lack of interest went beyond respect for Joaquín's claim to downright dislike of Melinda. He slept with Esperanza, seemingly content with her maternal commodiousness, until he moved into town. Rico thought everything would settle down after that, but she was wrong.

Joaquín became quieter and slower to smile, Melinda louder and quicker to laugh. Seth began avoiding her company, then Esperanza did too, so that during her pregnancy Rico was often alone with Melinda. In those last months of her confinement, and then after Elena was born, Rico felt grateful to Esperanza for taking on the responsibility of managing the household. She had taken on far more than that, but Rico was blissfully ignorant until Melinda chose to enlighten her.

It happened one afternoon when they were sitting in the shade beneath the cottonwoods behind the house. Rico was nursing her daughter and remembering more often than not the things Seth had said and done the night before. They had only recently resumed sex after a hiatus of several months, and Rico found as much delight in his lovemaking as she had in the beginning. Her memories elicited secret smiles that had no bearing whatsoever on anything Melinda happened to be saying.

Melinda wasn't dense. She knew the source of those smiles and could remember a time when she herself had smiled over her own memories of Seth. Now, however, that time was gone, and though she loved Rico as a sister, she couldn't resist pricking Rico's bliss with doubt. "Do you ever wonder," she asked in a tone of innocence, "what Joaquín and Seth do when they're alone?"

Rico laughed. "I'm sure it would bore us to tears."

"They're awfully close," Melinda said. "Does Seth talk about Allister much?"

Rico shook her head, suppressing a frown as she laid Elena in her cradle and pulled the netting over the top to keep the flies away.

"I suspect it's the same," Melinda said.

"The same as what?" Rico asked, feeling a nudge of discomfort.

"Men together." Melinda shrugged. "You know, like we were once."

"It's not the same," Rico argued.

"Why not?" Melinda asked flippantly.

"We shared affection, that's all. And comfort 'cause we had so little. It's not the same with men."

"How is it different?" Melinda asked, amused.

"You know," Rico murmured. Then lowering her voice even more, "The way men violate each other."

Melinda laughed. "Don'cha think Seth and Allister did that?"

"Why don't you ask Esperanza if you're so curious?" Rico answered sharply. "She knew Allister."

"She knows Seth, too," Melinda replied.

Rico stared at her.

"Shoot. I didn't mean to say that, Rico." Melinda grinned with feigned embarrassment. "Spilt the beans, didn't I. Jesus, I'm sorry."

Rico tried to pretend she'd known all along and didn't care. She shrugged, actually managed to laugh, then said, "Seth has so much hunger I'm happy for a little help once in a while."

Melinda snickered. "If you need any more help, let me know."

"Don't you think Joaquín would object?" Rico asked, appalled.

"He'd never find out," Melinda answered.

But Rico hadn't believed it. She felt certain Joaquín would sense the change not only in Melinda but also in Seth. It was Rico's greatest fear that something would destroy their friendship; without Joaquín's stabilizing influence, she suspected Seth would leave.

The happiness she'd brought home from church tarnished by her memory of Melinda's comments that day, Rico stood up and saw that the baby was asleep, then walked through the parlor and on into the kitchen seeking someone to unhook her dress. Melinda was at the table with a nearly empty bottle of Seth's whiskey. Knowing the bottle had been unopened, Rico warily sat down at the table and asked, "Is something wrong, Melinda?"

"Nope," she answered, shaking her head emphatically.

"Did you drink all that by yourself?"

"Yup. Felt bad bein' left behind. First I thought it was 'cause I ain't good enough to go to church, but I figured out now why I had to be left behind."

"Why?" Rico asked, confused.

" 'Cause ol' Seth," Melinda said in an earnest tone, as if all she wanted was affirmation of her great discovery, "couldn't walk into church with a harem, now could he?"

Slowly, Rico stood up. "You've had far too much to drink, Melinda. I think you should go sleep it off."

She shook her head. "I ain't done yet."

"Please go," Rico pleaded, "before the men come in."

"Why? You can't tell me Seth's never seen a drunk woman 'cause he's seen both of us drunker'n skunks. 'Member that time we shared him? Or did he halve us?" She laughed. "I can see why you need help pleasin' him. You was always drawin' the line short of what he wanted."

Rico turned to walk out but stopped when she saw Esperanza

and Lobo blocking the parlor door. Esperanza put her hand in the middle of the boy's back, impelling him forward. "Go outside and find your daddy, Lobo," she said. "Keep him and Joaquín out of the house for a while."

"Why?" Lobo asked.

"I'll explain later," Esperanza said, meeting Rico's eyes.

"All right," Lobo said, looking curiously at Melinda as he passed.

Esperanza pulled a chair out from under the table and lowered herself into it. "Sit down, Rico," she said.

Melinda tried to laugh but her voice broke with tears. "What is this, the ladies ganging up to throw the harlot out of town?"

Esperanza waited until Rico had sat down. A quick glance told her Rico wouldn't be much help. She looked back at Melinda. "Earlier you asked me to read your cards. I read them a little while ago when I was alone."

"What'd they say?" she asked with studied indifference as she poured herself more whiskey.

"I saw your death," Esperanza answered.

Melinda stared at her, then laughed. "You're layin' it on a bit thick, don'cha think? Why don'cha jus' come right out and say you want me to leave?"

"I already advised you to."

"How 'bout it, Rico?" Melinda jeered. "Do you want me to leave?"

"I don't understand," Rico whimpered, her eyes on Esperanza. "Will we all die?"

"What the hell're you talking about?" Seth asked as he strode into the room. He glared down at Esperanza, then at Melinda and the well-gone bottle of whiskey. He picked up the bottle and threw it out the door where it shattered in the dirt. "Think you had enough," he said.

In an effort to hide her tears, Rico stood up and moved toward the stove. Seth caught her arm and pulled her back, looking down at her with a frown of regret. Then he turned hard eyes on Esperanza. "What'd I tell you about those cards?"

"I have not disobeyed you," she answered without flinching.

They all looked at Joaquín coming through the door with Lobo.

"Sorry," Lobo said to Esperanza. "They wouldn't do it."

She nodded, thinking she should have known that when Lobo told his father the women wanted him out of the house, being Seth, he'd come find out why. She stood up and scooped the boy from the floor. "It's all right, Lobo. Now you and I will stay outside."

"No!" he protested. "I don't want to."

Softly, Seth said, "Go with Esperanza."

Joaquín had seen the broken whiskey bottle, and Melinda's drunkenness was as obvious as Rico's tears, though she gave him a hopeful smile. When Seth dropped his gaze and led Rico from the room, Joaquín felt ashamed. He listened to their bedroom door close, then looked at Melinda. "Get up," he said.

She laughed. "Not sure I can."

He crossed the room and yanked her chair out, caught her as she started to tumble, and lifted her to her feet. The whiskey on her breath reminded him of his mother and all the nights she'd tucked him into bed with the smell of liquor on her kisses. Joaquín had hoped to save Melinda from the sordid death his mother had earned working in brothels, and his heart ached at his failure as he led her from the house. When she stumbled as they walked across the yard, he wished he could simply put her to bed and let her sleep it off, but he knew the situation demanded a more drastic remedy. In his room, he set her in a chair and began gathering her belongings.

"So I'm to be turned out," she said, her voice slurred.

He kept quiet, trying to neatly fold her voluminous dresses to fit inside her valise.

She laughed at him. "You know what Seth would do with those? He'd throw 'em in the fire."

"I am not Seth," he said quietly.

She sighed. "What're you gonna do, Joaquín? Drop me off in a saloon, say that's where I found ya, sweetheart." She laughed bitterly. "Now that's something Seth would do."

Joaquín walked out without answering. As she sat on the chair looking at her closed valise and listening to him back a horse out of a stall, then the creak of leather as he saddled up, the finality of her leaving struck her with regret. If it hadn't been for Seth she could have loved Joaquín, but Seth was between them like a stallion flaunting his power to rule. Even now she was being kicked out because she'd become a problem to Seth. Joaquín would tolerate anything from her. He'd proven that by giving up his bed and sleeping in the loft without complaint. But she'd become a problem to the lord and master; she'd made his woman cry by telling her the truth. Though the suspicion that she'd said more than was actually true nudged at Melinda's mind, she dismissed it. Even if Seth hadn't touched her, she wanted him to. It wasn't fair that everyone else shared his bed and only she was shut out.

Joaquín returned and lifted her gently by her arm, then took her valise in his other hand and led her from his room, not bothering to shut the door. He put her on his black horse and swung up behind, his arm around her waist as he reined the horse out of the stable. When he dug in his spurs, the horse leapt to a gallop and jumped the fence. Even though Joaquín held her safely in front of him, Melinda clung to him with fright, then as they cantered along the trail, she clung to him with regret, knowing he had been a tender source of solace she had betrayed.

4

★

Rico watched Seth close their bedroom door then turn around and face her as he took off his jacket. He wore a shoulder holster with a Colt's .41 beneath his left arm.

"What was going on in there?" he asked, tossing his jacket across the footrail of the bed.

She picked up the jacket and hung it inside their chiffonnier, then quietly closed the door and looked out the window, seeing the white dove on the saguaro. "Don't you think it's surprising Joaquín's dove has stayed around?"

"Yeah," he said. "You didn't answer my question."

She shrugged. "Melinda got drunk."

"Why?"

"She was hurt that Joaquín wouldn't take her to church," Rico said, keeping her eyes on the dove.

"Joaquín stayed outside and watched the door. It wouldn't have looked real respectable for me to walk in with two women."

"That's what she said," Rico murmured. "That you didn't want to go with your harem."

He was quiet a minute then said, "If she told you I touched her, she lied."

Hearing him toss the gun and holster onto the bed, she turned around to watch him unbuttoning his vest.

"Is that what she said?" he asked.

Rico shook her head and sat down, pulled the pistol out and opened the cylinder with its five live shells and one empty chamber. She snapped the gun closed again as Seth threw his shirt into the laundry basket. He opened a drawer for another, shook it out and put it on, watching her as he buttoned it.

She thought about Esperanza doing the laundry, taking special care in ironing his shirts and stacking them in the drawer so he always had a fresh supply. Seth was particular about his clothes and changed shirts two or three times a day, and Rico was thankful she didn't have to keep up with the laundry as well as care for the baby and watch Lobo too. She met Seth's eyes and tried to smile.

He came closer but didn't touch her. Instead he lifted his .44 off the headboard and buckled it on walking across to look out the window as they both listened to a horse gallop away.

"Was that Joaquín?" she asked.

"Yeah, with Melinda. Looks like she's gone."

"How far?" Rico asked mournfully.

"You gonna miss her?"

"Yes," she said, not looking at him.

"You're not gonna tell me what's going on, are you?"

"There's nothing going on, Seth," she answered, meeting his eyes again.

"The hell there ain't."

She shrugged. "Melinda was drunk. I'm not going to believe anything she said."

"What'd she say?"

Rico knew accusations of infidelity would not stand her well with Seth. Whenever he expressed regret that he couldn't marry her, she always answered it was enough that they were together. Most of the time it was because it seemed he truly considered her his wife. At other times, though, reality came clear in how easily he could leave her. A wife would still be a wife whether wanted or not, but if Rico caused too much trouble she became an expendable problem. Since the only remedy had been stolen by his legal wife in Austin who refused to divorce him, Rico couldn't fault Seth. She smiled bravely and said, "I'll handle it."

He gave her a smile of admiration. "You want me to unhook your dress, or can you handle that too?"

"Please," she said, standing up and turning her back. She felt his fingers open the row of hooks and eyes, his breath on her neck, then his kiss on her cheek as he slid his hands around her waist inside her dress. She leaned into his strength, the enveloping protection of his arms, feeling the buckle on his gunbelt in the small of her back like a threat of doom. Death was everywhere; she could feel its humid presence swamping her home with an overpowering sensation of dread. From outside the window, Joaquín's dove cooed its rhythmic murmur of reassurance.

Melinda cried against Joaquín's shirt as they rode through the suddenly overcast afternoon. She tried to tell herself it was because of the way the light fell on the earth, golden sunbeams slanting from between the clouds at such a deep angle that they appeared to be a stairway to the sky, but she knew it was because she had lost this man who held her gently while getting rid of her.

When they reached the outskirts of town he reined up behind a house with yellow shutters on a back street. He swung down and tied his horse to a palo verde tree, then lifted her to the ground beside him. Carrying her valise and holding her elbow, he led her into the house and up the back stairs to a corner room. He pulled a key from his pocket, unlocked the door, then pushed it open, guided her inside, and set her valise on the floor.

"I have taken this room for you," he said. "You may stay as long as you wish; I will pay the rent." He handed her the key, his eyes dark with the same melancholy she felt. "It has a nice view of the desert," he said, then turned to go.

"Joaquín?" she whispered.

He turned back on the threshold and watched her in silence.

"Is that all?" she asked.

"What else would you like?" he answered gently.

"When did you rent this room?"

"Last week."

"Was it Seth's idea?"

He shook his head. "Seth hasn't mentioned you for a long time. That was how I knew you had become a problem to him."

"What about you, Joaquín?" she asked mournfully. "Are you gonna live in his shadow for the rest of your life?"

Joaquín smiled. "I am his shadow, and he is my abyss, but I don't expect you to understand that."

"Abyss?" she mocked. "Isn't that like death?"

"Yes, and all the wisdom it contains."

She laughed. "You're gonna be dead, all right. You oughta get Esperanza to read your fortune. It might make you think twice about being Seth's shadow."

"I have thought of it a thousand times."

"Yet you're still there!" she jeered.

"As you would be if you could. You are like his wife, full of ambition but without the discipline to achieve it."

"I'm like Seth's wife?" She laughed again. "Thanks, Joaquín." But when she turned away, she blinked back tears as she looked out the window at the desert stretching empty all the way to the mountains, then she looked at him over her shoulder with a teasing smile. "See you around?"

"Perhaps," he said.

Listening to his boots on the stairs, then the hoofbeats of his horse trotting away, she felt forlorn. The barest of breezes moved through the room as she sat on the bed and opened the crocheted bolsa Rico had given her as a birthday present the summer before. Inside was a tiny mirror which Melinda didn't look into, knowing too well what she would see. Almost as well she knew the contents of her coin purse, but she opened it anyway and counted all the money she had in the world: twenty-one dollars and seventy-two cents.

She heard a door open and close in the hall and then the tap of feminine footsteps and the rustle of a satin gown. Through the door Joaquín had left open, Melinda saw a woman stop and look in with discreet curiosity. The décolletage of her dress marked her for a lady of the evening, and beneath a cascade of auburn curls, her eyes were a clear pale green as she looked Melinda over. "New in town?" the woman asked.

Melinda nodded.

"Need a job?"

"I hadn't thought that far ahead," Melinda said, "but I guess I do. The man who left me here paid the rent but didn't give me any money."

The woman chuckled with sympathy then asked, "Ever work in a saloon?"

Melinda laughed. "That's where I met him."

"Well then," the woman said in a husky voice that rippled with camaraderie, "come by the Blue Rivers later, if you're interested in a job."

"The Blue Rivers Saloon?" Melinda asked with a mischievous smile.

The woman nodded. "Ask for Lila Keats. I'm the manager."

The afternoon was fading fast as Joaquín ambled toward home, the clouds steaked with crimson on the horizon, the silence around him heavy. He felt melancholy with failure, yet also relieved Melinda was gone, and satisfied that he had acted before the situation caused irreparable harm. She had originally come to the homestead to keep Rico company while the men were gone, so had been Rico's responsibility until Joaquín took her into his bed. Then suddenly Melinda was his, and when she turned sullen it had been his chore to get rid of her, even though he had long ago relinquished any claim.

He smiled now in the falling shadows of twilight, remembering the times he'd chastised Seth for resisting being stuck with a woman he didn't want but had slept with and so taken on. Now Joaquín knew how easily that could happen. It started with a tantalizing game that ended in bed, then suddenly the man was responsible for what became of the woman.

Joaquín was determined not to play that game again. If the time ever came that he brought another woman to his bed, he would marry her first. Even with that thought, however, he couldn't see himself a married man. His first loyalty belonged to Seth. If Seth decided to leave Rico and his children behind, Joaquín would go with him even if he himself had a wife and children. So he couldn't see taking on a family with any kind of clear conscience, and it was important to Joaquín to keep his conscience clear.

He had killed two men in his past, the first to protect Seth's wife and the second to protect Seth. Those deaths did not sit lightly, but what Joaquín felt was sorrow, not guilt, believing a man's defense of his family was no sin. The puzzle was why Joaquín's family was one and the same as Seth's, why their interests were identical and had been from the moment they met.

They were not kin, not even of the same race. They had grown up speaking different languages yet were brothers in a way stronger than blood. They understood each other without words, complemented each other's skills so they stood united against the world, maintaining a potent defense steeled by Seth's instinct for the kill tempered by Joaquín's need for mercy. Together they survived. Alone, Seth would have trapped himself in his own rage, and Joaquín would have martyred himself to his pious ambitions. Their finding each other was proof of God's care. Joaquín believed that, and he'd learned from Rico that Seth did too, but Joaquín and Seth had never discussed it. Though they talked of many things, the power that held them together was a knowledge too tender to threaten with words.

The world was poised on the cusp of night, the sunset still dying on the horizon, when Joaquín saw a buggy approach on the road ahead. As he studied the small black run-about pulled by a single horse, he couldn't sense any hostility from whoever rode in the shadowed interior, but he stopped anyway in the deeper darkness beneath a cottonwood and slipped the keeper strap off his pistol.

The buggy pulled abreast of him and stopped. Leaning halfway out to reveal himself, the preacher asked pleasantly, "Mr. Ascarate, isn't it?"

Joaquín smiled, thinking the Protestant padre had an interesting face, creased with a depth of understanding lightened by an ironic humor. "Buenas tardes, Señor Holcroft. I'm sorry I missed your sermon today. May I ask what scripture you quoted?"

"Job 3:26," Holcroft said, running it through his mind so he would get it right when he recited it.

"Yet trouble came." Joaquín laughed softly. "A good choice."

"You know the Bible?" Holcroft asked with surprise.

"I have studied it," Joaquín answered.

"We should have a discussion over brandy sometime." Holcroft immediately regretted mentioning that he imbibed spirits, then remembered he was talking with a Catholic and a gunman at that, so his smile deepened.

Joaquín had no suspicion the smile was related to the consumption of spirits. He credited it to Holcroft's remembering whom he was speaking with, and he liked the amusement in the padre's eyes. "Do you think we would learn anything?" he teased.

"Perhaps to understand what we know a little better," Holcroft answered.

Joaquín laughed again. "Seth told me he enjoyed meeting you."

"Was kind of him to say so. Maybe next Sunday you can join us."

He shook his head. "My job is outside. I don't need a church to worship God."

"I've always considered the fellowship of a church its most constant blessing."

Joaquín looked at the empty desert lit with the last glimmers of sunset. When he had made his decision to follow Seth, he hadn't realized how much human fellowship he would be sacrificing for the sake of his partner. He looked back at the padre. "Would you like to join us for supper?" Joaquín asked lightly, as if it weren't the first invitation ever extended from the homestead.

"I would be delighted," Holcroft beamed.

Joaquín swung down and tied his horse to the back of the buggy, then climbed in beside the minister. They smiled at each other as Holcroft turned his horse around on the road.

"I should tell you," Joaquín said, looking away again, "that I am returning from taking a woman to town. She had lived with us but became a problem. If you feel an oddness among us, it will be the newness of her being gone."

Holcroft smiled with understanding. "Will she be all right on her own?"

"I don't know," Joaquín said softly. "The path is just ahead, beyond those boulders."

Holcroft turned onto the trail marked by a huge saguaro growing from an outcrop of rocks. "I was visiting with the elder Mrs. Nickles, who's been ill," he said. "Mr. Nickles said this morning in church was the first time he'd met his neighbors." He smiled at Joaquín. "Abneth is a good man, more broad-minded than most. You would do well to win his friendship."

Joaquín said nothing.

After a moment the minister asked softly, "You were in the saloon when the killing happened, weren't you?"

"Yes," he said.

"Do you think it could have been avoided?"

"No."

Even more softly, Holcroft said, "That's an odd answer from a man who once wanted to be a priest." To his surprise, Joaquín laughed.

"Even the most disciplined zealot for life cannot abstain from death," he said.

"No, that's true." Holcroft smiled. "I came west to die. I had a lung disease and the prognosis was terminal. This land revived me. This air, this sky, these mountains towering with such sublime arrogance. There's power in land, any land anywhere, but the desert is shorn of ostentation so its power flows into us unhindered." He stopped himself, then gave his companion an embarrassed smile.

"I like the desert very much," Joaquín said.

"Have you always lived in it?"

He shook his head. "I was born deep in México."

"What brought you to this country?"

"I came seeking work."

"Did you find it?"

"Yes, and something more: the scaffold on which to hang my life."

"That is more," Holcroft agreed. "May I ask what it is?"

"Protecting Seth," Joaquín answered without hesitation.

"From his enemies, you mean?"

"He doesn't need me for that. I protect him from himself."

"Ah." The minister smiled. "How fortunate for both of you."

Joaquín watched him, wondering if he really understood, then asked, "What do you know of us?"

"Just the gossip around town." Holcroft shrugged. "I try to take it with a grain of salt."

"What do they say?"

He was unable to recall anything complimentary so answered honestly, "People fear what they don't know."

"We mean trouble for no one," Joaquín said earnestly.

"I believe you," Holcroft said, impressed with the intensity in the Mexican's dark eyes.

The outlaw's homestead was more humble than Holcroft had imagined: a small adobe home with a tiny casita in the yard, a modest stable with a corral holding fewer than half a dozen horses. Behind the house, cottonwoods loomed in the twilight, and a windmill creaked in a sudden breeze as the outlaw stepped through the dark door of the house—a barely discernable silhouette holding a rifle.

Joaquín jumped from the buggy while it was still moving and jogged toward the man in the shadows. By the time Holcroft pulled his horse to a stop, Strummar had set his rifle aside and was walking toward him.

"Evenin', Reverend," he said. "Glad you could join us for supper."

"Thank you," Holcroft answered, climbing down to accept the proffered hand.

The outlaw turned a playful smile on Joaquín. "For a minute I thought I was about to witness a wedding."

"More like a divorce," Joaquín answered wryly.

The outlaw laughed and slapped him on the back with affection, then grinned at Holcroft. "Come on in, Rev."

"I'll put the horses up," Joaquín said.

Holcroft stopped in his tracks, but the Mexican gave him an encouraging smile, as if knowing Holcroft felt vulnerable following the outlaw into his home, and the minister took reassurance from the gentle humor in the gunman's dark eyes.

The parlor was spartan, the wood floor bare, the only furniture a settee before the hearth. There were three closed doors and one threshold without a door. Holcroft followed his host through it into a brightly lit kitchen where Mrs. Strummar looked up from the stove with surprise.

"The rev's staying for supper," the outlaw said. "We got enough, don't we?"

"Of course." She smiled at their guest. "We're glad to have you, Reverend."

"Thank you," he said, turning to the large Mexican woman sitting at the table with Lobo.

"This is Esperanza Ochoa, the backbone of our family," the outlaw said, giving the woman a wink as he sat down. "This is Reverend Holcroft, Esperanza. Have a seat, Rev, you know my son."

"How do you do," Holcroft answered, nodding at the woman as he took the chair across from her, thinking she was still a beauty though no longer young. He smiled at the boy. "Hello, Lobo. Do you remember me?"

"Sure," he said. "You're the preacher."

The outlaw asked, "Did you pick up that broken glass?"

"Not yet," the boy said, drawing a pattern on the table with his finger.

"You gonna do it soon?"

Holcroft watched the boy look at his father. There was no fear in the appraisal but the challenge was clear.

The outlaw smiled at their guest and said, "If I had some whiskey, I'd offer you a drink."

"Esperanza's got another bottle in her room," Lobo said.

The outlaw laughed. "After you pick up the broken glass, why don't you fetch it for us?"

"I don't feel like it," Lobo answered.

"I will get it," Esperanza said, standing up and walking toward the door.

"Not the glass," the outlaw called.

She stopped and looked back at him, then at Lobo. "No," she said, going out.

Joaquín came in, dodging her in the door. He smiled at everyone, then crossed the room and picked up the dustpan from where it leaned in the corner behind the stove.

"What're you doing?" the outlaw asked.

"I'm going to clean up that broken glass," Joaquín answered.

"Lobo's gonna do it," the outlaw said.

Joaquín looked at Lobo watching his finger draw circles on the table. "When?"

"I don't know," the outlaw said. "When you gonna do it, Lobo?"

"When I get ready," he said, not looking at his father.

Joaquín put the dustpan back and took a chair at the table. "Too bad we can't offer the padre a drink."

"Blue left some whiskey by Esperanza's bed," Lobo announced. "She's gone to fetch it."

"You're a little loose with your information," the outlaw said softly.

Lobo looked around the table with a quizzical frown, meeting the eyes of each of the men. Holcroft wanted to reassure the boy that he wouldn't hold the information against the family, but he couldn't think of anything appropriate to say. They all sat in a silence broken only by the spoon as Mrs. Strummar whipped potatoes at the stove.

"Ay," Esperanza said, walking in the door. "All that broken glass, a person could get hurt." She set a half-full bottle of Magnolia Pike on the table, then brought three clean glasses from the cupboard.

The outlaw filled each glass and raised his in a toast. *"Salud,"* he said.

"Salud," Joaquín said.

"Salud," Holcroft echoed. He sipped the whiskey and smiled at the men, feeling comfortable in the kitchen full of the good smells of supper and the bustle of women at the stove, even the

pouting of the little boy who was now kicking one of the table legs.

"Quit it," the outlaw said. The boy instantly stopped, then watched his father ask, "How long you been in Tejoe, Rev?"

"A little over three years. As I was telling Joaquín on the way in, I came for my health, not expecting to live." Holcroft smiled. "But here I am."

The outlaw laughed. "I could say the same thing." Watching Lobo walk over to pick up the dustpan and carry it outside, the outlaw quickly looked away when the boy passed, then winked at the minister and said, "The desert has a way of reviving people, don't you think?"

"Yes, indeed." He smiled. "You have a fine son. Miss Perkins tells me he's her best student."

"Thanks," the outlaw said, standing up. "Excuse me."

Holcroft watched him walk into the parlor. Joaquín followed him as the women moved away from the window, and only then did Holcroft hear the hoofbeats of an approaching horse. Lobo came to stand just inside the door, holding the empty dustpan by his knee as he peered around the corner of the house. He looked back inside and whispered, "It's the sheriff."

"Lord have mercy," Mrs. Strummar murmured.

"They're coming in!" Lobo said, hurrying to finish his chore.

Holcroft stood up and smiled at the sheriff walking into the kitchen. Rafe Slater looked surprised to see him.

"Guess you two know each other," the outlaw said, settling himself at the head of the table again. "Have a seat, Rafe. You got another glass, Esperanza?"

She set it next to the whiskey, then retreated again as the outlaw poured the sheriff a drink. Joaquín remained standing by the door, his hands loose at his sides and his face shuttered against emotion. Holcroft glanced quickly at the women, huddled together before the stove. Mrs. Strummar was watching the sheriff with worry, while Esperanza glared at him with outright hostility. Lobo returned to stand in the door, his dustpan full of broken glass.

Sheriff Slater sipped his whiskey then gave the outlaw an awkward smile. "Guess you know why I'm here, Seth."

"What I don't know is what you're gonna do about it," he answered with an easy smile.

"There'll be an inquest tomorrow. It'd be helpful if you'd show up."

"You got a whole slew of witnesses. You don't need me."

"Can I take your statement now then?"

"This is it: the man called me out and I beat him."

Slater sipped his whiskey again. "You know who he was?"

The outlaw shook his head.

"Name was Bart Keats. His wife's working for Blue now. Guess I should say his widow."

"Sonofabitch," the outlaw muttered, meeting Joaquín's eyes.

"You know her?" the sheriff asked.

"I've met her."

"She didn't have anything to do with you killing her husband?"

The outlaw glanced at his wife before looking coldly at the sheriff. "What are you implying?"

"Nothing," Slater said, keeping his voice light. "Just asking questions. That's my job."

"I met her ten minutes before he called me out."

The sheriff sighed. "Well, like you said, there were plenty of witnesses as to how it happened. Why is the question."

"He said he was after the bounty," Joaquín said.

Slater twisted in his chair to study Joaquín a moment, then returned his gaze to the outlaw. "Mrs. Keats says you and her husband were associates back in Texas and there was bad blood between you. She said he came looking for revenge."

"I'd never seen him before last night."

The sheriff looked at his whiskey.

"You gonna believe her or me?"

"I'll take your word over hers," Slater said, "but it doesn't matter a whole lot. You acted in self-defense regardless of his motive. I just wonder why she'd lie."

"When you find out, let me know," the outlaw said.

Slater nodded. "Don't suppose you'd change your mind about the inquest even if I subpoenaed you?"

The outlaw shook his head.

Slater sighed again. "Well, I'll be going, then." He stood up. "Goodnight," he said to everyone.

"I'll walk you out," the outlaw said, leaving with him.

Holcroft looked around and saw Lobo still standing in the door with his dustpan. The boy's pale eyes met his, then Joaquín's. "What's it mean?" Lobo whispered.

"Nothing," Joaquín said. "The sheriff called it self-defense."

"He's not gonna try'n arrest Seth?"

"No," Joaquín said.

Lobo looked at Holcroft. "Seth wouldn't let him. I wouldn't either."

Holcroft didn't know what to say. On the one hand he admired the boy's loyalty, on the other he couldn't condone resisting the law.

"Neither would I," Joaquín said, meeting the minister's eyes.

"Nor I," Esperanza said.

"Don't leave me out," Mrs. Strummar added with a laugh.

Holcroft laughed too. "Let's hope it doesn't come to that," he said sincerely.

They all heard the sheriff's horse loping away, then from beyond the parlor a baby began to cry. After a moment the outlaw came into the kitchen carrying the infant against his shoulder. His wife moved across the room to take her, and Holcroft admired the family tableau, the gentle love in the outlaw's eyes as he smiled down at his daughter, quiet now in her mother's arms. Yet when he looked at Joaquín, the outlaw's gray eyes glinted with a cool anger, then softened again as he smiled at Lobo still holding his dustpan of broken glass. "You get it all?" he asked.

"Yes, sir," the boy answered.

"What're you gonna do with it?"

Lobo walked outside and dumped the broken glass into what sounded like an empty barrel. He returned the dustpan to its corner, then pulled a chair over to stand on while he washed his hands at the sink.

The outlaw lifted the bottle of whiskey. "Another drink, Rev?" he asked in a pleasant tone.

Holcroft shook his head, then watched the outlaw refill his own glass and slug down the shot. Quickly Esperanza whisked the bottle from the table. "Sit down, Seth," she said gently. "Supper's all ready."

As Reverend Holcroft drove his buggy back toward town later that night, he remembered the sound of the broken glass falling into the empty barrel, and it seemed the most cogent symbol of the outlaw's family. Love and loyalty were strongly evident, but beneath the surface of their fellowship cracks of fear threatened to shatter the courage of their smiles. Holcroft mused on the enigma of fear in his community.

Most everyone feared the outlaw and the repercussions of his presence, while his family feared the community as well as strangers who could destroy their home without warning. Yet the outlaw himself seemed fearless. Holcroft remembered his wink as Lobo left to perform the chore, the silent unity of father and son strung on a rope of battle the outlaw kept taut with control. Holcroft knew it required unceasing vigilance to raise a child without violence, a constant attention that kept its distance, allowing the child freedom to make choices yet never failing to judge the results, again from the distance of granting the child the same rights of integrity granted an adult. The ultimate aim was nurturing the growth of a man any town would be proud to count among its citizens. Seth Strummar was not such a man, but that he was so passionately involved in the raising of his son proved he could be, and Holcroft saw Lobo as his strongest ally in bringing the outlaw into the community.

5

★

Blue Rivers was twenty-five years old but that wasn't the only achievement he owed to Seth Strummar. Blue's silent partner had provided the financial backing to establish the Blue Rivers Saloon, and his reputation and patronage inspired more than a little of Blue's business. Blue was capable of gracefully acknowledging all that without losing any of his innate arrogance.

Despite a slight limp in his right knee, Blue walked through life with a leonine stroll of possession. His cocky self-assurance had initially drawn Seth into their friendship, and his mental agility and amiable disposition kept Seth there even after learning Blue's responses weren't as effective as his promotion of them. Blue knew Seth forgave him for being tardy when speed counted, relying instead on the constancy of his loyalty, because Blue's allegiance wasn't built on ignorance of any aspect of their partnership.

The Blue Rivers Saloon was the only establishment in Tejoe that Seth patronized. He had a private room where he could drink with men of his choice, and sometimes he mingled in the crowd around the gaming tables or drank at the bar knowing he was on home turf where no man could successfully challenge him and live to walk out the door. Blue hired his bouncers and barkeeps with the stipulation that if the time came when they were needed they would defend Seth Strummar, and an arsenal of loaded Winchesters was kept under the bar for that purpose.

Word of such circumstances wasn't kept secret. Everyone knew Seth Strummar could often be found in the Blue Rivers Saloon, and everyone knew if they made a move against him they would die. So it bothered Blue that Bart Keats had walked in on Saturday night and challenged Seth flat out. Blue wasn't surprised Seth had handled the man on his own; they had agreed the riflemen would be backup for disaster, but he couldn't figure why Keats had thrown his life away.

His connection with Lila was bothersome, too. Blue would have fired her except that he liked her too much. He knew it was too much in light of the short time he'd known her, and he suspected it was partly because she wanted him to like her and was doing her best to make it happen, but he no longer believed it was because she was desperate for a job. Joaquín had seen through her instantly, questioning why she'd come to Blue's in search of employment. At the time Blue had thought Joaquín was just down on women because he and Melinda were having problems. Even after Seth humiliated Lila by demanding she sleep with him then saying he wasn't interested, Blue credited Seth's hostility to resentment that a woman was nosing into their male sanctuary. He still thought those two motives were operational, but the death of Lila's husband made him realize his friends were closer to seeing the truth than he was.

There were two possible explanations. The one he wanted to believe was that Keats had followed Lila here and stumbled onto Seth, then made his decision on the spur of the moment to try for the bounty, maybe thinking with a thousand dollars in his pocket he'd look better in Lila's eyes. That had been her explanation and it left her guilty only of trying to escape an onerous husband. The other explanation was that Lila had agreed to meet him here as part of a plot. When introduced to Seth and Joaquín, she said she'd know them anywhere. Five minutes into the conversation she claimed to have seen Seth's wife and son in Austin. She had been interested in whether or not Joaquín knew Johanna. Then an hour later her husband tried to kill Seth for the bounty. If it was a plot, Blue wanted to understand it before he acted. He also figured there was no harm in enjoying Lila in the meantime, especially as she was trying so hard to please him.

He felt hungry to see her again, to admire the curves of her body in her elegant gown, the auburn flash of her hair and the wicked smile she wore as often as not, so he left his office and stood on the balcony looking down at the swirl of activity on the floor below. Among the tables of men playing poker wandered working girls, available for a laugh or a trip upstairs, and among their colorful flock Blue spotted Melinda.

She wore a yellow dress cut low in front, and her sun-streaked hair fell nearly to her knees, turning heads as she walked through the room, smiling and chatting like the professional she was. Knowing that neither Joaquín nor Seth was there because they always came up and visited him first, Blue was left with the undeniable conclusion that Melinda was working.

He called to Nib Carey who was standing at the head of the stairs. Nib was a bear of a man with a thick black beard and small bullet-hole eyes. When Blue nodded at Melinda and told Nib to bring her upstairs, Nib grunted and said, "I been waiting for that." Then he turned and walked heavily down the steps and across the room. Blue watched Melinda look up at him on the balcony as she listened to Nib, and he sighed as he turned back into his office.

Blue had avoided Melinda as a troublemaker from the start, recognizing she was the kind of woman who tried to trade cards in the middle of a deal. She'd repeatedly thrown herself in Blue's face and Seth's too, and Blue knew it had been just a matter of time before she went too far. He figured what she needed was a man ornery enough to make her toe the line, but Joaquín wasn't one to make anyone do anything, and Blue wondered what had finally happened to exile her from the homestead. It worried him, too, that whatever it was had happened the day after Lila's husband destroyed the carefully nurtured peace of his saloon. The coincidence seemed ominous with foreboding.

When she knocked on the door, he told her to come in then watched as she quietly closed and leaned against it, her mouth wearing a teasing smile while her eyes begged for mercy.

"What're you doing here, Melinda?" he asked.

"Workin'," she said. "Didn't Lila tell you?"

He shook his head.

Bravely she asked, "You're not gonna say I can't, are you?"

"I'm afraid I am. You should've known that."

"Don't, Blue," she pleaded. "What's to become of me?"

"There're other saloons all up and down the street, but my advice is to go back to Tombstone."

"I won't," she whispered. "I can't face it again."

"You'll make more money than in Tejoe."

"Do you think that's all I care about?"

He shrugged. "Seems to me you oughta be putting some aside for the future."

"I just need to get better at pickin' men," she retorted. "Joaquín didn't give me nothing."

"Were you there for wages?" Blue asked coldly.

"A partin' gift would've been nice!"

He shook his head. "You never did understand one whit of that man. He thought you were enough of a lady that giving you money would have been an insult. Besides, I can't imagine him just dropping you off on the street and saying adiós."

"He rented me a room," she admitted.

"For how long?"

"He said I could stay as long as I want," she answered defiantly. "Does that sound like he's tryin' to get rid of me?"

Blue shrugged again.

"Can't we wait and see," she argued, "if Seth takes exception to my workin' here?"

"We're talking about Joaquín," he said softly.

"They're the same man," she sassed back.

Blue turned around and looked out the window, thinking if he hadn't hired a manager this wouldn't be happening. He'd already lost control with Lila's presence: the saloon had seen its first gunfight the day of her arrival. Now one of his girls was a keg of dynamite waiting for a fuse.

Behind him, Melinda said, "They won't come to town tonight. At least let me finish the shift so I go home with a little money."

As he turned around and looked at her, he decided he could give her that much. "All right," he said. "But if they walk in the door, I want you out of here. Understand?"

"Thanks, Blue." She smiled, looking as though she'd give him her heart on a plate.

He knew it was an act, though. He didn't think Melinda had a heart.

Esperanza stood in her darkened doorway admiring the stars in the black sky. Lowering her gaze, she looked with affection at the small jumble of buildings that housed her family, though none of the people on the homestead were kin to her. She was the oldest, however, and had achieved a stature of wisdom among them. Her knowledge of harvesting medicine from the wilderness was valued, as were her meals and labor, her constant stance of giving comfort where she could.

The house across the yard was dark except for a single lamp in the kitchen. As she watched, it was extinguished, then Joaquín came out and started for his room in the stable. Softly she called to him. He came willingly, almost invisible in his black clothes, only the row of bullets in his cartridge belt catching starlight as he walked. She remembered the boy he had been when she first met him, how his eyes had shone with admiration for Seth, his every move aimed at winning Seth's approval.

Joaquín had become a man in the time between that first meeting and when she'd seen him again. He had taken Seth's wife to Austin and the journey had been long and difficult. Immediately afterward, he had started on his search to find Seth, and that journey too had been ripe with lessons. The next time Esperanza saw him, he and Seth were coming home to Rico with little Lobo. When during that visit Joaquín became angry with Seth, Esperanza had watched him challenge his former teacher with the courage of an equal.

For nearly three years now, Joaquín had willingly taken on the stigma of riding with an outlaw, earning his place by proving he could be lethal when necessary. Yet he had started out to be a priest, and his mission in life was to bring Seth to God. He worked toward that achievement by demanding Seth accommodate himself to his new partner's notions of virtue as much as he had accommodated Allister's habitual vice. Seth had told Esperanza all that in bed one night, laughing softly when he said Joaquín was determined to save his soul. She thought it an admirable ambition, and tonight she saw a chance to help the savior.

She watched him stop a scant distance away, a slight young man half a foot taller than she was, his dark eyes sad, his smile compassionate. She whispered, "Wouldn't you like to come in for a minute?"

He had never been inside her casita, and she could feel him following her with concern. She didn't light a lamp but turned to face him in the dark as she said softly, "I feel sad, Joaquín."

"Why?" he asked.

"So many things have been happening. Will you talk with me a while?" She didn't wait for his assent but took his hand and led him to sit beside her on the bed. "I feel lonely," she murmured, leaning against his shoulder. "I am happy with Seth's family, but sometimes it is hard to come to my casita alone."

"I know," he said, sliding his arm around her waist and holding her close. "Sometimes I am glad to hear the horses at night." She laughed softly, laying her cheek against his chest and listening to his heartbeat. "You are a good man, Joaquín. I have always felt close to you."

"I have loved you as a sister," he replied.

"Is that why you never come visit me at night?" she teased. "Because you see me only as a sister?"

"You are also a mother for Lobo," he said.

She sat up in surprise. "What about Rico?"

Joaquín shook his head. "Lobo is too much like Seth in the way he controls her. She answers Seth with sex but has no power over his son. You are the one he shares himself with. Rico is a competitor for his father's love."

"So you don't visit me," she asked, "because you see me as Lobo's mother?"

"No," he answered with a smile. "I've seen Seth come to your door in the middle of the night, and I've thought of doing that, but my manners made me wait for an invitation." He laughed softly. "I am half your age, Esperanza. Do you think I am experienced enough to please you?"

"Your wisdom humbles me, Joaquín," she said. "We have waited too long to share love."

When he leaned closer and kissed her, his hesitant caresses told her of the damage Melinda had done. Esperanza pulled him into her bed and cradled his slender body within her ample solace, suckling him through the night to a rebirth of self-confidence in his prowess.

In the morning she walked into the kitchen to see Seth at the window watching Joaquín return to his room in the stable. Seth turned around and grinned at her. "How'd it go?"

She sighed with exaggerated fatigue. "I didn't sleep all night."

He laughed and swatted her bottom as she walked to the stove to start the coffee. Rico came in carrying Elena, frowned at the swat, and said, "Don't let Lobo see you doing that."

"Doin' what?" Lobo asked, hobbling into the room carrying one boot.

"Go saddle the horses," Seth said. "I'll ride you to school this morning."

"Is Joaquín sick?" the boy asked with concern.

Seth shook his head. "I just thought I'd ride my son to school. Is that all right?"

Lobo grinned. "The kids have been wantin' to see you."

"Maybe I better dress up," Seth said.

Lobo laughed and ran from the house. Through the window, Seth watched him cross the yard toward the stable, then turned around and looked at Rico. "You got a problem with me touching Esperanza?" he asked with an incredulous tone.

"No," Rico said, concentrating on mixing the biscuits.

"Look at me," he said. When she'd raised her eyes to his, he said, "Esperanza ain't no threat to you."

Rico glanced at her watching warily, then looked back at Seth. "I know that," she said.

"Why don't you act like it then?"

"Why don't you act like it?" she retorted.

"What the hell is that supposed to mean?"

"When you've got your hands all over every woman in reach, what am I supposed to think?"

"What women?"

"Melinda, for one."

"If she said I touched her, she lied. I told you that already."

Rico nodded. "Like Lila Keats is lying?"

"Damn straight! You gonna believe them over me?"

"I don't want to!" she cried. "But I'm having trouble not believing something I hear so often."

"Is that my fault?"

She blinked back tears. "It might be. Why don't you think about it?"

"Okay, I'll think about it," he said. "Right now I'm gonna help Lobo with the horses and see if Joaquín wants to go with us. We'll get breakfast in town."

Both woman watched him take his hat from the peg and leave them behind.

Rico began mixing the biscuits again. After a minute she said with false bravery, "We'd make out."

"No problem," Esperanza agreed, setting the table for three, then remembering Melinda wasn't there. "You know where Joaquín took Melinda?"

"No," Rico said.

"He rented her a room in town. I don't think it was far enough, do you?"

"She'll probably work for Blue," Rico said.

"Uh-uh," Esperanza said. "He once told me she's trouble and he wouldn't want her in his saloon."

Rico laid the biscuit dough on the breadboard. "I'm beginning to suspect," she said with a smile of forgiveness, "that all the important conversations around here happen in your casita."

"It is the power of the cards," Esperanza answered with a twinkle in her dark eyes. "Their truth brings it out in everyone near."

6

★

The schoolyard was crowded with children, the girls playing jump rope or talking in clusters, the boys running in packs. They all stopped and watched as Lobo rode up with Seth and Joaquín. Sunlight fell through the trees and danced in patterns across the children's faces.

The girls wore short skirts, their hair in braids, their eyes wide with a curiosity that reserved judgment. In overalls or sporting suspenders on their trousers, the boys watched with excitement shining from their eyes.

Drawn outside by the sudden silence, the schoolmarm came to the door and saw Lobo with his father, a man she had never met but knew instantly because the boy was his spitting image. She nodded at the father, then at the Mexican who was usually waiting in the shadows beneath the trees when school let out, a dark figure on a black horse. Now the three of them sat their horses on the very edge of the yard. The outlaw tipped his hat, and all the children turned and looked at her then slowly looked at him again.

Lobo grinned up at Seth. "See you later," the boy said, kicking his horse toward the corral. He unsaddled and let the pinto loose with the others, a sorry collection of broken down mounts, mostly scruffy burros and ancient mules, then left his gear on the fence and sauntered through the silent schoolyard to the steps. He looked back and waved before walking in alone. When Miss Perkins began ringing the bell, the children filed inside.

Watching the kids look over their shoulders to catch a last glimpse of him, Seth noted how different they were from his son. Lobo dressed the same as he did, a store-bought shirt and vest over serge trousers and boots, while the other boys had homespun smocks and even now, so late in autumn, bare feet. In the corral Lobo's pinto shimmered like gold among the pitiful herd. His saddle was new, while the others on the fence had been patched so many times they were barely above worthless. Seth remembered, too, that Lobo had crossed the yard without greeting anyone. He'd walked in like a pansy bookworm who couldn't get along on the schoolyard.

Turning his horse away, Seth looked across at his friend. "What were *you* like in school?"

"I never went to school," Joaquín answered.

Seth thought about that a minute then asked, "How'd you learn your letters?"

"Johanna taught me."

Seth looked at the mountains hovering like a ridge of trouble on the horizon. "Think we'll ever see her again?"

"Do you wish to?" Joaquín asked with surprise.

"I'd kinda like to see Jeremiah." Seth smiled. "It pleases me she named him that."

"It was a wise choice."

"If she'd divorce me, I'd invite them all out here to visit. But the way it is now, I can't see putting Rico through that."

"It would be difficult," Joaquín agreed. "Besides, what if Johanna chose not to leave? Since she's your wife, what could you do?"

Seth laughed. "I could become a Mormon."

"Would you like that?" his friend asked earnestly.

"God, no. Imagine trying to keep more'n one woman happy."

"I haven't yet succeeded with one," Joaquín said.

Seth laughed again. "You're doing better'n I was at your age. Least your women leave without any bruises."

"I'm good at not doing things," Joaquín said, looking away.

Seth leaned closer and said, "We oughta go down to Tombstone for some carousing, Joaquín."

"Why Tombstone?" he asked unhappily.

Seth shrugged. "It ain't home."

"You're known there. I don't think it's a good idea."

"Let's go to Mexico, then. Some little pueblo south of nowhere. Stay drunk all week, share women, raise a little hell covering each other's backs."

Joaquín studied him a moment before asking, "Why are you restless?"

"Things don't feel the same," Seth said, looking at the distant mountains again. "Or maybe too much the same. Some days the only useful thing I do is feed the damn goat. Rico's unhappy over one thing after another, all of 'em falling in a chain that feels like it needs breaking. Besides, a bounty hunter found me and it won't be long before another one shows up. Maybe it's time to move on."

"Without Rico?" Joaquín asked with studied indifference.

Seth smiled into his partner's dark eyes. "Maybe she'll be happier somewhere else."

Joaquín shook his head. "I don't think moving is the answer."

"What is?"

"It's hard to say since you can't pinpoint the problem." When Seth remained silent, Joaquín asked, "What is it exactly you want?"

Seth twisted in his saddle and looked back as if he thought someone might be tracking him. "Real enemies instead of ghosts." He met Joaquín's eyes, then laughed at himself. "I spent a lot of years on the move. Maybe I just want to feel that kind of freedom again."

"What freedom?" Joaquín scoffed. "Being chased out of town

by lawmen? Sleeping with a pistol in your hand and one ear cocked for the approach of death? Assessing each new friend and situation as a potential trap?"

Again Seth laughed. "Doesn't sound like much the way you say it, but I like living with danger, knowing I have an edge over any man in front of me." He leaned closer and half-whispered, "I even liked shooting Bart Keats the other night. It came down clean and it felt good proving I can still cut it." He leaned back with a grin. "I liked feeling that again."

Softly Joaquín said, "Perhaps it will pass."

Seth looked at him sharply, then snorted in self-deprecation. They rode in silence through the outlying adobe homes of the pobres as they entered town on the main road. A few other riders passed, barely camouflaging their curious scrutinies, and with an oath of impatience at his notoriety Seth turned abruptly into an alley then asked his friend, "Don't you ever get restless?"

"Sí," Joaquín answered. "I think of Lobo when I do. He is only seven and needs us a few more years at least."

"We could take him with us," Seth pointed out.

Joaquín nodded. "Teach him to live with his life on the line at every step, to enjoy shooting men and carousing with drunken women? That sounds like a much better childhood than going to school and church on Sundays."

Seth swung down behind Blue's saloon and tied his reins to a pillar. "I like Holcroft," he said.

"So do I," Joaquín said, following him through the back door.

Their footsteps echoed in the empty saloon as they climbed the stairs. The door to Blue's office was open, and Seth stopped on the threshold.

Blue laughed, standing up from behind his desk. "Hey, come on in." When they had, he shook hands with each of them, then asked Seth, "You come to town for the inquest?"

"No," he said. "Was hoping you'd have breakfast with us."

Blue stared at him a minute, then laughed again. To Blue's

knowledge this was the first time Seth had come to town in daylight, and now he was proposing eating in a public cafe. "Let's go," Blue said. "I know the best breakfast in town."

They walked out the front door of the saloon and down the street to the corner, turning heads as they went. Another block east was a small restaurant called Amy's. The windows were curtained with red-checked gingham tied open with bright red sashes, and there was a sprig of purple primrose on each table. Blue led them to the corner and let Seth and Joaquín sit with their backs to the wall. A young woman came from the kitchen. Buxom and pink-cheeked with blond braids wound around her head, she grinned at him, then came over.

Blue stood up. "Amy, want you to meet some friends of mine. Seth Strummar and Joaquín Ascarate."

They both stood up and nodded at her.

"How do you do," she said softly, giving a tiny curtsey. "Please sit down, gentlemen. Coffee, all around?"

"Yeah," Blue said, "and three of your breakfast specials with lots of biscuits."

She laughed. "Got a fresh batch just coming out." She returned to the kitchen, calling back, "Only be a minute."

As the men resumed their seats, Blue saw that both Seth and Joaquín were watching behind him. He turned around to see the windows lined with the dirty faces of street urchins.

"Why ain't they in school?" Seth asked.

"They know too much," Blue answered with a snicker.

Amy came back carrying a tray loaded with plates of ham and eggs, a platter of biscuits, and three cups of coffee. After distributing the food among the men, she carried the empty tray over to the windows and closed the curtains, then returned to the kitchen.

"I like Amy," Joaquín said, digging into his food comfortably.

"She reminds me of some barkeeps I've known," Seth said. "The kind who stay in business by accommodating discretion."

"That's a nice quality," Blue said around a mouthful of eggs. "I wish Lila had a little more of it."

Seth lifted his cup and sipped at his coffee as he watched Blue over the rim.

"I've always been careful about the girls I hire," Blue said, buttering a biscuit. "Last night I went out and saw Melinda on the floor." He looked at Joaquín, who had stopped eating and was also watching him now. "I don't care for surprises like that," Blue said before taking a bite of the biscuit.

Seth set his cup down, flicked a glance at Joaquín, then asked, "What'd you do about it?"

"I fired her," Blue said, unable to read anything in Joaquín's dark eyes. "Meant to call Lila to task for it too, but we were busy last night so I let it slide. I'll talk to her today, though, and make sure she understands that I'm to clear everybody she hires."

"I'll talk to her," Seth said, picking up his knife.

They ate in silence a few minutes, then Blue asked, "When?"

"This morning. Where does she live?"

"La Casa Amarilla on the east edge of town."

"That's where I put Melinda," Joaquín said.

Seth laughed. "Least we know how she got the job."

"The inquest is at ten," Blue said. "She'll probably be there."

"I'm likely to catch her awake then," Seth said. "You going?"

Blue nodded. "Sheriff Slater asked me to since it happened in my place."

"You wearing a gun?"

"They won't let any in. Nib'll be right outside the door."

"What do you think of Slater?"

"He's crafty," Blue said. "I suspect he ran on the wrong side of the law at one time." He shrugged. "Tejoe doesn't need a top sheriff and he's up to the job."

"Think he's content with it?"

Blue shrugged again. "I haven't met many men his age who're

happy with where they ended up. He seems more content than most. Anyway, he's got an easy job and doesn't have to put himself out."

"Doesn't sound like much of a threat," Seth said.

"He ain't," Blue agreed. "But like I said, Tejoe doesn't need a tough sheriff. Last Saturday was the town's first killing."

Seth winced. "Don't guess they're real happy with me."

"You threw 'em a wild card going to church on Sunday. Nobody expected that."

"What do you think they'll do with it?"

Blue smiled. "I'll let you know after the inquest. You gonna be around?"

Seth shook his head. "Why don't you come out to the house for supper?"

"All right. I'll pick up Lobo at school on my way."

Seth stood up and dug into his pocket but Blue stopped him. "My treat," he said. "I'll let you get it next time."

"Fair enough. You want to keep Lila?"

Blue met his eyes a moment, then said, "Only long enough to find out why she came."

"We're in agreement, then," Seth said, extending his hand.

"Not unusual." Blue smiled, shaking with him. "She's in room fourteen upstairs." When he shook hands with Joaquín, Blue joked, "Don't let him get too rough with her," but Joaquín didn't smile.

Blue watched them leave, wishing he'd gone with them. At the door he saw the gaggle of urchins following them back to their horses, and it made him laugh. Ten years ago he'd been one of those street brats, and if Seth Strummar had ambled through his neighborhood, he would have followed him too.

Seth was uncomfortable with the parade of urchins behind him. When he and Joaquín reached their horses, he swung on then looked at the boys bunched at the end of the alley. "Ain't you got nothing better to do?" he asked them.

They shook their heads in silence.

He nodded, then reined his horse to approach them, Joaquín following along. As the boys parted to let him pass, Seth studied their faces, dirty and hungry, their eyes alive for any advantage they could find in the situation. He kicked in his spurs and loped away fast, thinking one of them might grow up to kill him.

La Casa Amarilla was a better-class lodging house on the edge of town. Seth thought Joaquín had done too well by Melinda in putting her there, but he kept his mouth shut as he always did about Joaquín's private business. They tied their horses in back and walked up the rear stairs to knock on the door of number fourteen. Joaquín looked at Melinda's door just down the hall and hoped she was asleep. If she was, they had a good chance to come and go in peace because it took a lot to rouse her. That intimate knowledge suddenly made him feel lonesome.

Lila opened her door, looked at Seth, then glanced at Joaquín. "Good morning, gentlemen," she said with a professional smile.

"Mind if we come in?" Seth asked.

The pretense of welcome fell from her face but she took a step back and opened the door wider. "Please," she murmured as they walked past her. She closed the door and moved to stand in the middle of the room. "I'm afraid I can't offer any refreshment."

Seth was looking out the window at their horses below, a corral beyond with only a burro in it, the desert past that, empty all the way to the mountains. In the room behind him was a deadly enemy, he felt sure of it. He turned around and met Joaquín's eyes, knowing his partner would stop him from going as far as he wished in questioning her. He looked at her, then at her bed, still unmade. "Sit down, Lila," he said, nodding at the bed.

She was wearing a dark blue dress that closed down the front with tiny black buttons, the skirt tight in the new fashion but without a bustle beneath the flounce of bows on her behind. Settling herself with difficulty on the soft mattress, she smoothed her skirt across her hips and thighs. From the window, Seth said, "Let's start at the beginning. What are you doing in Tejoe?"

She studied him a moment, looked at Joaquín leaning against the closed door, then back at Seth. "I'm working for Blue," she said softly.

"What brought you here?"

"I came to escape my husband."

"The same one I killed?"

"Do you think I had more than one?" she asked archly.

He shrugged. "Why'd you choose Tejoe?"

"I saw it on a map, bought passage on the train to Benson, then hired a rig to bring me here, having no idea what to expect other than a hole-in-the-wall where Bart wouldn't find me."

"Didn't take him long, though, did it? He walked into Blue's saloon less than twelve hours after you did."

"I didn't know he was following me."

Seth came closer until he towered over her. "Why do you think he would?"

"He loved me," she whispered.

"Uh-huh. Was hoping to get you back, I reckon."

"Maybe," she said. "I didn't get a chance to talk to him."

"Mind if I sit down?" He nodded at the rumpled sheets beside her.

A shutter fell across her eyes, making them colder. "Please," she murmured.

He took off his hat and sailed it across the room to land on a table by the window, then sat down and pulled her back to lie beside him, holding her waist. "You're a beautiful woman, Lila," he said softly. "I can see why a man would take a risk to make you his. But once that happened, I can't see him doing much to keep you around."

Her eyes flashed angrily as her belly quivered beneath his hand. "Apparently he felt differently," she retorted.

"You want me to believe Bart tracked you all the way from Austin, hot enough to be less than a day behind, walked into Blue's saloon expecting to hold you in his arms, then saw me and decided to change course?"

"I guess that's what happened. Like I said, I didn't get a chance to talk to him before he died."

"Did you want to?"

"No!"

Seth smiled. "That's the second time you've said you didn't get a chance. Seems to me you'd be saying you were spared having to talk to him." He began opening her dress.

She watched his fingers freeing her buttons, then met his eyes again, obviously frightened though trying hard to hide it. "What do you want?" she whispered.

"The truth." He untied the bow of her camisole and loosened its laces until he could slide his hand under the garment and caress her skin. "Do you know what the truth is, Lila?"

"In this case I don't," she said. "I hadn't seen Bart since I was in Austin six weeks ago."

Seth pulled his hand out and tugged the laces free, opened her camisole and bared her breasts. He covered one with his hand, feeling her heart pound against his palm.

She looked at Joaquín, watching with his dark, inscrutable eyes.

Seth took hold of one of her nipples and gently rolled it between his fingers, smiling as she bit her lip. "You're right to fear me, Lila. If you cross me, I'll kill you. Do you understand?"

"I have no intention of crossing you," she whispered.

"Then what're you doing in Tejoe?"

"I told you. I came here to escape Bart."

"Now that he's dead, why don't you move on?"

"I like it here," she said.

He raised his hand to her throat and slowly closed his grip. She lurched beneath him, trying to pry his fingers away from her neck.

"Seth," Joaquín said, his voice softly entreating.

Seth let go with a smile. "Maybe you'll change your mind about liking it here."

Her breath ragged, she taunted, "Why don't you just fire me?"

He glanced down at her breasts. "Blue's got the hots for you," he said, standing up and towering over her again. "Might as well let him work it out, though in my opinion he'd be wiser to shoot his cum down a privy." He chuckled and walked over to the window, turning his back.

She sat up swallowing her rage as she closed her dress. "Is that all you came to say, Mr. Strummar?"

Slowly he turned around to face her again, then shook his head. "Contrary to present company, Blue's particular about who works for him. The girls have to be young and pretty, of course, and they have to entertain all comers without prejudice, though who they take upstairs is up to them. He's not running a whorehouse but providing fresh entertainment for his patrons. Melinda's a little too experienced and she doesn't work for him. Next time you want to hire a girl, run her through Blue first."

"All right," she said, shrugging huffily. "You can't blame me. She's unusually pretty and was new to town. I'm sorry she didn't work out."

"You didn't know who she was before you hired her?"

"Who is she?"

Seth studied her. "You're either lying, stupid, or cursed with bad luck," he finally said. "None of 'em sounds good for Blue."

"Apparently he doesn't think so."

"He's been wrong before," Seth said, picking up his hat.

Joaquín opened the door and preceded him out. Seth turned on the threshold and gave her a barefaced smile of contempt. "Enjoy the inquest," he said just before he closed the door.

She stared at it, listening to their boots on the stairs, then their horses trotting away. With trembling fingers she rearranged her clothing and redid her coiffure, then pinned her bonnet on her head and picked up her gloves. She still had an hour before the inquest, so she walked across the hall and knocked on Melinda's door.

After the third knock, Melinda opened the door wearing her wrapper, her dark sun-streaked hair a tangle down her back.

Lila smiled. "May I come in?"

"Sure," Melinda said. Turning away, she opened the drapes. "Where're you goin' all dressed up?"

"The inquest," Lila said, settling herself on the only chair. "Why didn't you tell me you knew Seth when I offered you the job?"

Melinda looked at her sharply, then laughed as she crossed to the washbowl. " 'Cause I knew my only hope was to weasel my way in and then count on Joaquín defendin' my right to be there."

"What does he have to do with it?"

"We'd been livin' together the last two years." She splashed water on her face, then grinned up from the towel. "Sunday mornin' I drank a whole bottle of Seth's whiskey and he had Joaquín run me off."

"Must've been more to it than that," Lila said.

Melinda laughed. "Yeah, we go way back, Seth and me. I made a mistake hookin' up with Joaquín, though, and I'm glad I'm out of it." She sat down on the bed with a sigh, still holding the towel. "Don't know what I'm gonna do without a job."

"Maybe I can convince Blue to reconsider," Lila said thoughtfully.

Melinda studied her. "Why would you?"

Lila shrugged. "You're good at your job, and some men will want you just because you were Joaquín's once."

"Seth'll never go for it."

"Why should he care?"

Melinda smiled. "He keeps a tight rein on his world."

"Why are you a threat to that?"

"I'm not. But I said some things I shouldn't have when I got so drunk, and they made Rico cry."

"Who's Rico?"

"Seth's woman. He calls her his wife but he's got another one back in Austin."

Lila nodded. "I know."

That surprised Melinda, but she said, "I can't understand why he chose Rico over me anyway. Why d'ya think he'd want a woman who holds him back in bed? You'd think he'd want one who enjoys it when he lets loose."

"Perhaps he's afraid of what'll happen if he does," Lila said, remembering his smile when his hand closed on her throat. "I would be."

Melinda studied her with a growing suspicion. "Had you met him before?"

Lila quickly shook her head. "I'm familiar with his reputation, is all."

Melinda nodded. "Well, Seth doesn't really hurt women. He just uses us with relish."

"He hung one," Lila countered, "and knifed another in the heart."

"They crossed him," Melinda said.

Lila looked away, her lips pressed tight.

Melinda whispered, "You're not thinkin' of crossin' him, are you, Lila?"

"I wouldn't be so bold," she said, standing up. "I'll talk to Blue about your job. Would you like to meet me for lunch? Beck's Hotel, about noon?"

Melinda was inclined to refuse. She didn't want to be anywhere near a plot against Seth for fear she'd be caught in the crossfire. On the other hand, if she could unearth what that plot was, she would be in his good graces again. Maybe if she did keep working for Blue, in time Seth might even choose her on one of those nights he played around behind Rico's back. Smiling slyly, she said, "I'd be pleased to have lunch with you, Lila."

7

★

When Blue Rivers arrived at the inquest investigating the first violent death within the township of Tejoe, he found the courtroom crowded with men. They all watched him walk in, and no one failed to notice Nib Carey standing just outside wearing two gunbelts opposed across his hips. Blue saw a self-righteous anger in the eyes of the gentry. It was evident that they'd been expecting trouble in his establishment, and also that they had no intention of cutting him any slack. He took a seat by the door, wary of being trapped in the domain of the law.

Sheriff Slater came in and nodded at Blue, then looked over the others as he walked to the front. He stopped before the window beside the judicial bench and thrust his hands deep into his pockets. As he stared at the empty, barren courtyard, he wasn't thinking about what he was seeing but about the irony of being the lawman who might have to bring Seth Strummar to justice. Earl Boyd, a slight, dark man, came in a moment later. He and the Sheriff nodded at each other, then the court clerk set his satchel on the table at the front of the room and removed a sheaf of papers, several pens and a bottle of ink. He arranged them all neatly and stood waiting, watching the door.

Judge Hunnicutt came in wearing the black robe of his office. He was a tall man, florid and robust, nearly fifty and a widower who had come to the territory after losing his family and fortune to the Yankees. He had been appointed to the bench by a former comrade-in-arms, and he spent one week of each month in a different town in his jurisdiction. Tejoe was usually the quietest of his communities, its normal court calendar sparse with petty civil suits and misdemeanor criminal cases. This morning, however, the judge wasn't surprised to find the courtroom crowded.

Neither was he surprised to see no women in the audience. The men there were the owners of commerce, and their faces wore the hard expressions of an unmerciful intolerance they no doubt preferred their ladies not see. A killing threatened everyone's illusion of safety, and the men had gathered to mete out punishment, not compassion.

The clerk called the court to order as Judge Hunnicutt sat down behind the bench. He looked up to watch the widow come in. Realizing she was alone in her sex, she hesitated on the threshold until Blue Rivers rose and guided her to the seat next to his.

The clerk announced that the inquiry into the death of Bart Leroy Keats had commenced. First the sheriff took the stand and was sworn in. When Earl Boyd asked him to testify as to what he knew of the case in question, Rafe Slater said, "I was out of town at the time. I got home early Sunday morning and was informed by Doc Rawls that a stranger by the name of Bart Keats had been killed by Seth Strummar in the Blue Rivers Saloon the night before. That would be Saturday, the 13th of October, 1883. I talked to Blue Rivers, the proprietor of the saloon, and he told me that Keats had walked into his place of business about nine o'clock that night and drew down on Strummar, who then shot and killed him, the deceased, I mean. I rode out to the Strummar homestead and questioned him. Strummar freely admitted the killing, but said he'd never met Bart Keats before that night and did not know why

Keats had challenged him. I felt satisfied Strummar was telling the truth, and I have no more information to offer the court."

"Thank you, Sheriff," Earl Boyd said. "The court dismisses the witness and calls Dr. Hubert Rawls to the stand."

Dr. Rawls was a short man whose vest buttons were strained over his potbelly. Wearing a dusty black suit and carrying an equally disreputable hat, he settled himself into the chair after being sworn in, then looked at the judge and said, "I've been awake all night, Your Honor, tending the birth of a child, and have driven five hours to arrive here in time. I hope you'll forgive me if I'm not at my best."

Hunnicutt smiled. "You are forgiven. Proceed with your testimony."

"What is it y'all need to know?"

"Just tell us what you found when called to the Blue Rivers Saloon last Saturday night."

Dr. Rawls shrugged. "I found the deceased on the floor with a bullet in his chest." He reached into his vest pocket, straining the buttons even further, and extracted a slug. "This is it," he said, holding it up. "A .44 in near pristine condition. The heart, you know, is a powerful muscle that'll stop just about anything. Mr. Keats was prob'ly dead when he hit the floor." He grinned at the judge, fingering the bullet. "Figured I'd keep it as a souvenir."

Hunnicutt restrained a smile. "Since there's no doubt that bullet inflicted the fatal wound and came from Mr. Strummar's gun, I see no harm in your retaining possession. You may go home now."

"Thanks." The doctor stood up and scanned the room as he squeezed the bullet back into his pocket. "Important audience you got this morning, Judge," he said. "Think maybe I'll stick around after all." He trundled from the stand and found a seat in back.

The clerk called Blue Rivers. Blue stood up slowly, not seeing any friendliness in the eyes watching him. He crossed to the witness stand and was sworn in, then sat down and gave his testimony without any prompting. "About nine o'clock last Saturday night," he began, choosing his words carefully, "I was in my office when I noticed the saloon had gotten real quiet, so I went out to see why. I saw a stranger facing off in front of Seth Strummar. I asked the stranger what was going on. He said he was gonna kill Strummar. I was looking right at him, and Seth was behind him in my line of vision. I saw the stranger draw first, then Seth draw and fire." He stopped, scanning the faces watching in silence, then shrugged. "It was Seth's luck. That's all there is to it."

Sheriff Slater stood up. "I've got seven affidavits from witnesses who say the same thing, Your Honor. They're all here if you want to parade 'em onto the stand and hear it again."

Hunnicutt looked at the audience. "Will those men please stand up?" He watched them: three of the leading merchants, two members of the school board, a deacon in the Protestant church, and the town mayor; all upstanding citizens who patronized the Blue Rivers Saloon even though they knew it was backed by an outlaw. Maybe because it was, the judge mused, thinking sin was more enticing when it carried an edge of danger. In a stern voice he asked, "Do any of you disagree with Mr. Rivers' statement?"

They all shook their heads.

"Is there anything you wish to add?"

"Not to the facts," Maurice Engle said. He owned the county's major mercantile firm, was tall and dark with a craggy face and piercing blue eyes. "I got a question or two for Mr. Rivers, though, if I could have Your Honor's permission."

"Proceed," Hunnicutt said.

Maurice Engle scowled at the witness, then asked, "What brought Bart Keats to Tejoe?"

"I don't know," Blue answered.

"Had you ever seen him before?"

Blue shook his head. "He was a stranger to me."

"You're employing his widow."

"I hired her that morning. I didn't know her husband."

"Did you know she had a husband?"

"I didn't ask," Blue said.

Hunnicutt interrupted. "That's more than two questions, Mr. Engle, and I don't see how Mr. Rivers' personnel policies are relevant. Get to the point, please."

Maurice Engle shifted his mouth around as he watched the witness. "My second question," Engle said, "is how likely it is this'll happen again?"

"I can't answer that," Blue said.

"Somebody better goddamn well answer it!" Engle bellowed.

Hunnicutt pounded his gavel. "Any more profanity and I'll have you removed, Mr. Engle."

The merchant turned to the judge with entreaty for reason. "Keats was a bounty hunter, Your Honor. I got no quarrel with Strummar killing him. Any man'd do the same in that situation. But I got a quarrel with it happening in my town. This is the first killing we've had in Tejoe. We got a right to ask a few questions." He turned back to Blue. "I want to know why Strummar isn't here!"

The room was silent as Blue scanned their faces again. He looked through the open door at Nib, then softly told the merchant, "He would've had to come unarmed."

"Otherwise you're saying he'd be here?" Engle scoffed.

"I think so," Blue answered. "But he couldn't tell you anything more'n what I'm saying. We aren't any happier with what happened than you are."

Engle sat down with disgust.

Tom Beck, owner of the best hotel and also the town mayor, stood up and smiled at the judge. "May I speak, Your Honor?"

Hunnicutt nodded, suppressing a sigh. The procedure had strayed far from the business of an inquest but he recognized that it provided a needed forum for these men to air their views.

Beck politely addressed the witness: "Our concern is for the complexion of our community, Mr. Rivers. We've worked hard to build stability and prosperity for our families, and we can see how quickly all those years of work can be undone. Tejoe is not a poor town, we all know that. Our bank is quite plump, our stores stocked with merchandise, our establishments full of clientele. We are a thriving community, but the wrong element moving in now could turn everything sour. It was with trepidation that we heard the news of Seth Strummar's residence outside our town. When he kept to himself and was rarely seen, we all put our worry on a back burner and tried not to think of it, but we all knew he was a powder keg of potential violence. When you opened your saloon and word got out Strummar was your silent partner, we all felt that worry sputter on the stove. As time passed, we were beginning to think it would be all right. Then this happened. Now we're afraid, Mr. Rivers. Afraid of losing what we worked so hard to achieve because of one bad apple in the barrel."

"Seth's not a bad apple," Blue said. "He's put his past behind him and wants only to raise his children in peace."

Alfonso Esquibel, owner of the town's largest livery, stood up. "That is what we all want. But we do not threaten Strummar's peace. He threatens ours."

"He doesn't mean to," Blue said quietly. "You're right in that he backed me in the saloon, but we pay a good chunk of taxes on our business. He pays taxes on his wife's land, and the plumpness of your bank is due in part to the size of his account. I can't see he's hurt Tejoe any. What happened was unfortunate, but hopefully the results will discourage future contenders."

"I wish I could believe you," Esquibel retorted, "but violence breeds itself. Other bounty hunters will learn he is here, and now they will always come, thinking Strummar is a little older, a little slower, easier to take. It will happen until some kid comes along and beats him. You know it as well as I and every man in this room."

Softly, Blue said, "Seems to me you'd have some compassion for the man who has to face that."

Esquibel sat down as J. J. Clancy, owner of the Bank of Tejoe, stood up. He was dapper in his fancy suit, and he wore an amused smile. "I agree with Mr. Rivers entirely. Mr. Strummar has brought capital to our community, as discreetly as he has distributed it, and we are better off for his residency because there is a silver lining to the cloud of his presence. Reverend Holcroft mentioned it yesterday morning." He paused to nod at the minister across the room. "As everyone here has pointed out, our community is an affluent one. In some circles, gentlemen, we would be considered a plum to be plucked. It can only discourage criminals to know we have a citizen well capable of defending his interests."

Buck Stubbins, owner of the Red Rooster Silver Mine, stood up. "You're playin' with fire, Clancy. I told Rev'rend Holcroft the same thing yestiddy. You're thinkin' to use Strummar for your own purposes, but I'm here to tell ya that's like smokin' a cigarette sittin' on dynamite!"

The room erupted in vociferous agreement. Hunnicutt watched the minister stand up. After pounding his gavel, the judge asked, "Do you wish to say something, Reverend Holcroft?"

The minister walked to the front where he could look into the faces of his parishioners as he spoke. He nodded at Blue Rivers, a man he hadn't met before, then addressed the room.

"It seems to me there's truth in all the words spoken here today. I even agree to some extent with Mr. Stubbins. We are smoking a cigarette on a keg of dynamite, but the explosive isn't Mr. Strummar. It's the violence innate in all of us to some degree, and in the frontier around us to a great degree. Look at our neighboring city of Tombstone if you have any doubt. Killings there are frequent. It's the wealth of the mines that attracts the less desirable elements to our part of the country, a danger much larger than any created by the presence of one man. I met Mr. Strummar for the first time in church on Sunday, and later that day, by a fortuitous circumstance, I dined with his family. I was impressed by the care he is expending to raise his son to fruitful manhood, and by the love evident in his home. We are all children of God, gentlemen, and it seems to me that accepting Seth Strummar into our community can only benefit us. Believing the best of a man tends to bring it out in him, and from what I saw, Mr. Strummar has a lot to offer. Not only his wealth, as has been pointed out, and not only his ability to protect his holdings, which also has been pointed out, but in the example he provides our youngsters of a man who went astray in his youth but is trying hard to make amends and follow the straight and narrow now. I believe that if we give Mr. Strummar the benefit of the doubt, he will prove worthy of our confidence and be a credit to our community."

"That's easy to say from the pulpit," Maurice Engle shouted, "but on the streets where the rest of us live, Strummar is a scourge on this community that will only attract more of his own kind! I'm saying we oughta make it loud and clear that he's not wanted in our town."

The anger of his words was met in silence as each man contemplated the difficulties inherent in telling the outlaw to leave.

Sheriff Slater stood up. "The facts are these, gentlemen: we have no legal right to run Strummar out of town. He hasn't broken any laws in Arizona, and unless one of you wants to try'n collect the bounty from Texas, there ain't a thing we can do about him being here. Ain't that right, Judge?"

"Yes," he said. "Back to the business at hand, gentlemen. I find that Seth Strummar acted in self-defense when he shot and killed Bart Keats in the Blue Rivers Saloon on Saturday last. There are no charges to be filed. The remains are released for burial. Case closed." He pounded his gavel. "We will recess for half an hour before continuing with the calendar," he said, then stood up and walked out as the clerk echoed his last words.

Blue smiled at Nib through the door, and the gunman grinned in congratulation of the verdict, then Blue left the witness stand and walked back to where Lila was waiting. He knew it didn't look good to be so close to the widow, it tinged the killing with ulterior motives that weren't true, and he was sorry it had to be muddied because of him. But he also knew if he were to walk out and leave her on her own, the men would think less of him, so he took her elbow and guided her from the room, feeling the eyes watching them leave.

Outside the gate, Nib unbuckled the right-handed gunbelt and gave it to Blue. He strapped it on, then smiled at Lila. "Can I walk you home?"

"I'm not going home," she answered forlornly. "I'm going to the graveyard."

"Oh yeah," he said. "You want some company?"

She shook her head. "Sheriff Slater is escorting me. There won't be a ceremony and it'll be over soon. That's all I want, and to lie down before work."

Blue nodded. "See you tonight, then."

He walked away with Nib, but a block down the street Blue turned back and watched Lila waiting for the sheriff. When Slater came out, they fell in step beside each other without a greeting and walked in the other direction. Blue looked at Nib. "Do you get the feeling Lila knew Sheriff Slater before she got here?"

Nib's bullet eyes turned slowly away from the retreating couple to meet those of his boss. "Seems like they would've said hello or something, don't it?"

Blue nodded. "I'm going out to Seth's for supper tonight. I want you to watch Lila real close. If she does anything that doesn't seem connected to business, I want to know about it."

"All right," Nib said. "Won't be hard. She's easier to look at than most any woman I've seen."

Blue nodded again. "Makes me wonder what she's doing in Tejoe."

8

★

When Melinda met Lila for lunch, their presence created a stir. Not only because they were both brightly attired, Melinda in blue and Lila in green, and not only because they chose the table in front of the window, but because they were ladies of the evening and Hotel Beck was the best in town.

If they hadn't both been beautiful, Tom Beck would have thrown them out. He admired them sitting in the window of his dining room, however, and since their frocks were modest, if bright, and they comported themselves respectably, he allowed them to stay. He even went over and extended a welcome. Feeling tempted to invite himself to join them but knowing he'd never hear the end of it from his wife, he contented himself with offering them a bottle of his best burgundy. They accepted as if gifts from gentlemen were to be expected, then turned back to their conversation as if he'd already disappeared, which he quickly did.

As soon as they were alone, Melinda whispered, "So Seth's in the clear?"

Lila studied her across the sunlit table. "Why do you care so much?"

Melinda's laughter was tinged with bitterness. "Guess I shouldn't," she said, looking away.

"I would tend to agree," Lila replied, "unless you think there's a chance he'll leave Rico."

Melinda shook her head.

"Any woman can be pushed out," Lila murmured. "It only requires a carefully played hand."

Slowly Melinda turned her gaze back on the conniving woman.

Lila smiled. "The hard part is making him choose you when it happens. I've seen the plot ricochet so bad the man hates all women and won't have anything to do with any of us." She laughed softly, then asked in a conspiratorial tone, "If Seth left town, wouldn't it pull the rug out from under Blue?"

"I don't think so," Melinda answered warily. "The saloon's in Blue's name. Seth doesn't have any legal connection to it."

"Is that true?" Lila mused. "What about Seth's bank account? Does Blue have access to that?"

"I don't know," Melinda said. "Rico does."

"She can withdraw money without Seth's approval?"

Melinda nodded. "He set it up that way so in case he dies the money'll be hers."

"Avoiding probate." Lila's grin was gleeful. "That's smart, and it proves he trusts her."

Melinda shrugged uncomfortably. "Seth doesn't have any problem trusting Rico."

"Must be hard for him, though, after being a renegade so long."

"You don't understand their situation," Melinda said.

"I'd like to," she murmured, then added quickly, "It would help me do my job better."

"What does Rico have to do with that?"

"Nothing. But Seth's money has a lot to do with it."

The waiter approached with the wine. Melinda kept quiet until he had filled their glasses, taken their orders and left them alone again, then asked, "Did you talk to Blue about my job?"

"I didn't get a chance," Lila answered. "I went right from the inquest to the burial. It was melancholy." She sipped steadily at her wine a moment, then stared out the window with angry eyes. "Bart wasn't always such a fool. When I married him he had a lot of smarts. He's the one found Tejoe on the map when we heard Seth was living here, and it was his . . ." She stopped, then said hurriedly, "I had no idea he'd follow me."

"Seems odd you'd choose a place he knew if you really meant to escape him," Melinda countered, wondering what Lila had stopped herself from saying.

Lila laughed as if it were inconsequential. "He mentioned it once, that's all. I didn't think he even remembered it."

"There must've been other places he never mentioned."

"None where I knew the richest man in town." Lila smiled. "I learned a long time ago how a rich patron can make a real difference in a woman's life."

"So you did know Seth before," Melinda said softly, thinking she'd caught the woman in a contradiction.

Lila shook her head. "I figured once I got here I'd have him eating out of my hand soon enough."

"You intended to seduce him?" Melinda asked, astonished the woman would travel a thousand miles in search of a man she had never seen.

"Not necessarily seduce," Lila scoffed. "Just use him a little. You should do the same. I'm sure he has heartstrings you could pull."

Melinda delicately snorted with disdain. "Esperanza's the one who sealed my fate."

"Who's Esperanza?"

"An old friend of Seth's who lives with 'em."

"How did she seal your fate?"

"She read my cards and told me right in front of Rico. That's what made her cry, then Seth stormed in and blamed it on me."

"Esperanza tells fortunes?" Lila asked eagerly.

Melinda nodded. "Seth says he doesn't believe her cards, but her word carries a lot of weight out there."

"Do *you* believe her cards?"

"They predicted my death," Melinda said dourly. "Who'd want to believe that?"

"Not many. Is that why you left?"

She shook her head. "I made my mistake hookin' up with Joaquín. Once I realized that, I knew I had to leave 'cause I'd done the one thing to guarantee Seth would never touch me."

"Apparently he doesn't feel the same about Blue," Lila murmured.

"What d'ya mean?" Melinda asked sharply.

"I mean Seth came to my room this morning, pulled me into bed and had his way with me. Joaquín stood there and watched. As he was leaving, Seth said the only reason he's letting me stay around is because Blue has the hots for me. So Seth knows how Blue feels yet still took his pleasure."

"Joaquín watched?" Melinda whispered.

"With wide eyes," Lila said, then sipped her wine. "He's a handsome kid, dressed all in black with his black, black eyes. I'm surprised you couldn't get along with him."

"Joaquín gets along with everyone, but only Seth pleases him."

"Do I detect a nasty insinuation there?"

"Just that I didn't want to play second fiddle to God on Earth."

Lila laughed. "You'd rather play goddess, eh?" She softened her tone. "That's what I thought of Seth's wife in Austin: like a princess, so tiny and pretty, and both she and the child so well dressed and protected by an armed guard all the time." A cold glint lit her eyes. "I heard Seth gave Johanna fifty thousand dollars when they split up."

Melinda stared at her. "You think he has that much money?"

Lila nodded. "And plenty more right here in the Bank of Tejoe."

"That's why you came," Melinda whispered.

"Partly," Lila admitted. "I intend to get my hands on as much of it as I can. I mean, it's just sitting there waiting for someone to spend it. I might as well provide a need to be filled." She winked at Melinda, then gave a radiant smile to the waiter bringing their kidney pie. As she cut through the steaming crust with her fork, she asked, "Does Esperanza ever give readings to strangers?"

Melinda was wondering why she'd ordered kidney pie since she disliked the dish. At the time, she had simply echoed Lila's choice in order to get rid of the waiter, but now she felt ravenous and the aroma rising with the steam was unpleasant. When she watched Lila slide a forkful of meat into her mouth, the redness reminded Melinda of the blood and guts of Esperanza's loyalty to Seth. "She might," Melinda finally answered, "if you pay her. I don't think Seth ever gives her money."

Lila licked the bloody juice off her lips. "All women need a nest egg of their own, don't you think?"

"Something that'll still be there when the man isn't," Melinda agreed.

When Blue rode into the schoolyard that afternoon, he saw the three Nickles boys fighting Lobo. Watching the kid take it hard, Blue wasn't sure Seth would want him to interfere. Lobo was getting his licks in, he was just taking a lot more than he was giving. Finally one of the boys tripped him and he fell. They surrounded him with their fists and yelled "So there!" a couple of times. When they looked up and saw Blue watching, they turned and ran into the sandy arroyo reaching into the foothills.

Blue sat his horse and waited for Lobo to pull himself to his feet. The boy walked toward the trough with his head down, washed the dirt off his face and wiped his bloody nose on his sleeve, which made Blue wince anticipating Esperanza's reaction, then climbed the fence into the corral and saddled his horse.

He rode the pinto out and leaned from the saddle to latch the gate, closing two ancient mules inside. Only then did he look at Blue and say, "They belong to those fellows who were punchin' me. Think I should run 'em off?"

Blue shook his head.

"That's what an outlaw would do," Lobo said.

"Yeah," Blue agreed as they ambled toward the road. "But an outlaw would leave with the mules; he wouldn't have a home here and have to face those fellows again tomorrow."

"I'm bringin' a gun tomorrow," Lobo said.

Blue laughed. "You better talk to Seth about that."

"What am I s'posed to do?" the boy cried indignantly. "There's three of 'em and they always stick together."

"Try making friends with 'em," Blue suggested.

"Who wants to be friends with a bunch of pig farmers," Lobo muttered.

"You like bacon and sausage, don't you?"

"Yeah."

"Well, if it weren't for folks like the Nickles, you wouldn't have any. So what's wrong with being a pig farmer?"

"We could raise our own."

"Then *you'd* be a pig farmer."

"I don't like 'em!" Lobo cried with passion. "They ride stupid ol' mules and don't wear any shoes 'til it practically snows and never do wear boots! They're low class and I don't care to associate with 'em."

Blue studied him a moment, then said softly, "Seth paid a hundred dollars for that pony you're riding and another forty for the saddle. Your boots cost fifteen dollars and you outgrow 'em every year. It ain't the fault of the Nickles that they don't have money like that."

"It ain't my fault!"

"Maybe it is, in a roundabout way. You know where Seth got his money?"

Lobo sniffed and looked away. "He stole it," he said softly.

"From people like the Nickles. Only they lived in Texas and put their money in banks in Texas and Seth took it out. You know that, Lobo. So if I was you, I wouldn't go flaunting my daddy's ill-gotten gains in the pobres' noses. It ain't apt to build your popularity."

"I don't flaunt it," he argued. "I just want to have a race but nobody'll do it 'cause they know I'll win. I want to play craps but nobody else has any dimes. I want to sneak into the saloons and watch the poker but none of the other boys have the nerve. They say their ol' man'll beat 'em good if they're caught in a saloon. I hate 'em. They're all a bunch of pansies."

Watching him carefully Blue asked, "So who do you do those things with?"

"The kids in town," Lobo said.

"When?" Blue asked with astonishment, knowing Joaquín usually rode him back and forth to school.

"I wait 'til Seth's in bed with Rico, then I sneak out."

Blue looked at him hard. "You're asking for trouble, Lobo."

"A man's gotta have a life of his own," the child replied.

Blue decided Lobo was boasting of something he wouldn't dare do. "Are you trying to tell me you get a horse out of the stable without Joaquín hearing you?"

Lobo shook his head. "I keep one in the arroyo half a mile toward the road."

"What do you mean you keep a horse?" Blue asked, scarcely able to believe it.

Lobo shrugged. "I bought one and keep him staked in the meadow there. I move him every day, whether I go to town or not, and always make sure he has water."

"And Seth's never seen him?"

"Seth never goes anywhere," Lobo said with scorn, "except to town to visit your saloon."

Blue picked up the bitterness in the boy's voice. "It ain't easy," Blue said softly, "being who he is."

"It ain't easy bein' his son, either," Lobo retorted. "I'm learnin' to use it, though. At first the town kids thought I was a dandy, but I showed 'em otherwise 'fore they suspected who I am 'cause my name's Madera. Then when they found out I'm Seth Strummar's son, I saw it worked for me and I didn't deny it after that."

"Had you denied it before?"

"Yeah. Not 'cause I'm ashamed or nothin' but 'cause I got tired of explainin' why my name's different."

"Have you ever asked Seth about changing it?"

"He doesn't want me to, says I'll take grief all my life if I carry his name."

"Maybe he's right."

Lobo shrugged. "Yesterday he was talkin' about his brother. Did you know he had a brother named Jeremiah who died?"

Blue nodded, keeping quiet because he didn't know how much Seth had told the boy.

"Seth said I've got a brother named Jeremiah now, too. He lives in Texas with a woman named Johanna."

"What do you think about having a brother?"

"I don't think it's fair he gets to be a Strummar when Seth don't even live with him."

"Maybe it's one or the other," Blue suggested. "I bet Jeremiah would rather be called Madera and live with Seth."

"You think so?"

"I'd bet money on it."

Lobo snorted. "Life's fucked, ain't it?"

Blue was startled. "Who taught you to say words like that?"

"Seth!" Lobo chortled with glee.

When they rode into the yard, Seth walked out to meet them. He stood beside Lobo's horse, reached up and took the boy's hat off, then studied his face in silence a minute. "How'd you do?" Seth finally asked.

Lobo shrugged. "There was three of 'em, so I lost."

"To only three?"

Lobo stared at him in silence. Blue said, "One of 'em must've been twelve years old, Seth."

"I did the best I could," Lobo said earnestly. "But then one of 'em tripped me and I was down."

"Who were they?" Seth asked.

"The Nickles boys."

"What were you fighting about?"

Lobo looked away.

Seth watched him a moment, then asked, "You gonna answer me, Lobo?"

"They called you a killer," the boy said softly, hiding his eyes.

With a sigh Seth lifted his son into his arms. "Put his horse up, will you, Blue?" he asked, carrying Lobo toward the house.

"Sure," Blue answered, watching the kid's arms come around his father's back and hold on tight.

Blue edged his horse close to the pinto and picked up the reins, then turned toward the corral and saw Joaquín standing by the gate watching Seth and Lobo disappear inside the house. Blue clucked his horse forward and Joaquín opened the gate, then followed him into the stable and unsaddled the pinto while Blue tended his own horse. They worked in silence, comfortable with each other's company and bonded by their own memories of childhood fights. As they were leaving the corral, they saw Melinda in a hired hack coming into the yard.

9

★

Blue gave Joaquín a commiserating smile then walked into the house, leaving him alone. Melinda pulled the buggy to a stop in front of him. They looked at each other a moment before he asked, "Have you come to visit Rico?"

"Oh, you're cold, Joaquín," she retorted. "Is that all you have to say after living with me for two years?"

"You stayed in my room," he replied without rancor.

She glanced down at her gloved hands holding the reins, then met his eyes again with determination. "I had lunch with Lila Keats today. I learned some things Seth should know."

"Like what?"

She looked at the familiar collection of buildings she had lost as her home, the house brightly lit in the falling dusk, then back at him. "Aren't I even to be allowed in? I haven't become an enemy, Joaquín."

He shrugged. "It's not up to me whether Rico allows you in her home."

Trying to picture him watching Seth with Lila, Melinda wanted to ask if it was true but was afraid of his answer. "There was a time," she said softly, "when I thought you were incapable of cruelty."

"Have you changed your mind?" he asked with an amused smile.

She nodded. "You'd do anything for Seth. You've already committed murder for him."

Joaquín shook his head. "To challenge Seth with a gun is like swimming upstream with a pocket full of stones. I only added a little lead to those men's burdens. By being here you are adding weight to Seth's and I doubt if you will help anyone, including yourself." He smiled playfully. "But my opinion is only one of five. Go on in and test the water among the others."

"What did I ever do to make you hate me?" she whispered.

"I don't hate you, Melinda. I like you most of the time." He held his hand to help her down. "Are you going in?"

She took his hand, the familiar strength of which was hers only for polite duty now, then stood before him on the ground, looking up at him from so near. "I wish things had worked out dif'rent, Joaquín."

"I'll tether your horse," he said, backing away.

She sighed and walked alone toward the bright lights shining from the windows of the house. The front door was open to the cooling breeze of evening, and she stopped on the threshold, seeing a sliver of light beneath the closed door of Lobo's room. Then she heard Blue's easy laughter coming from the kitchen. She crossed the dark parlor and stopped again on the threshold.

Blue was at the table and Esperanza at the stove, Elena in her cradle fussing with quiet puckering sounds. Melinda smiled at Esperanza. "I've come in peace," she said hopefully.

Esperanza shrugged. "Sit down, niña, since you're here. You want some coffee?"

"Please," she said gratefully, taking the chair across from Blue. She pulled her gloves off and smiled at him.

"What're you doing here?" he asked.

She looked up at Esperanza setting a cup of steaming coffee before her, then asked, "If it would help Seth, would you read the cards for Lila Keats?"

Esperanza exchanged wary looks with Blue before answering. "How could that help Seth?"

Melinda suggested with sarcasm, "You could tell her the same thing you told me. That oughta make her clear out."

Esperanza shook her head. "I never lie about the cards."

Melinda felt stung. "Then it was true," she whispered, "what you saw for me?"

Esperanza nodded.

Melinda tossed her head in a gesture of defiance. "Tell Lila the truth then. Her future can't be any better'n mine since nearly every word out of her mouth is a lie. All I want to know is if you'll do it."

"Where?" Esperanza asked. "Not here."

Melinda smiled. "I'll let you know."

"When you do, I'll let you know if I choose to do it," Esperanza said.

Watching her move away to stare out the window, Melinda was unable to tell what Esperanza was thinking any more than what Blue's thoughts were. She sipped her coffee wishing she had some whiskey in it, but knew it would be ungracious to ask since her last escapade in this kitchen. When she thought back on that, she wondered what she'd hoped to accomplish. Cause a falling out between Seth and Joaquín, she supposed, but she couldn't imagine how she'd expected that to benefit her. Had she really thought either one of them would rescue the person who destroyed their peace? Yet that's what she wanted: to be rescued as Rico had been. Silently Melinda mocked herself, thinking maybe she had to prove she'd die for a man before that happened.

Rico came into the kitchen carrying a basin of water and a bloodied cloth. She stopped and looked at Melinda sitting at the table.

"Is someone hurt?" Melinda asked with sudden fear for Seth.

"Lobo got into a fight at school," Rico answered. She crossed to the door and threw the water out, then left the cloth and basin outside when she came back and washed her hands at the sink. Drying them on a towel, she faced Melinda and asked, "What are you doing here?"

Melinda laughed to cover her hurt. "I thought I was a friend," she said. "Everyone's treatin' me like an enemy all of a sudden."

"Maybe we don't trust you anymore," Esperanza said.

"Why? What'd I do other'n get drunk on Sunday mornin'?"

"You did more than that," Rico said softly. "You accused Seth unfairly."

"Sweetheart," Melinda said with genuine compassion, "if you don't know he's humpin' half the women in Tejoe, you ought to."

"I don't believe you!" Rico cried.

"Ask Lila Keats." Melinda turned her eyes on Blue. "I ate lunch with her today and she said Seth had his way with her this mornin'."

"Is that what you came to tell us?" Blue asked coldly.

She shook her head. "What I got to say is for Seth, and I'll wait."

Joaquín came through the back door but kept his distance, leaning against the wall. They all listened to the door of Lobo's room open, then the footsteps of the child crossing the parlor. When he came in alone, his face bruised and his lip split, he looked at Melinda at the table. "I thought you didn't live here anymore," he said, pulling a chair out beside Blue.

"Who won?" Melinda asked kindly.

Lobo shrugged. "There was three of 'em."

"Those are hard odds," she said, raising her eyes to his father coming through the door.

"Evenin', Melinda," he said with a sardonic smile. "You run out of liquor?"

Again she laughed to cover her hurt. "There's plenty of it in town, Seth. That's one thing I've got lots of these days."

"What're you missing?"

"Friends," she said.

"You think you have some here?"

She looked for a glimmer of regard behind his fun but saw only the cruelty of indifference in his pale eyes. "You're my friend," she said, entreating with her smile. "That's why I came."

He looked at Joaquín behind her, then at his wife. "Do we have any more whiskey, Rico?"

She moved quietly to take it from a cupboard then set the bottle and four glasses on the table. Seth poured a drink into three and held the bottle over the last as he looked at Joaquín. When he shook his head, Seth set the bottle down, nudged glasses toward Melinda and Blue, and picked up his own. "To friendship," Seth said, meeting Melinda's eyes with a bedeviling smile.

"To friendship," she murmured, sipping the whiskey.

"Tried and true," Blue muttered, downing his shot.

The kitchen was silent, everyone watching Melinda except Lobo, who was reading the label on the whiskey bottle.

"I had lunch with Lila Keats today," Melinda said to Seth. "I thought you'd like to know what I learned."

"I'm listening," he said.

She sipped at her drink, basking in his undivided attention. "Lila was askin' about your bank accounts, who had access to them, whether Blue or Rico could withdraw money, things like that." She saw Seth's eyes darken as he frowned. "Don't worry," she assured him. "I didn't tell her anything. She said you gave Johanna fifty thousand when you split, and that you had that much or more in the bank here in Tejoe." His eyes were darker than she'd ever seen them, a deep slate without light. "I asked if that's why she came and she admitted it was, then tried to pretend she meant to get her hands on it legally, through wages and all, but she told me both she and her husband found out you were livin' here when they were still back in Texas." Melinda sipped her whiskey again, seeing from Seth's eyes that she'd won a victory.

"I've never had fifty thousand dollars," he said.

"Where'd Johanna get it?" Melinda asked quickly, suspecting she wouldn't find out if she didn't pounce on it now.

"It was hers," he said absently, pouring himself another drink. He looked at Joaquín, then at Blue. "Sonofabitch," Seth whispered. "They're gonna rob the goddamned bank."

"Who is?" Blue scoffed. "Not Lila alone. And if that was their plan, why did Bart call you out? If they were after fifty thousand, why risk his life for the bounty?"

Melinda was still thinking about Johanna having all that money to herself, and she didn't hear what Seth said next.

"It ain't no fifty thousand," he said. "Most of my money's still in Santa Fe. Here in Tejoe I keep five tops, the other investors ten, maybe fifteen all together. You're right about Lila not being alone, though. But who and where are her compañeros?"

"Maybe Slater knows," Blue said. "He went with Lila to the burial today. I watched 'em and when they came together they didn't say a word. I figure, when you fall in step with someone without a greeting you're pretty good friends."

"I never did trust him," Seth said, pulling out a chair and straddling it backwards. "But I don't trust any badge so I didn't hold it against him." He sipped his whiskey then looked at Blue. "Would you figure him to hit his own town?"

"Maybe he's a patsy," Melinda said, "and Lila's gonna try'n frame him for the job." She paused, then added softly, "Or you."

Seth's eyes bore into her so coldly she had to work at not breaking her gaze. Finally he asked, "What makes you say that?"

"Just a hunch." She shrugged. "After your visit this mornin' she came to see me, and I got the feelin' then she was hatchin' a plot against you. That's why I agreed to eat with her, just to see what I'd learn."

"What gave you that feeling?"

"She seemed to know a lot about you. Guess it reminded me of how a person'll study his enemies to find their flaws."

"What'd she know?"

"Details about your past," Melinda answered guardedly. "And then there was something she said about your wife, how pretty she was, like a princess, that was it, so well dressed and with a body-guard all the time, and envy just rippled in her voice." She shrugged again. "It gave me the shivers."

Seth looked at Blue for a long moment, then at Joaquín, then at Lobo who was staring at him. He winked at his son. "Don't worry, Lobo, I ain't been outsmarted by a thief yet." He stood up and looked at Rico. "Think I'll ride into town."

"Now?" she cried.

"Why not?" he asked, already taking his hat from a peg by the door.

"Supper's nearly ready," she said lamely.

He laughed, then came back and gave her a quick kiss on the mouth. "We'll eat in town," he said, turning away.

She caught his arm, stopping him. "What're you going to do?"

Seth smiled. "Pay a call on the sheriff. Rattle his cage and see what falls out. We'll be back before midnight."

Joaquín and Blue followed him through the door, leaving the women alone in the kitchen with Lobo. Turning hard eyes on Melinda, Rico said, "If anything happens to Seth tonight, I'll never forgive you."

"Would you rather he lose all his money?" Melinda retorted. "Bein' as he ain't exactly employable, you'll be the one who goes back to work." She stood up with a sigh. "Honestly, Rico, you oughta come down off your cloud and look at the real world once in a while." She picked up her gloves. "I'll ride in with the men," she said, walking out.

Lobo stood up and started after her.

"Where are you going?" Rico cried. "Lobo, stay here!"

He ran. Making it outside before anyone caught him, he kept running past Melinda and all the way across the yard where he climbed the fence into the corral. Inside the stable the men were saddling their horses. Seth reached for the cinch under his sorrel's belly, then looked at Lobo sideways as he pulled the strap tight and tied it.

"Can I go?" Lobo asked softly.

Seth studied him, then warned, "We'll be late."

"I can stay awake."

"I'm gonna be busy. I won't be there to catch you if you fall asleep in the saddle."

"I'll be there for you, Seth," Lobo said proudly.

Seth chuckled with pleasure. "Don't make us wait for you."

Lobo ran to his pinto and backed it out just as Joaquín finished saddling his black. He stood a moment watching the boy tug the pinto's head down to get the bridle over its ears, then he swung on and ambled toward the door.

Joaquín didn't think the boy should come but wouldn't disappoint him by arguing about it now. Blue, following Joaquín out of the barn and across the corral, felt same. They looked at each other with a silent acknowledgement of their agreement as they sat just outside the gate waiting.

Seth swung onto his sorrel and sat there a minute, watching his son saddle the pinto. He thought maybe Lobo could pick up a few pointers in how to conduct a fight, though the meeting wasn't apt to involve anything harder than words, and in the best of circumstances their adversary wouldn't be the sheriff. But then he figured Lobo might as well learn young that because a man wore a badge didn't mean he upheld the law. Seth caught himself short, realizing he was thinking like a desperado again: because a man wore a badge didn't necessarily make him an enemy either. Trying to defend himself from this new vantage point of being on the right side of the law made Seth feel old, and watching Lobo jump to catch the stirrup didn't help. The boy wasn't even eight yet and had no business coming along. But like Joaquín, Seth wouldn't disappoint Lobo now.

They turned their horses out of the barn to join their friends just as Melinda climbed into her buggy. None of the men said any-thing about her accompanying them. Lobo trotted his pinto through the gate, Seth swung it closed and made sure the latch caught, then they all rode out at an easy lope, the buggy tagging along behind.

A huge moon cast long shadows across the pale desert as Seth and Joaquín led the way, followed by Blue and Lobo, the buggy wheels humming from the rear.

A mile up the road they met Abneth Nickles coming out of town. Seth reined to a stop and the others lined up alongside him, Lobo closest to the buggy. Nickles pulled his team of dray horses to a halt and smiled at his neighbor.

"Evenin', Abneth," Seth said. "I understand our boys got into a tussle today."

"I ain't heard about it," Nickles said, looking at Lobo. "Who won?"

"We'll let them tell you about it," Seth said, cutting off Lobo's reply.

"Fair enough," the farmer said. "Was glad to hear you were ex-onerated at the inquest this morning."

"Thanks," Seth said.

The men sat in a comfortable silence for a few minutes. The harness on the buggy horse rattled as it shook dust out of its ears, then Joaquín's black stomped one hoof with impatience. Seth asked, "You ain't seen any strangers around, have you? Group of men maybe camped out in the country keeping to themselves?"

"Not on my range," Abneth answered thoughtfully. "Course, I don't ride it much as I should. Noticed you're holding a bay all by itself in the arroyo 'tween your house and the road. Saw it from Juniper Peak t'other day. You got it quarantined or something?"

"There's a horse tethered there?" Seth asked sharply.

"It's mine," Lobo said.

Seth turned and studied his son.

"You know, come to think of it," Abneth said, "I did stumble on a campfire on the west slope of Juniper. Wasn't more'n a day or two old and looked like half a dozen horses stayed overnight. Might they be the men you're interested in?"

"Might," Seth said, dragging his attention away from his son. "If you catch sight of 'em, maybe you could send one of your boys over to let me know where."

"I'll do that," Abneth said. He smiled at the men. "Y'all make a formidable lineup. If I saw the four of you ride into my camp, I wouldn't think you'd come to talk. It's Kid Madera down there that'd shiver my timbers."

Seth laughed. "If you'd come over to the house for a drink sometime, maybe you wouldn't find him so intimidating."

"Thank you, Seth." Abneth smiled. "The hospitality's mutual, a'course." He peered into the darkness of the buggy, then shrugged. "Ma'am," he said, clucking his team forward.

Seth waited a minute before turning his eyes on Lobo. "You come ride with me," he said, nudging his sorrel along the road toward town. Joaquín hung back with Blue as Lobo kicked his pinto to catch up with his father. After a minute Seth asked, "What're you doing with a horse in the arroyo?"

Lobo ran through the lies he could offer but knew when he was found out it would only make everything worse. "I just wanted it," he answered.

"Don't you like the one you're riding?"

"Yeah," he said, suddenly afraid he would lose the pinto.

"Where'd you get a horse anyway?"

"I bought it."

"With what money?"

"Some I saved."

"You only get a nickel a week. Can't be much of a horse."

"It's okay," Lobo said.

"Who sold a horse to a kid like you?"

"Another kid."

"What other kid?"

"His name's Lemonade. He lives in town."

"Friend of yours?"

"Sort of."

"Where'd *he* get the horse?"

"I didn't ask."

"You know if you're caught with a stolen horse, I'm the one who'll get arrested?"

Lobo looked closely at Seth and realized he wasn't teasing. "Maybe it ain't stolen."

"Did you get a bill of sale?"

Lobo shook his head.

"I'll buy you another horse if you want one, Lobo," Seth said, "but I think we better get that one off our property first thing, don't you?"

"Yes, sir," he said contritely.

"Now," Seth said. "Why are you keeping an extra horse in the arroyo?"

"I like to ride him sometimes."

"To meet Lemonade in town, maybe?"

"Maybe."

"What do you do there?"

"Nothin'."

"What kind of nothing?"

"Play craps some."

"You any good?"

"I do all right," he answered cautiously.

"Is that how you bought the horse, with your winnings?"

Lobo nodded.

"How much did you pay for it?"

"Ten dollars," he said proudly.

"If I was my old man, I'd tan your hide right now. You know that?"

"I'm glad you're not," Lobo said.

"Maybe I ought to think of something else," Seth said. "Maybe

I ought to give that pinto to some kid who ain't such a good gambler."

"Why would you do that?" Lobo cried.

"It doesn't seem you need much help to get by in the world. Maybe I ought to start concentrating my attentions on Elena and teaching her what I know."

"She's just a baby, and a girl besides," Lobo scoffed.

"Yeah, but I got her from the start. Not like you. And when Elena grows up and I say jump, she's gonna jump. She ain't gonna hide horses in arroyos so she can sneak into town and do things she ain't supposed to in places she's not supposed to be in the company of people she'd better off not knowing. Anybody who acts like that, I figure trying to teach him anything is a waste of time."

"You did it when you were a kid," Lobo said. "You told me yourself."

"I was fifteen when I started gambling, Lobo. That's more'n twice as old as seven."

"I can't help that," he said stubbornly.

Seth laughed. "You keep pestering me to buy you a pistol. You think sneaking into town is showing me you're responsible enough to handle a sixgun?"

"Does that mean you won't?" Lobo asked, crestfallen.

"Not for a long time," Seth said. "And if I find out you've bought one on your own, I will take a strap to you. Do you understand me?"

"Yes, sir," Lobo said.

Joaquín and Blue kept a good distance behind, so the voices of Seth and Lobo were lost in the noise of hooves on the hard road and the creak and whir of the buggy wheels. After a while, Blue asked Joaquín if he had known about the horse.

Joaquín shook his head. "Did you?"

"He told me on the way from school this afternoon. I guess that fight rattled him and he let out a lot of stuff that surprised me. He rides into town at night after everyone's asleep and hangs out in the saloons."

Joaquín stared at Blue. "Alone?"

"With some street kids. Those we saw at breakfast, most likely."

Melinda laughed from inside the buggy. "Like father, like son," she said.

The men ignored her. Blue lowered his voice and asked, "Will Seth whip Lobo for it?"

"Seth never hits Lobo," Joaquín said with pride. "He vowed not to when he took him from his mother, and he has kept that promise."

Blue grinned. "So far."

"Perhaps," Joaquín conceded with a smile.

In front of La Casa Amarilla, Seth reined up beside the buggy. "We'll return it for you, if you like," he said to Melinda.

"Thank you, Seth," she cooed. "I'm afraid I promised to pay 'em when I got back but I haven't enough in my purse."

"I'll take care of it," he said, swinging off his sorrel. He gave his reins to Lobo, then offered his hand to help her down.

She clung to the first touch he had given her in years. His eyes were kind, and she thought she had a chance to kindle something if she played her cards right. She smiled up at him as she murmured, "Anything else I can do, let me know."

"Thanks," he said, then climbed into the buggy and slapped the reins, making the little horse lurch into motion.

She tried to catch Joaquín's eye to give him a smile, too, but he wouldn't look at her. Neither did Blue, though she got a smile from Lobo as he trotted past leading Seth's sorrel. Melinda stood outside the gate for a long time, savoring the memory of Seth's touch. Then she walked upstairs to her room and sat in the darkness, wondering how she could make him so grateful he would act to keep her in his life.

10

★

Rafe Slater was sitting in his office staring down the line of empty jail cells, well aware of the edge he walked that kept him on the keeper side of the bars. In his life he had done a few things against the law but nothing for which he felt shame, so he didn't figure he dishonored the badge he wore, though he didn't figure he especially deserved it either.

He was a native of Alabama and had fought for the Confederacy. After the war he felt a hollowness inside that no enterprise could satisfy, so he kept drifting and along the way improved his skill with weapons more in the interest of self-defense than procuring a livelihood. He had been pushing forty when he ambled into Tejoe, a small mining town in need of a sheriff, and he'd taken the job by appointment until the election when he was voted unanimously into office, there being no contender to oppose him. Tejoe's previous sheriff had died in his sleep in one of the cells, and Rafe had thought he had a good chance of achieving the same fate until Lila Keats blew into town.

Rafe knew the killing last Saturday was just the beginning of a chain of violence that could cost his life. He sure didn't want to tackle Strummar, but he found himself caught between a compromise of his duty and the cravings of his lust and didn't figure he had much chance of escaping retribution from both.

The thing of it was, his lust didn't have much power anymore and he'd slept with Lila more for old time's sake than anything else. Years ago, he'd ridden for her husband in Texas, back when Bart Keats had been Clay Barton and Lila had called herself Esmeralda. When Rafe finally cut himself loose from their gang of outlaws, he figured he'd done himself a favor, though the memory of Esmeralda often haunted him at night. She'd kept on haunting him until he walked into Blue's saloon and met her green eyes again. Then her memory didn't haunt him; her reality plagued him.

When she came to his office later that night, he felt an agonizing mix of desire and repulsion as he watched her walk in. Desire kindled by her still-vibrant beauty flaunted in his face, and repulsion born of a sure knowledge that she was trouble. Yet he'd allowed her to seduce him on the bunk of the farthest cell, and when she asked him to accompany her to the burial, he couldn't see how he could refuse since as sheriff he was required to be there anyway. But Lila hadn't paid any attention to the casket being laid in its grave; she'd thrown herself at Rafe right in front of the undertaker's crew until he promised to visit her in her room later.

Unable to fathom what she could be scheming now that she was on her own, he figured the least he had to know was her plan before he could act one way or the other. If he serviced her in bed while finding it out, he guessed that was all right, though making love to a woman who was only using him didn't come anywhere near to fulfilling his fantasies about her over the years. Neither was his pleasure augmented by the suspicion that whatever she had up her sleeve would result in his opposition of Strummar.

Now, staring down the long, dark row of empty cells, Rafe Slater had made himself melancholy with thoughts of his own death. When he heard the horses stop outside, he stood up and looked through the window, then inwardly groaned as he watched the four riders swing down and tie their reins to his hitching rail. Of all the people he didn't want to see right then, Seth Strummar was about the last. But Rafe arranged his face into what he hoped looked like polite welcome as he opened the door.

"Evenin', Rafe," Seth said. "Mind if we come in?"

Slater stood aside and let them all pass. Noting that Lobo had been beat up, Rafe hoped that was why they'd come to see him. Softly he closed the door. "Want some coffee? I could brew a pot."

"No thanks," Seth said, looking at the empty cells with their iron doors open as if in invitation.

Rafe figured he knew some of what the outlaw was feeling as he stared into their darkness. In an instinctive act of separating himself from that fate, the sheriff sat down and put his boots up on the corner of his desk. "Have a seat, why don'cha?" he offered.

Seth moved to the window instead. Joaquín and Blue were standing near the door as if already poised to leave, but Lobo walked over and peered into the closest cell with curiosity. Seth studied the street a moment, then turned around and met Rafe's eyes as he said, "We heard a rumor that someone's after the bank."

"Our bank? Here in Tejoe?" Rafe asked in surprise.

Seth nodded.

"They'd get more money in Tombstone," Rafe argued.

"Have to fight more'n one lawman to take it."

"That's true," he said.

"Nobody here to back you up," Seth said.

"I can deputize men when I need 'em."

"Who'd you have in mind?"

"Haven't thought about it," Rafe said carefully. "Never had the need."

"Maybe you better think about it," Seth said.

"Would you do it?"

"No."

"Joaquín?" Rafe asked, looking at him. The Mexican shook his head. Rafe shifted his eyes to Blue and again received a negative answer. "Why?" he asked. "You're the best guns in the county."

"We ain't lawmen," Seth said.

"You'd be protecting your own interests," Rafe pointed out.

"Don't need a badge to do that."

"No, I guess not," he said. "Who do you think is after the bank?"

"Lila Keats."

Rafe smiled, though he felt his heart go cold. "All by herself?"

"Figure she's got some men lying low."

"What're they waiting for?"

Seth shrugged.

They studied each other in silence. Finally Rafe said, "Don't make sense, Seth. If Bart Keats came here to rob the bank, why would he call you out? Few men could walk away from that, and even if he overestimated his abilities, why risk it if he was after the bank?"

"Lila knows," Seth said.

"I've talked to her more'n once and didn't pick up any hint of a bank job. Has she said something to one of you?"

Seth shook his head.

"Why don't you just fire her?" Rafe asked Blue. "Without a job she'd be forced to move on."

"You could roust her," Blue said.

"I got no cause," Rafe objected.

"I've been rousted by the law plenty without cause," Blue said.

Rafe studied him a moment, then shifted his eyes to Seth. "Are you boys asking me to roust her as a favor to you? Is that the kinda sheriff you want in your town?"

Seth's smile was whimsical. "I'd just as soon do without and let each man fend for himself, but that ain't the way the world's going. I got my money in that bank and I expect my sheriff to protect it."

Rafe couldn't resist a grin. "I'll do my best, and I'm sure it'll be enough since Strummar and Allister are out of business."

Seth laughed. "I ain't the only one with stolen money in that bank."

"I know that," Rafe said.

"Nobody else is gonna be any happier if they lose it."

"I know that, too. But maybe they aren't as adept at preventing it as you might be."

Seth stared at him hard. "We pay three hundred dollars a year in taxes to this county, give money to both churches and contribute to the schoolmarm's salary. I stay home the livelong day, and when I come to town I patronize my friend's establishment so as not to upset anyone. I don't aim to do more'n that along the line of becoming a good citizen."

"I doubt it'll be that easy," Rafe said, striving to keep his voice lightly undemanding. "You can stand 'em off from taking too much but you can't act like you're not connected to everything going on in this town. You're our most famous citizen. It's a little late to try'n pass unnoticed."

"You're not telling me what I want to hear, Rafe."

"You wouldn't like me if I did."

"Okay." Seth nodded. "What're you gonna do about the bank?"

"Come running when I hear shots, I guess. Can't arrest nobody for a crime that ain't happened yet."

"You can't stop one that's already come down either."

"You can keep the culprits from getting away. With any luck that's what we'll do. Then maybe we can send Lila Keats off to prison."

"Jesus," Seth said. "It'd be kinder to kill her."

"Are we talking about kindness?" Rafe smiled. "I lost the topic, if we are."

Seth turned away to look out the window again, and Rafe studied the men with him. Joaquín was as loyal a follower as a man could have. He'd stand by Seth even when he thought the outlaw was wrong. As for Blue Rivers, Seth had saved him from a hanging back in Texas and there weren't many debts stronger than that. The three of them made an impressive front against the world, each of them owning a top-notch ability with weapons as well as the kind of survival skills that only come from living outside society's protection. Lobo was their Achilles heel, the desire of both of the others as strong as the father's to see that the boy reached manhood without becoming a fugitive. In order to achieve that, Seth had to set an example, and the sheriff well knew it demanded changes that went against the grain.

Rafe studied the boy, his hair blonder than his father's but with the same lanky straightness, his eyes as pale, his mouth set in lines suggestive of a bitter amusement which looked uncanny on the child's face. Even the way he dressed was a copy of his father: quality boots, tailored trousers and vest and linen shirt. The only things missing were the gunbelt and jacket, emblems of authority denied the boy. Smiling at the bruises on Lobo's face, Rafe asked gently, "You get in a fight?"

"Yeah," Lobo said with defiance, making Seth turn around and look at him. "You gonna arrest me for disturbin' the peace?"

Rafe shook his head. "Haven't received a complaint from anybody. Guess you didn't disturb it enough, if getting arrested is what you're after."

"I'll never be arrested," Lobo boasted. "But any time you want to try, go ahead."

Seth took a step across the room and hit Lobo with the back of his hand, sending the boy sprawling into a cell. Except for his initial cry of surprise, Lobo didn't make a sound as he stared incomprehensibly at his father.

"Stand up," Seth said in a low voice.

Slowly Lobo pulled himself to his feet.

"Apologize to the sheriff," Seth said. "Beg his forgiveness for your smart mouth."

"You're shittin' me!" Lobo cried, his eyes indignant with betrayal.

"No, I ain't, Lobo."

He looked at Joaquín, then at Blue, then back at his father. "You never apologized to a lawman in your life!"

"I apologize for my son, Sheriff," Seth said, his eyes on the boy. "He's an ignorant fool who can't control what comes out of his mouth."

"You ain't bein' fair!" Lobo accused. "You're expectin' me to be better'n you."

"Damn straight," Seth said. "We're all waiting for you to act like a man."

Lobo looked at Joaquín again, hoping for help. When Joaquín gave him a small smile of encouragement, Lobo felt like crying. Seth had hit him, and now wanted him to crawl in front of not only Joaquín and Blue but the sheriff. Lobo knew nothing would be the same whether he did it or not. "I don't see I did anything wrong," he said, flat to his father's eyes, "and I refuse to apologize when it'd be a lie."

Seth laughed. "You little shithead," he said with affection. "You're too slick with your words. Go wait outside."

Lobo walked warily across the room, half expecting his father to hit him again, but Seth didn't move except to follow his son with his eyes.

When the boy was out the door, Seth looked at Joaquín, communicating without words how helpless he felt. Lobo was the same rebel he'd been as a child, and Seth well knew the end of that road and was doing his best to spare Lobo the grief. At the moment, though, he felt he'd failed. Joaquín shrugged as if to make light of the incident, but they both knew as well as Lobo that things were different now.

Giving the sheriff an ironic smile, Seth said, "Sorry," then left. Lobo was already on his horse, watching Seth come out, untie the reins to his sorrel and swing on. They looked at each other across the emptiness as Joaquín joined them.

Blue stayed on the boardwalk. "See you around," he said, giving Seth a playful smile. Blue watched the three of them ride away until they were lost in the dark, then he looked at the sheriff. "That's the first time Seth's hit Lobo."

Rafe winced. "Feel like it was my fault."

Blue shook his head. "Seth knew what he was doing bringing Lobo here. He's trying to teach him to get along with the law. Trouble is," he smiled again, "Seth don't really know how to do that himself."

Rafe laughed. "Truth be told, I didn't either 'til I pinned on a badge."

Seth and Joaquín rode abreast as they habitually did, and Lobo followed along a good distance behind. He seethed with anger at Seth, wishing he were big enough to hit him back and do some damage. Someday he would be. Until then he had to build his strength for the challenge he was born to conquer: being better than Seth Strummar.

They rode in silence the whole five miles to the cutoff and halfway home on the trail before Seth turned up the arroyo. Lobo followed with dread to where the horse he'd bought from Lemonade grazed on the stubby grass.

Seth reined up and looked around. "You picked a good spot, Lobo. Course you'd have to move the stake when the forage is this scarce."

"I moved it every day," Lobo said, still wary.

"You want to move it now?" Seth asked.

Lobo slid down and handed Joaquín his reins, feeling Seth's eyes on him as he walked over to the horse and untied the rope from the stake then led the horse back, reclaimed his reins and climbed onto his pinto. Without another word, Seth headed for the road again. Lobo looked at Joaquín, who gave him a gentle smile, then he followed his father, hearing their friend fall in behind.

For hours they rode south across the moonlit desert. In the distance the San Pedro River was like a satin ribbon reflecting the milky moonlight back at the sky. Twice they approached towns they didn't enter. The lights appeared on the horizon, gradually growing until they filled the desert, then were left behind to be quickly swallowed by the dark. They entered the third town. It was considerably smaller than Tejoe and seemed to consist of little more than the bawdy district. A nearby stamp mill shuddered the ground with its pounding.

Lobo rode between Seth and Joaquín along the street lined with adobe saloons. Their hitching rails were crowded though Lobo figured it must be nearly midnight. Seeing men in front of open doors watch them pass, he realized with a thrill that Seth was known in this town.

They turned off the street and rode through an alley to the back of a saloon where the men dismounted and tied their horses. Lobo still sat his pinto, waiting to learn if he would be allowed inside. Seth studied him a moment then said, "I'd leave you here if I could trust you to stay out of trouble. Since I can't, you're coming in. But you're not to speak unless spoken to. Understand?"

"Yes, sir," Lobo said. He jumped down and tied his horse beside the others, then looked up at his father with a smile.

Seth didn't smile back. He looked at Joaquín, then led them inside.

The room was a swirl of activity. Near the door, a man with his shirtsleeves rolled up was playing a piano, hammering the keys to be heard above the noise that seemed loud enough to lift the roof. Men shouted at the roulette wheel and joked with the painted women, who seemed to squeal at everything they heard. With Joaquín close behind, Lobo followed his father across to the bar, seeing men at the tables quickly look away when Seth turned to face the room. The keep came from the opposite end of the bar and leaned close to hear above the noise.

"Is Ayres around?" Seth asked, barely flicking his gaze at the keep before returning his attention to the room at large.

The keep nodded, walked from behind the bar and threaded his way through the tables to a door marked private. Lobo watched him knock then disappear inside. In a moment the man came back out and beckoned them over.

Seth walked away as if he'd forgotten Lobo. He tried to stand up proud as he followed his father, feeling so many eyes watching them, but when he looked at Seth's back he felt abandoned and it chiseled away at his courage. As if sensing how he felt, Joaquín laid a hand on his shoulder, and Lobo smiled up at his father's partner with gratitude.

The barkeep passed on his return trip, not looking at them, and Lobo saw that another man was standing in the doorway now. The man smiled and extended his hand. "Seth, good to see you." He turned and shook hands with Joaquín, saying, "Joaquín," then looked at Lobo. "Who's this?"

"Lobo Madera," Seth said. "This is Mr. Ayres."

Lobo felt a rankle of resentment that because his name was Madera this man didn't know he was Seth's son. But all he said was, "Pleased to meet'cha," as he held out his hand.

Ayres laughed and shook with him. "Come on in." He ushered them inside and closed the door, leaving them in quiet. While he was pouring shots of whiskey he asked, "What can I do for you, Seth?"

"Lobo's brought a horse he wants to sell," Seth said.

Ayres handed glasses to the men and raised his own in a toast. "Salud," they all said, downing their shots. "What kind of horse?" he asked Lobo.

"A bay gelding," he said.

"Is it a good one?"

"Pretty good," he said.

Ayres laughed. "Why are you selling it then?"

Lobo looked at Seth, who nodded, so Lobo said, "We think it might be stolen."

"Let's take a look," Ayres said. He led them all back outside into the relative quiet of the alley.

Ayres hesitated when he saw the horse. Thoughtfully he approached and examined the animal thoroughly, tracing the overgrown brand on the left hip with his finger, then he leaned on the horse's rump as he looked at Seth across its back. "Where'd you get it?" he asked.

Seth looked at Lobo.

"Bought him off a kid in Tejoe," Lobo said.

"This horse belongs to Fred Dodge," Ayres said. "He lost it chasing train robbers, was left afoot and had to walk back to town."

"What happened to the men he was chasing?" Seth asked.

Ayres smiled. "Two of 'em are sitting inside playing blackjack."

"They from Texas?"

"Matter of fact, they are. Think you might know 'em?"

"I'd like to find out."

"Where do you want it to happen?" Ayres asked amiably.

"Why not right here?"

"Now?"

"Seems easiest," Seth said.

Ayres looked at the horse belonging to Fred Dodge. "All right," he finally said, "but Fred's gonna be disappointed if you kill 'em before he can make an arrest."

"I'm just looking for information," Seth said.

"All right," Ayres said again. He stood up away from the horse and went inside.

Seth nudged the keeper strap off his pistol, then picked up Lobo, set him on the pinto and handed him the reins. "Just sit still and stay quiet," Seth said. He untied his sorrel, draped his reins over its withers and leaned casually with his left elbow on the saddle. Joaquín moved to his own horse and slid his rifle half out of its scabbard. He too draped his reins, ready to leave in a hurry. Lobo patted the warm neck of his pinto as if to calm the horse, but it was his own heart that was pounding.

The door opened and two men stepped out with Ayres. He closed the door and stayed in the shadows, listening.

"Evenin'," Seth said.

The men nodded warily, their hands near their guns.

"Name's Seth Strummar," he said. "This is my partner, Joaquín Ascarate, and the kid's Lobo Madera."

The two men looked at each other, then back at Seth. "Jim Tyler," one of them said, "and my brother Joe."

"I heard Bart Keats used to ride with you boys," Seth said, and Lobo felt a nudge of misgiving that the horse he'd bought from Lemonade might be connected to the killing.

Again the men looked at each other, then Jim said, "We din't have nothin' to do with what happened."

"You weren't there, I know that," Seth said. "What're you doing in Arizona?"

"It's a free country, ain't it?" Joe asked with an edge.

"Long as you follow the law," Seth said with a cool smile. "Selling stolen stock to kids ain't doing that."

Both brothers looked at the bay horse, then at Lobo Madera, then at Seth Strummar taking the part of a street brat. Jim said, "We sold that horse to a kid in Tejoe. What's it to you?"

"That kid's a friend of mine," Seth said. "And I take offense at anyone selling my friends stolen stock."

"Lemonade knew it was stolen," Joe scoffed.

"Lemonade's just a child," Seth said. "He sold that horse to Lobo here, who's a child too. Now all of a sudden Lobo's living with stolen property and that doesn't set well with me."

Joe shrugged. "We'll buy the horse back."

"It belongs to Fred Dodge," Seth said. "Ayres is gonna see it's returned."

"So what're you after?" Jim asked nervously.

"Nothing," Seth said. "I just wanted to get a look at you. If I see you in Tejoe, however, I'll feel different."

"Is that a threat?" Jim snarled.

"Yeah, it is," Seth said. Without taking his eyes from the men, he said under his breath, "Get moving, Lobo."

Lobo reined away, staring back over his shoulder. Joaquín swung onto his black and pulled his rifle from its scabbard. When he was abreast of Lobo, Joaquín raised the gun and rode looking backward. Seth stepped into his stirrup and slowly swung onto his sorrel, watching the men on the ground below, then he yanked his horse around and dug in his spurs. As he caught up with Lobo, he leaned close to slap the pinto's rump. "Move!" he said.

The pinto was already doing that but Lobo kicked in his heels and leaned into the whipping mane. He glanced at Joaquín ahead of him, sliding his rifle back into its scabbard with his horse at a dead run, then at Seth bringing up the rear, and Lobo laughed with excitement. They tore out of the alley onto the main street, turning heads whose faces flashed pale around coldly glinting eyes, then scuttled downhill off the road, galloping into the dark of the desert.

The cadence of running hooves was wild in Lobo's ears. He wished he could fire a gun to express the jubilation he felt, galloping at breakneck speed across the rocky soil. His heart pounded with excitement as he watched Joaquín choose their course with eagle eyes, hearing and feeling Seth's sorrel strain to stay behind his pinto pony. Lobo thought nothing could beat this thrill of being together against the world.

Joaquín was remembering that when he first started riding with Seth they always left town at a dead run, usually with bullets whistling around them. Joaquín didn't like going through it again. Most of all he didn't like the laughter from Lobo, worried that despite Seth's best efforts he was training his son to be a desperado.

A mile out of town they slowed to a walk that soothed them all into a somnolence, and before they were halfway home the young desperado had fallen asleep in his saddle. Seth pulled his son into his lap as Joaquín took the reins and led the pinto along. He smiled at Seth riding ahead with his son nestled against his chest. More than anything, Joaquín wanted to help raise Lobo to an honorable manhood, believing that achievement would balance the crimes of Seth's past and help fulfill his own aim to save Seth's soul.

When they reached the road into Tejoe, Joaquín reined to a stop. "Think I'll ride into town and visit Melinda."

Seth laughed as he took the pinto's reins. "See you in the morning." He waited until Joaquín had disappeared from sight, then he turned his horse and followed his friend toward town.

The hour was so late the saloon was almost empty, and the few men still there didn't seem to notice Seth carrying a child upstairs. He left Lobo asleep on the settee in Blue's office and went back to the balcony to look over the girls still on the floor. There was only one he hadn't had yet. When he smiled his invitation, she came up the stairs swishing her skirts and smiling too.

11

★

Joaquín jimmied the lock on the back door of La Casa Amarilla and crept silently up the stairs. With the blade of his knife he opened the lock on Melinda's door, latched it behind himself and turned to watch her sleeping.

The moonlight fell across the bed from the open window, and her hair was like a wayward dark stream flowing across the white sheet. When she stirred beneath his gaze, he moved quickly to cover her mouth. Her eyes flared with fear before they softened with recognition. Joaquín smiled and sat up away from her.

"What're you doin' here?" she whispered, sliding deeper under the covers.

"I need to talk with you," he said.

"Couldn't it wait 'til mornin'?"

He shook his head.

She smiled enticingly. "Did'ya come to talk with words or something else, Joaquín?"

He laughed gently. "Now that I'm no longer yours, you want me again?"

"I don't like being alone," she murmured.

He nodded. "What would it take, Melinda, to make you feel that you are not alone?"

"What d'ya mean?" she frowned.

"If you had Seth in your bed, would you feel you had lost your loneliness?"

She smiled again. "A man like him could overpower anything else in a girl's life."

"And to lose such a man? Would that also overpower anything else, even a husband?"

"I don't have a husband," she said.

"Lila Keats did."

Melinda studied him in silence a moment, then threw the covers off and stood up. In her transparent nightgown she walked across to the washstand and slowly poured herself a glass of water. Just as slowly she drank it down. When she turned to face him, she smiled as he raised his gaze from her body to meet her eyes again. "I can see you want me, Joaquín," she whispered in a baffled tone, "yet you stayed away from me all those months. Why?"

"You didn't want me," he said.

"I do now."

"Only because we are alone. If Seth were here you would prefer him. Or if Blue walked through that door, you would also choose him over me. I wonder if you would be content even then, or if you would covet me because I wasn't yours."

She threw her hair back off her face in the gesture of defiance he knew well. "You're sayin' I'll never be happy no matter who's in my bed."

"Not quite." He smiled gently. "It's just that I don't think the man in your bed has much to do with it."

"What does?"

"You tell me. What is it you really want, Melinda?"

She didn't answer but moved to the window and looked out on the moonlit desert. He walked across to stand behind her, lifting the weight of her hair away from her neck and kissing the damp warmth of her skin. "Tell me what you want, Melinda," he said softly, "and I will help you get it."

"Why?" she whispered.

"Because we both love Seth. Isn't that enough?"

She snorted with disdain. "So you admit you love him."

"I have never denied it," he said, turning her to face him. "But I didn't take your advice."

"What advice?"

"Don't you remember what you said the last night we slept together?"

She shook her head.

He sighed. "You said I should let Seth rape me to learn how it was done." He brushed her hair back, watching the memory tremble on her face. "Do you remember now?"

She looked at him, her eyes full of pain.

"Don't worry," he said. "The hurt you gave has been gone a long time. I don't understand why you want to be raped, why you would choose that over love, but I understand that we both want the best for him, and I came tonight seeking your help."

After a moment she asked, "What can I do?"

"I suspect Lila has a grudge against him, but he doesn't remember her, so maybe it was a brother or father. Find out if she ever used another name; maybe that would help Seth remember. Can you do that?"

"Yes," she said, then studied Joaquín with a mischievous light in her eyes. "Did you really watch him have his way with her?"

"I watched. I wouldn't say that's what happened."

"What would you say?"

"He frightened her."

"Oh yeah, he scared her, all right." She moved away to sit on the edge of her bed. "When she came over here she was shakin' like a leaf. If she's goin' up against Seth, it's takin' all of her courage to do it. What d'ya think could drive her so hard?"

"I don't know," he said.

She hesitated as if weighing her odds, then asked, "If I help, will you get Blue to give me her job?"

Joaquín too hesitated before asking, "Do you know he uses the girls who work for him?"

She shrugged. "Most men who own saloons do that."

"Do you know what he likes from his girls?"

"I can guess," she answered softly.

"Would you enjoy that?"

"As long as he didn't get too rough."

"Sometimes Seth watches. Did you know that?"

"No." She smiled impishly. "What about you, Joaquín? Do you watch, too?"

He leaned against the wall with a sigh. "I stay downstairs and watch the goddamned door." He laughed. "Sorry. It's an old joke."

"Between you and Seth?"

He nodded. "Would you like to know what it is?"

"Yes," she answered eagerly.

"It was when he was married. I convinced him it wouldn't be real unless sanctified by the Church, but when we went to the priest he refused to do it. I promised that if he performed the ceremony, I would dedicate my life to bringing Seth to God. Even then, when we were standing before the altar, the padre insisted Seth take off his gun and kneel. Seth didn't want to do it, but finally he looked at me with such humor in his eyes, such mockery and yet love, too, for my soul, and he handed me his gun and said, 'Watch the goddamned door.' " Joaquín laughed. "That's what I've been doing ever since."

She stared with bewilderment a moment then whispered, "Is that enough for you, Joaquín?"

"It is too much." He stood up straight and moved almost silently across the room as he said, "I will visit you again tomorrow night to find out what you learned." He turned back at the door with a smile. "Don't wait up for me."

The next morning Seth woke up in Lobo's room. At first he didn't know where he was, then he saw his son asleep and remembered putting the child to bed and stretching out beside him, telling himself he'd just lie down for a minute. Now he recognized that as self-deception. The question was why he'd chosen not to go to Rico's bed.

From the angle of sunlight, he guessed it was close to seven. He stepped into his trousers and gathered the rest of his clothes, then tiptoed across the room and eased the door open to peer out. Though he could hear the women working in the kitchen, the parlor was empty, the door to Rico's bedroom wide open. He looked back at Lobo, awake now watching him. "You best move or you'll be late for school," Seth said softly.

"Do I have to go?" Lobo asked.

"No. But the next time you ask to tag along on a late night errand, I'll have to say you can't 'cause you'll miss school the next day."

"I'll go," Lobo said.

Seth smiled, then eased the door shut behind himself.

Lobo looked at Seth's gun and hat hanging on the bedpost. Carefully he lifted the hat off, laid it on the pillow, and eased the pistol from the holster. It was a Colt's .44 that Lobo knew Seth had carried way back when he rode with Allister, when he'd been an outlaw and committed the crimes Texas still held against him. Lobo raised the heavy gun with both hands and sighted down the barrel, imagining how a lawman would look facing Seth Strummar's gun. He didn't mean to pull the trigger. He barely touched it. But the gun boomed in the early morning quiet, shattering the window glass and throwing Lobo backwards. He was sprawled on the bed with the barrel between his knees when Seth opened the door.

Lobo grinned. "Guess it's got a hair trigger."

Seth nodded. "I've told you more'n once not to touch it."

"I was just lookin' at it," Lobo said.

"Put it back."

Lobo did, then settled the hat carefully above it again.

"I'll let it slide this time, Lobo," Seth said, " 'cause I don't guess I should've left it there. But if you disobey me again, I'm gonna have to do something about it."

"You gonna hit me?" Lobo taunted, the cockiness in his voice undermined by a quiver of fear.

"If that's what it takes," Seth said. "Now go wash up for school."

Lobo approached cautiously, keeping his distance as he slid past his father in the door. Seth sighed and went into the room, settled his hat on his head and lifted the gunbelt off the bedpost, then walked back out. Rico was standing in the kitchen door watching him.

"Mornin'," he said, returning to her room. Tossing his hat and gunbelt on her bed as he walked to the washstand, he filled the basin from the pitcher. He disliked a cold shave but wouldn't ask for hot water, didn't want to talk to her at all, though he couldn't explain it any more than he could say why he was suddenly calling it her room instead of theirs. He scraped his razor across his whiskers, dunked it in the basin of water, then looked into the mirror to do it again and saw her standing in the door behind him. He kept on shaving until he was done, dried his face with a towel, and walked across to the chiffonnier for a clean shirt. It wasn't until he was buttoning it that he looked at her without having the mirror between them.

"I missed you last night," she said with a hopeful smile.

"We got in late, didn't want to wake you." He knew it was lame; he often came in late and not only slept in her bed but woke her with his attentions.

"What kept you?" she asked carefully.

"Rode down to Charleston on our way home."

"Any special reason?"

He turned his back as he opened his trousers to tuck in his shirt-tails, then looked out the window as he buckled on his gun and said, "Think I'll ride Lobo to school again today."

She crossed the room to stand beside him. "What happened last night?"

He ran through all the things he could tell her. Settling on the one that mattered most, he said, "I hit Lobo."

"Oh, Seth," she moaned with compassion. "What had he done?"

"It was what he said. Sassing the sheriff like a hundred two-bit punks I've known."

She reached up and tucked a strand of hair behind his ear. "Lobo only wants to be like you, Seth. Imagine how it confuses him when you fight it so hard."

"I'm right, he's wrong."

She smiled sadly. "How many times did your father say that to you?"

"With every lick of the whip," he admitted.

"Nothing's changed, Seth," she argued softly. "Just because it happened once doesn't mean all your efforts have been wasted."

"We'll see," he said.

She waited for him to touch her, but he kept studying the view outside the window as if he'd never seen it before. "What about Lila Keats?" she asked. "Did you learn anything useful?"

He shook his head. "I found out Lobo was keeping a horse in the arroyo between here and the road. That's what we went to Charleston for, to get rid of it."

"Keeping a horse? Why?"

"He's been sneaking into town after we're asleep, hanging out in the saloons and playing craps in the alley."

Rico sighed. "He's only seven."

"That's a helpful observation," Seth said.

She had to admit the justice of his sarcasm. "I guess I haven't been much help lately, have I?"

Finally he looked at her. "No, you haven't. All I've heard from you is one accusation after another."

"I'm sorry," she said. "I've been feeling out of sorts lately."

"Why?"

She hesitated, then plunged ahead, "We're going to have another child."

"Jesus Christ!" he exploded. "Elena's barely a year old!"

"That's a helpful observation." She smiled through her tears.

Seth whirled around, swept his hat off the bed and stalked toward the door. On the threshold he turned back and said, "Get rid of it, Rico."

"You don't mean that," she whispered.

"The hell I don't! I don't want any more responsibility!"

"Neither do I!" she shouted. "But I won't kill our child! I can't believe that's what you really want." She crumpled to the floor, hugging her knees as she cried.

He stared at her, then quietly closed the door and tossed his hat on their bed. Sitting on the floor in front of her, he pulled her into his lap. "Don't cry, Rico. You're right, it's not what I want. I wasn't ready for it, is all. We'll handle it, just like we've handled everything else. I mean, it's only another baby, right? What's so hard about a baby?"

"Nothing for you," she sobbed against his shirt. "You don't have to carry it for nine months and then have your insides torn out bringing it into the world. All you have to do is love us, Seth. Can you do that?"

"Yeah," he said, lifting her face to kiss the tears from her cheeks.

She met his eyes. "Are you sure? I need your love so badly."

He smiled. "Don't worry, Rico. I'll always be here to take care of you."

"Always?"

"As long as I'm alive."

"And you'll stay alive, Seth? For as long as we need you?"

"I'll do my best," he said.

She sighed deeply and leaned against his chest as they sat on the floor. Her hair was the golden color of sunlight, its wispy tendrils smelling of flowers. He closed his eyes and surrendered for a moment to the familiar comfort of holding her body, a feminine enclosure promising succor that thrived in his strength, withered in his weakness, survived only as well as he did.

A low knock came on the door. Sorry to be disturbed so soon, Seth said with a patient sigh, "Come on in, Lobo."

The boy pushed the door open and stood staring at them. "What are you doin' on the floor?" he finally asked.

Seth smiled. "We like it here."

Rico sat up and wiped her nose on her handkerchief, then she, too, gave the child a smile.

"I just came to say goodbye," Lobo said. "I'm leaving for school now."

"I'll ride with you," Seth said. "Wait for me outside."

"Okay," Lobo said, closing the door as he left.

Seth looked at Rico. "I'll get a board to cover the window in his room. It'll take a while to order new glass."

She nodded but didn't say anything.

"Guess we'll need a new bed, too, so we can move Elena out of the cradle when the baby's born."

Again she nodded, this time with a smile.

He laughed. "You're happy about it, ain't you."

"Yes," she answered. "But only if I get to keep you too."

He stood up with a sigh, looking out the window as he adjusted the weight of the gun on his hip. "Well, as long as Lila Keats doesn't get away with whatever she's got up her sleeve, reckon I'll be around." He gave Rico a smile, then walked through the parlor and across the yard to find out if Joaquín had made it home last night.

12

★

Lobo left them at the turnoff to the school yard. Seth sat watching after his son a moment, then he and Joaquín ambled on toward town. Though the sky was blue and the sun bright, the breeze carried the chill of winter. "Next January I'll be thirty-five," Seth said with a wry smile. "Never thought I'd live this long."

Joaquín smiled back.

"Rico's pregnant again," Seth said glumly. "She told me this morning."

"Congratulations!"

Seth snorted. "That makes four I know about. I think it's enough, don't you?"

"That is never for us to say."

"There's ways to stop it. Working girls know how to get rid of it when they want to."

"Yes," Joaquín snapped, his eyes suddenly angry. "I'm sure Rico knows all about it, and if she wanted such a solution, I am also sure she wouldn't take you into her counsel."

Seth smiled. "Don't get mad at me, Joaquín. I'm just making conversation."

"As lightly as you make love," he muttered. "You said you have four you know about. Were you trying for another at Blue's last night?"

Seth laughed. "It's a natural urge, you know. Not all of us can be monks in control of our baser instincts. Besides, what about your visit to Melinda?"

"I haven't made love to her since I knew we weren't right for each other. It's been well over a year now."

"You slept with her all that time without touching her?" Seth asked, incredulous.

"I slept in the loft," Joaquín said, looking away.

Seth laughed gently. "I only kept her around 'cause I thought you wanted her. Why didn't you speak up?"

"She needed us."

"And now she doesn't?"

"It was because her friendship with Rico went sour that Melinda had to leave."

Seth frowned. "Would you have given up your room forever?"

"It was only a bed." Joaquín shrugged. "The loft was just as warm."

"Not as warm as a bed shared with a woman."

Joaquín met his eyes. "I'm not the sort of man who finds rape a comfortable prelude to sleep."

"Seems to me," Seth drawled, "a woman sleeping in a man's bed can't fairly cry rape if he takes advantage of the situation."

"The world often seems different to you than to me," Joaquín replied.

"Can't argue with that," Seth agreed. "How long you gonna pay her rent?"

"Until I don't feel like paying it."

"Fair enough. If you didn't sleep with her last night, why'd you go see her?"

"To ask her help against Lila Keats."

"Is she gonna help us?"

"Yes. She asked a favor in return."

"Not surprising. What does she want?"

"For Blue to give her a job."

"I don't mind if Blue doesn't," Seth said, "but wouldn't you rather she go back to Tombstone?"

"And whore for a living again?"

He shrugged. "It ain't your fault you couldn't change her."

"We did change her, Seth. We showed her another kind of life, made her think it was hers, then dumped her back where we found her. I don't think it was right."

"What do you suggest we do about it?" he asked, straining for patience.

"Give her Lila's job."

"That's up to Blue," Seth hedged. "He doesn't like Melinda much, you know."

"That should make it easy to keep his hands off her."

"You laying that down as a condition of the arrangement?"

Joaquín nodded.

"I'll run it by him, Joaquín. But I ain't gonna push him to agree to it."

"If he knows it's what you want, he will agree."

"Can't see how he could since I don't. You're the one who wants it."

"Doesn't that affect your opinion at all?"

Seth sighed. "Looks like Melinda's got a job."

They found Blue in his office, and they all walked over to Amy's Cafe for breakfast again. By the time they were seated at the same corner table, the dirty faces of the street boys were pressed against the windows. Amy closed the curtains before coming over to greet them.

"Good to see you, Seth, Joaquín," she said, then with a warmer smile, "Mornin', Blue."

He smiled back. "Mornin', Amy. You got biscuits in the oven?"

"Just about to pop out," she said. "Specials all around?"

Blue nodded and watched her until she was gone, then grinned at his friends. "Never hurts to have a good cook on your side."

The men sat in a comfortable silence until Amy came back with their breakfast. She gave Blue a mischievous smile, then returned to the kitchen. He cut open a biscuit and spread butter to melt in the steam. "Look at that biscuit," he said. "Ain't it perfect?"

Seth laughed. "Sounds like you're in love, Blue."

"I'm in love with these biscuits, I'll admit that," he said.

"How about Lila?" Seth asked, cutting a wedge of ham. "Think you could part with her?"

Blue poured cream in his coffee and stirred it a while, then laid the spoon quietly in the saucer and met Seth's eyes when he said, "Anytime."

"What's the hesitation?"

He leaned back with a sigh. "We have a lot of wicked fun. You know what I mean, Seth. The kind I haven't had since I became a respectable property owner."

Seth sipped his coffee to camouflage his smile. "Joaquín suggested you give Melinda the job."

Blue glanced at Joaquín then looked at Seth. "I don't like her much."

"I think she'll do well by you," Seth countered.

Blue studied Seth, then Joaquín. Finally he gave Seth a sardonic grin and said, "Maybe the fun'll be more wicked with a woman I don't like anyway."

"That isn't what I had in mind," Joaquín objected.

"You staking a claim on her again?" Blue asked.

Joaquín shook his head.

"Then once she's in my employ," Blue said softly, "what happens between us is nobody else's business."

Knowing this wouldn't be the last time he'd have to intercede, Seth said, "Joaquín thinks Melinda needs us, and there's enough of a priest left in him to want to help her out."

"Help her do what?" Blue asked testily.

"Have a nice life," Joaquín answered.

"Managing my saloon?"

"So you will be free to indulge your wickedness until perhaps you become weary of it."

Seth laughed. "He'll save your soul, Blue, if you keep company with us much longer."

"Sounds like a fate worse'n death," Blue muttered, reaching for another biscuit. He carefully split it with his knife and spread the two halves with butter, thinking of the pink skin of the woman who'd made the biscuits. He had vowed to stay away from her because she deserved better than the likes of him. But as he met Joaquín's dark eyes across the table, Blue decided maybe his wicked days were over. "Okay. I'll hire Melinda as my manager and I give my word not to touch her. Does that please you, padre?"

Joaquín smiled. "Yes," he said.

When they walked outside, the urchins were still on the boardwalk. Seth looked them over then asked, "Is one of you named Lemonade?"

"He is!" several boys chirped, pointing their fingers.

The kid was a scrawny twelve, thirteen at the outside. His clothes were close to rags and he was barefoot, his face angular with a cupid's bow mouth and watery blue eyes under a shock of dirty brown hair. "Are you Lemonade?" Seth asked him.

The kid nodded.

"I heard you'd do a favor with discretion."

"Might," he said.

"Need you to take a ride with us. Are you free?"

"Where to?"

"Out in the country."

"What for?"

"Looking for something."

"What?"

"I'll tell you on the way."

"What's in it for me?"

"Five bucks and supper."

"Five bucks?" the boy asked with suspicion. "Jus' to help ya find something?"

Seth tossed him a gold piece, halfway expecting him to run with it. Lemonade pocketed the coin, however, and stepped forward. "I ain't got a horse," he said.

"We'll get you one," Seth said. He turned to Blue. "Can you handle your personnel problems?"

"Yeah," he answered unhappily.

Seth laughed. "Don't blame me. It was Joaquín's idea." He smiled at his partner, then the street urchin he had just taken on. "Come on," Seth said. "Let's get you a horse."

Blue watched them walk away, puzzled as to what Seth wanted with Lemonade. The kid was as dishonest as he was dirty, a punk about to cross the line into true criminality, and Blue wouldn't have conducted any business with him no matter how petty. He expected the kid to get away with the horse, if not a lot more, and he wondered if maybe he should have warned Seth. But apparently Seth had heard otherwise about Lemonade. That made Blue doubt himself, something he didn't do often. He had to concede he'd made a mistake hiring Lila, though, and couldn't help wonder if he hadn't made another by agreeing to replace her with Melinda, a woman he didn't even like. Now he was watching Seth walk away with the worst punk in town, and Blue could only think either he was losing his edge or Seth was, or maybe the world was changing around them so fast nothing fit right anymore.

Blue turned and saw the boys watching after one of their own walking away with a top gun. An honor like that could change a kid's life, set it straight again just because a man of Seth's stature had picked him out of the gutter. Seth had done that for Blue, saved him from being hanged and taken him out of the outlaw life. By setting him up in business, Seth had also given him a semblance of respectability, and Blue guessed there was a chance Seth could do the same for Lemonade. He turned away from the boys who hadn't been chosen and walked toward La Casa Amarilla, where two women lived across the hall of opportunity from each other.

Seth looked down at the filthy kid walking beside him. "Lobo tells me you sold him a horse," he said with a friendly smile.

Lemonade didn't believe the smile. "Ya mad about it?" he asked cautiously.

"No," Seth said. "Curious where you got it, is all."

"Bought it off some men," the kid said.

"Where?"

"Out in the country."

"Could you find the place again?"

"Sure."

"That's what I want you to do," Seth said.

Lemonade thought a minute, then asked, "What's gonna happen if they're still there? Ya gonna kill 'em?"

"Would that bother you?"

"No," he said.

"Then don't worry about it," Seth said.

They reached their horses at the back of Blue's saloon. Seth swung on and held a hand down for Lemonade. When he took it and leapt up behind, Seth had to suppress a cough at the kid's stench. He kicked his horse into a canter to create a breeze, then reined up in front of the general store. "Get down," he said gruffly.

Lemonade slid over the horse's rump.

Seth swung off and tied his reins. "We'll just be a minute," he told Joaquín, then jerked his head for Lemonade to follow him.

Inside, everyone stopped what they were doing and stared at the outlaw coming in. Lemonade stayed behind as Seth walked across to the counter, the metallic ring of his spurs accompanying the echo of his footsteps in the sudden silence.

Seth turned around at the counter and looked at the kid, then at Maurice Engle behind the register. Rumor said the merchant had once robbed a bank in Arkansas, and it seemed to Seth their common history should create a bond of camaraderie between them. But from the sour expression on Engle's face it was evident he didn't share that expectation.

"Can I help you, Mr. Strummar?" he asked with stiff politeness.

"Need some clothes for the boy," Seth said. "Something sturdy and not too expensive."

"Certainly," the merchant said, going to the shelves and taking a pair of dungarees down. "What color shirt?" he called. "Blue, brown or green?"

Seth looked at Lemonade.

"Green," the kid said.

Engle came back and laid the garments on the counter, pushing them gingerly toward Seth. "Anything else?"

"Socks and drawers and some boots, I reckon," Seth said. "And you might as well throw in a handkerchief. Maybe he'll learn how to use it."

Engle's smile was cool. He added the items to the pile and asked, "A belt?"

"All right," Seth said, knowing the milking was about to commence.

"How about a hat?" Engle asked.

Seth smiled at Lemonade. "You want a hat?"

"Sure!"

"Go pick one out." Watching him move eagerly to the display, Seth called, "Don't touch any of 'em."

When Lemonade chose a slouch in fine, black beaver, Engle gloated as he found the right size in the row of boxes on a high shelf. He set the box on the counter and asked, "Will he be wearing them home, Mr. Strummar?"

"No, he needs a bath first. And you best throw in some kinda medicine for lice. What do I owe you?"

"Thirty-seven-fifty," the merchant said, wrapping the bundle with paper that crackled in his hands.

Seth took the bills from his wallet, then fished into his pocket for the fifty cents. He slid the money toward the merchant, but Engle wouldn't meet his eyes. Seth looked at Lemonade and said, "You can carry it."

At Esquibel's livery, Seth bought the cheapest horse and the sorriest saddle the hostler had. Esquibel was so cowed he didn't even bother to haggle but agreed to Seth's first offer. Again, when the money was exchanged, the businessman wouldn't meet Seth's eyes.

Waiting for Lemonade to saddle and mount his new horse, Seth looked at Joaquín, whose dark eyes were warm with affection. Seth smiled, thinking it would be a cold world without his partner.

When the three of them had ambled a short distance out of town, Seth reined up and looked across at the kid. "The clothes are yours, the horse and saddle are mine. You run off with 'em and I'll hang you as a horse thief. Do you understand me?"

"Yes, sir," Lemonade answered.

"All right," Seth said. "Now I'm taking you home. My wife and daughter and another lady live there. I expect you to act like a gentleman. You think you can do that?"

"Yes, sir," he said again.

"Tonight after supper," Seth said, "we'll go looking for your friends, so don't get too comfy in my home. If you do a good job, I'll give you the horse on the condition you skedaddle and I never see you again. Agreed?"

"Yes, sir," the kid said with a smile this time.

"All right," Seth said. "Let's go."

When Lobo came home from school that afternoon, he saw a strange horse in the corral. The horse was too scrawny to be one Seth would buy, and Lobo approached slowly, wondering who was visiting. Then he saw Lemonade hunkered in the shadow of the stable. He was wearing new clothes, even boots, and a hat better than Lobo's. Lobo reined up and stayed on his pinto. "What're you doin' here?"

"Seth brung me," Lemonade answered, squinting into the sun. "What for?"

"Says he needs my help to find some men."

Lobo thought about that a minute, then said, "The ones who sold you the horse?"

"Yeah," Lemonade said. "Is Seth gonna kill 'em?"

"I'll kill *you* if you say that again," Lobo snarled.

"Take it easy," Lemonade wheedled. "Bein' as I'm gonna be along, I think it's a fair question."

"Why don't you ask *him,* then?" Lobo snapped. He jerked his horse around and trotted to the gate, opened it and rode through, then latched it behind himself.

Lemonade climbed the fence and followed him into the stable. "Nice place ya got," he said.

Lobo swung down and lifted the stirrup to untie the cinch. Being only seven, he had to reach the full stretch of his arms to pull the saddle off, then heft with all his strength to throw it across the rack. Breathing hard he turned around and looked at Lemonade. "Did Seth buy you those clothes?"

"Yeah," the older boy said proudly.

"That horse too?"

He shook his head. "Only if I do the job good."

Lobo went back to his pinto, tugged its head down so he could pull the bridle over its ears, then slapped it out into the corral with the other horses. Looking at his friend again, he asked, "Do I get to go along?"

Lemonade shrugged.

"Sonofabitch," Lobo said. He started out then turned back to look at Lemonade still standing there. "Why don't you come up to the house?" he asked. "What're you doin' down here in the barn anyway?"

"Waitin' for ya," Lemonade said.

"Well, come on," Lobo said, letting him catch up so they walked abreast out of the stable.

They climbed the fence and crossed the yard toward the house. Lobo felt strange walking in with a friend at his side. That the friend was working for Seth made it feel even stranger. He wondered why nothing was ever normal in his family. As they walked through the parlor he tried to imagine how Lemonade was seeing it.

They had hardly any furniture, just the settee covered with an old Indian blanket in front of the hearth. There were no portraits on the wall or flowers on the mantle, none of the stuff typical in other peoples' parlors. Then Lobo remembered that Lemonade usually slept in Engle's warehouse, and if he didn't sneak in before the last door was locked he slept outside. If it was cold, Alfonso Esquibel let the boys sleep in the loft of his livery, but when it was warm he said they carried bugs and ran them off with a pitchfork if he caught them in his hay.

Hearing quiet laughter from the kitchen, Lobo caught a fleeting look of envy on his friend's face.

"Sounds like a party," Lemonade said, "but I don't guess they'll let us drink."

Lobo didn't bother to answer. When he entered the kitchen, the men were at the table, the whiskey in plain view, while the women worked at the stove. Lobo sat down in his usual place as if nothing were different.

"Sit over here, Lemonade," Joaquín said, pulling a chair out beside him.

"Thanks," the kid mumbled, sitting down and not looking at anyone.

"How was school?" Seth asked.

Lobo shrugged. "All right."

"You talk to the Nickles boys?"

"Yeah."

"What'd you say?"

"I'll give 'em more any time they want it!"

"What'd they say?"

"That their father whipped 'em for it."

Seth sipped his whiskey. "How'd that make you feel?"

"He shouldn't't've done it!" Lobo cried indignantly. "It was between them and me."

"Guess Abneth didn't see it that way," Seth said. "It's a funny thing about being a father. You feel responsible for what your children do, but I don't expect you to understand that for another ten years or so."

"At least," Rico said, giving Seth a teasing smile.

Lobo hated seeing it, the way Rico could make his father's eyes light up just by smiling in a certain way. He couldn't figure what was so great about her. Esperanza did the laundry and kept the house clean while Rico spent a lot of time alone with Seth in their bedroom. Lobo knew what they were doing in there and that his father liked it. He just couldn't figure why Seth liked Rico. All she did was parade around with Elena as if the baby was a badge of honor.

Lobo didn't even especially like his sister. She was cute when she laughed, but most of the time she was just a bundle of crying and diapering as far as he could see. Sometimes, though, Seth sounded as if he liked her better than Lobo. There were too many women on the homestead, in Lobo's opinion. He wished Rico and the baby weren't there and it was just the men and Esperanza. She did the work and was a constant source of comfort, never a problem. Lobo thought she was pretty near perfect, whereas Rico was always coming between him and Seth.

Like right now. Seth was watching her at the stove rather than paying attention to his son. Lobo felt angry that Seth was playing with him by not saying straight out whether he could go along to find the outlaws. Losing patience, he jeered, "Why don't you just tell me?"

Still, it took Seth a minute to drag his eyes off Rico. Then he gave Lobo an amused smile. "You want to go?"

Lobo was tempted to deny it just to spite him, but Esperanza was faster.

"No, Seth!" she protested. "He is too young."

Seth looked at Rico. "What do you think?"

"I agree with Esperanza."

"Joaquín?" Seth asked.

"I, also," he said softly.

Seth smiled. "Lemonade?"

Lobo held his breath.

"We might need someone to hold the horses," Lemonade suggested.

"Yeah, we might," Seth agreed, smiling at Lobo. "What do you think, Joaquín? If we leave him back with the horses, he should be up to the job, don't you think?"

"*Sí,*" Joaquín said in a flat tone. "He is up to the job but defenseless if shot at."

"What have you got to say, Lobo?" Seth asked.

"I want to go," he said.

"Why?"

Lobo ignored everyone else as he met his father's eyes. "I want to be a man."

Seth smiled. "Okay, you're in." He looked sharply at the women. "That's it," he said.

Esperanza turned her back and Rico shook her head.

"If supper ain't on this table in five minutes," he said, "we're going without."

"At least you can feed your son," Esperanza huffed, "before you keep him up 'til dawn for the second time in a row."

"We were home by midnight," Seth said.

"It was four-thirty," she answered, lifting the whiskey from the table. "I looked at my clock."

"Next time I'll come bang on your door so you be sure and not miss our return."

She smiled. "That would be thoughtful. Then I could sleep peacefully, knowing my family is safe at home."

Seth laughed and slapped her bottom as she moved away, then met Rico's eyes. "Well, hurry up," he said. "I don't think I can stand all this feminine censure much longer."

13

★

Esperanza eased the corral gate open as quietly as she could, then opened the stable door, too, with care for her silence. She moved through the familiar darkness to saddle Rico's palomino, knowing it was the only horse on the place she had any hope of controlling.

Carefully she led the palomino through the barn door and corral gate, leaving both open so she wouldn't risk waking Rico when she returned. Esperanza stepped into the stirrup and pulled her bulk into the saddle, sat gathering the reins a moment as she stared at the dark house, then slowly eased the mare out of the yard. Only when she was beyond the mountain did she urge the horse into a lope that cut distance fast.

She had never been to the tenderloin, but she followed the music of the tinny pianos through the quiet of the sleeping town. The street was illuminated with light spilling from the saloons, and Blue's was easy to spot. Its sign was the most brightly lit, its hitching rail crowded with the best quality horses, and the din escaping from inside carried the loudest laughter with its ribald music. Esperanza tied the palomino in a shadow and pulled her shawl close over her breasts as she stepped onto the boardwalk. Years had passed since she'd approached a saloon, and even back then she hadn't been alone. She stopped warily at the edge of the batwing doors and peered in.

The front room was the least congested. Only a few men were drinking sociably at the tables, a few more bellying up to the bar. The sweeping staircase separated them from the gaming room in back. The tables there were crowded, and beyond them, on a small stage against the far wall, an old man played a piano. A singer sat on top of it with her skirts drawn up above her knees. Remembering the lustful stares of men in saloons, Esperanza almost turned around and went home.

It had been easier when she was young and could laugh at the greedy hunger in men's eyes. She and all her sisters in the profession had known how men's insatiable need could provide a living, and they'd used that knowledge with a frivolous disregard for anyone's opinion of women who satisfied men for money. Now that she was older she couldn't ignore how the men's eyes demeaned those very women, naming them receptacles of pain.

Esperanza, however, was no longer one of those women. It was true Seth often came to her bed in the middle of the night, but her staying at the homestead wasn't dependent on servicing him. Sometimes she even felt he made love to her more because she wanted it than because he did. She was forty-four, after all, and Seth certainly had his choice if variety was his only motive. But Esperanza suspected he had taken on the duty of her satisfaction because he felt responsible for Ramon kicking her out. Seth would never tell her that, of course, just as she would never tell him she felt responsible for his having hanged Oriana.

In Esperanza's mind, people were responsible for what they didn't prevent as much as for what they caused to happen. And though she'd loved Seth from the beginning, she hadn't warned him of Oriana's existence or the poison Allister's letters had planted.

When Oriana used that weapon to destroy what was left of the men's friendship, she was able to do it because of Esperanza's silence.

Determined not to fail again, Esperanza resolutely entered the saloon. A few men glanced at her and looked away without even curiosity, though the barkeep studied her with suspicion. She smiled as she approached, then stood on tiptoe to lean across the bar and ask for Blue. The keep raised his eyes to the second floor. Esperanza followed his gaze and saw a burly, bearded man watching from the top of the stairs. The man nodded and walked deeper into the shadows of the balcony. He came back with Blue, who stood at the railing a moment before coming down and crossing the room toward her. He nodded at the keep, then took her elbow as he steered her toward the door.

"What are you doing here, Esperanza?" he asked softly.

"I came to see Lila Keats."

Blue stopped and studied her a moment. "Where's Seth?"

"Hunting," she answered with a smile.

"Is Joaquín with him?"

"Lobo, too. I don't like leaving Rico home alone, so I must hurry." She let her gaze drift across the women in the gaming room. "Is Lila Keats here?"

"Upstairs," Blue said.

Esperanza looked at him sharply. "Is hard for a manager to watch the floor from behind a closed door, no? Or perhaps you wish more that she watch the ceiling?"

Blue chuckled deep in his throat. "You know Seth wouldn't like you being here."

"If I wish to earn a few dollars telling fortunes, are you gonna make me take my business down the street?"

"No," he said reluctantly. "But I'll give you money if that's what you're after."

"It is more'n that," she admitted.

He nodded. "You best watch your step. It's hard to predict what Lila's gonna do. If you give her dire news, she may not jump the way you expect."

"I will only say what the cards reveal," Esperanza answered.

Still he hesitated. "Okay," he finally said. "I'll send her down, but as soon as you've read her fortune, Nib'll take you home."

"I got here on my own, and I can get home that way, too."

"I don't doubt it, but I'm still gonna send Nib with you."

She shrugged. "Suit yourself."

"I intend to. You stay down in this end of the room."

"How can I get business from here?"

He looked around at the solitary drinkers and the few clusters of men engrossed in conversation. "I'll send some of the girls over. How much you gonna charge?"

"One dollar." She smiled. "Is a fair price to know the future, don't you think?"

He studied her morosely. "I'll tell Gus to keep an eye on you. If you need help, he's there at the bar."

"Thanks," she said.

He nodded and walked away. She watched him take a girl aside and give her a silver dollar from his pocket. The girl stared apprehensively at Esperanza a moment, then warily walked toward her.

Lemonade led the way into the mountains, followed by Seth, Lobo, and Joaquín. They caught an old Indian trail heading southeast, then climbed an arroyo onto a plateau, traveled the ridge south and stopped on the edge of a natural bowl gouged out of the range. From a spot in the far end of the valley, the smoke of a campfire rose gray into the black sky.

"That'll most likely be them," Lemonade said softly.

"How many?" Seth asked.

"Was five last time."

"Was Bart Keats one of 'em?"

Lemonade nodded. "I was there when ya killed him. I saw him come in and was tryin' to vamoose 'fore he seen me, then when he called ya out I stopped and watched, knowin' it wasn't me he was after."

"Why'd you think it might be?"

Lemonade squirmed in his saddle, looked back at Lobo, then squinted unhappily at Seth. "Do I have to tell?"

"You're working for me now, Lemonade, and I need to know everything I can."

Again the kid twisted in his saddle to look at Lobo. "I din't do it to hurt ya, Lobo."

"What'd you do?" he cried, already angry that Lemonade had been there to see Seth shoot Bart Keats.

Lemonade looked at Seth again. "It was Bart told me to sell Lobo that horse."

"Why?"

"He promised he wouldn't harm Lobo none, but that he wanted ya caught with stolen prop'ty."

"Didn't you think hurting me would hurt Lobo?"

Lemonade's eyes flashed with fun. "I figgered ya was up to it, Mr. Strummar. 'Sides, I went into the Blue Rivers that night to tell ya 'bout these men."

"What were you gonna say?"

" 'Bout the horse and all, and how they was up to no good agin ya. I figgered maybe I could get a job from it."

"Why didn't you tell me before you sold Lobo the horse?"

"I din't have no proof! The horse was the ev'dence."

"Okay," Seth said. "You and me are going down to that camp and you're going in alone. I'll be close enough to hear everything said, so watch your mouth. I want to know when they're gonna move on the bank. Understand?"

Lemonade nodded.

"Mention of the bank doesn't surprise you, does it?"

"Nope. I heard 'em talkin' 'bout it."

Seth looked at Lobo. Disappointed in his son's gullibility, he blamed himself for not teaching the boy to be more suspicious of people's motives. But Seth also felt a begrudging admiration for Lobo's spunk, so he let that emotion shine through his smile. Giving Joaquín a playful wink, he said, "You men wait here. The fewer we are, the less noise we'll make." He turned back to Lemonade. "Let's go."

Lobo watched his father and Lemonade disappear in the forest, then listened until he couldn't hear their horses anymore. Joaquín swung off and sat on a boulder, his silhouette dark in the moonlight. Finally Lobo dropped down from his pinto, tied it near Joaquín's black, and found himself a boulder with some loose sand in front of it that he could kick at. The horses shuffled their bits and shifted their weight with a dull clump of hooves. Varmints scurried beneath the underbrush. An owl hooted from across the valley. Otherwise it was quiet.

Lobo felt hollow, knowing he'd let himself be used against Seth. Remembering how proud he'd felt while doing it, often wishing his father could see him win at craps or sneak in the back doors of saloons, only proved his total idiocy. He looked across at Joaquín and said, "I fucked up bad, didn't I?"

Joaquín smiled forgiveness. "It was a mistake," he admitted.

"Seth won't ever buy me a sixgun," Lobo said, kicking at the sand. "When he found out I'd been goin' into town, he said it proved I wasn't responsible enough for one. What's he gonna say now? That I proved I'll never be responsible?"

"Never is a long time," Joaquín said.

"Why do people hate him so much?"

Joaquín shrugged. "Usually they do not even know him, but hope to use his fame for their purpose."

"I wish he wasn't famous then," Lobo said, digging his heel into the soft sand.

"The past will fade and people won't remember so often,"

Joaquín said gently. "Even terrible mistakes can be forgiven in time."

"I wish Seth's brother hadn't died," Lobo muttered.

As always, Joaquín felt stabbed with sorrow at the thought of Jeremiah. "Why do you say that?"

"I'd like to ask him what Seth was like as a kid, maybe then I could see if I'm doin' all right."

"You're doing fine," Joaquín reassured him.

"How did Jeremiah die?"

"What did Seth tell you?"

"Not much," Lobo said, leaning forward with his elbows on his knees, as Seth often did. Lobo looked at Joaquín with eyes the same smoky gray as Seth's, except unlike the man's, the child's eyes were full of need. "Tell me, Joaquín."

Regretfully he said, "Jeremiah was lynched."

"By who?" Lobo gasped.

"Townspeople."

"Why?"

Joaquín looked into the dark valley. "Why some things happen is a mystery, Lobo. I have thought of it many times but never found an answer. I will tell you what I know. Jeremiah was eighteen. Seth was only three years older, but he had been riding with Allister a few years by then. They had stopped in Austin and were spotted by some Texas Rangers who tried to arrest them. In making their escape, a Ranger was killed and another man, too. The people of the city were angry that such a thing could happen on their streets. They went to the home of your grandfather looking for Seth. He wasn't there, but they were so caught in their rage, they hung Jeremiah instead."

"Had he done anything wrong?" Lobo whispered.

Joaquín shook his head.

"What did Seth do?"

Joaquín sighed. "He took his vengeance against the leader of the mob."

"Did he hang him?"

Joaquín nodded.

Lobo's eyes were fierce. "He deserved it."

"Perhaps."

"What would you have done?"

"I would have left him to God."

Lobo stomped away to peer over the edge of the precipice. He knew how badly Seth must have felt about Jeremiah's death because he knew how he'd feel if Seth died because of his mistake. Suddenly the world seemed a vicious place to Lobo, the games of self-defense his family played no longer fun but precautions of deadly earnest. He had been told that when a stranger rode into the yard he was to make for the nearest door, and once inside to stay away from the windows. Yet as dangerous as Arizona was, Texas was worse.

Texas wanted to hang Seth. The state still offered a thousand dollars to any bounty hunter who killed him. Lobo wasn't sure why. He knew his father had been an outlaw with Ben Allister, that they had robbed banks and Seth had saved enough of the loot that he didn't have to work. Lobo also knew Allister had been a rough desperado, and that he and Seth had killed men in the years they rode together. But all that had been before Lobo was born.

He tried to imagine what Jeremiah had looked like, then remembered he had a brother named Jeremiah, too. Lobo felt confused by his kin, they were so disconnected and spread out. He had lived his first years on a ranch in Colorado with his mother, Esther, and her husband, a man named Angel Madera who had given Lobo his name. Lobo had been happy there, but it had nagged at him that he was missing out on knowing his father. Then one night Seth walked into the house. As soon as their eyes met, Lobo knew they were together and nothing would ever change that again. He hadn't realized, however, what it would mean to leave Esther.

He still missed her, and even Angel. Once in a while he thought of their other son, who was his brother in the same way Elena was his sister. Now Seth had told him he had yet another brother living with kinfolk in Texas. Lobo had never met any of them: Seth's father, a man named Abraham Strummar who lived at 600 Grackle Street in Austin, and Seth's wife and son, Johanna and Jeremiah Strummar, a whole other family who got to carry Seth's name.

Lobo turned back around to Joaquín. "Did all that happen in the same house Seth's father lives in now?"

"I think so," Joaquín said.

"Wasn't Abraham home?"

"Yes, he was."

"Why didn't he stop 'em?"

Joaquín smiled at the four-foot tall Strummar demanding an answer to that question. "A mob is a frightening foe," he said. "It is the ugliest of human faces."

"So he was afraid!"

"Yes," Joaquín said sadly, "he was afraid."

"And let 'em do it!"

"He watched helplessly."

"Seth wouldn't have."

"No. He would have died saving Jeremiah."

Lobo walked back over and sat on his boulder, digging the heel of his boot into the sand until he hit rock. "If Seth had died savin' his brother, I wouldn't be here. Neither would my brother Jeremiah."

"That's true." Joaquín smiled. "And we wouldn't be sitting here talking."

Lobo laughed. "Where would you be?"

"México, probably."

"But you're an American now."

"The older I get, the less American I feel."

"Why?"

"Their hunger is insatiable."

"What's that mean?"

"You, for instance," Joaquín teased. "You have a horse as good as mine and dress as well as Seth, two women fussing over you like mother hens, a beautiful baby sister and a ranch of a thousand acres to roam freely, yet you sneak into town and gamble for more."

"I don't do it to get stuff but to have fun," Lobo argued.

"When I was young, getting stuff was all we did because we never had enough, and having fun was an accident that happened when we felt so bad we didn't care anymore. Many of the boys you think you are playing with are working, as I was at your age."

"Hangin' out in alleys ain't the same as a job," Lobo protested.

"It is if you're there to earn your supper," Joaquín said.

Lobo looked into the darkness where his father and friend had disappeared. "Lemonade's like that. Some days he doesn't eat at all."

"You should try it some time," Joaquín suggested. "Then you would understand what drives half the world."

"Do you think Lemonade was tellin' the truth when he said he didn't think I'd be hurt?"

"Yes," Joaquín answered without hesitation.

"What makes you think so?"

"He wouldn't lie to Seth."

Lobo laughed. "I can't. Can you?"

"No," Joaquín said with a smile.

Esperanza watched Lila Keats walk down the stairs sticking pins back into her coiffure. Even from that distance, Esperanza could see how perfectly the green of her dress matched the hue of her eyes, a color Esperanza distrusted. When Lila came close and stood above the table, her smile seemed as hypocritical as the cool aspect of her gaze. "Are you Esperanza?" she asked.

Esperanza nodded.

"Have you come to tell my fortune?"

"If you wish it, señora."

"And if I don't, you would leave feeling content with your night's work?"

"A few moments ago, I would have said yes," she replied, suppressing a shiver at the chill in the woman's eyes.

"But no longer?"

Esperanza shook her head. Gathering her shawl, she rose to her feet and started for the door.

"Wait!" Lila commanded. When Esperanza reluctantly turned back to face her, Lila mocked, "Don't you wish to tell my fortune?"

Again, Esperanza shook her head.

"Come, come," Lila scolded. "Isn't that why you're here?"

"I came in the hope of making money," Esperanza answered, "but some visions are not worth the price."

"Not worth five dollars in gold?"

"I charge only one."

"I will pay you five."

"You will not influence the cards with generosity."

Lila shrugged.

"Are you certain," Esperanza asked, "that you wish to see the future?"

"Do you think my fortune so unsavory?"

Esperanza nodded.

The green eyes darkened. "Come, vieja. Stop trying to frighten me and show me the truth if you can."

"The cards will reveal it."

"Well, let's have it then," she said, yanking a chair away from the table and sitting down.

Slowly Esperanza returned to sit in the facing chair. She pulled the deck of cards from her pocket, unwrapped them from their silk scarf and laid them on the table. "Shuffle them with a pure heart, señora, and divide the deck in two."

Lila expertly shuffled and cut the deck. Esperanza rejoined it with the top on the bottom, closed her eyes a moment, then dealt four cards face up in the form of a cross. She studied the message a long moment before raising her gaze to meet the green eyes watching so intently.

"Well?" Lila demanded.

Esperanza touched the king of swords. "This man behind you is cruel and capable of great malice. You should not oppose him."

Lila laughed. "His name isn't Seth Strummar, by any chance?"

"The cards do not share names," Esperanza answered, "but I feel this man is dead."

Lila paled, then laughed again. "What harm can he do me then?"

"Sometimes behind you does not mean his influence is past, but that he is riding hard to overtake you."

"How can he do that if he's dead?"

Esperanza shrugged, then touched the five of cups. "This card covering you signifies loss. And because this card," she touched the nine of wands, "is before you, the loss will be great. I feel the chill of the grave, so death is close. Perhaps it is not yours but the king's. For you I see defeat through deception."

Lila hugged herself as if she, too, felt the chill. "And the last card?"

"Reveals the aspect of what is coming," Esperanza said. "The Tower signifies misery, and again, deception. You would be wise to watch your tongue in the days ahead. All of these influences come from inside you and can still be avoided."

Lila stared at her for a long moment then asked coldly, "Did Seth tell you what to say?"

Esperanza shook her head. "I never lie about the cards, señora. Your best hope is to carry the weight of what is yours. Only then can you reclaim justice."

Lila smiled. "Justice can still be mine?"

"If you resist treachery."

"If I do, then how would you read these cards?"

Esperanza studied the message again. "If you conduct yourself with honor, the king will not overtake you but will be left behind where he belongs. Your joy will be clouded but only for a time, then the loss will be of your sorrow."

"And all I have to do is conduct myself with honor?"

Esperanza nodded.

"Since vengeance is an honorable endeavor," Lila said smugly, "it seems my future is rather bright after all."

"The indications are grim, *señora,*" Esperanza warned. "Be cautious."

"Thank you," Lila said. She stood up and smacked a five-dollar coin on the table. "Tell Seth his trick didn't work."

Esperanza watched her in silence.

"You can tell him something else, too," Lila gloated. "Tell him I came to return the favor he did me years ago. I'm sure he'll understand what I'm talking about."

"He does not remember you," Esperanza said.

"You expect me to believe that?" she jeered, then whirled and walked away.

After watching her climb the stairs without looking back, Esperanza reached to the top of the deck and turned up the next card, the signifier if the seeker asked further questions. It was the Beast, predicting that Lila Keats would not outwit death. Esperanza sighed deeply, then left the gold coin glimmering on the table and walked into the darkness where Rico's horse stood tied to the rail. She had barely pulled her weight into the saddle when Nib came through the door and caught hold of her reins.

"I've been told to see you home safe, Señora Ochoa," the gunman said. "You wouldn't want me to fail my boss, would you?"

She shook her head with a smile, thinking only the grace of Seth's protection allowed an old whore to be treated with such respect.

Seth tied his sorrel a safe distance away from the glow of the campfire and left his spurs in his saddlebags, then rode behind Lemonade the rest of the way. When they could see the men in the circle of light, Seth slid down quietly and laid his hand on Lemonade's leg, meeting the kid's eyes with warning that it was a rough game they were commencing. Lemonade smiled with childish confidence, then walked his horse slowly forward, calling out, "Howdy, Mr. Norris!"

"Lemonade, is it?" a gruff voice asked as a short, husky man stood up.

Seth could see his face plain but didn't recognize him.

"What'cha doin' here?" Norris asked.

"Jus' got lonely," the kid answered. "Mightn't I have some coffee?"

"Reckon." Norris studied the kid as he tied his horse to a tree and approached. "Got yourself new duds."

Lemonade grinned, hunkering down by the fire. "Decided I was comin' up in the world so I best look like it."

"You still ain't got a gun," Joe Tyler snickered from where he lay in his blankets.

"I'm workin' on it," Lemonade said, filling a cup with coffee.

Seth could smell it from where he was standing behind a tree. He studied the men in the erratic light from the fire: the Tyler brothers he'd met in Tombstone, Norris, and another man half-shadowed in his blankets. Seth didn't recognize any of them from his past but knew their breed.

"How much longer ya gonna be around?" Lemonade asked.

"What's it to you?" Norris answered. He still hadn't sat down, was still watching the kid warily.

Lemonade shrugged. "Thought I might ride along when ya go."

Norris snorted. "Come back in ten years and maybe I'll consider it, if you're still alive."

"If *you're* still alive," the man in the shadows said.

Norris glared at him. "You're goin' the way of Bart, you know that?"

"Uh-uh," he answered. "I ain't so stupid as to go against Strummar. Seems to me you're the one doing that." He stood up and came forward to squat by the fire and pour himself a cup of coffee, then sipped at it without looking up, his face hidden by his hat.

"I ain't even gonna see him," Norris said.

"You got that right," the man said, blowing noisily on his coffee, " 'cause you'll be dead 'fore it happens." He looked up with a grin, revealing a long, narrow face beneath the brim of his hat. He was a stranger to Seth.

"When you agreed to come on this job," Norris said, "you didn't ask for a list of depositors."

The man smiled coldly. "Guess I'll have to in the future."

"Does that mean you want out?" Norris asked.

"Guess it does," the man answered. "I'll mosey now, if it's all the same to you."

"It ain't," Norris said. "We already lost one man. We can't pull it off bein' two short."

The man shrugged. "I'm cutting out."

"The hell you are!" Norris bellowed. "You make a move, Webster, and I'll blow you to kingdom come."

Webster stared at him a long moment, then chuckled. "Seems to me Bart already did that to our chances. Or maybe I should say Strummar blew 'em to hell with Bart."

"I saw it," Lemonade said proudly.

"You did?" Jim Tyler asked with interest. "How'd Bart look?"

"At first he jus' looked mad," Lemonade said, staring into the fire as he remembered. "Then he looked kinda sick."

Tyler snickered. "Lead in your heart's apt to make anybody sick."

"How'd Strummar look?" Norris asked.

"Bored," Lemonade said.

Webster and Norris laughed, but Joe Tyler growled, "That's how he looked in Charleston, like he was tired of us even though he'd never seen us before."

Lemonade studied Joe thoughtfully, then said, "Maybe he is."

Seth smiled, thinking Lemonade was a smart kid.

"You know," Webster said in a conversational tone, "I heard J. B. Ayres is an undercover agent for Wells Fargo."

The fire crackled in the silence.

"Where'd you hear that?" Jim Tyler finally asked.

"Around." Webster shrugged. "You ever hear anything like that, Lemonade?"

He shook his head. "I don't believe it, neither."

"Why not?"

" 'Cause when they dragged that man Lafferty outta his place and lynched him, Ayres stood there with a shotgun and watched it happen. Any kinda lawman would've stopped it."

"No man can stop a mob," Norris scoffed.

"I'd try," Lemonade said. "If it was mine to do, I would."

"You ain't even got a gun!" Joe hooted. "How you gonna help us in Tejoe?"

"When're ya goin'?" Lemonade asked.

"We don't know," Webster said with a mocking glance at Norris. "We're waiting to hear from the boss lady."

"But we gotta be ready," Joe taunted. "And you ain't, are you?"

Lemonade shook his head, then stood up as he looked at Norris. "If I get me a gun, can I ride with ya?"

"Come back when you got one and ask again," Norris said.

All the men watched Lemonade mount his horse and ride into the dark. Seth moved quietly to intercept the kid. They smiled at each other when they came together again, but didn't speak until after Seth had retrieved his sorrel and they were back with Joaquín and Lobo, who had heard them coming and were already mounted.

"What happened?" Lobo asked.

"Not much," Seth said. He met Joaquín's eyes and communicated without words that they'd discuss it later, then reached across and slapped Lemonade on the back. "You handled 'em real smooth, kid."

"Thanks," he said, smiling proudly at Lobo, who didn't smile back.

"Let's go home," Seth said. Turning his horse, he kicked it into a fast trot down the mountain.

14

★

When the men returned, all the horses were in their stalls and the homestead slumbered peacefully. Seth told Lemonade he could sleep in the loft, then asked Joaquín to come to the house. Lobo went to bed, and while Seth checked on Rico, Joaquín heated the coffee left from supper.

Coming back into the kitchen just after Joaquín had filled the cups, Seth took a bottle of whiskey from the hutch and joined him at the table. "They're waiting for word from Lila," Seth said, adding whiskey to his coffee. He offered the bottle to Joaquín, who shook his head.

"Fellow named Webster," Seth continued, "tried to get out of it but Norris backed him down. Apparently he's the ramrod. The other two are the Tyler brothers we met in Charleston." He stopped and drank half his coffee, refilled the cup with whiskey, and took another sip.

"What will you do now?" Joaquín asked.

Seth smiled. "I'd like to run Lila out of town but it doesn't seem neighborly to push her off on someone else."

"What other choice do we have?"

"Slater can arrest her and send her to prison." He drained his cup, then asked with sarcasm, "Ain't that the civilized thing to do?"

"But she hasn't acted yet, so he must wait for her to rob the bank and catch her while she's doing it."

"She won't likely be there," Seth said, refilling his cup from the bottle. "Those clowns up on the mountain are gonna be the ones who're caught."

"If they are taken alive, they will testify against her."

"We'll still have to nab her before it comes down to make sure she doesn't get away."

"A few minutes, perhaps," Joaquín agreed.

Seth smiled playfully. "Let's take it a step closer and make it happen."

"What do you mean?"

"Let's visit Lila and convince her to give the word. When they walk in the door, the sheriff'll be there to welcome 'em." He chuckled at his cleverness. "It's perfect."

"Maybe too perfect," Joaquín said. "There is more to her plot than robbing the bank. You're forgetting they put Lobo on a stolen horse. When he wasn't riding it to town, it was a trap waiting to be sprung on your land. And don't forget Melinda's suspicion of a frame-up. If you are with Lila when she gives the word, it will be difficult to prove you weren't in on it. She is after more than money, Seth."

"Smells like vengeance, doesn't it?"

Joaquín nodded.

"It would explain why Bart challenged me. Maybe he didn't intend to but just went to see Lila, then saw me and couldn't stop himself."

Softly Joaquín said, "It seems you would remember people you had touched so deeply."

Seth chuckled with affection. "If you were a priest, Joaquín, I'd turn Catholic just to receive your absolutions. Anybody who can call the things I did 'touching people deeply' has a silver tongue, that's for damn sure."

"Maybe if we knew Lila's maiden name," Joaquín said, watching Seth sip more whiskey.

"A woman like her uses a dozen names."

"I asked Melinda to find out."

"I doubt if Lila let anything slip." Seth thoughtfully sipped at the whiskey until his cup was empty again. "I'm gonna keep Lobo home tomorrow. Think I'll keep Lemonade here, too. I may need him again."

"I don't think he's a good influence on Lobo."

Seth laughed bitterly. "Neither am I."

He reached for the bottle, but Joaquín took hold of it first. "It is never wise to get drunk," he said gently. "You told me that in El Paso."

Anger flared in Seth's eyes, then was quickly replaced with the familiar glint of self-mockery that made Joaquín ache for his friend. Seth smiled and stood up. "You're right. See you in the morning." He touched Joaquín's shoulder on his way out of the room.

Joaquín smiled as he listened to Seth open and close the bedroom door, then he blew out the lamp and walked across the yard to the stable. He intended to saddle Rico's palomino and let his black rest, but when he went to smooth the blanket on, he discovered the mare's back was wet with sweat. He puzzled over that a moment, then saddled his black after all.

In the dark bedroom, Seth sensed Rico was asleep and moved quietly to undress. As he slid under the covers, she turned unconsciously to take him in her arms, and the warmth of her body aroused him. He slid his hand beneath her nightgown, across the rise of her hip to nestle in the crook of her waist, then felt her kiss on his cheek. Smiling that she never refused him, he kissed her with gratitude, and also with guilt that he didn't do right by her love. He used the girls in Blue's saloon at will, and when his hunger wasn't strong enough that he felt inclined to participate, he sometimes watched another man use the girl. In Seth's mind all that was disconnected from Rico, but he knew she didn't see it that way. Breaking their embrace, he lay back alone.

"What is it, Seth?" she whispered.

He sorted through his mind for an approach to what he wanted to say. Finally he asked, "Why is it important to you that I be faithful?"

She took a long moment to answer. "I don't like to think of you with other women," she said softly.

"What difference does it make? It's got nothing to do with us."

"Unless you find one you prefer over me."

"That ain't gonna happen."

"It happened to Johanna."

"Johanna was a child I had no right to marry," he retorted with impatience. "What she and I shared wasn't like what you and I have."

"What *do* we have, Seth?" she asked carefully.

"If you don't know, my saying it won't make much difference."

"It will to me."

He rolled onto his belly and hid his face in his folded arms as he thought back over his life, remembering the loneliness he'd felt when whores were his only feminine companions. He turned his head to look at Rico. "A man ain't complete without the love of a woman, and you love me for what I am, not my reputation or even my money. You have your own money, and you're not half-bad with a gun either." He chuckled. "Despite all your carrying on, you don't need me. I guess that's why your wanting me around means so much."

Knowing what she was risking, she said, "That's not true, Seth. I do need you."

"You say that," he scoffed, "and you may even believe it, but it ain't true."

She hesitated, then asked, "You know what I did when you left me before?"

"No," he said, feeling bad that he'd never thought about it.

"I tried to kill myself," she said.

"Say that again," he said, sure he'd misheard her.

"I lied about the scars on my wrists. I did it to myself, because I couldn't face life without you."

He jerked out of bed and backed away until he hit the door. "I can't carry that, Rico."

She sat up, knowing they had to have it clear between them or everything that followed would be a lie. "I'm not saying I'd do it again," she explained. "I have Elena now, and soon another child who'll need me. I'm just saying that without you there would be an emptiness in my life no one else could fill."

"Why did you lie to me?"

"Because when you first asked about the scars, you would've left if I'd told you the truth."

"I've never lied to *you.*"

"Not even about Lila Keats?"

"Jesus Christ!" he exploded. "What's she got to do with anything?"

"Melinda told me you had your way with her."

"I unbuttoned her dress and played with her body to scare her. If that's having my way, I guess I did, but there wasn't any pleasure in it."

"That's not a pretty picture, Seth," she whispered.

"That's why I didn't take you along. All of life ain't pretty."

"No. Some of it's sordid."

"Like what I did with Lila Keats?"

"I don't care about that."

"What then?"

"Melinda implied things," Rico said gently, "about you and Allister. She said they were the same with you and Joaquín."

"What kinda things?"

She struggled to find the words. "Even saying it sounds ugly."

"What are you trying to say, Rico?"

"I did it with Melinda," she said, hoping to help him.

He was silent as her meaning came clear, then he said, "I never fucked Allister and I've never fucked Joaquín. Is that what you want to know?"

"Don't be angry, Seth. It hadn't occurred to me until Melinda brought it up."

"Was kind of her," he muttered. "And I'm glad to learn you have so much faith in me."

"Please, Seth. It's just that I felt like a fool when she told me about Esperanza. I thought maybe I was blind about this too."

"Don't you trust your own judgment more'n that?"

"It gets confusing when half the time I have to deny what my senses tell me."

"Like what?"

"Smelling perfume on your clothes when you come home from Blue's."

He shrugged. "A lot of women work there."

"You must get pretty close to pick up their perfume."

"They're just whores, Rico. There's no goodness in what I do with them."

"Why do you want it then?"

If he had been dressed he would have left rather than answer that question. But he was naked standing against the door, and it made him hesitate long enough to appreciate her courage. Finally he said, "Old habits, I guess."

"Habits you learned from Allister?"

"Everybody gives him a lot of credit for who I am."

"Don't you?"

"Allister's dead."

"Then let him go," she pleaded. "Don't pass onto your son the lessons he gave you." When Seth was silent, she asked, "Don't you think Lobo knows what happens in Blue's saloon?"

"How could he?"

"He spends a lot of time trying to figure out why you're different from other fathers. It was Allister who made you different."

"Bullshit!"

"Is it? If you'd never met him, your first killing would've been forgiven. You would never have robbed those banks or killed all those men. And something else: your brother would still be alive."

"You think that was Allister's fault?"

"Yes," she said. "Whose fault do you think it was?"

"Mine. I should've stopped that mob."

"No one can stop a mob, Seth."

"I could've. Well, maybe not then. I wasn't smart enough then, but I could stop 'em now."

"It isn't happening now," she said sadly.

"No," he admitted. "Nothing's happening anymore. I'm just an old man who only fights with his wife."

"You're considerably more than that." She smiled, then sighed. "You've often said you'd marry me if you could. Is that the truth?"

"Yeah."

"Marriage is being true to each other. Can you give me that?"

"What, exactly?"

"I want you to stop hurting yourself by abusing the women at Blue's."

He frowned. "Abusing them? Well, maybe," he conceded. "But if I stay away from 'em, what am I gonna do with my grief, Rico?"

"Give it to me," she answered. "I can handle the part that's truly yours. Why don't we let the rest die of neglect?"

"You think it will?"

"Yes," she said.

Hungrily he approached the bed, then stood looking down at

her. "All right. I give my word not to touch another woman for carnal pleasure. Will that satisfy you?"

"If you also give your word not to watch other men do it."

He was surprised he had assumed her ignorance of that, given their history. He chuckled, sliding under the covers to hold her again. "You continue to amaze me," he murmured into her hair.

"And please you?" she whispered.

He answered her with a kiss, hoping she wouldn't notice he hadn't given his word on the second part of her request. Rico did notice, but for the time being she felt content with her partial victory.

La Casa Amarilla was dark as Joaquín tied his horse in the shadow of a cottonwood a short distance away. He walked slowly toward the rooming house, suspecting he was there as much to fulfill a need of his own as to help Seth. When he had jimmied the locks between them, Melinda greeted him with a smile that said she'd been waiting, and he felt pleased with the thought.

He crossed the room lit only by starlight and sat on the edge of her bed. "Buenas noches," he said, amused with himself for falling back on his native tongue.

"Buenas noches," she repeated, then laughed softly. "You're quiet as a cat, Joaquín. I didn't hear you until you were outside my door."

"To move in silence is a useful skill," he answered modestly. "And not so difficult if I remember to take off my spurs."

She laughed again. "Blue came to see me today. He offered me a job."

"Did you accept it?"

"Yes," she whispered, sitting up and leaning close to kiss his cheek. "Thank you, Joaquín. He told me it was your idea."

He shrugged. "We discussed it together, the three of us."

"Ummm," she said, knowing the truth. "When I said I hadn't

enough frocks, he gave me an advance on my salary so I could order some from the dressmaker. Wasn't that generous?"

"Yes," he said. "Have you placed your order?

"I gave the woman a small amount to begin. Tomorrow I'll put the rest in the bank." She giggled. "I'll have a bank account, Joaquín, for the first time in my life." She slid closer and put her arms around him. "I'd like to thank you for what you've done."

He shrugged out of her embrace and moved a scant distance away. "Did you find out any more about Lila Keats?"

"Blue told me she was dangerous and he thought it best I stay away from her."

"So you haven't seen her since we talked last?"

Melinda shook her head. "I spent most of today at the dressmaker's choosin' patterns and material. I had a lot of fun, Joaquín," she cooed, sidling up close again. "Wait 'til you see my gowns, I'm gonna be so beautiful."

"You don't need fancy dresses for that." He gave her a smile, then said, "I should go now."

"Don't hurry away," she said, sliding onto the floor in front of him and reaching to unbuckle his gunbelt. "Let me thank you first."

"No," he said, catching her hands.

"Why?"

"I don't use women that way."

"Not even the girls in Blue's saloon?"

He shook his head.

"Why not?" she asked, astonished.

"I feel sorry for them."

She climbed onto his lap, pushing him back to lie beneath her. "Do you feel sorry for me?"

"No," he said, "but I don't want to love you either."

She pulled her nightgown off over her head so she was naked on top of him. "You just now said I don't need fancy dresses to be pretty," she teased.

Her breasts were lovely in the starlight, but he said, "For over a year we slept a short distance apart and you never wanted me."

She sighed, resting her weight on his hips as she unbuttoned his shirt then ran her cool palms over his chest. "I do now, Joaquín."

He knew he should resist but the perfume of her hair overpowered his resolve. When she unbuckled his gunbelt, he let her pull it out from under him, then listened to its quiet thud on the floor. Taking hold of her waist, he lifted her off and nestled her in the blankets, kissing her mouth as he dipped his fingers inside to discover she was wet.

She laughed deep in her throat and whispered, "Now that's something Seth would do."

Joaquín retreated to the far side of the bed.

"Jesus, I'm sorry," she moaned. "I said the wrong thing again. Forgive me, Joaquín."

"Why did you say it?" he asked, his desire gone.

She shrugged. "It just slipped out."

"It wasn't an accident," he said. "It has already happened twice. The last time I left, and this time I will, too. But first I want to know what you expect when you say something like that."

"I want to make you mad."

"Why?"

"It's how you get started in this game. You know, things get a little rough, then the sweetness comes." She stared at him a moment. "You've never hit a woman, have you?"

"Not for fun," he said.

She laughed. "Well, that's why I have to say it, Joaquín. When I mention Seth, I'm tryin' to make you mad enough to hit me. But you always get up and leave instead, just like you're doin' now."

He stood by the bed buttoning his shirt.

"Don't leave," she pleaded. "I don't want to be alone."

"I have to go home."

"Because Seth needs you?" she asked with sarcasm.

"Yes," he said.

"Will you always choose him over a woman?" she taunted.

Joaquín walked around the bed, buckled on his gunbelt, then raised his eyes to hers. "Seth and I shared a woman once. Her name was Rosalinda. She was like you in more than her name, though, because she also wanted men to hurt her, and she was good at making it happen. I do not think you want to be like her, Melinda. Or perhaps it's that you are not yet like her, but you are on the same road. Do you know what happened to Rosalinda?"

She shook her head.

"She asked to be hurt one time too many and Seth killed her." Joaquín settled his hat low above his eyes. "You should learn to seek love from men, and to accept it when you find it." Quietly he walked to the door, slipped out and was gone.

Melinda stared bleakly at the emptiness he'd left behind. But as she listened to the hoofbeats of his horse diminish in the distance, she thought he'd be back another night. If not, the next time he came into Blue's she would tease him until he laughed in the old way again. She knew how to please men, and he was just one more.

Across the hall, Lila Keats heard a creak on the stairs and then a few moments later a horse loping away. She rolled over and shook Rafe's shoulders. "Wake up," she hissed. "You idiot, someone's been here."

Sheriff Slater stood up and pulled on his pants, then walked over to the window as he buttoned them. Studying the dark desert, he said, "I don't see anybody."

"He's gone now." She started picking his clothes off the floor and throwing them at him. "You should be, too."

He turned around in time to catch the crumpled wad of his shirt and vest. "I'm going," he said. "You can stop throwing my stuff."

She sat down on the bed and glared at him.

When he looked down to button his vest, he saw the silver star of his badge. "Seth's onto you, Lila," Rafe said, "so if your boys try for the bank, you best be gone."

"What do you mean 'try for'? Who's gonna stop us?"

"I am."

"Since when?"

"I'm telling you, Lila. Bart spoiled the pudding when he called Seth out."

"Good old Bart," she muttered. "It was an appropriate legacy, don't you think?"

"Maybe it was," he said, sitting on her bed while he pulled on his boots. "Maybe he was telling you to walk the straight and narrow for a change."

"That's something he never tried," she retorted.

"Maybe he regretted it. And think about this, Lila." He turned to face her across the rumpled sheets. "Bart didn't have a chance in hell against Seth and knew it. That means he chose to die right in front of you. Don't you think there was a message in that?"

She shrugged. "I didn't even know it was him 'til it was over."

"Yeah, well, that was sort of Bart's luck all the way through, wasn't it." He stood up and lifted his gunbelt off the floor then buckled it on, watching her.

"Seth made him crawl," she spit out. "That's what ruined Bart."

"Seth says he never met the man."

"He's lying!" she shouted.

"Take it easy," Rafe said. "You want to wake the whole house?"

"He remembers me," she whispered hoarsely. "And he remembered Bart, too. He couldn't forget us after what he'd done."

"What'd he do?" Rafe asked, looking around for his hat. He found it but didn't put it on.

She glared as if she hated him as much as the man she was thinking about. Finally she said, "Made him eat shit. The human kind."

Rafe swallowed hard.

"Ben Allister is the one who crammed it down his throat," she said, "but Seth Strummar told Allister to do it."

"What'd Bart do to Seth?"

"Nothing! He talked to a federale, just passing the time of day, that's all. Seth said it looked like Bart didn't know the difference between a desperado and a dog so he made him eat shit, saying that's how dogs learn to recognize their own kind."

Rafe sniffed loudly as if a sudden stench pinched his nose. "Allister's been dead almost ten years, Lila. When did all this happen?"

"What difference does that make? You know what Seth did afterwards? He took me to his room and played with me all night. Now he says he can't remember us!"

"Who'd want to remember something like that?" Rafe muttered. "You'd be better off forgetting it, too. Anyway, Seth ain't the man he was, and Bart ended his part Saturday night. I can't see what's it got to do with you."

"He raped me!" she hissed. "The other morning he lay with me on this very bed and I thought he was going to do it again. I think he would have if Joaquín hadn't been with him."

"He didn't though, that's what counts. Anyway, I can't see that a woman living with outlaws has much claim to virtue. I seem to remember you sashaying between beds freely enough."

"I took my pleasure," she said. "Bart wasn't any good after what happened. If I hadn't been there, he might've gotten over it. But I begged Seth to stop and all that did was increase Bart's humiliation. As if that wasn't enough, Allister made Bart watch Seth drag me into his room. They destroyed my husband as surely as if they'd killed him. Seth did kill him! Bart was a fool to challenge Seth, though, I admit that. We came here for the money and Bart thought he could let the other slide, but I guess when he saw Seth again he couldn't. I don't care about that. I haven't cared for Bart in years, but I'll never stop hating Seth Strummar. I'm going through with our plan and I'm gonna live soft the rest of my life on his money."

"Aren't you forgetting your partners? There ain't enough in that bank to set you all up."

"They're just making wages, whatever they think is going on."

"You're in over your head, Lila. Soon as you make your move, I'll arrest you." He smiled. "But I promise to visit you at night long as you're in my custody."

"You'll be in jail too," she threatened.

He shook his head. "A man can't be arrested for loose talk, only for what he does." He put his hat on. "That's why you're still free: it goes for women, too." He opened the door, looking back over his shoulder. "My advice is to get out of Tejoe while you still can."

By the time he reached his office, Rafe Slater was feeling melancholy. He lit the lantern at its lowest wick and poured himself a drink, then put his feet on his desk and stared down the dark corridor of empty cells. He knew it was a fine line which side of those bars he was on, as well as for Seth, Blue Rivers, and even Joaquín. Rafe had inherited wanted posters on all three of them when he took the job. The posters were old and the money probably wasn't there anymore, except for the thousand-dollar bounty against Seth. That was for killing a Ranger and Texas wasn't likely to drop it soon, but Texas Rangers weren't real popular in Arizona.

Rafe remembered the scene when he'd told J. J. Clancy that Seth Strummar expected the bank to be robbed. "What's he doing about it?" the banker had demanded angrily.

"He told his sheriff," Rafe answered. "And I'm passing it along so maybe you can take precautions."

"He stands to lose as much as the rest of us, more than most," Clancy bristled indignantly. "Why doesn't he take precautions?"

"I don't guess he figures it's his job," Rafe said.

"But he has the experience," Clancy argued.

"What d'ya expect him to do? Stand around the lobby with a rifle?"

"It would certainly discourage thieves."

"I don't think that's what Seth wants to do with his life. He could keep his money at home if he did."

"So what are you doing about it?" Clancy barked.

"Not much I can 'til something happens. Being as I don't have the budget for a deputy, I thought you might want to put on a private guard."

The banker frowned. "For how long?"

"Hard to tell." Rafe shrugged. "I'd be careful picking him, though. Don't hire a stranger."

"Do you think I'm an imbecile?" Clancy shouted.

"No, sir," Rafe said, swallowing his bile at the man's tone. "Just trying to help out."

"Trying and doing aren't the same, though, are they?" Clancy asked with a sneer.

Rafe had pounded his boot heels in anger all the way back to the tenderloin. Blue bought him a drink and let him run on about the arrogance of the rich longer than he deserved, then Lila came down and he watched her falling all over Blue until he couldn't stand it anymore. He'd returned to his office and gotten drunk alone, staring at the empty cells as he was doing now.

Tonight the prospect was too melancholy, and finally he walked outside and began his midnight rounds. As he passed the Protestant rectory, he saw a light in the parlor. On impulse, Rafe stopped and knocked on the door.

Homer Holcroft opened it fully dressed. "What a pleasant surprise, Rafe." Homer smiled, opening the door wider. "Won't you come in for a nightcap?"

"Thanks," Rafe said, then followed the pastor into his study, accepted a drink, and carried it over to the window.

He stared out in silence so long that Homer finally said from behind him, "You're pensive tonight. Is something bothering you, Rafe?"

He turned around and studied the minister. Deciding to take a cautious tack, Rafe said, "I was surprised to see you at Seth Strummar's the other day."

Homer chuckled. "I was returning from visiting the elder Mrs. Nickles when I encountered Joaquín on the road. He invited me home for supper."

"Didn't know you knew him."

"It was the first occasion I'd had to talk with him. I liked him, though. As I did Mr. Strummar."

Rafe nodded. "I like 'em too. You know who Lila Keats is?"

"The widow of the man killed in the Blue Rivers Saloon?"

"Yeah. She came here to take vengeance on Seth."

"For what?" Homer asked softly.

"Something that happened a long time ago, when he was still riding on the wrong side of the law. Bart Keats was, too, and according to Lila, they had a falling out which was bad enough that it's festered all this time. At least for them. Seth claims he can't remember either one of 'em."

"What was it he did?"

"That don't matter. Thing of it is, I know something's gonna happen but legally I can't act 'til it does. Makes me feel helpless just waiting for it to come around."

"Have you warned Seth?"

"He warned me."

Homer frowned thoughtfully then asked, "Is it going to be bad for the town?"

"Yeah, if Lila's friends succeed."

"Is there anything I can do?"

"Can't think of it if there is," Rafe answered with a smile, then turned around and stared into the darkness again. After a long moment he said softly, almost as if he wished the minister wouldn't hear, "It's my fault it's happening."

Homer waited a moment before asking, "How is it your fault?"

Rafe sighed and turned to face him again. "Remember six months ago when I took a holiday?"

"You visited your family," Homer said.

"My family's dead. I just used that as an excuse to get away for a bit. Rode halfway across New Mexico to El Paso, ran into Lila there, Lila and Bart."

"You knew them before?" he asked cautiously.

Rafe nodded. "You see, Homer, there was a time when I was an outlaw too. Oh, I never had Seth Strummar's class but I broke the law more'n once. Back in those days I was in love with Lila, only she called herself Esmeralda then. When I saw her in El Paso I had a lot of those old feelings, and I figured she'd be tickled to learn I was wearing a badge now, so I told her that, her and Bart. She was tickled all right, especially when I told 'em Seth Strummar was living right outside our town. 'Cause Bart, see, he had this notion Seth had saved all the loot he stole with Allister, and Lila came up with the idea that Seth had it on deposit here in Tejoe." He shrugged. "I didn't persuade 'em otherwise. I let 'em think what they wanted, and even that I'd help 'em if I could. I was just talking through the wine, you know how it is. I never expected 'em to show up." He laughed grimly. "But they did."

"It seems to me," Homer said slowly, "if you know for a fact they're about to rob the bank, you could arrest them."

"Who? Lila? You think anyone would believe it? And I haven't seen hide nor hair of her partners. I told Clancy my suspicions and he hired Bob Tice to stand around the lobby with a rifle, but Bob's about the worst shot in town." He sighed deeply. "Tell you the truth, I feel like taking another holiday, this one permanent, head west to California and forget I ever took an oath to uphold the law. I asked Seth and Joaquín and Blue Rivers if they'd let me deputize 'em but they all refused, said they weren't lawmen. Well, I don't feel like one either. I feel like a damn fool waiting to get caught in his own trap, and it ain't a good feeling."

"No," Homer agreed. "When do you think Mrs. Keats is going to act?"

Rafe shrugged. "It's bound to be soon. Blue fired her today so she hasn't any excuse to stick around. Not that she needs one. Like

I said at the inquest, until a person breaks the law they're free to live where they please." He looked into his empty glass, then smiled wryly at his friend. "Well, I'll go finish my rounds. Thanks for listening, Homer. I feel a mite better, and maybe something'll open up so I can see what I should do."

Homer smiled. "Solutions often present themselves at the oddest moments. I'm sure when the time comes, you'll do what's right."

Holcroft walked the sheriff to the door and tried to send him on his way with an encouraging smile. But Homer's smile disappeared as soon as he was alone. As he poured himself another drink, he admitted ruefully that he wasn't much different from Lila Keats since he, too, wanted to get his hands on Seth Strummar's money. That he intended to use it for the good of others was in his favor but didn't change the fact that he was in competition with thieves to obtain the use of funds already stolen. He remembered Joaquín saying his purpose in life was to protect Seth from himself. Assuming that included plots of revenge stemming from the outlaw's past, Homer decided to seek the Mexican's advice.

Early the next morning, Holcroft drove his buggy to the turnoff from the east road toward the schoolyard. He knew Joaquín usually rode Lobo to school, but the time came and passed without their arrival. When Holcroft heard the school bell ring, he drove into the yard and watched the children file into the building. Seeing neither Lobo among them nor his pinto in the corral, Holcroft turned his buggy east toward the Strummar homestead.

The corral there was empty. When the door of the house opened and Esperanza walked from under the shadowed portal, Holcroft clucked his horse forward to meet her in the center of the yard.

He smiled. "Good morning, Esperanza. I've come to see Joaquín."

She shook her head. "The men left before dawn to hunt deer in the mountains."

"Lobo, too, I suppose?"

She nodded.

"I went by the school hoping to catch Joaquín." He sighed. "Well, there's nothing to be done. Even if I could track them, my buggy couldn't follow where they go."

She smiled. "You couldn't track them."

"No, I suppose not," he conceded.

"Would you like to come in for coffee?"

"Very much. Thank you."

She trundled ahead while he tied his horse to the corral then followed across the yard. At the door he turned back and watched a white dove cooing from the highest branch of a saguaro. The homestead seemed so peaceful, the dove an emblem of love, it was difficult to remember that it was owned by a man reputed to be the worst killer in the Southwest.

Holcroft crossed the parlor and entered the kitchen just as Esperanza was taking an apple pie from the oven. Near the back door was a cradle with the sleeping infant. Esperanza smiled, sliding the pie onto the counter. "Sit down, Señor Holcroft. In a few minutes this will set and I can cut you a slice."

"Thank you, it smells delicious." He sat down and watched her fill a cup with coffee. "Did Mrs. Strummar accompany the men?"

Esperanza shook her head. "Rico goes riding alone every morning."

"An unusual woman," he murmured.

"Yes," she said, setting the strong coffee before him. "She is carrying a child and I argued against it, but she said she needs time to herself."

Holcroft puzzled over that a moment, then latched onto the familiar sentiment. "A child! How wonderful for them. Their third?"

"Only second," she said, sitting down across from him. "Lobo is not hers."

He nodded. "Usually when a child has a different name, it's because of the father. But Lobo is obviously Seth's son."

"He is a little Seth, no doubt of that," Esperanza said with a twinkle in her eyes.

"Have you been with the family long?" Holcroft asked.

"Two years," she said. "But I have known Seth much longer."

Holcroft blew on his coffee to cool it. Trying to stifle his curiosity, he said obliquely, "You're obviously fond of him."

"My life is his."

The commitment stated so simply gave the minister pause. He smiled. "Joaquín said the same. Mr. Strummar must be an extraordinary man to inspire such loyalty."

"He is," she said.

Holcroft sipped his coffee, then carefully set the cup in its saucer. "The sheriff came to see me last night. It was because of what he told me that I was looking for Joaquín. I was hoping we could help each other."

"Do what?"

"I'm not sure." He smiled. "Do you know Lila Keats?"

"I have met her."

"Sheriff Slater said Seth claims he doesn't remember her. Is that true?"

"If Seth says so."

Again he was impressed with her loyalty. "The sheriff said she used to go by the name of Esmeralda." He watched Esperanza's eyes darken with recognition. "Does that ring a bell?"

"I heard Allister speak of her once."

"What did he say?"

She shrugged, veiling her eyes. "It was a long time ago."

"The sheriff is worried, Esperanza, that Mrs. Keats has brought trouble to our town. Do you think there is anything I can do to avert what he sees coming?"

She shook her head. "Lila Keats will die. How many people die with her is in God's hands."

"Surely there's something we can do?"

"Forgive me, Señor Holcroft," she said with an edge of anger, "but a minister is like a woman in this world. Our power lies in the men we can petition. For us on this homestead, that man is Seth. If he weren't trying to live under the law, Lila Keats would be no problem. It seems the law gelds men by placing their power in the hands of a sheriff who cannot act without legal cause, so people like Lila Keats are free to spread their poison until they break the law. Isn't that what the sheriff told you?"

Holcroft nodded.

"So there is nothing to be done," she said.

He studied her uncomfortably, then asked, "Are you saying we are all impotent before the virility of evil?"

"That is what the law has made us."

"But surely, Esperanza, you see rule by law as a good thing?"

She shook her head. "I believe in the rule of a strong man. Seth is such a man. Your lawmen are weak, your judges without honor, your laws written by the rich to protect themselves. I believe in the power of the gun. It requires skill and courage to be its master, and in my heart I do not believe a man without skill and courage deserves to survive. By submitting to the rule of law Seth has crippled himself, and all of us who love him are helpless when he is threatened. Do you know what Seth does?"

Holcroft shook his head.

"He drinks. That is what the law has done to him. He numbs his mind so he can keep himself harmless, so his son can survive into the next century by learning to live under the rule of lesser men." She shrugged. "They call it progress. Myself, I would rather go backward. But I will go where the people I love go. That is the only choice we have."

Homer was disturbed by her vision. "That's a grim view of the world, Esperanza."

"It is how I see things."

"Would Seth agree with you?"

"If he did, he would take his family far into the wilderness where the law hasn't yet found its way."

Feeling a glimmer of hope, Holcroft asked, "What does he expect to find in civilization?"

"Redemption for his crimes," she answered.

"Don't you consider that a worthy goal?"

"Ah sí, but his method is mistaken. By raising his son to be a good citizen, Seth is hoping to redeem himself. But Lobo cannot redeem Seth. Only he can do that. Yet the only remedy the world will accept is for Seth to surrender his freedom. That he won't do, so he offers his son instead." She smiled sadly. "But Lobo doesn't want to be Seth's peace offering. He wants to be a man who moves with power. In the wilderness that is possible. In the civilized world such a man is sacrificed for the rule of law. So while Seth is striving to offer his son for his sins, Lobo is striving to become an equal of his father. Both will fail."

"You're making me melancholy, Esperanza," Holcroft said.

"You asked for my thoughts." She smiled. "You and I are the same, are we not? My name means hope, and isn't that what religion offers: the hope that God will set everything right after death? But in this life we can only comfort those close to us. Is that not true?"

"Yes," he said.

"Bueno." She laughed. "How about a piece of pie to nourish you for your journey home?"

Rico rode her palomino high into the hills, feeling better than she had in weeks because she now knew it was her pregnancy that upset her equilibrium. She hoped for a second daughter. Seth's love for Elena was a joy to share, and Rico looked forward to watching the girl grow to be a woman beneath Seth's appreciative eye. Lobo, however, was worrisome. As he approached manhood, his challenge of Seth would grow stronger, and Rico was afraid another son might break Seth's resolve to raise his children without violence.

He had a deep well of it which she knew he controlled with severe discipline. She supposed it had been born under the whip wielded too vigorously and too often by his own father. Yet Rico didn't blame Seth's father; she blamed Allister, the seasoned outlaw who had taken Seth on at eighteen and taught him, not only to pillage and rape, but to expend any regret he felt by inflicting more hurt. After watching Allister's solution suck him into an early grave, Seth was trying to change, at least to the degree that he didn't inflict his hurt on his family.

Rico believed if she could help him understand that what he did at Blue's was the last vestige of all he'd learned from Allister, Seth could finally leave those lessons behind and be the man he would've been without Allister's influence. Already his love for Elena was teaching him that the girls working for Blue were other men's daughters who didn't deserve what he gave them. Blue, of course, saw it the same way Seth always had, but Joaquín was Rico's ally.

She spurred her mare to gain the final ascent onto a cliff overlooking the railroad to Benson. Stretching to the distant mountains, the desert was empty except for the two lines of iron slicing the wilderness. A boy carrying a bouquet of roses walked on the wooden cross ties. He was about ten years old and dressed in city clothes, the roses deep red in the bright light of noon. As she watched, he looked up and saw her. He stared a moment, then gave her a shy smile. Wondering who he was, she turned her horse and caught the trail leading down, an ancient path left by Apaches who had once claimed this desert as home.

Now she owned the land bounded by the railroad, and she curiously approached the boy who was crossing the edge of what was hers. He stood watching her come, his face freckled, his smile tentative. When she reined to a stop beneath the embankment of the tracks, she was looking up at him as if he were already a man. He offered her a rose from his bouquet, and she stretched from the saddle to accept it, held it to her nose in gratitude a moment, then smiled at him.

"You're Lobo's stepmother, aren't you?" he said.

She nodded. "Who are you?"

"Rick Clancy," he answered.

"Your father owns the bank in Tejoe," she said.

"Yeah. I'm taking these flowers to my mother. They come from Mrs. Nickles' garden."

Rico laughed to think of roses growing on a hogranch. She thought she and Mrs. Nickles might be friends if things were different, if she weren't the supposed wife of an outlaw whom people shunned.

"I've seen you in town," the boy said, "when you come to Engle's Mercantile to buy supplies."

"And you know Lobo from school," she said.

"Yeah," he said. "But we're not friends."

"Why not?"

He looked down the long line of rails shining in the sun. "My father told me to stay away from him. All the kids were told the same."

"Did he tell you why?" she asked, feeling sad for Lobo.

The boy's dark eyes met hers. "He said Lobo's a bad seed, but it doesn't make much sense to me." He looked at the roses withering in the heat. "My mother said different, though."

"What did your mother say?" Rico asked with a smile.

"That it's not Lobo's fault what his father did, and he won't have a chance to be good if nobody'll be his friend. That a person needs friends to get along in the world, and maybe if the outlaw had better friends when he was young, he wouldn't have done the things he did."

Rico smiled again. "I think I'd like your mother."

"She said the same of you. After you came to church, she told my father at supper that you looked like a lady coming in on your husband's arm, and that maybe everybody should forget the past and bring you all into the fold." He smiled awkwardly. "She talks like the Bible sometimes."

Rico smiled back. "What did your father say?"

"He doesn't think the same. I can't make much sense of the world, they see it so different." Again he looked down the iron rails toward town. "My father'll whip me when I get home because I ditched school." He looked at the roses, then back at Rico. "Lobo told me his father never whips him. Is that true?"

She nodded.

"I wish he was my father then. I don't like my father much, and it's plain Lobo likes his a lot."

"You'll like him better when you're a little older," she said. "Things will make more sense then."

He shook his head. "I don't see how a man can love his son and take a whip to him too."

"He's only doing what he believes is right," she said gently. "Just because a person's grown doesn't mean they never make mistakes."

The boy watched her a moment, then said, "Sometimes I think about how to hurt him back. You know what's the worst thing I could do?"

She shook her head.

"Grow up like the outlaw. Then no one could whip me."

"Seth regrets the things he did," she said quickly. "In his mind he whips himself, and that's worse."

The boy frowned in puzzlement. "Can't see how it could be."

He looked at the flowers again, then gave her a smile. "I have to get home now. Tell Lobo hello for me, will you?"

She nodded and watched him trudge off between the rails. When he was just a speck in the distance, she saw him leave the tracks and cut across the desert toward town and the whipping he knew was waiting. Sadly Rico turned her horse and headed home, lifting the rose to smell its fragrance.

15

★

It was late afternoon when Seth and Joaquín came down from the mountains with the two boys and the carcass of a deer. The yearling buck had been draped across Lemonade's horse, and he rode behind Lobo.

At the homestead, the men left the carcass with the women and rode into town. The boys, too, were supposed to stay with the women and help if they could, but as soon as the men were gone, Lobo and Lemonade followed them. From a safe distance they watched Seth and Joaquín leave their horses in the high-plank corral behind Blue's saloon.

"What about supper?" Lemonade asked, feeling the pangs of hunger.

Lobo shrugged. "I'm thinkin' more of where we can leave our horses and get to 'em in a hurry if need be."

"There's the corral behind the courthouse," Lemonade suggested. "If we tie 'em to the fence, they can reach the water trough easy."

"Okay," Lobo said, reining around toward the right alley.

The courthouse corral was empty except for the sheriff's horse, a huge bay that snorted warily as the boys tied their reins to a rail. When Lobo pumped the handle to fill the trough, the sheriff's horse came over with its head down, blowing great sighs that raised dust from the hard-packed dirt of the corral. Lobo stopped pumping and leaned on the fence as he watched the horse drink.

"You can tell the caliber of a man by the horse he rides," he told Lemonade, who looked sheepishly at his own rather sorry mount. "You should've kept that bay you sold me," Lobo went on. "Did you know it belonged to a lawman in Tombstone?"

Lemonade shook his head. "Just as glad I din't keep it, if that's the truth."

"You callin' me a liar?" Lobo asked, standing up straight to face him.

Lemonade laughed. "For such a little tyke, ya sure are ready to fight at the drop of a hat."

"I ain't little," Lobo argued.

"How old are ya?"

"Almost eight."

"Well, I'm fourteen. Reckon I could beat ya pretty easy."

"You want to try?"

"No," Lemonade said with disgust. "Ain't we gonna get any supper?"

Lobo looked at the back of the courthouse. "When I was in the sheriff's office the other night, I saw a basket of apples in the corner. Reckon we could snitch some if he ain't around."

Lemonade groaned. "I'd rather snitch from 'most anybody but the sheriff. If he catches us, it ain't far to jail, is it?"

"He won't put us in jail for stealin' apples," Lobo scoffed.

"How d'ya know?"

" 'Cause he and Seth are friends, for one reason."

"Yeah? Give me another."

"He's afraid of Seth."

"Who isn't?" Lemonade agreed.

"I ain't," Lobo said.

"How 'bout when he hits ya. Ain't ya afraid then?"

"He never hits me," Lobo said, unable to look at his friend.

Lemonade knew he was lying but let it pass. "Let's go get some of them apples. If'n we're caught, reckon I'll find out, huh?"

"We won't get caught," Lobo said.

They climbed the fence into the corral and ran across to the stables. The door leading to the long aisle in front of the cells wasn't locked. Neither were the cells; all their doors stood wide open. As the boys moved through the dark shadows toward the office in front of them, Lobo walked nonchalantly, figuring if anybody was there he'd just say they'd stopped by to say hello. He knew he could ask for an apple and be pretty sure of getting one, but stealing it seemed a lot more fun. The office was empty, however, and the bushel basket still in the corner as he remembered.

Lemonade picked out the apple he wanted, then bit into it as he watched out the window for the sheriff. Lobo turned around and looked at the cell Seth's blow had sent him sprawling into. He even walked inside and stuck his wrists through the bars as if he had been in there so long he was bored. "Please, Sheriff Slater," he joked, "don't hang me. I promise I won't ever steal apples again."

Lemonade laughed and walked over to the case of Winchesters against the wall. "Now here's something worth stealin'," he said, then took another noisy bite of his apple.

Lobo went over and stood beside him, both of them appraising the chain that ran through the trigger guard of each rifle. It was closed with a padlock. "You any good at pickin' locks?" Lobo whispered.

Lemonade snorted. "If Seth caught ya with one of them rifles, I know for a fact he'd hit ya so don't try'n tell me dif'rent."

"I wouldn't let him see me," Lobo argued.

"Like ya weren't gonna let him catch ya with that horse?"

"Abneth Nickles told on me is the only reason I got caught."

"Well, a seven-year-old kid totin' a 'spensive rifle's gonna get told on too," Lemonade said.

"I'm almost eight," Lobo reminded him, looking around the office. He walked behind the sheriff's desk, sat down and put his feet up. "Wonder what it'd feel like to be a lawman."

Lemonade laughed with ridicule. "Seth Strummar's son wearin' a badge. That'd be somethin'!"

"Yeah," Lobo said. He lowered his feet and opened a drawer. Seeing a stack of wanted posters, he lifted them out and flipped through them. "Look at all this money just for catchin' somebody."

"Ain't that easy," Lemonade said. "Those men are killers, like as not." He walked across to look over Lobo's shoulder at the posters the kid was rifling through.

Lobo stopped and pulled one out. SETH STRUMMAR, it said across the top. ONE THOUSAND DOLLARS, DEAD OR ALIVE, FOR THE MURDER OF A TEXAS RANGER. POSITIVE IDENTIFICATION REQUIRED. "There it is," he whispered.

"A lotta money," Lemonade said.

"I'd kill the man who tried to collect it."

"Uh-huh. You and who else?"

"Joaquín."

Lemonade pulled the next flier out of the pile and held it up, grinning at his friend. JOAQUÍN ASCARATE, ALIAS SAMANIEGO. WANTED BY THE TERRITORY OF NEW MEXICO FOR ATTEMPTED MURDER AND LARCENY OF A HORSE.

"Gosh," Lobo whispered. "I didn't know he had one, too."

"Here's another," Lemonade crowed, pulling one out with BLUE RIVERS, DEAD OR ALIVE printed across the top. "Jesus," Lemonade said. "Blue killed a judge. Did ya know that?"

"Sure. It was a fair fight but they was gonna hang him anyway, so Seth rescued him from the Rangers in Isleta. Didn't you ever hear that?"

Lemonade shook his head.

"That's what I mean," Lobo boasted. "There's no way Seth would let me be arrested for nothin'."

"Huh," Lemonade said, knowing he wasn't included in that protection. "Maybe we best get outta here, Lobo."

"We only came 'cause you was hungry." He smiled. "If you've had enough to eat, we can go anytime."

"I'll just get one more apple," Lemonade said.

Lobo folded the three posters together and stuffed them into his back pocket, then replaced the others in the drawer and slid it closed.

"Don'cha think he'll miss 'em?" Lemonade asked.

Lobo shrugged. "Won't know where to look if he does."

Lemonade turned around and peered through the window again. "Here he comes!"

"Shit," Lobo said. Spinning on his heel, he ran into the corridor.

Lemonade was right behind, but they'd only made it into the deeper shadows when the front door opened. Lemonade pulled Lobo into the darkness of a cell where they huddled in a corner, trapped until the sheriff went out again.

Melinda left the dressmaker's and walked down the street toward the bank. After giving the seamstress half the cost of the dresses, she still had a hundred dollars in her purse. Since Joaquín had paid the rent on her room for the rest of the month, she planned on putting the full amount in her account and eating off Blue until payday. That hadn't been part of their arrangement but she figured she could milk him good as long as Joaquín was taking her part.

She smiled fondly, remembering Joaquín's sweetness. How he ever hooked up with the likes of Seth Strummar was a mystery she didn't have to understand to use to her advantage. By plying Joaquín's leverage, she might end up half owner of the Blue Rivers Saloon and eventually have enough money to buy Blue out. Then she'd be the one welcoming Seth into her domain. For that to happen, though, her nest egg had to accumulate interest from the beginning, and she meant to add to her account every payday.

Seeing Lila Keats go into the bank, Melinda quickened her pace, wanting to crow about the coup she'd pulled. She smiled as she walked through the door and saw Lila standing at a counter filling out a transaction slip. Melinda walked over and stood close enough to see that Lila was only doodling, making Melinda wonder who she was trying to impress with her presence in the bank. When Lila looked up, Melinda smiled and said, "Afternoon, Lila."

She laughed. "Heard you got yourself a job."

Melinda nodded. "Figure I'll last longer'n you."

Lila shrugged. "My working days are over."

"You find yourself a sugar daddy?"

"Yeah, I did. His name is Seth Strummar." Lila looked at the clock on the wall. "Excuse me," she said with sarcasm. "I have someplace else to be."

"Ain't that just too bad," Melinda said, blocking her path. "Are you tryin' to tell me Seth's keepin' you now?"

Lila laughed, looking past her as the door opened.

Melinda glanced over her shoulder and saw three men come in with their guns drawn. "Holy shit," she whispered. "I walked right into it."

"Don't stick your neck out and you won't get hurt," Lila warned.

Bob Tice had been watching the two woman talk, distracted by their beauty. He flicked his gaze at the men who had just come in, not expecting them to be of any interest, but their guns told him otherwise.

"Hands up!" Norris barked, pointing his pistol at the guard.

Tice raised his hands, wishing he had the rifle he'd left leaning in a corner.

Webster came close and took the sixgun out of Tice's holster, then said with a grin, "Go stand with the ladies."

Tice moved over against the wall with the women, the only other people in the bank besides the teller, who was staring with an open mouth.

Joe Tyler stayed by the door, nervously glancing outside at his brother holding the horses, as Norris went behind the counter and stuck his gun in the teller's face. "Open the vault," Norris said in a pleasant tone.

"I can't," the teller said.

"Open it or die," Norris said calmly.

The teller looked at the guard.

"You best do it," Bob Tice advised.

The door to the office opened and J. J. Clancy stood framed on the threshold. "What's going on?" he demanded.

Norris laughed. "Came to make a withdrawal, Mr. Banker. Why don't you open the safe?"

Clancy hesitated, loath to give in so easily.

"You best do it," Tice said again.

"All the money in the world ain't worth your life," Norris agreed.

Still Clancy hesitated. "You won't get away with this," he warned.

"Who's gonna stop us?" Norris mocked. "You do it now and both you and your teller'll still be alive. One more minute and one of you's gonna be dead."

Clancy looked at Bartles and saw sweat beading on the teller's upper lip. "He can't," Clancy told Norris. "No sense in hurting him."

"No sense a'tall if you move." Norris grinned. "If you don't, a little blood's a prime spur to action, don'cha think?"

"He has a family," Clancy argued.

"Don't you?" Norris asked.

Slowly Clancy moved toward the vault, trying to think of a solution. Only last month a drummer had come through and tried to sell him a time lock, but he'd scoffed at the notion that Tejoe needed such protection. Realizing the robbers couldn't know he hadn't bought one, he toyed with the idea of trying to convince them he had. His mind was a blank, though. He couldn't remember one thing the drummer had said that might sound convincing. "You're stealing the money of Seth Strummar," was all he could think to say. "You sure you want him for an enemy?"

Norris guffawed as if at a joke. "Ain't a more famous thief in the West, Mr. Banker. I figure he'll admire our pluck. 'Sides, everybody knows his money was stolen once, so it don't make no nevermind we're stealing it again."

"It's not just his money," Clancy pointed out.

"All money's the same to us," Norris said. "Get busy."

Clancy looked at the two women, recognizing one of them. "You're Lila Keats," he said.

She smiled. "I came to make a withdrawal."

"I didn't," Melinda said.

"You come to make a deposit?" Webster asked, eyeing her purse.

"I came to stop you," she said.

Lila thought that was funny. She laughed when Webster tore Melinda's purse off her arm. He rummaged inside, found the hundred dollars, and held it high as he grinned at her.

"You sonofabitch," Melinda yelled, grabbing for it.

Webster hit her with his gun. She fell with a cry as blood poured from a cut in her forehead.

Norris frowned. "That enough blood for you, Mr. Banker, or you want some more?"

"I'll see you hang," Clancy threatened.

"If you don't open that safe right quick," Norris answered, "you ain't gonna live to see nothin'."

Believing him, Clancy knelt on the floor and spun the dial. His hands were shaking so badly, however, that when he'd turned the combination and yanked the lever, the lock held. "Just a minute," he wheedled.

"You got one more chance," Norris said.

Clancy looked over his shoulder at Lila Keats. "The sheriff told me you were planning this," he told her.

She smiled. "I guess he was hoping to ride clear after it was over."

"You saying he's in on it?" Clancy asked, astonished.

"He's not here stopping it, is he?"

"Hurry up," Norris said, jabbing his pistol into the banker's neck.

Clancy told himself to concentrate as he spun the dial again. He didn't like the dark bore of the gun leveled at his jugular any more than he liked the chill of Mrs. Keats' smile. He had one more number to find when he heard the other woman moan. Looking over his shoulder to see the blood oozing from her forehead as she sat up, Clancy felt ill. He couldn't breathe well, and it amazed him that the men holding guns were smiling as if they were having a good time. He wanted to strike out at the ugliness of their arrogance. It wasn't that he'd worked so hard to accumulate the money they wanted, but his depositors had. Not Strummar, of course, though he wasn't the only man in town whose livelihood had come from a shady source. Clancy heaved the lever down and opened the door, revealing the town's lifeblood neatly stacked and bundled.

"Goddamn," Webster whispered, moving closer to his new-found wealth.

Melinda touched her wound, then looked at the blood on her fingertips as she struggled to think. She knew her money was in the hands of the thieves and she'd never see it again. That didn't bother her so much as the thought that Lila Keats would get it after all. Melinda looked up at the woman standing just above her, but Lila was watching the safe and smiling at the sight of all that money.

Webster was smiling at it too, though he was supposed to be watching the guard. Bob Tice began inching toward the rifle he'd left leaning in the corner.

Joe Tyler was watching the street. Nobody was coming so he gave his brother a wink to say everything was going according to plan. Thinking of the good times ahead, Webster laughed as he watched Norris rake the bundles of bills and sacks of coins into his saddlebags.

Lila looked down at Melinda and gloated, "You be sure and tell Seth I got what's mine. Tell him my name was Esmeralda when he knew me before, and the man he killed wasn't Bart Keats but Clay Barton. I think he'll remember us now."

Melinda grabbed hold of Lila's skirts. "Why don't you tell him yourself?"

Lila tugged at her dress. "Let go," she snapped.

Melinda held on. The waistband tore, then caught again, and Melinda laughed because the seamstress had done a good job and doublestitched the skirt to the bodice.

Norris turned with the bags heavy in his hands. "Let's go."

"What about them?" Webster asked, nodding at the banker and teller watching with ashen faces.

Joe Tyler was already outside, taking his reins from his brother.

Bob Tice reached his rifle just as the banker's son came in from the alley. Rick Clancy stopped, bewildered by the chaos in front of him: one woman bleeding on the floor and holding onto the skirts of another who was kicking her, two men with guns on his father and Mr. Bartles. Mr. Tice was raising his rifle, the front door wide open and empty. In panic, the boy ran toward the sunlight.

Tice fired at Norris but missed. Webster whirled and pulled the trigger, not taking time to aim, hitting the kid instead of the guard. Rick Clancy sprawled and slid face down toward the ribbon of sunlight just inside the door. Norris shot the guard, who fell over backwards as the banker bellowed in anguish.

"Help me!" Lila screamed, kicking at Melinda.

Norris ran. Webster did too, spraying bullets at Clancy and Bartles who ducked behind the counter. Knowing she could betray them, Webster saved his last shot for Lila Keats. She grunted as the bullet pierced her side, then she swung her fist at Melinda. "You goddamned bitch! Let me go!"

Melinda hung on. "Not 'til Seth sees what I've done for him."

Bob Tice knew he had failed. Only the woman was left, struggling to escape. In a last ditch effort to redeem his honor, he took aim at the purple bodice of her dress, but he slumped into death as he pulled the trigger, so his bullet went low and hit Melinda's heart.

Bartles huddled behind the counter, hugging himself with fright as he listened to the horses gallop away. When he heard footsteps, he raised himself to a crouch and peered over the counter in time to see Clancy fall to his knees beside the body of his son, lifeless in a pool of blood. "Lord have mercy," Bartles whispered.

When Lila whimpered as she tried to pry open Melinda's hands, Clancy rose and hurtled himself across the room. "You'll hang!" he sobbed, wrenching Lila free of the dead woman's grasp. "Let's get the goddamned sheriff!" he yelled to Bartles.

The teller followed as his boss dragged the bleeding woman through the door, then Bartles stood stunned on the boardwalk as Clancy half-carried the woman down the street. Men were coming out now, their faces stern with expectation of danger. They looked at the banker hauling the shrieking woman toward the sheriff's office, then at Bartles standing alone.

"What happened?" Maurice Engle yelled from in front of his store.

"Robbed the bank!" Bartles shouted.

"Them just now?"

"Killed Rick Clancy, too!" he yelled. *"She* was in on it." He nodded toward the woman leaving a trail of blood behind as she was dragged up the street.

Tom Beck opened the door of his hotel and stood a moment watching Clancy and the woman, then looked at Engle. "What happened?" Beck asked.

"Robbed the bank!" Engle shouted angrily.

"Who?" Beck asked, stunned.

"Her," Bartles said, thrusting his chin after Clancy. "The others got away."

"Killed Rick Clancy!" Bartles repeated, then added, "And Bob Tice and a woman, too!"

Men jostled him out of the doorway as they pushed into the bank to see for themselves.

"Sonofabitch," one man whispered.

"Lord Almighty!" another said.

"Where's the sheriff?" Engle demanded of Bartles.

"That's where Clancy's gone," he answered.

Engle bolted back across the street and inside his store, then came out carrying a shotgun. "We'll need a posse," he yelled, running toward the sheriff's office. "Get your guns, men!"

Bartles followed, his feet like wood. He could see the entire length of the block ahead of him: ladies staring from the boardwalks at Clancy and the woman, men ducking through doors and coming back out with guns, accumulating in number until they were a wave of rage rolling toward the sheriff's office. When someone took hold of Bartles' arm, he turned around to see Blue Rivers beside him.

"What happened?" Blue asked in a low voice, as if soliciting his confidence.

Bartles had often admired Blue, his easy nonchalance as he rode rein over his saloon, his wholesome good looks and confident walk. Feeling flattered that Blue had singled him out, Bartles told what he knew.

Sheriff Slater had heard the shots and hesitated a moment too long. Standing in front of the rack of Winchesters, he'd barely managed to unlock the chain on the rifles when Clancy burst in dragging Lila Keats, followed by twenty men rabid with outrage. "The bank's been robbed," they all yelled at once, "an innocent child killed!"

The woman was hideous, a painted face screeching betrayal as the men shoved her into the front cell and slammed the door. Holding her bloody side, she snarled, "Rafe Slater knew all along! He told me and Bart how rich the bank was! We came here to rob it under his protection!"

The eyes of the men turned on their sheriff.

Rafe shook his head. "She's lying," he said weakly.

"We need a posse!" Tom Beck said.

"Gotta have the law for that," Engle said.

"The law was in on it!" Clancy shouted. "Slater told me it would happen." His face crumpled as he bit back tears. "They killed my boy, you bastard!" He lunged for Slater.

Beck caught and held the banker. "That doesn't make sense, Clancy. He wouldn't have told you if he was in on it!"

"He's in on it!" Lila confirmed. "He was just trying to cover himself when it came down. It's his fault the boy's dead."

"We elected you to protect us!" Clancy yelled, struggling within Beck's grip.

"Let's hang him!" Engle uttered. "Then catch the others."

"Put him in jail," Beck argued. "Isn't that easier?"

"He knows this jail inside out," Engle answered. He reached across and disarmed Slater, then tore the badge off his vest. "I say hang him!"

"Deserves it sure as hell!" someone shouted from the back.

"Wait a minute," Rafe pleaded. "Think about what you're saying, Maurice."

"Nothin' worse than a sheriff who hits his own town," Engle retorted. "What do you say, Clancy?"

"Hang him!" he sobbed.

"The sooner we're done," Engle growled, "the sooner we go after our money!"

"Hang him!" Lila echoed. "Robbing the bank was his idea!" Weakening from loss of blood, she sat down hard on the bunk and laughed, a curdled sound.

"You gonna take her word over mine?" Rafe asked incredulously.

The men all looked at her collapsed on the bed, then at the blood dripping into a pool on the floor beneath her.

"The woman is dying," Esquibel said. "No one lies facing Judgment."

Men grabbed the sheriff and jostled him onto the street.

"You're making a mistake," Rafe argued.

"Our mistake was trusting you," Engle said. "But we're gonna rectify that damn quick."

Rafe tried to meet the eyes of the men crowding him along, but no one would look at him. Men he had eaten lunch with in Amy's Cafe, drank with in the Blue Rivers Saloon, men he had sat with in the courtroom to mete out justice, in the council chambers to decide town policy. Their faces were closed against him now, their eyes blind to what they were doing, shuttered to the agony of remorse he knew would be theirs with dawn, a regret so powerful they couldn't allow themselves to contemplate it in the heat of action.

Like a stampede to disaster, the mob surged down the street toward Esquibel's livery. Women in shadowed doorways watched with pale faces. A child stood on the boardwalk with his hands stuck straight down at his sides and his mouth open in silent terror as the men swept past. Flinging open the corral gate and swarming inside, they frightened the horses so the herd escaped into freedom. Rafe Slater watched after the animals with envy as he was pushed under the crossbeam outside the loft and a dozen men shouted for a rope.

Esquibel brought a horse from inside, and Rafe was lifted onto its back by men he had thought were friends. Feeling the animal's warmth between his thighs, he thought it was the last thing he'd remember, then someone put the noose around his neck and he felt the rough rope prick his skin with the promise that soon he wouldn't remember anything.

Across the heads of the noisy mob, he saw Blue Rivers standing in the empty street. Rafe smiled to let Blue know he understood there was nothing one man could do, it was just his luck this time. Blue lifted his hands in a gesture of helplessness, then turned and hurried away. Rafe stared at Blue's retreating back, not wanting to miss his last glimpse of a friend across the bestiality boiling around him.

Esquibel yelled from the loft that the knot wasn't right, and Engle shouted for him to hurry up because the horse was scared. The horse, Rafe thought, they're worried about the horse.

Lobo and Lemonade had huddled in the back cell as the mob stormed into the sheriff's office and took him away. Slowly Lobo crept into the silence left by their departure and looked at Lila Keats dying in the first cell, then he ran for the tenderloin hoping Seth hadn't gone home.

Inside Blue's saloon, the tinny piano blocked all sounds from the street. Lobo saw Joaquín at the bar. Joaquín saw him, too, and Lobo was dimly aware of the anger on Joaquín's face, then that the anger was replaced by alarm.

"Where's Seth?" Lobo shouted.

"Upstairs," Joaquín said softly. "What is it, Lobo?"

Lobo ran up the stairs. The music quit and his footsteps sounded frantic in the sudden quiet. At the top he stopped, confused by all the closed doors along the hall, then he heard Joaquín behind him. "Where?" Lobo cried.

Joaquín grabbed him. "Tell *me,* Lobo!" he commanded.

But Lobo wouldn't. "Where is he?"

Joaquín looked at a door and it was enough. Lobo twisted free, lunged for the door, and flung it open to see his father drinking at a table with Nib Carey. There was a woman on Nib's lap. Her dress was open, her breasts bare between the dark wings of cloth. She lurched to her feet, backing away as she covered herself. Slowly Seth stood up, his eyes colder than Lobo had ever seen them.

"This ain't no place for a child," Seth said.

"A mob's got the sheriff!" Lobo shouted. "Someone robbed the bank and they think he was in on it. They're gonna lynch him, Seth!"

Silence in the room. Seth's eyes a cold slate gray. The woman looking sick, Nib Carey astonished, Seth standing there wearing a gun but not moving.

"They'll lynch him!" Lobo wailed. "They'll hang him, Seth, and he didn't do nothin'! Ya gotta stop 'em!"

The woman murmured, "Honey, no man can stop a mob."

"You would've done it for Jeremiah," Lobo told his father. "It's the same, ain't it? Ain't it?" He felt Joaquín's hand on his shoulder but shook it off. "Ain't you gonna do nothin', Seth?"

Seth's gray eyes softened with hurt. "You shouldn't be here, Lobo."

"So what?" he screamed. "Ya gotta stop 'em!"

Into the silence footsteps rang out ascending the stairs, then Blue ran into the room. He opened his mouth to speak but didn't, seeing Seth and Lobo staring at each other.

Seth asked his son, "You expect me to defend the law?"

"Who else can do it?" Lobo answered.

Reverend Holcroft sprinted up the street toward the livery. Minutes earlier, Tulia had told him what happened, chattering in Spanish at first then finally using English to say the town had gone mad over the death of the Clancy boy.

"I told you!" she crowed. "The outlaw has doomed us all."

Holcroft didn't contradict her. He ran outside, following the hideous siren of the mob to disaster. "Wait!" he wanted to yell as he ran, but he couldn't find the breath.

Tom Beck caught hold of him at the corral gate and pulled him aside. "You can't stop them," he said sadly. "They're bent on doing it, Reverend."

Holcroft took one more faltering step, then stopped, appalled at what he was seeing. He looked around for help and saw Lemonade behind Beck.

"Ya best pray," the boy said cheerfully.

Holcroft stood on the other side of the fence from the frenzied agitation of the mob, feeling sick. Never had he seen humanity so ugly. He wanted to do as the boy said, drop to his knees and beg God to stop what he was seeing, but his knees wouldn't bend.

Esquibel called from the loft that the knot was ready now, and Rafe Slater almost laughed that all his striving to go straight had ended with a noose. A hush fell over the men as Engle told Clancy to let go of the horse's head and get out of the way, but Clancy was staring up the street and didn't move. Twisting around to follow the banker's gaze, Rafe felt the rope prick his neck with tiny feelers of warning that soon his life would be over. He heard gunfire, then saw Seth galloping his sorrel toward the corral, Joaquín on his black like a shadow, both of them firing rifles over the heads of the mob.

Homer Holcroft fell to his knees with a prayer for mercy.

"Back off or die!" Seth shouted, aiming his rifle at Engle about to slap the condemned man's horse.

Engle met the cold gray eyes behind the gun and took a step away, his hand frozen in the air. "This is right what we're doing!" he yelled. "Don't interfere where you don't belong!"

"I ain't," Seth said. "I don't like lynching in my town."

"They killed my son!" Clancy shouted.

"Robbed the bank, too!" Engle added. "Cleaned it out and got clear away!"

"Seems to me you oughta be chasing them," Seth drawled with disgust, " 'stead of committing a crime yourself."

"They're gone!" Engle retorted. "Slater's caught and we're gonna teach him an irrevocable lesson."

"He'll be dead," Seth said. "You're the ones facing a hard lesson."

"You say that to us!" Esquibel shouted from the loft. "You who has hung not only the man who killed your brother but the woman who killed your partner!"

"I know all about lynchings," Seth agreed. "I'm sparing you some of the knowing I carry."

"Don't listen to him!" Engle bellowed.

Seth fired a shot over the roof of the barn. "I got eight bullets left and Joaquín's got twelve. We'll kill at least half of you before you stop us. Is that what you want?"

"What will you gain?" Engle sneered. "You'll be dead, too." When Strummar met his gaze, Engle took another step away. He saw that the outlaw knew about the bank in Arkansas and thought him a hypocrite.

Seth shifted his gaze, lowered the sight on his rifle, and pulled the trigger. The sheriff's horse jerked as the severed rope fell free, and the men gasped at the accuracy of the shot. As the irony of who they were opposing came clear to them, the mob was restored to a collection of individuals.

Seth laid his rifle across his lap and waited for the next move.

Alfonso Esquibel challenged him. "Let me ask you this, Señor Strummar. We had no trouble before you arrived. Now we try to rid ourselves of trouble and you interfere. Why should we listen to a man who has lived outside the law all his life?"

Seth studied the faces waiting for his answer, then spoke directly to Esquibel. "If you think I give your town a bad name, what do you reckon this'd do to it? That ain't the worst, though. A man can learn to live with the ill feelings of his neighbors, but all the times you wake at night in a cold sweat 'cause of what you've done, the times you look in a mirror and 'stead of your own reflection see your victim's face blacken above the noose, see his boots kicking for ground that ain't there, what his feet'll find is your soul, and I guarantee you won't like the kick of his death." Seth stopped and scanned the faces again. "I made a lot of mistakes in my life. This ain't one of 'em."

"What'll happen to Slater?" Engle jeered.

"We'll put him in jail and you can hold him for trial."

They all stared in silence at the outlaw enforcing the law. Rafe Slater sat with his hands tied behind him, bareback on a horse whose bridle was held by the banker.

Clancy's face crumpled with grief. He leaned heavily on the head of the horse, clutching a cheekstrap in each hand as he sobbed on the animal's nose.

Joaquín lowered his rifle and slid it into the scabbard. He edged his horse into the crowd, then leaned to touch the banker's shoulder. Clancy looked up and met the gentle eyes of the man who had once wanted to be a priest.

"Go comfort your wife," Joaquín said with sorrow.

In silent acquiescence, Clancy turned and stumbled away.

"All of you go home," Seth said to the rest of them. "Give it to your wives. They'd rather have it than a husband with blood on his hands."

In humbled silence, the men dispersed. Joaquín pulled his knife and cut the rope holding the sheriff's hands, then smiled across the now empty corral at Seth.

Homer Holcroft stood up, seeing Lobo standing in the open gate. He embraced the boy, whose body trembled as much as the minister's knees. With pride shining in his eyes, Lobo whispered, "Seth stopped 'em."

"Yes," Holcroft said.

Blue walked into the corral. "Holy shit!" He laughed. "I ain't never seen anything like it."

Seth slid his rifle into its scabbard, then smiled at the sheriff. "First time I've defended the law," Seth said.

Rafe yanked the noose off and threw it into the stable. "You've restored my faith in humanity."

Seth laughed. "You got any whiskey in your office?"

Rafe nodded.

"Let's go have a drink before we tuck you in," Seth said, turning his horse to amble away. At the gate he stopped and looked down at his son standing with the minister.

"God bless you," Holcroft murmured.

Seth snorted in self-deprecation, then held his hand for his son, who took it and leapt up behind him.

Blue swung on behind Joaquín, and they followed with Rafe and the minister. They tied their horses in front of the office and went in. With shaking hands, Rafe opened a new bottle of whiskey as Seth stood looking into the cell at Lila Keats dead on the bunk. Blue was explaining what had happened as he'd heard it from the teller, but Seth was only half-listening. He tried the cell door and discovered it wasn't locked. After hesitating a moment, he walked in to look at Lila more closely.

He could see she had bled to death from a wound just below her ribs that wouldn't have been fatal if she'd been tended by a doctor. Seeing her face of despair on the bed beneath him, a memory flashed in Seth's mind, bringing back his recollection of Lila and Bart Keats, though that hadn't been their names and they'd all been a century younger.

Joaquín came in and stood beside him. Nodding down at the woman with a baffled frown, Joaquín said, "She would have escaped if not for Melinda."

Seth thought about Melinda having the will to hold on to Lila's skirts even as she died.

"If I hadn't tried to help her," Joaquín said, "Melinda wouldn't have been in the bank."

"Maybe," Seth said, wanting to squelch his partner's guilt. "Then again, she might've ended up like Lila, living for vengeance 'stead of giving her life to fight it."

"She gave her life fighting for us," Joaquín said.

Seth gave him a playful smile. "Which proves you have good taste in women."

Joaquín was affronted by the joke. He stared at Seth with new eyes across the dead women between them.

"Seth," the sheriff said, offering the bottle of whiskey from the other side of the bars. "Don't have enough glasses." He shrugged in apology.

Seth walked out of the cage and accepted the bottle. As he drank, he saw the chain reaching through the trigger guards of a dozen rifles in their rack. The lock had been opened and the end of the chain dangled free, catching light on the last link as it twisted in the sun like an empty noose. Seth shuddered. Something had been finished in the cell behind him, and he shivered with dread of what would replace it.

He knew only that he had a job in front of him, and the fact that he would rather be home with his family was as peripheral to his purpose as the suspicion that Joaquín had just broken free from whatever power held them together.

When Seth passed the bottle to Blue, he took a sip, then asked, "What'll you do now?"

"Reckon I'm going after my money," Seth said.

"You want me to ride along?"

He shook his head. "I'll take Nib, if you can spare him."

"Sure," Blue answered hesitantly. "But don't you want me to go?"

Seth looked at Joaquín still standing in the open door of the cell, his dark eyes fierce with vengeance, a drive Seth knew well. He looked back at Blue. "Figure Joaquín's got more of a claim. I need someone to stay with the women."

"All right," Blue said.

"What about me?" Lobo asked hopefully.

Seth shook his head. "Tell Rico I'll be back soon as I can." He looked at Reverend Holcroft. "Can you take charge of the sheriff?" When he nodded, Seth said, "Let's move."

16

★

Outside the sheriff's office, Seth saw Maurice Engle, Tom Beck, J. J. Clancy, Alfonso Esquibel, Buck Stubbins, and Abneth Nickles walking toward him. He and Joaquín swung onto their horses, then sat looking down at the townsmen bunched a few yards away.

"Ya goin' after the robbers?" Stubbins asked gruffly.

Seth nodded.

"Any objection to our riding along?" Engle asked with sarcasm.

Except for Abneth Nickles, Seth hadn't received an overture of friendship from any of them. "I suggest you go home and stay out of it," he said, reining his horse around.

"Wait!" Clancy yelled.

Seth turned back.

"We got a right to ride along," Stubbins said.

"It was our money, too, señor," Esquibel argued.

His voice shrill with emotion, Clancy yelled, "Five hundred dollars to whoever gets the man who killed my son."

"Hold it!" Seth shouted. "Since none of us has a badge, I think you should let me handle it."

"It's our money you'll be handling," Engle growled.

Seth shrugged with contempt. "Suit yourself," he said, then turned his horse and trotted out of town with Joaquín. After a moment, Nib Carey loped down the road after them.

The six men stood their ground watching the dust settle.

"I'm going," Engle finally said.

"Me, too," Stubbins grunted.

Esquibel appraised them quickly, then said, "I, also."

Beck, Clancy, and Nickles gave their assent by following the others back to the stable where Esquibel supplied them mounts from the ones remaining in the stalls.

The hostler looked regretfully into the distance where his corraled horses had escaped, thinking he should be chasing them, not bandits. He was also risking the mounts he put under the posse, and abandoning his business to scavengers and vandals while he was gone. He would have stayed home and placed his bet on the outlaw retrieving the money except that he didn't want it falling into the hands of Engle or Stubbins. Esquibel had picked up enough gossip to know they were riding the edge of bankruptcy, and he felt certain one or both of them would skim off the top and lie about how much they'd recovered. So he went along hoping to make sure that didn't happen.

Beyond the edge of town, Seth saw Lemonade waiting beside the road, his clothes so new they were still stiff. Seth reined up and smiled at him.

"Can I go, Mr. Strummar?" the kid asked hopefully.

Seth evaluated the horse he'd bought the kid and didn't think much of it. Then, too, Lemonade didn't own a gun. Stacked up against those flaws was the kid's ability to be cheerful in dire straits, a quality shining with charm next to the gloom coming from Joaquín. Seth asked the kid, "You know where the dunes are?"

"Yes, sir," Lemonade said.

"Go to the homestead and trade horses. Tell Rico I said you could take one of the chestnuts. Take the one with the blaze rather than the star; it's better trained to the saddle. Tell Esperanza I need food for four men for three days, fill all the canteens on the place and bring 'em. And tell Rico I said to lend you the Winchester I keep in the wellhouse. You got all that?"

"Yes, sir!"

"Don't forget bullets for the rifle. Meet us at the northeast edge of the dunes quick as you can."

Lemonade yanked his horse around, kicked in his heels and galloped back toward town.

Seth looked at Joaquín and Nib. "Let's try'n stay ahead of the good citizens. Agreed?"

Joaquín nodded, his face hard.

"You bet'cha!" Nib said.

They all touched their spurs to their horses' flanks and headed south toward the dunes.

Through the open door of Esquibel's livery, Buck Stubbins watched Lemonade ride past. He'd heard about the outlaw buying new duds for the kid, and Stubbins guessed Lemonade was going to the Strummar homestead for supplies. As he pulled his cinch tight, Stubbins muttered to Engle, "What d'ya reckon, Maurice? Think Strummar's on the level 'bout helpin' us?"

Engle swung onto his horse and smiled grimly. "If he turns outlaw again we can shoot him down easy enough, him and his Mexican shadow."

Abneth Nickles jerked around. "I ain't gonna let that happen! Strummar's taking a risk helping us, and you know it. He's got my support clean down the line."

Engle scanned the faces of the five men watching him. "I'm just saying that if Strummar reverts back to old habits, we got him outnumbered."

"I'm not making a move against Strummar," Tom Beck said. "He could kill us with his eyes closed."

"I've always maintained," Clancy said, struggling for dignity while he felt devastated with grief, "that Strummar is the man with the most experience in this sort of thing."

"Don't forget," Esquibel warned, "he has not only Ascarate behind him, but also Nib Carey. Those men are professionals."

Engle sneered. "Maybe you oughta stay home, Alfonso."

Esquibel shook his head. "I am interested in my money, the same as you. I also think the outlaw has the best chance of success, so I will follow, not oppose him."

"Seems to me," Stubbins said, swinging onto his horse, "that'll depend where he leads us." Not waiting for a reply, he reined down the road, intending to get his money back any way he could. The rest of the men followed with sour faces.

Maurice Engle rankled with resentment that he'd been outmaneuvered. Though he was beginning to feel a smidgeon of gratitude that the lynching had been stopped, he had no intention of letting Strummar lead the posse.

Alfonso Esquibel and J. J. Clancy had been humbled by the outlaw's act and felt profound gratitude for what he'd done. Their only intention was to take custody of the money once it was retrieved.

Abneth Nickles had arrived in town after everything was over. Impressed with Strummar, and wary of Engle and Stubbins, Nickles disapproved of the banker offering a reward, doubting that blood money to promote civic action would foster the reign of reason. He suspected, too, that contemplating the reward might tempt someone to try for the thousand dollars Texas still offered for Strummar, dead or alive. So Nickles rode along to help the outlaw if he could. Otherwise his first loyalty was to his family, and he intended to stay out of the fray.

Tom Beck went along because he had a vague notion that it was incumbent on his duties as mayor. The posse had scant claim to legitimacy without a sheriff, and the fact that it was led by an outlaw made it even shadier. Beck wasn't any kind of warrior, however, but a hotelier. He, too, felt grateful that Strummar had stopped the lynching. Such a sordid event could discredit a town and poison its future overnight, so in Beck's estimate, Strummar had already saved Tejoe. The loss of the money was survivable.

The six men traveled at a tense trot, covering the miles quickly. Except for Nickles, they were businessmen accustomed to walking on floors and sitting in chairs, winning their living with words and signatures on paper. Now they were embarking with various degrees of determination on a cross-country chase, carrying only weapons and water. Before them a dust storm obliterated the horizon. They rode blindly into the abyss, pursuing a man who knew the way.

At the dunes, the road forked east and west, and the strong wind showered the posse with tiny, cutting crystals of sand as it erased even their own tracks. In the distance, Nickles spotted Strummar and his men riding huddled into the storm. He pointed them out to Beck, who nudged Engle. Stubbins caught them all staring in the same direction and saw the riders just before they disappeared in the blowing sand. He led the posse in a gallop after them, but Engle wanted to be first. He spurred his horse into a dead run, passed Stubbins, and had to rein up hard to keep from crowding Nib Carey off the road. Nib swore under his breath and jerked his horse out of the way, glowering at the merchant.

Strummar turned to look at the posse bunching up behind him. He squinted against the sand, his hat pulled low above his eyes and a bandanna across his face.

Engle kicked his horse past the Mexican to ride abreast with Strummar, then leaned close to shout above the wind, "Where're they headed?"

Strummar pointed with his chin. "Chiricahuas."

"Think they're still together?"

"Were before the wind came up."

Engle looked back and saw that all the posse had covered their faces with handkerchiefs now, so he did the same, then looked at Strummar again. The outlaw's eyes were the cold gray of knife blades, making Engle feel unwelcome. Keenly aware of the Mexican riding right behind him, Engle felt it imperative to establish some degree of authority. To his way of thinking, merely riding alongside the jefe achieved that.

Seth knew why Engle was there, and he was willing to humor the merchant until he got in the way. Joaquín also knew, but in his experience claiming a place you couldn't hold only made a fool of a man.

For an hour, they rode through the swirling dust peppered by sharp crystals of sand. The horses walked into the wind with their heads down, their manes and tails buffeted by the wind. At the edge of the dunes, Lemonade waited on a palomino. With his face covered with his new, white handkerchief and his crisp clothes and shiny boots, he looked the image of a storybook highwayman. As the posse approached, Lemonade fell in on the other side of Seth.

Seth nodded a welcome but said nothing. Gunnysacks of food and canteens of water were tied to the kid's saddle, and the Winchester was snug in the scabbard. As for the horse, Rico had loaned him her mare rather than one of the chestnuts, animals trained more to harness than riders. That meant she supported Seth's endeavor and had made her contribution, slight as it was, to his success. Letting his mind drift along the pleasant currents of Rico's pleasing ways, Seth jerked back with the realization that he'd been woolgathering the comforts of his woman instead of concentrating on the task at hand long enough that the terrain had changed around him.

The wind carried only dust now, dry and stifling. An improvement over the stinging sand, it was still debilitating. The posse was soon winding between red rocks carved into eerie visages by the constant wind as the horses ascended the Chiricahuas through the thickening light of dusk. Halfway up, piñons crowded the trail. The men pocketed their bandannas and slapped the dust from their clothes with their hats as the horses snorted and shook their ears, clanking their bridles. Accustomed to the solitude of a renegade, Seth thought the posse sounded like an army moving into the mountains. In the cold dark of a moonless midnight, they entered the yard of an isolated homestead.

Seth swung down and handed his reins to Lemonade, then approached the cabin, stopped and hollered, "Hey, Dan! It's Seth Strummar. You home?"

His voice rose up against the mountains, echoed faintly in the distance, then was lost to the cold wind sighing in the trees. The door opened a crack, and a grizzled codger peered out at the men in his yard. "Hey, Seth," he said in a voice hoarse from disuse. "What'cha doin' ridin' with so many?"

"Tracking four men," Seth said. "They robbed the bank in Tejoe."

Dan studied him morosely. "Ya mean this is a posse?"

Seth nodded.

"Ya can come in," Dan said, "but I don't want the whole herd."

"You mind if they rest in your barn? Get out of the wind for a spell?"

Dan looked across at his barn and studied it for a long while, as if he didn't know every sliver and notch in it. Then he looked at the men sitting their horses, their faces chapped and wind-burnt. "Reckon," he finally said. "But no fires!"

Seth looked at Nib Carey, who nodded and led the posse toward the barn. Joaquín swung down and gave his reins to Lemonade. Maurice Engle dismounted and did the same, then arrogantly met Seth's eyes. Disliking the merchant, Seth merely turned and walked into the dim, smoky cabin of Hermit Dan.

The old man knelt before the hearth, building the fire up strong as the men filed in, first Seth, then Engle, then Joaquín closing the door. Dan carried a grinder over to a hundred-pound sack in a corner, dumped in several handfuls of coffee beans, closed the lid on the grinder and worked the crank as he looked at Seth. "I know Joaquín," Dan said. "Who's the other'n?"

"Maurice Engle," Seth said.

Dan snuck quick glances at Engle. "Sit yourselves," he finally said.

Engle sat at the table in the middle of the room. Seth pulled a chair into an empty space between the far wall and the table, straddling the chair backwards to face Joaquín, who remained standing by the door. Lemonade came in and looked at everyone as Hermit Dan looked at him.

"Name's Lemonade," Seth said with a smile.

Dan nodded, then snickered. "S'prised to see ya ridin' with a posse, Seth."

"Life's full of surprises, ain't it?"

"Allister'd be tickled," the hermit said.

"Reckon he would," Seth agreed.

" 'Member the time he Pecos'd that fella in Seven Rivers?"

Seth nodded.

"Why'd he come at ya shootin' like that?"

"Never found out," Seth said.

Dan looked at Joaquín. "Allister killed 'im fair. Then they was left with the corpse, though. Corpses ain't good things to have to account for. So Allister lassoed the feet and drug it away. Few minutes later he come back and says he Pecos'd 'im." Dan giggled through his broken teeth. "Threw 'im in the river, is what he done."

Joaquín smiled politely, feeling too hurt to laugh. But he thought if a river happened to be nearby when he caught up with Melinda's killers, he might Pecos them, too.

Seth asked, "You ain't seen the men we're after, have you, Dan?"

He shook his head. "Ya'll never catch 'em with so many. These mountains're riddled with overlooks, they'll see ya comin' and skedaddle. Ya oughta move like the Apaches, quiet and few."

"I'd prefer it," Seth said. "But those men feel they have an interest in the money."

For the first time, Hermit Dan looked straight at Engle. "Ya oughta trust Seth. He'll not double-cross ya."

"Never said he would," Engle muttered, throwing Seth a surly frown.

Seth shrugged. "I don't care if you come along, Engle. But what do we need the others for? I'd bet money most of 'em can't shoot well enough to win third prize at a county fair."

"All right," Engle said. "Let's each keep a backup, one man. That suit you?"

"Who do you want?"

"Stubbins."

Seth nodded, already having assessed the miner as the most aggressive of the bunch. "I'll keep Joaquín," he said, then called to Lemonade, "Go ask Stubbins to come in, and tell Nib to take the rest of the men home."

"What about me, Mr. Strummar? Can I stay?"

"I don't care," Seth said, looking at Engle. "You got any objections?"

When Engle shook his head, Lemonade grinned and ran out to deliver the message.

Hermit Dan dropped the ground beans into a huge blackened pot he filled with water from a bucket. Kneeling before the hearth, he hung the pot on the trivet and swung it over the flames, then stayed there, tending his fire.

Seth smiled at Joaquín, trying to soften the grief obviously consuming his thoughts. "We'll sleep here tonight," Seth said. "Get an early start in the morning."

Joaquín nodded.

"Is it all right with you, Dan," Seth asked, "if we bed down in your barn?"

The old man stood up and squinted across at him. "No lanterns. No smokin'."

"Agreed," Seth said.

A few minutes later, Buck Stubbins came in alone, though Nib

Carey stood outside the door holding the reins of his horse. Seth walked out to talk in the shadows of the hermit's porch.

"Ya sure this is what ya want?" Nib asked. "Neither one of those men is your friend."

Seth smiled. "I ain't their friend either."

The posse was already shuffling tiredly across the yard to the trail down the mountain. Abneth Nickles waved at Seth. He waved back, wishing the farmer was staying instead of Engle.

"I'm worried about Joaquín," Nib whispered, blunt because they didn't have much time.

Seth evaluated the apprehension in the depth of Nib's bullet-hole eyes. "Appreciate it," he said.

"Any message for home?"

"Tell Blue thanks." He smiled. "And give Rico my love."

Nib nodded and turned away to mount his horse.

Seth took a step closer and spoke softly. "Tell Lobo I'm proud of him. Will you do that, Nib?"

"Sure," he said, gathering his reins. "Good luck."

Seth watched Nib ride away at the tail end of the posse, then went back inside and stopped by the door to lean against the wall near Joaquín. Stubbins and Engle were whispering between themselves at the table. Hermit Dan was crouched before the hearth, pulling the coffeepot out of the flames. Meeting Joaquín's eyes, Seth winced and said, "It wasn't your fault."

"What wasn't?"

"Melinda's death."

"Nothing I did helped her."

"You did your best. Can't expect more from a man."

"God expects the impossible," Joaquín retorted bitterly. "Yet even when I achieve it, He destroys my accomplishment before I have time to catch my breath. I'm beginning to suspect I missed my calling."

Seth studied him carefully. "You wish you'd become a priest?"

Joaquín shook his head. "If we had followed your plan, the men we are now tracking would have been arrested when they walked into the bank. No one would have died. Whose plan was better? Mine that sought to save lives and avoid complicity? It cost the lives of four people and prevented nothing."

"It wasn't our job to stop those men."

"It is now," he said, his dark eyes angrier than Seth had ever seen them.

"We took it on," he admitted.

"Whatever happens next," Joaquín bit off, "four people are dead because I held you back."

"You didn't kill them," Seth said, straining to keep his voice low. "Seems to me you're shouldering more than your share of blame."

"We have already agreed," Joaquín muttered, "that the world often seems different to you than me."

"This ain't the time to fight about it."

"I will not fight your instincts again. I hope to develop more of my own."

"This ain't the time for practice either," Seth argued. "You go off half-cocked, you could get yourself in as much trouble as the desperados we're chasing."

"Are we not already outlaws?"

"Yeah, in some circles. Most, I reckon."

"Then whatever we do will be outside the law. I see no need to draw the line finely."

"I see the need. Will you grant me that?"

"Yes," Joaquín said. "But if a chance comes that even hints at a cause to kill those men, I will not hesitate."

"Neither will I," Seth agreed.

Lemonade came through the door, carrying bags of food. He looked at the two men huddled over the table, then at Seth and Joaquín watching him. "You want I should make supper, Mr. Strummar?" he asked.

"You know how to cook?"

"Enough for what we got."

Seth smiled. "Be sure you make plenty to share with our host."

Hermit Dan brought them cups of coffee, then leaned against the wall nearby, all of them watching the kid hunkered in front of the fire laying slabs of jerky in a skillet. Dan said, "My eyes are goin', did'ya know that, Seth?"

He shook his head with sympathy.

"Usually, this time of year, there's deer in the oak thickets down b'low. Think maybe ya could kill me one 'fore ya ride out? Would get me clear through winter, almost."

"I'll go down at first light," Seth said.

Hermit Dan smiled. "I'm glad ya come visitin', Seth. Though you're movin' in strange comp'ny. Those two at the table look shady to me."

Seth chuckled. "One of em's the owner of the biggest mercantile firm in the county, and the other owns the Red Rooster Silver Mine. Those are high-class gentlemen, Dan."

"You talking about us, Strummar?" Engle asked huffily.

"Just telling Dan what upstanding citizens he's got at his table tonight." Seth finished his coffee and moved away from the wall. "Hey, Lemonade, did the women pack me any whiskey?"

"Yeah, they did," he said, bringing it over to the table.

Seth broke the seal and pulled the cork. "To successful partnerships," he said, lifting the bottle then taking a swig.

He offered the whiskey to Engle, who stood up and raised the bottle, took a sip and passed the bottle to Stubbins. He did likewise, then extended it toward Joaquín. As Seth watched to see if he would come out of his self-imposed exile, Joaquín pulled himself away from the wall, advanced into the half-moon of light thrown by the fire, and accepted the whiskey. Holding Seth's eyes with his own, Joaquín took a sip and offered the bottle to Lemonade.

He looked at Seth, who nodded, so the kid took the bottle, raised it in agreement to the toast and sipped, then gave the whiskey back to Seth. He recorked it and set it on the mantle, smiling at

Dan, who wet his lips in anticipation of the gift. Then everyone but the hermit sat down and watched Lemonade finish cooking supper. Dan stayed by the wall, nervous at having so much company. After the meal, the visitors walked out to bed down in the barn, and only then did Dan come out of his corner to eat.

Dawn was still a rosy smudge above the ridge when Seth and Joaquín carried rifles down the slope behind the hermit's cabin. From the distant pines an owl hooted its melancholy murmur of vigilance, but the men hadn't yet spoken. Walking quietly through the dense underbrush, Seth glanced at Joaquín and asked, "How'd you sleep?"

Joaquín looked over with surprise. "I didn't."

"You gonna sleep on the trail?"

"Don't worry about me. I am not your concern."

"The hell you ain't! I need you, Joaquín. Don't get independent on me in the middle of this."

"Don't you trust my judgment?" he retorted sarcastically.

Hearing the barn door creak open, they both turned and watched back through the sparse forest of juniper among the tangle of rabbitbrush. After a moment, Lemonade appeared and stared down at them. Seth beckoned the kid closer, then smiled at Joaquín. "This is the grand adventure of Lemonade's life, and neither one of *us* wants to be here."

"I do," Joaquín said. "Men who commit such acts must be brought to justice, and I intend to see that they are."

Seth studied him, then pointed out warily, "I used to commit such acts on a regular basis. I had more finesse and didn't leave so many bodies behind, but I hurt plenty of people. Those men are no different from me and I feel damn uncomfortable tracking 'em. I don't need God's avenger for my partner right now."

"Now or ever?"

"Ever, if it comes to that." They could hear Lemonade crashing through the brush, and Seth lowered his voice. "I know you're hurting, Joaquín, and I understand how you feel, but let's keep it simple: we're after vengeance and restitution. Any notion that we're delivering justice is suicide."

"Do you not feel justice has its own power?" Joaquín asked archly. "Isn't that what you felt when you hung the man who lynched your brother? Can you honestly tell me you didn't see yourself as the hand of justice at that moment?"

"That was different," Seth muttered.

"Why?"

" 'Cause what Pilger did was a deliberate act. What happened to Melinda was bad luck. She got in the way, is all."

"That makes it worse," Joaquín said with disdain. "To kill randomly, with no regard for whoever has the misfortune to be in your way, is barbaric."

"No more'n what you'll be doing."

"My aim is not random."

Lemonade came up beside them and asked with a grin, "Where we goin'?"

Looking away from the dour face of his friend to the beaming enthusiasm of the kid's, Seth smiled. "We're gonna bag Hermit Dan a deer," he said, leading them downhill.

"Will you let me shoot it, Mr. Strummar?"

"Can you do it?"

"Sure!"

"I don't see why you shouldn't then." He caught Joaquín's eye but couldn't get a smile out of him.

The sky was a luminous dark blue, the morning star glimmering alone with the crescent moon, the horizon now a wedge of crimson thickening fast. Within the oak grove were two does and a yearling buck, glossy and plump as they grazed on the fallen acorns scattered among the crisp, yellow leaves. Seth handed his rifle to Lemonade and whispered, "Get the buck."

Lemonade raised the gun and took his time aiming. One of the does lifted her head and looked straight at the men. Nobody moved. She stared, chewing a minute, then the buck raised his head and stared at them, too. When Lemonade pulled the trigger, the three deer turned on their toes and bounded in the other direction. Lemonade pulled the trigger again and again, but missed. Joaquín raised his rifle and dropped the buck with one shot.

Amazed, Seth asked Lemonade, "Who taught you to shoot?"

"Nobody," he admitted.

"I believe that. We just used six bullets to bag one deer and prob'ly woke up every man within a hundred miles. Next time I ask if you can do something, don't lie to me."

"No, sir, I won't," Lemonade promised, undaunted.

Seth smiled at Joaquín. "Good shot."

"Thanks," he said.

"Lemonade, get us a pole," Seth said, starting toward the carcass.

"What're we gonna do with it?" the kid asked.

Seth stopped and looked at him with fresh amazement. "We're gonna tie the buck to it and tote him back to Dan."

"A big stick, then," he said.

"Yeah," Seth said. He watched the kid go into the forest, then said to Joaquín, "I was never that ignorant. Or that bad a shot, either."

Joaquín shrugged. "There's not much chance to shoot deer while living in town, or need to carry a carcass, either."

They walked through the carpet of golden leaves to the fallen deer. The bullet had gone into the back of its head. Seth gave his friend a teasing smile. "I call that a righteous killing, Joaquín."

"A lucky shot of desperation," he admitted wryly.

Seth laughed, pulled his knife and slit the deer's belly open, stepping back as he cut the innards loose with his blade and they swamped steaming onto the ground. By the time Lemonade came with the pole, the carcass was ready to be loaded. They tied the feet over the bar, and each man toted an end. Lemonade carried the rifles.

"If I hadn't come along," he said, "ya would've had to tote your guns and the deer, too."

"We've done it before," Seth said, still disgruntled at being lied to. "What's your real name, anyway?"

Lemonade was quiet.

"You don't have to tell me if you don't want," Seth said.

"Warren Walker," the kid said.

"How'd you get the handle 'Lemonade'?"

"It started out as a joke," he said, glancing at Joaquín.

"They usually do," Seth said. "You want to share it? I could use one right now."

"It sounds silly," Lemonade hedged. " 'Specially considerin' who ya are."

They walked in silence a few minutes, climbing the slope back toward the cabin, then Lemonade said, "It was at a orphanage in Topeka. I liked lemonade a lot so this lady who worked there started callin' me the Lemonade Kid." He laughed awkwardly. "It jus' stuck, is all."

Seth chuckled.

"I told ya it was silly," Lemonade said defensively.

Seth shrugged. "If I'd known I was riding with the Lemonade Kid, I would've minded my p's and q's a little sharper."

"Aw, Mr. Strummar, ya don't mean that. Ya wouldn't change your ways for nobody, would ya?"

"Nobody but women and children and a partner who's always giving me trouble," he muttered.

Lemonade glanced over his shoulder at Joaquín, who didn't appear to be listening. It seemed a troublesome partner might be replaced, and Lemonade's failure to make the kill didn't diminish his opinion of himself as a likely contender.

17

★

As they were hanging the deer from a tree in the yard, Hermit Dan came out of the cabin and stood nearby. Seth nodded for Joaquín to take Lemonade inside.

"I need you in the cabin, Lemonade," Joaquín said, walking away.

Lemonade looked at Seth securing the deer, then followed Joaquín.

Dan came closer. "Fat buck," he said with approval.

"Joaquín shot it," Seth said. He walked over to the water trough by the corral and cleaned his knife, dried the blade on his pantleg and slid the knife back in its sheath on his belt, then returned to the old man admiring the deer. Seth waited, not looking at him.

"I know those men," Dan whispered.

"Do you know where they are?" Seth asked softly.

The old man shook his head. "One of 'em, Dirk Webster, is keepin' comp'ny with Micah Wells' wife." He snickered naughtily.

Seth smiled. "You don't miss much for being a hermit."

"These mountains are infested with men! Must be a dozen of 'em livin' in this range. Can't be no decent hermit."

Seth laughed. "I know what you mean."

"I bet ya do," the old man said, his eyes bright with scorn. "Ridin' with a posse chasin' robbers!"

"It was my money they took. Can't let 'em get away with it."

"Pshaw!" he scoffed. "If ya collected all the blood's been spilt over money, ya'd have to be Noah to survive the flood." The glare of his eyes softened. "Did Joaquín lose someone?"

Seth nodded.

"I knew it! He's got vengeance in his eyes. Ya watch 'im, Seth. He ain't under your wing no more."

Seth sighed, turning around to watch Stubbins and Engle come out of the barn. "Where is the Wells ranch?"

"Toward the ass end of the Pedregosas. On a mesquite flat bordered by a ridge blockin' the view of Mexico."

"How far south?"

"Hundred miles." Dan smiled. "As the crow flies."

"Guess we better move," Seth said, sighing again.

An hour later, they rode out with Seth in the lead on his sorrel, followed by Engle and Stubbins, both on dark bays, then Joaquín on his black and Lemonade on Rico's palomino at drag. The trail wound down the west side of the mountains toward the valley floor fifty miles south of the dunes. An expanse of ancient lake bed, the valley below was immense and flat, the only trees stubby mesquite. All morning the men rode down the shady side of the mountain. At noon they stopped to let the horses graze on the last of the grass, then continued their descent with the afternoon sun in their eyes.

At dusk, they camped in an arroyo that opened on the valley. Towering into the darkening sky, red rocks stood like sentinels carved by sand and wind into visages of reptilian monsters with human faces. Joaquín settled his horse off by itself and left his gear in camp before walking back up the arroyo toward the mountains.

Seth watched him go, then looked at Lemonade waiting for instructions.

"You ever hobble a horse?" he asked the kid.

Lemonade shook his head.

"Ain't too many lessons more important," Seth said. He swung down and pulled his hobbles from his saddlebags, dumped his saddle and blanket in the sand, then knelt by the sorrel's forefeet. Nudging them together, he whipped the leather straps into position and tied them fast. "Let's see you do it," he told the kid.

Lemonade swung off the palomino and found the hobbles in the saddlebags, pulled the saddle and blanket off, then crouched near the hooves. The palomino backed away and stopped with its forelegs spread wide.

"Pick 'em up," Seth said. "A good horse'll let you handle its feet."

Lemonade grabbed a fetlock and pulled the hooves together, wound the strap around and tied it. Seth came over and looked down at his work. "It's too loose," Seth said. "This mare could be halfway to Mexico by morning." He knelt in the sand beside the kid, untied the hobbles and started over. "Quick loop, see, another one, yank it tight and catch the hold. You can undo it just as quick, which sometimes is important."

"Yes, sir," Lemonade murmured.

Seth looked at him. "I'd hate to lose this mare."

"I'll take good care of her," the kid promised.

"All right," Seth said, standing up.

They took the bridles off, slung their saddles and blankets on their backs and returned to camp. Joaquín's gear was in a small cove of rocks affording a good view. Seth dropped his gear there, too, but when Lemonade started to put his down, Seth stopped him.

"You sleep over there," he told the kid, nodding at the far side of the camp. "Joaquín'll be here with me, so watch our backs. And keep your gun where you can reach it at all times. Understand?"

The kid nodded.

"Do it, then," Seth said. He turned and walked up the arroyo, seeking solitude. From a distance, he watched Stubbins and Engle collecting enough wood for a bonfire. Seth shook his head at the company he was forced to keep, then sat down in a deep shadow beneath the wall of the arroyo.

His eyes never stopped moving, scanning his surroundings for any hint of danger. It was a habit established so long ago that he was rarely conscious of performing it, yet tonight Seth felt keenly aware of himself as a pinnacle of defense isolated against the proverbial wall.

With each year, the restrictions on his life grew more severe. He guessed it was the natural result of having spent his youth raising hell, though that hadn't been his aim. It had been to live as he damn well pleased, and he'd done that. It was only now when the repercussions of his past threatened to destroy his carefully constructed sanctuary that he realized to what degree he'd turned the world against him: even acting in defense of the law didn't mitigate the fact that he was a fugitive from both sides of it. His best hope for survival was to stay low and out of sight. Leading posses wasn't doing that.

If not for Joaquín, Seth would have gone home and abandoned the chase to the good citizens. Despite his training and ability, however, Joaquín was a novice at vengeance. To achieve it without provoking the law's retribution would be tricky, and Seth figured the cut would be so close they'd need a sharp edge which he meant to provide if Joaquín didn't.

Within the shadow of the wall, Seth watched the townsmen build the fire so high it could be seen for miles, then stand around it, perfect targets from any angle. When Joaquín finally came back down the arroyo, Seth stood up, and they watched each other as Joaquín came closer.

"How you doing?" Seth asked softly, falling in step beside him.

"Fine," Joaquín answered, though the torment in his eyes denied it.

As they walked back toward camp, Seth shared the tip Hermit Dan had given him.

Joaquín listened in silence then asked, "If you were running from such a crime, would you visit a woman?"

Seth smiled. "There were times I did. Guess I figured if I was about to die, I'd just as soon have my ashes raked."

"Is that all a woman is to you?" Joaquín mocked.

"It's all they were then," Seth answered, uneasy with his friend's new quickness to anger.

Stubbins and Engle were sitting on their saddle blankets on the north side of camp, Lemonade alone with the now-dark valley yawning behind him. Seth sat down next to Joaquín, both of them lounging against their saddles from the comfort of bedrolls. As he studied the townsmen across the fire, Seth wondered what would happen if they got lucky and actually caught the men they were tracking.

He would get his money back, he knew that. Given free rein, he'd probably kill the thieves doing it. In this instance, however, Joaquín's claim had precedence. On the other hand, if Seth let Joaquín kill them, he risked losing his best friend to the same swamp of death Joaquín had pulled him out of. The best solution he could come up with was to deliver the thieves to the law, but sending men to jail went against the grain with Seth.

Neither did he like riding with Engle and Stubbins, both of them as shifty-eyed as any men he'd ever met. They expected the worst, kept themselves on guard against it, and barely managed to be civil. Seth had spent a good chunk of his past in the company of men he wouldn't turn his back on, but he'd enjoyed himself. It surprised him that the businessmen were inept at establishing common ground. Even when he looked straight at them, they were so buffaloed it took several minutes for them to garner the courage to look back. When he finally had their attention, he said, "I think we oughta agree on what we hope to accomplish."

"Get our money!" Stubbins barked.

Seth mentally winced. That Stubbins would answer before considering all the angles didn't bode well for his performance in a showdown. Seth looked at Engle.

"The same," Engle said, his eyes narrow and crafty. "Isn't that your intent?"

Seth nodded. "But these men won't give it up without a fight. Are you willing to kill 'em?"

In the silence broken only by the fire, Engle and Stubbins looked at each other. Stubbins nodded. Engle looked back at Seth and said, "They killed four people. We'll be delivering justice."

"I don't attach that word to my thinking," Seth said. "What we gotta consider is that none of us has a badge or any legal sanction to interfere with those men."

Again, Engle and Stubbins looked at each other, then Engle asked, "Are you saying if we kill them we could be charged with murder?"

Seth nodded.

Lemonade stood up and crossed to kneel before the fire, then slowly added more branches to the pyramid of wood. Engle and Stubbins stared into the flames. Seth and Joaquín kept their eyes on the forest so as not to blind their vision. The pyramid fell and Lemonade quickly leaned logs to catch the heat.

Stubbins cleared his throat. "If we take 'em alive, what'll we do with 'em?"

"You can escort 'em to Tombstone and hand 'em over to the U. S. marshal," Seth said.

"Not a ride *you* care to take, is it?" Engle taunted.

"You knew that before you came along."

"That's precisely why we're here."

"You're here," Seth said, " 'cause you don't have a prayer in hell of finding 'em on your own."

"Let's just say we think your odds are better," Engle drawled, "being as experienced as you are."

"Let's just say that," Seth agreed, striving to keep the conversation pleasant.

"Who gets Clancy's reward?" Engle asked.

Seth looked away to disguise his contempt. "If you collect it," he said, meeting Engle's eyes again, "that makes you a bounty hunter. That's nothing I want." He paused a moment, then said, "If you try to collect the reward after you've killed 'em, though, you'll be confessing to murder." He looked at Joaquín. "We'd be better off taking 'em alive."

From the shadows where he lay listening, Joaquín shrugged.

Lemonade sat back on his heels, proudly watching the fire blaze into the black sky.

Finally Stubbins said, "I'll go along with that. Except ya forgot to mention what happens to the money."

"I'll take it back to Tejoe," Seth said.

"You expect us to let you ride off with it?" Engle asked incredulously.

Seth smiled across the flames. "Look at it this way: if I held a gun to your head and told you to hand it over, you'd do it. So let's just agree now and save ourselves the trouble."

"We'll think on it," Stubbins muttered.

Seth laughed. "What's for supper, Lemonade?"

"Jerky and biscuits, same as last night."

"Only one thing's missing," Seth said.

"What's that?" the kid asked warily.

"Coffee's always first."

"Yes, sir," Lemonade said, digging into the supplies.

"Don't reckon you oughta call me sir," Seth said, smiling again at Engle and Stubbins. "Name's Seth Strummar, reviled far and wide for doing the same thing these gentlemen did once upon a time. Only I flaunted my crimes before the world. Good citizens hide theirs in shame."

"I ain't ashamed of nothin'," Stubbins said. "I was wearin' a Confederate uniform when I stole that Yankee gold."

Seth didn't bother to question if the gold ever made it into the Confederate treasury. "How about you, Engle?" he asked. "You ashamed of robbing that bank in Arkansas?"

"No," he said, meeting Seth's eyes. "I deserved a fair shake and I took it."

"That's the same as me," Seth said.

"Nowhere near the same," Engle scoffed. "I did it once and didn't hurt anybody. You made a career not only of robbing banks but of killing men who got in your way."

Seth smiled. "It's what I'm good at."

"Nobody'd argue with that," Stubbins muttered.

"Had a lot of fun, too." Seth laughed, rubbing it in.

There was a silence broken only by the crackling of the fire, then Engle asked in a confidential tone, "You ever think about doing it again?"

"No," Seth said.

"I've heard it's easy to hold up trains," Stubbins said. "Stop 'em in the middle of nowhere and get away on your horse. They can't chase ya 'cause they're stuck on them steel rails!" He laughed. "Sounds like easy pickin's to me."

"I've heard some of the takes are real plump, too," Engle said.

"Hell, even just a coupla thousand would make a dif'rence to me," Stubbins said. " 'Specially if we don't recover what was in the bank."

"How much you figure it was?" Seth asked.

"Twenty," Engle answered. "That's what Clancy told me. How much was yours?"

"Five," Seth said.

"I'm out four," he said.

"Six for me," Stubbins growled. "I'd jus' moved money down from Santa Fe to pay for openin' a new shaft. Minin's gettin' so goldarned mechanized it costs a fortune to turn a profit. Makes me wonder if workin' for a livin's worth it." He squinted across the fire at Seth. "Ya don't have to worry about that, do ya, Strummar?"

"I was born with a six-shooter in my hand," he said.

Stubbins laughed. Engle chuckled nervously. The coffee boiled over. Lemonade pulled the pot out of the flames, filled a cup and handed it to Seth, then poured another and carried it to Joaquín. Hearing him say "Gracias" in his soft voice, Seth yearned to have his partner back.

Lemonade gave full cups to Engle and Stubbins, then they all sat sipping their coffee while the kid divided the supper and passed it, too, around.

As they were eating, Stubbins said, "Don't see how they could catch a man robbin' a train like that. If he only did it once. Made sure the take was worthwhile, then sat back fat and sassy while they combed the hills for desperados."

After a minute, Engle said, "It could be done."

"Ain't it gonna hurt ya, Strummar?" Stubbins asked in a sympathetic tone, "if we don't recover the money?"

"It'll set me back," Seth admitted, knowing where the conversation was headed.

"Well, sayin' we have bad luck and lose it," Stubbins said. "Would ya consider pullin' a train job, just once, to recover our loss?"

Seth smiled. "I might."

Engle laughed nervously. "We could pull it off, the four of us. Even use the kid to hold the horses. And we have the perfect alibi: we're hunting bank robbers. Nobody'd suspect us."

"I know which runs are worth it," Lemonade said. After glancing shyly at Seth, the kid told the townsmen, "A while back in Tombstone I heard the freight agent say ev'ry third Wednesday the payrolls for the big mines come in from El Paso."

"That's tomorrow!" Engle whispered exultantly. "I'd say it's fate that we do it."

"What d'ya say, Strummar?" Stubbins asked.

Seth leaned forward and poured himself more coffee, then sipped at the boiled tar, watching the townsmen over the rim of his cup. "If I did it," Seth said, swishing the coffee to settle the grounds, "I'd kill my partners afterwards so they couldn't give evidence against me." He smiled at Engle and Stubbins, then grinned at Joaquín. "Ain't that what you'd do?"

"It would be the wisest choice," Joaquín answered.

Seeing that Lemonade felt chagrined for having gone along with the plan, Seth winked at him, then stood up and tossed him the empty cup. "Think I'll check on the horses," Seth said, walking into the shadowed arroyo.

Engle muttered, "He'd do it, too."

Stubbins looked at Joaquín. "Would he kill his partners in a job?"

Joaquín shrugged.

In the morning, the men rode out in a tense silence. Only Lemonade felt pleased at the prospects of the day. After running errands for the likes of Bart Keats, being Seth Strummar's backup was an immense promotion for the orphaned street urchin. But he figured he'd already made enough mistakes that Seth wouldn't hesitate to count him out. Missing the deer had been Lemonade's first mistake; agreeing to rob the train was a far more serious miscalculation. Lemonade hadn't caught on that Seth was joshing the townsmen, and he knew that to replace Joaquín as Seth's partner required anticipating the jefe and making himself indispensable.

That he was scheming to usurp Joaquín's place wasn't the only reason Lemonade felt wary of the Mexican. Joaquín had changed from a source of kind encouragement to a cold front of anger that challenged anyone within range, including Seth. Having managed to overhear pieces of their conversations, Lemonade understood Joaquín was grieving for the woman killed in the bank, but that had little meaning in Lemonade's life. Never having loved anyone, he couldn't imagine the loss. Neither had he ever owned anything it would grieve him to part with, until now. Seth had not only bought Lemonade his first new clothes and put him on a horse, the jefe had also loaned him a Winchester, and Lemonade meant to earn it before the game was up.

Riding directly in front of him, Joaquín had a low opinion of Lemonade. The kid was poised on the threshold of true criminality, lied about his abilities and exhibited a sham of arrogance that begged to be redressed. Though missing the deer should have taken the wind out of his sails, Lemonade prattled on undaunted, even including himself in the train robbery talk as if he were an equal. Joaquín couldn't figure why Seth kept the kid around. Lemonade was handy for grunt work, but Joaquín wouldn't bet a brass peso on his loyalty.

Yet Seth seemed to be pulling the kid close, as if he thought there was a man worth saving inside the cocky punk. Seth didn't often single people out for his largess. When he did, Joaquín had to concede that it paid off handsomely. After knowing Blue Rivers a matter of weeks, Seth had risked his life to save Blue from hanging. Joaquín had argued against it and refused to help, so Seth had done it alone. Now Blue was their strongest ally and closest friend in Tejoe. Remembering all that made Joaquín doubt himself more severely than ever.

For years he had been content to be Seth's shadow. Believing the depth of their friendship justified being partner to a man the world considered a vicious killer, Joaquín had become the staunchest advocate of Seth's proclaimed desire to live within the law. It had been an interesting role, full of complexities and an ironic humor, but it was gone now, lost to the profound betrayal Joaquín felt at Melinda's death.

He suspected the fault was his for trying to change others when he was the one who needed to change. Rather than strive to share the blessings of Christ's benevolence, Joaquín intended to strike with the wrath of Jehovah. The thieves had wronged him. Not only by killing a woman he cared for, but by killing an innocent child they had outraged his tolerance of brutality. He thought he would never breathe freely again until they bore the full brunt of what they had done. Which meant justice in Joaquín's mind: suffering and loss equivalent to what had been inflicted. Beyond that, he couldn't contemplate what his life would become, who he would be or where he would go. He only knew he was no longer a shadow to be relied upon no matter what.

Seth was well aware of the change in Joaquín's loyalty. He wanted to approve but wished it hadn't come when he himself felt so vulnerable. Suddenly Joaquín was a wild card in the deal. Having learned the finer points of lethal maneuvers from Seth, he was more than ten years younger and had the edge all along the blade, and Seth sure didn't want his former partner as an opponent. He knew this shift was tricky. He'd been through it with Allister and didn't guess the usual result was a deepening of friendship. Yet that's what Seth wanted: to take Joaquín home better friends than when they'd left.

Buck Stubbins didn't feel friendly toward either Seth or Joaquín. Still smarting from the outlaw's joke the night before, Stubbins might have shot Strummar in the back if not for his compañero riding behind. Ascarate's dark eyes seemed to miss nothing. They were mean, too, hard and cruel, as if he would just as soon shoot as look at a man. Stubbins didn't like Mexicans much anyway, and this one struck him like a viper coiled for attack.

No happier than Stubbins, Engle also felt humiliated by the joke. It burned like acid in his throat that Strummar was always playing the high and mighty. If he wasn't so damn good, he wouldn't have a chance in hell of getting away with it, but that was the catch: Strummar was more than a thief, he was a legend. Songs about him were sung in cantinas across the Southwest. Having heard some of the songs, Engle had admired the outlaw before meeting him.

After Strummar moved to Tejoe, however, Engle's romantic illusions of an outlaw's charm died fast. From their first encounter, he'd hated Strummar's arrogance: the cold way his eyes bore into a man, allowing no respite of courtesy; how his hand lingered loose by his .44, the polished bone of its grip a testament that he used it daily; the aggressive way he occupied space, defining limitations and enforcing them, making men back off just by looking at them hard. The outlaw rankled with a balls-to-the-wall approach to life, and any sane man recognized the danger in his company.

Yet Engle was following him into the wilderness. Everyone had long ago given up the pretense that Strummar was tracking sign. He'd heard a tip from the hermit and wasn't sharing it, but the outlaw obviously had a destination in mind. Engle thought it would be smart for bandits to have an accomplice lead the posse on a wild goose chase. Even if Strummar wasn't connected to the robbers, he'd lost five thousand but stood to gain twenty, and there was nothing to prevent him from killing his partners, as he'd threatened the night before. Engle couldn't help wonder if that had been a joke or a warning, and it bothered him that he couldn't read Strummar's intentions.

In late afternoon, they approached a homestead in the middle of a clearing cut from the mesquite forest. The house was a low adobe with a covered well, a water trough and a hitching rail in the hard-packed dust of the yard, with a corral and stable about a hundred yards off. The corral was unshaded and empty, the white dust bright in the sun.

Seth looked across at Engle. "If I got my directions right, Micah Wells lives here. I'd rather you do the talking. I'll just listen and watch." He let that settle in a moment, then asked, "Can you handle it?"

Engle nodded, staring at the house. "Shall I tell them the truth?"

"About everything," Seth said, "except why we're here. Just say we lost the robbers' trail heading south, so we stopped to ask if anyone's seen 'em. Then say our horses are tired and ask to stay the night. They should be amenable. If not, we'll know they're hiding something."

Engle asked with sarcasm, "So I'm to pretend I'm the leader of this posse?"

Seth smiled. "Let's see how you do." He reined his horse back to ride alongside Joaquín as they ambled into the yard behind Engle and Stubbins, Lemonade tagging along at the rear. Seth leaned close to his friend and whispered, "Remember: watch the wife."

Joaquín nodded.

They all sat their horses in the middle of the yard while Engle hollered, "Anybody home?"

18

★

The door opened and a skinny woman came out. Her dress had once been blue but was now a faded gray from having been washed and dried in the sun too many times. Her dark brown hair was wound into a thick bun on top of her head, and strands had escaped to frame her face with wispy curls. Her eyes were sharp with suspicion, her mouth closed in a hard line beneath jutting cheekbones. She carried a rifle.

The merchant tipped his hat. "Afternoon, ma'am. I'm Maurice Engle, and these men are citizens of Tejoe. We're a posse chasing bank robbers. Do you think we might come in for supper? The Township of Tejoe will reimburse you for the expense."

Seth muttered to Joaquín, "That's a line I'd never think to use." When Joaquín laughed softly, Seth thought maybe his friend's hurt was easing and reason reasserting its welcome claim.

The woman said, "The sheriff of Tejoe is Rafe Slater."

"Yes, ma'am, that's true," Engle said. "He wasn't able to come along."

"Why not?"

"The unpleasant fact," Engle intoned, "is Rafe Slater is now in jail for having aided the thieves."

"That ain't been proved," Seth shouted from the back.

The woman looked at him, at Joaquín, Lemonade and Stubbins, then back to Engle. "I'll ask," she said, returning inside and closing the door behind her.

Engle twisted in his saddle and glared at Seth. "You gonna contradict everything I say?"

"Slater ain't been proved guilty," Seth said.

"If we don't catch these men," Engle retorted, "there won't be anyone to testify against him. Since he's a friend of yours, maybe it would behoove you to let them go."

"Maybe it would behoove you to take 'em alive," Seth answered.

The door opened and the woman reappeared, still clutching her rifle. "Put your horses in the barn," she said. "My husband broke his leg, so you'll have to tend them yourself. You can wash up at the trough." She went back inside, closing the door again.

Jessica Wells was thirty-two years old, had been married ten years, and was childless. Although she had once been pretty, her good looks were fast being lost to the ever-present wind blowing through her home, a house of mud on a parched plot of land in the middle of nowhere. The closest town was Tombstone, a wild and sinful city where prices were outrageously high. Usually when Micah rode into town he went alone, coming home a day later smelling of whiskey and cheap perfume. Jessica wasn't angry when that happened, only envious.

She had been easy pickings for a man who liked his woman safely married to someone else, and Dirk Webster had met with no resistance when he wandered onto the Wells' ranch and sought a warmer welcome than his host offered. Keenly aware of the transitory nature of her romance, Jessica cherished Webster's visits, which were erratic and announced by his artful imitation of a meadowlark. She thought it a beautiful summons, and always smiled when she heard it.

A discreet affair of the heart seemed a harmless diversion in the labors of her life—a life she had no intention of leaving, a husband she valued though their passion had long ago died. She thought, too, that the problem was not with her but Micah, and if she could give him a child after all this time, maybe some essence of love could be restored to their marriage. Of course, her husband must never know the child wasn't his, and Jessica did her utmost to ensure he didn't learn of her lover. They had devised a message with candles: a taper in the east window was a request that he wait, a promise she would come; in the west window, a flame was a forlorn expression of regret. It broke her heart to place the candle in the west window but she had done it, then lain awake beside her husband yearning for the pleasure she was missing.

Since Micah's leg had been broken, he spent his days on the settee with the cast propped on a chair, querulously recounting everything wrong with his life. Twice Jessica had been forced to light the candle in the west window because Micah was drinking and would neither go to sleep nor let her escape. He needed an audience for his tirades; as his wife, it was her duty to listen.

For hours she had endured his whining complaints while part of her mind never stop craving her lover's caresses. She had sat demurely in the parlor, fetching another bottle from the kitchen when her husband asked, saying little and agreeing with everything because he wanted to argue and she didn't. She wanted to be lying on a blanket beneath the stars, feeling her lover's hands on her naked skin.

She worked now to prepare supper for the strangers. First she tied an apron over the front of her dress, filled her big kettle with water from the bucket and set the kettle on the stove, then stoked up the fire to burn hot. She took the axe from the woodbox and walked out to the chickens, caught and beheaded a rooster. Returning to the kitchen, she poured the now hot water back into the bucket and carried it out to a stump. The rooster still ran headless around the yard, so she looked at the strangers unsaddling in the corral.

The tall one seemed familiar but she couldn't place him. Memory nudged with the Mexican, too, but it was faint and she couldn't catch the connection. The man who had talked to her—Maurice Engle, he'd said his name was—struck her as shady. Bad-mouthing the sheriff of Tejoe didn't sit right with her. She had liked Rafe Slater and would have entertained him as her lover if given the chance. But Tejoe was too far away. Its sheriff didn't often ride across two counties to the southern edge of the territory.

She didn't see how these men could be a posse if none of them had a badge. Neither would she hold her breath waiting to get paid by the Township of Tejoe. She caught the rooster now flopping on the ground and carried him to her bucket of hot water. After immersing his body, she bent to the task of plucking the chicken, inhaling the sour smell of wet feathers and feeling certain the strangers brought trouble.

Pal came over and lay down to watch her, knowing he'd get the innards when she was done. He was a gentle mutt with a fluffy yellow coat and soft brown eyes. "What do you think, Pal?" she asked the dog. "These fellows are up to no good, wouldn't you say?" The dog whined. "Yeah," she said, looking up from her task of yanking feathers that came out with a wet slide then a jerk, a steady rhythm from her fingers denuding the bird.

The men were washing at the trough now with their sleeves rolled up; splashing their faces, slicking their hair back, beating the dust out of their hats against their legs. She noted the kid kept his rifle nearby. The others didn't, but then they all wore sixguns on their hips. When they started toward the house, she looked down at her work, listening to them cross the yard, only the tall one and the Mexican wearing spurs, until the door closed behind them.

When she carried the chicken into the kitchen, she could see them through the open parlor door. The Mexican was leaning against the far wall, watching her. She turned to her workboard and attacked the chicken with her butcher knife, Pal at her feet waiting for the innards. A clink of glass from the parlor told her the men were drinking, and she snorted with disdain. These strangers were as dangerous as rattlesnakes yet the first thing Micah did was get drunk with them. Looking at her rifle leaning by the back door, she wondered if the gun was close enough. She didn't stop cutting up the chicken, though. She finished and fed Pal outside, then washed her hands. Wishing she could ask someone to fetch a pail of water, she remembered the kid and decided he was still young enough to be commandeered. She walked to the door of the parlor, stopped on the threshold and waited to be recognized.

Micah looked up, his face flushed with the pleasure of company. "What is it, Mrs. Wells?" he boomed.

"I was wondering," she said softly, lowering her gaze to the floor, "if the boy could fetch some water and wood for the kitchen."

A silence followed her words. If any communication passed between anyone, it was inaudible. When she heard the boy walk toward her, she looked up and fixed a polite smile on her mouth as she scanned the faces of the men. They were all watching her, except the Mexican, who was watching them.

The kid stopped and said, "I'd be glad to help any way I can, ma'am."

"Thank you," she said to the room at large, then turned and led the boy into the kitchen. She handed him the bucket. "You can fill this first. And be quick about it."

He laughed going out the door. She stood looking after him, wondering how long it had been since anyone had laughed in her kitchen. Shaking off her reverie, she set to work. By the time the boy came back, she was paring potatoes.

"What else?" he asked as he set the bucket on the floor.

"What's your name?" she replied, studying him. He was well dressed, so obviously not alone in the world.

"Lemonade," he said.

"Is one of those men your father?" she asked cautiously.

"Nope. I'm workin' for Mr. Strummar."

"Seth Strummar?" she whispered, putting it together, the memory that had nudged when she first saw them ride up: the tall man with gray eyes on a red horse, his Mexican partner on a black, both of them with the blood of murder on their hands.

Lemonade grinned, tickled by her reaction. "Is there somethin' else I can do for ya, Mrs. Wells?"

"Yes," she said, dragging her mind back to the task at hand. "There's a stack of split by the woodpile. Would you bring it in, please?"

Again she watched him leave, this time feeling a strong forboding of dread. She couldn't think of any reason an outlaw would ride with a posse. So that was no posse in her parlor. At least that much was clear. Hearing the men laugh over their whiskey, she smothered her anger at her husband beneath the concentration of labor. She poured water into a pot, dropped in the quartered potatoes, and set the pot on a back burner to boil, started the chicken frying in her large skillet, then mixed a double recipe of biscuits. She was rolling them out when the boy came back, his arms laden with wood. She jumped when he dropped it into the box. "Goodness," she said.

"Sorry." He laughed. "I thought ya'd be expectin' it."

"I'm accustomed to being alone," she said.

He nodded, then asked willingly, "What else can I do for ya?"

"You could set the table," she suggested.

"Where's the stuff?"

She crossed to the hutch, took out a clean tablecloth, and handed it to him. Then she went back to the stove and turned the chicken. She added more wood, heating the oven for biscuits, and poked at the chicken again with her tongs. When she looked at the boy, he was fussing with the tablecloth, trying to center it perfectly. It was touching to see him struggle with a task she performed without thinking. Finally satisfied with the way it fell, he looked up and saw her watching. They smiled awkwardly at each other.

"The silverware's in that drawer behind you," she said.

He turned around and opened the drawer, then stood staring at the neat array of utensils arranged in their slots.

"We'll need six of each," she said. "And six plates from the shelf above."

"All right," he said, but there was hesitation in his voice.

She concentrated on moving the chicken around in the skillet. When she looked up again, he was putting the silverware on the table, the three pieces bunched together to the right of each place. She set her tongs down and went to help, lining up the knife and spoon on the right and placing the forks the correct distance to the left.

Watching her mend his ignorance, he liked that she didn't accompany her lesson with a lecture. When she finished the last setting, she met his eyes and asked softly, "What are those men doing here?"

"We're chasin' bank robbers!" Lemonade boasted.

"Do you know their names?"

"Sure. Hal Norris, Dirk Webster, and Joe and Jim Tyler. I know what they look like, too. That's part of why I'm along."

She studied his face, thinking it wasn't fair a child had the power to ruin a person's life. "Will your testimony be the only evidence against them?" she asked, trying to sound merely curious.

He shook his head. "There were plenty of witnesses. Mr. Clancy and the clerk were in the bank when it happened. They both lived through it. Four people died, though. The Clancy boy, the guard, and two women. One of the ladies was in on it."

"God in heaven," Jessica whispered, sinking into a chair. "When did this happen?"

"Day before yesterday. Some say the sheriff was in on it, too. The townsmen was gonna lynch him but Mr. Strummar stopped 'em. Jus' rode into the corral and told 'em all to go home. Can ya beat that?"

"No," she murmured, thinking of Dirk.

"The Clancy kid was only ten," Lemonade said, adding spice to the gossip, death meaning no more to him than that. "And the woman what was innocent, she held onto the other one so she couldn't get away. Died holdin' onto her skirts so they had to pry her hands loose."

"Lord have mercy," Jessica moaned.

"Ya all right?" he asked worriedly. "Ya ain't gonna faint or nothin', are ya?"

She shook her head. "A terrible thing," she managed to say.

"The robbers got away with the money. That's what we're after. We're aimin' to take the men alive if we can."

"Is that true?" she whispered.

"I wouldn't lie to ya."

"No, of course not," she said with an apologetic smile.

Pulling herself to her feet, she returned to the stove, slid the biscuits into the oven, then stared at the chicken sizzling and snapping in the grease. The boy watched her as if still worried she might faint. "You can put the plates on the table," she said, remembering almost too late to start a pot of coffee.

When she looked up again, he was setting cups beside each plate. She drained the potatoes, slid them into two bowls and set one at each end of the table, took the salt and pepper and crocks of butter and marmalade from the pantry and set them on the table, then arranged the chicken on a platter and set it before her husband's place. She surveyed her work, returned to the oven for the biscuits, piled them onto a platter and set it, too, on the table, then looked at the boy. "Tell the men supper's ready," she said.

He left eagerly. She took a deep breath, entered the parlor, walked across to the settee, and offered her shoulder to help Micah up. He leaned on her heavily before he caught his balance between the cast and the cane, then he jerked away as if he didn't need her. She followed him meekly into the kitchen. After repeating the procedure to lower him into his chair at the table, she slipped out the back door.

Seth and Joaquín watched her go, both of them already seated. They glanced at each other, then Joaquín stood up. "I wish to check on my horse," he said, leaving through the parlor.

Seth smiled at their host and said, "He's fussy about his mount."

Once outside, Joaquín skirted the house until he came into view of the back. Mrs. Wells was there, leaning against the wall and hugging herself as if she were cold. A yellow dog, tethered to a stake, lay nearby. Joaquín hunkered down in the dark shadow thrown by a cluster of mesquite. Their lacy leaves bobbing in the wind whispered as softly as a harlot's negligee as he watched the woman, knowing she was yearning for her lover. Joaquín remembered the sweetness of that hunger, a satisfaction he had once found with Melinda. Remembered, too, her fear of being alone, and he shuddered to think of her in a grave. With a start he realized she would be buried long before he returned.

A meadowlark sang from beyond the clearing. He didn't really hear it until the woman took notice. She raised her head at the sound and walked away from the house, threw a worried look back at its lights shining through the dusk, then disappeared in the mesquite thicket east of the yard. Quietly Joaquín followed her. The path wound through the low trees with needle-sharp thorns. He kept himself crouched in the shadows, pausing every few moments to listen. A quarter mile into the thicket, he heard voices and stopped, waited, then crept closer.

An arroyo suddenly opened, a giant gouge dropping into the lower plains. In its mouth, the woman stood talking with a man whose horse grazed in the shadowed canyon. Mrs. Wells was pleading. Her tone reached Joaquín before he caught her words: "The boy told me they want to take you alive, Dirk. Maybe that's your best chance."

"The hell it is," Webster growled. "Forget it, Jessica. I ain't surrendering."

"But all those people died!" she cried softly. "The law won't forget something so bad. They'll catch you, Dirk, and then there'll be no mercy."

"We only killed half those people. Their goddamned guard killed the other two."

"Two or four, what difference does it make?" she asked frantically. "One is a hanging offense, Dirk."

"We didn't kill no women," he muttered.

"That means you killed the child," she moaned. "For God's sake, surrender and beg the mercy of the law."

"It ain't got none, Jessica. If I'm not lynched, I'll hang. Even if by some miracle I escape that, they'll lock me in prison. Is that what you want?"

"No," she whimpered.

"I'm near starved. Can you bring me some food without attracting attention?"

"It'll be a while," she said. "They're all in the kitchen eating."

"Where do they think you are?"

She shrugged. "I'll bring whatever I can soon as they're done." Suddenly she clung to him, their words too muffled for Joaquín to hear. He watched, aching with his own loss, as they kissed hungrily in the darkening arroyo. When she finally tore herself free, Joaquín stepped back into the mesquite and watched her pass within a yard of him. He waited until he heard the kitchen door open and close, then he followed the path toward the arroyo, walking with the nonchalance of assumed possession.

The moment he cleared the trees, Webster saw him and froze. Keeping his hand close to his gun, Joaquín laughed lightly. "Buenas tardes, señor. Are you with the men visiting at the house?"

"Yeah," Webster said.

"I work for Señor Wells. It is unusual to have so many guests at one time. You are keeping guard, eh?"

"That's right," Webster said.

"You wouldn't have any tobacco, would you?" Joaquín asked with a friendly smile.

Webster reached into his vest pocket, pulled a pouch of makings out and tossed it over. Joaquín shook the tobacco into a paper, rolled it tight and licked the seal. Privately swaggering for taking the risk of occupying both hands while facing his foe, he struck a match on the sole of his boot and took a long time holding the glare to his face as he lit the cigarette. Exhaling a billow of smoke, he tossed the makings back. *"Gracias,"* he said.

"So what d'ya do for Wells?" Webster asked.

"Vaquero," Joaquín said with a dismissive shrug.

"You must know this country pretty good then."

"Sí," he said as if bored.

"Ride the range near everyday, don'cha?"

"Sí," he said again, puffing on the cigarette, which was making him dizzy. "Are you looking for something, *señor?"*

"Friend of mine was s'posed to meet me nearby. You ain't seen a man traveling alone, have you?"

Joaquín shook his head. "I have seen no one I didn't know for days now, except you."

Webster began rolling himself a smoke. When he had the bag of tobacco in one hand and the paper in the other, Joaquín lazily dropped his own cigarette and ground it out with the heel of his boot, then drew his gun.

Webster's hands stopped.

"You are under arrest," Joaquín said, "for robbing the bank and killing four people in Tejoe."

"You got a badge?" Webster growled.

Joaquín smiled. "I have a gun, señor, and it would give me great pleasure to kill you, so I suggest you not hesitate when I ask that you raise your hands."

Webster dropped his makings, the paper fluttering away on the wind as he complied.

"Now with your left—very slowly, *señor*—take out your gun and toss it gently toward me."

Webster hefted his pistol to land with a thud in the sand, then asked, "Who the hell are you?"

"Joaquín Ascarate, *a su servicio.*"

Webster thought a minute. "You ride with Strummar?"

"We ride together."

"Is he in the house?"

"*Sí.*"

"Who else?"

"Other men. Some of us wish to kill you. Some wish to deliver you alive to the law in Tombstone. It is up to you what happens."

Webster assessed him. "What if I cut you into the take?"

"What would I get?" Joaquín asked.

"The Tylers already took their share back to Texas. Norris and I got fourteen left. We'll give you four and split the ten."

"Only four?" Joaquín asked playfully.

"All right!" Webster barked. "I'll give you my five."

"That is not all I would be taking. The blood of murder is on your money. Do you think that is something I wish to own?"

Webster stared at him a long moment. "If you kill me, you will own it. If you really don't want it, what's to prevent me from riding away?"

"I will not shoot unless you provoke me," Joaquín said. "Melinda provoked no one, yet she is dead by your gun, so I would not consider killing you murder."

"Melinda? The other woman in the bank?"

Joaquín nodded.

"The guard killed her. I swear it."

"Do you think that lessens your guilt?"

"Yes! I'd never shoot a woman."

"But a child?"

"Norris hit the kid. It was chaos in there all of a sudden. You've been in tight situations, you know how everything can turn wrong in the blink of an eye."

"You will die in less than that," Joaquín said, "unless you walk now ahead of me to the house."

"All right," Webster said.

Joaquín knelt to pick up the pistol, keeping Webster covered as he groped on the ground. But he couldn't find the gun and glanced down. Webster kicked sand and Joaquín lurched back, raising his arms to shield his eyes. He heard a rifle fire, then a grunt, shook his head and refocused in a matter of seconds. Webster lay on the sand, thrown backward by the force of a bullet, blood spreading across his chest. In his hand was the pistol Joaquín had lost. He stood up and reholstered his gun as Seth dragged a silently resistent Mrs. Wells toward him. In Seth's right hand was a Winchester, still smoking.

The woman moaned when she saw Webster, then she fell against Seth's chest and sobbed in helpless abandon. Seth tossed the rifle to Joaquín, meeting his eyes with an honest assessment that judged him short. They could hear the dog barking and the men shouting guesses of where the shot had come from.

Seth took hold of the woman's shoulders. "Snap out of it, lady," he said, shaking her roughly. "You got one minute to tell us everything you know or you won't be Mrs. anybody for long."

She leaned away as far as his grasp allowed, her pale face streaked with tears.

"Where're his partners?" Seth asked.

She shook her head.

He slapped her, then raised his hand to do it again, expecting Joaquín to object. Joaquín said nothing and Seth's palm came down hard against the woman's cheek. She cried out and fell to her knees. When Joaquín stood immobile, apparently indifferent, Seth felt a cold chill of loss.

They could hear the other men crashing through the brush, searching for them. Seth lifted the woman to her feet. "You best say it before they get here," he warned, "or you'll be telling it to your husband."

Fear filled her eyes. "Dirk was to meet Norris at somebody's cabin," she whimpered. "He just came back to say goodbye." She stopped and looked at her dead lover, grief hollow in her face.

As the others came running into the mouth of the arroyo, Micah Wells bellowed from the porch, "What the devil's going on?" His wife jerked free of Seth's grasp and turned away to hide her tears.

Stubbins stomped over to the corpse and stared down at it a moment, then asked, "Who was he?"

"Dirk Webster," Lemonade piped up.

"Who killed him?" Engle asked.

"I did," Seth said. "He was getting away."

"That right?" Engle asked Joaquín.

He looked at Seth a long moment before he said, "*Sí.* I was careless and Webster gained the advantage. He would have escaped if Seth hadn't shot him."

Engle looked back and forth between them a moment, then at the woman. "What do you know about it?"

"Nothing," she said, shaking her head as if in a daze. "I was out walking and just happened to be near. Everything was over by the time I arrived."

"Ya best go to the house, little lady," Buck Stubbins said kindly. "This ain't no place for ya."

She walked away without looking back.

After a moment, they could hear Micah Wells angrily demanding that his wife tell him what happened. Their voices moved into the house and the door closed, then the four men and a boy stood in the silence of the arroyo lit only by brittle starlight.

"What'll we do now?" Stubbins asked.

"You could try searching his horse for the money," Seth wryly suggested.

As Engle and Stubbins moved eagerly to do it, Seth stepped closer to Joaquín. "Did you learn anything?"

"He asked if I had seen a man traveling alone," Joaquín answered, staring into Seth's eyes as if he could find a key to survival in their depths.

Seth frowned. "One man?"

Joaquín nodded. "The Tyler brothers have gone back to Texas. Webster offered me a cut, saying he and Norris had fourteen left."

Seth studied Joaquín's face. "You think he'd trust Norris with the money?"

Flicking his gaze at the townsmen searching the horse, Joaquín asked, "You don't think they'll find it?"

Seth shook his head. "Webster would've hidden it under a rock before bringing it here."

"When he made his offer," Joaquín said softly, "it didn't sound as if they had split it yet." He shifted his gaze to the corpse. "I should thank you for saving my life."

"Only if you mean it."

Joaquín met his eyes again. "I was lucky you happened along just then."

"I followed the woman back out," Seth said.

Stubbins left the horse and searched the clothes on the corpse, but both he and Engle came up empty-handed.

"Sonofabitch," Stubbins complained. "Ya sure ya didn't kill an innocent man, Strummar?"

"Yeah, I'm sure," he retorted, losing patience. "Ain't he one of 'em, Lemonade?"

"Yes, sir. That's Dirk Webster."

"Well, he didn't have any money," Engle said.

"So Norris has it," Seth said. "Webster told Joaquín the Tyler brothers are already gone, but he and Norris were supposed to meet up someplace."

Stubbins and Engle looked at each other, then Engle asked with sarcasm, "You didn't find out where?"

"Webster was not stupid, *señor,*" Joaquín replied with equal sarcasm.

"What'll we do now?" Stubbins asked Seth.

"Nobody travels cross-country unseen. We'll hit the cantinas and scavenge another lead. Are you up for that?"

Again the townsmen looked at each other, this time longer. Stubbins looked back at Seth. "If that's what it takes."

Seth looked at Engle.

"I'll go," he said.

"All right," Seth said. "I suggest we finish our supper and move out. That agreeable?"

"Will you tell us where?" Engle asked, bristling with resentment.

"Sulphur Springs seems a good bet," Seth said, ignoring the hostility. He looked at Lemonade. "Go ask Wells for use of a shovel and where he wants the grave, then dig it. When it's ready, come get us and we'll help tote the body."

"Yes, sir," Lemonade said, trotting toward the house.

Seth watched the townsmen until they, too, moved across the yard and went inside. He looked at Joaquín and said, "That was an old trick to fall for. You should've left the gun and come back for it later."

"Thanks for pointing out my error," Joaquín snapped.

"Might keep you alive next time," Seth said. He walked over and looked down at the corpse, feeling somewhat better to see he'd hit the heart despite the haste of his aim. After a moment, Joaquín came over and they both stood staring down at Webster. In the distance, they could hear the shovel working. Seth asked, "Would you feel better if you'd killed him?"

"No," Joaquín admitted.

"I don't feel a thing," Seth said, meeting his friend's eyes. "Maybe it's better this way."

"Which way?"

"Letting me spill the blood."

"Do you think I would gain anything by that?"

"I already got a death warrant on my head, but you don't. Seems to me that's worth preserving."

"You think I should live my life in the safety of your protection?"

"Maybe I want to live mine in the safety of yours. Maybe if you become known as a killer, we'll have to split company for the sake of finding a moment's peace."

"Is peace what you're after?" Joaquín mocked.

"Yeah, but I'm having a hard time pinning down what you're after."

"I already told you: I am serving justice."

Seth nudged the corpse with his boot. "Is this a piece of it?"

Joaquín looked down at the dead man between them. "It would have been better to take him alive."

Seth shrugged. "I'd rather die from a bullet than a noose."

"There is a difference, though," Joaquín said. "His death is the result of my careless mistake and his desperate move against the deadly Seth Strummar. It was a game of skill and error. Justice had no time to be heard."

"If I hadn't come along, would you have heard it?" Seth asked, straining to keep sarcasm from his voice.

"I would be dead," Joaquín conceded. "To be both just and dead carries little weight."

Seth laughed. "I'll agree with that."

They both looked down at the corpse again. "One thing we know," Joaquín said, "is that Webster believed Norris is waiting for him somewhere nearby."

"If he was right, that means we have to scour this corner of the territory hoping we're close enough to do something about it when Norris makes a mistake."

"And if Webster was wrong?"

"Then Norris is already across at least one border, maybe two, and we're setting off on a trek admirable only for its ambition."

Joaquín nodded. "I will do what it takes. Will you?"

Seth hesitated, then smiled. "I'll back up whatever you want."

"You have a family," Joaquín pointed out. "Perhaps you should think of them."

Seth looked north, thinking of the warm comforts of Rico's bed, the commodious friendship of Esperanza, the baby Elena with her flashing blue eyes, and Lobo, who had been angry at being left behind. Meeting the dark eyes of his friend, Seth said, "None of 'em are more kin to me than you are."

Joaquín gave him an awkward smile. "This is something I must do. It is not yours."

"We're partners, ain't we?" Seth asked painfully.

"I am releasing you," Joaquín said with soft determination.

Seth looked away. After a moment he gave his friend a playful smile. "We can be partners on this job, can't we?"

"Perhaps," Joaquín answered solemnly. "We'll see."

Lemonade's voice cut between them. "The grave's ready," he shouted, ebullient with happiness at his achievement.

19

★

Lobo was unhappy at being left behind. The first moment he could slip away, he took his pinto from the stable and rode hard for the dunes. He also took a Winchester carbine from Joaquín's room and two boxes of .44 cartridges, a full canteen of water, and a fistful of jerked venison wrapped in a bandanna along with a dozen oatmeal cookies.

By the time he got there, the wind had swept the dunes clean of tracks. He sat his pinto feeling his hopes dwindle until he spotted fresh dung half-buried in the sand. He chose his direction on the chance the horse had been pointed the way it eventually walked. A mile further on, he came across more dung dropped on the move. He knew that meant the odds were good he was on the right trail.

The women didn't realize Lobo was gone until Nib Carey arrived at the homestead for breakfast. Though both he and his horse were tired from just having returned from the mountains, Nib pursued the boy, expecting to catch him within hours. At the dunes he, too, saw the dung and a few traces left by the pinto's hooves, so Nib spurred his horse into a lope across the ancient lake bed of Sulphur Valley, heading east toward the Chiricahuas.

At noon, Lobo was outside the cabin of Hermit Dan. He sat his horse and hollered, as Seth had told him to do. Lobo's shout echoed against the far ridge and bounced back; otherwise only the wind moving in the trees made any noise. His eyes searched the shadows around the cabin until he spotted the carcass of a deer hanging under a tree. Behind him the corral was empty, the looming barn silent. "Dan!" he called again. "It's Lobo Madera."

The door cracked open and the hermit peered out, then stepped into the sunlight and smiled up at the boy. "Trackin' your daddy, ain't ya?"

"Yes, sir," Lobo said.

"Left early this mornin'. Kilt me a deer 'fore he went."

"Where was he goin'?" Lobo asked, trying not to sound impatient.

The old man shifted his mouth around as he considered the situation. He knew Seth wouldn't want Lobo crossing the country alone, but the boy riding so hard to catch his daddy made Dan feel sad. Finally he said, "It's a long ride after 'im, Lobo. Ya best get down and let your horse breathe a spell."

"Will you tell me where Seth went?"

Hermit Dan nodded. "Give ya vittles for your inner man, too."

Neither of them moved for several long moments. Dan chuckled. "Ya got your daddy's eyes, damn if ya ain't, Lobo. He went to the Wells ranch in the southern valley, thinkin' one of 'em he's chasin' might be visitin'. So don't go in flappin' your lips, if you're a-goin'. Make better time on a rested mount, though."

"How far is it?" he asked.

"Hundred miles, down the mountain into the inferno."

"Thank you kindly for the invitation." Lobo swung his leg over and jumped from the stirrup. "I sure am hungry."

"Put your horse up," Dan said. Camouflaging his relief, he quickly went back inside the cabin.

Lobo led his pinto into the barn, unsaddled and tossed an armful of hay into the manger, then stood a moment listening to the creak and moan of the roof in the wind. Empty except for him and his pinto, the barn was a cavernous structure built to hide stolen stock. Seth had told him that, saying once upon a time Hermit Dan had taken a bite of nearly every steer rustled between the two territories.

It seemed to Lobo that during that mythical "once upon a time" only outlaws, Indians, and a few settlers to provide sport had lived on the frontier. As a baby, he'd heard stories of how exciting an outlaw's life was, but now that he was older he understood there was no future in being an outlaw. Most of them died young to begin with, and those who stayed alive were hermits to one extent or another. Even Seth, though he had a family and rode into town, acted as if the world were an ever-shrinking corral of threat. That's why he never went anywhere but Blue's saloon, and why he stayed in the shadows when someone rode into the yard until he knew who they were.

Now he was crossing the country, wide open for any number of catastrophes to fall on his head. As much as Lobo accepted that Seth's survival was a gambling proposition, he meant to defend his father against the enemies he could fight. If that made him an outlaw, too, then Lobo guessed he was born to it because he was Seth Strummar's son.

Lobo and Hermit Dan sat at the table over bowls of chile beans and a skillet of cornbread, eating with a purpose that excluded conversation. The shuttered cabin was dark, the only light coming from the fire blazing intermittently above a somnolent glow of flickering coals in the hearth. When Lobo looked up, he saw a bottle of whiskey on the mantle. It was the same brand Seth bought, and seeing it made Lobo yearn for his father with a painful ache of anger aimed at himself. He thought if he hadn't been so stupid about sneaking into town on the sly, Seth might have taken him along.

Lobo knew he was just a kid, but he meant to prove his worth so Seth wouldn't leave him behind again.

Hermit Dan gathered the dirty dishes and carried them to the corner kitchen, then stayed in the shadows, having exhausted his tolerance of intimacy by sharing a table with the boy. He liked Lobo, though, and thought he should do his best to send the boy home.

"Ya know," Dan said in his husky voice, "Seth won't like ya disobeyin' 'im. If he wanted ya along, he would've took ya."

"Reckon," Lobo mumbled.

"But you're a-goin' anyway?"

"Looks like it," he said, peering into the shadows to meet the old man's eyes.

"What d'ya aim to do when ya catch up?"

"I'm gonna help him."

"He may need ya," Dan admitted with regret. "He's alone with them men."

Lobo preened under the implied praise, then caught the flaw in the hermit's words. "Ain't Joaquín with him?"

Dan shook his head. "There's a bone 'tween 'em. I don't know how it happened, but they ain't together no more."

"What do you mean?" Lobo cried, stunned at the thought of Joaquín not being their friend.

Dan shrugged. "Ya'll see for yourself. If ya go, I mean."

"I'm goin'," Lobo said.

Hermit Dan studied the boy in the flickering light of the fire, his blond hair so angelic, his pale eyes so fierce. Dan had traded Seth a deer for a lead on one of the men being tracked. It was an equitable exchange, worthy of their mutual respect, but Dan never gave anybody something for nothing. Yet he decided to give the other man to Lobo as a buffer against Seth's anger. "I gave your daddy one man for the deer," Dan muttered. "I hear tell the other un's hidin' at Deadman's Cabin." He let that sink in a moment, then said, "Ya might mention it when ya see 'im."

"Where is it?" Lobo asked eagerly.

"South side of Guadalupe Pass," Dan whispered, "clear t'other side of the Pedregosas in New Mex Terr'tory." He paused, then said, "Nobody knows what happened to him what built the cabin, not even his name. He's nothin' more'n a dead man now."

Lobo stood up. "The trail southeast?"

"After ya get outa the Chiricahuas. Ain't ya gonna sleep none?"

"No," Lobo said. "Thanks for dinner."

Dan chuckled. "There be no doubt you're a Strummar. Ya got that drive."

"It's nothin' to do with the name," Lobo said defensively.

"No, it ain't," Dan agreed.

"Thanks for everything," Lobo said.

He walked into the sunlit yard and across to the barn where his pinto sighed when he threw the saddle on its back. "Yeah, I know, Bandit," Lobo said as he tightened the cinch, "but it can't be helped."

He swung on and trotted down the trail, keeping up a good clip as he shortened the distance between himself and his father.

Nib Carey arrived at Hermit Dan's at sunset. While he sat his lathered horse in the yard and hollered three times, Nib could have sworn someone was watching him from somewhere, but no one answered his summons. He stepped down, loosened his cinch and watered his horse, even gave it some feed, and still no one appeared. The silence was broken only by ravens squabbling over a deer carcass hanging from a tree.

Nib cautiously pushed the cabin door ajar. The room was tidy, the dishes washed and put away, the floor freshly swept, the blankets on the bed tucked tight. He went back outside and stared into the forest all around. Seeing the carcass again, he knew the hermit would be wanting to butcher the deer and salt it down, so wouldn't have gone far. Nib hollered once more, trying to keep the anger from his voice. Not wanting to shout Seth's name into unknown ears, he yelled, "I'm lookin' for Lobo!"

The echo of his voice was answered only by the raucous complaints of ravens quarreling in the trees. After unsuccessfully searching the yard for tracks he could identify as Lobo's, Nib stood up straight and scanned the fringe of forest again. Nothing moved except the pines bouncing in the wind and an occasional flash of shiny black as ravens glided between perches.

Nib trounced himself thoroughly as he rode back down the mountain, letting his tired horse pick its own pace. He should have taken a fresh horse and ridden hell out of it to catch the kid. Now Blue would be mad, and Nib might even lose his job. Seth would be mad when he got home, and mad, too, if the kid caught up with him. If Lobo didn't catch up, if he got lost or died somehow, Nib would be the point of failure in Seth's carefully constructed defense of his family. But Lobo could have gone any direction from the cabin, if he had ever been there. Nib had lost him. It was as simple and humiliating as that.

A hundred miles south of where Nib was riding, the border route between Tucson and El Paso met the road to Nogales. The crossing was graced with a scattering of adobe hovels and blessed with a spring. Its water was life-sustaining but unpalatable, giving the town, if such it could be called, the name of Sulphur Springs. It was owned by Raul Ortega. He offered for sale food, lodging, dry goods, whiskey, weapons, ammunition, horses, and the company of women.

Seth figured Raul's Cantina was as good a place as any to pick up gossip of the nature he was seeking. He led the posse to stable their horses in Raul's Livery and walk the block of town to the cantina. Stubbins and Engle bellied up to the bar, sharing a bottle of whiskey, while Seth and Joaquín took beers to a corner table. Lemonade stood awkwardly just inside the door. Flipping him a nickel, Seth said, "Buy yourself a beer."

"He is only fourteen," Joaquín objected.

Seth smiled, pleased to hear Joaquín correcting him again. "It's only beer."

"I don't trust him sober," Joaquín argued. "Will you give me a reason why you want him along?"

Seth sipped his beer and watched Lemonade talking to the barkeep. "Because he tells anyone who'll listen what we're doing, so every man through here tonight will know who I am and why I'm here without my having to say a word. If any of 'em have something to share, they'll let me know." Seth smiled at Joaquín, trying to break through his hostility. "It's a trick I learned from Allister: you let the green kid blow your horn, and all you have to do is watch and see who's interested."

"The green kid," Joaquín replied sharply, "is risking his life every time your name comes out of his mouth."

Seth grinned. "Nobody's twisting his arm."

"You are using his ignorance, leaving him open to danger when he is incapable of protecting himself."

"He dealt himself in. If he's gonna play, he may as well learn how."

"Does that mean you would defend him?"

"If he's acting in my interest."

"And if he isn't, you will let him die because he failed to understand a situation you put him into?"

"I didn't put him anywhere," Seth snapped. "He came along."

"You allowed it. I'm surprised you didn't bring Lobo."

"Why don't you buy yourself a woman, Joaquín?" Seth suggested. "It would do you good."

"It won't be difficult to find more pleasant company," Joaquín retorted. He took his beer over to the far end of the bar and leaned with his back to the wall.

Left alone, Seth felt weary at being jefe again. He was too old to be riding the trail, definitely too old to change colors and uphold the law. Too slow to face professionals in their prime, that was the truth of it. If he had a predictable backup, or a troop with any degree of loyalty, he might feel more optimistic. But fighting the men he needed to lead, he had no control over what lay ahead and he knew it. Knew, too, that he was vulnerable because he felt divided.

Half of him wanted to go home to his women, lovely Rico and cantankerous Esperanza and the bundle of sweetness called Elena, while half of him wanted to indulge in the rambunctious bedding of a whore to ease his tension. Half of him wanted to camp in the wilderness with Lobo and watch the stars fall; half of him wanted to grind Norris' face in the dirt to prove no man got away with stealing money from Seth Strummar. There were two many halves pulling him in too many directions, and he felt disgruntled.

A bevy of whores came in to milk the new arrivals. The women were colorful and gay, laughing as they dispersed among the men. Seth saw Raul Ortega lead a young beauty through the door. They stopped on the threshold as Ortega pointed Seth out to the girl. She smiled shyly. Nodding his thanks at Ortega as she walked toward him, Seth stood up and held a chair for her, then sat back down and admired her, thinking not all the repercussions of being jefe were unpleasant.

She raised her head under his scrutiny, her exotic features framed by curly black hair falling loose to her shoulders. She was Creole, a breed Seth hadn't seen since the last time he'd been in east Texas. Her skin was cocoa-colored, her cheeks flat and her nose delicate over her sensuously full mouth, her eyes black fire glistening from beneath long lashes she used in the way Spanish girls flirted with fans. He guessed her age at sixteen, and that she was either new to the profession or extremely well trained. "What're you drinking?" he asked.

She turned to the barkeep, expectant of his attention, and signaled with three fingers together. Then she turned back and demurely looked at her lap. Seth nodded with a smile, knowing now that she was a spy. There had been a time when he liked nothing better than spending a few hours with a woman who wanted something from him, a time he would have enjoyed pushing the limits of her desire to please him. Now he thought she would at least provide some diversion while he waited, since he wasn't keeping any secrets.

Two vaqueros came in and stood at the bar between where Engle was with Stubbins and where Lemonade stood alone. Seth watched Stubbins assess the newcomers so aggressively they shied away, which was no way to gather information. Engle was more interested in the woman on his arm. Seth appraised her, trying to plumb the man by his taste in whores. It was a hard call. She was pretty and obviously dumb, if not deliberately stupid, but there were times when Seth had chosen a dim-witted woman because she wouldn't interfere with his thinking. Which wasn't what he wanted now. He watched the barkeep deliver two beers and a shot of tequila, setting them quietly on the table without meeting his eyes. Seth looked at the woman assigned to him. "What's your name?" he asked.

"Heaven," she said in a whispery voice.

He smiled and lifted the tequila. "Is this for me?"

"If you wish."

He drank half of it down, then slid the glass toward her. "We'll share."

"Gracias," she said, downing the raw tequila as easily as he had.

He watched Maurice Engle walk out the door with the woman. Stubbins had managed to overcome his clumsy approach and was talking with the vaqueros now. Lemonade listened, sitting crosslegged on the bar and watching the door, his Winchester at his knee, his beer mug empty. Joaquín still had his back to the wall, his hat shadowing his face. The woman with him—small, dark, and plump—laughed often. For a moment, Seth envied Joaquín's youth and bachelorhood and clean slate, then he smiled at the ancient child sharing his table. She smiled back as if guessing his thoughts, but he knew whores were adept at performance.

Seth caught Lemonade's eye. The kid jerked his chin at the vaqueros and shook his head. Stubbins broke away from them, came over and sat down without an invitation. He looked at Heaven a long moment, then shifted his eyes to Seth. "How long we gonna be here?"

"Where do you think we should go?" Seth asked.

"After Norris!"

"Which way?" Seth replied, answering the man's hostility with calm for the sake of peace. Stubbins was so brash he constantly rode the edge of being provoked, and Seth didn't want him to fall over that edge and force a confrontation the miner would lose.

"Ain't ya got any idea?" Stubbins asked impatiently.

"I'm thinking on it."

"That means ya don't," he muttered.

"It's too bad Webster didn't leave us a map."

Stubbins glared at him. "Ya think that makes me afraid of ya?"

"Don't see how it should change your opinion one way or the other."

"Would've been better to take him alive," Stubbins said, as if the idea were his own.

"Would've been worse to let him get away," Seth answered.

Stubbins sniffed loudly, scanning the cantina as he frowned. "Reckon," he said.

Seth winked at the ancient child, and she gave him another wise smile that was almost convincing. He figured if he got drunk enough she would become one hungry ear dripping with desire. Not intending to get that drunk, he made a mental note to congratulate Ortega on his acquisition.

Stubbins asked, "What would ya do in Norris' boots?"

Seth pretended to mull the question over, as if he hadn't been pondering exactly that for the last two days. As he sipped his warm beer, he saw Joaquín lift a lock of the woman's hair to fall behind her shoulder. Seth smiled, thinking what the kid needed was a good lay to take the edge off his grief, then he looked back at the owner of the Red Rooster Mine. "I'd go to Mexico," Seth said.

"He could be there now," Stubbins complained.

"Yeah, he could," Seth agreed.

"Why ain't we? If he crosses the border he'll disappear."

"We got information he ain't left yet."

"From Webster?"

Seth nodded.

"So we're sittin' here tryin' to catch his wind?"

Seth laughed. "That's about it."

Stubbins laughed, too. "Don't seem a respectable occupation for a man."

"I prefer the running, myself," Seth said.

"What's the dif'rence?" Stubbins asked, suddenly friendly.

"The man out front is making the decisions. All we can do is ride the repercussions."

"We got choices," Stubbins argued.

"Can't see too many right now."

He sniffed his agreement, then asked, "Ya think Norris has all the money?"

"The Tyler brothers took six."

"So there's fourteen left?"

"That's what Webster said."

"There's the reward Clancy put up. That's another five hundred."

Seth shrugged. "Webster said Norris killed the boy. Norris'll say Webster did it. Hard to prove either way."

"We can say anything we want, then," Stubbins muttered.

"That's always true," Seth said. He watched Joaquín walk out with the woman, not even glancing his direction. Seth's only consolation was knowing Blue and Nib were home with the women and children. Stubbins left the table and went outside alone. Seth looked at Heaven. She flashed her crescent eyes and asked, "Would you like more tequila?"

"Why not?" he said, watching her signal the keep again.

By midnight, the cantina was rowdy with vaqueros and drifters. The whores were busy, and more than one resentful glance was thrown at Seth for having a woman to himself. The resentment was contained only because everyone knew who he was. They also knew the Mexican leaning against the far wall was his compañero, that the two surly men and the boy at the bar were with them, and why they were there. The law in Arizona, however, was scattered and scant, and most men approved of vigilantes. Provided, of course, their actions didn't result in a miscarriage of justice.

Ortega's regular patrons had heard rumors that Seth Strummar was living in their part of the country. Now they were seeing him for the first time. They noted Ortega had given Strummar his personal concubine, and they all noticed that the outlaw hadn't touched the girl, though he seemed to be enjoying her company. The Mexican was like a lizard, standing immobile for hours, his eyes missing nothing.

No one missed seeing the vaquero stop beside Strummar's table. Holding his mug of beer, he petitioned shyly in Spanish for permission to sit down.

Seth smiled into the broad mestizo face of a man so recently removed from peonage that his every gesture was imbued with humility. *"Siéntese,"* Seth said in his clumsy Spanish, then caught his partner's eye with a glance that yesterday would have summoned Joaquín, but Seth didn't watch to see if it still worked. He smiled at the vaquero and waited with hope.

Joaquín came over and sat down. Seth watched their faces, hearing the murmur of Joaquín's Spanish as he leaned with his arm on the back of the vaquero's chair and spoke softly.

"Sí," the vaquero said.

Joaquín kept speaking, his Spanish too quick for Seth's ears. The vaquero nodded several times, glanced once at Seth, studied Heaven as if he weren't seeing her, then met Joaquín's eyes and spoke in a fluid whisper.

"¿Está seguro?" Joaquín asked.

"¡Sí!" the vaquero affirmed.

"Gracias," Joaquín said solemnly, touching the vaquero's shoulder like a priest delivering a benediction.

Seth restrained a smile, then glanced at Heaven. Her face had come alive with yearning aimed at Joaquín, which made Seth smile after all.

Joaquín reported, "There is an abandoned cabin on the land where this man works. He says yesterday it was no longer abandoned."

"Did you find out where?"

Joaquín nodded.

Seth smiled at the vaquero. "Gracias, señor. Le diga no otra persona, ¿entiende?"

"Sí," the vaquero said. "Nadie."

Seth smiled again. "Si necesita ayuda de yo, soy a su servicio."

"Gracias, señor," the vaquero said, standing up and bowing. He kept his knees rigid but couldn't help himself from backing the first steps away. Then he went to the bar to glory in his notoriety for having spoken with the outlaw.

"I'm going outside," Seth said to Joaquín. "Can you keep the lady company for a while?"

Joaquín shrugged, not looking at her.

"Thanks," Seth said. "She's a speciality of the house so we can't let her loose with the rabble." He smiled sardonically. "Help yourself if you feel inclined. I'm passing, myself."

"Sí, ya lo creo," Joaquín muttered with sarcasm.

"It's true," Seth said. "I promised Rico—swore fidelity to the marriage bed."

Joaquín laughed with disbelief. "I would like to see you keep that promise."

Seth stood up. "Stick around and you will."

Finally Joaquín looked at the woman. "Take your time," he said to Seth.

Seth laughed and walked out. Every eye in the room followed him, and he stepped into the darkness relieved to be away from the constant scrutiny. Heading north along the edge of the road, he deeply inhaled the cool, night air after so many hours of breathing tobacco smoke and kerosene fumes inside the cantina.

He knew he needed sleep more than anything, which meant the best plan would be to stay at the crossroads and ride out in the morning. If Norris was in the cabin yesterday, odds were good he would give Webster one more day and be there tomorrow. But he would be rested and wary. Best to face him sharp with fresh horses, ready for anything. The plan made sense, and Seth realized that if he could get Stubbins and Engle to fall for it, he could give them the slip. By tomorrow he and Joaquín would have the money and be on their way home. Whatever happened in between would be nobody else's business.

He started back toward the cantina, then remembered Joaquín was with the ancient child and decided to give them more time. Lemonade came outside and stood a moment, letting his eyes adjust to the dark. When they had, the kid saw Seth and joined him. They ambled down the road together, the boy carrying his borrowed rifle proudly, the man feeling the weight of his sixgun heavier than he used to.

Thinking he'd leave the kid behind with the others, Seth asked, "What'll you do when this is over, Lemonade?"

"I hadn't thought on it," he answered with a grin.

"You remember the deal we made?"

"Yeah," he said, looking worried now.

"I want to keep it," Seth said.

"Ya mean ya want me to skedaddle?" Lemonade asked, crestfallen.

"That pretty well fits it. Reason I brought it up now, I don't want you doing something thinking there's a job for you out of it. There ain't."

"No chance?" the kid asked.

Seth shrugged. "Not that I know of."

After a moment, Lemonade asked with chagrin, "I fucked up with the deer, din't I?"

"You missed the deer, there's no arguing that. But you did the part I hired you for fine. We're playing a different hand now, is all."

"I wish you'd let me stay, Mr. Strummar," he said, trying not to plead.

"You can stay for this job. I ain't saying you can't. But there's no payoff for you at the end of it."

Lemonade turned around and stared back at Sulphur Springs, a squat huddle of lights across the distance. "If I left on my own," he asked, "would ya let me take the mare?"

"No," Seth said. "But I'll buy you a horse from Ortega as good as the one you left at my place."

A man inside the cantina laughed. Distorted on the breeze, the guffaw sounded like a plaintive cry of loneliness from where Seth stood in the dark. Feeling isolated on the edge of society was a familiar sensation for Seth, as well as for Lemonade. On the strength of that unspoken bond, the kid pushed for an opening. "Will ya tell me, Mr. Strummar," he asked, "why it is ya don't want me around?"

Seth considered his answer carefully. "You lied to me for one thing. Hard to trust a man who lies."

"That wasn't really a lie," Lemonade argued. "It was more like a brag."

"If that deer had been a sheriff," Seth retorted, "we'd be dead."

"Ya ain't ridin' against sheriffs no more," Lemonade pointed out.

"Outlaws shoot back, too," Seth said, surprised at having made that slip. "What I'm saying," he said gruffly, "is we're playing a dangerous game and you don't stand to gain anything by surviving it. No one would hold it against you if you went your own way."

"I stand to gain a lot, Mr. Strummar," he pleaded. "I'm riding with ya and learnin' from that. For the rest of my life, I'll be proud to say I knew ya. It's all I got goin' for me, that and the clothes ya bought. I'd sure like to stick it."

Seth despised the pitiful tone of Lemonade's appeal, but if his plan worked the kid would be left behind with the others. There was no sense kicking him out when he could spoil the play. "Well, as long as you're here," Seth said, "run back inside and tell the men we're staying the night, to get themselves rooms and be ready to ride at dawn. Can you do that?"

"Yes, sir!" the kid said with vigor.

"Don't shout it from the door. Tell each man quietly. Learn to control your mouth."

"Yes, sir," he said meekly.

Seth took a coin from his pocket. "Get yourself a room, too."

Lemonade laughed. "Thanks, Mr. Strummar!"

Watching Lemonade run back to the cantina, Seth remembered the gaggle of street urchins he'd plucked the kid out of. When he'd first seen those vultures, Seth had wondered if one wouldn't grow up to kill him. Now he couldn't help wonder if he wasn't training Lemonade to do it.

A few minutes later, Seth saw Engle and Stubbins come out and walk to the hotel across the road. Seth stood in the dark for an hour, enjoying the quiet, the stars, and the rising new moon. The land was a humid presence around him, a desert oasis with the faint scent of sulphur evaporating off the spring, and he felt a moment's compassion for Heaven. Such an accomplished beauty deserved a better place to call home, and a better man than one who shared her at whim. Carried on a sudden breeze, the sulphur smell was strongly unpleasant as he watched Lemonade cross the road to the hotel. Seth waited until the cantina's hitching rail was empty, then walked back through the dark to the lighted door.

Only the keep behind the bar, and Joaquín and the ancient child engrossed in conversation, were still there. Seth walked across to their table and sat down. They watched him, their faces as smooth as river stones. Regretfully he said, "I think we should move out while the good citizens are asleep."

After a moment, Joaquín said, "I will go." He didn't move.

"I'll be in the stable," Seth said, then left them alone to make their private adieus.

He chuckled as he saddled his sorrel, thinking if there were ever two people meant for each other, it was Heaven and Joaquín. Their educations meshed, allowing for the difference in sex, of course. Seth thought they would be a dynamite team in any scam a couple could pull, then had to admit they weren't thinking of schemes these days. They were playing it straight, catching thieves and going home when it was over. At least he was.

Finished with his own, Seth saddled Joaquín's horse, too. When he was done, Joaquín still hadn't shown up. Seth swung onto his sorrel and led the black down the road to the cantina. He stopped outside and whistled softly. Nothing happened for so long he was about to dismount and go in when Joaquín sauntered out the door. He took his reins with a smile and slapped his horse so it leapt to a gallop while he swung on with the agility of youth, forcing Seth to dig in his spurs to catch up.

They galloped along the road heading east, then slowed to a trot when they cut south toward the mountains. Seth looked at the newly blossomed Don Juan riding beside him where a monk had been. "It's a good thing you raked your ashes before meeting Heaven," he teased, "or you'd still be back in Sulphur Springs."

Joaquín looked across as if he hadn't really seen Seth before. "The girl and I went for a walk," he said.

"You didn't fuck her?" Seth asked with surprise.

Joaquín shook his head.

"How'd you resist Heaven, then?"

"Ortega gave her to you, not me."

"I gave her to you."

Again Joaquín looked at him with a baffled curiosity. "How can you love Rico and see every woman as a piece of meat?"

Seth laughed. "We're all just people who go bump in the night."

"And sometimes," Joaquín said, leaning close to point his finger like a gun at Seth's chest, "we go bang in the night, too."

Seth laughed again, ignoring the gesture he would not have tolerated from any other man. "Love and death," he quipped. "They're the only things that matter."

"Are they?" Joaquín asked. "What about honor and dignity? Do they not matter?"

"Most people seem to get along without 'em."

"Melinda got along without them," Joaquín replied angrily. "So does Heaven. But it is not their choice."

"Ain't mine," Seth said.

"Wasn't it yours with Lila Keats?"

"Lila brought herself down," he retorted. "Which is what I see you doing."

Joaquín was quiet for a long stretch, then said, "The abuse of women is the worst sin. It amazes me I have ridden so long with a man who enjoys it so much."

Seth reined up sharp and turned his horse head-on to face his former partner. "That's right. I've done things to women that would make you puke. I've killed more men than you've got fingers and toes, and I robbed nearly every bank in Texas. You knew that the moment we met. It's a little late to be getting so goddamned self-righteous. You've used whores and killed men. Now 'cause you're chasing thieves for a crime you never lowered yourself to commit, you think you're the scythe of God out to right wrongs. Well, I'm wrong, Joaquín. Why don't you start with me?"

They stared at each other across their horses' ears. Joaquín said, "I have no wish to kill you."

"You think you could?" Seth scoffed.

"I have no wish to find out."

"Maybe I do."

"Would it make you feel better?"

Seth remembered Allister asking how it would feel when one of them looked down on the other's corpse. Remembered, too, that he had challenged Allister to that final confrontation by stealing his women. Now Joaquín was challenging Seth, again over women, but with a whole new twist. He smiled painfully. "Don't try to kill me 'cause I'm a whoremonger, Joaquín. I gave it up."

"I have no desire to kill you," he answered.

"What are we doing then?"

"Wasting time," Joaquín said, reining his horse around and kicking it into a trot again.

Seth caught up. "Where we going?"

"Deadman's Cabin."

"That sounds promising. Where is it?"

"On the south side of Guadalupe Pass. Have you been there?"

"Yeah, it's rough country."

"*Sí*," Joaquín agreed. "It's all badlands, though, isn't it?"

Seth smiled. "No rest for the wicked."

Joaquín shook his head. "I want to catch Norris and give back what he gave Melinda. After that, I will be satisfied."

"You'll let the Tyler brothers go?" Seth asked hopefully.

"They are not worth a trip to Texas."

"I agree," Seth said. He turned in his saddle and looked back, nudged by a suspicion of being followed.

"What is it?" Joaquín whispered.

"Don't know," Seth said, facing forward again with a puzzled frown. "Let's quit talking and move."

20

★

Lobo rode into Sulphur Springs an hour after dawn. He saw Rico's palomino in the corral and felt a moment's jubilation before he noticed neither Seth's sorrel nor Joaquín's black were there. He sat puzzling over that a minute, tired and hungry from having ridden all night. The town was a cluster of low adobes permeated by the sour smell of rotten eggs. As he watched, a door opened and Lemonade stopped abruptly on the threshold and stared at him.

"Well, lookee here!" Lemonade called back over his shoulder. Then to Lobo, "Howdy, Lobo. Ya lookin' for Seth?"

Engle and Stubbins came to the door. The merchant smiled but the miner didn't. "What in tarnation ya doin' here, Lobo?" Stubbins demanded sternly. "If your daddy wanted ya along, he would've brung ya."

"Hold on," Engle said. "Took a lot of courage for the boy to ride this far. We shouldn't chew him out for having gumption. You hungry, Lobo?"

He nodded.

"Well, step down and come on in. Your daddy'll be surprised to see you, no doubt about that."

"Is he here?" Lobo asked.

Engle smiled. "He's not up from bed yet. Had company last night; I'm sure you know what I mean."

Lobo nodded again, swung his leg over and jumped to the ground.

"Why don't you put his horse up, Lemonade?" Engle suggested kindly. "He looks plumb tuckered."

"Thanks," Lobo said, handing his reins to Lemonade. He followed Engle into the house, Stubbins coming along behind.

There was no one else in the dining room, only three plates set at the table, but the food looked good. Hotcakes with honey and fatback and coffee. Lobo sat down and dug in without waiting for a second invitation. Engle and Stubbins sat down and watched him. After a few minutes, Lemonade came in and sat down, too, all of them watching Lobo.

Engle asked, "What brought you here?"

"Lookin' for Seth," Lobo answered, his wariness returning with the coffee and food in his stomach.

"What made you think to look here?" Engle asked.

Lobo looked at Stubbins, who seemed grim, then at Lemonade, who seemed amused. "Seth ain't here, is he?" Lobo asked the kid who had once been his friend.

Lemonade shook his head. "Him and Joaquín left last night after we was all asleep."

Lobo laughed at the townsmen. "So he shook you off, like a dog shakes fleas."

Engle reached across and slapped him.

Stubbins was on his feet. "I'll have none of that!"

"He's a smart-mouthed son of a killer!" Engle shouted.

"He's still a kid," Stubbins retorted with disgust. "I don't go for roughin' up chil'ren."

Engle didn't seem to care what Stubbins went for. The merchant was glaring at Lobo as if ready to hit him again when Lemonade said with disdain, "Ya oughta jus' ask 'fore ya rough him up."

"You ask," Engle sneered.

Lemonade looked at Lobo. "D'ya know where Seth is?"

Lobo looked at the two men watching so intently. "Maybe."

"Don't play games," Lemonade warned. "These gen'lemen are in earnest."

"Believe that, kid," Stubbins growled.

"If Seth wanted you with him," Lobo sassed, "he would've taken you."

"Ya little snot!" the miner yelled.

Engle laughed. "Why don't you hit him, Buck? You'll feel better."

Lobo looked at the door.

"There's no chance we'll let you go," Engle said. "Make up your mind to that."

"What do you want with me?" Lobo asked.

"We want the money your father's after," Engle said in a reasonable tone.

"If he said he'd bring it back, he will."

"He lived his life provin' otherwise," Stubbins grumbled.

"But he always keeps his word," Lobo boasted.

"Then why doesn't he want us there?" Engle argued. "Why did he leave us behind, if not to get away with the money?"

Lobo shrugged. "Maybe you slowed him down. He's accustomed to crossin' the country pretty fast."

The two men stared at him for a long moment of silence, then Stubbins asked in a patient tone, "Where's he goin', Lobo?"

"If I tell, will you take me along?"

"Hell, no! A manhunt's no place for a child."

"Then I won't tell," Lobo said, looking at Engle, "but I'll lead you there."

"It's a deal," Engle said.

"Wait a minute," Stubbins protested.

Engle snickered. "Strummar'll trade the money for his kid in the blink of an eye. What're you complaining about, Buck?"

"I don't like usin' a kid."

"No one's gonna hurt him." Engle looked at Lemonade. "Go saddle the horses and fill the canteens."

Lemonade glanced at Lobo, then left to do it.

Lobo asked Engle, "Can I help him?"

"No," Stubbins said. "Stretch out on that settee there and close your eyes. I'll wake ya when it's time."

Lobo looked at Engle, who nodded, so he laid down and closed his eyes. The next thing he knew Lemonade was shaking him awake.

"Ya been sleepin' for hours," the kid said with scorn. "Mr. Engle told me to wake ya now."

Lobo looked around the room, remembering where he was. Then he studied Lemonade's face, trying to figure if he was still a friend.

"Ya best move," Lemonade said.

Lobo slowly stood up and stretched, trying to collect his thoughts. He knew only that he wanted to be with Seth, so he picked up his hat and followed Lemonade into the bright light of noon.

Engle and Stubbins sat their horses in the road, Rico's palomino standing beside Lobo's pinto. Sight of the golden horse made Lobo feel protective of his stepmother in a way he hadn't before. Knowing she would cry over the loss of the mare but be undone by the loss of the man, Lobo swung onto his pinto and looked at the carbine in his scabbard.

"Take his rifle, Lemonade," Engle said with strained patience. "He's a Strummar, after all."

Lobo watched to see if Lemonade would do it. The kid grinned sheepishly as he came forward and slid the carbine free. He shrugged as if had no choice, but Lobo didn't see it that way. He glared icily at Lemonade until the kid took a step back, his smile wavering.

Lobo reined his pinto around and trotted east toward the badlands, hearing the three horses fall in behind. Hermit Dan had described their destination as a cabin on the south flank of a pass. Studying the mountains looming in the distance, Lobo realized his odds of finding that cabin were slim.

Thirty miles southeast, Seth and Joaquín were bellied down on a rock overlooking Deadman's Cabin. A bay gelding stood in the unshaded corral with one rear hoof crooked, his head lowered as he slept in the sun. Occasionally a sparrow chittered from the scrub brush or a fly droned close, attracted to the moisture of the men's sweat, but otherwise everything was silent. Not a breath of wind moved off the mountains towering starkly red all around, and the thin column of smoke from the cabin's chimney rose straight into the blue sky.

Joaquín searched the scene in front of him for a clue to success. "Any ideas?" he asked.

"I was cornered in a cabin by five Rangers once upon a time," Seth said.

"How did you get out?" Joaquín asked, watching him now though Seth still studied the terrain.

"Set fire to the cabin, crawled underneath and made it to my horse. About the same distance as here."

"You set fire to your sanctuary?" Joaquín asked in amazement.

"I destroyed my cover as a way out. My sanctuary was a horse moving fast between my legs."

"Why were the Rangers chasing you?"

"I held up a high-class poker game in Austin." He smiled. "Pissed off a few legislators, I reckon."

Joaquín looked away. "What did you do with the money?"

"Spent most of it on women without honor or dignity." He met his partner's dark eyes with a playful smile. "Let's see how close we can get, then take it from there."

"All right," Joaquín said.

They approached the cabin from opposite sides, walking silently with their rifles cocked in their hands. As they peered in opposing windows and met each other's eyes across the lethal terrain of enemy turf, Joaquín was struck by Seth's profound alienation. He was a pariah to outlaws as well as the law, and the brutal fact was that his life had been lived and there remained only the repercussions to ride until a young man keen on a reputation killed him. Joaquín shuddered with lucidity: he saw Seth reduced to bones, a skeleton mouldering in the privacy of a grave, if lucky.

In that moment, the existence of the human soul seemed a mirage, a dream born of a yearning so powerful that Joaquín had hung his life on the scaffold of its need. For years he had sustained himself by striving to bring Seth to God, yet the road of that journey led instead to a vision through a window of absolute mortality. Joaquín was now in a territory which wanted him for crimes different only in degree from those committed by the man he sought to kill. That man had as much right to kill him, and Joaquín knew the outcome of what lay ahead would turn on luck and skill, not virtue.

Seth nodded at their prey with a smile acknowledging the honest moment just passed, and he was again the outlaw Joaquín had chosen to follow away from the priesthood: irreverent and in control. Joaquín looked at the man in the cabin—intent on preparing his midday meal—and remembered Webster saying the guard had shot Melinda, which meant she'd been caught in the crossfire as Seth said, only not of the bandits but of the law trying to stop them.

Though Joaquín tried to tell himself it didn't matter, that the bandits were still responsible, it was uncomfortably easy to put himself in their place. At any time in the last few years, if Seth had asked him to help rob a bank, Joaquín might have done it. If in the course of such a robbery, the guard had been so inept as to shoot an innocent bystander, Joaquín wouldn't accept the blame. It was the guard's mistake, which was the banker's mistake for hiring an incompetent. But the banker had paid with the life of his son, so maybe there lay the justice. It put enough doubt in Joaquín's mind that he decided he'd do what he could to deliver Norris to the law.

All Seth wanted was the money. Alive, Norris could produce it. Dead, he was the doom of success. Under normal circumstances, Seth could count on his partner to follow his lead. Now he was worried Joaquín would jump the gun, knowing the money had never once entered his thinking. Catching Joaquín's eye, Seth jerked his head at the door.

They approached from different sides, shifted their rifles to their left hands, drew their pistols and cocked them with their thumbs, then met each other's eyes across the empty space they intended to fill with undefeatable threat. A cognizance of the years they had ridden together flashed between them, a memory of meeting in a sunlit yard, of Joaquín taking Seth's weight when he was wounded and couldn't stand alone, an afternoon spent sharing whiskey and arguing over vengeance, their reunion and midnight talk of what it meant to be a man, another time when Seth came seeking the same courage Joaquín had sought from him. Now they stood opposed across a door to chaos, knowing everything about each other except the future of their friendship.

"Ready?" Seth whispered.

Joaquín nodded.

Seth kicked the door open and jumped in to land solid on both feet with his guns on Norris. "Don't move," Seth said.

Joaquín came in just as Norris jerked around in front of the stove.

"Don't try it," Seth warned.

Norris looked back and forth between them. "Who're you?"

"Seth Strummar," he said.

"Joaquín Ascarate," he said.

"Goddamn," Norris muttered. "It ain't right," he complained, his voice gaining volume. "Thieves catchin' thieves ain't right, not where I come from."

Seth smiled. "Maybe you should've stayed there."

Norris looked at him hard. "So you're Strummar, huh?"

"That's right."

"And you've come after your money."

"That's right, too."

"How 'bout I split with you, bein' as I think I earned it, seein' how things turned out?"

"I agree you paid heavy," Seth said.

"Damn straight," Norris said. "The guard was the one started shootin'. We had it smooth 'fore he opened up."

Seth shrugged. "That doesn't change the fact that I'm taking the money back to Tejoe. All of it."

Norris glanced between them again. "What'll you do with me?" he asked nervously.

"Kill you if you don't drop your gunbelt," Seth said.

"If I do?" Norris asked warily. "How long will I be alive?"

"How long will he be alive, Joaquín?" Seth asked, not taking his eyes off Norris, who was sweating as he waited for the answer.

Finally, Joaquín said, "At least as far as the law in Tombstone."

"There you are," Seth said to Norris. "What're you gonna do?"

"Do I have your word?" he asked in a quavering voice.

Seth laughed. "I wouldn't take your word, Norris. Why would you take ours?"

Norris looked frantically at Joaquín. "Do I have your word you'll deliver me safely to Tombstone?"

"I will do my best," Joaquín said.

Seth laughed again. "That's as good as you're gonna get, Norris. Make up your mind."

"All right," he said, reaching with his left hand to unbuckle his gunbelt. He let it dangle a moment, then gently fall.

"Move away from it," Seth said.

Norris did.

Joaquín picked it up and tossed it onto the bed under the far window.

"Now," Seth said, holstering his sixgun then sitting down at the table and laying his rifle in front of him, "what's for supper? I'm starved."

Norris looked at a kettle on the stove. "Shot a rabbit," he said nervously.

Seth grinned. "Ain't that the way? You pull off a big heist and still have to eat lean 'til you feel safe enough to spend it."

"Yeah," Norris mumbled.

"Where *is* the money?" Seth asked casually.

Norris looked at Joaquín, then back at him. "Webster has it."

"Webster's dead," Seth said. "I killed him yesterday. He didn't have any money on him."

"He was supposed to," Norris wheedled. "Maybe the Tyler brothers have it."

Seth shook his head. "They've already gone back to Texas, taking six thousand with 'em. Webster told us you had the rest."

Norris looked at Joaquín.

"Those were his dying words," Seth said. "I wonder what yours'll be."

"Wait a minute," Norris protested, his eyes on Joaquín. "You gave your word."

"I also gave my word to help Melinda," he replied testily. "If not for that, she wouldn't have been in the bank and would not have died. If I were you, señor, I would not put much faith in my word: it tends to ricochet out of control."

"The guard killed the woman!" Norris cried. "I've never shot a woman!"

"Nor a child?" Joaquín scoffed.

"Webster shot the kid! He overreacted, pulled the trigger too quick, aimin' at the guard. The kid was in between, is all."

"Webster told us it was you," Seth said.

"You've done the same, if not worse!" Norris accused. "How can you turn me over to the law?"

"That ain't my part of it," Seth said. "All I want is the money."

Norris looked back and forth between them. "You mean, if I give you the money, you'll let me go?"

"I won't," Joaquín said.

Seth smiled. "Sorry, Norris."

"Sonofabitch," he muttered.

"Seems to me," Seth said, "giving us the money is your best bet."

"Don't seem that way to me!" Norris retorted. "Soon as you have it, you got no reason to keep me alive."

"My inclination," Seth said, "is to kill you right now and count the money a loss, knowing anyone else who thought to rob me would think twice. But Joaquín's thinking is all tangled up with justice." Seth grinned at Norris. "Doesn't that word send chills down your spine?"

Norris nodded.

"So you see," Seth said, "Joaquín and I ain't partners in this deal. But we're going along unless one of us gets in the other's way. You turn the trick, Norris. You don't give me a reason to kill you, Joaquín wins. You give me a reason, I win. But there ain't no way you're gonna win. Unless you think if you stick it through a trial you might find mercy. In which case you best side with Joaquín and not give me a reason to kill you."

Norris just stared at him.

"Where's the money?" Seth asked.

"Outside."

"Let's get it," he said, standing up.

Norris looked at Joaquín. "All of us?"

Seth laughed. "Don't you trust me, Norris?"

He shook his head.

"But you trust Joaquín. Why is that?"

Norris studied him, then said, "He has the eyes of a priest."

"And what's a priest ever done for you?" Seth teased.

Norris shrugged. "Prayed for me, maybe."

"Think it did any good?"

"Guess we'll find out," Norris said.

21

★

The rabbit had been eaten and a fresh pot of coffee was simmering on the stove. Norris sat with his hands tied behind him, his legs and body tied to the chair, watching Joaquín, who stood between the door and a window. The Mexican seemed to be drowsing, leaning against the wall with his Winchester beside him, his face hidden by his hat.

Strummar was out there with the money, settling their horses into an arroyo. He thought like an outlaw, all right, Norris told himself. Even while acting for the law, Strummar hid in defense. Didn't let anything rush him, either. Most men, once they had the money, would have ridden hard for home. Strummar was letting their horses rest. He was smart, no doubt about that, and Norris was unhappy with his situation.

He kept chastising himself for being caught by surprise. His only defense was that few men won against Strummar, but that argument did nothing to bolster any hope of escape. Despite Ascarate's promise to deliver him alive to Tombstone, Norris had no doubt the Mexican was lethal. Even when relaxed, he was like a fist clenched for a blow. Norris suspected he would attack on the least provocation, but provocation was required. He wasn't sure with Strummar.

The outlaw had claimed to be accommodating his partner's notion of justice, but he'd also said they were going along until one of them got in the other's way. That smacked of mutiny to Norris, and he considered it piss poor to be caught in a power play that had nothing to do with him. He was the trick, like Strummar said—a dummy who would turn the game but couldn't win it for himself.

Norris weighed the benefits of throwing what little he had behind the man he chose to win. On one side was Seth Strummar, a renowned bandit and cold-blooded killer. On the other, Joaquín Ascarate, famous for abandoning the priesthood to follow Strummar. With the discipline of a zealot and the training of a desperado, Ascarate tracked men under the banner of justice. He wanted Norris alive, while Strummar was profoundly indifferent.

If he were watching from the sidelines, Norris would root for Strummar because the outlaw had risen above sentiment and lived life honestly. But the honest truth was the world didn't need Norris. He knew that. So did Strummar. Ascarate, however, believed even the worst sinner was a child of God, worthy of salvation. Norris smiled, thinking maybe the Mexican's holy crusade wasn't so bad if he could be moved to mercy. "Hey, Joaquín," he whispered.

The Mexican looked up, his dark eyes inscrutable.

Softly Norris said, "They'll lynch me in Tombstone. You know that, don't you?"

Ascarate shrugged. "That will be the marshal's problem."

"I'm your responsibility. You can't just turn me over to be lynched."

He shrugged again, watching the yard.

"It's the same as murder," Norris wheedled. "You might as well kill me here."

The Mexican turned around with an amused smile. "Do you think that argument is in your favor?"

"If I can get you to see it's the same thing. You don't strike me as a man who wants blood on his hands."

"You have already proved you are such a man."

"Those deaths were a mistake! I didn't go in there intendin' to kill anybody, let alone women and children. It blew up in my face. Webster was too quick and too sloppy. It was out of control 'fore I could catch it."

"Are you saying," Ascarate drawled with disdain, "that you expect me to let you go?"

"Strummar said he would. All *he* wants is the money."

The Mexican looked away, and Norris knew he'd hit a sore spot. Striving to drive a wedge into their already splintered partnership, he said with an insinuating warmth, "It's hard to figure why you're ridin' together. I ain't ever met two men more different in what they value."

"I doubt if you understand what I value, *señor.*"

"Oh, I think I got a pretty good picture. Any man who'd ride for justice, after all, must be operatin' from some basic assumptions. Things like love should reign triumphant, kindness and mercy should shower on the heads of sinners, all of Christendom should be a gentle place to live." He paused to smile. "That sound about right?"

"I see nothing wrong with it."

"There ain't nothing wrong," Norris agreed, " 'cept it's not true."

"It could be," Joaquín said, looking out the window at the horizon tinged rose with the beginning of dusk. He hadn't expected independence to be this mournful recognition of solitude. He'd expected strength, not doubt, courage, not fear, and he knew the man whispering behind him was like a viper circling for the exact point to pierce poisoned fangs into his intent.

"If Strummar got what he wanted," Norris said, "it'd be every man for himself and there wouldn't be no law."

"What do *you* want, *señor*?" Joaquín asked sharply.

"To ride away free. Ain't no secret about that."

"And you think the deaths of four people should be forgotten as an unfortunate accident?"

"It's the truth! Strummar killed men the same way. You ride with him. What's the difference?"

"His crimes are in the past."

"Three days ago is in the past."

"Three days ago Melinda was alive."

"So this is a personal vendetta," Norris accused. "That makes you no better'n Strummar. You're both actin' for yourself, and all that talk about justice is nothin' but hot air!"

Joaquín drew his pistol as he walked forward. He pressed the barrel of his gun between the viper's eyes and slowly cocked the hammer with his thumb. "You are right in thinking you will be lynched in Tombstone. If not lynched, you will hang. If I pull this trigger, I can easily call it justice. You will not be alive to call it anything."

"For God's sake!" Norris cried.

Joaquín chuckled, lifted his pistol and eased the hammer back. "I am in no hurry. Perhaps death is a void of nothingness after all, and this time with us will be your only hell."

In a cold sweat, Norris watched the Mexican resume his post by the window and assume the same nonchalant pose—one knee crooked and his boot flat against the wall, his face hidden by his hat except when he scanned the view—giving no indication that anything had happened since he'd been there a few moments before. Norris decided to keep quiet.

Lobo wasn't talking much either. Having told Engle and Stubbins only that he needed to go to Guadalupe Pass, they'd found the way.

Now they sat their horses staring at the peaks rising from both sides of the chasm through the mountains, and Lobo had no idea where to go.

Lemonade eased the palomino alongside Lobo's pinto. "What're we lookin' for?" he asked confidentially, as if they were still friends.

Lobo figured he had to tell or they'd never find it. "A cabin," he said.

"Where at?" Stubbins barked.

Lobo shrugged. "On the south side. That's all I know."

"Shit," Engle muttered.

"That ain't no problem," Lemonade piped up. "We'll jus' wait 'til dark and watch for smoke."

"Seth won't build a fire when he's bein' tracked," Lobo said.

"He doesn't know we're here," Engle argued. "He probably thinks he lost us and is feeling real sassy about now. I'll bet he has coffee for supper."

"We should look for a trail leadin' up," Stubbins said. "The only reason anybody'd build a cabin out here is a mine. In this terrain, that means we gotta gain some elevation."

"All right," Engle said. "You lead the way, Lobo. If we stumble across 'em, they won't shoot with you up front."

Lobo kicked his tired pinto along the trail winding through the pass. The mountains were rocky and red in the sunset, treeless even on top, a dry comfortless vision against the fading blue sky. Engle and Stubbins were both in foul moods, Lemonade was treacherous, and Lobo no longer believed he'd done the right thing. Tired and disarmed, he was bringing his father nothing but trouble, not least of which was himself. Now Seth would be forced to make his decisions in the interest of protecting his son.

Even worse was the thought that Seth might not be there. Hermit Dan hadn't told him about the cabin, so maybe Seth didn't know. Maybe he was fifty miles away, looking somewhere else. That meant Lobo was riding unarmed into an outlaw's lair with two businessmen and a former friend who was now a traitor, and Lobo felt stupid for coming.

Seth saw them from the ridge. Studying the pass through his spyglass, he spotted the four horses when they were still distant specks interesting only because of their steady progress closer. After watching them for an hour, standing under a ledge as he studied their pace through the shadowed canyon, he recognized the pinto first, then the palomino. He had seen those two horses together so often he didn't think he was making a mistake, but he studied the pinto's rider a long time before admitting it was Lobo. Seth laughed with pleasure, then frowned and muttered, "What the hell?"

When the canyon was lost in the shadow of the peaks behind him, he turned to his sorrel and rode back to the cabin. He left his horse with Joaquín's in a box arroyo a couple hundred yards from the corral, an enclosure small enough that he could seal it with piles of dead brush, and carried the saddlebags of money to the water trough filled by a tiny trickle from the windmill. Listening to the blades slowly creak in the breeze of twilight, he washed the dust from his face as he considered the situation.

The game had changed. Any room for play was lost with Lobo's arrival, and Seth wished he'd already killed Norris. Then when Engle and Stubbins got here, the hand would be dealt. Now there was a prisoner to jinx the deal when all anyone cared about was the money. Except Joaquín. Seth wasn't sure what his former partner wanted, but he knew if a play came down and he had to decide which way to jump, Lobo complicated the decision considerably. Scanning the trail his son would ride in a few hours, Seth rolled down his shirtsleeves and buttoned his cuffs, then settled his hat on his head, feeling apprehensive.

The hardest challenge before him was to conduct himself in a manner his son would admire. It was a stipulation Seth had never placed on his behavior before, certainly not in the middle of a skirmish, and to be facing it without Joaquín's loyalty seemed a breach of their contract. Joaquín had promised to help raise Lobo. Now here they were at a crossroads where Seth had to shine as a fatherly example. Without the partner he had come to depend on, he had to perform with grace in a game he'd survived by playing with no rules. Suddenly he had a lot of them, and victory demanded more than survival.

Seth slung the saddlebags over his shoulder and walked across the yard to the cabin. Inside, he moved to the stove and poured himself a cup of coffee. "The good citizens are coming," he told Joaquín, then blew on the coffee to cool it before adding, "Lobo's with 'em."

"How did that happen?" Joaquín asked.

"I don't know," Seth said, "but it'll save me a trip back for the palomino."

Joaquín looked out the window. "How soon will they be here?"

"Little after dark. I figure they'll see our smoke and find us easy."

Norris was nearly beside himself, tied helpless in the chair. "Why do you want 'em to find us?" he cried.

Seth gave the captive a cold smile. "They have my son. What do you think I'd be willing to trade for him?"

"Who are they?" Norris asked querulously.

"Good citizens acting in the interest of their community." Seth finished his coffee and set the cup aside, walked to the window and said softly, "I'll stand guard a while."

After watching Joaquín cross the yard and disappear in the rocks to see for himself, Seth turned around and smiled at Norris. "I'd say your odds just dropped through the floor. Clancy put up a reward for the killer of his son, and these fellows are businessmen. If they kill you, they get paid for their trouble."

"The reward's yours," Norris said with frantic geniality. "Webster shot the kid. Didn't you say you killed Webster?"

Seth shrugged.

"You got the money," Norris argued. "You said that's all you wanted. They'll kill me. If not these men, I'll be lynched in town. None of it was my fault. In the middle of a job, things happen. You got four men who ain't necessarily compatible, the somewhat predictable defense force and totally unpredictable bystanders. Anything can happen. It was bad luck, but none of it was my mistake! I got caught in a disaster. You understand that, I know you do!"

"What makes you think so?" Seth asked pleasantly.

"I've heard tell of banks you robbed with Allister where people died, innocent people, same as now."

"If you aim your pleas at someone who cares," Seth said, "you might have better luck."

"No one else is here," Norris muttered.

Seth laughed. "Reckon I'd be talking, too," he said. "Being as you ain't got nothing but words to fight with."

"I can't believe Seth Strummar's gonna turn me over to the law!"

"Yeah, I'm having trouble believing it myself," he said, watching out the window again.

"Why do it, then?"

"I told you," he said impatiently. "This is Joaquín's game. I'll play it unless I see you getting away. Then I'll kill you. Other than that, I ain't taking any action."

"Will you stand by and let the good citizens kill me?"

"I don't know," Seth said. "That depends on how it falls."

"You sound like it's gonna happen!"

"They were hot to do it when we started out. Can't imagine their mood's improved since."

"What about your kid? You gonna let him watch 'em kill me?"

"He's here," Seth said. "Reckon he's gonna see what happens."

Norris took no comfort from the conversation. He sat through the lengthening shadows of dusk in the silence of despair. The only conclusion he could draw was that Webster had been right and any man who crossed Seth Strummar was a fool. They all should have vamoosed like the Tyler brothers. But Webster had wanted to see his sweetheart, and Norris to recover from the shock of what he'd helped do. Now Webster was dead, and Norris had dim hopes for a future long enough to see the next sunrise.

It was dark when the good citizens arrived. Strummar and Ascarate had heard them coming and left Norris alone in the cabin, tied to the chair like a stuffed pigeon in the light. Unable to see anything outside, he heard the horses crest the ridge, snorting and sighing with weariness after the climb.

Seth was on a perch overlooking the yard, his Winchester in his lap. Joaquín was behind a boulder on the other side, his rifle in position along the ledge of stone. Lobo came into view first. Seeing that the child was tired and felt ashamed, Seth coaxed silently for Lobo to put some distance between himself and the others.

Lobo nudged his pinto close to the wall of rock directly beneath Seth. Warily, the boy looked around, then up to meet his father's eyes. Seth smiled, though he knew he should be mad. Lobo wanted to laugh but looked away before someone followed his gaze.

Lemonade was watching Engle and Stubbins, who stared at the brightly lit, apparently empty cabin.

"What d'ya think?" Stubbins whispered.

"It's a trick," Engle said. "The question is, what do they want us to do?"

"Go inside," Stubbins said.

"Why?" Engle asked. Looking around nervously, he saw Seth.

"Evenin'," Seth said.

Stubbins and Lemonade jerked around to look at him too. Lobo vainly searched the opposite side of the yard for his father's partner, remembering what the hermit had said about Joaquín being different now. Lobo wanted to know if that meant *he* was different to Joaquín, a man who had been his friend half his life. Feeling the presence of his father on the cliff above him as his only sure connection, Lobo clung to it. Without speaking to or looking at each other, they both breathed acknowledgment of their bond.

"Why'd you go off and leave us?" Engle bellowed.

"Figured we'd be more effective," Seth answered in an easy tone.

"Ya got the money?" Stubbins barked.

"Yeah."

"And Norris?" Engle asked.

"In the cabin."

"Alive?" Stubbins asked.

"Was when I left."

"How about the money?" Engle asked.

"It's with me," Seth said.

Lobo watched Lemonade angling to be in tight with whoever came out on top. Looking at Seth on the ridge, Lemonade's eyes glinted with ambition, and Lobo realized you couldn't be friends with anyone who blew with the wind. He'd heard Seth say that about someone else, but Lobo understood it now: a man could be like a tumbleweed or a tree; it was his gumption that decided whether he had something to offer or was just drifting through. The orphaned street urchin was drifting through with both hands open, and Lobo suddenly remembered he had been the one to bring Lemonade into Seth's circle.

Lobo wanted to look up at his father but didn't because he knew that would be wasting a pair of eyes, so he watched the others for any move toward attack. The only aid he could give would be warning, but it might make the difference.

Stubbins asked, "Ya intend on takin' the money to Tejoe?"

"Yeah," Seth said.

"When?"

"In the mornin'," Seth said. "Our horses are tired."

"Why don't you come down, then?" Engle asked.

"I like it up here," Seth answered. "Why don't you put your horses away and make yourselves at home?"

"Is there grub?" Stubbins asked.

"No more'n you brought."

"Will ya come in and eat with us?"

"Reckon," Seth said. "I'm getting pretty hungry."

"All right," Engle said. "Why don't we all go in together?"

"I want to talk to my son."

"He's coming with us," Engle said.

"The hell he is," Seth said.

A rifle cocked in the opposing shadows, and Lobo finally spotted Joaquín behind the boulder.

"Why don't you gentlemen step down?" Seth suggested.

Engle and Stubbins did, keeping their hands away from their guns.

"Lemonade," Seth said, "put their horses up."

The kid leaned from his saddle to gather the reins, then led the two horses toward the corral.

"Wait," Lobo said. He kicked his horse alongside Engle's and took his carbine back, then laid it across his lap.

Seth said, "Go on in and start supper, gentlemen. We'll be along."

Engle and Stubbins turned reluctantly and walked into the cabin. Seth watched them a moment, seeing their silhouettes move around the brightly lit room, then he looked at his son. "Come up here," he said.

Lobo dismounted, tied his horse to a creosote bush, and climbed the rock with his carbine in one hand. He settled cross-legged, holding the rifle in his lap as Seth was doing, noting there was a plump set of dusty saddlebags at his father's side. Finally, Lobo met Seth's eyes.

"How'd you find me?" Seth asked, his voice noncommittal.

"Hermit Dan sent me. I was hopin' to catch you in Sulphur Springs but I ran into Lemonade and the others instead."

"Hermit Dan sent you here?"

Lobo nodded. "He said one deer was worth one man, not two."

Seth chuckled. "The old coot."

"How'd you come to be here?" Lobo asked, relieved to hear him laugh.

"Saloon gossip." Seth smiled. "I oughta tan your hide, you know that?"

"Reckon," Lobo admitted.

"If you knew it was wrong, why'd you do it?"

"I wanted to be with you."

"Someday you will be, Lobo," Seth said gently. "But you're still a child. I wish you could understand that."

"Does that mean I should stay home with the women, 'cause I'm a child?"

"Yeah, pretty much."

"How can I learn to be a man if I'm always home with women?"

Seth looked away, into the cabin at Engle and Stubbins cooking supper as comfortably as if they were two prospectors who had lived together for years. What impressed Seth was how easily they dropped their guard. Knowing he wouldn't be that relaxed alone with Joaquín, Seth looked back at his son. "I don't want you to be the kind of man I am, Lobo. I want better for you."

"There ain't none," Lobo said.

Seth studied him a moment, then nodded at the cabin. "See those good citizens down there? They're not thinking of anything but filling their stomachs. Oh, in the back of their minds, they're rolling the problem around, knowing pretty soon they'll have to deal with it again. Right now, though, they're making supper. If I was to move against 'em, now is when I'd do it. They wouldn't think that was fair. They think they should eat first, then resume the skirmish. That's what makes 'em amateurs. You think that makes 'em less than me?"

"Yes, sir," Lobo said quietly.

Seth shook his head. "It means they're doing other things with their lives besides maintaining a constant defense, keeping an offense that changes with every shift of the wind. I live like an animal, Lobo, aware with all my senses all the time. There's a lot to admire in being sharp, but I never had any time for daydreaming. You ever think about that? No time to close my eyes and forget the world. No chance to love a woman with my full attention. Well, you're too young to know about that. Which is exactly my point. You're a child, Lobo, and you don't belong here."

"I think I do," he said.

"I don't want you here," Seth retorted.

Lobo glanced down, fighting tears. "You want me to get on my horse and go home?"

"You know I can't let you. If that's what you were gonna do, why didn't you stay there?"

"I want to be with you," he said again.

Seth leaned close with menace. "I want you to stay alive, Lobo. Is that so hard to understand?"

"I want the same for you," he answered bravely. "Why can't we be together?"

Seth sighed. "Com'ere," he said, laying his rifle aside and pulling his son into his lap. The sky was a myriad of stars clustered thick in the west, dimming near the rising moon. The mountains towered overhead, gouged with hidden canyons, while the pass below was lost in oblivion, a whole piece of the world that had disappeared.

Seth asked softly, "Did Nib tell you I was proud of you?"

"No, sir. I didn't see Nib."

"Well, I am. Do you know what for?"

"Helpin' to stop the lynchin'?"

"That's what you did. But what I admire is your drive to act when you see something's wrong. That takes courage and it can't be taught."

Lobo thought a moment, listening to his father's heartbeat. "Are you sayin' I should follow my conscience?"

"It'll hold you in good stead."

"That's what I did by decidin' to find you."

Seth chuckled, the sound rumbling in his chest. "I'm glad you're here. I was feeling lonely."

"Why?"

"I'm too old for this. Reckon I'm ready for a rocking chair on the porch."

Lobo laughed at the notion, and Seth took more pleasure from the sound than he'd felt in days.

After a moment, Lobo asked, "Is Joaquín still our friend?" He felt his father tense behind him.

"Why do you ask that?"

"Hermit Dan said he wasn't."

Seth was quiet, then said, "Joaquín was hit hard by Melinda dying. I don't suppose you can understand that."

"Rico cried," Lobo said.

"Did she?" Seth asked softly.

"And there was gonna be a big funeral for Rick as soon as Mr. Clancy got home."

"Did you know the boy?"

"Jus' from school," Lobo said. "But it felt strange seein' him dead, and Melinda and Mr. Tice, and Mrs. Keats in the jail. I felt like I'd seen dead folks before, though."

"You had," Seth said. "Coming down from Colorado, remember?"

Lobo nodded. "This wasn't like that. Did I ever meet Allister, when I was a baby and don't remember?"

"No," Seth said.

"I feel like I did."

Seth looked down at the top of his son's head. "When Allister died, you were about a month from a seed growing in your mama's belly."

"Did he know I was there?"

Seth shook his head. "Neither did I."

"It might've made a difference."

"How do you figure?"

"Maybe he wouldn't have tried to kill you, if he'd known you had a son who'd get him back for it."

"He didn't try," Seth said. "He wanted me to kill him."

Lobo twisted around to look up at his father. "Why?"

Seth smiled. "Maybe 'cause he didn't have a son to keep him alive."

Lobo laughed with delight.

"Let's go eat," Seth said. Setting his son aside, he retrieved his rifle with his left hand and picked up the saddlebags with his right.

Lobo could tell they were heavy. Carrying his carbine, he jumped off the rock and started toward the cabin.

Seth was thinking about Allister and Joaquín, wondering what they would have thought of each other, opposed as they were across nearly every facet of life. He wondered what it would have been like if they'd met, whether that meeting could have come off without a fight, and where he would have fallen between them, a man caught short by the disparity of his past and his present. Under the false assumption that his enemies were in the cabin, he jumped from the rock into the business end of a Winchester.

Lobo heard Seth jump down behind him, then remembered he had to put his pinto up and turned around to see Lemonade holding a rifle on Seth. Lobo didn't move.

"I'm takin' that money," Lemonade said. "Ya can toss it over real easy, Mr. Strummar, or I can take it off your corpse."

"You're gonna have to kill me to get it," Seth said in a low voice.

"Ya don't mean that," Lemonade answered with cocky assurance. "But I want to thank ya. Your tryin' to send me away, sayin' I wouldn't get no payoff at the end, got me to thinkin'. None of ya gen'lemen need that money. I'm jus' startin' out and I do. So I'm takin' my payoff, along with Lobo's pretty pinto all saddled to go."

"I'll kill you," Seth said.

Lemonade grinned. "I don't believe ya will, not in front of Lobo. Toss that money now, real gentle so I don't have to shoot."

"I already know you can't hit the broad side of a barn," Seth scoffed.

"I'm standin' right nigh close to it, though, ain't I?"

Lobo stood frozen, wondering what he should do.

Seth threw the saddlebags hard.

Lemonade stepped aside and let them pass, not lowering the aim of his rifle. "I know ya'd track me, Mr. Strummar. So reckon I'll have to kill ya after all." He giggled nervously. "I'm gonna be famous."

Seth reached for his sixgun, sure of his kill even if the kid got lucky. A carbine fired and Lemonade fell. For a long moment of denial, Seth watched a blotch of blood spread over Lemonade's shirt. Moving as if through mud, he holstered his sixgun and retrieved the rifle he'd loaned the kid who tried to kill him. Then he forced himself to turn around and look at his son holding a smoking gun.

A few minutes earlier, Joaquín had gone inside the cabin to check on Norris. Seeing the townsmen eating at the table, Joaquín leaned against the wall and watched.

Norris watched, too, glancing at the Mexican once in a while but finding no encouragement in his stance of waiting. The good citizens seemed indifferent to their captive's fate.

"What do you think?" Engle whispered to Stubbins.

He shrugged, wiping his bowl with a crust of biscuit. "Not much we can do."

"We can take the money away from Strummar," Engle muttered.

"Us and who else?" Stubbins asked with disgust.

"He's got his kid now. He'll give us the money if we raise a stink. Probably be glad to get shut of the whole deal."

"I don't think so," Stubbins said.

"What *do* you think?" Engle asked with strained patience.

Stubbins looked at Norris, then at Joaquín. Raising his voice he asked the Mexican, "What d'ya reckon's gonna happen here?"

"Seth will take the money to Tejoe," Joaquín answered. "One of us will take the prisoner to Tombstone."

"Ya volunteerin'?" Stubbins jeered.

"If no one else will do it," Joaquín said.

Engle snarled, "Do you expect us to let a known bandit ride off with the entire contents of the Bank of Tejoe?"

"That's right!" Norris said.

"Shut up," Stubbins growled. "Ya got no say."

"Seems to me I'm in pretty deep," Norris said.

Engle sneered at Stubbins. "Unless you can think of a way to get the money from Strummar, Norris is all we got to show for our trouble."

Stubbins kept quiet.

"Both of us together could get it away from him," Engle argued. He looked at Joaquín. "Would you stop us?"

"I will kill no one over money," he said.

"Are ya tellin' us to try?" Stubbins asked, exasperated.

Joaquín shrugged. "That is your decision, is it not?"

"Will you stand with Strummar?" Engle demanded. "That's all we need to know."

"What if I lied to you?" Joaquín asked with a playful smile.

"What're we gonna do?" Engle asked Stubbins. "Let Strummar ride off with the money?"

They both glowered at the prisoner, who was keenly aware he had caused their problem.

When the gun fired outside, Joaquín raised his rifle and cocked it at the townsmen. They lurched to their feet, half-crouched over their chairs. "Put your guns on the table," Joaquín said.

"Would you shoot us?" Engle mocked.

Joaquín pulled the trigger and splintered wood at Engle's fingertips, then recocked his rifle.

Engle jerked his hand back with a yell. "All right!" he said, not moving.

"I suggest you do it now, *señor*."

"All right," he said again, glancing at Stubbins.

The miner was already unbuckling his gunbelt. "I surrender," he muttered, glaring at the Mexican. "Wash my hands of the whole deal. If Strummar comes back to Tejoe with the money, I'll celebrate. Until then, I'm goin' home to lick my wounds."

"Stay where you are," Joaquín said.

"Am I a prisoner?" Stubbins demanded gruffly.

"At the moment, yes."

From outside, Seth called, "Joaquín?"

"Sí," he shouted. To the townsmen, he said, "Back away from the table."

Engle and Stubbins moved against the far wall, their guns left behind.

Seth appeared on the threshold, took his cut of the room, then called over his shoulder, "Come on in, Lobo."

Watching him leave his rifle and the saddlebags of money on the table, then cross to the stove and pour a cup of coffee, Joaquín saw that Seth was different. "What was that shot outside?" he asked.

Seth stared into his cup for a long moment before answering. "Lemonade pulled a gun on me," he finally said, scanning all the faces watching him. "He died."

"Jesus," Engle whispered.

"He was only a kid," Stubbins muttered.

"His bullet could've killed me just as dead," Seth said. "Any of you would've done the same."

Lobo came through the door and stood in the light. "You want me to get the horses, Seth?"

It took Seth a moment to look at his son. When he did, Joaquín knew from the hurt pride in his eyes what had happened: Lobo had killed Lemonade, in defense of Seth. Joaquín felt stunned at the enormity of his own failure. In the name of justice, he had abandoned his alliance with Seth and left a child to fill the empty place in their broken partnership.

Seth asked, "You still taking Norris to Tombstone?"

Joaquín nodded, knowing the break was irrevocable.

In a voice rough with feigned indifference, Seth asked, "Will you ride as far as the cutoff with us?"

"Sí," Joaquín answered gently.

Seth gave him a bittersweet smile, then nodded at Lobo, who spun and disappeared. Everyone in the cabin listened to his footsteps running away. Joaquín crossed the room and cut the ropes holding Norris to the chair. He lumbered stiffly to his feet, his hands still tied behind him.

Seth shouldered the saddlebags, picked up his rifle, and collected the two gunbelts. He smiled with melancholy at Norris bound for justice, then looked at Engle and Stubbins. "I'll leave your weapons a mile down the trail," Seth said. He started for the door, but turned back and studied their faces for another long moment. "It's been interesting, gentlemen." He smiled wryly. "See you in Tejoe."

By the Same Author

BLACK ENGLISH: Its History and Usage in the United States
ALL-AMERICAN ENGLISH

AMERICAN
TALK

Where
Our Words
Came From

Random House New York

AMERICAN
TALK

J. L. Dillard

Library of Congress Cataloging in Publication Data

Dillard, Joey Lee, 1924–
    American talk: where our words came from.

Bibliography: p.
Includes index.
1. English language in the United States.
2. English language—Slang.   3. Americanisms.
I. Title.
PE2846.D5   427'.9'73   76–10645
ISBN 0–394–40012–7

Manufactured in the United States of America

9 8 7 6 5 4 3 2

FIRST EDITION

Contents

Acknowledgments

Students and colleagues at several universities have provided material for this book. Dr. Ian F. Hancock of the University of Texas, Austin, has been especially helpful with detailed information on little-known language varieties. Margie I. Dillard assisted in all stages of preparation of the manuscript.

The most important influences, however, have been the writings of scholars concerned with aspects of American English who work outside the linguistic mainstream. Among these, perhaps the most important is Ramon Adams, whose *Western Words* is the most useful guide one can find to the language of the cowboy and certain other frontier groups, and whose *The Rampaging Herd* is the best bibliography on the subject. Other material on the language of the pioneer is contained in the works of historians like Philip Ashton Rollins, Everett N. Dick, and Josiah Gregg. Walter McCulloch's *Woods Words* contains important information on the speech patterns of the Northwest.

Among books more explicitly concerned with linguistic matters, a few, generally overlooked by researchers, have proved to be invaluable. Brian Foster's *The Changing English Language* has material on the German influence on American English that made it unnecessary for me to deal with that topic and encouraged me to look rather to Dutch. Lilian Feinsilver's *The Taste of Yiddish* makes any further attempt to cope with the influence of Yiddish superfluous. Joanna Carver Colcord's *Sea Language Comes Ashore* treats nautical influences more thoroughly than any other work has done.

The Dictionary of Americanisms and the older *Dictionary of American English* (often strikingly similar in content) are, if not absolutely complete, near enough to discourage competition. Together with *The Oxford English Dictionary,* they are essential tools for anyone working in this field. In fact, unless a bibliographic attribution of another nature is made in the text, it should be assumed that any citation in this book comes from one of these sources. However, unless otherwise stated, all interpretations are my own, and divergences from long-accepted opinion are intentional.

Introduction

This book is part of a continuing effort to determine the origins of and influences on the language spoken in the United States of America. As such, it has a direct relationship to my two earlier books, *Black English* and *All-American English*. In those books I attempted to show how Pidgin English and the Creole that results when a pidgin becomes the native language of a group were of basic importance in separating American English from British. In this book, I carry that investigation farther by considering the detailed workings of language-contact influences on the vocabulary and phraseology of American English.

Methodologically, the book follows the premise that an earlier period can be best understood by examining the records of intelligent observers who were there. It does not assume that such observers were perfect, or that their descriptions were always comparable to those of modern social scientists. It does, however, insist that their observations be taken into account in any general picture. If a great number of eighteenth- and nineteenth-century observers recorded the speaking of Pidgin English by American Indians, it does not matter if some twentieth-century armchair theorist decides that a pidgin was never spoken in the continental United States. The evidence is there.

It is generally accepted that in the Americas some words were added to the English language, some were changed in meaning, and others retained archaic meanings that they lost in British English. But according to the conventional position, the "basic" grammatical structure of

the English language was unaffected. Recently, however, the emphasis in linguistics has shifted to semantics, or the study of meaning, as the most important level of language. And the semantic change in American English, including as it does influences from many other languages, is marked. If semantic structure is more basic to language than inflectional endings, then American English has changed more, not less, than it would have if a few new inflectional endings (something like *we arop, you arel,* to accompany *I am, he is,* etc.) had been picked up.

Some of the familiar examples of semantic change are worth examining. It is well known, for example, that *corn* was a general term for grain in England, but in America it came to be applied, first in the phrase *Indian corn,* to what might otherwise have become *maize* in the colonies. In 1838, Harriet Martineau wrote:

> It occurred to me that some of our commonest English writing must bear a different meaning to Americans, and to us. All that is written about cornfields, for instance, must call up pictures in their minds quite unlike any that the poets intended to create. "Waving corn" is not the true description to them; and one can scarcely bring one's tongue to explain that it means "small grain." Their poetical attachments are naturally and reasonably to their Indian corn, a beautiful plant, worthy of all love and celebration. But the consequence is that we have not their sympathy about our sheaves, our harvest wain, our gleaners; for though they have that, their harvest *par excellence* is of corn-cobs, and their "small grain" bears about the same relation to poetry with them as turnips.

Anyone who has ever heard a class in sophomore literature snickering over Keats's line "She stood in tears amid the alien corn" knows that Martineau was not exaggerating.

Martineau's linguistic sensitivity allowed her to perceive that American English had been *differentiated* rather

than corrupted. This is preferable, from a linguistic point of view, to making value judgments about "good" and "bad" language. Martineau is linguistically superior to Charles Dickens, who wrote in *American Notes* (1842) : "I need not tell you that the prevailing grammar [in America] is more than doubtful, and that the oddest vulgarisms are received idioms."

Dickens even went so far as to assert that American language forms were not intelligible to British visitors. In Chapter II of *American Notes* he reports that he did not understand what was meant when a waiter asked him if he wanted his dinner *right away*. He or any other Englishman would have understood the word *right* and the word *away*. What was wrong was the combination of the two. In the same author's *Martin Chuzzlewit* (Chapter XXVII), Martin does not understand the American Mrs. Hominy when she asks, "Where do you hail from?" There are other reports of the difficulty Englishmen of the period had with American expressions.

Today, when a more-or-less popular interpreter of culture tries to differentiate between American and British English (as most of them do at one time or another), he usually leans heavily on terms like *jargon* for American usage. Richard Freeman, reviewing *All-American English* in the New York *Post* for May 27, 1975, represented the tradition almost perfectly by asserting that we are not as coherent or as jargon-free as the "average literate Englishman," but that we manage to achieve a certain "dash and color" which can be compared to "Renaissance English" or "the language of Elizabeth [I]."

When a professional dialectologist goes about describing the differences between American and British English, he eschews terms like *jargon*. He stresses a few vocabulary items and ways of pronunciation as the major differences— a car's *bonnet* instead of *hood*, *chemist's* for *drugstore*, etc., and "ah" rather than "a" in *path, bath, dance, fancy*.

Most of us are not really convinced by the professional dialectologist—the difference just has to be greater than that. So unless we have to take a test on Dialectology 101 or a Ph.D. oral this semester, we go back to the impressions of the popular observer, which appeal to us without our being able to say exactly why. We *know* that the reviews in the (London) *Times Literary Supplement* have something that the reviews in the (New York) *Times Book Review* don't. But we don't always try to explain the difference.

Freeman's reference to Elizabethan English may be instructive, although not necessarily in the way one might expect. Anyone who has studied either Renaissance literature or the history of early modern English must be aware that Englishmen in the "great age" of English literature were not so confident of their own superiority. They were still somewhat servile toward foreign models—especially toward writers who had achieved the great feat of living a few centuries earlier. Renaissance Englishmen said things about the "rudeness" and "barbarousness" of English, and they worried about how to make it the equal of contemporary Romance languages. (There were even a few ambitious souls who dared to think of making it equal to Latin or Greek!) For the majority of sixteenth- and seventeenth-century Englishmen, the language of Shakespeare was no vehicle for great, permanent literature, but rather an inferior tool fit only for transient expression. From William Caxton, the fifteenth-century printer and translator, to Francis Bacon two hundred years later, important writers expressed reluctance to write in their native tongue and made elaborate excuses for using "this rude and comyn Englyssh." Many, like Roger Ascham in *Toxophilus* (1545), asserted that they stooped to English only because they wished to appeal to readers who would not be able to understand Latin.

Wholesale borrowings from other languages, most especially from French after the Norman Conquest, left English

with a supply of terms like *timorosity, odible, jurate,* and *adminiculation.* These words were especially abundant in works of the Euphuistic style, which Shakespeare parodied beautifully in the speech of the pedant Holofernes in *Love's Labour's Lost:*

> I abhor such fanastical phanasimes, such insociable and point-devise companions, such rackers of orthographie . . .

When it comes to clichés and stale comparisons, nothing can approach the Elizabethan sonnet sequence, which features skin white as snow, eyes like stars, and teeth like pearls. Today we are more familiar with Shakespeare's parody than with what it parodies:

> My mistress's eyes are nothing like the sun
> Coral is far more red than her lips' red . . .

Perhaps the key word is *cliché.* The first use of a "used-up" expression is not hackneyed; it is the lack of originality that finally makes the expression objectionable. (Milton was not using a cliché when he wrote *paint the lily,* but all of us who misquote him and say *gild the lily* obviously are.) At any rate, this is what our literature and rhetoric teachers would have us believe. But if hackneyed expressions turn up in Old English poetry, it's all right. They're called kennings then. To call the ocean *the swan road* is to use a kenning, but to refer to Detroit as *the motor city* is cliché. We would not dare to suggest that an American sportswriter should be judged by the same canons of criticism as an Old English poet.

Allusiveness—suggesting a great deal more than is actually said—is one of the strong points of what we call poetic diction. The pleasure that a certain kind of reader finds in the kenning *ring giver of heroes* (meaning 'a king') derives as much from its allusiveness as from anything

else. To that reader, it recalls how Germanic leaders of the so-called Heroic Age rewarded their warriors with armbands ("rings") of gold. Whether there is any formal beauty to the phrase, apart from its allusiveness, is questionable. But no quantitative measure would reveal less allusiveness in the horribly mundane "Somebody give me a cheeseburger" (Skeet Miller Band, "Living in the U.S.A."), at least when responded to by a culturally indoctrinated person like a television-raised American teenager. The outsider, who has not internalized the system whereby MacDonald's hamburger chain beats this phrase into the consciousness of millions, will not get the point. But the non-initiate will not find much in *ring giver of heroes* either.

All but the best of us, if we write or talk naturally, are going to use some of the characteristic clusters of words called clichés. Clichés are stale metaphors, our rhetoric teachers tell us. On the other hand, a lot of seemingly plain English words are historically fixed combinations: *daisy* from *day's eye, window* from *wind eye,* to give only the two most familiar ones. Nothing seems as plain and unfigurative as a walrus, but the most elementary student of the English language knows how to derive it from two words virtually equivalent to *whale horse.* To be sure, language historians call these "frozen" rather than stale metaphors. If a metaphor is lucky enough to be frozen early in the history of a language, it may never be accused of being a cliché.

However, with all the British visitors observing and commenting, early American English didn't have the chance that Old English or even Middle English did to freeze its metaphors. Objections were made to them in the very early days, and schoolteachers set about—unsuccessfully—to eliminate them. About the only success the teachers had was in driving such "jargon" out of studies of the history of American English. Linguists who were lin-

guistic relativists were, paradoxically, hypersensitive to the criticism of the schoolteachers they professed to scorn, and they usually tried to pretend they had never heard of the trite expressions the freshman English handbooks condemned.

So here we are, or rather were. The words didn't really show any great difference between American and British English, even when a little bit of data about pronunciation was added. The sentences, on the other hand, were too complex to deal with; they were, as Noam Chomsky and others have demonstrated, at least potentially infinite in number. You can't put an infinite number of items in a dictionary. And you can't deal historically with a comparison between the sets of sentences that, say, an Englishman and an American produce. You can't even prove that they are different, although common sense tells you that they must be. Within such a context, it is impossible to use documentary evidence, as historians have always done. Language history therefore tended to become a matter of pure speculation for a while—great for linguistics, but terrible for history.

The answer to the dilemma lies in precisely the parts of the language the specialists have tried to suppress. If we study our much-maligned jargon and clichés, we will find out something about our language history.

Most rhetoricians object to the "colorless" nature of typically American jargon. *That's the way I put it up* for 'That's the way I construct my theory' was a typical Westernism, according to Albert D. Richardson's *Beyond the Mississippi* (1867), an excellent source for frontier language materials. This is not the stuff of great poetry, and most freshman English handbooks would condemn it; but it is an authenticated Westernism, and as such it has as much interest for the historian of language as a more literary expression. Alfred Holt's *Phrase Origins* (1936) declares that "a cant expression . . . was 'Nantee palaver'—

nantee standing for Italian *niente,* nothing." This expression is not so well documented as *put it up,* and the statement could be regarded as questionable. On the other hand, it has been established that *palaver* was widely used in the West, and its distribution in Pidgin English should make us wary of rejecting Holt's evidence. In view of what so many other observers reported of frontier American usage, the very word *cant* should awaken a certain interest.

Jargon is important to the historian of American English for another, very special reason. Virtually every lingua franca, and certainly every pidgin, has been stigmatized as jargon. Generally, speakers in a multilingual contact situation have to use a language in which they do not have native proficiency; therefore they seldom scale the heights of rhetoric. Everyone calls the contact language used by the Indians of the Northwest *Chinook Jargon,* perhaps because so many people understand it. Pidginists and students of lingua francas have railed against the use of the term jargon. But languages don't need any defense against such attacks. If everyone says there's a connection between pidgins and jargon, there probably is. And if early observers insisted that American English was full of jargon and that the pidgins were jargons, perhaps both statements are true. Furthermore, the early observers may have put their fingers on something basically important about American English and its development.

Pidginisms have remained in strange places in the American vocabulary. Weseen's *Dictionary of American Slang* (1934) calls *no go* 'lack of agreement' general slang, and *no likee* 'poorly received, unsuccessful' theatre slang; both are certainly pidgin in structure. As the various chapters of this book will show, pidgin expressions show up sporadically in the usage (I prefer to avoid the word slang) of cowboys, trappers, and other frontier American groups. One might ask what theatre people have in common with motley groups like Black and Chinese forced-labor units.

had the general sense it has today. *Stake a claim* referred to the process of establishing one's exclusive rights to a potentially rich piece of mining land, and a *claim jumper* was one who ignored the marking of such rights. Today, the former phrase could apply to giving a girl an engagement ring, and the latter to someone else who dated her anyway. A person with a successful (mining) claim might *make a stake* 'earn some money, make a fortune'. If his prospects of doing so were good, a wealthy nonprospector might *grubstake* him—advance the money needed for his living expenses in exchange for a share of the eventual strike. Of course, even pay dirt would *peter out* after a time.

There is much overlapping in the usages of these essentially nomadic groups, and it is risky to say dogmatically that a term came "originally" from one group or the other. There were no lexicographers in the logging and mining camps, and the first attestations we have were written down after the words and phrases had been in daily use for a period of years. Mencken (Supplement II, p. 761) points out how a word like *tenderfoot*, first used by cowboys for a cow new to the range, was popularized by miners. Walter McCulloch and Ramon Adams may claim the same phrase for the loggers and the cowboys, respectively, and my approach has been to conclude that both are probably right.

The interactions of the nomadic groups produce some fascinating possibilities for the future language historian. For example, there is the term *stiff* 'person, hobo' used by those who rode the freight trains during the Depression. It entered into many compounds, like *mission stiff* 'parson'. But the original usage was apparently on the Western ranches in the 1870's. There is some evidence that *stiff*, in this sense only, is a phonological variant of *stuff* (compare the way a young Northerner and an old-fashioned Southerner pronounce the second syllables of *Alice* and *Dallas*). *Stiff* in this sense meant 'corpse', and the *stiff man*

on the ranches was the hand who disposed of carcasses by burning them. To call a man a *stiff* was to suggest that he had little worth, and the humorists of the hobo jungles found it an appropriate term. A tramp carrying his belongings over his shoulder in a bundle tied to a stick was a *bindle* (phonological variant of *bundle*, as with *stiff* and *stuff*) *stiff*, and a certain kind of cow was *brindle stuff*.[30]

There is too much of this for one book and one man. Others may find more complete and more satisfactory explanations; they may find groups even more fascinating than the cowboys and the mountain men. I have stuck to them because of my admiration for such guides as George Ruxton, Ramon Adams, and Philip Ashton Rollins. But it seems safe to say that whoever works with the Western territory and nomadic groups again will not find an exclusive pattern of Eastern words moving west.

7

Color Our
Talk Black

The mountain men and the cowboys were typically American in being mobile. Their opposites, the farmers and sheepherders, stayed put. The Blacks, whose influence on American English has been considerable, belonged to both groups. They produced fur traders like Jim Beckwourth and cowboys like Bill Pickett. As slaves on the Southern plantations, they also constituted the group most tied to one spot. It was not until the migrations to Northern cities after World War I that they joined to any great extent in the pattern of American mobility. That migration is famous because it included the movement of New Orleans jazzmen up the Mississippi to Chicago and then to New York. The second great exodus came during and just after World War II.

As the playmates of Southern white youngsters in pre–Civil War days, Blacks imparted a great deal of their own dialect to the white population, and words like *goobers* 'peanuts', *juke* 'a house of ill repute', *jazz* 'frenetic activity (basically associated with music)' became basic parts of American English. *Cooter* 'turtle' is known to whites in South Carolina, Georgia, and Mississippi; the Africanism *buckra* 'white man' means 'poor white trash' to even more residents of the Deep South. *Geechee*, used as a virtual synonym for *Gullah* on the Sea Islands of South Carolina and Georgia, means 'typically Black' to the Negro com-

munity on Cape Cod and 'mulatto' to the whites of north-
western Louisiana. But the Blacks' primary contribution is
the compounds they made out of familiar words.

As far as we can judge from historical documentation,
the Negro on the Southern plantation—and, in the seventeenth and eighteenth centuries, on many Northern ones
too—spoke a special variety of English that linguists would
call a Creole—that is, a pidgin that has become the first,
or only, language of a population group. Many attestations
represent Blacks on the Southern plantations saying things
like:

> boccarrora make de black man workee, make de horse
> workee, make ebery ting workee; only de hog. He, de
> hog, no workee; he eat, he drink, he walk about . . . he
> lib like a gentleman.[1]

This Creole variety of English was analogous to the variety
of Dutch spoken in New York–New Jersey (Chapter 2)
and to the "Gombo" variety of French spoken in Louisiana
(see Chapter 3). It has gradually changed in the direction
of Standard English (become decreolized) as the Black
group has been acculturated, slowly, into the American
mainstream; but just as the process of acculturation has
not been completed, neither has the decreolization.

By the 1920's, the sophisticated adult Black male of
Harlem was better known for this kind of talk than for
pidgin:

> She laid the twister to her slammer on me, ole man,
> understand, and I dug the jive straight up and down,
> three ways sides and flats.

This seems to have nothing whatsoever in common with
the pidgin quoted above, except perhaps for the comment
of its author Dan Burley:

Such jargon is reminiscent of Tibet, Afghanistan, as unintelligible to the uninitiate as listening to a foreign dictator's harangue over a shortwave broadcast.[2]

Here's our old friend *jargon* again—just what everybody called Pidgin English, whether spoken by Chinese, Indians, or Blacks.

But it would be wasteful to go to Tibet or Afghanistan to find an analogue to this kind of "jargon." It would be cheaper, and more relevant, to go to Trinidad and listen to a couple of tesses limin' Old Talk—that is, to a couple of hip chicks from Trinidad talking the way they talk among their peers:

> Jane: Nuh, man. You jokin. She horn he till de mark
> buss. Then he buss lash in she licks like fire and
> she buss durt. She friennin wid Johnny now.[3]

Many Harlemites would look down on the Trinidadians, but there is more in common between the speech of the two groups than meets the untutored eye or ear. The history—especially the early history—of English in Trinidad (or in Jamaica or any of dozens of other islands) is strikingly like that of Black English in the United States. Furthermore, even "jive talk" phrases like *play it cool* 'take it easy' or the ubiquitous term of address *man*[4] are as well known in Trinidad as in Harlem. There is perhaps a greater concentration of "jargon" phrases in the conversation imagined by Burley than in that by Otley, but this may be a matter of greater contrivance on the part of the former.

Like the slaves on the Caribbean islands, the slaves in the plantation South found it necessary to use a code vocabulary in order to conceal certain messages from their masters. (For historical reasons too complex to go into here, African languages were no longer available for such disguise purposes.)[5] Because religious meetings were tolerated

more extensively than other slave assemblies, the disguised messages were most often transmitted through the medium of religious songs ("spirituals"). Although the white masters thought the "darkies" were expressing simple religious devotion, they were actually conveying invitations to the meetings of an African cult of liberation.[6] *Steal away to Jesus* was a code phrase amounting to an invitation to a meeting of the cult.[7] *Judgment Day* was the day on which the revolt was scheduled to take place.[8] *Jerusalem* was Courtland, Southampton County, Virginia, where revolt leader Nat Turner was incarcerated after his capture. "Home," "Canaan," and "heb'm" were veiled allusions to Africa, in some cases specifically Liberia.[9] A song about a brother "a-gwine to Glory" referred to one who had successfully boarded a repatriation ship.[10] An occasional white church dignitary found out that "the spiritual singing of the Negroes was according to the African cult,"[11] but the disguise worked remarkably well. However, after Turner's forces proved unequal to the gigantic task they had undertaken, the double meanings of the spirituals lost their force, and for some they came to express truly pious sentiments. But the tradition of double (or even multiple) meanings remained alive a long time, for at least some members of the Black community. And, as is well known, Black militancy, even after it had lost its back-to-Africa emphasis, remained close to religion, whether to a Christian sect, a Muslim group, or some more exotic faith. The concept of *soul*, combining as it does the Black protest movement with religious spirituality, would have been impossible if historical conditions had been different.

It is not certain that this tradition of disguise language arose simply as a reaction to the challenge of the slave environment or in the service of the African cult. There have been long traditions of allusiveness and disguise communication in African cultures.[12]

Part of this hidden usage results, as Karl Reisman has shown conclusively for Antigua, from ambivalence in the face of prejudice on the part of the "upper" white culture. When a mainstream culture deprecates his traditional values, the Black has often adopted that culture's disapproving terminology (on the surface) but given it his own meaning. Reisman has shown that *ugly* 'Afroid in facial features' is virtually the same as *beautiful,* given the proper context, for Antiguans. Since non-European things would be "bad," the most characteristically African traits of Black culture would be "bad"—but the Black felt a certain attraction for them anyway. *Bad* (especially when pronounced *ba-a-ad*) can mean 'very good, extremely good'. In such a context, *That woman is a bitch* is extremely complimentary, as is *She a tough bitch.* Dalby cites "frequent use of negative forms (often pronounced emphatically) to describe positive extremes in African languages."[13] And Black American linguist Grace Holt Sims calls the process "using The Man's language against him as a defense against sub-human categorization."[14]

For reasons like these, Black talk can frequently be misunderstood. *Mean* can carry the sense 'excellent'; Mean Joe Green, the defensive tackle for pro football's Pittsburgh Steelers, is mean in both senses—a defensive lineman has to love to hit running backs hard in order to be good at his job. *Uptight* is one of the most expressive of these chameleon words. It may mean either 'attractive, good' or 'unattractive, bad'. Early jazzmen associated it with preparedness: "I got my boots laced up tight (and am, supposedly, ready to go places)." Of course, too much preparedness could easily ruin the spontaneity needed for a jazz performance. A person who has his evening planned too exactly, who refuses to improvise with the group, is really "uptight."

Both *hot* and *cool* participate in this reversal. In the 1950's, jazzmen decided that being too *hot* 'frenetic, over-

active' had left them open to exploitation, and *cool* 'detachment, ability to gauge the situation before acting' came to be the appropriate term. But coolness could go too far, as in Don Lee's fine poem about the Black who was so cool "he even stopped for green lights" and who failed to realize that in the end, "to be black is to be very-hot."

Some of the uses of *shit* within Black communication reflect the same kind of reversal. A successful pimp, a deejay who makes it, or any other person successful in the ways open to Blacks can be said to have *gotten his shit together*—that is, to have acted efficiently with regard to his most valuable (not least valuable) possessions or traits. Although the relationship between Black speakers and the drug trade is a two-way street,[15] and it is far from certain what the direction of influence has been unless there are clear-cut African or Creole analogues, the use of *shit* to mean 'heroin' (that is, something extremely costly, represented by something that can be had for less than nothing) probably represents a similar reversal.

Closely related to this reversal, and sometimes almost indistinguishable from it, is the use of indirection. Verbal games like *signifying, put-on, mocking the sender, doing the Tom Jones*, and *gamesmanship of Muhammad Ali* were examples of this kind of inversion:

> Blacks intentionally behave in ways which whites perceived as inappropriate but by which they were flattered, elevating "whitey" to a status they both knew he didn't occupy, invoking praise and ridicule in the same terms. The patrolman became a police "chief," the ex-private was elevated to "cap'n," the ex-captain to "colonel."[16]

Whether in terms of indirection or not, the plantation slave's need for a disguise language could take other forms than simply trying to fool the master concerning secret meetings. It could also be useful for communicating secret messages of a more personal nature:

Sometimes while loading corn in the field, which demands loud singing, Josh would call to Alice, a girl he wanted to court on the adjoining plantation, "I'm so hongry want a piece of bread"; and her reply would be "I'se so hongry almost dead." Then they would try to meet after dark in some secluded spot.[17]

The terminology of food—and especially of baked products —as disguised expressions for sexual intercourse is a strikingly pervasive theme in what little we have that can be considered reliable from the plantation literature and in jazz and blues lyrics. *Cookie, cake,* and *pie* are commonplace terms with this type of association; Guy B. Johnson reports that "in order to express superlatively his estimate of his sweetheart's sexual equipment, [the Black] often refers to it as *angel-food cake.*"[18] Harold Courlander, in *Negro Folk Music, U.S.A.*, attests the same meaning for *pie* and *custard pie.*[19] Johnson also reports the use of *bread* in that significance and postulates a "vulgar" second meaning for the title of the song "Short'nin' Bread":

> One turned over [in bed] to the other an' said,
> "My baby loves short'nin', short'nin' bread."[20]

If so, this would be a rather coarse, undistinguished kind of routine sex. *Corn bread* conveys the same meaning. *Biscuit,* on the other hand, betokens a finer product of baking and a more refined sexual experience. A *biscuit roller* is an especially talented lover, either male or female. Another blues song reports the wife who has "corn bread for her husband, biscuits for her backdoor man."[21]

The best known example of this kind of sexual disguise terminology, however, is *jelly roll.* In a real sense, this is an Africanism—or what is more significant in understanding Black Talk, the shaping of European material to an African pattern. David Dalby has shown that the term involves "Mandingo *jeli* 'minstrel' (often gaining popular-

ity with women through his skill in the use of words and music)" and hypothesizes "convergence with English *jelly* and *jelly roll* (as items of food)."[22] Although the food reference may be dominant insofar as the white listener is concerned, Black texts show a fascinating awareness of both halves of the referential pattern:

> Jelly roll, jelly roll ain't so hard to find,
> There's a baker shop in town makes it brown like mine.
> I got a sweet jelly, a lovin' sweet jelly roll.
> If you taste my jelly it'll satisy your worried soul.[23]

> I ain't gonna give nobody none of this jelly roll.
> Nobody in town can bake sweet jelly roll like mine.
> Your jelly roll is good.[24]

The Southern whites' awareness of this meaning is shown by novels like Thomas Wolfe's 1929 *Look Homeward, Angel*. White characters used the term, although always referring to Black women. Newsboy Eugene Gant, trying to collect, has a memorable conversation with a Black customer who cannot pay:

> "I'll have somethin' fo' yuh, sho. I'se waitin' fo' a white gent'man now. He's gonna gib me a dollah." . . .
> "What's—what's he going to give you a dollar for?"
> "Jelly Roll."[25]

Within Afro-American culture, however, there is a deeper level to *jelly roll* than even Dalby has suspected. In the Caribbean, *jelly* is used to refer to the meat of the coconut in a still viscous stage. The *Dictionary of Jamaican English* reports the meaning 'an unripe cocoanut sold in the streets and the jelly eaten.' This meaning is cited as early as 1834; there are no known earlier attestations of the specifically Black meanings. To look at, this "jelly" closely resembles semen. A jelly roll, then, is, in one

sense a (rock and) roll that produces jelly. From there, there is an easy transference—although there is no suggestion here that such was the historical process—to intercourse:

Jelly, jelly, jelly; jelly stays on my mind,
Jelly roll killed my pappy, it drove my mammy stone
   blind.[26]

On a simple level, it is the woman whose contribution makes intercourse sweet, and the vagina, shaped like the bakery product, is the referent for *jelly roll*:

Ain't been to hell but I been tol'
Women in hell got sweet jelly roll.[27]

The truly hip male lover, however, knows how to make himself the more desirable one; he is a *sweet-back man,* and what he contributes becomes the jelly roll, which the female in her turn may long for:

When your man comes home evil,
Tells you you are gettin' old
That's a true sign he's got someone else
Bakin' his jelly roll.[28]

Like *rider* (as in both "Easy Rider" and "See, See, Rider") *jelly roll* is a bisexual (or, in more modern terms, unisexual) term. In the end, it simply means the process of intercourse, appreciated from the viewpoint of either female or male.

The hippest of the hip, the best of the jazzmen and the pimp, merited the name Jelly Roll. According to the biography by the late folklorist Alan Lomax, Ferdinand LeMenthe, who renamed himself Morton and made jazz history as leader of the Red Hot Peppers, inspired his

nickname during a comedy performance onstage when the other Black comedian, using a pastry metaphor, proclaimed himself "Sweet Papa Cream Puff right out of the bakery shop." The only way Morton could top that one was to call himself "Sweet Papa Jelly Roll, with stovepipes in my hips and all the women in town dyin' to turn my damper down."[29] Lomax also makes it clear that prostitution was economically more important to Morton than music, enabling him to live the flashy life of a pimp and to wear diamond fillings in his teeth.[30]

The language of the pimp, besides being aggressively hip, is one of the more notable examples of trade jargon that couldn't help filtering out to square America. The prostitute's customer is no *sweetback man* or *sweet man*, but a *trick*, a term probably derived from nautical usage in the sense of 'a task',[31] or a *john* 'a dupe, someone to be deceived'.[32] With him, the prostitute will not *get her nut hot* 'become sexually stimulated' or *get her nut off* 'experience orgasm'. (In white terminology, *getting the nuts off* refers to the male orgasm exclusively.) A pimp prefers a woman who is *qualified* 'an experienced whore' but occasionally has to use a *turn out* 'a recently recruited prostitute'.[33] *Turn out* is another term adapted from nautical usage, where it is strictly a verb and means 'begin activity'. Its opposite, at sea, is *turn in* 'cease activity' or 'go to bed', a term that seems to have no special function among Black pimps and prostitutes.

Despite the familiarity of prostitution in the Black ghetto—or perhaps because of it—it plays an important role in the verbal insult ritual called *the dozens*:

> At least my mother ain't no cake—everybody get a piece.[34]

The dozens is one of many ways in which the verbally superior ghetto male utilizes his superiority. Whether or

not he intends to recruit her as a prostitute, he may *rap* to a *chick* 'make an aggressive verbal approach to a young woman'. *Rapping* refers to any kind of self-confident, aggressive discourse style. The older plantation Black was forced to depend more upon *tomming* (speaking in the manner of Uncle Tom) and *jeffing* (playing up to the white man's expectations—a wild guess about the etymology has put it as a reference to President Thomas Jefferson or to Confederate leader Jefferson Davis).

In plantation society, the field hand spent most of his time in arduous work under the supervision of the overseer. Malingering was severely punished. After work, his contact with whites might be limited to the "pateroller" (patrol officer), who would run him in if he were off his own plantation without a pass. With either of these white men, the Black frequently adopted the verbal strategy of *copping a plea* 'admitting guilt so humbly and persistently as to embarrass the accuser'. British visitor J. F. D. Smyth, whose slave Richmond had failed in his task of minding the master's fishing pole, heard this example in 1784:

> now, massa, me know me deserve good flogging, cause if great fish did jump into de canoe, he see me asleep, den he jump out again, and I no catch him; so, massa, me willing now take good flogging.[35]

As might be expected, Smyth did not flog or even punish his slave.

Another verbal strategy important to surviving slavery and degraded social status was *loud talking*, getting at an otherwise invulnerable offender by speaking up about his offense in an embarrassing context. (To be really effective, the loud talker should also employ *signifying*, indirect statement or suggestion.) With what sociologist John Dollard in *The Shadow of the Plantation* called "the sexual advantage," Southern owners would undoubtedly have

spawned a much greater number of mixed-blood children if slave women had not known the strategy of subtly calling attention to hereditary resemblances in the presence of the owner's wife.

With the end of slavery and a partial shift in the American caste structure, the disguise function and the coping function of Black verbal performance became less essential than they once were. A positive value is still attached, however, to verbal strategies; to "belong" in the Black community is partly a matter of using the slang. Among adolescent male groups like Manhattan's Morningside Heights Thunderbird gang, a hierarchy of verbal skills is to be observed.[36] On the fringes, *lames* engage in futile attempts to *run with the gang*, 'use the slang', and play the dozens, but can't quite keep up. *Squares* don't know there's any running going on, and *sissies* would be appalled at the activities or the language of the group.

The hierarchy of verbal skills is clear-cut. There is, however, another hierarchy in another kind of verbal skill. In reading, the order of proficiency is exactly reversed, with the sissies at the top and the leaders of the gang at the bottom.[37] In a nation in which literacy is virtually requisite to employment, ghetto language ability correlates highly with joblessness and negatively with success.

More advantaged middle-class Americans, almost all of them white, have been attracted to the language of the ghetto and to some of the more superficial of its values. These whites have become known by the name *hippies*, originally a derogatory term for a would-be *hipster* who couldn't quite make it. (Dalby has shown that *hip* is an Africanism, citing Wolof *hipi* 'to open one's eyes, to be aware of what is going on'.) Much of the hippies' slang comes from the Blacks. The hippie defines himself as the opposite of the *redneck*, who has fewer resemblances to Black culture. Since the hippie got into Black-influenced music after the bop revolution of the 1950's led by Charlie

Parker, Dizzy Gillespie, and Charlie Christian, he uses *cool* as the term of universal approbation. Smoking marijuana, commonplace among jazz musicians even in the days before it was illegal, is another strong distinguishing characteristic of the hippie; to be *cool* is likely to mean, for him, 'to be favorable toward the use of marijuana'. "Smoking" is not, however, an indispensable feature; anyone who promotes the hippie life style without attracting "hassles" from authority figures like the police, school officials, or parents may be "cool." There is a feeling among some hippies that to smoke marijuana ostentatiously, not as a matter of *doin' your own thing,* is uncool.

But the aesthetic principles of the cool movement that culminated in Miles Davis are completely foreign to the hippies. Their music comes from another part of the Black tradition, rock and roll. It is loud—almost always amplified electronically—and frenetic, but the term *hot* is not used to refer to it. For the hippie, *rock* is an etymologically unexamined musical term. There is little doubt, however, that it reflects a sexual metaphor: "My baby rocks me with one steady roll." *Roll,* the silent partner in the combination insofar as hippies are concerned, is an active one for the Blacks:

> Say, you must be wantin' me, baby, to break
>   my back — No!
> Sweet mama rollin' . . .
> Sweet mama rollin' stone.
>
> Tell me, mama, how you want your rollin' done.
> Sweet mama rollin' . . .
> Sweet mama rollin' stone.[38]

Hippies use rock music as, among other things, background music for drug consumption, producing a condition labeled *stoned* 'totally involved', taken over from the originally Black intensifier in phrases like *stone blind* and

my stone friend. For Blacks, on the other hand, the music serves for dancing. Historically, names like Camel Walk, Buzzard Lope, Fish Tail, Snake Hip, Giouba, Dog Scratch and others have revealed African associations.[39] In the Jazz Age of the twenties, the related Black dance, the Charleston, revolutionized American white ballroom dancing, and further developments like *jitterbugging* have put their stamp on almost all popular entertainment.

However, the apparent recent increase in Black influence is partly illusory. The drug culture, at least as great an influence as the Black, is responsible for song titles like "Yellow Submarine" (downers) and "Eat a Peach" (hallucinogenic mushroom). The jazz scene of the twenties had *viper* 'a marijuana user', which the hippies have not picked up, and *roach* 'a marijuana cigarette', which they have—with the semantic change that it is now the unsmoked remnant of a "joint." The simple report studies of hippie language that have been made so far permit no real conclusions as to the degree of influence, but it seems a safe guess that about fifty percent of it is Black. Hippies continue to address each other as *man*, for example, but few have changed to *dude* with the Black fashion.

Much of the "hip" slang is not so strikingly new as is often believed. A great deal of it is paralleled in the speech patterns of plantation Blacks in the nineteenth century, although in most cases some semantic change has taken place. There is, for example, the participle *busted,* long familiar in white slang in the sense 'broke, without funds' which was replaced in the sixties by the meaning 'arrested'. A person who had been busted was likely to be *on ice* 'in prison'. Although the hippies and their associates might use *busted* for even such minor infractions as traffic violations, the most characteristic use of the term was for being picked up by the vice squad for prostitution or drug use. Harrison's "Negro English" of the 1880 records the expression *to get busted* 'to fail', which could lead by easy

semantic transference (the subject failed to evade the fuzz) to the present meaning.

The contemporary use of *heavy* to mean 'arcane, profound' also has its plantation progenitors. In the inner city today, *heavy knowledge* (also *heavy stuff* or *heavy shit*) generally refers to a kind of occultism associated with the Black Muslims, their concept of Allah, and their racio-political line of reasoning. As collected by Labov, Cohen, Robins, and Lewis, it is highly eschatological in nature:

> Dig that—the *laast* days of that *ye-ear* when all people— we'll have succeeded in becomin' a dominant people under Christ Revelation, when all people will come to know our knowledge, wisdom, 'n' understanding that we are the sons of men.[40]

In spite of the demonstrated fact that *heavy* knowledge was the latest thing in Harlem hipness in the 1960's, neither the term nor the attitude should have been a surprise to anyone halfway conversant with Afro-American anthropology. In *Suriname Folk-Lore* (1936), Herskovits and Herskovits reported the use of the same term in a strikingly similar sense among the Blacks of Paramaribo, Surinam:

> Thus comment is made that *Kromanti* dancing is *hebi*— "difficult"—that is "strong," or "dangerous." . . . The *Kromanti winti* are conceived as powerful spirits, who when they possess human beings, cause them to speak African words not intelligible to the uninitiated.[41]

Gullah folk-tale collector Ambrose Gonzales lists *hebby* 'great' in the Glossary to his *Black Border* and cites *uh hebby complain'* 'a great outcry'.

Hippies and other derivative and imitative groups are not always aware of the Afro-American cultural patterns in which Black slang is rooted. Nor do they have access to

the out-of-awareness sense of tradition that a ghetto Black can draw upon. They have "picked up on" the in-group identification feature of Black slang but have not mastered either the cultural background or the productive devices. A few inversions exist among the motorcycle gangs, as the world learned when Hell's Angels made the headlines and it was discovered that the girl friend of a member was his "ol' lady." Beyond that, there is little that expresses the spirit rather than the letter of Black verbal performance. Whites play the dozens, especially in the South, but their insults tend to be ritualized and stereotyped rather than creative as among Blacks. In this respect, the adult white player of the dozens reaches about the level of a preteen beginner in the ghetto, who memorizes a few responses (if someone says to him, "You favver ain't no man," he is able to respond, "You muvver like it") as an initial stage of learning to "play."

Playing the dozens had a real value for the Blacks in that it provided a way of retaining self-respect even under humiliating conditions like slavery. The origin of the term is lost to history; perhaps the best guess is that *putting* [a slave] *in the dozens* meant classifying one with that part of the human merchandise which had been damaged in the middle passage so that he could not even be sold as an individual but had to be offered with eleven others. But the earliest recorded example shows how an African on a slave ship managed a verbal comeback to a white slaver whom he would not have dared to challenge on any other terms. Told that a recently captured monkey of large size and unusual color could be his wife, the African replied, "No, this no my Wife, this a white Woman, this fit Wife for you."[42] William Smith, the captain of the slave ship, considered that "this unlucky Wit of the Negroe's . . . hastened the Death of the Beast, for the next Morning it was found dead under the Windless."

Until commercial exploitation made jazz and some of its

vocabulary known in the 1920's, Black language forms had been very little known. Because their musical terms and their expressions for private and personal interaction were unfamiliar, Blacks were assumed to use the same vocabulary as Southern whites. In fact, they were considered rather more Southern than the whites of Alabama or Louisiana, since the whites traveled a great deal and the Blacks did not. As a nonmobile part of the population, Blacks were supposed to speak the nearest thing we had to a truly regional dialect. Those who sampled their language concentrated on farm terms (*string beans* or *snap beans; slop bucket, swill pail* or *swill bucket; hay stack, hay barrack,* or *hay doodle; corn husk* or *corn shuck; wish bone* or *pulley bone; corn bread, corn pone,* or *johnny cake*). They found, predictably, little or no difference from Southern whites, since the whites owned the farms and the agricultural implements that the sharecropping blacks had to use and were able to control the terminology. With the expansion of linguistic research into other domains, motivated by the sometimes harsh criticism of the new sociolinguists, much greater differences are being discovered. It has been found, for example, that in a given area only certain Black speakers will say *Higo* (*Here go*), 'here is' or 'here are', and *Dago* (*there go*), 'there is' or 'there are'. Whereas a middle-class child, describing the falling of a rock into the water, will say that it *"goes* splash!" the speaker of Black English Vernacular will report that it *"say* splash!" Black speakers use zero copula (*he sick* for *he is sick*) and the unmarked possessive (*he book* for *his book*) more than even white children who have been in extensive contact with Blacks. And the Black vernacular has phrases like *You been know dat!* 'You've known that a long time' that most white speakers don't even understand.[43]

The attitudinal change that made the Black vocabulary from something almost unknown into a part of almost

general American English usage was the result of an important sociological phenomenon, the revolt of middle-class youth in the 1960's.[44] Thus, although Blacks were present in great numbers before 1665, their greatest influence on the American vocabulary took place around 1960. As everyone knows, a great part of that impact has reached England.[45] Indeed, some of it has come back to America from Great Britain through the medium of British rock groups like the Beatles and the Rolling Stones. The full scope of the Black influence, and what has happened to the Black terms in their migration first to the Northern cities and then to the entire world, would make another book in itself.

8

Advertisers, Politicians, and Other Hucksters

Since at least as early as the beginning of the nine-teenth century, Americanization of English has been associated in many people's minds with the debasement of the language, and American advertising has been cited as one of the major debasers. Advertising jargon is no recent development. Even before the end of the eighteenth century, if we can trust the records, American housewives were being tempted to extravagance by advertisements in newspapers—and husbands were being driven to despair by their wives' expenditures. In "Account of a Buyer of Bargains" (1797) a husband reports

> I had often observed that advertisements set her [his wife] on fire, and therefore . . . I forbade the newspaper to be taken any longer.[1]

In 1803, an "English gentleman lately returned from America" reported his "Animadversions on the Present State of Literature and Taste in the United States":

> One third of the American newspaper is filled with un-couth advertisements written, in general, in language, and abounding in phrases, wholly unintelligible to the English reader.[2]

The phrase "unintelligible to the English reader" is probably one of the exaggerations typical of such statements; but obviously something was happening to the language of the United States, and it was expressed as directly in advertising as in anything else.

Many other observers reported the prominence of advertising in the public functions of American English, that being one of the domains in which it gained an early advantage over competing languages. Benjamin Franklin, for example, complained about the persistence of German in Pennsylvania. German speakers imported books from their homeland, and of the six publishing houses in Pennsylvania, two published exclusively in German, one published half in German and half in English, and two (from Franklin's point of view, "only" two) published exclusively in English. Street signs had inscriptions in both languages, and in some places only in German. But advertisements, "intended to be general," were printed in English as well as in German.[3]

To disseminate the advertisements, early Americans had nothing like the electronic media (radio, movies, television). There were, nevertheless, methods other than newspapers and magazines. One of the most successful was the traveling medicine show, with a certain amount of entertainment thrown in so that a crowd would gather to listen to the pitch. Some of the shows involved the services of minstrels, both black and white. Where the commercial-theatre minstrel show used white performers in blackface, the medicine show was multiethnic and multicolored. It included an Indian component from very early times.

The Indian medicine show peddled "Indian" herb medicines along with free entertainment. Indians would arrive in a New England town and boil medicinal herbs in front of their tents. One of the earliest groups was the Kickapoo Indian Medicine Company—surely an inspira-

tion, at some remove, for the Kickapoo Joy Juice of *Li'l Abner*'s Lonesome Polecat and Hairless Joe.

The Indian medicine show apparently began as a white enterprise. Some clever fellow was able to exploit the popular belief in Indian "medicine"—and, of course, the popular half-understanding of that concept. (See Chapter 6.) One John E. Healey, who named himself variously "Doc." or "Col.", conceived the idea of having real Indians give the pitch for "Indian Herb Medicine." Such employment—or exploitation—of Indians in the medicine shows was a forerunner of sentimental Indianism in many phases of advertising, from the use of statues of Indians in front of cigar stores to brand names that suggest the American aborigine.

The term *medicine show,* rather surprisingly, does not appear in the historical dictionaries before the citation from Herbert Asbury's *Sucker's Progress* of 1938. Given Asbury's skill in re-creating an epoch of the past, it seems impossible that he invented the term rather than using an authentic phrase from the period. We know that the show itself existed much earlier. It utilized Indian *medicine men* (1806), who did a *medicine dance* (1805), by which they evoked the "Great Spirit." They sang *medicine songs* (1791), smoked *medicine pipes* (1833), carried *medicine bags* (1805), talked *medicine talk* (1791), and even lived in *medicine lodges* (1814).[4] The Indians who conducted these curative ceremonies were *powwows* (1624) or *powwow doctors,* the latter phrase sometimes becoming *power doctors* by folk etymology. If the shows in which they participated were not called *medicine shows,* even though the term is not attested for that date by the historical dictionaries, something is strangely amiss.

The importance of medicine in early American advertising can be explained in part by the scarcity of physicians on the frontier. Many people tried to cure their own

illnesses or resorted to whatever remedies might be offered. There was a remarkable growth of medical quackery in the second half of the nineteenth century, producing medicines like "J. L. Curtis's Original Mamaluke Liniment, A sovereign remedy for man and beast" in the Dakota Territory in 1859, and Dr. Williams's Pink Pills for Pale People in the South immediately after the Civil War. Other patent medicines were produced by or attributed to a virtuosic but otherwise unknown Dr. Robertson: Celebrated Stomachic Elixir of Health, Vegetable Nervous Cordial (or Nature's Grand Restorative), Celebrated Gout and Rheumatic Drugs, and Worm Destroying Lozenges. Dr. Godbold's Vegetable Balsam of Life was apparently the work of another great medical mind. The expansion of American newspapers, providing a good medium for promoting the sale of popular remedies like these, contributed to the expanding market for patent medicines.[5]

The herb-medicine tradition was commercially important over a long stretch of time. Louis Hebert, reputedly the first Canadian apothecary, was painted consulting with an Indian over herb remedies in 1605. In view of all the modern concern about tobacco as injurious to health, it is startling to find that early America counted the plant among Indian herb medicines. In fact, in the seventeenth century, Europeans considered it a kind of miracle drug from the New World.[6] Some propaganda from the opposition, which in the very early days conceived of tobacco as "stunting a child's growth," seems to have eliminated that idea from popular favor, but in the eighteenth century the concept still cropped up now and then. Even into the nineteenth century the Clingman Tobacco Cure Company of Durham, North Carolina, advertised tobacco cakes and ointment as a cure for bunions, snake bite, scarlet fever, lockjaw, and most other ailments. In the twentieth

century, the belief persisted in rural areas that blowing smoke into the aching ear would cure earache.

The debate over smoking and health has always, it seems, been with us, and ad men have always been around to confuse the issue. In the 1940's Old Gold cigarettes advertised "Not a cough in a carload," thus undoubtedly reflecting the apprehension some people felt about the use of "the weed." (*Cigarette cough,* although not represented in the dictionaries, was certainly around by the 1930's.) The Old Gold advertising campaign must have been effective; Lucky Strike found it necessary to adopt a countering tactic: "A treat instead of a treatment."

The cigarette industry's first response to the health question was the adoption of a filter. The term *filter* began to appear in cigarette advertising in the 1940's, and for most Americans unless there is another specific context given, "Does it have a filter?" is automatically assumed to refer to a cigarette. A grimly resigned addicted public adopted *coffin nail* (1901) to describe the cigarette, *cigarette fiend* (1890) to describe the smoker, and *nicotine fit* (not recorded in the historical dictionaries) to describe the withdrawal symptoms of a smoker trying to quit.

Tobacco consumption has been the subject matter of perhaps the biggest, best-planned, and most expensive advertising campaigns in American history. When in 1952 a columnist wanted to compare the "selling" of the Eisenhower-Nixon team to an especially effective advertising campaign, she referred to "patently rehearsed ceremonials borrowed from the tobacco ads."[7]

After tobacco and medicine, politics is probably the biggest customer of American advertising. Vance Packard put it rather strongly:

By 1952 the Presidency is just another product to peddle through tried-and-true merchandising strategies.[8]

Only occasional politicians like Adlai Stevenson (one of the losers) kept objecting that "the idea that you can mechanize candidates for high office like breakfast cereal . . . is the ultimate indignity to the democratic process."

Actually the "merchandizing" is no new phenomenon. "Tippecanoe and Tyler, Too," the 1840 campaign slogan of General William Henry Harrison, is squarely in that tradition. Harrison's opponent in that race, New Yorker Martin Van Buren, called "Old Kinderhook" because of his birthplace, used the chance similarity of his nickname's initials to the newly popular colloquialism *O.K.* in a clever but eventually ineffective attempt to profit by some sloganism of his own. The term was an Africanism, as David Dalby has shown, picked up from the slaves,[9] but the aggressiveness of Van Buren's campaigns caused even some etymologists to think that his adherents had invented and popularized the expression. The appeal of frontier sloganism was never more perfectly exploited than in Harrison's campaign, which became known to history as the *hard cider campaign*. His adherents were *hard cider* democrats or *hard ciderites* (both from 1840); his program *hard ciderism* (1841); and his congress the *hard cider congress*.

It turned out, however, that the log cabin, which also came into use during the 1840 campaign, was a more potent political symbol than hard cider. The term *log cabin* was originally used to describe a type of housing that seems to have been first used, perhaps by Swedish immigrants, around 1750. Thanks to politicians it came to symbolize solid American frontier virtues. The fact that Abraham Lincoln was born in a log cabin added to his appeal; his administration interrupted a long succession of generals and wealthy landowners in the Presidency. In the comic strip *Li'l Abner*, the wealthy prospective candidate who was reared in the world's largest log cabin by his politically ambitious parents captures the spirit—and some of the absurdity—of this part of our folklore.

Ever since 1840, a slogan has been essential to a presidential campaign. Although the statement has been contested,[10] there seems to be no real doubt that "Fifty-four forty or fight" contributed a great deal to the 1844 campaign of James Polk. The slogan promised, of course, to extend the Oregon Territory far into what is now Canada or to wage war. Polk did neither. Americans are, however, accustomed to the failure of both political and advertising slogans. Both Woodrow Wilson and Franklin D. Roosevelt won second terms as Presidents who "kept us out of war," and war was declared during the second term of each. For that matter, not every little boy who eats his Wheaties becomes a champion athlete. In both domains, politics and advertising, slogans have become a kind of phatic communication. The catchiness of the slogan is the important thing, not the semantic content of the words.

Both Abraham Lincoln and Franklin Roosevelt, facing reelection in wartime, made capital of the rural proverb "Don't change horses in midstream" as a campaign slogan. Horses were an important factor in American life when Lincoln ran, but not when Roosevelt used them. His slogan was part of the rather self-conscious appeal to frontier life that has remained a large part of the vocabulary of politics. Rather than stressing the supermodern, as other public-relations efforts usually do, politics depends largely on allusion to the American past. It uses the homey vocabulary of the backwoods in such phrases as *pump priming, slice of the melon,* and *log-rolling.* "Distribution of governmental largesse to political adherents" is a pale description alongside *pork barrel.*

The last expression, meaning 'a barrel in which pork is kept', was used as early as 1801, but even that citation refers proverbially to "minding our pork and cider barrels"—thus symbolically to property in general. The figurative meaning 'funds for local improvements designed to

ingratiate congressmen with their constituents' is not attested before 1913, but it must have existed earlier since *pork barrel bill* is recorded for the same year. Contacting his most important constituents is *getting back to the grassroots* for the American politician, even one whose voters are predominantly urban. The *full dinner pail* is one of the few expressions appealing to both urban and rural workers equally.

Both rural and urban voters expect the politicians to *talk turkey*. The phrase is attested, although with little explanation, from 1835. *The Life and Adventures* of Black Indian trader James P. Beckwourth (published in 1856 but reporting events of twenty years or so before) quotes a Pawnee Loup Indian whom a white man was trying to swindle in a proposed treaty as saying that the document "talked all turkey" to the white man and "all crow" to the Indian tribe. *Talk turkey* in that sense means something like 'tell me what's in it for me that is really worth having'.

If he fails to get reelected, a congressman is in for a session as a *lame duck*. This term has been in use in British English since 1761, in the sense of 'a disabled person or thing', specifically in Stock Exchange slang for 'one who cannot meet his financial obligations; a defaulter'. In the sense of 'an office-holder who has not been reelected', it is purely American, first attested in 1863. It is especially applicable to a congressman who has lost the election and is participating in a short legislative session. *Dead duck*, perhaps an analogical development from the other *duck* term, was originally political. It was used from 1867 on in the sense of 'one who is without influence politically, bankrupt, or played out'. More recent usage applies it to a defeated or hopeless person—more or less like the Western *gone coon* or the rural *gone goose*. Ranching terminology is not especially important in the American con-

gress, except for *maverick*. A *dark horse candidate* probably refers to horse-racing rather than to ranching.

In keeping with the old-fashioned emphases of political terminology, Indians have retained an important place in the vocabulary. Tammany Hall, for example, was named for a Delaware Indian chief, although most Americans I have questioned about it thought it referred to an Irishman. The original Tammany was famous for his love of liberty and for his wisdom. William Mooney, who founded the Tammany organization and named it after the Delaware Tamanend, introduced the affectation of using Indian titles in 1789. The thirteen trustees of the organization, called *sachems,* symbolized the thirteen original states; the president of the organization was the *grand sachem;* and the President of the United States, up to the time of Andrew Jackson, was the *great grand sachem.* In the 1920's Al Smith was known as "the Tammany brave."

Words like *caucus,* from the Algonquian, still play an important part in national legislative action. Others, like *mugwump,* are further from their original Indian meaning. *Mugwump* is perhaps the extreme case, having gone from meaning 'a very important person' to signifying 'a fence sitter' (mug on one side, wump on the other). But losing the original meaning is not unusual in the field of political terminology: Boss Flynn of Chicago inspired the expression "In like Flynn," because he always won; but when movie actor Errol Flynn got into some much-publicized trouble with what we would now call groupies in the mid-forties, the phrase came to mean something quite different. Semantic changes take place easily in the domain of politics, and it matters little what language the terms originally came from.

There are enough Indian terms in politics to make them seem quite normal. It was nothing unusual, for example,

when the powerful New Orleans Ring organization, which had kept the city under white supremacy rule throughout almost all of the third quarter of the nineteenth century, regrouped under the name of the Choctaw Club after it was defeated by a reformist group. The familiarity of non-Anglo-Saxon terms in politics probably facilitated the adoption of words of problematic origin like *scalawag* and *snollygoster,* and the free and easy word-forming of the multilingual early American society no doubt expedited the adoption of new compounds like *carpetbaggers.* A compound like *muckraker* seems, in the American context, especially appropriate to 'one who makes charges of corruption on the part of politicians and governmental figures'. *The Oxford English Dictionary* cites one example of *muckrake* 'to rake refuse together' in British English, but the figurative meaning is strictly American. The noun *muckraker,* in the American sense, is attested as early as 1871 and enjoyed a real vogue in the early twentieth century applied to writers like Lincoln Steffens. *Muckraking,* in the phrase *muckraking reformers,* is first reported in 1906.

Except for a certain amount of scientific terminology in the claims made by popular drugs (now greatly restricted by federal law), advertising, like politics, has preferred to recombine everyday vocabulary elements into new compounds rather than to use Latin- and Greek-derived elements as scientists do. Our soaps, medicines, cigarettes, and politicians have sold better when they were advertised in a homey, slightly old-fashioned vocabulary. Most of our really big promotional schemes, whether in business or in politics, have been rural- and frontier-oriented.

Why should this be so, when our society prides itself on being mechanized and technological? Why do we go to the drive-in window at the bank in an automobile whose name commemorates the premechanical days of the frontier? Automobiles with names of more effete reference,

like Grand Prix, El Dorado, Riviera, Monaco, and Malibu are not unknown, but the market is dominated by Bronco, Pinto, Charger, Colt, Mustang, Maverick, Cougar, Wildcat, Bobcat, Hawk, Falcon, Skylark, and Rabbit (with which Volkswagen gets into the American spirit of things). Hornet, the old Hudson, is so much in the spirit of things that American Motors has recently revived the name. The Indian past is also evoked, largely for its exoticism, in automobile names. Pontiac, the name of an Indian chief, has long been with us, and Chevrolet has recently come up with a Cheyenne model. But the most blatant commercial use of Indian lore has been Ford's Thunderbird. This creature with an extra head on its abdomen was especially important to the Haida of the Northwest Coast, whose carvings of it are still extant. Conspicuous consumption in automobiles (the lean little T-bird of the 1950's was designed as a second car for people who found their Cadillacs too cumbersome to park downtown, although its contemporary namesake is decidely overstuffed) is bizarrely consistent with a pretense of arcane knowledge about Indian tribal customs.

Why does so much history survive in the terminology of an assembly-line product whose prophet, Henry Ford, proclaimed, "History is bunk?" Why do we have football teams named Longhorns, Mustangs, Lions, Cowboys, Plainsmen, Badgers, Bruins, Golden Bears, etc., in the "athletic" entertainment carefully tailored for our television screens, and only one with a "business" name like the Packers? (The New York Mets, Jets, and Nets are perhaps symptomatic of another trend developing, but they haven't been around long enough for the onomastic pattern to become clear. Whether the name had anything to do with it or not, the Shreveport Steamers didn't last even one entire season.) It would be easy to explain this phenomenon in terms of "the American spirit" or "the enduring ideals of the frontier," but the answer is prob-

ably more mundane—culture lag. The frontier itself was the biggest promotional scheme in our history. We have carried over the habits of the past rather than consciously innovating.

Those who moved westward did not do so simply because they spontaneously felt the urge. It may not have been only Horace Greeley's "Go West, Young Man" that did the trick, but his and other slogans probably had as much to do with it as the desire for adventure. The real advance guard, like the mountain men, was motivated both by the desire for what gain could be realized from the sale of furs and by the easy availability of Indian women, a welcome contrast to the frigidity of the Puritan girls back home.[11] It is no accident that a promise of sex (the girl in the bikini may go with the car or the Coca-Cola) is a major part of the best advertising techniques. But for the larger groups who ventured out toward the Oregon Territory and other areas, it took a promotional scheme of fantastic proportions to instil any urge to move away from the comforts of the East.

With the movement for territorial expansion and free land, the country entered upon one of the greatest advertising campaigns in history—the "booming" of the West. (The verb *boom,* from a noun originally Dutch, was first applied to a river, in the meaning 'rush strongly', around 1831; by 1884, *booming* meant 'splendid, grand'; the sense of 'in a period of great economic activity' came shortly thereafter.)* This was a campaign in which orators and politicians participated as much as railroad companies and land salesmen, departments and bureaus of agriculture and other farmers' organizations, boards of trade, and chambers of commerce. Countless speeches were made in support of it, and promotional activity included inspirational literature in immigrant handbooks, railroad

---

* See Chapter 2 for material on the ultimate derivation of *boom.*

guides, state and regional gazetteers, rural almanacs, real estate directories, and government reports.

The people involved in these activities were *boosters.* This term, in the sense of 'one who supports or promotes given interests', arose in the West in the 1890's and soon spread to general advertising and chamber of commerce activities. The booster was the type Sinclair Lewis satirized so brilliantly in *Babbitt* and *Main Street,* but without dissuading Americans from "boosting"—in fact, Lewis' conscious exaggerations seemed to give them some new ideas. The opposite of the booster was, of course, the *knocker,* who dared to see that every money-making or expansion scheme wasn't perfect. Even the churches were against knocking. In the 1930's, Southern Baptist Sunday school children sang, to the tune of "Everybody Ought to Love Jesus," "Everybody Ought to Be a Booster":

> Everybody ought to be a booster, a booster, a booster.
> A booster never knocks, and a knocker never boosts.
> Everybody ought to be a booster.

Lincoln Steffens had one of his cartoonists do a picture of a burglar, caught in the act and menaced by a policeman's club, saying "Don't knock; boost."

Americans have continued to revel in the kind of ballyhoo by which the West was won. Historically, there can be little doubt of the importance of this promotional rhetoric. B. A. Botkin has put it exceptionally well.

> Besides manifest destiny, free land, and state pride, the West had another string to its bow—the long bow which it drew in order to live down its wild and woolly reputation and to attract settlers. It was the myth of a land flowing with milk and honey—part of the American dream of a promised land of plenty, opportunity, and "beginning," which had first attracted settlers from the

Old World to the New and was now transferred to the fabulous, far-off West. To make its assets outweigh its endurances, orators, promotors, and guidebooks painted this unknown country in the rosy hues of fairyland.[12]

The promotional terminology, in its very hyperbole, was directly comparable to advertising today. The West was called *the land of Nature's bounty*, or *God's country*. Perhaps the most characteristic slogan to draw expansion-minded settlers to the West was "The sky's the limit." Individual states had their own slogans. Oklahoma was the Boomer State, or Boomer's Paradise. Illinois and Kansas each called itself the Garden of the West; New Mexico was either the Land of Heart's Desire or the Land of Sunshine. An act of the legislature changed Arkansas from the Bear State to the Wonder State. California proclaimed that it was the state of perpetual sunshine—and radio comedians of the 1930's and 1940's told a million jokes about their homes being washed away by "liquid sunshine."

Early and late, it was the advertising man who sold the frontier. The Wyatt Earps and Bat Mastersons really had nothing to do except be more superlative than anyone else at slinging a gun—or at holding the pose reasonably well until a publicity man came around to tell the world about them. By now dozens of debunking biographies have been written about these sometimes bogus frontier heroes, but the country has not wanted to forget the legendary—as opposed to the historical—frontiersman. Products bearing the name of Davy Crockett became a commercial success about one hundred years after his books had been best sellers.

It is, therefore, not in the least surprising that advertising and ballyhoo continue to stress the frontier spirit, cattle country, and the rural. A skeptic may wonder just

what a cigarette has to do with all those Western men on horses, but the ads apparently sell cigarettes. Probably not even prizes given for so many box tops have sold as much breakfast cereal as the commercials accompanying serialized Wild West stories on radio and television.

Soap is one of the few commodities that can vie with politics, whiskey, automobiles, and tobacco in competing for the advertiser's minute and dollar. Soap seems an exception to the stress on rural and frontier associations; soap commercials emphasize the mild, new formulas, so different from the lye soap great-grandmother used to make. The ubiquitous soap or detergent advertisement on daytime television (and, earlier, on the radio) justifies the term *soap opera* for the teary dramas that act as come-ons for the soap salesman's pitch. Even that term, however, has a Wild West predecessor: *horse opera,* used of Western and cowboy-type entertainments in general and attested as early as 1857; *soap opera* does not appear until eighty-two years later.

Crass and vulgar as it may be, the triumph of sloganism in American popular communication is overwhelmingly convincing. If you don't believe it, try this simple experiment: Ask fifteen or twenty people, in an interview situation, to quote either a singing commercial for Coca-Cola or two lines from any work by Walt Whitman. Unless you bias the interview by speaking only to Whitman specialists, even university professors will be much more familiar with the soft-drink commercial.

Brand names have played a part in the coinage of new words in American English. Everyone knows how the Kodak Company and Frigidaire suffered because their brand names became common terms for cameras and refrigerators, or how a leading soft-drink manufacturer tried to resist the use of *coke* as a common noun. In everyday usage, *levis* refer to denim trousers without any necessary

connection to the trade name from which the term originated. *Simonize* 'to clean and wax the enameled surface of an automobile' has virtually parted company with Simoniz, the trademark from which it originated. In the later nineteenth century, Merry Widow was a brand name for rubber prophylactic devices. By around 1930, *merry widow* designated such a contraceptive, and a reference to Lehar's operetta would bring snickers in rural America. The term became obsolete in the 1940's, possibly because the product couldn't compete with Trojans. The name of the University of Southern California football team inspired its share of leers during the forties and fifties, and the familiarity of the brand name made Homer's *Iliad* an obscene text to some.

The richness of compounds (noun modifying noun, as in *sherry cobbler* and *baby sitter*), which the earliest observers found in American English, is today nowhere more in evidence than in the common nouns borrowed from advertising. Many phrases that originated there are now part of our basic vocabulary: *do-it-yourself, back-to-school* (*sale*), *wash-and-wear* (or *drip-dry*), *ready-mix* (*cement* or *cake*), *all-purpose* (*gloves* or *soap*), *handy-wipe, off-the-rack.* The phrase *ready-to-wear* has developed since the 1930's, superseding phrases like *ready for wearing.*[13]

The commercialism of American life is openly and frankly manifested, as it has been in almost no other culture of the past or present. There is obvious hypocrisy in our sentimental attitude toward the Indian in our advertising, but probably no more than in the Renaissance English sentimentality toward the Arthurian legends, dealing with a Celtic people long ago conquered and subjected to exploitation. The positive thinking that our advertisers and commercial people took over from the boosters of our frontier past dominates every aspect of our life. When the American merchandizer doesn't want to fool with returned bottles for soft drinks, he labels them *Disposable* or *No*

Return. When the ecology movement forces him to change that policy, he continues to accentuate the positive by calling them *Money-Back Bottles.* Nothing else would be possible in our society. It's the American way.

Notes

Chapter 1

[1] Sabir was virtually ignored for a very long time, although there have been a number of articles recently. Hugo Schuchardt, "Die Lingua Franca," *Zeitschrift für Romanische Philologie*, 1909, is the classical source. An even more specialized work is Kahane, Kahane, and Tietze, *The Lingua Franca in the Levant: Turkish Nautical Terms of Italian and Greek Origin*, Urbana, Illinois, 1958. The most important article linking Sabir to the New World pidgins and creoles is probably Keith Whinnom's "The Origin of the European-based Pidgins and Creoles," *Orbis*, 1965.

[2] In addition to the works listed in footnote 1, there are tantalizing hints in books like J. C. Hotten's *The Slang Dictionary* (1887, reprinted 1972): "The vulgar dialect of Malta and the Scala towns of the Levant—imported into this country and incorporated with English cant—is known as the Lingua Franca, or bastard Italian" (p. 2). Schuchardt also makes the point that the earliest form of Lingua Franca was predominantly Italian in vocabulary, probably because of the early prominence of the Italian city-states in Mediterranean shipping. The possible relationship of Lingua Franca to English "slang" or "cant" has been developed in an article by Ian F. Hancock (see Bibliography).

[3] *Hakluytus Posthumus, or Purchas His Pilgrimes*, Vol.

18:277 ("The Voyage of Monsieur de Montis into New France, written by Marke Lescarbot," A.D. 1606).

⁴ Robert A. Hall, Jr., *Pidgin and Creole Languages,* Cornell University Press, 1966, p. 100.

⁵ See Hall, *Haitian Creole,* 1953; and Jules Faine, *Le Creole dans l'Univers,* 1939. Both of these take the notion of the actual linguistic content as representing "Norman" French more seriously than I am inclined to do.

⁶ See Michael Silverstein, "Dynamics of Recent Linguistic Contact," in I. Goddard (ed.), *Handbook of North American Indian Languages,* Vol. XVI (forthcoming). A summary of some of Silverstein's main points will appear in Emanuel J. Drechsel, "An Essay on Pidginization and Creolization of North American Indian Languages, with a Note on Indian English, *International Journal of the Sociology of Language,* 1976.

⁷ See Whinnom, *op. cit.,* and Paul Christophersen's two articles in *English Studies,* 1953 and 1959.

⁸ The extremely diverse nature of American Indian languages can be appreciated after an examination of a work like Franz Boas, *Handbook of American Indian Languages,* 1911, 2 vols.

⁹ J. Dyneley Prince, "An Ancient New Jersey Indian Jargon," *American Anthropologist* 14:508.

¹⁰ *Ibid.*

¹¹ Lorenzo Johnston Greene, *The Negro in Colonial New England, 1620–1776,* Columbia University Studies in History, Economics, and Public Law, No. 494, p. 198.

¹² William Fitzwilliam Owen, *Voyages to Explore the Shores of Africa, Arabia, and Madagascar,* London, 1833, I:29.

¹³ See *Black English,* Random House, 1972, Chapter III.

¹⁴ Justin Winsor (ed.), *The Memorial History of Boston, Including Suffolk County, Massachusetts, 1630–1880,* Boston, 1882, p. 477.

¹⁵ "A Merchant of Boston," *The Present State of Eng-*

land, quoted by Kittredge, *The Old Farmer and His Al-manac,* 1912, p. 354.

[16] Cf. *me no stomany* 'I don't understand' and *Now me stomany that* 'Now I understand that' in Sarah Kemble Knight's *Journal* (1704).

[17] It is a linguistic commonplace that American Indian languages, like some other non-Indo-European languages, have "whisper" vowels, without the vibration of the vocal chords in the way that we tend to regard as essential to vowels. (For the approximate effect, try pronouncing *a day* or another phrase consisting of *a* plus a monosyllabic noun by whispering the article and pronouncing the noun with full voice.) This is an accepted fact, but apparently no studies of borrowings from American Indian languages have given any special attention to it.

[18] William Safire, review of *All-American English, New York Times Book Review,* May 18, 1975, p. 4, treats this opinion as though it were beyond question. George Philip Krapp, *The American Language* (I:106) counted "all of the words of Indian origin, exclusive of personal, place, and other proper names . . . that have had at some time or another greater or less currency as English words." He came up with more than 230 words. Most recent treatments contain some phrase like "about fifty words of Indian language origin."

[19] *American English,* 1958, p. 32.

[20] Christopher Ward, *The War of the Revolution,* Macmillan, 1952, p. 143.

[21] Quoted in Morris Bishop, "Four Indian Kings in London," *American Heritage,* December 1971, p. 74.

[22] Jack D. Forbes, *The Indian in America's Past,* Prentice-Hall, p. 39.

[23] Peter Wood, *Black Majority,* Knopf, 1974, p. 59.

[24] Forbes, *op. cit.,* p. 99.

[25] Page Smith, *John Adams,* I:5.

[26] Quoted in Forbes, *op. cit.,* p. 199.

27 Meridel LeSueur, *North Star Country*, New York, 1945, p. 156.

28 Richardson, *Beyond the Mississippi*, 1867, p. 486.

29 *The New World Negro* (ed. Frances Herskovits), Indiana University Press, 1966, p. 284.

30 Hans Nathan, *Dan Emmett and the Rise of Early Negro Minstrelsy*, University of Oklahoma Press, 1962, p. 11.

Chapter 2

1 Melville J. Herskovits, "Gods and Familiar Spirits," in *The New World Negro* (ed. Frances Herskovits), Indiana University Press, 1966, p. 284.

2 O. G. T. Sonneck, *Report on the Star-Spangled Banner, Hail Columbia, America, and Yankee Doodle*, Washington, 1909, p. 111.

3 Geoffrey D. Needler, "Linguistic Evidence from Alexander Hamilton's *Itinerarium*," *American Speech*, October 1967, p. 210.

4 Smith, *John Adams*, I:54.

5 Needler, *op. cit.*, p. 215.

6 For an illuminating account of the contemporary situation, see Jan Voorhoeve, "Varieties of Creole in Suriname," in Dell Hymes (ed.), *Pidginization and Creolization of Languages*, Cambridge University Press, 1971.

7 *Crumbs from an Old Dutch Closet*, The Hague, 1938, p. 39.

8 This is approximately the dialect of *Uncle Tom's Cabin*. Since Mrs. Stowe knew New York better than Natchitoches Parish, Louisiana, it is probable that she projected the dialect of her own area into the region about which she had scanty knowledge. For a much better rendition of the Louisiana Black dialect of the nineteenth century, see Kate Chopin, *Bayou Folk*.

[9] Frances D. Gage, transcript quoted in Elizabeth Cady Stanton, Susan B. Anthony, and Matilda Joslyn Gage (eds.), *History of Woman Suffrage,* Rochester, New York, 1889, pp. 165–66.

[10] *Dialect Notes,* 1910, p. 459.

[11] Gertrude Leffert Vanderbilt, *The Social History of Flatbush,* New York, 1881, p. 53.

[12] *Ibid.,* p. 55.

[13] Prince, *op. cit.,* p. 464.

[14] Saxby V. Penfold, *Romantic Suffern,* Tallman, N.Y., 1955.

[15] Edwin Newman, *Strictly Speaking,* Bobbs-Merrill, 1974, p. 157, quotes this as an example of "bad" English, in a context of insistence that American English is undergoing some kind of deterioration. On the same page, Newman refers to Muhammad Ali's *flustrated,* evidently as an example of the same kind of "corruption." Actually, neither form is especially unusual in Black English. A story on a Black convicted murderer in the Houston *Chronicle* for November 14, 1965 (Section 2, p. 2), quoted him as complaining about his "life of flustrations."

[16] See Ian F. Hancock, "A Provisional Comparison of the English-based Atlantic Creoles," *African Language Review* VII (1969):7–72. Since this theory about relexification of Pidgin English with Dutch etymons is controversial even among professional creolists, I have continued to refer in this book to a Pidgin Dutch origin for Dutch Creole.

[17] A representative treatment is that of D. C. Hesseling, *Het Negerhollands der Deense Antillen,* Leiden, 1905. Popular belief that Virgin Islands speakers spoke "Danish" Creole, because the islands were owned by Denmark and because the plantation owner group was largely Danish, greatly overestimates the influence of Europeans on the language of the West Africa–derived population.

[18] Van Loon, *Crumbs from an Old Dutch Closet,* p. 46.

¹⁹ See the statement of Captain Marryat, in a context of commenting on names for cocktails, quoted in Chapter 5.

²⁰ Matthew St. Clair Clarke, *The Life of David Crockett, the Original Humorist and Irrepressible Backwoodsman, An Autobiography,* New York, n.d.

²¹ Samuel P. Orth, *Our Foreigners: A Chronicle of Americans in the Making,* New Haven, 1920, p. 153.

Chapter 3

¹ This particular *y'awl* is probably a calque (a filling in of an African structure with English material) from *unu,* the West African second person plural pronoun also used in Gullah, Jamaican Creole, and the dialects of many other West Indian islands. Jay Edwards ("African Influences on the English of San Andres Island, Colombia," in Hancock and DeCamp [eds.], *Pidgins and Creoles: Current Trends and Prospects,* 1972) points out that in the Creole English of San Andres both *you all* and *unuaal* occur. Edwards asserts: "In the white plantation English of Louisiana, the form *y'all* functioned precisely as did the *unu* of the slaves. The use of *y'all* (semantically *unu*) was probably learned by white children from black mammies and children in familiar domestic situations" (p. 14).

² Hans Kurath, *A Phonology and Morphology of Modern English,* Heidelberg, Carl Winter, 1964, p. 120.

³ See, for example, the diphthongal treatment in George L. Trager and Henry Lee Smith, *Outline of the Structure of English,* 1951.

⁴ John Peale Bishop, *Collected Essays,* 1933, p. 99.

⁵ Mima Babington and E. Bagby Atwood, "Lexical Usage in Southern Louisiana," *Publications of the American Dialect Society* 36 (November 1961):11.

⁶ Herbert Asbury, *The French Quarter,* p. 100.

[7] Charles Gayarré, "The New Orleans Bench and Bar in 1823," *Harper's Magazine,* Vol. 77 (1881).

[8] *Ibid.,* p. 889.

[9] *Ibid.,* p. 888.

[10] *Ibid.,* p. 889.

[11] Cable, *Old Creole Days,* p. 99.

[12] Gayarré, *op. cit.,* p. 894.

[13] Harnett T. Kane, *The Bayous of Louisiana,* William Morrow, 1943, p. 322.

[14] The first two of the quotations are from Chopin's *A Night in Acadie,* 1897, pp. 190 and 203, respectively. The third is from the short story "Loka" in the collection *Bayou Folk,* 1894.

[15] Ramsey, *Cajuns on the Bayous,* 1957, p. 160.

[16] *Ibid.,* p. 51.

[17] *Ibid.,* p. 49.

[18] Sarah Searight, *New Orleans,* Stein and Day, 1973, p. 101.

[19] Kane, *The Bayous of Louisiana,* p. 325.

[20] See, for example, William W. Chenault and Robert Reinders, "Northern Born Community in New Orleans in the 1880's," *Journal of American History* XC (1972).

[21] Kane, *Queen New Orleans,* New York, 1949, p. 134.

[22] *Ibid.,* p. 235.

Chapter 4

[1] Herbert Asbury, *Sucker's Progress.* This book is exceptionally good on gambling terminology—better than *The Dictionary of Americanisms,* which quotes it extensively. The reader will easily determine that I have been frequently guided by Asbury's work. Additional material of great interest is to be found in his *The Barbary Coast.*

[2] Searight, *New Orleans,* p. 29.

[3] Asbury, *Sucker's Progress,* p. 156.

[4] *Ibid.,* p. 117.

[5] Matsell, *Vocabularium, or the Rogue's Lexicon.*

[6] Rollins, *The Cowboy,* 1936, p. 179.

[7] Barton, *Comic Songster,* 1838.

[8] St. Louis *Reveille,* 1845 (2 May I/6).

[9] Asbury, *Sucker's Progress,* p. 80.

[10] *Ibid.,* p. 205.

[11] Rollins, *op. cit.,* p. 79.

[12] "Poker, Pawns, and Power," in Neil Postman, Charles Weingartner, and Terence P. Moran (eds.), *Language in America,* Pegasus, 1936.

Chapter 5

[1] Mrs. Frances Trollope, *Domestic Manners of the Americans,* Vintage, 1949, p. 279.

[2] Library of Congress Record LP 20, recorded by John A. Lomax.

[3] Trollope, *op. cit.,* p. 241.

[4] *Davy Crockett's Almanac of Wild Sports in the West, Life in the Backwoods, and Sketches of Texas,* Nashville, 1837, I:40.

[5] Tyrone Power, Esq., *Impressions of America During the Years 1833, 1834, and 1835,* London, 1836, I:57.

[6] Ian F. Hancock (personal communication) supplied the information on *kaktel* in Krio.

[7] Searight, *New Orleans,* p. 248.

[8] "A Domestic Origin for the English-derived Atlantic Creoles," *Florida FL Reporter,* 1972.

[9] *The Look of the West,* London, 1860.

[10] James H. Cook, *Fifty Years on the Old Frontier,* University of Oklahoma Press, 1954, p. 188.

[11] Ed. Samuel Cole Williams, New York, 1930, p. 6. On the subject of Indians and whiskey, there are many interesting and revealing Pidgin English attestations like this

one from Thomas Simpson Woodward's *Reminiscences of the Creek or Muscogee Indians,* 1851:

> My friend, you French Chief! me Whiskey John . . . heap my friends, giv me whiskey, drink, am good. White man my very good friend me, white man make whiskey, drink him heap, very good, I drink whiskey . . . You me give one bottle full. I drink him good. Tom Anthony you very good man, me you give one bottle full. You no drink, me drink him all, chaw tobacco little bit, give me some you [p. 70].

[12] Horace Greeley, *Overland Journey from New York to San Francisco in the Summer of 1859,* New York, 1860, p. 201.

[13] Philip Ashton Rollins, *The Cowboy,* 1936, p. 189.

[14] Everett N. Dick, "The Long Drive," *Collections of the Kansas State Historical Society,* Vol. XVII:47.

[15] "Nautical Sources of Krio Vocabulary," *International Journal of the Sociology of Language* VII (1976).

[16] John C. Duval, *The Adventures of Big-Foot Wallace,* 1870, p. 294.

[17] Rollins, *The Cowboy,* p. 79.

[18] Pp. 170–71.

[19] Norman W. Schur, *British Self-Taught, with Comments in American,* Macmillan, 1973.

Chapter 6

[1] *Diary in America with Remarks on Its Institutions,* Philadelphia, 1839, II:30.

[2] Winfred Blevins, *Give Your Heart to the Hawks: A Tribute to the Mountain Men,* Nash Publishing, 1973, p. 53.

[3] *Collections of the Massachusetts Historical Society,* Second Series, VIII:231.

[4] I:14.

[5] I, Series I, 504.

[6] Constance L. Skinner, *Adventures of Oregon: A Chronicle of the Fur Trade,* Yale University Press, 1920, p. 102.

[7] Murray Morgan, *Skid Road: An Informal Portrait of Seattle,* New York, Viking, 1960, p. 7.

[8] Ruxton, *Life in the Far West,* 1848, III:99.

[9] A. B. Guthrie, *The Way West,* 1847, p. 95.

[10] Quoted in Everett N. Dick, *Vanguards of the Frontier,* 1940, p. 59.

[11] Marryat, *op. cit.,* p. 38.

[12] Supplement I:595.

[13] Supplement II:347.

[14] Neihardt, *Black Elk Speaks,* p. 5.

[15] *Life in the Far West,* pp. 165–66.

[16] Skinner, *op. cit.,* p. 103.

[17] Bliss Isley, *Blazing the Way West,* London, 1939, p. 100.

[18] *Life in the Far West,* p. 19 (Ruxton's footnote 33).

[19] Blevins, *op. cit.,* p. 52.

[20] *Life in the Far West,* p. 8.

[21] P. 217.

[22] *Owen Wister Out West, His Journals and Letters* (ed. Fanny Kemble Wister), University of Chicago Press, 1958, p. 153.

[23] *Ibid.,* p. 159.

[24] See Philip L. Durham and Everett L. Jones, *The Negro Cowboys,* Dodd, Mead, 1965; and William Loren Katz, *The Black West,* Doubleday, 1971.

[25] Julian Mason, "The Etymology of *Buckaroo,*" *American Speech,* 1960.

[26] Wister, *op. cit.,* p. 155.

[27] Vance Packard, *The Hidden Persuaders,* David McKay, 1957, p. 167.

[28] Ramon F. Adam's *The Cowman Says It Salty,* Uni-

versity of Arizona Press, 1971, contains a very detailed treatment of the quaint and proverbial language of the cowboy. See also his *Western Words* (1941 and 1968). Many of the materials dealt with in the 1971 work are not known outside the cattle trade, and therefore would not be relevant to this treatment.

[29] For the language of miners, see especially Lincoln Barnett, *The Treasury of Our Tongue,* Knopf, 1964, pp. 188–89. The speech of roughnecks in the oil fields is treated by Lalia Phipps Boone, "Patterns of Innovation in the Language of the Oil Field," *American Speech* 24 (1949): 131–37. Walter McCulloch's *Woods Words* is an outstanding source for the language of the lumberjack of the north woods. There appears to be no adequate treatment of the speech of railway workers.

For miners, although Mark Twain and one or two other well-known writers provide valuable primary data, the most useful original source would seem to be James F. Rusling's *Across America; or, the Great West* (New York, 1875), pp. 72–73. Rusling lists and explains *square meal, shebang, outfit, go down to bed rock, panned out, pay-streak* (not in *A Dictionary of Americanisms,* although it has *pay dirt* from 1856), *peter out,* and *you bet!*

[30] John A. Lomax, "Cowboy Lingo," in Wilson M. Hudson and Alan Maxwell (eds.), *The Sunny Slopes of Long Ago,* Publications of the Texas Folklore Society XXXIII, 1966, p. 117.

Chapter 7

[1] Benjamin Franklin, "Information to Those Who Would Remove to America," in *Writings* (ed. Smythe), VII:606.

[2] Dan Burley, "The Technique of Jive," reprinted from

Dan Burley's Original Handbook of Harlem Jive, in Alan Dundes (ed.), *Mother Wit from the Laughing Barrel,* Prentice-Hall, 1973. *Twister to the slammer* is obviously 'key to the door'. *Dig the jive* means 'perceive what is going on'; it combines the Africanism *dig* (Dalby cites Wolof *dega, deg* 'understand') and what Burley considers a development from English *jibe.* Dalby, however, cites Wolof *jev* 'to talk about someone in his absence'. In all fairness, it should be admitted that neither of these is very convincing. Burley translates *straight up and down, three ways sides and flats* as 'for all she was worth' (*i.e.,* the man to whom the girl gave her door key played her for all she was worth).

³ C. R. Ottley, *How to Talk Old Talk in Trinidad,* Port of Spain, 1965. Ottley gives the following translation:

> She took her revenge out of that one by clandestingly [sic!] bestowing her favours on another until her infidelity came to light. He flogged her. She left the house. She has now transferred her affections to Johnny.

Till de mark buss [i.e., burst] is an unusually transparent example of the relationship between an Afro-American dialect and its Pidgin-Creole background. In WesKos Pidgin English, for example, *pass mark* is an absolute intensifier ('extremely', 'excessively'). *Pass* itself is the normal function word of comparison, something like English *than. Till de mark buss* would be '*WAY* past the mark'! (Obviously, Ottley's very free translation does not indicate those relationships.)

⁴ In the Caribbean, this term is used to both male and female interlocutors (as is *hombre* in Puerto Rican Spanish, for rural speakers). Outsiders frequently misunderstand its import. A psychiatrist named Edwin A. Weinstein (*Cultural Aspects of Delusion: A Psychiatric Study of the Virgin Islands,* Free Press, 1962) was misled by this

use of *man* and by the well-known Creole identity of masculine and feminine pronouns into a fantastic over-statement of the relationship between language and social structure. Less sophisticated observers frequently suspect widespread homosexuality.

[5] Lingua Franca versions of Twi, Yoruba, Wolof, and some other prominent coastal West African languages were in use during the early period. According to Turner, *Africanisms in the Gullah Dialect* (1949), some texts of African-language songs were in use on the Sea Islands in the twentieth century. William A. Stewart (personal communication) suspects that Turner strongly overstated the restriction to the Sea Islands.

[6] Miles Mark Fisher, *Negro Slave Songs in the United States,* Citadel, 1953, *passim.*

[7] *Ibid.,* p. 66.

[8] *Ibid.,* p. 89.

[9] *Ibid.,* p. 111.

[10] *Ibid.,* p. 49.

[11] *Ibid.,* p. 38.

[12] The works of Herskovits cited in this chapter and elsewhere make this point forcefully, but perhaps the most convenient source of concentrated information on the subject is Donald C. Simmons, "Possible West African Sources for the American Negro Dozens," *Journal of American Folklore* LXXVI (October–December, 1963).

[13] Dalby, *op. cit.,* p. 177.

[14] Grace Sims Holt, "Stylin' Outa the Black Pulpit," in Kochman (ed.), *Rappin' and Stylin' Out,* University of Illinois Press, 1972, p. 153.

[15] This point, as well as the complicated relationship between Black speech and underworld usage, is well treated in Nathan Kantrowitz, "The Vocabulary of Race Relations in a Prison," *Publications of the American Dialect Society* LI (April 1969):23–34.

[16] Holt, *op. cit.,* p. 157.

[17] Harold Courlander (ed.), *Ethnic Folkways* 417, notes, p. 11. This use of *bread* is also attested by Guy B. Johnson, "Double Meaning in the Popular Negro Blues," in *Mother Wit from the Laughing Barrel*, p. 261.

[18] Johnson, *Ibid.*

[19] Courlander, *Negro Folk Music, U.S.A.*, pp. 129–30.

[20] Johnson, *op. cit.*, p. 261.

[21] This familiar blues motif can be heard in (e.g.) "Cornbread Blues," sung by Texas Alexander on OK 8511 (recorded December 8, 1927).

[22] Dalby, *op. cit.*, pp. 181–82.

[23] Peg Leg Howell, "New Jelly Roll Blues," Columbia 14210 (recorded August 4, 1927).

[24] Quoted in Johnson, *op. cit.*, p. 261.

[25] P. 252.

[26] These traditional lines are here transcribed directly from "Jelly, Jelly," sung by Billy Eckstein with Earl Hines and an orchestra, recorded in Hollywood on December 2, 1940, and rerecorded on Camden CAL-588.

[27] This is a slight variation on the traditional pattern (thus for *hell* can be substituted *Atlanta, New York, Miami, Texas,* or any other place name). As reported by Alan Lomax (*Negro Folk Songs from the Mississippi State Penitentiary,* Tradition Records TLP 1020, Side B, Band 4), it goes:

> Well, hain't been to Georgia, boys, but,
> Well, it's I been told, sugar,
> Well, hain't been to Georgia, Georgia,
> Well, it's Georgia women, baby,
> Got the sweet jelly roll.

[28] Quoted in LeRoi Jones, *Blues People,* William Morrow, 1963, p. 104.

[29] Quoted in Alan Lomax, *Mr. Jelly Roll,* p. 136.

[30] P. 155 (including footnote). On the association of

early jazzmen with pimps and prostitutes, see any standard treatment. Max Jones and John Chilton, *The Louis Armstrong Story,* Little, Brown, 1971, p. 56, give a characteristically restrained account of Louis' early dabbling in that activity. In *Satchmo: My Life in New Orleans* (1954), Armstrong reveals, "I always felt inferior to the pimps" (p. 199). Such statements document the importance of the pimps in the ghetto community, although of course they do not prove that the pimps were as much an asset to American life as creators like Armstrong. Skill in *walking that walk* (sometimes called the *Pimp Strut*) and *talking that talk* (using the slang and excelling in other typically Black aspects of verbal performance) is, by all published accounts, a requisite for a successful career in procuring.

[31] See *All-American English,* p. 163.

[32] Dalby, *op. cit.,* p. 182. Dalby cites Mandingo *jɔn,* 'a person owned by someone else'.

[33] Robert Beck ("Iceberg Slim"), *Pimp: The Story of My Life,* Holloway House, 1969. Note that Beck writes of the "master pimp who turned me out"—i.e., introduced him to the practices necessary for successful pimping. Beck and other writers on pimping use a lot of slang phrases *(pull my coat to* 'inform me of') that seem peripheral to a treatment like this because they are not a part of general Black ethnic slang.

[34] Johnson, *op. cit.,* p. 309.

[35] J. F. D. Smyth, *A Tour of the United States of America,* 1784, p. 121.

[36] William Labov, Paul Cohen, Clarence Robins, and John Lewis, *A Study of the English of Blacks and Puerto Ricans in New York City,* U.S. Office of Education Cooperative Research Project No. 3288, final report, 1968.

[37] *Ibid.,* II:164–166.

[38] Quoted in Frederic Ramsey, *Been Here and Gone,* p. 129.

[39] Marshall Stearns and Jean Stearns, *Jazz Dance*, Macmillan, 1968, pp. 24–30.

[40] *Op. cit.*, II:146.

[41] P. 285.

[42] William Smith, *A New Voyage to Guinea*, 1744, p. 53.

[43] William Labov, probably the leader of the linguists who long resisted the notion that there could be any syntactic differences between Black English and Standard English, admits this point in *Language in the Inner City*, University of Pennsylvania Press, 1972, p. 53.

[44] Probably the best-written description of this phenomenon is in Eldridge Cleaver, *Soul on Ice*, Delta, 1969.

[45] The most suggestive article on this subject is John M. Hellman's " 'I'm a Monkey,' The Influence of the Black American Blues Argot on the Rolling Stones," *Journal of American Folklore* 86 (1973):367–73. For the development of some of the onomastic suggestions of this article, see Chapter II of my *Black Names* (Mouton, forthcoming).

Chapter 8

[1] Mathew Carey, *The American Museum, or Repository,* 1787.

[2] *Monthly Magazine* XIV (Supplement 1804):626.

[3] *Works,* ed. Jared Sparks, Vol. 7:71–72.

[4] James Harvey Young, "American Medical Quackery in the Age of the Common Man," *Journal of American History* 47 (June–March 1960–61). The above material is a partial paraphrase of some of Young's materials, with certain data (especially the dates of the earliest attestations) added. Although he does not say so, Young clearly assumes that *medicine show* came into English at about the same time as the other phrases. As the discerning

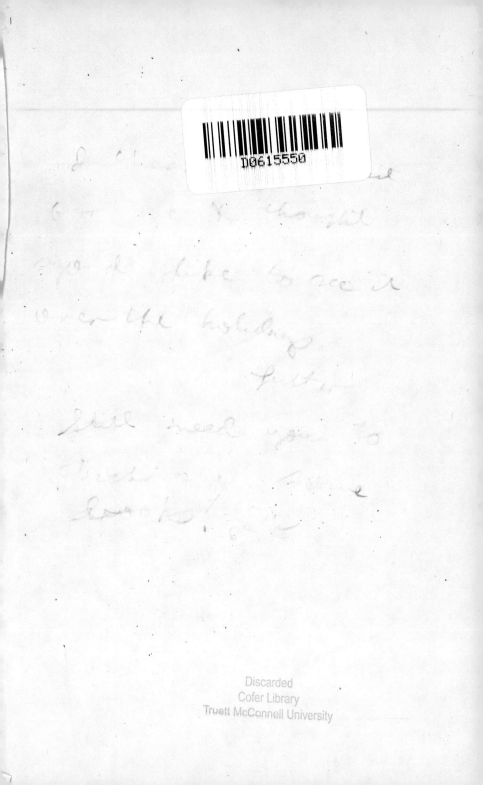

❧ THE GETTY FAMILY ❧

PART TWO

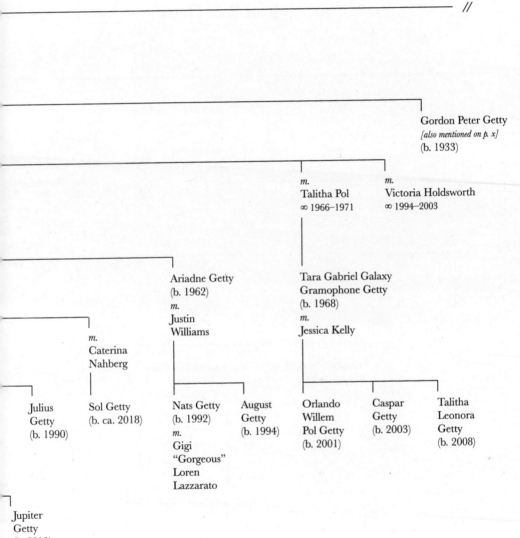

//

Gordon Peter Getty
[also mentioned on p. x]
(b. 1933)

m.
Talitha Pol
∞ 1966–1971

m.
Victoria Holdsworth
∞ 1994–2003

Ariadne Getty
(b. 1962)
m.
Justin
Williams

Tara Gabriel Galaxy
Gramophone Getty
(b. 1968)
m.
Jessica Kelly

m.
Caterina
Nahberg

Julius
Getty
(b. 1990)

Sol Getty
(b. ca. 2018)

Nats Getty
(b. 1992)
m.
Gigi
"Gorgeous"
Loren
Lazzarato

August
Getty
(b. 1994)

Orlando
Willem
Pol Getty
(b. 2001)

Caspar
Getty
(b. 2003)

Talitha
Leonora
Getty
(b. 2008)

Jupiter
Getty
(b. 2019)

Jean Paul Getty
(1892–1976)

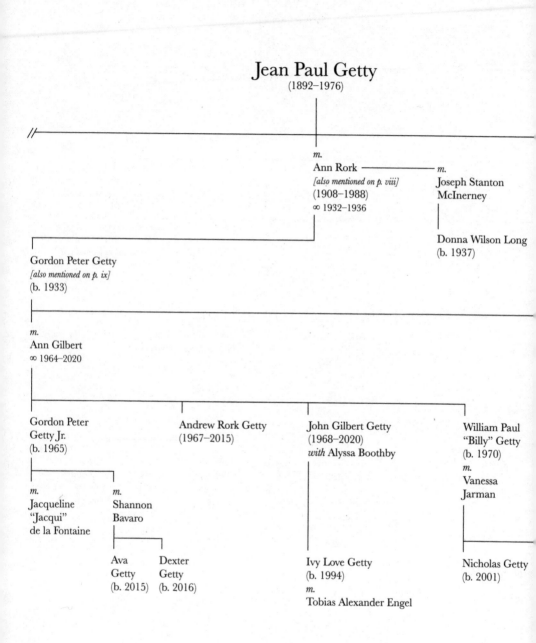

m.
Ann Rork ——————— *m.*
[also mentioned on p. viii]   Joseph Stanton
(1908–1988)   McInerney
∞ 1932–1936

Donna Wilson Long
(b. 1937)

Gordon Peter Getty
[also mentioned on p. ix]
(b. 1933)

m.
Ann Gilbert
∞ 1964–2020

Gordon Peter   Andrew Rork Getty   John Gilbert Getty   William Paul
Getty Jr.   (1967–2015)   (1968–2020)   "Billy" Getty
(b. 1965)   *with* Alyssa Boothby   (b. 1970)
                                                                    m.
                                                                    Vanessa
m.   *m.*   Jarman
Jacqueline   Shannon
"Jacqui"   Bavaro
de la Fontaine

              Ava   Dexter   Ivy Love Getty   Nicholas Getty
              Getty   Getty   (b. 1994)   (b. 2001)
              (b. 2015) (b. 2016)   *m.*
                                           Tobias Alexander Engel

THE GETTY FAMILY

PART THREE

m.
Louise Dudley "Teddy" Lynch
(1913–2017)
∞ 1939–1958

Timothy Ware Getty
(1946–1958)

with
Cynthia Beck

Nicolette
Michelle Beck
(b. ca. 1985)
m.
Michael Lee Hays

Lula Elisende Hays

Kendalle
Pauline Getty
(b. ca. 1989)

Alexandra
Sarah Beck
(b. ca. 1992)

Alexander Getty
(b. 2003)

Veronica Louise Getty
(b. 2008)

Introduction

Dynasties are notoriously difficult to maintain. By a common benchmark, a family can't really be considered a dynasty until it has endured for four generations with its fortune and social rank still standing. When a family does cross that threshold, to keep them all on track at least one of the heirs generally needs to produce something original.

With its fourth generation ascendant, the Gettys tick all the boxes, though they are an unconventional dynasty. This is only fitting considering their independent-minded patriarch, J. Paul Getty. Descended from Scots-Irish stock, he was born in 1892 in Minneapolis; as a teenager, he moved with his family to Los Angeles. In 1916, he struck out as a wildcatter in Oklahoma, where he hit black gold. He built his petroleum empire stealthily, while working out of suitcases in a succession of hotel suites he occupied as he roamed around Europe for decades. Something of a one-man band, he bested many of the so-called Seven Sisters, the corporate oil oligopolies, including Standard Oil. Rich as he became, he was never an Establishment guy. To the world at large he was relatively obscure until 1957, when *Fortune* magazine named him, at age sixty-four, "the Richest American." With his estimated net worth in the range of $1 billion, he eclipsed Rockefellers, Mellons, Astors, and Du Ponts—members of dynasties that had been established several generations earlier.

Becoming "an overnight financial freak," as he later observed, he was catnip for the press, which lapped up his foibles, especially his frugality. In the beginning, the stories were comical. Everyone enjoyed the one about the World's Richest Man—as Getty was soon enough surmised to be—installing a pay phone for "the convenience" of guests at his residence, Sutton Place, the sixteenth-century mansion twenty-three miles outside of London that he bought in 1959. (After sailing from New York to London in June 1951, for what was supposed to be a few months, he never set foot again in America.)

But after the drug-related death of his firstborn child, George Franklin Getty II, in May 1973, and—just five weeks later—the kidnapping of his eldest grandson, J. Paul Getty III, the saga of the Gettys took on a decidedly darker tone.

"The Tragic Dynasty." "A Cautionary Tale." "The Getty Curse." Newspapers and magazines printed such headlines again and again, turning the Gettys into a poster family for dysfunction. They lived up to this billing in the 1970s and 1980s: JPG's third son, J. Paul Jr., battled drug addiction and depression for many years, as did some of Paul Jr.'s children, including Aileen, and Paul III, who suffered a stroke in 1981 that left him a paraplegic until his death in 2011.

Then there were the family's legal battles, most of which revolved around the source of their immense wealth, the Sarah C. Getty Trust. Begun in 1934 at the behest of J. Paul Getty's mother, for whom it is named, it was initiated with capital of $3.5 million to provide primarily for her grandchildren. Throughout his life, Getty plowed his profits back into it and, in turn, borrowed from it to grow his business empire. In the 1960s, Getty's fourth son, Gordon, challenged his father in court over the trust, resulting in a seven-year-long suit that the younger Getty lost. Following the patriarch's death in 1976 at age eighty-three, the clan was dragged into the public eye again, this time thanks to the astounding bequest he made—valued then at $750 million—to his recently opened namesake museum in Malibu. A few years later, lawsuits erupted between family members over the sale of Getty Oil. After Texaco bought it for $10.1 billion—the biggest corporate acquisition in history—the relatives litigated for another eighteen months over management of the trust, the coffers of which at that point swelled to $4 billion.

It was irresistible material for numerous journalists, biographers, and filmmakers. In his 1995 book *Painfully Rich* (later republished under the title *All the Money in the World*), John Pearson described the Getty Trust as "probably the most destructive major fortune of our time" and pondered "why it has apparently devoured so many of its beneficiaries." Director Ridley Scott used Pearson's book as the basis for his 2017 film *All the Money in the World*, which plumbed the grisly details of the kidnapping. The five-month ordeal was an immensely traumatic event for family members, and it continues to haunt some of them. Yet in the film, the biggest villain was J. Paul Getty—not the kidnappers who brutally cut off their victim's ear and abused him before they finally released him. Overall, Getty was depicted as a monstrous figure—coldhearted, greedy, humorless, lonely, reclusive. The ultimate misanthrope.

Could J. Paul Getty have been such a thoroughly irredeemable person? Was his family so cursed?

The Getty family tree is a complicated one. During his five short-lived marriages, Getty produced four sons who lived into adulthood (his fifth and youngest boy died at age twelve); between them, they fathered nineteen children, sixteen of whom survive as of 2022. They, in turn, have produced a generation of around forty Gettys—JPG's great-grandchildren. About fifteen great-great-grandchildren have been born.

In this book, I examine the patriarch, his wives, and their descendants, reassessing some of the narratives about them that have taken root and grown—often in the fertile soil of tabloid websites. You will see that while some of the myths are based in reality—a number of Gettys have been decimated by addiction and depression—the majority of its members today are thriving. A more nuanced look at the family is thus called for.

Geographically, the descendants spread out and have lived in North America and South America, as well as Europe, Asia, and Africa. Following the lead of their international forebear, they've become a global dynasty. Some of his grandchildren might be modern-day versions of Henry James or Edith Wharton characters, having assimilated (in some cases by marriage) into European nobility. Others remain true Californians, some marrying into Hollywood royalty.

"They're weirdos, all of them, in different ways," a gentleman who has been friends with many of them told me. "In a good way," he added. "Their wealth and position in the world has allowed them to delve deeply into the things that they are interested in. So many other extremely rich people who could do whatever they want, do exactly what everybody else does. The Gettys are idiosyncratic. They all have a streak of wildness—and sometimes mental health issues."

Looking at the Gettys today, I found creative, accomplished, and philanthropic individuals. Perhaps most surprisingly—in view of what is usually written about them—a number of them indeed appear to be well-adjusted and happy. Tragedy has revisited the family on more than a few occasions, but it would be inaccurate to describe the whole of such a large clan as cursed. And a lively batch of young Gettys are starting to make their marks on the world.

The Gettys are a surprisingly tight-knit clan. Every summer, the extended family holds an annual meeting, usually in Italy; at another point in the year, typically, many of them get together in New York or take a trip elsewhere. In December, a gala party for Gordon's birthday draws many Gettys to San Francisco, where their political power is on display; in addition to family, longtime close friends and political heavyweights Nancy Pelosi, Dianne Feinstein, Kamala Harris, and Gavin Newsom are also regulars.

Though Sutton Place itself was sold long ago (at last report, it was owned by Uzbekistan-born oligarch Alisher Usmanov, the eighth-richest man in Britain), the Sutton Place name continues to figure prominently in the life of the clan, existing virtually in various of their domain names, IP addresses, and SEC filings, and terrestrially within an unmarked building on an elegant street in London's Mayfair that houses their family office, the well-staffed nerve center for all matters Getty.

"They have this sort of army of people around them," said one Londoner familiar with the family. "To an extent, then, the real world never really impinges on them. They are quite elusive and difficult to pin down. But they really care about things and want to do things properly. They don't just lend their names to a cause. At the same time, they are one state removed from the real world. When you've had that amount of money for that long, that's where you are."

Even though it has at times threatened to tear some of them apart, the legacy of the Sarah C. Getty Trust continues to bind them. In 1985, after the settlement of the family litigation in the wake of the sale of Getty Oil, $1 billion was reserved for taxes, leaving them with $3 billion, which was partitioned into four separate trusts (each worth $750 million). How rich are they today? In 2015, *Forbes* pegged the Getty family's net worth at $5.4 billion in a ranking of "America's Richest Families." But a number of Gettys hold foreign passports; at least eight of them reportedly have carried Irish passports, which have sometimes been granted in exchange for making investments in Ireland. According to several financial experts I consulted, given the extraordinary growth of the stock market over the past decades, the family's combined net worth could easily be in the neighborhood of $20 billion. (The Getty Museum's endowment, which also began around 1985 with its $750 million bequest, soared to $9.2 billion in 2021.)

"They could have done *way* better," one prominent investment manager said of the Getty family. "If they actually did smart things, and managed their taxes well, which you would expect from a respectable family trust with the resources and brainpower they'd have access to, their compound annual growth rate could have been higher than 11 percent, putting them in the $150-plus billion range."

Much of the Gettys' wealth has been shielded behind their trusts, which have provided family members with large distributions. But according to the Sarah C. Getty Trust's terms, its capital will be divided between the heirs upon the death of J. Paul Getty's last living son. So, immense windfalls await Sarah's great-grandchildren when Gordon's time comes.

Diverse as the Gettys are, they can be divided—for journalistic purposes—into two camps: the "public" ones and the "private" ones. Aside from a few flamboyant individuals, much of the family remains remarkably private. Some of them intensely so. There are many Gettys you never read about and probably have never heard of.

Some have become well-known through their achievements in business, philanthropy, and society, or have been made notorious through tragedy. Even when these "public" ones speak to the press (or, in the cases of younger Gettys, post on Instagram), they generally focus on a specific undertaking or cause. They are not inclined to cooperate with reporters attempting to pull together a big picture of the clan. You can't blame them. They don't want to read another "Tragic Dynasty" tale. A good deal of what has been written about them has been, if not inaccurate, then off the mark. And they want their achievements to be taken on their own merits.

As the new generations of the four branches of the family mature and go in different directions, a wide-angle lens is needed to look at them. One also has to debunk some of the myths that have grown around them.

I began my research into the family by delving into J. Paul Getty's personal papers, housed at the Getty Research Institute, one of the monumental travertine-clad buildings at the Getty Center in the Brentwood neighborhood of Los Angeles.

In his correspondence—including love letters to and from some of his wives—and his diaries, which span from 1938 to 1976, a figure emerges quite different from the one that has hardened in the public imagination, a man capable of humor and affection. His diaries are also a fascinating record of wealth and power in the twentieth century. Each day—in a sort of proto-Warholian fashion—he made note of business transactions great or small; the people he saw; pieces of art that caught his attention and prompted him to open his checkbook; his bodily functions and ailments.

His social life was nonstop. Well into his seventies, he was routinely out dancing at nightclubs until two in the morning, if not later. (So much for his reported reclusiveness.) One also finds note of many visits from his children, grandchildren, ex-wives, and numerous mistresses. According to accounts from the women themselves, as well as Getty, he maintained warm relations with all of his exes until the very end.

There are also details of his fervent efforts to build his art collection and his museum, shedding light on the astounding cultural and philanthropic legacy he left. His bequest to his museum was the largest donation to a cultural institution in history—which no doubt emboldened critics to mock it in its early years, particularly for its design in the form of a Roman villa, which the intelligentsia derided as "Disney-like," even as the public adored it.

When J. Paul Getty died, he left his descendants with colossal riches as well as his unconventional DNA. Wealth is often squandered; genes can split in many directions. Despite considerable tragedies, the Gettys have survived, and even thrived. Now, as its younger branches spread out, can they endure as a contemporary dynasty?

I.

THE PATRIARCH

1

Sutton Place

It was the dawn of a new decade and a new era—a day early in 1960—as J. Paul Getty marched through the Tudor labyrinth of Sutton Place. Twenty-three miles southwest of London, it had been built 440 years earlier by a courtier of Henry VIII. Just now, it had been rebooted as the nerve center of Getty's worldwide petroleum empire, and his seventy-two-room home. Telex machines clattered with reports of stock market gyrations on Wall Street and the flow of oil from Arabian deserts. Bustling about were members of Getty's executive and domestic staffs, the latter headed by Francis Bullimore, his unimpeachable butler.

Getty, wearing one of his customary Kilgour, French & Stanbury dark three-piece suits, and bearing the mournful mien that made him always look, his longtime aide Claus von Bülow observed, as if he were attending his own funeral, trod through the 165-foot oak-paneled Long Gallery, draped with sixteenth-century Flemish tapestries. When Getty reached his private study, where Dutch Old Masters hung on the Honduras mahogany paneling, he shut the door.

He then unlaced his John Lobb oxfords and jumped onto a long antique settee.

"Come on," he beckoned to the other person in the room, his solicitor, Robina Lund, a brainy twenty-three-year-old Scotswoman employed by the starchy firm of Slaughter and May. The dealer who had just delivered the settee had vouched for its sturdiness, promising it was "strong enough to jump on," explained Getty (who stood five feet eleven and weighed 180 pounds, with a muscular build from years of weight training).

"So let's try it!" he said to Lund.

"What if it breaks?" she wondered.

"I'll send it back," he said.

Recalled Lund, "So for a good five minutes we bounced up and down, and I nearly killed myself laughing as he did an Indian war-whoop each time he went in the air."

At the sound of a knock on the door, the pair were back into their shoes in a flash. As Bullimore ushered in the next appointment, a pair of businessmen, Getty reassumed his customary countenance. "Paul gravely shook their hands," Lund remembered.

People can be so different behind closed doors. J. Paul Getty had so many doors. That day, as he settled into Sutton Place, the richest man in the world had reason to feel giddy. This was at last a permanent home—something this sixty-seven-year-old hadn't had since childhood. Over the previous decades, he'd been a virtual stranger to the households where his five wives and five sons lived. His had been a nomadic existence, unspooling in a succession of hotel suites, mostly in Europe, where his ear was glued to the phones on which he conducted business, and where he washed his own socks and underwear.

Resolutely low-profile, Getty ensured that his photo seldom appeared in print outside of the *Oil & Gas Journal* and publications of that ilk. The anonymity suited him well, allowing him to stealthily acquire stakes in companies he sought to take over, and, when he had the time, to conduct amorous meetings with an array of women.

But his cover had been blown on October 28, 1957. His first inkling came when he found the lobby of the Ritz, the hotel in

London where he was then living, swarming with journalists, all clamoring to see "the richest American." *Fortune* magazine had just published the results of a thorough and novel investigation that identified all citizens with fortunes exceeding $75 million. Getty was not only at the top of the seventy-six-person list—which was divided into five tiers—but far above the rest. His name alone appeared in the $700 million to $1 billion category. The $400 million to $700 million class included four members of the Mellon family as well as John D. Rockefeller Jr., Dallas oil magnate H. L. Hunt, and Miami real estate mogul Arthur Vining Davis.

Four Du Ponts, as well as Joseph Kennedy, Howard Hughes, Fort Worth oil wildcatter Sid Richardson, and steel heiress Mrs. Frederick Guest (the former Amy Phipps), made the $200 million to $400 million category; six Rockefellers (John D.'s kids), Vincent Astor, Doris Duke, and Mrs. Edsel Ford were bunched in with Texas oilmen Clint Murchison, John Mecom, and James Abercrombie at the $100 million to $200 million level; Henry Ford II, Mrs. Horace Dodge, Marjorie Merriweather Post, and John T. Dorrance Jr., son of the Campbell Soup formula inventor, were among those bringing up the rear, with $75 million to $100 million apiece.

The compilation, *Fortune* wrote, "only serves to emphasize the tremendous changes that American wealth has undergone in both numbers and character over the past twenty years. . . . No longer among today's Very Rich are the Morgans, the Goulds, the Guggenheims."

This rich roster was republished in newspapers worldwide. "Topping the list is Jean Paul Getty, Minnesota-born oil man and owner of the Pierre Hotel," wrote the *New York Times*, in its front-page, above-the-fold story.

For the rest of his life, Getty expressed rueful feelings over this "outing."

"I was thenceforth a curiosity only a step or two removed from the world's tallest man or the world's shortest midget. . . . I had become a sort of financial freak, overnight," he observed.

Yet he did invite some of those journalists who thronged the Ritz lobby up to his suite. "In a two-hour interview," wrote the *New York Times*'s reporter, "he traced the origins of his fortune, spoke lovingly of his extensive art collection, and imparted some thoughts on world affairs." Nonetheless, Getty claimed to the paper that being named the richest man in the USA was "a distinction I'm not particularly interested in. I don't think there is any glory in being known as a moneybags. I'd rather be considered an active businessman."

In 1963, he concluded that the *Fortune* piece had marked "a turning point" in his life, "in the sense that it had the effect of ending my existence as an ordinary private citizen and made me, for better or worse, a public figure, or at least a person about whom the public curiosity was whetted."

Most materially, the article prompted him to finally acquire a permanent residence. Stalkers and concerns for his security had come with fame, making hotel life problematic. Perhaps, too, he decided it was finally time to settle down. A home at last? In his own way and unique vocabulary, he envisioned it initially as "a sort of liaison base." He weighed the merits of various capitals in Western Europe (midway between the Middle East and California, twin centers of his empire, this was the place for him). Paris was his first choice. But then, one evening in June 1959, just after he'd arrived back in London, a friend drove him into Surrey to a small dinner party at Sutton Place, hosted by its owner, George Granville Sutherland-Leveson-Gower, 5th Duke of Sutherland—Geordie, to friends.

While Sutton Place and His Grace's lineage were both ancient, they hadn't, in fact, been connected so long. Geordie, one of the largest landowners in Scotland, had bought the manor in 1917 from descendants of its builder, Sir Richard Weston. (Weston's young son, Francis, had the misfortune of being beheaded by Henry VIII after the king decided that Francis had engaged in more than tennis matches with Anne Boleyn, his second queen, during royal visits to Sutton Place.)

With numerous other roofs to keep in repair, Geordie was ready to part with the twenty-seven-bedroom, redbrick pile on 700 acres. Getty made the lowball offer of £60,000, which was promptly accepted.

Although it took several months to install acres of new curtains, linens, and upholstery, Sutton Place came largely furnished—Bullimore included. A native of Norfolk, England, he had served as butler to Joseph Kennedy when he was the American ambassador to the Court of St. James's, and to Henry Ford II, before the Duke of Sutherland hired him at Sutton Place. Getty described him as "benevolently despotic."

Another indispensable employee was the footman, Frank Parkes—Bullimore's longtime companion. While guests were likely unaware of their relationship, it was evident to everyone that Parkes's floral arrangements were second to none. Some visitors even compared them favorably to the legendary florist Constance Spry's.

A rotating cast of other lively characters inhabited Sutton Place too: Getty's numerous lady friends and mistresses. Among them were Penelope Kitson, a well-bred English divorcée; Mary Teissier, a lady of Russian and French extraction with regal bearing; Rosabella Burch, a seductive Nicaraguan widow; and Lady Ursula d'Abo, née Manners, a daughter of the 9th Duke of Rutland (as well as the niece of the celebrated Lady Diana Cooper).

His protestations against the press notwithstanding, Getty warmed up to reporters. The gates of Sutton Place were opened to a variety of glossies, from *Town & Country*, with which he discussed entertaining ("The English are simply marvelous at giving a party. They're never blasé. . . .") to *Cosmopolitan*, with which he discussed, naturally, his success with women and his failure at marriage. ("You have to face facts. If you've tried to fly an airplane and crashed five times, you had better give up. It's too dangerous.")

But it was a fifty-five-minute BBC program, *The Solitary Billionaire*, aired in February 1963, that probably created the most indelible public image of J. Paul Getty. A documentary, it was also something of a precursor of reality TV. It began in the dining room, with the camera panning, and panning, down the immense seventy-foot length of the silver-plate-laden refectory table (previously owned by William Randolph Hearst), until finally coming upon the aptly named title character, who was dining in solitude. "An absolute monarch, his real wealth incalculable—remote and mysterious as someone from another planet," the announcer intoned. Trailed by Shaun, a forlorn-looking Alsatian (the four-legged kind), Getty proceeded to take the horn-rimmed host and interlocutor, Alan Whicker, on a tour of the manor, even offering him a demonstration of his fitness regimen, in which Getty, still clad in a three-piece suit, did overhand presses with a bar-bell, a Renoir in the background. Quizzing Getty about his already famous frugality ("There are a great many stories, Mr. Getty, of your *care* with money"), Whicker inquired about that phone booth that had been installed "to prevent guests from abusing your hospitality." "Well," Getty answered, "I think right-thinking guests would consider it a benefit. It's rather daunting if you are visiting someone, and you have to place a long-distance call and charge your host with it."

Just three weeks later, Getty made an entry into his diary verifying his celebrity status: *My name was mentioned on the Lucy show on TV tonight. Lucy was expecting a blind date.*

Throughout the sixties and seventies, Getty produced several publications of his own, through which he clearly intended to build and burnish his legend. *My Life and Fortunes*, a memoir published in 1963, struck a Horatio Alger–like note from its first sentence: "In 1914, a brawling, bare-knuckled frontier atmosphere still prevailed in Oklahoma."

Getty had a knack for coining memorable maxims. "The meek shall inherit the earth—but not its mineral rights," he declared. Then there was his advice when asked for his recipe for success: "Rise early, work hard, and strike oil."

From 1961 to 1965, he wrote monthly columns for *Playboy* in which he expounded on the themes of "men, money, and values in today's society," which were subsequently published in book form under the title *How to be Rich*. He opted not to publish these essays in any of the "staider" magazines, because they had lesser reach among his intended audience of "young executives and university students," he said. "[Whereas] Mr. Hefner's frisky and epidermal periodical attracts the nation's highest readership among men in these two categories. And it was precisely these individuals whose thinking-processes the articles were designed to prod and even jolt."

(A seventysomething Getty recalled a private chat in which he delighted in regaling a thirtysomething Hef with tales of his youthful sexual exploits, to the latter's chagrin. "Younger people," explained Getty, "are discomfited by the suggestion that members of their swinging generation are not, after all, the first to have enjoyed amorous adventures while still in their teens.")

In *The Joys of Collecting* (1965), Getty delivered a didactic art primer, with anecdotes and advice that aimed to convey to the reader "the romance and zest . . . that make art collecting one of the most exhilarating and satisfying of all endeavors."

A decade later, in the last years of his life, he wrote another memoir, *As I See It*, which appeared just after his death. Here, there's a different tone. It's not so sunny. A good deal is pessimistic and defensive. Family tragedies had taken their toll.

"The idea that people who are reputedly wealthy must be miserable seems to gladden countless hearts," he wrote. "After a time, a person who is wealthy grows a tough impervious skin. It is a protective carapace essential for survival."

During his lifetime, then, Getty cultivated his image as a rich skinflint. Following his death in 1976, it was easy to turn him into a caricature—one of the twentieth century's premiere Scrooges. But in the succession of articles, books, and films that appeared in the years to come about him—and, inevitably, his heirs—the narrative grew darker and more unsympathetic.

In one of the first biographies, *The House of Getty*, published in 1985, English journalist Russell Miller established a tone on his dedication page: "To my family, with heartfelt thanks that our name is not Getty."

Perhaps it was Getty's somber countenance that caused him to be depicted as such an ogre. But appearances can be deceiving.

"If he looked gloomy, it was because he had three facelifts," Gillian Wilson, the longtime curator of decorative arts at the J. Paul Getty Museum, explained to me. "So when his face lost all its plasticity, there was a great collapse and he looked rather gloomy. It took a great deal of effort to put a smile on and he didn't bother. But he was perfectly happy."

Though he was ruthless in business, people who actually knew Getty—whose eyes were described as "penetratingly blue"—liked him, his ex-wives and former mistresses included. Over time, some of them have stepped forth to offer their views.

One year after his death, Robina Lund wrote an affectionate memoir, *The Getty I Knew*. But she held back from revealing that she and Getty (forty-four years her senior) had become lovers in the early sixties, about a year after he hired her away from Slaughter and May and made her his English legal advisor and press officer. Their romance continued until his death.

Four decades later, the releases of *All the Money in the World* and the FX TV series *Trust* prompted Lund, now a retired octogenarian in Aberdeenshire, Scotland, to disclose the full extent of her relationship with Getty, which included two failed pregnancies, and to defend him. "Both [depictions] were gross distortions . . . complete fabrications, and obscene at that," she said in a podcast with her niece, Glenda D. Roberts, a psychotherapist. "I want people to know the truth. He's been maligned, to a disgusting extent. He was lovable and very loving . . . very caring, very gently affectionate. The only person he was mean with was himself."

More recently, she shared other fond memories of Getty with me: "What were the things I liked most about him? His kindness and empathy, especially toward people in genuine trouble; his modesty; his sense of humor and enjoyment of fun; his intellect and knowledge; his respect for women and their intellects; his willingness to debate with opposing views." Lund also recollected Getty's "very good 'party tricks.' He was, for instance, a superb, but not malicious, mimic."

In 2014, ninety-eight-year-old Lady Ursula d'Abo came forward with her own defense, in her memoir *The Girl with the Widow's Peak*. "He really was the most charming man, made into this monster by journalists," she wrote. (She was a widow in her early fifties and he was in his late seventies when she began seeing him around 1970.) "Very few people saw the kind, cozy side of Paul as more often than not he was on his guard when he mixed in society. He was clever and used to study Latin grammar at breakfast. He made you feel like you were the only person in the world when you were with him. He had a great sense of fun."

Lady Ursula, who was one of the six maids of honor at the coronation of George VI in 1937, passed away in 2017, a few days short of 101, survived by three children from her second marriage. Her eldest, John Henry Erland d'Abo—who, during his school days at Eton, spent many breaks at Sutton Place—has also stuck up for his mother's old flame. "He was absolutely not as portrayed. The movies were very inaccurate," d'Abo said. "He could be difficult. But *all* very rich people are difficult.

"You liked him," he continued. "He was funny, with a very, very dry sense of humor. He was always interested in trying to ameliorate his knowledge in matters that he didn't understand. When I see [Getty's grandson] Mark today, he is the spitting image of him."

When Jean Paul Getty was born, in Minneapolis on December 15, 1892, his parents, George and Sarah, were just beginning to rise out of the harsh circumstances that their families had endured for generations. Wealthy though they became in later life, they retained forever that particularly strict brand of Scots-Irish frugality, as did their son.

It is curious that, despite George and Sarah's Anglo-Saxon, Calvinist background, they chose the Gallic spelling for their son's first name. (He was always called by his middle name, however.)

George Franklin Getty, whose ancestors had come over from the north of Ireland at the end of the eighteenth century, was born in 1855 in Maryland. His father, John, a struggling farmer, died of diphtheria when George was six, forcing him to do what farmwork and errands he could to bring in pennies.

Rescue came from an uncle, a preacher, who brought him to Ohio for education. Resolute George worked his way through Ohio Normal University, where he met Sarah McPherson Risher—a stern-looking woman almost three years his elder. They married in 1879.

In Sarah, a fellow Methodist whose ancestors had fled Scotland for Ohio in 1746, he found his match. In fact, she may have been even more determined and ambitious than he was. He planned to become a teacher, but she steered him to law, providing $100 from her dowry to finance his studies at the University of Michigan. Their funds had to be stretched in 1880, when a daughter, Gertrude Lois, was born to the couple. Two years later, George earned his law degree, and opened his own practice.

His career was off to a promising start, but Sarah thought they could do better in Minneapolis. In 1884 they arrived in the bustling midwestern city. His legal business, which catered to the insurance industry, began to thrive. But the young family was shattered in 1890 when Gertrude perished in that winter's typhoid epidemic. Sarah was stricken too. She recovered, but her hearing declined. Though George hadn't been infected, the loss of his child shook his faith and led him to convert to Christian Science.

In 1892, when she was forty, Sarah gave birth to Jean Paul. Always to be an only child, he grew up much loved by these overprotective parents. Yet—firm, devout people that they were—they never gave him physical affection.

"My parents," Paul wrote, "knew the now apparently-lost art of showing their child great love and affection without being overly indulgent or permissive."

Paul's solitary childhood, and the Getty fortunes, were transformed in 1903, when George was called to Bartlesville, later to be part of Oklahoma but then in Indian Territory, and in the early years of its oil boom. There to settle an insurance claim for one of his clients, George lifted his sights. He invested $500 in a lease to the oil rights of "Lot 50." Within a few months, multiple wells to which he had rights were gushing.

By 1905 the Gettys were wealthy people, and they relocated, at Sarah's behest once more—this time to Los Angeles. At 651 South Kingsley Drive, adjacent to a still-unpaved section of Wilshire Boulevard, George constructed a fine two-story stucco house. The architectural style: Tudor.

Paul was a voracious reader, but his academic record was hardly stellar. Structured environments like schools didn't bring out the best in him. He did well enough at Harvard Military Academy and then at the University of Southern California, where he studied economics and political science, but his more stimulating and formative experiences came through his summer jobs, working for his father's company, Minnehoma Oil (the name being an elision of Minnesota and Oklahoma). Later, Getty senior bought or established other companies, including George F. Getty Inc.

After earning his stripes as a roustabout (a laborer who performs the heaviest and dirtiest work on a drilling site), Paul rose up to become a tool dresser (an assistant to a driller). A "toolie" was required to be a crack technician and skilled blacksmith in order to do his tasks of sharpening drilling bits and tools and keeping them in optimal order.

To master this craft, Paul convinced a leathery veteran known as Grizzle to take him under his wing. "Such was his reputation in the fields that when he pronounced that he considered me a qualified toolie, it carried more weight than any dozen university diplomas," Getty wrote.

But the strongest influence in Paul's life, and, to an extent, his parents' too, lay a continent and an ocean away. Early on, the Gettys developed a profound reverence for Europe. Its art and refined culture were beacons to them. As a family, they undertook three grand tours, each one lasting at least a few months. The first, in 1909, when Paul was sixteen, took them to England, France, Germany, Switzerland, Monte Carlo, and Holland.

In 1912, Paul convinced his parents to send him to Oxford to continue his education. The US, he said, was "insular, isolationist . . . it largely ignored what transpired outside its borders." Before reporting to Magdalen College in Oxford, he spent two months traveling through Japan and China. A year later, upon finishing his exams, he embarked on a yearlong solo trip that took him across Scandinavia, Russia, Greece, Turkey, and Western Europe. When he reached Paris in June 1914, his parents were waiting; another family grand tour had been organized. But their itinerary was altered by the assassination of Archduke Ferdinand in Sarajevo later that month, by which time they had reached London, where they awoke to learn that Austria had declared war on Serbia. Arranging passage back to the States was difficult, as most ocean liners were being pressed into service as troop transports.

George eventually prevailed upon the Cunard Line, and on September 12 the Gettys set sail back to America on the *Lusitania*. Several months later, the ship sank to the bottom of the Atlantic after being hit by German torpedoes.

Prior to World War I, it was uncommon for West Coast families, even wealthy ones, to undertake such extensive European travel. Certainly, few of Getty's fellow wildcatters harbored such worldly curiosity. It's interesting to compare Getty to his peers on that *Fortune* rich list, such as Sid Richardson. Born one year apart, they were exact contemporaries. But Richardson rarely strayed far from Fort Worth. "I don't want to go nowhere outside the US," he declared.

Getty was also a whiz at languages. He became fluent in German, French, and Spanish; he got along commendably in Italian, Russian, Greek, and Arabic—which he taught himself so he could negotiate better terms in the Middle East. He could also read Latin and ancient Greek.

Once back in California, Paul expressed his desire to become a diplomat or a writer. To entice Paul into the oil business, his father advanced him $10,000. Paul could invest it in whatever oil fields he chose, but most of the profits would go back to Minnehoma—save 30 percent, which Paul could keep. Within a year, oil was flowing from wells he had taken leases on. At twenty-three, he had made his first million.

In the ensuing decade, J. Paul Getty also devoted a good deal of his energy to another vocation: marriage. Unlike his business career, which he pursued till almost his dying breath, this one had a compressed and finite time frame, though his strong interest in women endured till the very end.

By 1958, he had five failed marriages behind him—each to a woman about half his age. The first four marital unions were particularly short-lived: his maiden trip to the altar came in 1923 and his fourth divorce decree was issued in 1936.

In *My Life and Fortunes*, he shoehorned in a speedy summary of weddings. His opening sentence: "Then, in October 1923, two months before my thirty-first birthday, I took my first plunge into the troubled seas of matrimony."

Jeannette DeMont, a nineteen-year-old beauty of Polish extraction, had just graduated from high school in Los Angeles. He described her as having "a vibrant and magnetic personality and remarkable degree of intelligence." They eloped to Ventura, then returned to Los Angeles and surprised his parents with news of the wedding. In a house he rented not far from George and Sarah, marital life began well enough.

Jeannette was soon pregnant. But after the birth on July 9, 1924, of his first son, George Franklin Getty II, named after his father, "jarring notes of dissension and discord crept into the relationship." Two months after George was born, Jeannette filed for divorce.

Getty accepted the blame, and pinpointed the problem, in his inimitable fashion: "No wife wants to feel she is being neglected for an oil rig." In fact, Jeannette had diagnosed the same problem. "I married you, not your oil rigs," she pouted.

That conflict—between the demands of business and the responsibilities of marriage—was the crux of all his subsequent divorces, he maintained.

After their separation, Getty admitted to feeling "stunned and dismayed." There are discrepancies, however, regarding the date the divorce decree became final. In his memoirs, Getty says it was February 15, 1925; other sources have said it arrived September 22, 1927.

In any event, Paul soon enough resumed a warm rapport with his ex-wife, the start of a pattern. "Once the acrimony that accompanies any divorce was dispelled, Jeannette and I re-established a friendly relationship, and have remained friends ever since," he wrote in 1963.

In the aftermath of the divorce, Paul had little time for reflection. It was a banner year for Minnehoma Oil. Several wells were gushing.

By the spring of 1926, with his fortunes flush, he took a break. Driving in his Duesenberg to Mexico, he enrolled in Spanish language and history courses at the National University of Mexico City, where he met Allene Ashby, seventeen, the tall, slender daughter of a Texas rancher, who was there with her elder sister, Belene. Getty recalled being "enchanted" by the "vivacious, attractive, and brilliant" Allene when they took romantic horseback rides together. Within weeks, they drove to Cuernavaca and, impetuously, were wed. If some sources are correct about the date of his divorce decree from Jeannette, the marriage was bigamist.

At the same time, Paul became very close to Belene. There is some conjecture as to how close—we will return to that a bit later.

For now, suffice it to say it was a splendid summer. But when it drew to a close, he and Allene realized they had little in common, that they'd made a mistake rushing into marriage. In September, they parted amicably, though they kept in touch; apparently they also kept the marriage—Getty's only one that did not produce a child—a secret from some family members. "Somewhat later," according to Paul, "Allene got around to suing for divorce." *That* decree came finally late in 1928—in the nick of time for his third wedding.

After Paul steered the Duesenberg back to LA, the thirty-four-year-old millionaire resumed his established patterns, another of which was bunking again on South Kingsley Drive. "I always went back and lived at my parents' home between marriages," he told *Cosmopolitan*. "I had a great love and respect for them both. They had a marriage any two people could be proud of. . . . I could never achieve that, I'm sorry to say."

When the spring of 1927 wheeled around, these septuagenarians and their son embarked upon another grand tour. Accompanied by George's devoted Japanese valet, Frank Komai, they crossed the continent by rail, then sailed on June 7 from New York aboard the SS *Resolute*. By all accounts the next months were idyllic, their itinerary encompassing London, Paris, Strasbourg, Baden-Baden, Venice, Rome, Naples, Augsburg, Munich, Innsbruck, and Cortina d'Ampezzo.

As summer came to an end, Paul waved the trio off as they boarded the SS *Olympic*. In no rush to return to America, he rented a *petit meublé* in Paris for six weeks. It was during this time that Getty made a decision to thenceforth spend five months a year in Europe, a vow he broke only when it was made impossible by war in 1939.

Tearing himself away from Paris in October 1927 wasn't easy, but his father was ailing (George had a stroke in 1923 from which he never fully recovered), so Paul's attention was needed more than ever at the Getty businesses. An agreement was reached for the son to buy 30 percent of the stock in his father's company for $1 million, "which would give me a considerable voice in the management of the company." It was another demonstration of the Gettys' capacity to simultaneously negotiate contracts and familial relations.

With business on an even keel, Paul returned to Europe in the summer of 1928. One of his first stops was Vienna. Dining at the Grand Hotel, he became infatuated with a flaxen-haired, blue-eyed beauty at a nearby table. The future third Mrs. J. Paul Getty was Adolphine "Fini" Helmle. Seventeen, she was seated with her parents. "Romance blossomed despite the strictly chaperoned climate in which it was nurtured," Paul recounted.

Herr Dr. Otto Helmle—a wealthy engineer who headed the Badenwerk industrial complex in Karlsruhe, Germany—was not amused by a twice-married thirty-six-year-old American courting his teenage daughter. But Getty's charms won out. Young Fini, convent girl that she was, was determined enough to override her father's diktat.

In December, Paul arranged for her and her mother to sail to Havana, where he and Fini were married (the ink on his divorce decree from Allene perhaps barely dry). Once wed, the pair enjoyed a two-month honeymoon in Miami and Palm Beach, and then a leisurely cross-country drive back to Los Angeles, where Fini was introduced to Paul's parents, surprised again.

George and Sarah took an immediate liking to Fini, which was fortunate, since Paul, too busy with work to find a new house, deposited his new bride with them on South Kingsley Drive. Fini, who spoke little English, became pregnant in the spring. Lonely, she sailed that summer back to Germany for the birth of their child. Paul promised to follow as soon as he could. In October 1929, just as he was ready to embark from New York, the stock market crashed. He reached Berlin just in time to be beside Fini for the birth, on December 19, of his second son, Jean Ronald, whom he would call Ronny.

Getty's happiness over becoming a father again was tempered by his new father-in-law's opposition toward him. Helmle issued an ultimatum that Paul would have to live permanently in Germany with his wife and child, or he would insist Fini get a divorce. Paul remained in Europe for several months, trying to work things out. But in April a cable reached him with the dire news that George had had another stroke and his condition was serious. Getty departed immediately for California.

Amidst the drama surrounding the death of George F. Getty at age seventy-five on May 31, 1930, and the early months of the Depression, Helmle pressed the divorce case forcefully. By the time the decree was finally issued in August 1932, Getty had to agree to a large financial settlement, which left him bitter at Dr. Helmle, though not at his daughter. "I was forced to admit ruefully to myself that, in Dr. Helmle, I had encountered a businessman who was most certainly my equal," Getty wrote. (Grief and loneliness may well have propelled Helmle's actions: his wife, Fini's mother, had died unexpectedly in the early 1930s during what was supposed to be a routine operation.)

As war clouds gathered in Germany, Fini and Ronald moved to Switzerland for safety. Dr. Helmle, a Catholic and a staunch opponent of Hitler, was imprisoned. Eventually he was released, but his fortune was seized by the Nazis. In 1939, Fini and Ronald fled to Los Angeles.

Back in Los Angeles, even as Paul faced the enormous financial repercussions of his father's death and the divorce negotiations, he began his next romance. Things being as complicated as they were, it would take some time to get to the altar for this wedding.

In 1930, Ann Rork was twenty-two. In fact, Ann and Paul had first met at a restaurant in Hollywood when she was a spirited fourteen-year-old. Some electricity between them was evident, but her parents forbade them to see each other.

Her father was producer Samuel Edwin Rork, who made movies with Douglas Fairbanks Jr., Rudolph Valentino, Will Rogers (Ann's godfather), and silent picture "It girl" Clara Bow—who was also reputed to be his lover, which was perhaps what prompted Ann's mother, onetime starlet Helen Welch Rork, to relocate with Ann to Boston.

Eventually Ann found her way back to Hollywood, where she got parts in a few early "talkies," and somehow reconnected with still-legally-wed Paul in 1930. Gossip that they were dating began to circulate around Hollywood, prompting Paul to transfer their romance out of town. In early 1931 he took her to Berlin, where he dealt with continuing divorce drama; in August he brought her to New York, where he established her in a series of hotels and apartments, while he continued to live in Los Angeles.

They took two more trips together to Europe, including a summer holiday to Italy during which, on September 7, 1932, she gave birth to Getty's third son, at sea. They were en route from Naples to Genoa.

Owing to miscommunication with the notary in the port of La Spezia, where Paul and Ann disembarked with their precious little bundle, confusion over this son's name has persisted. His father asked for him to be named Jean Paul Getty Jr. But the Italian clerk wrote down "Eugenio Paul" on his birth certificate. Once in America, that turned into Eugene. When he returned to Italy as an adult, he officially changed his name to J. Paul Getty Jr. To make things more befuddling, he adopted the anglicized spelling of his first name: his obituaries referred to him as John Paul Getty Jr. In any event, his first name was never used—during his lifetime he was just Paul, or Sir Paul, to pretty much everybody.

Once the divorce from Fini was at last sealed, wedding number four took place on December 2, 1932, in Cuernavaca, Mexico (just like marriage number two). "I embarked upon yet another marital venture," the groom recorded. Now legally wed, Ann and Paul moved into a beach house he bought in Malibu, though Paul continued to keep his clothes at his mother's house. Sarah, for her part, was frosty to poor Ann. As usual, business pulled Paul away. By the birth on December 20, 1933, of Gordon Peter, the marriage was on the rocks, and the couple separated. She continued to live in Malibu and later sued for divorce, as he decamped to New York. Their divorce decree came in 1936.

Ann, described by contemporaries as "madcap," went on to compile a colorful and impressive marital résumé of her own. In the club car of the train bound for Reno, Nevada, where she was heading to obtain her divorce from Paul, she met Herbert Douglas Wilson, an Ohio-born stockbroker. Their marriage lasted less than a year, but before it ended in divorce it produced a half sister for Paul and Gordon, Donna Wilson Long. (A resident of Palm Beach, she is an equestrian and an artist with an active social life.) The records vary, but 1941 appears to be the likely year of Ann's wartime marriage to Jay Ruppert Ross, an aviator who volunteered for the British Royal Air Force. Four years later, she married Joseph Stanton McInerney, an attorney, with whom she settled in San Francisco. Though this marriage was not to endure either, she remained in the Bay Area, where she brought up the children.

During their childhoods, Paul Jr. and Gordon could enjoy the camaraderie that came with being the only pair of full siblings born to J. Paul Getty. Like all the Getty sons, they seldom saw their father, or their half brothers. "Oh, this is your brother Ronald. Do you know him?" Paul Jr. was asked by his father during a rare get-together at the Getty Oil offices in Los Angeles, when the boys were on the verge of puberty. In fact, they hadn't yet met.

In the autumn of 1931, Ann Rork, temporarily domiciled in Manhattan, pined for her lover a continent away.

"Darling," she addressed J. Paul Getty in a letter postmarked September 18, 1931, from 38 E. Fifty-Ninth Street in New York City and mailed to him at the Subway Terminal Building in Los

Angeles. "The letter I wrote yesterday is now void and I am again on top of the world. . . . There is now hope of my being able to become pregnant. . . . You have no idea sweetheart how badly I want a family. . . . I'm so happy that you're phoning tonight."

Over the next months, she wrote him a series of poignant letters. His replies are not in the archives of the Getty Research Institute. But, if one can judge only by the ardor of Ann's missives, it is hard to believe that the recipient was the cruel, coldhearted misanthrope some have accused him of being.

The letters do, however, confirm one stereotype: Getty was cheap. He was putting her up in far from royal style, in the depths of the Depression. Cans of sardines were sometimes all she could afford for dinner in her room, unless a friend treated her to a meal out.

A letter of October 8 indicates she wasn't in it, as it were, for the money:

"In spite of the fact that you are a very wealthy man I live as would become the sweetheart of a striving young poet, but, my love has not flown nor will it ever," she assured him.

Yet in the same letter, she chided her beau. She has caught wind that he has been veritably bragging to her friends and family—including her mother—how parsimonious he has been with her: ". . . by much propaganda I had them ready to love you for being so good to me. Then you turn around and admit that you kept me without bus fare for months! . . . So please stop that conversation. . . . Remember I'm one of the few people in the world that have gone to the pain of trying to understand you and that you make things very difficult for me by alienating people whose high opinion of you is necessary to my happiness."

Not to say it is all penury. She wrote excitedly of shopping for pretty hats, coats, and shoes—but on sale, or at wholesale. But then, on October 2, she wrote, "Sweetheart Angel—I learned something last night. It's no fun to look beautiful when the man you love isn't there to see you."

On occasion, she partook of glamorous Manhattan society. "Expect tonight will be gala. Condé Nast is having a party after the concert at his penthouse and Mrs. Stotesbury is having one at the Casino. Mrs. Hearst also wanted to entertain. . . ."

She also curled up with some good new books: "I'm reading Ernest Hemingway's *The Sun Also Rises* and it fills me with the most terrific nostalgia for Europe. When can we sail?"

Mostly, however, she pines for her "Angel Mine," as she often addresses him.

"Oh darling, I love you so, miss you so."

"I love you, only you, ever you."

"I'm so frightened. Oh why aren't you here? I need you so badly. . . . Oh please dear come to me."

"It's raining cats and dogs—very depressing. But your wire makes me believe I'll never be unhappy again."

On October 31, it was all blue sky and sunshine ahead, when Getty phoned her to say they would be departing the following week on a round-the-world voyage: "I'm simply breathless over the itinerary. . . . I'm practically packed—will finish Sunday. . . . Oh blessed to be with you again Thursday—I'm afraid I'll burst!"

Two years and two babies later, it didn't end happily ever after for the couple. But in her letters to Getty in the years after their breakup, it is clear that they remained mutually affectionate.

By May 2, 1934 they had traded coasts—she in Santa Monica and he in New York, at the Hotel Biltmore. She wrote, "Try to eat regularly and if you get too tired go away for a few days."

"Dearest Paul," she wrote on February 25, 1941 (five years after their divorce decree). "Such fun to speak to you yesterday, and such a temptation to accept your suggestion of Acapulco." Before signing off, she asked him: "Do you suppose I'll ever get over missing you? . . . hoping you are happy—Always, A."

On July 7, 1941, she sent a letter from the Lake Placid Club in the Adirondacks, where she was participating in the summer ice-dancing competitions that were all the rage. "The boys seem to be having a wonderful time at camp," she opened, before reeling off her plans for the remainder of the summer, which included Newport and East Hampton. In closing, she said, "I do miss you darling. Be a little careful about a girl that works at Saks. All the saleswomen are pointing her out to their customers as a girl that won't be working there much longer because of Mr. Getty. Love—A."

There is another touching, and illuminating, file of correspondence in the Getty archives: letters written by J. Paul Getty to Allene and Belene. They were discovered by Belene's granddaughter, Christine Banks, a Carlsbad, California, cosmetologist, after the death in 1984 of her grandfather Orell "Frank" Smoot. Belene Ashby Smoot predeceased him by four years, at the age of seventy-six; they'd had one child together. Allene died in 1970 at age sixty-one, never having remarried or had children.

While rummaging through her late grandfather's desk, Banks found stacks of uncashed checks made out to Belene, stock certificates, and notes, all with the name Getty on them—a name she'd never heard of. After a good deal of research, including visits to staff members at the Getty Center, she learned who J. Paul Getty was, and that in his will he'd left Belene $183,281 of Getty Oil common stock, and $300 a month for the remainder of her life. Over the previous forty years, he had also been sending her regular checks, letters, and a dozen roses on her birthday every year.

Christine Banks nonetheless concluded that her grandmother and Getty had not been lovers, though others have drawn that conclusion. In any event, he maintained great fondness for both sisters his entire life, as his letters attest. (Unfortunately for Christine, none of Getty's beneficence reached her. While Belene "never spent one penny of it," she recalled, her daughter—Christine's mother, Donna—blew through it on "spur of the moment" spending that included several time-share condominiums. Donna died "virtually broke.")

Paul's first letter to Allene was postmarked from Los Angeles on November 20, 1926—a few months after they parted in Mexico. "I was indeed glad to hear from you. You broke a long silence. Of course, I am not mad at you," he wrote. "I have too many trials and tribulations in my business ventures to relish silly anger. . . . Trusting to see you very soon."

"Hello Infant," began a sunny letter he composed to her on June 26, 1927, from "Le Beau, Paris," where he and his parents, on one of their grand tours, had very much enjoyed the Grand Prix that day. "But I would like it much better if you were here," he told her. "Do take care of yourself and Beanie and don't see too much of your friend . . . Did you get the cable and allowance all right? I will send you the other fifty a little later," he finished the letter, signing off "With loads of kisses."

A short Western Union cable sent to her two months later indicates he sought to resume their romantic relationship: "Dearest Precious, Expect your first letters in New York. Love you, please leave now."

There is no record of the two ever seeing each other again. In a letter sent June 24, 1928, from the Grand Hotel Wien, Paul mentioned meeting someone he doesn't name, but doubtless he was referring to Fini: "I found the girl I wanted to see, in Vienna." Yet he maintained his warm tone toward Allene: "I have certainly missed you. . . . The 28th is your birthday—just think how smart you will be—nineteen—it doesn't seem possible . . . Please write me."

Three months later, a letter from Paris is full of shock:

"I just received your letter. . . . Are you really in a sanitarium? . . . I got such a nice letter from you in early June. I have always been very proud of you and liked the way you do things and then, like a bolt from the blue, came the letter you wrote June 15th. It was so terrible. I'll never get over it. . . . But if you have really been ill I am terribly sorry. . . . I had expected to come home about July 4th, but when I got your letter in Vienna, I decided that I didn't want to come back at all. This summer I just figured you out of the picture. Can you blame me? Once such letter, and then not a line for six weeks, from you or Beanie?"

The Ashby-Getty correspondence continued for decades, but henceforth all the notes were addressed to Belene, who, like her sister, lived in the Los Angeles area. "Dearest Beanie," he wrote on August 9, 1950, from the Grand Hotel Victoria-Jungfrau, Interlaken: "Your letter just came. I am glad Allene is feeling better . . . use your discretion about the gift, tell her it was from me, if you want to. I hope to be back in October."

In a February 1969 letter from Sutton Place, Paul thanked Belene for her "very welcome Valentine" as well as for some photos from that distant summer. "The Mexico City pictures brough back vivid remembrance of our sojourn in Mexico 1926. What a wonderful time we had and how jealous Van turned out to be!"

One year later, he reached out to her following Allene's death: "I have been trying to phone you. . . . It is tragic to think that poor Allene has gone. She had so much to cope with in her life. I know that nothing I can say will be helpful. We both know what a sweet person she was."

He wrote again in October 1971: "Dear Beanie, it has certainly been much too long since we have seen each other and I am planning to be back some time next spring. I wish you were here to go on a long walk with me and the dogs. I think often of you and the many years of unbroken friendship." Over the forty-three years since Paul's divorce from Allene, and his three subsequent marriages, his fondness for the Ashby sisters had persisted.

Before getting to the story of J. Paul Getty's fifth and final wife, let's rewind to 1920, and go back to the subject of business.

Getty began his career as a wildcatter—an independent operator—

and he kept that mentality all his life. He usually went against the grain of prevailing trends, fashion—and big corporations. In the twenties, while many were feverishly buying stocks as values soared, Getty sank his money into buying leases on lots, betting that he would strike oil.

On the question of where to drill, Getty certainly had good instincts, but he put his faith in science—petroleum geology, to be specific. It was a field of study then in its infancy. Many old-time oilmen sneered at the notion that "some damned bookworm" could help them find oil. While Getty didn't consider this branch of study an infallible science, he realized its potential. "I felt that, as with all things in nature, there must be some logical order to the manner in which petroleum was distributed within the earth's surface," he noted. "I was convinced that geology provided the oil prospector with certain generally fairly reliable guides and indicators to aid him in the search for oil."

When the Depression came, Getty, not freighted with collapsed stocks, was in an advantageous position. He went from strength to strength, now snapping up stocks at a fraction of the value of the oil in the ground.

He began assembling holdings in a number of companies, then sought to gain controlling interests in them. Among the first was Pacific Western, one of the largest oil producers in California, which he acquired in 1931. The ultimate prize would be Tide Water Associated Oil, then America's ninth-largest oil company, with over 1,200 service stations as well as refineries, storage, and marketing arms. It would provide the centerpiece of his master plan to become a fully integrated oil company. But in the first decades of the twentieth century, the idea of Getty acquiring Tide Water was akin to David slaying Goliath.

He began circling it covertly, his great white whale, buying up Tide Water stock quietly so as not to alert its management to a takeover threat or drive up the share price.

Concurrently, he had to deal with his mother. To Getty's shock, his father had left virtually his entire $15 million estate in her hands. Ironically, while Paul became a world-famous tightwad, his father felt he was a spendthrift; he also disapproved of his son's multiple divorces. Thus Paul had to contend with Sarah as well as with the board of George Getty Inc. At Christmas 1933, she offered to hand over her shares to him. A letter from mother to son illustrates the businesslike way in which Gettys communicated amongst themselves:

> *This offer shall remain open to and until 12 o'clock noon, December 30, 1933, and if not accepted by you in writing on or before that date and hour shall be considered as withdrawn by the undersigned and shall be wholly terminated and at an end.*
>
> *Very truly yours,*
> *Sarah C. Getty.*

Soon after, he succeeded in easing her out of the company and gaining full control. In return, she insisted that they establish a family trust. "I want to be certain that you and your sons are financially secure and protected against the possible catastrophe which may result from speculation," she reasoned. The paperwork was drawn up in December 1934; she contributed $2.5 million and he put in about $1 million. The Sarah C. Getty Trust commenced its work.

While the trust was meant to provide for all her descendants, there was one glaring inequity: Ronald was virtually excluded from it (he would receive just $3,000 a year—though his children would eventually share in the trust) because Paul, bitter at his former father-in-law for his role in the divorce from Fini, felt that the wealthy Helmle could shoulder the financial care of Ronald. But the loss of the Helmle fortune during World War II put Ronald at a great financial disadvantage compared to his brothers.

By the terms of the trust, Paul, its sole trustee, could borrow from its funds for purposes that would grow his business, such as buying stocks. In turn, he plowed his profits back into the trust. The capital grew and grew.

Days after signing the trust's documents, Getty boarded a train traveling up the California coast, bound for America's Valhalla, San Simeon, where press baron William Randolph Hearst and his mistress, Marion Davies, had invited him to a house party to ring in the New Year. On January 1, 1935, Getty received a long-distance call from New York that gave him the most momentous stock tip of his life. Though at first it sounded like a disaster.

A friend, Jay Hopkins (later the founder of General Dynamics Corporation), broke the news that the Rockefeller-family-dominated Standard Oil of New Jersey was transferring its large block of Tide Water shares to a new holding company, Mission Corporation, through which shares would be distributed to its own stockholders. Effectively, that would put gaining control of Tide Water out of Getty's reach forever.

But Hopkins had an inside track: he knew that John D. Rockefeller Jr. was somehow unaware of the reasons behind Standard's transfer, and that he was willing to sell his Mission shares. Having committed a fortune to building Rockefeller Center in Manhattan just as the economy collapsed, the Rockefeller family was then stretched a bit thin—for them.

Getty was only too eager to buy John D.'s shares, but he assumed that Standard's management would quickly talk Rockefeller out of selling.

"Not a chance," Hopkins told him. "He's aboard a train bound for Arizona. They can't reach him, and I have his authorization to sell."

Getty closed the transaction on the spot, which gave him his breakthrough leap forward in his quest for Tidewater (now one word), though he would not gain clear-cut control until 1951.

(In the 1970s, Getty slyly recalled what happened after Rockefeller debarked from the train and Standard Oil managers got hold of him: "They said, 'Oh, Mr. Rockefeller, we were very anxious to get in touch with you. We wanted to tell you to be sure not to sell your stock in Mission Corporation because we're in a big proxy fight.'" Informed that he had, they pressed him for the identity of the buyer. "'I understand he's a very nice young man, but I can't remember his name,' said Rockefeller. And they all said: 'His name wasn't Getty, was it?' He replied: 'Yes, I think it was.' They answered: 'Oh my God.'")

Fresh from his triumph at San Simeon, Getty had yet to work out the details of his divorce from Ann. Amicable as she might have been, her lawyers were less accommodating. Legal proceedings, which Paul described as "noisome," dragged on in Los Angeles. It must have seemed a good idea to get out of town. So, breaking one of his old habits, instead of moving back in with his mother postdivorce, he opened a new chapter of his life in New York.

Flush as he was, he opted for once to splurge, taking a sublease on one of Manhattan's most palatial apartments. Its address was prophetic: 1 Sutton Place South.

The furnished penthouse he rented there would become a pivotal influence in his life, for it belonged to a great connoisseur, Mrs. Frederick Guest. One of Getty's fellow *Fortune* listees some decades later, the former Amy Phipps was the daughter of industrialist Henry Phipps, Andrew Carnegie's partner, and the wife of English aristocrat Freddie Guest, a cousin of Winston Churchill. In 1947, Amy and Freddie's son married Lucy "Sissy" Cochrane—C. Z. Guest, who became a celebrated style icon.

The 6,400-square-foot aerie atop Sutton Place—the building itself had been commissioned around 1920 by Amy's father—featured wraparound terraces and seventeen rooms, including a pair of boiserie-lined forty-foot drawing rooms. But it was the contents of the apartment—Amy Guest's magnificent collection of eighteenth-century French and English furniture—that so inspired Getty.

"This, I suppose, more than anything, motivated me to begin . . .

my own collection," Getty explained. "I suddenly became aware that fine furniture was no less fine art than a painting or a piece of sculpture. . . . It wasn't that a spark was struck. It was rather like a blazing torch was applied, and my collector's urge flared high."

It was a propitious time to embark upon a collecting career. In the depths of the Depression, there were great bargains to be had. Getty became well-acquainted with the leading art dealers and auction houses in New York and Europe and methodically studied art history and the art market. He began to acquire museum-quality pieces of fine and decorative art, items that propelled him on the road to the museum he founded decades later.

During this New York interlude, he picked up another trophy, the Pierre Hotel. A forty-two-story tower at Fifth Avenue and Fifty-Ninth Street, it had been lavishly erected in 1930 at a cost of $6 million. In the distress of 1938, Getty snapped it up for a relative song, paying only $2.35 million.

Romance returned to his life one night in May 1935, when friends brought him to the New Yorker, a smart supper club on East Fifty-First. They'd just been ushered to a ringside table when a raven-haired chanteuse appeared in the smoky spotlight and hit it with "Night and Day." It was the future fifth Mrs. J. Paul Getty, Louise Dudley Lynch, age twenty-two. "I was hopelessly smitten," he said.

Teddy, as everyone called her, was no nightclub vamp. Born in Chicago to a prosperous merchant family, she'd been raised in Greenwich, Connecticut, and her name was listed in the *Social Register*. Financier Bernard Baruch was an uncle. Unbeknownst to the patrons at the New Yorker and most anyone, she harbored serious ambitions to become an opera singer.

As soon as she finished her set and the applause died down, she found herself looking into "the bluest eyes of an immensely charming man," she recalled.

"This is Paul, my friend from California," said her friend Betzi Beaton, who happened to be one of Getty's tablemates.

Dispensing with further chat, he swept Teddy into his arms. "Let's dance," he said.

"I closed my eyes and let my body follow his. We moved as one," she remembered. "He was a fabulous dancer."

"You're very beautiful, Teddy, and your voice is too," he said when the music ended, in the semidark. "You know, you should study opera. You'd be a great Carmen, or Tosca."

Transfixed by this mysterious stranger, she caught her breath and asked, "And what do you do, Paul?"

"He's in oil," Betzi cut in.

"*Oil?* What show is that?" Teddy asked.

Within months, they were engaged. In January 1937, when he brought her to meet Sarah in Los Angeles, she passed muster.

This time, it was his fiancée's schedule as much as his that delayed the wedding. At his encouragement, she threw herself into serious vocal study, which he paid for in exchange for a promise of 10 percent of her future earnings—her idea, she maintained. She also began traveling to give concerts and recitals. At last they sailed to Italy and were married in November 1939, in the Palazzo Senatorio, Rome's palatial city hall in the Campidoglio overlooking the Forum.

But there was no honeymoon. She wanted to stay on in Italy to continue her studies, and he had business in California. So, after a postwedding lunch at the Ambassador Hotel, he rushed for the train to Naples, where he boarded the *Conte di Savoia* to New York.

Although World War II had begun, Italy was then still neutral. After Italy joined the Axis, Teddy extended her visa by signing on as a correspondent for the *New York Herald Tribune*—which the National Fascist Party cited as the grounds for her arrest in December 1941. Suspected of being a spy, she was interned in Siena. In June 1942, she was released and repatriated aboard the Swedish boat *Gripsholm*, along with a group of American diplomats.

In her absence, Paul and his eldest son had joined the war effort. Paul moved to Tulsa, Oklahoma, where he revved up production at the Spartan Aircraft Corporation, an asset of one of the many companies he had bought. George enlisted in the army. Commissioned as an infantry second lieutenant, he served in the Pacific theater.

The year 1941 ended on a sad note. At Christmastime, Sarah died, age eighty-nine. *How I miss her! No one ever had a better mother,* Paul wailed in his diary. Decades later, he observed, *The years have done little to lessen my sense of loss.*

Following Teddy's arrival on the *Gripsholm,* she reunited with Paul in Tulsa, moving into his stucco bungalow near the Spartan factory. Her first morning, she woke to find a note in a familiar scrawl: "Darling . . . I'm at the factory. . . . Have a good breakfast. Love."

But he was a tiger in bed: "He was as demanding and passionate as I. Strong and well-built from years of weight-lifting. . . . But it was also his mind, his sensitivity, that aroused me. I could never say no to this man . . . who so perfectly satisfied me sexually," she recalled in her memoir, *Alone Together: My Life with J. Paul Getty,* published in September 2013, days before her one hundredth birthday.

After the war ended, she set up housekeeping in a beach house in Santa Monica that Paul acquired. "Paul was always leaving, for somewhere," she recalled. But when he was home it was lovely. Sometimes they went over for dinner with their next-door neighbors, Marion Davies and William Randolph Hearst. Just the four of them, and "WR" would run pictures too—often Marion's old films.

About this time, another great bargain came to Getty's attention: 64 oceanfront acres in Malibu (now Pacific Palisades), part of an old Spanish land-grant ranch. Snapping up the property, he drafted plans to rebuild the two-story cottage standing on the grounds, which came to be known as the Ranch House. While he never lived there (he stayed only a few nights), it was where his increasingly large shipments of art and antiques were sent. In the 1970s, the J. Paul Getty Museum rose on the site.

In June 1946, Teddy gave birth to Timothy. Two months premature, Timmy, as he was known, weighed five pounds and suffered from anemia. "I rejoiced at his arrival," wrote Paul in his first memoir. At fifty-three, he had his fifth son.

"But this pleasant, peaceful interval did not last long, for in 1948 I was on the threshold of seizing the greatest opportunity and taking the biggest gamble of my entire career," he later reminisced. Getty was not being hyperbolic. For he was about to enter . . . the Neutral Zone.

To almost everyone else in the world, the Neutral Zone was nothing but a barren wasteland—a 1,500-square-mile tract of desert between Saudi Arabia and Kuwait. No evidence existed that oil lay underneath it. Once again Getty relied on his instincts and science. He commissioned the finest geologist he knew, Dr. Paul Walton, to make an aerial survey over the territory. After landing, Walton sent Getty a terse cable: STRUCTURES INDICATE OIL. In 1949, Getty offered the king of Saudi Arabia unheard-of terms for a sixty-year concession on the Saudi side. In addition to $9.5 million in cash, Getty agreed to pay $1 million per year for the entire term, whether or not oil was struck, plus the hefty royalty of 55 cents a barrel. Most of the oil industry laughed, predicting that the expenditure would be Getty's ruin.

Four nerve-racking years passed before he saw a drop of oil. During that time, to facilitate the drilling operation, he had to invest another $18 million building infrastructure where absolutely none existed. The longed-for first strike came in 1953, and with it the stunning realization that vast deposits were waiting to be tapped. Still, before a dime could be made, Getty had to solve the massive challenges of how to transport and refine all this petroleum. He spent $600 million building an entire fleet of supertankers and state-of-the-art refineries. As the Neutral Zone assets began to be exploited, Getty's fortune doubled.

Back in Santa Monica, Teddy made a reluctant choice. "I'm the kind of woman who needs a husband," she told Paul. "But, Teddy, you *do* have a husband. It's just that I can't always be home," he responded.

She asked for an end to the marriage in January 1951. That June, when he sailed to Europe for his annual European stay, did he have any idea he would never see America again?

The couple attempted a reconciliation in 1955, in Paris, but it didn't take; their divorce decree was issued in 1958. Later that year, she married a long-standing friend, William Gaston, with whom she had a daughter, Louise "Gigi" Gaston, before the marriage ended in divorce in 1966.

For the remainder of the 1950s Getty was a true nomad, operating out of one hotel suite after another, from which he oversaw his empire, and occasionally his children. Number-one son George, who had been summoned in 1949 to the Neutral Zone, was sent back to America, where he became president of Tidewater and seemed destined to one day ascend his father's throne. (Tidewater finally merged with Getty Oil in 1967.) In 1951, George married Gloria Gordon, a pretty brunette debutante from Denver, the granddaughter of a Colorado senator. The following year, their daughter Anne Catherine was born—Paul's first grandchild. Her sisters Claire Eugenia and Caroline Marie followed in 1954 and 1957.

Ronald graduated in 1951 from the University of Southern California, where he studied business, then became Tidewater's vice president of marketing before being sent to Hamburg, where he utilized his German skills running Veedol, Tidewater's motor fuel operation.

Paul Jr. and Gordon both graduated from St. Ignatius High School in San Francisco, then enrolled at the University of San Francisco, another Jesuit-run school. Life in their mother's house on Clay Street was relaxed. But the "madcap" Ann was not always the most stable parent. The brothers spent a good deal of time on nearby Jefferson Street at the home of William "Bill" Newsom III, their St. Ignatius classmate. It was the start of an intimate family friendship, spanning generations, between the Gettys and the Newsoms, including Bill's son, Gavin, who became the fortieth governor of California in 2019.

During the Korean War, Paul Jr. served in the army, stationed in Seoul. In the wake of the conflict, Gordon was called up for active duty at Fort Lee, Virginia. Both sons subsequently entered the family business, at the bottom. They pumped gas at Tidewater stations before entering the Tidewater training program. In January of 1956, Paul Jr. married his childhood sweetheart, Abigail "Gail" Harris, a swimming champion and the adored only child of a prominent federal judge, George B. Harris.

During their younger years, none of J. Paul Getty's sons had grown up in luxury in their respective maternal households; their absent father had paid just reasonable alimony and child support. So when the October '57 issue of *Fortune* appeared with its list, the brothers were as stunned as anyone, if not more. *"Holy mackerel!"* said Gordon. "Paul and I were surprised. We didn't have any idea." The following year, their father planned to send Paul Jr. to the Neutral Zone; but after meeting Gail and one-year-old Paul III, he reconsidered sending the new father off to that harsh clime. So Gordon got shipped there instead, while Paul Jr. was dispatched to Getty Oil Italiana.

Timmy had been enduring a long series of painful operations after the diagnosis of a brain tumor. After some six years, the cancer was cured, but he was left with severe facial scars. Doctors suggested cosmetic surgery. In August 1958, the twelve-year-old underwent an operation in New York, which was supposed to be routine. Instead, it was fatal. Teddy flew home to Los Angeles with his body. Getty was in Lugano, Switzerland, at the villa of his good friend and fellow art collector Baron Heinrich "Heini" Thyssen-Bornemisza.

Getty has been widely castigated for not returning to America to see his son during his illness, or to attend his funeral. Getty never again boarded a plane after 1942, when a harrowing trip from St. Louis to Tulsa instilled in him a morbid fear of flying. (In later life, boarding an ocean liner became almost as daunting to him.)

Eventually, in the 1970s, Timmy's body was moved to a grave site on a bluff overlooking the Pacific Ocean, on the grounds of the Getty Museum, where he was interred next to his father and eldest brother. Not a mausoleum, it is a simple, low slab of marble engraved only with their names and dates. In the first paragraph of his book, Russell Miller described the burial plot as "forlornly unvisited."

Yet a number of Getty grandchildren and great-grandchildren have described it as an especially meaningful place, which they visit regularly. Getty Museum employees have considered it a very special spot too. "It's a small space at the end of a quiet, tree-lined path," said one curator. "It is so modest—there is no structure, no religious symbols. But with its view to the ocean, the feeling of tranquility and peacefulness is utterly magical. I used to take people there because it was so beautiful, and we had so much to thank [J. Paul Getty] for. When I worked there, many of the staff had known him and bore him in mind."

However, as the image of J. Paul Getty as Scrooge solidified, the narrative of his family as a little-loved "cursed dynasty" took root. To what extent were these depictions anchored in fact? For some insight, it is enlightening to read Getty's diaries from the last sixteen years of his life—the Sutton Place years. When he moved in in 1960, his sons ranged in age from twenty-seven to thirty-six. Six of his grandchildren had already been born. According to the journals, all of his progeny visited Sutton Place regularly in these formative years. Getty wrote about them with affection.

The journals also provide entertaining snapshots of daily life for the richest man in the world. Typically, Getty stayed up until three or four in the morning, strategizing and placing calls to the Middle East. Rising around 10 a.m., he worked through the day, breaking only for lunch and for a walk or a weight-lifting session in the late afternoon. Evenings were social. He hosted dinners at Sutton Place, or frequently drove into London. An average evening—a Tuesday in March 1963—began with drinks at the Ritz, followed by dinner at the fashionable Mirabelle, dancing at the groovy new Garrison Room, and nightcaps back at the Ritz at 2:30 a.m. The cast included Aristotle Onassis, Drue Heinz (wife of condiment magnate H. J. Heinz II), the Marquess of Blandford (the future Duke of Marlborough), Bindy Lambton (the future Countess of Durham), and a member of the Livanos shipping dynasty. *Wonderful music. We did the Twist and enjoyed it. Live bands are out. Records are better,* JPG noted. (Once back to Sutton Place, his nocturnal phone calls to the Middle East would begin.)

In the mid-sixties, his preferred hangouts included the 400 Club in Leicester Square and Trader Vic's, the Polynesian-themed tiki bar in the basement of the Hilton on Park Lane, where he was partial to the mai tais. On October 26, 1967, he noted a new favorite: *I like Annabel's. It is the best nightclub in London.*

His close companions included the Duke of Bedford and members of such dynasties as the Guinnesses, the Rothschilds, and the aforementioned Lambtons and Mannerses. Today, Getty's heirs socialize with many of theirs. "Our families are part of the same landscape. So we're sort of wrapped up with each other," said fashion icon Daphne Guinness of her family and the Gettys.

Snobbish as English aristocrats can be, they're practical. So Getty's reception in England contrasted with his initiation in Italy earlier in the decade. A number of Italian blue bloods had been welcoming enough, prompting Getty in 1965 to purchase La Posta Vecchia, a palatial sixteenth-century seaside villa at Palo Laziale, close to the Italian capital. He launched an extensive renovation, but his ardor for Italy cooled the following year, when he hit a Roman roadblock.

Charming as those Italian princes and counts could be—with their ancient titles but often-depleted bank accounts—they had limits on how far foreigners could get, even the richest (*especially* the richest, perhaps). Getty had been a guest at the inner sanctum of Italian nobility, the Circolo della Caccia, housed in the Palazzo Borghese in Rome, but when he made a bid for membership in 1966, he was blackballed. The rejection stung.

In England, the Queen Mother and other members of the royal family and the aristocracy congregated at Sutton Place. Getty also enjoyed the full spectrum of London's social and cultural offerings. An avid movie buff, he attended seemingly every gala premiere, including *Cleopatra* (he noted: *I thought Elizabeth Taylor good, Harrison, excellent as Caesar*), *Dr. Strangelove*, *The Night of the Iguana*, *My Fair Lady*, *Doctor Dolittle*, and *Funny Girl* (*Barbra Streisand is terrific*).

An animal lover, he never missed a Crufts show, the premiere international dog competition. The subjects of some of his most loving diary entries are his fearsome canines—Shaun, above all. He also doted on his lions, Nero and Teresa, who were kept in large cages on the grounds of his estate. Scratches and bites from these animals often sent guests and staff running to the local hospital, where the attendants automatically asked, "Sutton Place?" when the wounded turned up.

In the course of each year, Getty unfailingly noted the anniversaries of the births and deaths of family members: *Walk and think of Timmy. Timmy! Papa was born 116 years ago. Mama was born 112 years ago. How I still miss her!* In another tribute, he named one of his supertankers after her. The 80,000-ton *Sarah C. Getty* was christened in Dunkirk in 1963. Shaun's passing was dolefully acknowledged as well. *I pick two roses and put them on Shaun's grave. I was devoted to him. Gone 3 years.*

His ex-wives and girlfriends pop up frequently—on the phone, in the mail, at the door.

Dear Belene ph at 8am.

Sent red roses to Jeannette.

Fini and Marion arrive. Both look well. To Annabel's for dinner, but I never saw it look so empty.

Ann Light ph from Palm Beach, inviting me for Xmas.

SP [Sutton Place], *to lunch, Ann looking well and is chic. Her last husband left her 30 million.*

Teddy, her 8 year old daughter, Gigi, her sister Nancy and Nancy's daughter for lunch. Teddy looks as well as she did in 1955.

Getty's sons and their growing families appear often. Although he was surely an absentee dad when his boys were young, he established relationships with them as they reached adulthood. And he became a doting grandfather.

George and Gloria's brood beguiled him on their visits. *Charming girls,* he notes of Anne, Claire, and Caroline. He is *very glad to see them,* and always regretting when it's time for them to leave. *My 3 girls leave for Los Angeles at 11:05. Sad.*

Following George's 1967 divorce from Gloria and his subsequent 1971 marriage to Jacqueline "Jackie" Riordan, a wealthy widow with two sons and a daughter, the new blended family was welcomed into Sutton Place. *Geo and his bride arr. I like her,* he wrote in the fall of 1971. The next spring, there's a visit from *Jackie and the Riordans.* By this point, George's girls are reaching their teenage years and moving with the times: *Geo's daughters dress in hippy style and are pretty.*

In October 1964, Ronald, then thirty-four, married Karin Seibel, the blond, twenty-one-year-old daughter of a businessman from Lübeck, Germany. Fini was a witness in the civil ceremony at that Baltic seaport, which was followed the next day by a wedding mass at the Maria Grün Roman Catholic church outside Hamburg. The honeymoon couple began paying visits to SP, including one during which Mr. and Mrs. John D. Rockefeller Jr. joined them for lunch. The diary notation of a visit with Ronald and Karin's firstborn, Christopher, who came into the world in 1965, is classic Getty: *Ronny, Karin, and Baby Chris here . . . a fine little fellow. . . . Chris plays with the puppies, Sugar and Spice. Valuation of Getty Oil is 2 billion, 7 million dollars net. I have 79% of it.*

News of the couple's first daughter, Stephanie, was also noted enthusiastically, in 1967: *Ronny and Karin have a baby girl!* Cecilia and Christina followed in, respectively, 1970 and 1975.

Meanwhile, Paul Jr. and Gail embraced parenthood too. Following the birth of Jean Paul III in 1956, Aileen, Mark, and Ariadne were born over the next six years.

Diary, December 27, 1963: *Father Albion baptizes Ariadne Joanne Noel Getty, 18 months old . . . Mary* [Teissier] *and I were godparents. Touching ceremony. The little girl is very good and pretty.*

Her parents' marriage did not last, however. *To SP. My dear son Paul here. He flew from NY. Gail has left him,* Getty writes sadly on June 6, 1964.

Getty became fond of his son's second wife, Talitha Pol, a stunning Dutch beauty whom Paul Jr. married in 1966. They paid visits to SP, along with their son. Born in 1968, he was christened with three middle names: Tara Gabriel Galaxy Gramophone. *Paul, Talitha, and Tara my 15 month grandson here. He is a fine platinum blond.*

But as Paul Jr. and Talitha succumbed to heroin addiction, a particularly common scourge at the time among members of their class, their marriage unraveled—beginning the cycle of tragedies that would befall the family.

Mckno [Getty's right-hand man] *here. He tells me Paul Jr has a dope problem.*

Gordon ph I tell him about Paul's weakness.

Papa's birthday. . . . Talitha arrives. . . . Dinner at SP. Talitha complains that Paul is idle and always about the house.

Ph that the lovely Talitha is no more. [She died of a heroin overdose in Rome.] *Shocked and sad. Ph McKno. Paul phs and I try to comfort him.*

Paul ph from Palo [Getty's Italian villa] *and lost his temper. I didn't know this side of his character. I ph back and Gail replied. I think Paul is mentally ill.*

Shortly after, Paul Jr. fled to a house in London that he had acquired, where he became a virtual recluse. Through this stormy time, the valiant Gail watched over the children, including Tara, whom she took into their apartment in Rome. Gail and the children continued to pay visits to SP. In April 1972, Getty's eldest grandson, Paul III, arrived for a stay on his own. They watched a Spencer Tracy and Kate Hepburn movie (*a great pair,* Grandpa noted). But a concerning note was registered: *Dinner and supper with Paul III. I don't approve of his smoking cigarettes.*

Gordon, Getty's youngest son, was the last to marry and begin a family. Before he did, he gave his father a run for his money—literally.

Disgusted with Gordon, the old man veritably spat into his diary, uncharacteristically, on February 13, 1963. *He cables he will sue for declaration of his rights to the 1934 trust.*

Gordon, considered the most absent-minded son, with the worst head for business, was the one who challenged his father by requesting an increase in the then relatively meager income he was receiving from the trust. The trust had always paid its dividends in stock, thereby sheltering its funds from taxation. Gordon wanted cash. If he succeeded in changing the terms of the trust, severe penalties could be levied on the Getty fortune.

While Gordon's lawsuit against his father dragged on for seven years, normal family relations carried on, per the Getty way.

Talked NZ [Neutral Zone] *with Gordon.*

Cable from Gordon in Squaw Valley that he married Ann Gilbert [the daughter of a Sacramento Valley rancher]. *She is unknown to me. I hope they will be happy. Jeannette ph last night.*

With Paul and Gordon to National Gallery to see my Raphael and Veronese. Robina joined us.

Ann, Gordon's bride arr. She seems a nice girl. Gordon and she seem happy and devoted to each other. Wish them a happy marriage.

Snow still covers the ground. Talk business with Gordon, Claus. . . . Walked a mile with Shaun.

Read business reports. Played tennis for 25 minutes with Gordon.

Gordon Getty Jr. born today. Ph. Gordon in NY to congratulate. [After the birth in 1965 of Gordon Jr., known as Peter, came three more boys: Andrew Rork, born 1967; John Gilbert, 1968; and William Paul "Billy," 1970.]

Usual mail. . . . Gordon files trust suit. Ph Hayes, Maltby.

To London, excellent dinner at Wilton. . . . Then went to Annabel's. Gordon, Ann, Papamarkou [Alexander "Alecko" Papamarkou, a Greek-born stockbroker, who figured prominently in the later life of the clan].

Then to SP. Watch the men on the moon. Dinner with caviar, gift of the stunning wife of Gordon.

Ann ph that Gordon might drop his suit.

Gordon Ann and 2 children arr.

Ann Getty and Mr. and Mrs. Pelosi here.

Gordon and Ann ph yesterday. He said he is dropping his claim re stock dividends and he thought it best to do so.

That December, some two hundred guests gathered at the Dorchester Hotel in London to celebrate J. Paul Getty's eightieth birthday. The gala was hosted by his close friend Margaret, Duchess of Argyll. The daughter of a wealthy Scottish industrialist, "Marg of Arg," as she became widely known, was one of the most fascinating and alluring women of her time. The 1930 Debutante of the Year, she was wed first to golfer Charles Sweeny; soon after, Cole Porter immortalized her in his most famous song, "You're the Top."

> *You're Mussolini,*
> *You're Mrs. Sweeny,*
> *You're Camembert.*

In her 1975 memoir, *Forget Not*, Margaret reflected on Getty. "Paul has been my very dear and staunch friend for many years . . . and has been unwavering in his loyalty," she wrote, alluding no doubt to the many people—including her own child, Frances—who shunned her following her scandalous 1963 divorce from the 11th Duke of

Argyll, wherein the judge excoriated Margaret for being "a highly sexed woman." (Frances, who Margaret had with Sweeny, became a duchess herself upon her marriage to Charles Manners, the 10th Duke of Rutland—a brother of Lady Ursula d'Abo. Though Margaret and Frances held sway as one of Britain's rare sets of mother-and-daughter duchesses, the ladies remained permanently estranged.)

When Paul's milestone approached, "I felt that he deserved the best possible birthday," Margaret recalled. Although her friend was "essentially gentle and shy" and "fundamentally a modest man," she nonetheless pulled out all the stops for a splendid evening.

It began when Richard Nixon phoned from the White House to extend his congratulations. His daughter Tricia came to the Dorchester in his stead. Other attendees included Umberto, the former king of Italy, Ambassador Walter Annenberg, and Getty's fellow oilman Nelson Bunker Hunt, as well as Ann and Gordon.

At midnight, as a giant birthday cake was wheeled into the ballroom, bandleader Joe Loss launched into a custom rendition of Porter's classic:

> *You're the top, you are J. Paul Getty*
> *You're the top, and your cash ain't petty*
> *You're a Franklin Fellow with a Paris medal as well,*
> *Got your own museum, let's sing a Te Deum to such a swell*

> *You're the top, you are like Jack Benny,*
> *You're the top, wouldn't waste a penny. . . .*

The evening was the pinnacle of a life of extraordinary accomplishment. From here, it was downhill for J. Paul Getty—not financially, but emotionally and physically. His *annus horribilis* was about to begin.

2

The Tragic Years

New Year's Day 1973 began on a fresh note. J. Paul Getty ventured into London for a haircut and manicure at the Ritz. But dense fog made the drive back to Sutton Place uneasy, and then there was a worrisome portent. *Had increased tremor in hands and jaw today,* he recorded.

It began to be reported around this time that Getty had Parkinson's disease, but he persistently denied it, even to himself. *To dentist. . . . While waiting read Time and read that I've Parkinson's!* he scoffed.

His handwriting deteriorates around now. His shaky hand renders the pages of his diary increasingly difficult to decipher (until October 29, 1974—from which point secretaries wrote them from Getty's dictation).

The pace of his social life lessened. However, he and Ursula had an enjoyable visit in late April to the County Durham estate of his good friends the Lambtons, where the grounds held surprises: *U and I to Biddick. Bindy and the children welcome us, also a black Labrador, a greyhound and 3 or 4 others. . . . Bindy drives us through the Safari Park in a Land Rover. An ape nearly got inside.* But not long after, Getty received a phone call that must have been serious from Lord Lambton on May 21—

the day he wrote Prime Minister Edward Heath a letter tendering his resignation from the Cabinet. A few days later, the sex scandal that precipitated his departure exploded in the press and rocked Great Britain. (Norma Levy, the sought-after dominatrix with whom Lambton had been caught in bed, later told the *Daily Mail* that her gilt-edged client list had also included the Shah of Iran, Greek shipping tycoon Stavros Niarchos, the 11th Duke of Devonshire, and J. Paul Getty. For the septuagenarian Getty, she would don a white robe, then lie down in an open coffin for about an hour, playing dead. "Jean Paul would just stand over me in his underpants, just looking at me," she recounted.)

From Getty's journal, it appears that he offered Lambton the use of Posta Vecchia as a refuge from the storm: *Tony Lambton ph re Palo. He will be there May 31.* (Lord Lambton soon acquired a glorious seventeenth-century Italian villa of his own called Cetinale—located just a few miles from Orgia, the refuge of Gail Getty—where he enjoyed a splendid exile, and the younger members of the families became neighbors. Recently, producers of *Succession* rented Cetinale from Lambton's son, Ned, to serve as the location for the Roy family's epic season-three finale.)

Pleasures aside, the pressure was rising at Sutton Place. Getty Oil was risking huge sums of money to explore in difficult new territory, so far without success. *North Sea well news is bad,* JPG wrote on April 16. That winter and spring, there was a high volume of communication with number-one son. The diary is peppered with *ph Geo, Geo ph, Geo arr, Geo lv,* and the like. In February, George arrived from Los Angeles for a two-week stay at SP.

Since the merger with Tidewater, George F. Getty II had served as executive vice president and chief operating officer of the Getty Oil Company. (Paul was president.) In the view of many, George modernized the combined company and made it a success. And outside the company, he was a respected civic leader (the Los Angeles Philharmonic's chief fund raiser), and he enjoyed his real passion—

thoroughbred horses, which he bred and raced. "He got more joy and happiness from seeing his horse win a race than from anything else money could buy," a friend recalled. (The winners in his stable included Gentle Thoughts, Injunction, and Natashka.)

But he always had trouble measuring up to his father, whom he habitually referred to as "Mr. Getty." "He's president in charge of success and I'm vice president in charge of failure," George said glibly.

Following his split from Gloria in 1967, he stayed in LA and she relocated with the girls to the San Francisco Bay Area. Like her father-in-law's ex-wives, she felt her husband had put business ahead of their marriage. After his 1971 remarriage to Jacqueline Riordan, George moved into her mansion in Bel-Air. He was under increasing pressure, which sometimes led to drinking binges, which probably contributed to his weight gain, for which, in turn, he was prescribed medications. He developed a masochistic tic of stabbing his hands with a letter opener.

Various accounts of what happened the night of June 5, 1973, have been told. At dinner, George drank a few glasses of wine. Later he ran to the kitchen, grabbed a barbecue knife, and inflicted a superficial wound across his upper abdomen. Blood was drawn, but his vital organs weren't punctured.

Jacqueline placed three calls: to Dr. Kendrick Smith, Getty Oil's in-house doctor; to Stuart Evey, the Getty Oil vice president who was George's most loyal right-hand man; and to the Bel-Air Patrol, the wealthy community's private police force. Just after midnight, the patrolmen arrived first, which panicked George. He ran to his bedroom and locked the door. Evey and Smith got there soon after. After about an hour of trying to communicate with George, they broke down the door and found him on the floor. He was snoring, blood dripping down his stomach.

Evey then asked Dr. Smith not to send George to the nearby UCLA Medical Center. Reporters monitored admittances of celebrity patients there; the incident would likely hit the news. So George was taken on a longer ambulance ride to the smaller and quieter Queen of Angels Hospital downtown. After being admitted there under an assumed name, again at Evey's insistence, George seemed to be stabilized and merely in need of recovery from an alcoholic stupor.

About 2 a.m., Evey went to sleep on the floor beside George's bed. A few hours later he was woken by the staff swarming over George, who had fallen into a coma. Shortly after, Jacqueline arrived. She showed Evey two empty pill bottles that had contained barbiturates. She had discovered them in the bathroom when the doctor and Evey were with George in the bedroom, but her fear of scandal had prompted her to withhold them at that moment.

To control George's appetite, his doctor had prescribed amphetamines, which revved him up in the day but made sleep difficult. The same doctor prescribed barbiturates to help him sleep. Uppers combined with downers and then even a small amount of alcohol can be fatal. George died a few hours after Jackie arrived at the hospital.

"Mr. Getty's death was the result of a slowly increasing personal stress which was triggered into an acute reaction by alcoholic intoxification and which manifested itself in violent and self-destructive behavior," the coroner concluded. "We believe Mr. Getty took the pills in the brief time he was in the bathroom, that the pills were ingested on impulse. . . ."

In 2004, Evey published a memoir, *Creating an Empire*, in which he explained his fateful choices that night. He didn't view his actions as a "coverup." Loyalty and deep affection guided him: "Everything I did was to protect the image of the one person in the world to whom I owed everything in my adult life," who had been "like a brother to me—not just my boss, not just my mentor."

George's death sent Evey into a deep depression. "For five long years, I simply went through the motions of showing up for work and being alive. I drank. I disappointed myself." (In late 1978, however, Evey, who was then in charge of Getty Oil's nonpetroleum businesses, turned his life around after a former minor-league hockey announcer walked into his office and pitched "a crazy idea" for a twenty-four-hour all-sports cable network. In those pre-CNN days, the idea had been turned down by eight other companies. Evey persuaded the Getty board to invest $10 million for an 80 percent stake in this "crazy idea"—ESPN. Evey later explained that memories of outings with his old friend at the racetrack guided his decision to back ESPN, which was launched in 1979. "I did this primarily because I thought George Getty would like it," he said before he died in 2017.)

It fell to Evey to phone J. Paul Getty to tell him his son was dead. He reached Paul at the home of the Duchess of Argyll, where she was giving a dinner for the Turkish ambassador. Getty took the call in the duchess's library. After he hung up, "he beckoned me in . . . to say, 'George is dead,'" she recalled in *Forget Not*. She stayed up with him until about 3 a.m. He could do little but stare blankly into space and say repeatedly, "George has gone. He is with God."

Tragic! Shattered, he inscribed in his journal. *I walked to church and said a prayer for my dearest son. . . . George was a splendid son.*

Family visits provided intervals of comfort: six days after George's death, Ronald and Karin arrived with their children. *We walk about and watch the lions.* Two weeks later, Gordon and Ann and their boys came to stay. Paul Jr.'s son Mark was there too. *A fine boy.* They watched TV: Wimbledon and Watergate.

On July 10—just thirty-five days after George's death—came the next catastrophic event. The scrawl in the diary is almost impossible to read: *Message for Paul . . . that Paul . . . is kidnapped.*

A group of Calabrian mafiosi had snatched sixteen-year-old Paul III, Getty's eldest grandson, as he was walking home about 3 a.m. on a dimly lit street in Rome.

Along with the ear that Little Paul eventually lost, the most indelible element of the narrative was J. Paul Getty's initial refusal to pay the $17 million ransom demanded by the kidnappers, which he announced in his statement: "I have fourteen other grandchildren, and if I pay a penny of ransom, I'll have fourteen kidnapped grandchildren." From then on, it was more or less cemented in the public imagination that J. Paul Getty didn't care about his progeny, that he was heartless.

Entries in his diary over the next five months contradict that narrative. *I hope that he is not kidnapped and that he is OK,* Getty wrote when news of the abduction reached him. There were numerous strategy meetings and conversations with advisors and family members, including Gordon: *Indoors all day. Long discussion of Rome. . . . Crisis in Rome.*

I shudder at the boy's peril, Getty wrote after a newspaper in Rome received an envelope with Paul III's right ear.

Monitoring the press coverage, he took issue with some reports: *Rome TV news . . . castigating me for heartless refusal to . . . Actually I am putting up all the money. Ph Robina.*

On December 16, a day after Paul III was released, amidst frenzied global media coverage, he spoke to the young man on the phone. *Talk to her* [Gail] *and then to Paul,* he wrote in his diary. Most published accounts have said that the grandfather refused to talk to his grandson.

Excruciating as the five-month-long ordeal was, the Gettys have had to endure having it "told" again and again, in the forty years since, with creative license.

One of the few people still alive who was actually there at Sutton Place was Robina Lund. She agreed to share her views with me in writing, from her home in Aberdeenshire.

J. Paul Getty was far from heartless, she wrote. But he deliberately crafted the *perception* that he was heartless:

"Paul III was his eldest and favourite grandson. He loved all of his children and grandchildren but was also well aware of the frailties of some of them although he never publicly criticized them. His public refusal to pay any ransom was deliberately made to save ALL the other family members from immediately becoming potential hostages. There were many people and journalists who understood and agreed with the approach and so publicized, on JPG's behalf, his 'disinterest' and refusal to pay. The public fell for it and so did the kidnappers."

(No other Gettys were kidnapped, but seven weeks after Paul III's release, publishing heiress Patricia Hearst, nineteen, was abducted in Berkeley, California. The following year, Samuel Bronfman II, a twenty-one-year-old heir to the Seagram liquor fortune, was taken and held for ransom in New York. Throughout the 1970s, Italy suffered an epidemic of kidnappings—hundreds of individuals from wealthy families were abducted by organized gangs.)

Lund also described how misperceptions surrounding Getty—"the gross distortion of facts and characters"—have been perpetuated:

"Many [journalists] and, later, authors who could not get an interview with him (especially after his death when he couldn't answer them back or, more importantly, sue them for defamation!), built their works of fiction based on previous publications and news-clippings or interviews with grudge-holders, their aim, of course, being to make money. Scandals sell; hagiographies bore. . . . Many, particularly the later authors and film-makers, none of whom had ever met JPG, did not want to know the truth about him. 'Never let the truth get in the way of a good story.'"

She even deflated the other Getty Ur-myth. The infamous pay phone was *her* idea, she says. During the gala housewarming party that Getty threw at Sutton Place, AP and UPI reporters had kept a phone line open to Los Angeles for six hours. Costly as transatlantic calls were then, the bill amounted to over $40,000 in today's money. On another occasion, when Sutton Place was open for a charity function, a visitor phoned Tokyo for three hours. At the next directors' meeting of the Sutton Place Property Company, the holding company that she had formed to run the estate, Lund called for the removal of the phone extensions in the public rooms and installation of a pay phone. "NOT, please note, a red telephone box!" she wrote. Located in the downstairs cloakroom, for use by the press and the public who were not JPG's personally invited guests or company employees, it was removed after eighteen months, she added.

Four days after the kidnapping drama concluded, Gloria and her daughters—the Georgettes, as they are sometimes called—arrived at Sutton Place for the holidays. (Gail soon took Little Paul and his siblings away to the Austrian Alps for two months, to help them recover from the ordeal.) On the verge of their twenties, George's offspring were making their own decisions, which Grandpa wasn't always of one mind with. *Claire wants to go to school in Rome. I don't agree.* But it appears they had a happy visit, opening Christmas presents, having dinners, and watching TV. *Upstairs, Downstairs* was his current favorite. *Hudson, the Butler, hopes to marry a young girl.*

Walk 40 minutes. Nero roaring, he wrote in the last log of that tumultuous year. *U and Gloria, Claire and Caroline watch 1974 come in. We are in 1974. We drink a glass of champagne.*

In these early years of the 1970s, despite his declining health and family traumas, Getty remained laser-focused on the plans for his namesake museum, which was rising out of its building site on the Malibu coast. He micromanaged its construction remotely, via drawings, models, photos, and films that were sent the six thousand miles to him.

At the same time, his newly hired curators made regular trips from Malibu to Sutton Place, bringing with them photographs of treasures they hoped to convince him to buy. Among the frequent visitors was Gillian Wilson. Born into a middle-class family in England, she moved to Los Angeles in 1971 at age thirty to begin her job as the J. Paul Getty Museum's first curator of decorative arts. Essentially self-taught, and anything but prim (she had a fling with the Rolling Stones drummer Charlie Watts), she assembled an unrivaled collection of eighteenth-century European furniture and decorative arts for the Getty, building on the holdings J. Paul Getty acquired personally.

"It was big and freezing cold. He always saw you at the most peculiar hours," Wilson recalled of her visits to Sutton Place. "He would stay up until very late ringing Saudi Arabia and places like that. At three in the morning—and you were jet-lagged—Bullimore would fetch you: 'Mr. Getty will see you now.' Every so often [Getty] wanted to show you his oriental carpets in the Long Gallery. He would get on his hands and knees. So I had to as well. I remember thinking, *This is rather peculiar—here I am crawling along with the richest man in the Western Hemisphere in the middle of the night.*"

On January 16, 1974, just weeks after Paul III's release, the J. Paul Getty Museum opened at last. It was the culmination of Getty's life as a collector, the legacy he wanted to leave to the world. The cultural elite greeted it with scorn.

The complaints from the critics focused not on the art but on the building. In the late sixties, when he settled on the design, Getty went against the grain of prevailing fashion and trends, as usual. At the high noon of modernism, he chose to build a replica of an ancient Roman villa, and a colorful one at that. "I refuse to pay for one of those concrete-bunker-type structures that are the fad . . . nor for some tinted-glass-and-stainless-steel monstrosity," he said.

Ten days before its doors opened, the *Los Angeles Times*'s art critic weighed in with a preview: "L.A. intelligentsia . . . will find that the Getty outstrips any existing monument to expensive, aggressive bad taste, cultural pretension, and self-aggrandizement, south of Hearst Castle."

Other critics piled on, ridiculing it as "Pompeii on the Pacific" and "an intellectual Disneyland."

"For the majority of the architectural establishment who still at least give lip service to the canons of the Modern Movement [it] is not only disgusting but it is downright outrageous," another author summed up.

Getty tried to downplay the drubbing ("certain critics sniffed at the new museum," he wrote), but, according to biographer John Pearson, the poor reviews "genuinely shook him." Soon enough, however, the public vindicated him. By March, 100,000 visitors had besieged its gates, backing up traffic on the Pacific Coast Highway for miles. Ever since, it has been one of California's most popular destinations. (In 1997, the J. Paul Getty Trust expanded its operations substantially, with the opening of its acropolis-like campus in Brentwood, designed by Richard Meier at a cost of approximately $1 billion. The two sites, which charge no admission fee, typically draw two million visitors a year.)

In time, even the intelligentsia came around—some of them, anyway. One fan of the villa was Joan Didion, who described it as "mysteriously and rather giddily splendid" in a 1977 *Esquire* piece (subsequently published in her collection *The White Album*) in which she pondered how differently elite and popular audiences had responded to it.

"The villa . . . manages to strike a peculiar nerve in almost everyone who sees it. From the beginning, the Getty was said to be 'vulgar,'" she wrote. "To mention the museum in the more enlightened of those dining rooms . . . is to invite a kind of nervous derision, as if the place were a local hoax, a perverse and deliberate affront to the understated good taste and general class of everyone at the table.

"The Getty is a monument to 'fine art,' in the old-fashioned didactic sense. . . . The place resists contemporary notions," she continued. "As a matter of fact large numbers of people who do not ordinarily visit museums like the Getty a great deal, just as its founder knew they would. There is one of those peculiar social secrets at work here. On the whole 'the critics' distrust great wealth, but 'the public' does not."

Another positive but more concise assessment appeared in *The Andy Warhol Diaries*. "Went to Getty Museum. . . . It was thrilling. Bought a book on painting ($17)," the artist wrote on September 21, 1978.

Despite the harsh reviews, his physical decline, and lingering traumas, 1974 and 1975 were mellow for the old man. His final two full years were filled with visits from his progeny and various ex-wives.

Teddy continued to make her customary visits to Sutton Place, with her daughter, Gigi. "We came every summer," recalled Gigi, who became an equestrian and a filmmaker in Los Angeles. "Paul was more of a father to me than my own father. He played toys with me and, when I turned thirteen, he taught me how to mix a rum and coke. I have only very fond memories of him." (Gigi had watched him enjoy his beverage of choice in previous years and asked for the lesson; she didn't imbibe, except for a sip.)

The Georgettes and their mother, Gloria, were guests at Sutton Place numerous times. Claire delayed college and traveled around the world. Between countries, she returned to Sutton Place for long stretches, and she sometimes brought foreign friends back with her. *Claire and a nice Italian man friend of hers were here for a swim and dinner,* JPG noted in July of 1975. She also joined lunches and dinners Getty hosted for his wide variety of friends, ranging from Jacques Cousteau and Zsa Zsa Gabor to Charles Wrightsman, Getty's fellow oilman and art collector, who came with his wife, the divine Jayne.

Getty also took Claire to meet the head of the Mitsubishi Oil Corporation, a strategic partner of Getty Oil. (A couple decades on, Claire's sister Anne, an environmentalist, went to battle against Mitsubishi.)

Gloria, on her own, sometimes overnighted at Sutton Place en route to France, Scotland, or some other holiday destination. Other times, George's second wife, Jacqueline, arrived with her son, Mike. At a loss after George's death, Jackie, a slim blonde, had taken up

George's equestrian hobby, and found great satisfaction in it. In June 1975, one of her three-year-olds pulled off a sensational victory at Royal Ascot, running in one of the week's most prestigious races, which Paul was delighted to attend: *Her horse Blood Royal won the Queen's Vase in a thrilling fashion. I had five pounds on it.*

Mike, a graduate of USC, also got hooked on the sport of kings. Over the years, he had great success with his horses, including Are You Kidding Me, Dunbeath, and Bates Motel (Mike's also a film buff).

Getty's second son, Ronald, and his family came to visit from their home in South Africa. Summer afternoons, they enjoyed the lovely weather by the pool. *They are very nice looking children and well behaved,* the old man noted in June '74, of Cecilia, Stephanie, and Christopher, who ranged in age from four to ten. By their next visit, in January, the brood had expanded. *The special attraction is a young lady aged 4½ months,* he wrote delightedly of Christina, his sixteenth grandchild.

Karin and the children usually arrived and departed by air, while Ronald always voyaged by sea. Like his father, he had developed a fear of flying.

Getty biographers have portrayed Ronald as being bitter at his father over his exclusion from the Sarah C. Getty Trust (caused by Paul's anger toward Ronald's rich maternal grandfather). But the diaries indicate Ronald had certainly some warm feelings for his father. In these final years, Ronald made efforts to coax him into returning to America at last. With their shared terror of airplanes, the son was empathetic. *Ronny wants me to go with him on the* [ocean liner] *France and I would like to. But business!* Getty wrote in August 1974. And in early 1976: *Talked to Ronny. He would like me to come with them on the boat which goes to Miami via Lisbon and Nassau. It is 24,000 tons. I would like to but I have a Government Participation meeting January 21st.*

Ronny's mother—Paul's third wife—also arrived, with a girlfriend, for a weekend: *Fini and Marian arr at 8 last night after a stormy Channel crossing. . . . Both look well.*

Paul Jr. was not allowed at Sutton Place. Big Paul refused to see him until he kicked drugs. Paul III, then eighteen, married his German girlfriend, Martine Zacher (who later became known as Gisela), and the couple moved to Los Angeles. The patriarch was delighted to hear about the birth of their son, Paul Balthazar, in January 1975, from Paul III's maternal grandparents: *I received a cable from Judge Harris: 'Boy born to Martine and Paul, Congratulations, George and Aileen.' This makes me a great-grandfather.*

The rest of the brood visited frequently: *Gail and the 3 children to tea. We all remark how nice Mark, Aileen, and Ariadne are.* They were in their teenage years—or, in the case of the baby of the family, just beginning them. *Had a birthday lunch with a cake with candles for Ariadne,* he wrote on July 23, 1975. *She is 13 today. I gave her ten pounds in cash and a wooly bear, which she liked. She found another ten pounds in the bear. She is a nice child. She said, 'Now I am a teenager.'*

There were lovely afternoons with them on the grounds: by the pool (*they all swim like porpoises*), the garden (*we walked and admired its beauty. The Rhododendrons are out in all their glory*), or farther afield (*Went Blackberrying . . . there is a good crop this year*).

Their eight-year-old half brother visited with his maternal grandmother: *Tara and Mrs. Pol to lunch. . . . Tara is a handsome boy and has good manners.*

Gordon and Ann were back and forth from San Francisco, together and separately. Gordon was at Sutton Place for his father's final weeks, in the spring of '76. *He looks good,* Paul observed of him that April. The couple's four boys, home in California, ranged from age five to ten.

Getty's last wife kept tabs remotely: *Teddy phoned from the Algonquin Hotel in New York just for old time's sake. I remember the Algonquin back in 1935.*

With his face looking more funereal than ever, Paul got a chance to see himself in a way that only a few have experienced. *Miss Simpkins and Miss Fraser here from Madame Tussaud's to make a wax replica of me,* he reported in late '74. A few months later, he was pleased, at least with his placement and apparent popularity. *Saw my image in wax. It is next to Katharine Hepburn. There are big crowds.*

By the beginning of 1976, his body was in considerable pain, especially in his neck, leaving him challenged. *Bullimore helped me put on my socks and shoes and fasten the neck button on my shirt.* Parkes, the underbutler, suffered a stroke at the same time. Getty noted: *We were told it would be a long time before he is ready to work again.*

That spring, Getty was informed he had prostate cancer. He never acknowledged this in the journal; he just described his pains, which made sleeping in his bed difficult. He began spending nights in an armchair in his study.

In his final weeks, he rallied to have several conversations with Gail. The trial of Paul III's kidnappers was finally about to start in southern Italy. She and Little Paul were determined to attend and face the perpetrators. Security was a big concern. JPG made arrangements for them to stay at Posta Vecchia and in another villa he owned on Gaiola, an island off Naples.

Gail called to say they are leaving tonight for PV and then on the 11th will go to Gaiola, he wrote May 7.

The trial was a grim ordeal for Paul III and Gail. It lasted ten weeks. Finally, a three-judge court convicted only two of the nine defendants.

J. Paul Getty never learned the verdict. He slipped away quietly on June 6, 1976—three years to the day after George's death—in the chair in his study, next to the settee upon which he had once jumped so boisterously.

Upon his death, J. Paul Getty was no longer the richest man in the world. But he was up there.

There were two vast piles of wealth to sort out—Getty's personal fortune and the Sarah C. Getty Trust. In theory they were separate, but they were very much intertwined, because the value of both lay in Getty Oil Company stock.

His personal fortune consisted of 12 percent of the company's stock, valued then at $750 million. Three days after his death, it was revealed that virtually all of this (save for some bequests to his lady friends) was bequeathed to the J. Paul Getty Museum. In Malibu, the staff nearly fainted collectively. Getty had never let on that he would leave them anything approaching this. The rest of the art world was equally staggered. Overnight, this eccentric little museum became the best-endowed cultural institution on earth. (While George, Ronald, and Gordon served on its board for periods over the years, the family has never been involved in the management of the museum.)

The Sarah C. Getty Trust held a 40 percent stake in Getty Oil, worth about $2 billion. In theory, the trust's path was preordained: the vast distributions it would provide to the heirs in the coming decades, until the death of J. Paul Getty's last surviving son, at which time the principal would be divided up among the heirs.

Within a few years, disagreements in the family led to titanic battles over the fate of Getty Oil and the trust. Once again, the Gettys were exhibited as a poster family for dysfunction. As the media painted it, the Gettys were at each other's throats. It was brothers against brothers, nieces and nephews against uncles, cousins against cousins. Pure rancor. Those headlines kept coming—"the Tragic Dynasty," "the Getty Curse," "the War between the Gettys"—which, in turn, provided many Gettys with ample reason for never wanting to speak to the press.

When there are this many zeros involved, however, it's rare when there isn't litigation. Some of Getty's contemporaries left far messier estates. Howard Hugues, who died one month before Getty, didn't leave a legitimate will, a situation that led to years of bizarre courtroom battles among his many would-be heirs. More than thirty-five years after the death of H. L. Hunt, a bigamist who produced fifteen children from three overlapping relationships (a clan that makes the Gettys seem like the Brady Bunch), some of his heirs were still litigating over their trusts. It would take nearly a decade to settle all the complicated financial issues for Jean Paul Getty's heirs, his company, and his museum.

II.

BRANCHING OUT

3

The Georgettes

While the demands that came with being J. Paul Getty's firstborn son ultimately took their toll on George F. Getty II, his early years were placid. Born in 1924, he grew up in the verdant community of San Marino outside Pasadena, where his mother, Jeannette, settled with her second husband, stockbroker William H. Jones, who was a kind stepfather to George.

After attending the Webb School in nearby Claremont, George enrolled at Princeton University, though the war interrupted his studies. He enlisted in the army in 1942 and received a second lieutenant's commission in the infantry in 1944. He spent sixteen months in the Pacific.

Thenceforth he was under his father's command, and dispatched to a variety of harsh locales, including the Neutral Zone and West Texas. On a break home in California, he got engaged as the second half of the twentieth century dawned.

"Vivacious" was a word used to describe Gloria Alice Gordon. In March 1951, the *Los Angeles Times*'s society page buzzed with the news ("Betrothal Announced") that this dimpled, Denver-born debutante, now a senior at Marymount College, was "the summer bride-elect of George Franklin Getty II."

The couple's June wedding at the Church of the Good Shepherd in Beverly Hills was also avidly covered: "The bride's radiant brunette beauty was accented by her period gown fashioned with a fitted bodice and portrait neckline. . . . The full skirt of pleated ruffles of taffeta and tulle completed the bridal gown. On her dark curls was a tiny crown of Chantilly lace delicately frosted with pearls from which floated a veil of illusion." After the ceremony, the guests, including her maid of honor and five bridesmaids, continued to the reception in the Crystal Ballroom of the Beverly Hills Hotel, before the newlyweds departed for their honeymoon cruise on the Mediterranean.

Being the wife of a rising young oil executive (especially the first-born son of J. Paul Getty) entailed a considerable number of moves over the next decade, as her daughters were born. A November 1952 issue of the *Princeton Alumni Weekly* carried this news from the Class of '46: "A young Texas miss arrived in Midland on Thursday, Oct. 9. The young lady's name is Anne Catherine Getty. . . . Her father is a Texan-for-Ike, manager of the Mid-Continental Division of the Pacific Western Oil Company."

Two years later, around the time Claire Eugenia was born, the family moved to Tulsa, and later to New York. In 1957, when Caroline Marie arrived, they relocated to San Francisco, where, according to the *Oil & Gas Journal*, "George F. Getty II is making the family name synonymous with the oil business." By the fall of 1958, they were Southern Californians. "The attractive honorees, George and Gloria, have moved to Our Town from New York (via a short stopover in San Francisco) and will make their home here," the *Los Angeles Times* wrote.

All those moves must have been taxing for Gloria. She and George separated in 1965; their divorce decree came a few years later. She relocated with the girls to Hillsborough, the mannerly community south of San Francisco on the Peninsula, while George remained in Los Angeles. By the time he remarried—to Jacqueline Riordan in 1971—Gloria had moved to the livelier shores of Newport Beach in Orange County. Gloria joined "the new sea set" and bought a little motorboat, which she christened *Titanic*. It blew up on its maiden voyage. "She went ahead and called its replacement, a whippy little motor launch with a bright blue-and-white fringed canopy, the *Titanic Too*," it was reported.

On June 9, 1973, three days after George's shocking death at age forty-eight, he was buried on a bluff overlooking the Pacific Ocean on the Getty Ranch in Malibu, where the J. Paul Getty Museum would rise. Caroline was fifteen, Claire eighteen, and Anne twenty.

After the girls finished school, Gloria returned to the San Francisco Bay Area. At Trader Vic's, she was accorded her own table in the Captain's Cabin, "the most sacred region where only the best-known are seated," the *San Francisco Chronicle* noted.

She traveled in Europe. In the summer of 1984 she attended a starry gala, a benefit for United World Colleges, at Sutton Place, which had been purchased by Milwaukee-born timber heir Stanley J. Seeger. Familiar as the surroundings were, the art and the crowd were different. Under the ownership of Seeger, a reclusive gay collector of modern art, a Francis Bacon hung where a Gainsborough had been; instead of the Queen Mother, Prince Charles and Princess Diana were on hand. (Two years later, Sutton Place was bought by yet another rich, eccentric, gay American—Koch Industries heir Frederick Koch, who also rivaled Getty in extreme frugality.)

In the aughts, Gloria could be found at the Balboa Cafe, now under the management of young up-and-comers Billy Getty, her nephew, and Gavin Newsom; in 2002, she was seen encouraging fellow patrons like Will Hearst to sign a petition for homeless reform that fledgling mayoral candidate Newsom hoped to get on the ballot. In 2013, she and her offspring attended her former brother-in-law Gordon Getty's gala eightieth birthday party. Her daughters had grown up to become exemplary citizens—and very private ones.

On an afternoon in November 2019, as a nor'easter lashed Manhattan with forty-mile-per-hour gusts and torrents of rain, the recipients of the Carnegie Medal of Philanthropy climbed the marble steps of the ornate New York Public Library.

In the world of philanthropy, a Carnegie Medal is the equivalent of an Academy Award. Like some of J. Paul Getty's forebears, Andrew Carnegie had arrived in America from Scotland penniless. In 1889, when Carnegie had amassed a fortune from steel that put him on par with robber barons such as John Jacob Astor, Cornelius Vanderbilt, and Jay Gould—whose excesses spawned the Gilded Age—he published a manifesto, "The Gospel of Wealth." Influenced by his strict Scottish heritage, he urged his fellow millionaires to embrace social responsibility and to donate their money to organizations that would address the root causes of poverty and social ills. He gave away $350 million, the bulk of his fortune, to such efforts. It was the birth of modern philanthropy.

Biennially, the international network of institutions that Carnegie endowed recognizes philanthropists who embody his spirit of giving. Medals have gone to some of America's most recognizable names, including Brooke Astor and Michael Bloomberg, as well as the Mellon, Rockefeller, and Gates families.

The 2019 class of medalists included financier Henry Kravis and George Lucas, who in his acceptance speech quoted "my friend Yoda," to make the point that "everyone has the Force inside them— the light and the dark . . . and hopefully we're able to move it a little more toward the bright side."

Next up to the podium was a petite sixty-seven-year-old brunette whom few Americans would be able to identify—Anne G. Earhart. According to her citation that night, her efforts over the decades to protect the environment place her "prominently within the ranks of today's great conservationists."

Many in the audience probably had no idea what the G. stood for. (Her biography in the program didn't mention it.) In her acceptance speech, J. Paul Getty's eldest grandchild said simply, "I knew that when I inherited a large sum of money, that some good should come of it." (There was also a certain triumph for a Getty grandchild to be accepting an award named after Carnegie, who is credited with coining the adage "Shirtsleeves to shirtsleeves in three generations"—a warning that wealth gained in one generation will likely be lost by the third.)

"I joke that it was the Catholic nuns who gave me my perhaps overdeveloped sense of responsibility," Anne also stated that afternoon. According to her biography, her schooling was at the hands of the Sisters of the Immaculate Heart.

The few times that Earhart's name has appeared in the press, the words "intensely private" invariably have run alongside it. The same goes for her sisters. While almost all the members of the extended Getty family could be described as private, the descendants of Gloria and George F. Getty II have the strongest aversion to being in the public eye, even as they've been models of social responsibility.

As Anne continued her remarks, she made one more personal reference. "I want to ensure that my grandson and all of his generation will get to see the wondrous sights that I have been privileged to see," she said, referring to four-year-old Finn, who was in the audience with his mother, Sara Earhart Lowell, then thirty-eight, and her brother, Nicholas Earhart, thirty-four.

One of those wondrous sights, she recalled, was a baby gray whale with which she came eye to eye four decades before. She had been on a boat when a pod of whales broke the surface and a pair of enormous orbs the size of baseballs focused on her. "To be with an animal that has chosen to come up and look at you in the eye is a transcendental experience. . . . It is magic," she recalled in *A Force for Nature: The Story of the NRDC and Its Fight to Save Our Planet,* by John H. Adams, founder of the National Resources Defense Council.

That encounter took place in Laguna San Ignacio in Baja California. Some 450 miles south of the Mexican border, it is a narrow 16-mile inlet of sparkling jade-green waters, surrounded by a 6 million-acre desert reserve teeming with pronghorn antelope, bighorn sheep, and mountain lions. One of the most pristine places on earth, it is here, every winter, that thousands of gray whales conclude their epic journey from their summer feeding grounds in the Arctic Circle. Despite having been hunted nearly to extinction along this route in the nineteenth and twentieth centuries, these forty-ton, forty-five-foot-long marvels continue to undertake the 10,000-mile migration (the longest-known of any mammal in the world) to Laguna San Ignacio, where they mate and calve in the warm, salty waters, and are renowned for their friendliness. They often nuzzle up to boats; a mother will sometimes even nudge her curious offspring forward, to afford them a look at the strange creatures aboard the vessels.

After her trip to San Ignacio, Anne left California for several years, as a rare newspaper item about her, published in the *Los Angeles Times* on June 6, 1980, reported: "Anne Catherine Getty, daughter of Mrs. Gloria Getty of Newport Beach and the late Mr. George F. Getty II, married John Edwin Earhart in Corona del Mar. The newlyweds are living in Paraguay, where he is with the Peace Corps. He is the son of Mr. and Mrs. Edwin Earhart of Rogue River, Ore."

While living in South America, Anne gave birth to Sara in 1981; she also became an environmental advocate. After seeing devastating destruction of land in Paraguay and Brazil, she studied environmental issues and began engaging with leaders in the conservation movement.

In 1983 the family relocated to Connecticut, where John earned a master's degree in forestry from the Yale School of Forestry and Environmental Studies. By 1985, when Nicholas arrived, they were back on the West Coast, in Seattle and finally Laguna Beach, where they settled. (She and John divorced in the 1990s.)

By then, Anne and her sisters were young women of great means, being the beneficiaries of their father's income from the Sarah C. Getty Trust. (Because of his early death, the girls came into substantial wealth two decades before some of their cousins.) Though the value of the trust doubled after the sale of Getty Oil, the trio had initially opposed the deal. After they did acquiesce to the sale, they continued to press a lawsuit against their uncle Gordon, the sole trustee, over his management of the trust (his brother, Paul Jr., joined them in this action). Reserved and youthful as the women were, they were no pushovers.

The upheaval began in 1982, six years after J. Paul Getty's death. Until then, Getty Oil had continued to be run by its management, headed by chairman and chief executive Sidney R. Petersen, a company veteran. All along, however, there had been a power behind the throne: the iron-willed C. Lansing Hays, Paul's longtime attorney, and a trustee of the Sarah C. Getty Trust. Gordon was cotrustee, but habitually deferred to him in the running of the trust as well as Getty Oil, where the management largely deferred to Hays too.

Hays's death in May 1982 set off the extraordinary drama. In essence, Gordon now became sole trustee, which gave him increased power over Getty Oil and the trust.

For the first time, Gordon developed a serious interest in the management of the company. After studying it, he wasn't happy with what he saw. The value of its stock had declined significantly. He wondered why it was underperforming. Getty Oil's management and board, which had long considered Gordon a docile, rather eccentric character—an absent-minded professor type, the member of the family least cut out for business—were taken aback.

At the height of the merger mania then sweeping Wall Street, Gordon began to chat with bankers and other oil companies, which put Getty Oil in play. In late 1983, Pennzoil was on the verge of consummating a deal for the company when Texaco swept in, setting off one of the most sensational takeover battles ever. Texaco ended up buying Getty for $10.1 billion, the biggest corporate acquisition in history. (Pennzoil then launched a colossal and ultimately successful multibillion-dollar lawsuit against its rival that bankrupted Texaco. *That's* a whole other story: the Getty family wasn't a party to that suit, their billions from Texaco having already been banked.)

During the run-up to the sale of the company, Getty Oil management schemed to neutralize Gordon. They sought to enlist other family members to challenge Gordon's position as sole trustee in order to block the sale, eventually drafting Paul Getty Jr.'s youngest son, Tara, then fifteen years old, for the role.

But the strongest challenge to Gordon came from the Georgettes. Loyal to the memory of their grandfather and their late father, they didn't want to see the family legacy dismantled. Nonmaterialistic, too, they thought they were rich enough. "Why, Uncle Gordon, since the trust has so much money already, are we trying to get more?" they asked him during a meeting. "A very interesting philosophical question," he replied. "But it is my duty to maximize the wealth and income from the trust and to prevent it from falling into a weak minority position." (These conversations were drawn from depositions Gordon had to give when the young women later brought legal action against him.)

In January 1984, the sale went through, because Gordon got the museum, with its 12 percent of the stock, to vote with him. The fortunes of both the museum and the family doubled. With the trust now worth $4 billion, some heirs questioned how it was being managed by Gordon, the sole trustee. For the next eighteen months, branches of the family litigated. Finally, in 1985, a judge agreed to a plan to partition the Sarah C. Getty Trust into four separate trusts, so each branch could oversee its own. But the matter was still far from settled. A major legal hurdle had to be cleared, which was accomplished when the California State Legislature enacted a new law that allowed family trusts to be split upon agreement of all the beneficiaries. Bill Newsom helped steer it through in Sacramento, from the statehouse to the desk of Governor George Deukmejian, where it was signed. But getting all twenty-six living Getty heirs to sign the eighty-nine-page agreement to divide their Trust took another three years, largely due to disagreements over tax issues.

"Were my nieces and Paul mad at me? Believe it," Gordon wrote in a preface to *Logic and Economics: Free Growth and Other Surprises*, an economics primer he self-published in 2018. He placed the blame for the family friction on the attorneys, however. "Lawsuits get that way. Lawyers on both sides say nasty things," he wrote. But amicable family relations continued, according to his account: "Problem solved. The Trust was split into four in 1988, and an unhappy chapter ended. My nieces and I are as close as ever. So were Paul and I until his death."

While cordial relations between nieces and uncle did resume, this distaff branch of the Gettys—George's daughters and their children—veered in its own direction, largely going its own way. To use a whale metaphor, they stay in their own pod, while the other three branches of the family swim together, more or less.

In 1986, Anne established the Homeland Foundation, which initially focused on helping disadvantaged women. When environmental causes became her primary focus, she renamed it the Marisla Foundation. (The Marisla Seamount is a group of three underwater peaks rising from the sea floor eight miles off the coast of Baja California; Marisla is also Anne's daughter's middle name.)

The Marisla Foundation emerged as a particularly effective leader in marine conservation, working to mitigate habitat destruction, pollution, and overfishing. While her efforts have made Anne a hero to conservationists, the public knows little of her philanthropy, by her choice. In the early nineties, for example, she provided about $400,000 to the NRDC so it could lead the opposition to a proposed billion-dollar toll road that would plow through the idyllic San Joaquin Hills near Laguna Niguel south of Los Angeles. The battle lasted years. Area residents who also opposed the highway were surprised when the *Los Angeles Times* revealed that the Earharts had been footing the bills for the resistance.

It was also reported that funding from Anne's foundation typically came with a request that the recipients never talk about the couple or the foundation. It was a deal that grassroots activists in California were happy to keep. "I'd say we'd be in deep trouble without them," said one of them. (Despite Earhart's efforts, the road was ultimately built.)

As Anne's children grew up, Laguna San Ignacio became a favorite family destination. They camped in the desert and voyaged out to see the whales. "I love this land of high winds, desert, and mangrove and water alive with whales, porpoises, and pelicans," she also recalled in *A Force for Nature*.

In 1994, Anne learned that this paradise was coming under attack. The Mexican government planned to build the biggest salt-production plant in the world here, in partnership with the Mitsubishi Corporation. Their joint venture, Exportadora de Sal SA (ESSA), had already built a sizable saltworks in Laguna Guerrero Negro, a hundred miles away.

Anne's grandfather and the Japanese firm had a long history, going back to 1924, when the fuel department of the Mitsubishi Trading Company secured exclusive rights to sell in the Far East the petroleum products made by the Getty-owned Associate Oil Company of California. In 1928, Mitsubishi entered into a broader joint venture with Tide Water. There was an interruption after Pearl Harbor, but by 1950 the companies resumed their partnership. By the 1970s, Getty Oil owned 49.7 percent of Mitsubishi Oil; the affiliate was a significant part of Getty business. But disaster struck on Christmas Eve 1974, when the rupture of a storage tank at Mitsubishi's Mizushima refinery resulted in the largest oil spill in Japan's history—an event that was environmentally devastating and financially costly. Some eleven million gallons poured into the scenic Inland Sea, creating a huge slick.

In the wake of this calamity, Mitsubishi's top executives paid a visit to Sutton Place in April 1975, when Anne's middle sister, Claire, happened to be in residence. Getty was concerned about the damage. *This is an anxious time*, he wrote. *Mr. Watanabe, Mr. Nimura arrived at noon. Long discussion about Mitsubishi and the catastrophe. They say it might cost a hundred million dollars. I recommend a dyke to be built around the 3 Mitsubishi refineries.*

The troubles notwithstanding, *Mr. Watanabe is very charming*, he noted. *Claire was with me. Mr. Watanabe was very fond of George. George liked Japan very much and so do I.*

Anne—who since the 1984 sale of Getty Oil had no financial interest in Mitsubishi—got wind of plans for the San Ignacio plant, which would cover 130,000 acres and include a mile-long pier, in a roundabout way. A local fisherman, Don Pachico Mayoral, had somehow gotten his hands on a set of blueprints. A guru-like figure in the small community, Pachico lived on the edge of the lagoon in a wooden shack with a sand floor and no telephone. He showed the blueprints to an American PhD candidate, Serge Dedina, who was at the lagoon carrying out research for his dissertation on gray whales; Dedina in turn alerted Anne. She sprang into action. She enlisted the NRDC to spearhead the largest coordinated global environmental campaign to date. During the ferocious five-year-long battle, her support went unreported.

In early 1995, the *Los Angeles Times* broke the story of the impending peril; it punched holes in the environmental impact statement that had been prepared, which had concluded that the proposed project's impact on the whales would be "insignificant," discounting the likelihood of toxic chemicals contaminating the lagoon and not contemplating how the pumping of 462 million gallons of seawater out of the lagoon a year might reduce the salinity of the water. Its high salt content is thought to make the whales more buoyant, and account for why females with calves gather there.

The Mexican government, eager for the plant's projected $100 million in annual revenue, blasted the "disinformation." Mitsubishi wouldn't return reporters' calls or respond to the frightened population who lived near the lagoon—a small community of fishermen and people who work in the ecotourism business.

The NRDC gathered an international coalition to raise awareness of the situation: environmentalists, fishermen, artists, intellectuals, writers, and dozens of world-renowned scientists, including nine Nobel laureates. They focused on getting consumers around the world to care about this remote spot that most had never heard of. Editorials appeared in newspapers worldwide. In the *Los Angeles Times*, Robert F. Kennedy Jr. and NRDC senior attorney Joel Reynolds raised the cry for "the one place on earth where the last of the gray whale species can breed and calve undisturbed by human intrusion." A campaign of boycotts, disinvestment initiatives, petition signings, and letter and postcard writing was orchestrated. Some 700,000 postcards were mailed to Mitsubishi car dealerships worldwide.

Mitsubishi's public relations offensive included full-page newspaper ads touting the plant as "a partnership with nature." Then, in December 1997, Baja fishermen made a gruesome discovery: ninety-four highly endangered giant black sea turtles floating dead downstream from Laguna Guerrero Negro. An investigation found that they had been poisoned by a spill of toxic salt brine wastes from the ESSA plant there.

In March 2000, Mexican president Ernesto Zedillo helicoptered to the site with his family and a group of friends. They boated on the lagoon to view the whales, then camped onshore for a night. A week later, he announced the cancellation of the project. "This is a place that has had minimal interference by humans—one of the few places like that left on the planet," he reasoned.

"We came to appreciate a number of arguments by people that this is an area that should be left as is for ecotourism," a Mitsubishi spokesman commented.

It was a watershed victory that broke new ground in environmental activism, and was soon viewed as a case study in how to conduct a grassroots campaign—developed with multilayered sophistication—in the era of globalization.

A decade later, NRDC president John H. Adams reflected on the battle in his memoir. "Multifaceted campaigns like this are hugely expensive, and this one cost millions of dollars," he wrote. "It could never have happened without the support of Anne Earhart, the president of the Marisla Foundation. Anne's philanthropic strategy was to look for people with passion and give them whatever they needed to get the job done."

When Anne received her Carnegie Medal, Serge Dedina—now the mayor of California's southernmost city, Imperial Beach, and the director of his own nonprofit, Wildcoast—recalled her support. "Anne has this really quiet presence. Not everybody knows the work she does. But she's out there, kind of like a coach, pushing everybody forward. She's like that surfer on the beach that watches the gnarliest waves on the biggest day of the year, and instead of watching it from the beach, she decides to paddle out."

She inspires others to paddle out too, he added, because they know she has their backs: "She is always there for you when you are an activist in a heavy situation."

As she concluded her remarks that night at the New York Public Library, Anne explained how her meeting with the gray whales had set the direction of her philanthropy: Initially she focused on marine mammals because they were her passion. Soon enough she realized that these animals were "the canaries in the coal mine, as they filled up with the toxins that were dumped into the oceans, the plastics that were becoming ubiquitous in the sea, and the specter of climate change."

Some progess has been made, she allowed—gray whales are still swimming the 10,000 miles to Laguna San Ignacio to mate. But with warming water in the Arctic endangering their feeding grounds, this is "an all-hands-on-deck moment," she declared: "We are not separate from these sentient beings. . . . We need to understand we are one community and now is the time for service to that community in any and every way that we can."

With annual giving of around $50 million, Marisla has in recent years provided funding to more than six hundred nonprofits that work to address global environmental challenges. According to a Carnegie release, Earhart-funded philanthropy has helped preserve 4.5 million square miles "and counting" of ocean.

A board member of another conservation foundation described Marisla as "absolutely top-notch. . . . They really do their homework and pick the most worthy grantees to support. They go the extra mile and do things no other foundation does, like providing enhanced security to environmental defenders. In many parts of the world, these people are in real danger.

"They are caring, thoughtful people," he added. "Anne is quite soft-spoken. She doesn't speak often [she prefers to remain in the background, leaving most of the public work to Marisla's executive director Herbert M. Bedolfe III]. But when she does, she speaks forcefully, and is very well-informed."

Sara Earhart Lowell shares her mother's interests. After graduating from Laguna Beach High School and the University of California, Santa Cruz, where she double-majored in environmental studies and Latin American history, she worked as a tour guide in Laguna San Ignacio. For her master's degree in marine affairs, which she earned in 2008 from the University of Washington, her thesis examined the impact of ecotourism on the Laguna population. An Orange County resident, she has served as the Marisla Foundation's marine program director since 2016. She oversees efforts to create protected marine areas, advance sustainable fisheries, and protect coastal lands in California, Hawaii, Baja California, Chile, and the broader Pacific.

Another thing mother and daughter have in common is an aversion to the press. "We prefer to keep a low profile," Sara said, turning down a request for an interview. Her brother, Nicholas, expressed reticence as well. "I'm just not comfortable appearing in a book about my family [or] talking about my kinfolk," he wrote in a polite email. Furthermore, he felt that people "would take no pleasure in reading about the pallid and humdrum events of my daily life. It mostly consists of writing, fly-fishing, and golfing."

J. Paul Getty with Teresa, one of his pet lions, at Sutton Place in the 1960s

Getty Research Institute, Los Angeles

THE FIVE WIVES OF J. PAUL GETTY

Jeannette DeMont
Getty Images

Allene Ashby
Institutional Archives,
Getty Research Institute, Los Angeles

Adolphine "Fini" Helmle
Getty Images

Ann Rork
Los Angeles Times Photographic Archive
Department of Special Collections/
Charles E. Young Research Library/UCLA

Louise Dudley "Teddy" Lynch
Getty Images

J. Paul Getty with Robina Lund
Dezo Hoffman/Shutterstock

Sutton Place, southwest of London, was built in the early 1500s
and acquired by J. Paul Getty in 1959.
Print Collector/Getty Images

J. Paul Getty with Margaret, Duchess of Argyll, en route to his eightieth birthday party in London, December 1972

Pierre Manevy Express/Hulton Archive/ Getty Images

ABOVE: George Franklin Getty II

Express/Hulton Archive/Getty Images

LEFT: Ronald Getty with his father at Goodwood, England, circa 1970

Keystone-France/Gamma-Keystone/Getty Images

Christopher Getty and Pia Miller at their wedding in Bali, 1992
Collection of Christopher Getty

Isabel Getty at Royal Ascot, June 2019
David M. Benett/Getty Images/Ascot Racecourse

MOROCCAN WAKE-UP

MR. AND MRS. PAUL GETTY, JUNIOR, HAVE SHAKEN TO LIFE A DESERTED HOUSE IN MARRAKECH, MADE IT IMAGINATIVE, RARE – WITH A LITTLE MYSTERY

"This house is really a stage," Talitha Getty said of the nineteenth-century ramble of rooms, courtyards, and terraces that she and her husband came upon on their honeymoon about four years ago and bought: "Things happen here spontaneously." The spontaneity of this holiday house for the Gettys, who live most of the year in Rome and London, depends on their care as they gradually, joyfully restore its old graces, its harems and friezes, and add treasures of their travels. *Above:* On the terrace overlooking the souks, the towering Koutoubia, and the snowy Atlas Mountains, Paul and Talitha Getty, wearing Moroccan caftans. *Left:* The Riad, or main courtyard, its fountain floating flowers, its paths glistening with tiles specially made for the Gettys, and with the flare of lanterns: "We light the house with a hundred candles and lanterns," said Mrs. Getty, who lights this house, too, with a continuum of friends.

Paul Jr. and Talitha at Palais de la Zahia, Marrakech,
as seen in the January 1970 issue of *Vogue*

Patrick Lichfield/Vogue/© Condé Nast

Wormsley Manor in Buckinghamshire, England was acquired by Paul Jr. in 1985.

Christopher Simon Sykes © Condé Nast Shutterstock

Sabine Getty and the *Talitha*

Jason Schmidt/Trunk Archive

Paul III on a forty-foot ketch, embarking for Catalina Island, 1977, photographed by Jonathan Becker

© *Jonathan Becker*

Tara and Jessica Getty at Wormsley, 2011
© *Dafydd Jones*

Balthazar, at right, with (from left) wife, Rosetta, and children Grace, Violet, June, and Cassius at the CORE Gala, Los Angeles, January 2020

© *Kevin Mazur/Getty Images*

Paul III and his wife, Gisela, at home in Los Angeles with their children
Balthazar and Anna, 1977, photographed by Jonathan Becker

© Jonathan Becker

LEFT: Julius Getty and his father, Mark, at the opening of the Julius Getty Gallery, London, 2019
Jeff Spicer/Getty Images

RIGHT: Alexander and Tatum Getty, San Francisco, 2012
© *Drew Altizer*

BELOW: Sabine and Joseph Getty with daughter, Gene, at home in London, 2019, photographed by Simon Watson
© *Simon Watson*

Aileen Getty and Christopher Wilding,
photographed by Firooz Zahedi
© *Firooz Zahedi*

Aileen at a Fire Drill Friday,
Washington, DC, December 2019
Collection of Aileen Getty

Honoree Aileen at the
amfAR Inspiration Gala,
Los Angeles, 2013, with
her sons Caleb Wilding
(at left) and Alexander
Wilding with his wife,
Alexandra
Jason Kempin/Getty Images/amfAR

Ariadne Getty with her children Nats and August
at home in Beverly Hills, 2018

Emily Berl/The New York Times/Redux

Gigi Gorgeous and Nats Getty at their wedding
in Montecito, July 12, 2019

Alex Welsh/The New York Times/Redux

Gordon and Ann Getty at the memorial service for his father
in San Francisco, 1976, with their sons Peter, Andrew, John, and Billy

Steve Fontanini/Los Angeles Times Photographic Archive/Department of Special Collections,
Charles E. Young Research Library, UCLA

Ann Getty departing her mansion in San Francisco,
aided by footman Frank Parkes (left) and butler Francis Bullimore,
photographed by Horst for *Vogue*, 1977

Horst P. Horst/Vogue/© Condé Nast

"Nico" Earhart is a writer and adventurer. He has posted a number of his pieces on his website and blog, the Wind-Blown Golfer. Since graduating in 2008 from the University of Denver, where he majored in international/global studies, he has made Colorado (his maternal grandmother's birthplace) his home. From there he travels to the Australian outback, the Alaskan Great North, and other far-flung locations to write about his sporting pursuits, including fly-fishing and surfing but primarily golfing. "There are no limits to where my golf bag and I will go," the bio on his site says.

A foodie too, he apprenticed at a restaurant in Italy, then returned home to the Rocky Mountains to continue his culinary progress, which he described in his piece "Coming to Fruition."

During his six months in Northern Italy, he had worked eighteen-hour days without compensation, mostly in a damp, chilly basement—peeling potatoes, hand-rolling gnocchi, "and dispatching and butchering every woodland creature under the canopy." It was all worth it: the twenty-four-year-old chef upstairs was that good.

"And now, here I was back in the U.S., ready to grab the Denver culinary scene by the throat," Nicholas continued. His foray into a Colorado kitchen, under the thumb of a sadistic chef, was short-lived, but it made for an engaging piece.

"Claire Getty, daughter of Mrs. Gloria Getty of Hillsborough, was feted at a family dinner marking her election as senior class president at Castilleja School in Palo Alto," the *Times* of San Mateo, California, reported in 1972, in one of the rare newspaper items about George II and Gloria's middle daughter. "Claire plans to attend the University of Salzburg in the fall, where she will study music and languages and will be accompanied on a pre-college trip to Europe by her sisters. . . . En route, the three girls will stop in Denver to visit their maternal grandparents. . . . They will also plan a stop in London with their paternal grandfather, J. Paul Getty."

Like other Gettys before her, Claire was captivated by European art; given her interests, her grandfather's masterpiece-laden house alone provided much to study. She spent a few years in Europe during the mid-1970s, during which she gave birth to her first son, Beau. According to John Pearson's book, Beau was born "as a result of a love affair with an Italian she met at Perugia University."

In 1980, she was living in Washington, DC, and enrolled at Georgetown University's School of Foreign Service. As she pursued her degree in international economics, which she received in 1983, complicated issues surrounding Getty Oil and the management of the Sarah C. Getty Trust were demanding her attention too. She was the first of the sisters to contact their father's younger brother to question the control he was beginning to assert. "Dear Uncle Gordon," read a handwritten letter she composed to him. "I do not mean to be critical of you, but I think you would admit that your business management background is limited."

Nevertheless, she, like her sisters, wanted to stay out of the papers. "If you want a story, try my uncle Gordon. He enjoys publicity. We don't," she said to a reporter who managed to get her on the phone around that time.

While an undergraduate, she also helped found a major new museum in Washington.

Art collector and patron Wilhelmina Cole Holladay had long harbored a dream to open a museum of works by female artists, which would be run by women. Throughout the 1970s, she organized countless meetings, trying to drum up enthusiasm as well as financial backing for her pie-in-the-sky idea. Thus far, it hadn't crystallized. But it was about to.

"An experience with a new neighbor brought it to a head," Holladay wrote in her 2008 memoir, *A Museum of Their Own*. "A young woman who had come to study at Georgetown University moved in the house next door to ours on R Street NW. Claire, who turned out to be an attractive girl; her fiancé, a former member of the Peace

Corps; a darling three-year-old boy; and their Great Dane brought to our quiet street a lively household." (Claire's future husband, Noel Perry, a Rhode Island native, had served for two years as a Peace Corps volunteer in Yemen.)

Holladay first met the couple after their dog left a mess on her driveway, which Holladay's husband stepped into.

"That evening the doorbell rang, and there on the threshold stood two sweet young things, almost in tears. 'We're so sorry,' Claire blurted out. 'We just want to be good neighbors.'" A few weeks later, Claire was at her front door again, this time in a panic. Beau had fallen and cut his head. Wilhelmina called her grandchildren's pediatrician, and all was soon fine. A grateful Claire asked Wilhelmina what she was involved in. Informed about the museum idea, Claire perked up. "I find that fascinating," she said, as Holladay elaborated in an oral history she conducted with the Smithsonian Institution's Archives of American Art.

As it happened, a meeting was on the calendar for the next Tuesday with a group of young women, a junior committee; Holladay invited her neighbor to drop in:

"Claire attended, became excited, and declared, 'A building is needed.' I replied, 'Someday, my dear.' She said, 'You know, Mrs. Holladay, I really want to help.' And I said, 'Well, tell me what committee you want to be on and we'll do something about that.' And she said, 'No, I mean I really want to help.' And I said, 'Well, that's wonderful, my dear . . . we'll talk about it.'"

With that, Claire had to rush out to a class, at which point one of the other girls piped up, "Is that Claire *Getty*? As in J. Paul?"

"It had never occurred to me," Holladay recalled.

Soon enough, after a discussion Claire had with her financial advisor, she pledged $1 million to start a building fund; she got her sister Caroline to come across with the same amount. (Gloria became involved in fund-raising events too.) The gifts were instrumental in finally making the museum a reality. In 1983, a 70,000-square-foot former Masonic Temple was purchased for $5 million. After extensive renovations of the 1908 building, a few blocks from the White House, the National Museum of Women in the Arts opened in 1987. It is still the only major museum in the world dedicated exclusively to recognizing the achievements of women artists.

In 1995, Claire earned a PhD in art history from Stanford University, after working on it for a decade. Along the way she and Noel had been raising Beau and the four boys they had together in the 1980s. Byron was born just three months before she began graduate school at Stanford. Twins Somerset and Sebastian arrived next, and finally Winslow, the baby of the family.

When the family settled into their home in the community of Woodside, near Stanford, they spearheaded a drive to plant three hundred little oak trees along a forlorn stretch of Cañada Road, at the entrance to the town.

The university embarked on a major project to rebuild its art museum. When it opened in 1894, the neoclassical Leland Stanford Jr. Museum was the largest privately owned museum in America. It was built by Jane and Leland Stanford as a memorial to their only child, a lover of European art who died of typhoid at age fifteen.

The museum had bad luck. The 1906 earthquake wrecked much of it. During World War II it was closed altogether. Portions were rebuilt in the 1960s; then the 1989 Loma Prieta earthquake decimated it again. When it finally reopened in January 1999—renamed the Iris & B. Gerald Cantor Center for Visual Arts at Stanford University—Dr. Claire Perry was its curator of American art. She curated its inaugural exhibition, *Pacific Arcadia: Images of California, 1600–1915*, which was based on the dissertation she wrote for her doctorate. (Oxford University Press published the accompanying 256-page catalog, the first of several books she has written.)

Pacific Arcadia illustrated how, over five centuries, the idea of the

"California dream" came to be. The notion of abundance, the promised plenty of the Golden State, was at the heart of the show. To mount the show, Claire sifted through masses of images—paintings, drawings, maps, photographs, newspaper and book illustrations, printed ephemera—before ultimately selecting the works to display. Perhaps not unlike the way her grandfather prospected for oil, digging through layers and layers of sand and shale before finally striking black gold, she mined for ideas. She focused on how, beginning in the seventeenth century, with the creation of elaborate maps and depictions of fertile valleys and other natural wonders, the concept of the Golden State had been marketed and promoted by merchants, railroad owners, financiers, and real estate speculators in order to lure settlers. They presented the state as the ultimate fulfillment of the American dream and established it as a land of infinite possibilities in the mind of the American public.

Claire investigated American culture in other exhibitions and books. *American ABC*, which opened in 2006 at the Smithsonian American Art Museum in Washington, DC, scrutinized childhood in nineteenth-century America. In 2011, *The Great American Hall of Wonders*, also at the Smithsonian, examined nineteenth-century America through the lens of its technological innovations and native ingenuity. *California: The Art of Water*, a 2016 show at the Cantor Center, where Claire is now a guest curator, examined the state's complicated water story through works by a diverse roster of artists, including Albert Bierstadt, David Hockney, and Ansel Adams. For the exhibition, she successfully lobbied to have the walls of the galleries painted swimming-pool turquoise.

Like others in her family, Claire supports environmental causes, and in doing so she has tangled with powerful interests. In the fall of 2010, a ballot initiative that would have suspended California's greenhouse gas law, Proposition 23, was gaining steam. Big money from oil-related interests—including $1 million from Koch Industries— was pouring in to stoke the Yes campaign for the measure. It seemed like a David vs. Goliath situation, in which the environmentalists would be crushed. Claire stepped up to help fund the No campaign with two $250,000 contributions over the next weeks. The tide turned, and the measure failed in the November voting.

Since his days building water projects in rural Yemeni villages with the Peace Corps, Noel Perry has been a green advocate too. He established Baccharis Capital, one of the early "socially responsible" venture capital funds, which has invested in education and health-oriented consumer products, including organic foods. An amateur painter and sculptor, he founded several nonprofits, including 100 Families Oakland. Dozens of multigenerational families from across the city were brought together in workshops over ten weeks, where they were taught to paint, quilt, and sculpt. "Possibilities happen when you get around a block of clay: people learn about themselves and others—how to work together. . . . It's mind-expanding," Perry told a community newspaper, which described him as "intensely private."

Both Claire and Anne married men who shared their aversion to publicity. "We are private people and trying to remain that way. People hate rich people," one of the husbands once explained.

The oak trees that the Perrys helped plant on Cañada Road grew into a veritable forest. When Beau, their eldest, grew up, he planted something of a forest of his own, underwater. A mariculturist, he is the largest grower of seaweed on the Pacific Coast of North America.

"I have loved seaweed all my life. As a surfer I've spent an eternity bobbing up and down amidst California's kelp forests—often getting it tangled around my legs, fins, or leash. Sometimes I'll even chew on a nice-looking frond while waiting for the next set of waves," he wrote on Instagram.

"Travelling the coast you can find surf spots with a variety of kelp beds—giant kelp, bull kelp, sea palm, the list goes on and on—and they feel as different to me as beech, redwood, or oak forests. When the water is clear you can see them waving in the current under the board, parting occasionally to reveal the vibrant life beneath the canopy—fish, crab, lobster, urchins, anemones, octopi. . . ."

Following in his mother's footsteps, Beau earned his undergraduate degree in 1999 at Georgetown, where he majored in foreign service and international relations and affairs. At the Presidio Graduate School, he got an MBA in sustainable business. Like his aunt Anne, he traveled to Baja California. Instead of the plights of whales, it was the effects of overfishing and destructive seafood farming practices that alarmed him.

Blue Evolution, the company he founded in 2013 in Los Altos, another San Francisco Peninsula town, began propagating seaweed in onshore tanks in Baja. In 2014, he expanded and went north, heading to Alaska's Kodiak Island, in perhaps the same pioneering spirit with which his great-grandfather arrived in Bartlesville. Perry was among the first entrepreneurs who saw the potential to cultivate seaweed in these waters.

His company contracts with local fishermen, transforming them into sea farmers in winter—the growing season for seaweed and the off-season for fishing. Blue Evolution provides them with the seed stock, which it makes by extracting spores from wild kelp; the seedlings are grown on pieces of string known as seed pipes, then given to the farmers, who wind the string along long ropes that are suspended from a floating frame in the ocean. After the "planting" is done in late November, the ribbons of kelp grow up to a foot a day. Weaving and protecting the lines is arduous. Beau has also involved members of the Indigenous population: the seaweed, once harvested, is processed at a facility in Kodiak owned by the Sun'aq Tribe.

Now the largest commercial seaweed hatchery in the US, Blue Evolution is at the forefront of sustainable marine aquaculture. Some of its seaweed is blanched and frozen and sold to restaurants and food service operations throughout the country. The company also sells a line of seaweed-infused products, including pastas and pop-corns, under its own label. "Blue crops" have the potential to change the climate equation. Seaweed requires only sunlight and seawater to grow—no expenditures of energy, fresh water, fertilizer, or pesticides. And seaweeds naturally detox the ocean through photosynthesis, helping to combat marine acidification and global warming.

In May, Beau and his cohorts haul up the fruits of their labors—tons and tons of slimy green bunches. "Harvesting dawn to dusk. I'm really proud of the crop this year and the hard work put in by all. Major increase and improvement over last year," read a 2019 tweet from @beaugperry ("Dad, sea farmer, surfer, Founder and CEO of Blue Evolution"). Two years later, *Vegworld* magazine reported that his eight-year-old animal rights activist son was already supporting his plant-powered endeavors.

In a family so press averse, Byron is something of an outlier. In 2011, when he was twenty-seven, he founded an unconventional media enterprise out of his apartment in Bangkok.

His trajectory began when he was an undergraduate at George-town. English was his major, but he took a journalism class his senior year. "Something clicked," he said.

After graduation, he worked as a fact-checker for *San Francisco* magazine, then as a copy editor and writer in Los Angeles at *Variety*, where his responsibilities included coming up with the pun-laden headlines for which the publication is known.

When he got laid off during the crash of 2009, he embarked on a trip to South America and Asia. Southeast Asia appealed to him, so he looked for a job there, and landed one with the *Phnom Penh Post*, Cambodia's leading English-language newspaper. He wasn't stationed in the capital city, but in sleepier Siem Reap (home of the historic Buddhist temple Angkor Wat), where he found his stories riding around on his bike.

He moved on to Bangkok, Thailand, where the city's brashness and quirkiness fascinated him. "I saw there was an opportunity. Nobody was covering all the really weird, crazy stuff happening, in English," said Byron, a burly, bearded fellow with an easygoing manner.

He started a local-news website, which he called Coconuts Bangkok. ("Brands named after fruits have done pretty well," he reasoned.)

Launching it on a shoestring, he wrote and produced everything himself the first year. He got traction through posts he shared on Facebook. Thanks to a couple of small, successful angel-investor rounds, he was able to expand operations. Coconut Media is now an English-language news and video network that reaches up to 26 million people per month in eight cities across Southeast Asia, with a staff of about twenty-five. Coconuts TV, its video production arm, makes documentaries and films that have appeared on networks such as Discovery and streaming platforms including Netflix.

Coconuts takes an irreverent approach to most of its coverage, but has also produced insightful coverage of democracy protests in Hong Kong, the catastrophic floods in Bangkok, and Covid-19's impact across Asia, among other stories.

Byron's brother Sebastian has been a creative collaborator. He produced and hosted several films. *Highland*, a docuseries about Thailand's cannabis legalization movement, was acquired by Netflix, while *Hijab Riders*, a look at a group of women shaking up the male-dominated world of motorbike racing in Malaysia, received an award for Excellence in Video Reporting from the Society of Publishers in Asia. In *Nagaland: Twilight of the Headhunters*, Sebastian took viewers on a journey through Nagaland, an isolated corner of India sandwiched between Myanmar and the Himalayas, where he tracked down some of the last living Naga headhunters, as well as the new generation of Naga.

The other Perry brothers live in the Bay Area. Somerset, another Georgetown graduate, received his JD from the University of California, Berkeley School of Law in 2013. Since 2015, he has been deputy attorney general in the Environmental Section of the California Department of Justice. Winslow, the baby of the family, an intern at UCSF Medical Center, directed *The Edge of Purpose*, a forty-one-minute documentary, in 2019, which focused on nine people from different backgrounds who followed their passions as they built unique routes to success.

In this very discreet branch of the Gettys, the most private one of all has been Caroline, George and Gloria's youngest daughter. Though she's now in her early sixties, her name has appeared in the press only a handful of times.

In 1976, she was mentioned in a society column covering a wedding in Walla Walla, Washington: "Flying in for the party are Gloria Getty and her daughter Caroline (a student at Reed College)."

Academically rigorous Reed College, founded in 1908 in Portland, Oregon, was a haven for antiwar activists, hippies, and nonconformists of all stripes during the 1960s and '70s. Sweatshirts worn by many students during that era bore their unofficial motto: "Communism, Atheism, Free Love."

In 1989, Caroline was accorded a distinction she probably didn't like—being the youngest person on the Forbes 400 list; at age thirty-two, she ranked as the 322nd-richest American, with $330 million. (Her sisters, ranked alongside her, possessed equal fortunes.)

The anonymity she has enjoyed since was broken only around 2002, when a series of headlines began appearing in California papers about a "mystery donor" who had contributed $1 million to an advocacy group, the Nature Conservancy, enabling it to campaign on behalf of three state ballot propositions, all intended to protect clean water, open spaces, and farmland, among other wholesome things.

Self-appointed "watchdog groups" began digging around for the identity of this secret donor, whose contributions were made under the names of mysterious-sounding LLCs, one of which was named, yes, Rosebud.

Caroline was eventually outed as the donor, and identified as a resident of Corona del Mar in Orange County. After she gave the Nature Conservancy permission to confirm that she had written the checks, her troubles were hardly over. The California Fair Political Practices Commission filed a thirteen-page lawsuit against her, seeking $520,000 in penalties and asserting that she had used the LLCs (another was named Wild Rose) as conduits to disguise that the money was coming from her personal trust account. "Panel Accuses Getty Heiress of 'Campaign Money Laundering,'" blared a headline in the *Los Angeles Times*.

She refused to admit any wrongdoing, but in March 2004, a settlement was reached. Getty agreed to pay a $135,000 penalty. Her lawyer issued a statement saying that she and her company settled the case to resolve the matter and "recommit their full attention to California's critical conservation needs." The attorney also called on the state to clarify its vague campaign reporting requirements "so that other civic-minded and well-intentioned individuals won't be discouraged from supporting the environment or other worthy causes."

One can understand, then, why Caroline and her sisters prefer to remain anonymous.

4

The Ronald Line

Of J. Paul Getty's five sons, Jean Ronald, the second, was the only one born and reared on European soil. (His younger half brother Paul Jr. came into the world on European waters, off the coast of Italy, but he was quickly bundled up and brought back to Los Angeles.)

In the wake of the stock market crash, Paul barely made it to the Berlin hospital before Fini, his third wife, went into labor on December 19, 1929. Four months later, when his father was stricken, Paul raced back to Los Angeles alone. As war clouds gathered, Fini and Ronald remained in Germany as long as they could, then took refuge in Switzerland. In 1939, after the Nazis arrested her anti-Hitler, staunchly Catholic father, they fled to California.

Ten-year-old, German-speaking Ronald was a European at heart, and remained so all his life. He established the most predominantly international branch of the family. It is also the only one that has no public record of tragedies or substance addictions. Ronald's progeny appear to possess, overall, the sunniest dispositions in the extended family.

Their oceanic crossings sometimes went in surprising directions. Homesick Fini had broken up with Paul (their divorce decree came in 1932) in order to raise Ronald in Germany. The war forced them to return to California for safety—but, after peace was restored, she didn't repatriate. She remained a Los Angeleno until her death in 2009 at age ninety-nine.

Living in Beverly Hills, she never remarried, but she was no loner. "I think she had lots of boyfriends," recalled her grandson Christopher. "She kept herself very trim and fit. In her mid-eighties, she had better legs than many girls I was dating."

Ronald, by most accounts the quietest of the brothers, graduated in 1951 from USC, where he studied business. Capitalizing on his German-language fluency, Paul sent him to Hamburg to run Veedol, Tidewater Oil's German subsidiary.

In 1964, in a church near Hamburg, thirty-four-year-old Ronald— six feet four, dark-haired, with a pencil mustache—said "Ja" when he married Karin Seibel, twenty-one, the blond daughter of a Lübeck businessman. They had met three years earlier at a ball in Hamburg— where the couple remained for a year following their wedding, and had Christopher, the first of their four children. English was Ronald's third language. After German, he learned French when the family relocated to Paris. Over the next decade, as the family moved back and forth between Europe, California, and South Africa, Karin gave birth to Stephanie, Cecilia, and Christina in, respectively, 1967, 1970, and 1975.

Thanks to his parents' acrimonious divorce and the wealth of his maternal grandfather, Ronald was virtually excluded from the Sarah C. Getty Trust (though his children are beneficiaries of it). The unforeseen loss of the Helmle fortune during the war put him on a considerably lower financial footing than his half brothers. But he was still a multimillionaire, thanks to gifts from his paternal grandmother, Sarah.

In the late 1960s and early 1970s, he executive-produced and financed a few movies, including *Flareup*, a thriller starring Raquel Welch, which was released by MGM, and Warner Bros.' *Zeppelin*, a World War I aerial spectacle starring Michael York and Elke Sommer. The films had respectable runs and generated a fair amount of buzz, thanks to their high-profile stars and the last name of the producer. But it was the pursuit of profit, not glamour, that motivated him to invest in movies, as the normally press-shy Ronald said in a few interviews he gave ahead of the October 1971 premiere of *Zeppelin*. He revealed little else. "I've been an avid moviegoer for many years. . . . I don't believe in following the crowd," he said in a sit-down with the *Los Angeles Times*, in which he was described as "unostentatious in manner."

In the early 1980s, he invested tens of millions into a large hotel development near Los Angeles International Airport. It was ill-timed, coinciding with the onset of a deep recession and a glut of newly built properties on the market. In order to keep the development afloat, Ronald personally guaranteed its debts. Nevertheless, the project went bust, after which creditors pursued him over the next decade, eventually leading him to file for bankruptcy in 1992 in San Juan, Puerto Rico, where he and Karin had moved. After they resolved their financial difficulties, the couple settled in Munich, Germany, where Ronald died at age eighty-one in 2010.

As a widow, Karin took up residency in America again, moving to Miami Beach, where her youngest daughter, Christina, resides. Meanwhile, Stephanie and Cecilia (who is called Cecily by family and friends) straddle the hemispheres: each divides her time between South Africa and various locations in Europe (England, Germany, Austria).

During his young adult years, Christopher lived in California, New York, Brazil, Russia, and England, among other places. A few years ago, he settled in Rome.

So, while some Gettys remain elusive due to their penchant for privacy, with others perhaps it's a factor of their peripatetic natures.

While they crisscross the globe, groupings of Gettys alight in certain places at certain times, such as the London "Season." Commencing in May with the opening of the Chelsea Flower Show, the Season's a succession of splendid events, including the Royal Ascot races and Wimbledon, that draws the beau monde to London.

The V&A Summer Party, held in the Victoria and Albert Museum's courtyard garden, is perhaps the Season's smartest invitation. The June 2019 edition, hosted by Nicholas Coleridge, head of Condé Nast Britain, drew a microcosm of England's elite, including former prime minister David Cameron, three dukes, four Windsors, Dame Joan Collins, Lord Andrew Lloyd Webber, singer Kylie Minogue, artist Grayson Perry, and actress Cressida Bonas (an ex of Prince Harry's). Among the Gettys in attendance: San Francisco–born Ivy Getty, twenty-four, Gordon's granddaughter (dashing around with American paper heir Peter Brant Jr.); Mark's middle son, Joseph, and his fashion-plate wife, Sabine (*Vogue* pronounced her elegant cream three-piece Yves Saint Laurent suit "ravishing"); and a Getty relation by marriage, Princess Marie-Chantal of Greece.

As readers of glossy magazines in the 1990s will recall, Marie-Chantal and her sisters, Pia and Alexandra—daughters of "duty-free" billionaire Robert Miller and his wife, Chantal—made the most brilliant marriages since the Cushing sisters some fifty years earlier.

Pia, the eldest, got to the altar first, with Christopher Getty. In 1992, they tied the knot on a mountaintop in Bali. Native attendants dressed the bride and groom in brightly colored sarongs and elaborate golden headpieces; Balinese tribesmen transported them on ornate litters up to the temple. Scores of children showered them with rose petals. One of the hundred friends and family members who attended the ceremony described it as a "fantasy production worthy of Cecil B. DeMille." (A minister from Boston conducted a quiet Christian-faith service beforehand.)

Three years hence, nearly every crowned head in Europe gathered in London for the wedding of Marie-Chantal to Crown Prince Pavlos of Greece—a critical mass of royals hardly seen since the wedding of Queen Elizabeth and Prince Philip, who were among the guests. The monumental festivities celebrating the union included a ball featuring a re-creation of the Parthenon.

Within a few months, Alexandra marched down the aisle with Prince Alexander Egon von Fürstenberg, scion of a thousand-year-old dynasty begun during the Holy Roman Empire, at Manhattan's St. Ignatius Loyola Church, where the pews were crammed with a good portion of the *Almanach de Gotha*.

As the 1990s unfolded, the young couples enlivened Manhattan society significantly. After Marie-Chantal threw a rollicking Roaring Twenties–themed party at the Cotton Club in Harlem to celebrate Pavlos's thirtieth, Pia one-upped her with a cross-dressing party for Christopher's next birthday, at their house in Southampton. The sisters, like most of the female guests, wore tuxedos and top hats, while the brothers-in-law transformed themselves into *la dolce vita* icons— Pavlos was Gina Lollobrigida and Christopher Anita Ekberg.

The elder two Miller sisters did not meet their Prince Charmings by chance. They were carefully matched up by longtime Getty family consigliere Alecko Papamarkou.

J. Paul Getty met him in the 1960s at Woburn Abbey, where both were guests of the Duke of Bedford. Papamarkou, then a young BBC Radio journalist, became a stockbroker, as well as a frequent visitor to Sutton Place, where he and Ann Getty hit it off on her visits from San Francisco. The Princeton-educated son of a Greek government minister, he became a close friend and investment advisor to the family. With his gregarious personality, he amassed an unrivaled list of friends in high places, becoming, in the words of writer and bon vivant Taki Theodoracopulos, a fellow Greek, "the Sir Edmund Hillary of social mountaineering." As Papamarkou invested his clients' money, he also enriched their social and personal lives. What good is having all the money in the world if you don't know how to spend it, or, worse, if nobody knows who you are? As lore has it, it was a teen-age Marie-Chantal who, having heard about Papamarkou, lobbied her father to hire him, which he did. He subsequently stood as her godfather when she converted from Catholicism to the Greek Ortho-dox religion before her marriage.

"Alecko was the ultimate connector—whether it was people's business or romantic lives," said Marie-Chantal. "He was great with the guys, he was great with the women, and he mixed together their children. He made sure people were connected."

According to Marc Leland, a financial advisor to Gordon Getty (who spoke before Papamarkou's death), "He manages to balance an enormous amount on the head of a pin. He is one of the few people who can talk everyone's language: money managers, major investors, socialites. . . ."

Christopher and Pia Getty—amicably divorced since 2005—were unable to make it to the V&A that evening in 2019 as they were making their way back from day two of Royal Ascot with the eldest of their four children, Isabel, an artist and musician who was born in 1993. The proud parents had viewed an artwork Royal Ascot com-missioned Isabel to create, or remake, as it were. She was asked to paint one of the benches along the track in the Royal Enclosure. Just above it sat the Queen, Prince Charles and the Duchess of Cornwall, and other members of the royal family. Isabel transformed the bench with crosshatching inspired by the forms and colors of Viennese Secessionists Egon Schiele and Gustav Klimt.

Per the strict rules for visitors to the Royal Enclosure, the Gettys were in regulation attire—top hat and morning coat for him; dresses "of modest length . . . with straps of one inch or greater" and fanci-ful hats for the ladies. A mass of violet-hued feathers extended from Isabel's bonnet.

The same week, Christopher attended a cocktail party in honor of

American supporters of Prince Charles's charities at Clarence House, official residence of the Prince of Wales and the Duchess of Cornwall. Square-jawed and wearing horn-rimmed glasses, he was handsome and affable, chatting about his new apartment in Rome.

That weekend, an exhibition of photographs by Nick Knight opened at Albion Barn in Oxfordshire. Afterward gallerist Michael Hue-Williams hosted a lively lunch on the bucolic grounds for a fashionable group. Isabel was among them, now clad in a fringed suede jacket, jeans, and biker boots.

Born in New York City, where she spent her early childhood in her parents' six-story townhouse on the Upper East Side, she's a picture of transatlantic poise. "To my English friends, I'm a foreign friend. To my American friends, I'm English," she said. At age eight, around the time her parents separated, Isabel moved with her mother to London; enrolled first at Harrodian, she later boarded in Switzerland at Le Rosey, Pia's alma mater, where she was a member of the choir and the school band. For college it was back to the States. Isabel arrived at New York University thinking she should study law or business, but music, she decided, made her happiest. She transferred to NYU's Clive Davis Institute of Recorded Music. But despite her boarding-school vocalizing, the idea of performing solo frightened her. Of all people, it was Diana Ross who helped her get over her stage fright. It was May 2013, at Farmington Lodge, Marie-Chantal and Pavlos's eighteenth-century manor house in England's Cotswolds, where four hundred guests had gathered to celebrate her maternal grandfather's eightieth birthday. At one point, Ross, the gala's entertainer, pulled Isabel onstage. *It's Diana Ross passing you the mike—you better bloody sing,* she remembers thinking to herself in panic. Isabel deftly belted some classic Supremes lines. "It was pretty epic," she recalled.

After graduating from NYU in 2016, she moved back to London, celebrating with a *Midsummer Night's Dream* theme party for three hundred friends at One Marylebone (she went as a fairy in a gold Oscar de la Renta gown), and temporarily reclaiming her room in her mother's Knightsbridge mansion. Pia, who is regarded as the bohemian one among her sisters, had just launched a film production company, Pia Pressure, which aims to support emerging talent—particularly female—from underrepresented backgrounds. Toward that goal, Pia (who has directed multiple documentaries) created the Pia Pressure Award. That year, it was bestowed on two young British filmmakers—Johnny Kenton and Debs Paterson—who each received a $35,000 grant.

That fall, Isabel landed on the cover of *Tatler*, wearing a silk-velvet coat by Etro ("The Heiress: Glamour, Talent, Two Fortunes . . . Yes, Isabel Getty Has It All," read the cover lines), and then on Dolce & Gabbana's runway in Milan, where she walked in the designers' Fall/Winter 2017 show.

With two friends—Ali on guitar and James on keys—she formed a band, Jean Marlow. (Its first name was a nod to actress Jean Harlow, the last to sixteenth-century English poet Christopher Marlowe.) Isabel identified herself—the group's singer-songwriter—as Izzy Getty. "I still had terrible stage fright. It's easier—there is more freedom—in going by another name. I liked the concept of creating this other persona when I go onstage." Getty's voice is soft, slightly raspy; the band has a soulful, grunge, soft-rock sound. "We're die-hard acoustic musicians," said Isabel. On Spotify and iTunes, they have released several EPs, with titles including "Spin" and "Run Leon," for which she drew the album art. In 2020, following a stay in Los Angeles, where Isabel had retreated during the lockdown months, the group released "Santana Winds," a hypnotic ballad inspired by Southern California's fierce and sometimes evil autumn winds.

"There was so much destruction going on," she recalled a year later, by phone from Gstaad, Switzerland. By this time, things were considerably brighter. Working remotely, she had been helping her father manage real estate investments, primarily in Germany and Portugal. She had just returned from Mykonos in Greece, where she and her South African–reared cousin Vanessa Waibel staged a high-spirited bachelorette weekend for their San Francisco relation Ivy Getty. Photos of the girls—at one point in matching pink hot pants, dancing stageside at Jackie O', the fashionable beach club— splashed across Instagram and the *Daily Mail*. (Ivy's elaborate wedding that November would draw much coverage too.)

"They are like sisters—we grew up together," Isabel said of Vanessa and Ivy. (Living thousands of miles apart is no hindrance in this family.) "I'm very close to a lot of my cousins. . . . I feel very fortunate—a lot of people don't get along with their families."

Isabel acknowledged that her family has had its troubles. But she puts them in perspective. "Everyone has tragedies in their families. It's just that ours have been more public. There has been a lot of suffering, but that's why it's important to stay grounded and together."

That September, Isabel moved back to New York to study for her MBA at Columbia Business School, while simultaneously pursuing her musical career. "I've always followed my own path. I don't like to be dependent on anyone," she said. "I want to make my own way."

Christopher is not the first Getty to reside in Rome. "This is where my grandfather would spend the winters. He felt very happy here," he said. It was during those stays that J. Paul Getty visited the Capitoline Museums and became inspired to found his museum in Malibu. "This classical civilization, this humanist tradition, is what they aspired to," Christopher said, referencing also his paternal great-grandparents. "They were austere Scottish peasants who hooked into this worldview."

The city continues to cast its spell on their descendants. Aside from the obvious charm of Roman life, Christopher said he also enjoyed the disorder endemic to it. "They give you just the right amount of grit," he said.

He was eleven when his grandfather passed away, but memories endure. "Sutton Place was the most fun place in the world," he recalled. Every night before dinner, they would watch the lions being fed. Family meals were punctuated by amusing banter about which truants might be thrown to the beasts. There was a golf buggy he could sneak off with, to tear around the grounds. But once, as he was plowing through the prized rose garden, he looked up at the house and saw his grandfather staring down from a window. That night at dinner, not a word was said about it, surprisingly. But the next morning, when Christopher jumped into the buggy for another spin, the battery had been removed.

"That was him," he said. "I remember him as a very calm man. He was not a shouter. He was very easy—easier than many grandfathers I've come across. That was my view as a child, and sometimes a child has the best view."

The world's richest man was "almost a bit of a hippie," he added. "He could have been a beachcomber . . . he was never part of the Establishment . . . he was not a mainstream character."

The tougher one was Grandmother Fini, who, he noted, remained true to her Germanic stock till the end: "She didn't have any sense of humor!"

Christopher's middle son, Conrad, a graduate of Harrow in England, was attending Berkeley, where he was excelling in math—a first for a Getty, Christopher claimed—as well as physics, which was a subject Conrad's great-uncle Gordon enjoyed discussing with him during their weekly dinners at Gordon's mansion in Pacific Heights.

While his youngest, Max (short for Maximus), is an undergraduate at NYU, the eldest son, Robert ("Bob"), is a budding filmmaker. He has directed several short movies, including a horror flick, *Unbaptism*, in which two priests find themselves trapped by evil when they arrive at a remote house to investigate paranormal activity, and *Untitled Chat Show*, a comedy about a failed talk show pilot in 1978 (which carries a credit for Pia Miller in the role of "hippie").

"They're all coming along nicely," Christopher observed of his offspring. He expressed the same sentiment about the close-knit cousinage to which they belong. (Marie-Chantal and Pavlos have five children; Alexandra and Alexander, who were divorced in 2002, have three.) "They're all good kids . . . they run in a pack," he said. All of them attended the lavish ball that Marie-Chantal and Pavlos threw in 2017 for the twenty-first birthday of Princess Olympia, their eldest. Held at Farmington Lodge, it drew a stunning assortment of the royal, the rich, the young, and the beautiful. It was "the party that had everything," the *Daily Mail* reported.

Even as perceptions persist that the clan is riven with strife and factions, the reality, according to Christopher, is different. "Everyone is interested in what other people are doing, and wishing them well," he said.

Members communicate over joint investments too. Christopher was among the founding investors in some of the family's marquee ventures, including Conservation Corporation Africa, Getty Images, and PlumpJack, which began with a small wine store in San Francisco and now produces some of the best Cabernet Sauvignon in the world. "I was the first investor," he said, as he ordered a bottle of excellent Amarone.

A talent for viniculture runs in the family. Christopher's middle sisters, Stephanie Getty-Waibel and Cecilia Getty-du Preez, produce some of South Africa's most internationally lauded bottles, alongside their respective husbands, Alexander Waibel and Pierre du Preez.

Considering their avocation, it's not surprising that a friend of the women used wine vocabulary to describe them—as well as their youngest sibling, Christina: "The girls are all very bubbly and attractive. At first blush, they might seem like dizzy blondes, but they all have depth."

Both the Getty-Waibels and the Getty-du Preezes divide their time between Europe and South Africa's Constantia Valley, where they own adjacent wine-growing estates located on the mountainous slopes overlooking Cape Town and its breathtaking bay.

Alexander Waibel's family history in South Africa goes back to 1950, when his maternal grandfather, Dr. Manfred Thurnher, relocated operations of BMD, the enormous textile business begun by his wife's family, from their native Austria. The reins of the company eventually passed to Manfred's son-in-law, Dieter Waibel, who had five children with Manfred's daughter Rosemarie. Alexander was the firstborn.

In the 1960s, the Cape Town region became a second home for the family when they purchased their 150-acre estate in the valley, where they built country houses and enjoyed rustic life. In fact, the land had been farmed for grapes by Dutch settlers beginning in 1680. Then the acreage was left to lie fallow for centuries.

In the late 1990s, after a mountain fire devastated much of the landscape, Dieter, a lover of Bordeaux wines, hatched the idea to bring the land back to its earlier function. Alexander and Stephanie joined the venture.

It was a mammoth undertaking to clear the ravaged land and plant their vineyards on the steep slopes. Their inaugural Sauvignon Blanc was released in 2007; sales of reds began three years later. When Alexander took over the operation, he and Stephanie stuck faithfully to his late father's vision of creating world-class Bordeaux-style wines. Under their label, Constantia Glen, four premium wines are produced: two reds (Constantia Glen Three and Constantia Glen Five) and two whites (Constantia Glen Sauvignon Blanc and Constantia Glen Two). The numerals reflect the number of Bordeaux varieties in each blend.

With their three daughters—Marietheres, Sigourney, and Vanessa—the Waibels could be a wine dynasty in the making (there is a strong tradition of matrilineal succession in this branch of the family). "They . . . will be the true beneficiaries of what we were doing," said

Alexander, referring to his offspring as well as future generations. "Perhaps they will nod and remark that we knew what we were doing."

Mousy, as their eldest is called, started stomping grapes and pitching in on the farm at the age of ten. Now, on the verge of thirty, she's Constantia Glen's export manager. "I watched Constantia Glen grow from an idea to something bigger," she wrote in a Facebook post. "The fact that I could be part of that process makes me so proud and happy to still be involved in the farm today." Sigourney, meanwhile, is studying for her doctorate in neurotechnology at Imperial College London.

In 2000, another devastating fire swept through the area, and from its ashes sprang Beau Constantia, a vineyard created by Stephanie's sister and brother-in-law.

Coming from a Sunday lunch at Stephanie and Alexander's, Cecilia and Pierre, a South African–born investment banker, noticed a FOR SALE sign on a burnt-out goat farm—a property on even steeper slopes.

They planted vineyards over the 55 acres they acquired, on which they built a modern glass and concrete home, for themselves and their daughter, Lucca, and son, Aidan, born in the first years of the new millennium. They have literally produced a family of wines: Cecily, their Viognier, debuted in 2010 (it received a very respectable 92 points from wine authority Robert Parker). The portfolio grew to include Pierre, a Sauvignon Blanc; Lucca, a Merlot/Cabernet Franc blend; and Aidan, a spicy red blend of 35 percent Shiraz, 23 percent Malbec, 23 percent Petit Verdot, and 19 percent Merlot. In memory of Pierre's mother, there is also Stella, a Shiraz, while Karin, a Blanc de Noir, celebrates Cecilia's German-born Floridian mother.

After the death of her husband, Ronald, in 2010, Karin moved to Miami Beach, where her youngest, Christina, has lived since her wedding in 2002 to investor Arin Maercks, with whom she had three children before their divorce around 2013. An attentive grand-mother, Karin has taken well to the South Beach lifestyle, according to one Miamian, who described her as "a live wire." The apple hasn't fallen far from the tree. "She's the life of the party," said another local of Christina. "She has a big personality. But she's down-to-earth too. She doesn't have the airs of someone who grew up in Europe. She's not stuffy."

Given her outgoing character, Miami is an appropriate place for her. "Her impact here is being 'the Miami Getty.' San Francisco is full of Gettys, but she's our only one. Though ninety-nine percent of Miami doesn't know what a Getty is," said a resident.

Along with her fiancé, Juan Pablo Cappello, a Chilean-born law-yer and tech entrepreneur who is the father of three girls, Christina is a cofounder and investor in NUE Life Health, a business start-up that will use psychedelic drugs such as ketamine to treat mental illness. "With one in five women in the United States relying on an anti-depressant to get through the day, and with our losing twenty-two veterans a day to suicide, we felt compelled to launch a different kind of mental wellness company," Christina said.

A supporter of worthy institutions such as the Bass Museum of Art and Nicklaus Children's Hospital, Christina is a regular at char-ity events. She also sends out, biennially, one of South Florida's most coveted invitations—to her "Bad Santa" party, which she usually throws at her house on Sunset Island (where neighbors have included Enrique Iglesias and Lenny Kravitz). In 2018, it outgrew the prem-ises; Christina and Juan Pablo transferred the party to Soho Beach House Miami. Traditionally, the party has been a good-natured exer-cise in flouting the boundaries of taste, with strippers, dancers, Play-boy Bunnies, and bawdy Christmas tree ornaments—"pornaments," as one guest called them.

"It's something we all look forward to," said one prominent Miamian. "It's all in good fun. She just wants her friends to enjoy themselves. She could care less if anybody thinks it's in bad taste. She doesn't care about impressing people."

That outlook, according to someone who knows a variety of Gettys, is a hallmark of the family: "They don't give a fuck about what other people think of them. They're not snobs and they don't think in terms of something being 'correct' or 'incorrect.' In a weird way, they are liberated from that paradigm."

III.

THE PAULS

5

Paul Jr.

Born at sea in 1932, J. Paul Getty Jr. was brought up first in Los Angeles. Around 1945, as he entered his teenage years, he moved to San Francisco. His mother, the madcap Ann, and her fourth husband, attorney Joseph Stanton McInerney, settled Paul and his brother Gordon—fifteen months Paul's junior—into a rambling house on Clay Street. But perhaps *settled* is a word that never applied to the young Gettys. Within a few years, McInerney was gone, and sometimes their gregarious, artistically inclined mother was absent as well, leaving the boys—the only full siblings born to J. Paul Getty—to their own devices. "They were raised by a mother who wasn't always available," recalled Bill Newsom III, their St. Ignatius High School classmate and lifelong best friend.

Paul Jr. was considered the best-looking and most charming of all the Getty brothers. Tall and thin, wearing horn-rimmed glasses, he liked music and literature, which he studied at the University of San Francisco before his army service in Seoul during the Korean War. Abigail Harris, whom he married in January 1956 in a modest ceremony at Our Lady of the Wayside Church on the San Francisco Peninsula, was the outgoing one. Pretty and athletic, Gail was the adored only child of a federal judge. The pair had known each other since childhood, when she attended the Convent of the Sacred Heart; they were sweethearts during her years at Dominican College in Marin County. From the start of their marriage, she tried to curb her husband's drinking. "Paul had been grounded by Gail in the cause of temperance," Bill Newsom remembered about the young couple, who set up housekeeping in Marin County, where they had their first child, J. Paul Getty III, in November 1956.

Everything changed when the young Californians landed in Rome in 1958, just as Federico Fellini began preproduction for *La Dolce Vita*, which would immortalize the decadent, ravishing world of the ancient capital in its postwar years when it was released in 1960.

They had been summoned to Italy by the patriarch, in order for Paul Jr. to begin working at Getty Oil Italiana. But by 1964 the younger Getty had lost interest in business. He began to embrace the counterculture movement—complete with long hair, beard, and a hippie wardrobe that exasperated his father. And the couple had drifted apart. Gail had fallen in love with Lang Jeffries, a handsome American actor who had come to Rome to shoot a television show. (Gail and Lang were married in Rome in 1966, and divorced five years later.)

Though Paul was saddened, their separation was amicable. Bill Willis, a handsome, lanky, gay Tennessean, heard a knock on the door of the antiques emporium he'd opened at the top of the Spanish Steps in the early 1960s. "I'm Paul Getty Junior and this is my wife, Gail," the oil heir said cheerfully. "I'm looking for an apartment for her, because we're separating."

Gail wanted no alimony, but things were more complicated when it came to ironing out details of financial support for their four small children—Paul III, Mark, Aileen, and Ariadne. To figure it out, Paul Jr. and Gail asked Bill Newsom to journey to Rome from San Francisco. Bill—who was also Paul III's godfather—had just graduated from Stanford Law School and become an associate at Lillick,

Geary, Wheat, Adams & Charles. Now he had to choose between staying at the law firm or coming to Rome.

He never regretted his decision to resign. "I saw the world and really got around and had a marvelous time," Newsom said in a series of oral history interviews he recorded in 2008 and 2009 for the Bancroft Library of the University of California, Berkeley. During his several months in Rome, he recalled meeting "some crazy interesting people," such as writer Gore Vidal, and "a lot of freakish people," including the circle of actors around Fellini. "I'm glad I didn't stay at Lillick, Wheat," he said.

The business of negotiating the settlement was resolved pretty easily, on the backs of a few envelopes, over some pleasant dinners. Coming up with rational numbers was challenging, though. Paul's annual trust income was then just $56,000 after taxes. But calculating a sliding-scale percentage of the income he would one day inherit, the figures became "astronomical."

Gail remained a frequent visitor to Sutton Place and in high standing with her former father-in-law: *I am very pleased with Gail and her children,* wrote Paul Sr. in his journal. And on other occasions: *Gail and Paul, Mark, Aileen, and Ariadne arr at 6 from Rome. I admire them. We pass time happily. I am proud of my darlings.*

On a trip to England in 1965, Paul Jr., then thirty-three, met Talitha Pol. She had been born twenty-five years earlier in Java, where her Dutch parents, Willem and Adine Pol, were traveling. When the Nazis invaded the Netherlands, the couple were unable to return home. In Bali, where they sought refuge, they were captured by the Japanese and interned in atrocious prisoner-of-war camps. After their release, Adine died in 1948. Willem then married Poppet John, daughter of the Welsh postimpressionist painter Augustus John.

Poppet was a warm stepmother as Talitha grew up in the family's homes in London and Ramatuelle, in the South of France. Talitha's beauty—almond eyes, alabaster skin, and red-gold hair—blossomed. But people sensed a fragile, wounded quality in her.

After studying acting and dance at the Royal Academy of Dramatic Art, she landed a few parts. She was an extra—one of the thousands—in *Cleopatra* (1963) and had a credible role in Michael Winner's drama *The System* (1964).

About town in London, people were enthralled with Talitha. "Everyone fell in love with her," tastemaker Nicky Haslam recalled.

Talitha even transfixed men not normally attracted to women. She was the only woman who ever "erotically stirred" Rudolf Nureyev. According to the legendary dancer's biographer, Julie Kavanagh, he told several friends he wanted to marry Talitha. "What he was actually seeing was an exquisite, androgynous reflection of himself," Kavanagh wrote.

It was thanks to Nureyev that Talitha and Paul Jr. met, at a dinner party in London hosted by Claus von Bülow, right-hand man to Paul Jr.'s father. When Nureyev couldn't make it at the last minute, von Bülow filled his seat with Paul Jr.—who was instantly smitten by Talitha. Their wedding, a year later in Rome, took place in the same damask-lined room inside the Palazzo Senatorio, atop the Campidoglio, where Gail had married Lang four months before and where Paul's father had married Teddy three decades previously. Talitha wore a white hooded minidress trimmed in mink and carried a white lily, a symbol of purity and commitment; Paul, in a dark suit, sported a silk tie with a large lily printed on it. (Six months earlier, von Bülow himself had headed to the altar, with the former Martha "Sunny" Crawford. Two decades later, when he was on trial for attempting to murder her in Newport, Rhode Island, Getty provided him with millions for his bail and defense costs.)

Bill Newsom recalled his first encounter with Talitha, in the terraced penthouse she and Paul Jr. had moved into in one of Rome's most ancient quarters:

"They had a beautiful place on the fifth story in a narrow, narrow sixteenth-century building. I arrived there and there was a canary out of a cage and Talitha . . . shushed me and said, 'Quiet.' And for the next five minutes crawled around in a skimpy costume, very skimpy indeed. A bikini or something. And crawled around trying to trap the canary and finally did it. And then only after that did everybody say hello.

"She was perhaps the most beautiful woman I've ever seen. That sounds extravagant. Put it this way: I've never seen a better-looking woman. And she was very, very nice. A lovely woman."

Newsom's new acquaintances also included Getty's close friend Alessandro Ruspoli. "A strange, strange fellow. An older man with a teenage wife and a lot of rich stories about them," the lawyer recalled.

Dado, as this gentleman was called by his legion of friends and admirers, was born to a plethora of hereditary titles. To name a few, he was 9th Prince of Cerveteri, 9th Marquis of Riano, and 14th Count of Vignanello. He was also, it was widely believed, the inspiration for the lead character in Fellini's 1960 film *La Dolce Vita*, played by Marcello Mastroianni.

Reared in his family's stupendous palazzo on the Via del Corso and at their massive, moated castle in Lazio that dates back to 847, he bestrode many worlds. While respecting the strict codes of the "black aristocracy"—nobles historically aligned with the pope, particularly in an 1870 conflict—from which his family descended, with its lineage of saints, popes, and warriors, Dado glided stylishly through café society, the culturati, and the opium dens of the Far East, where he also was a student of yoga, transcendentalism, and the occult. (Orson Welles gave him lessons in hypnotism.)

At one point, Ruspoli shared a villa on the Côte d'Azur with director Roger Vadim and Jane Fonda, where Paul Jr. and Talitha were guests. Fonda described the group as "some of the most decadent types I'd ever met—lovely, charming and sensual." From Dado's three marriages and another relationship, he produced five children, one of whom, Bartolomeo, later married Paul Jr.'s daughter Aileen.

"Dado was the best-looking man of his generation, the ultimate prince-intellectual," recalls his friend Taki. "He was extremely well-read, poetic, a big seducer."

Bill Willis, who became great friends with Paul Jr. and Talitha, not only planned the couple's honeymoon in Morocco, he tagged along. When it was over, "none of us wanted to leave," Willis recalled. Perhaps it was he who located the Palais de la Zahia, built in the pink-walled city of Marrakech centuries before by the ruling pashas. Its sumptuous days were long gone—it was then a maze of disheveled rooms, courtyards, terraces, and gardens—but Paul decided it would make a good wedding present for his bride, and that Bill could fix it up for them.

Willis, who had studied briefly at both Columbia University and Stella Adler's acting school in New York, was yet another American who sailed to Europe with dreams. "Bill yearned for civilization," influential antiques dealer Christopher Gibbs said. In Morocco, he found his calling. La Zahia was soon magically restored at his hands, its rooms faced in *zellige* (glittering, richly patterned mosaic tiles) and *tadelakt* (glazed and pigmented plaster).

Zahia means "pleasure" in Berber. Now the palace was living up to its name again. Up and running, it was imbued with that splendid combination of decadence and efficiency that only the very rich can pull off. "There was a marvelous secretary," remembered a woman who lived in a neighboring house. "She ran the house with such precision, at the same time she'd also be there cutting up hash cakes for us all. There was hash for the novices, opium for the advanced."

La Zahia was only used for holidays, though. Home was still the couple's penthouse in Rome, now filled with many treasures from their frequent travels to Thailand and elsewhere in Asia. It was on these trips that the couple descended deeper into drugs.

La Zahia became the ultimate destination for haute hippies and some of the singular people of the era. The Gettys' guests included the Doors' Jim Morrison and his girlfriend Pamela Courson, Yves Saint Laurent and Pierre Bergé, writers William S. Burroughs and Gore Vidal, director Michelangelo Antonioni, and Marlon Brando, who stayed for months. Paul and Talitha's "One Thousand and One Nights" parties sometimes carried on for days.

For the Rolling Stones, it was practically a home away from home. In the mid- to late sixties, Morocco was to them what India was to the Beatles. While John, Paul, George, and Ringo ventured to the ashram of the Maharishi Mahesh Yogi in Rishikesh, Mick, Keith, and Brian gravitated to La Zahia, burnishing its legend.

Brian Jones arrived first, with his girlfriend Anita Pallenberg, a German-Italian force of nature who had grown up in Rome. Keith Richards and Mick Jagger followed. The stoned Stones found bliss at La Zahia. "We would climb up on the roof, where we could see the snowy mountains above and the garden below, full of palm trees, squawking birds, and fish in tanks," recalled Gibbs, their close companion. Paul and Talitha "had the best and finest opium," wrote Keith. "We enjoyed being transported."

Paul and Talitha were catalytic figures within a circle of remarkable people. But who met who first? Paul and Anita knew each other as youngsters in Rome; through her boyfriend, the avant-garde painter Mario Schifano, she got the jump on meeting the most celebrated people of the day, including the two pivotal figures who arguably invented "Swinging London"—Gibbs, and his great mate Robert Fraser. Tastemakers extraordinaire, both were gay, drug-toting, Eton-educated, upper-class rebels. Anybody really cool in town, including the Beatles and the Stones, as well as artists visiting from New York and Los Angeles, hung out in Mayfair at Fraser's art gallery and flat, and in Chelsea at Gibbs's shop and his apartment on Cheyne Walk.

And who found which drugs first? Willis was the discoverer of cocaine; he turned Fraser on to it, who in turn introduced the Stones and the Beatles to it. When it came to LSD, Fraser led the way. "Robert was your gentleman junkie," said Richards. "With Robert, it was always the crème de la crème, it was pure."

Fraser, whom Paul Jr. called "an icon of his time . . . the most infuriating friend I've ever had," turned everybody on to the new movements in art—pop art, particularly—which galvanized their creativity. "He was the best art eye I've ever met," said Paul McCartney in *Groovy Bob: The Life and Times of Robert Fraser*, by Harriet Vyner.

In the late 1960s, this group, through their combustible, often drug-fueled interactions, helped usher in a new era of social liberation. They led the way in breaking down the class barriers and distinctions that had long stood, particularly in England. A key ingredient in this new social mobility was music, and musicians.

"Suddenly we were being courted by half of the aristocracy," Richards recalled in his autobiography, *Life*. "I've never known if they were slumming or if we were snobbing. They were very nice people. I decided it was no skin off my nose. If somebody's interested, they're welcome. . . .

"It was the first time I know of when that lot actively sought out musicians in such large numbers. They realized there was something blowin' in the wind, to quote Bob [Dylan]. . . . They felt they were being left out of things if they didn't join in. So, there was this weird mixture of aristos and gangsters, the fascination that the higher end of society had with the more brutish end. . . . The rough mixed with the smooth."

A key figure in it was snappy young Tara Browne, a son of Dominick, the 4th Baron Oranmore and Browne, who sat in the House of Lords, and the fabulously wealthy brewing heiress Oonagh Guinness.

Guinnesses and Gettys—scions of beer and oil fortunes—could relate well to one another. Over generations, addictions and tragedies have plagued both of these astronomically rich, accomplished, and eccentric dynasties.

While still a teenager, the precocious Tara socialized with Truman Capote, Salvador Dalí, Samuel Beckett, Jean Cocteau, Lucian Freud, John Huston, and Humphrey Bogart as well as Jimi Hendrix, David Bowie, the Stones, and the Beatles. (Paul McCartney dropped acid for the first time in his London townhouse.)

"Tara was absolutely central to it," said Jane Ormsby-Gore, daughter of the 5th Baron Harlech, about the contemporary scene. "We were meeting people from different walks of life, but we needed someone in the middle saying, 'Oh, so-and-so, have you met such and such?' And that was what Tara did."

Tara's twenty-first birthday, in March 1966 at Luggala, his mother's glorious 5,000-acre estate in County Wicklow, Ireland, drew two hundred of Britain's brightest young things, including most of the above named (and the Lovin' Spoonful, who performed). A photograph of Paul, Talitha, Bill Willis, Anita Pallenberg, Brian Jones, and Tara on the emerald mountaintop, with silvery Lough Tay far below, shows them bursting with glee, and stoned out of their minds, as the wind howled. It was a defining moment.

One evening around midnight a few months later, the Lotus Elan convertible that Tara was behind the wheel of smashed into another vehicle in London. Shortly afterward, at home in his country house, John Lennon read the coroner's report in the *Daily Mail*. He sat down at his piano and began writing "A Day in the Life":

> *I read the news today, oh boy*
> *About a lucky man who made the grade . . .*
> *He blew his mind out in a car*
> *He didn't notice that the lights had changed*
> *Nobody was really sure if he was from the House of Lords . . .*

It was the final song on what has been called the band's greatest creative achievement and the best album of all time, *Sgt. Pepper's Lonely Hearts Club Band*, which was released in May 1967 with a cover art-directed by Fraser.

In the view of many of those who knew him, Tara Browne's death augured a sea change.

"It was like a death knell sounding all over London," said Marianne Faithfull in *I Read the News Today, Oh Boy*, a biography of Browne by Paul Howard.

The good vibes—the freewheeling, optimistic, sunnier, London-centric portion of the sixties—gave way to an American-driven youth culture, which was darkened by Vietnam, Charles Manson, Altamont, assassinations, and the really destructive kind of drug usage.

Earlier in 1967, a police raid at Redlands, Keith Richards's house in England, left him, Mick, and Fraser facing serious drug charges as well as a hostile press. They bolted to Morocco. Brian and Anita joined them. En route, she fell into Keith's arms, the start of their twelve-year relationship; while tripping on LSD, they all ran into Cecil Beaton, who photographed them, and then came along to the Gettys'. "While watching the native dancers, Mick was convulsed by the rhythm, every fiber of his body responding to the intricacies," Beaton wrote in his diary.

Brian was captivated by Berber music, full of chanting and complex percussive rhythms. After he found a large troupe from the Gnawa tribe in the Atlas Mountains, Paul invited them all to come to dinner and to perform in Zahia's banquet hall. But Brian was so stoned for most of his stay he barely got out of bed; then, enraged after a fight with Anita, he ripped out La Zahia's one phone line.

The celebration Paul and Talitha threw to usher in 1968 was particularly epic. It drew Stones and Beatles. "Paul McCartney and John Lennon were there, flat on their backs. They couldn't get off the floor, let alone talk. I've never seen so many people out of control," the American writer John Hopkins recorded in his diary on January 1.

That May, Talitha, then twenty-seven, gave birth to the couple's son, whom they christened Tara Gabriel Galaxy Gramophone Getty. It was the Age of Aquarius, but the name still elicited chuckles worldwide. "Rich Kid with Silly Name," ran a headline in the *San Francisco Examiner.* In the story underneath, Talitha explained: "Every name has a precise significance and my son will be very proud of them when he grows up. Tara is an Irish aristocratic name; Galaxy means galaxy and he was born under the stars. He will be undoubtedly fond of music so we named him Gramaphone [*sic*]." (His first name was an homage to Tara Browne, who was also the namesake of Tara Richards, Keith and Anita's third child, who died in infancy.)

In October, Talitha appeared in an uncredited cameo in *Barbarella*, the camp sci-fi sensation directed by Vadim, starring Fonda, and featuring Pallenberg in the role of "the Great Tyrant."

In 1969, *Vogue* dispatched a team to La Zahia, including photographer Patrick Lichfield, a cousin of Queen Elizabeth's. "During their brief Moroccan vacations the Gettys' house comes sensuously alive," *Vogue* reported. "Orangewood burning . . . music of Strauss, Wagner, The Beatles . . . cushions embroidered a century ago by Christian slaves in Essaouira . . . dancers, acrobats, storytellers, geomancers, and magicians . . . never fewer than fifteen or twenty for dinner . . . by the light of candles ('the shadows have to be alive') among roses wound with mint and pyramids of tuberoses. While Salome is playing in the background, snake charmers charm and tea boys dance, balancing on their feet trays freighted with mint tea and burning candles."

Nothing secured the couple's mythic stature more than the picture that Lichfield shot on the roof; it became one of most iconic photographs of the twentieth century—an image seemingly no fashion designer since has not tacked onto his or her mood board. With the minaret in the distance and the sky darkening, Talitha crouches in the foreground, clad in a vibrant coat over white harem pants and boots, rings on every finger. Paul Jr. lurks in the background, brooding in a hooded sand-colored djellaba, out of which he peers inscrutably.

That's the take from the portrait session that has been most widely reproduced (licensed by Getty Images). The shot that *Vogue* actually ran in the January 1970 issue is markedly different: he is in the foreground, standing next to Talitha, smiling broadly and wearing a hoodless and very colorful printed silk robe.

But the portrait is really about her. It captured her look—her bohemian chic and posh-hippie style; her extravagant eclecticism, with its mix of couture pieces and ethnic finds, which has become an essential reference point for innumerable fashion designers in the last half century.

As the January *Vogue* hit the stands, Talitha and Paul were spiraling further downward due to their drug addictions. They separated, and Talitha embraced sobriety back in London, where she and infant Tara moved into a house that Paul Jr. acquired on Cheyne Walk, along the Thames. Queen's House, as it was called, was built in 1707 and had a haunted, romantic aura.

In July 1971, she flew to Rome to talk things over with Paul Jr. Paul woke up in the apartment one morning to find Talitha unresponsive. Cardiac arrest was listed as the cause of death, but, according to most media reports, she died of a heroin overdose. She was thirty years old. (In the months just before and after her death, Jim Morrison, Janis Joplin, Jimi Hendrix, and Edie Sedgwick would self-destruct as well.)

Talitha and Paul's impact on style has been strong and enduring.

In 1967, when thirty-one-year-old Yves Saint Laurent first met her in Morocco, the youthquake that had shaken London had yet to hit Paris; couture still maintained a certain rigidity.

He was enthralled by Talitha's air of sexual freedom, the easy, fluid movement of her body; he had never seen anything like her. "My vision completely changed," he said, after her death.

Both he and Pierre Bergé were then still "terribly square," Thadée

Klossowski, a member of YSL's inner circle, told author Alicia Drake in her book *The Beautiful Fall.* "Yves was shocked and immensely titillated."

In 1983, when Diana Vreeland mounted her landmark Yves Saint Laurent show at the Metropolitan Museum in New York, the first exhibition the institution had ever devoted to a living fashion designer, Saint Laurent paid homage to Talitha and Paul in his catalog essay:

"Like F. Scott Fitzgerald, I love a dying frenzy. . . . Decadence attracts me. It suggests a new world. . . . In my own life, I've seen the last afterglow of the sumptuous Paris of before the war. . . . And then I knew the youthfulness of the sixties: Talitha and Paul Getty lying on a starlit terrace in Marrakech, beautiful and damned, and a whole generation assembled as if for eternity where the curtain of the past seemed to lift before an extraordinary future."

The fascination has only continued. "Forty-six years later, we still seek to emulate her mysterious allure," *Vogue* observed recently.

In addition to altering the direction of fashion, these Gettys put their stamp on interior design. Yves and Pierre were so captivated by La Zahia that they bought properties in Marrakech and asked Bill Willis to decorate them: Dar es Saada ("House of Happiness," in Arabic) and then Villa Oasis (on which Willis collaborated with Jacques Grange, the eminent Paris decorator). Willis became a revered figure in Marrakech, where he remained until his death in 2009 at age seventy-two. He worked his magic there for a very select list of clients—Marella Agnelli, Marie-Hélène de Rothschild, and a few other grandees. While his name never became widely known—something to do with his relatively small body of work along with his love of cocaine and his willfulness—his influence traveled far: the international style-setters who visited his clients' houses were paying close attention.

"Bill created the Marrakech look, and it started with that house," said Grange, referring to La Zahia.

According to Bergé, Moroccan history can be divided into two epochs: "'Before' and 'after' Bill Willis," as he wrote in his foreword to *Bill Willis*, a 2011 monograph written by Marian McEvoy. "Today there is not a single Moroccan house that does not owe something to him. He became a tireless student of Morocco, laying bare the country's soul like almost no one else."

(La Zahia has belonged to French *intellectuel engagé* Bernard-Henri Lévy since 1998, when he bought it from actor Alain Delon.)

Following Talitha's death, J. Paul Getty Jr. withdrew from the world. Debilitated by addictions, depression, and a growing list of physical ailments, he secluded himself on Cheyne Walk, when he wasn't checked into the private London Clinic. When Paul III was kidnapped in 1973, and when the young man suffered his stroke eight years later and required expensive care, Paul Jr. was so enfeebled that he couldn't deal with his responsibilities. The ever-valiant Gail held everyone together. She moved into Queen's House with Paul for a time, while the three younger children went to schools in England.

After the death of his father in 1976 and the 1984 sale of Getty Oil, Paul was not just another peculiar, reclusive invalid: he was a filthy-rich one. As he struggled to regain his health, much of the time still at the London Clinic, he began making donations of all stripes, large and small. He sent checks to battered women's shelters, striking coal miners, a down-on-his-luck concert pianist. He sent his Bentley to the north of England to pick up a cat burglar's dog made homeless after its owner was sent to prison. Much of the giving was done very quietly.

But in 1985 Great Britain collectively gasped at the news that he had given £50 million to the National Gallery. Other gigantic gifts followed: £20 million pounds to the British Film Institute; £5 million to St. Paul's Cathedral, the masterpiece of Sir Christopher Wren.

Paul made a number of other gifts that enabled important works of art to remain in Britain, out of the clutches of wealthy foreign collectors and museums—the J. Paul Getty Museum included. *The Three Graces*, an exquisite sculpture that the 6th Duke of Bedford commis-

sioned Antonio Canova to create in 1814 for Woburn Abbey, his family seat, was one such example. In the early 1980s, the heir of the 13th
Duke of Bedford (who had been J. Paul Getty's close friend) tried to
give the statue to Britain in lieu of taxes. After his offer was rejected,
the Cayman Islands–based company that bought it sold it to the Getty
Museum for about $12 million. Public outcry and a tumultuous, five-
year-long legal battle followed, during which the government with-
held its export license while various parties tried to raise funds to buy
it. Paul Getty Jr. offered to contribute $1.5 million toward its pur-
chase on behalf of the Victoria and Albert Museum and the Scottish
National Gallery. This transpired at the height of the paranoia in the
art world over the so-called Getty factor, whereby—as some feared
and others hoped—the newly loaded Malibu museum would send art
prices soaring as it veritably plundered Europe of its patrimony. When
Paul Jr. stepped up to help keep the Canova and other treasures in
Britain, the London papers had a field day. Some reports suggested
that he was motivated by spite for his late father and his museum. Just
as it seemed the deal to "save" the Canova was sealed, the director of
the Scottish National Gallery gave credence to this view in a television interview. Outraged, Getty rescinded his offer. After the director apologized profusely, Getty reinstated his pledge, and the marble
remained in Britain.

A new Maecenas had appeared in the land; he was still a fragile one,
though. But one day in 1985, one Briton took Paul in hand: Prime
Minister Margaret Thatcher marched into the London Clinic and
dispensed a dose of her particular brand of strong medicine: "My dear
Mr. Getty. Now, what is the matter? We must have you out of here."

Within the next two years, Getty received an honorary knighthood
from the Queen and was named Arts Patron of the Year; he was to
receive the award from the Prince of Wales during a gala dinner at the
Savoy Hotel. Still wobbly, Getty got cold feet. Just forty-five minutes

before he was due to arrive, Christopher Gibbs had to call the organizers to break the news that Mr. Getty couldn't make it. Nineteen-year-old Tara was deputized to accept the award on his father's behalf.

Eventually J. Paul Getty Jr. did come out of his shell. His rehabilitation finally jelled, thanks in large part to a woman. But an English country estate, a boat, and the game of cricket also helped make the last decade of his life pretty glorious.

The woman was Victoria Holdsworth, a willowy beauty he had known for many years who became his close companion. The daughter of a Suffolk farmer who had been a commander in World War II, she had been married three times previously and had two sons. In 1994, they boarded a Concorde to Barbados (his first trip outside Britain in eighteen years), where they embarked on the *Talitha G.* Six years earlier, Paul Jr. had purchased the 262-foot superyacht, which had been commissioned in the 1920s. Only now was she emerging from the restoration he'd ordered—one of the most painstaking in the annals of yachting. In December 1994, on her teak deck, Paul, then age sixty-two, and Victoria were married.

By then, Getty also owned Wormsley Park, an ancient manor in Buckinghamshire on 2,700 sublime acres. Dating from 1086, it passed in 1574 into the hands of the Scropes, a noble family, and belonged to their descendants, the Fanes, until 1985, when Paul bought it, at Gibbs's suggestion. Gibbs and a dream team of talent including interior decorator David Mlinaric spent seven years bringing the neglected property back to its original glory, and then some. With the addition of some extraordinary new elements, including a four-acre lake and one of the finest private libraries anywhere, Wormsley was a magnificent country seat ready for a new dynasty.

The library, constructed of flint, was built from scratch in the style of an ancient castle, though it includes state-of-the-art climate control and other technologies. Inside its baronial reading room, the fifteenth-century-style hammerbeam roof of English oak is painted in gilt and midnight blue, depicting the conjunction of the planets at the hour of Paul's birth, at sea off the coast of Italy.

It was a worthy home for his peerless collection of rare books and manuscripts. In the 1960s, before he came into his fortune, Paul Jr. started to collect seriously, sometimes buying from dealers on credit. Whatever money he had seemed to go to books. After his father died, he had the wherewithal to fully pursue his obsession. His collection, one of the best in the world, spans the seventh to the late twentieth centuries; it includes illuminated manuscripts, early printed books, and historic bookbindings. Highlights include the First Folio of Shakespeare's *Comedies, Histories, and Tragedies* (which he bought from Oriel College, Oxford, for £3.5 million), the first printed edition of Chaucer, and the psalter used by Anne Boleyn (a guest at Sutton Place, remember).

In 1999, over one hundred masterpieces from the collection traveled to New York, where the Morgan Library showcased them in a major exhibition, *The Wormsley Library: A Personal Selection by Sir Paul Getty, KBE.*

For many of its visitors, however, Wormsley's greatest delight is its cricket ground.

Cricket became much more than a game to Paul. It was a big part of his recovery, and his reemergence into society. "I came upon cricket at a time when I was deeply depressed and it had a lot to do with bringing me out of that state," he said in a rare interview, with ESPN.

Mick Jagger introduced him to the sport when Getty was still secluded on Cheyne Walk. Jagger, who lived a few doors away, was one of the few visitors allowed into the house. If cricket was on the telly, Mick wanted to watch. Over cups of tea, he began to explain the game's many subtle idiosyncrasies and arcane rules. Paul was hooked. And it wasn't just the game itself. He loved the surroundings of this quintessentially English pursuit. "There's a whole way of life about it which I adore," he said.

England's great aristocratic estates traditionally included cricket grounds, along with a team supported by the lord of the manor. But no one had built one of these costly follies since the war years—until Getty. Then he outdid everybody. He had his modeled on the Oval, the nation's most sacrosanct pitch, in south London. At Wormsley, it is flanked on three sides by glorious countryside. The fourth side, looking toward the wooded Chiltern Hills, is elevated on a large grassy bank, allowing perfect viewing, with a delightful mock-Tudor pavilion for the players.

"It's so perfectly cut into the landscape," says one English lord who is a regular there. "It's not just one of the most beautiful cricket pitches. It's one of the most beautiful things. Full stop." (Getty was so mad for the game, it was even played on the deck of the *Talitha G.*)

The inaugural match in 1992 was attended by Her Majesty the Queen Mother and Prime Minister John Major. An invitation to one of its summer matches, particularly to see the home team, the Sir Paul Getty XI, at bat, remains one of the most coveted in the realm— "The most enchanting, exclusive, and enthralling place in England to hear willow on leather," as *Tatler* recently declared. (Cricket bats are made of wood from willow trees.)

In March 1998, three months after he was granted British citizenship, J. Paul Getty Jr. became a full-fledged knight of the realm. "Now you can use your title. Isn't that nice?" the Queen said to him after she dubbed him with her sword, making him a Knight Commander of the Most Excellent Order of the British Empire, for his services to charity. A photo of Sir Paul and Lady Getty outside Buckingham Palace after his investiture appeared the next day on the front page of the *Times* of London. Getty was even the subject of an editorial inside the paper under the headline "Model Billionaire," which read: "This reclusive Briton, once trapped in the world of wealth and family tragedy, has imperceptibly become an English institution himself."

6

Mark

One morning in 2005, Londoners woke to find one of their most beloved icons massacred.

A classic red British Telecom box lay overturned in Soho Square, half of it bent almost ninety degrees, a pickaxe protruding from it. It appeared to be bleeding.

The "blood" pooled around it was paint. It was all the handiwork of then little-known street artist Banksy. His pranks would soon escalate about as fast as his prices. Without ado, however, the Westminster City Council ordered the nuisance carted away. Whether the piece amounted to a violent attack on a cherished national institution or a cheeky satire on modern life and technology was a question pondered by a few.

Three years later—Valentine's Day 2008—*Vandalized Phone Box* (lot 33A) appeared on the block at Sotheby's in New York during the (RED) Auction, a gala event spearheaded by musician Bono and artist Damien Hirst, to raise funds for AIDS programs in Africa. (The biggest charity auction ever, it collected $42.5 million.)

Lot 33A, carrying an estimate of $200,000 to $300,000, sparked heated competition. A determined anonymous bidder fended off all challengers until the hammer fell at $605,000.

It took another three years for the item to resurface, on the grounds of Wormsley, not far from the cricket ground.

"I had to have it . . . it was killing the phone box story with a phone box that was being killed," Mark Getty—Paul Jr. and Gail's third-born child—eventually confessed. "A marvelous joke and metaphor."

Indeed, in the public imagination, the much-mythologized Sutton Place pay phone had become synonymous with "the tragic dynasty." Putting a stake through the heart of *that* was well worth the 600K (and the money did go to charity).

The timing of its purchase that night at Sotheby's was propitious too. Just ten days later, Mark, then forty-seven, accepted a $2.4 billion buyout offer from a private equity firm for Getty Images, the scrappy start-up he cofounded in 1995, which revolutionized the photography industry. Gettys were not just inheriting fortunes now, they were making them again.

Broad-shouldered, red-haired, Rome-born Mark (whose first language was Italian) had become a pillar of the British Establishment. But every summer in Tuscany, he's still "Marco." He's gone since he was five, when his mother bought a primitive farmhouse. Weekends and summers there in the remote wooded hills near the village of Orgia provided a safe haven and a sense of normalcy, especially during the maelstroms that hit the family. In July 1973, Mark happened to be away in San Francisco visiting his maternal grandparents when his brother was abducted.

From age fourteen onward, he was educated in England—at Taunton, a relatively relaxed prep school in Somerset, and then at Oxford, where he studied politics and philosophy.

As Mark's father recovered his health and became one of the leading philanthropists in Great Britain, Mark and his siblings mixed easily among different strata of British society, including the aristocracy. "They just swam in, seamlessly, which is very rare for Americans," observed one peeress. "People liked them because they were just themselves. The kids were all very nice and cool. But the Gettys also knew the rules of England. They made the right decisions about which schools to go to. They had all those cricket matches. It was all very pukka. The Gettys just got it."

Mark, an Anglo-Saxon and Italian mash-up, found his match when he met Domitilla Harding in 1980 in Rome. Born in New York (in 1960, like Mark), she was brought up in Rome by an American father, a businessman, and an Italian mother who descends from one of Italy's great papal dynasties, the Lante della Roveres. Their family tree includes Pope Sixtus, who built the Sistine Chapel, and his nephew, Julius II, who commissioned Michelangelo's frescoes. Julius also restored part of the ancient Basilica dei Santi XII Apostoli, where Domi, as she is known, and Mark were married in 1982.

The couple spent the first years of their marriage in New York, where Mark worked in investment banking at Kidder, Peabody. In 1986, they acquired their own summer property in Orgia, close to Gail's. Atop a steep hill, they found a hamlet of six rustic farmhouses—a *borgo*, as it's called in Italy. It had been abandoned for years, except for an elderly, eccentric hermit squatter. After buying one of the stone houses, they slowly—over fifteen years—were able to acquire the entire property, as they tracked down the various owners and gained the deeds. As they spread out from house to house, the family expanded too. After Alexander, who was born in 1984, the couple had Joseph in 1988 and Julius two years later.

As the boys grew up, Getty cousins and other relatives descended on the property every July and August. A bit of work was mixed in during the holidays—the kids were given Italian lessons, and a number of family members pitched in to help Domitilla with Miss Italy, the fashion line that she operated for a decade. Anna, her niece, was the fit model; Gisela, Anna's mother, and Ariadne, Mark's sister, took the photographs that were posted on the website, which Alexander set up.

Traditionally, wealthy Anglo-American expatriate families in Italy, like the Actons in Florence, have kept fairly aloof from Italians and spoken the language poorly, if they did at all. The Gettys all speak beautiful Italian (Mark speaks with a Sienese accent) and they mix with a wide variety of Italians—aristocrats, locals, artists, and intellectuals.

For everyone in the family, but for Mark in particular, the high point of summer was (and still is) the Palio di Siena. Held in the Piazza del Campo, Siena's magnificent medieval square, it lasts only about ninety seconds as ten jockeys—each representing one of the city's *contrade* (districts)—career bareback for three laps. Possibly the most dangerous horse race in the world, it is doubtless the most splendid.

Brief as the races are—one is held in July and one in August—the Palio consumes the passions of the Sienese all year long, as they scheme and prepare for the competition, an eight-hundred-year-old tradition full of intrigue and pageantry. Only citizens of Siena can fully participate, but an outsider is allowed to take part as a *cavallaio*, a horse breeder. When he was about twenty-five, Mark bought his first horses, a pair of Anglo-Arabians named Amore and Barbarella. For the next nearly thirty years, with fifty-some horses, he never missed a year—or won a race.

By the early 1990s, Mark and Domitilla were living primarily in London, where he worked in the corporate finance department of Hambros Bank. Not that he needed the work. By now, the Gettys were all awash in cash, as their trusts swelled following the sale of Getty Oil. But without a family business, and with each of four branches now managing its own trust, they had become a splintered tribe, and there was a sense of loss.

At the same time, Mark and a Hambros colleague, South African–born Jonathan Klein, hatched plans to launch an investment fund of their own. Mark persuaded relatives from three of the four Getty family branches (George's daughters being the exception) to back them. His father, his uncles Gordon and Ronald, and thirteen cousins put up about $30 million in seed capital. (Other investors joined them, including Hambros Bank and RIT Capital Partners, the investment trust run by Lord Rothschild.) The idea was to make money, but at the same time it presented an opportunity to knit the family back together.

An initial investment in Conservation Corporation Africa, a fledgling game-reserve and ecotourism operator based in South Africa, got off to a good start, for the business and the Gettys: the relatives got along, and Mark's role as the peacemaker in the family solidified.

Looking for something big to make a splash in, Mark and Jonathan homed in on the stock photography business, then an inefficient but lucrative seller's market.

Getty Images got off the ground in March 1995, when they paid $40 million for Britain's Tony Stone Images, with its library of 1.1 million photos. Building on that cornerstone, they snapped up one stock firm or archival collection after another, in a bid to consolidate the fragmented field.

With the digital era in its toddler years, photo researchers still located images by dint of cumbersome quests through mazes of independent photo stock agencies. After it consolidated collections, Getty Images enabled researchers to use computers to retrieve images—initially in the form of snail-mailed glossy prints, later via digital technology.

In October 1995, Getty gained stiff competition from Bill Gates: Corbis, a firm he had founded in 1989 to make digital artworks to decorate people's homes, acquired the vast Bettmann Archive, making the two companies archrivals.

Two years later, *Forbes* published an interview with Mark about his new company and "the arcane field of stock photography." The article's quizzical tone suggests that the public, and some journalists, didn't yet understand what Getty was onto: "You may chuckle when you hear what industry the younger Getty has delved into: stock photos. This is the business of pulling used photographs out of file folders and lending them to book publishers, movie studios, advertising agencies, and the like."

With Getty Images now in possession of about 25 million images, their costly challenge was how to distribute and market them. It was not unlike the situation Mark's grandfather faced when he first struck oil in the Neutral Zone. Where he had to build railroads, supertankers, and refineries, Mark had to digitalize his images and build thick cables and data centers for downloading them.

"Intellectual property is the oil of the twenty-first century," Mark told the *Economist*. "In the oil business, the capital is in the ground; in the intellectual-property business, it is in people's heads."

Late in 1997, Getty Images' quest to build out its digital infrastructure was jump-started with its purchase of Seattle-based Photo-Disc, a pioneer in web-based photos, which also led the company to relocate its headquarters from London to Seattle, joining the emerging tech megalopolis.

The same year, far from any digital domain, photographer Slim Aarons, eighty-one, heard a knock on the door of his farmhouse in Bedford, New York. It was Mark. "He was wearing this little windbreaker and I thought he was a guy looking for a landscaping job," Slim recalled in a *Vanity Fair* profile.

After a storied career photographing old money scions and high society ringleaders for such publications as *Holiday, Town & Country*, and *Life*, Aarons was retired, his work little valued. When *A Wonderful Time*, his photo album of the rich at play, was published in 1974, it sank. Vietnam, Nixon's resignation . . . Slim was out of step with the times.

When he realized that this young "fella" wasn't a gardener, he invited Getty up to his attic to look at his life's work. Mark made an offer on the spot for the entire collection, and the deal was sealed with a handshake. "He gave me what I call 'fuck you' money," the photographer said happily.

With Getty Images' distribution and marketing, Aarons's oeuvre became another touchstone for the fashion world. Not unlike Mark's stepmother, Talitha, in fact. Style-wise, they were just polar opposites. While Talitha became a patron saint of posh hippiedom, Aarons—"the Jimmy Stewart of photography," as fellow lensman Jonathan Becker called him—made WASP style look crisp and cool. "I don't think there's any American designer who doesn't have a copy [of *A Wonderful Time*]," said designer Michael Kors.

"Wonderful guy," said Slim about Mark. "Grandson of the old man himself. Direct line right down."

In 2001, Mark and his uncle Gordon made a £10 million donation to the National Gallery in London, in honor of Paul Jr., who had virtually saved the institution sixteen years before with his £50 million gift. Shy as he was, his name wasn't carved anywhere on the building. Now, after this new donation from his son and his brother, one of the main entrances on Trafalgar Square was remodeled and named the Sir Paul Getty Entrance. A bronze bust of him there greets visitors. (In 2009, Mark was appointed chair of the institution's board of trustees, considered the most prestigious charitable post in Britain.)

The next year, the family name returned to the Big Board, after a decades-long absence, when stock in Getty Images began trading on the New York Stock Exchange under the ticket symbol GYI.

In April 2003, Sir Paul Getty, age seventy, died at the London Clinic, where he had been undergoing treatment for a chest infection. Five months later, an epic memorial mass for him took place at Westminster Cathedral. The 1,500 attendees comprised a who's who of the British Establishment—including Baroness Thatcher and scores of English cricket champions.

The Getty family—all branches—appeared in full force. In addition to Mark, Domitilla, and their three sons, there was Paul's first wife, Gail, and his widow, Victoria; Gordon and Ann with their son Peter; Donna Long, Gordon and Paul's half sister; Gloria, Paul's brother George's first wife, with her daughter Caroline; brother Ronald's son Christopher with his wife, Pia; Paul III and his former wife, Gisela, with their daughter, Anna; Caleb Wilding, Aileen's son; and Ariadne with husband Justin and their children, Nats and August.

In his eulogy, Christopher Gibbs spoke about Paul's battles with addictions and depression: "While we must not ignore the woes of his life, it is how he turned them around and put them to work which deserves fanfare."

Having inherited Wormsley, Mark took the reins and moved into the massive estate with his family, though the younger boys were off at boarding school (the esteemed Dragon School in Oxford), and Alexander soon left the nest. He set off first for Africa, where he helped out at Conservation Corporation's Zuka Private Game Reserve, then moved to New York, where he studied at the School of Visual Arts and worked as a video technician for Getty Images.

As Getty Images expanded, the digital media landscape continued to shift. With the rise of the internet came demand for lower-resolution, and lower-priced, images. Madison Avenue went into a slump and the financial crisis was looming. Thinking that the company would fare better under private ownership, without public investor pressure, Getty Images in 2008 accepted a $2.4 billion buyout from Hellman & Friedman, a private equity firm. Mark remained as chairman, and collected about $38 million. His relatives also became even richer—with their collective stake, they reaped a $281 million windfall. All of them remained as minority shareholders.

Four years later, the company accepted a $3.3 billion buyout from the Carlyle Group, the Washington-based private equity firm, which provided capital to continue competing against rivals old and new.

Despite being an information-age chief, Mark has no social media accounts and guards his privacy acutely. He considers the press a necessary evil to which he occasionally speaks. Inevitably, every article about him includes "the tragic background paragraph," as he peremptorily termed it to a reporter for *Management Today*, a British business publication, with whom he sat down for an interview. Then there's "the trite association of money and tragedy," he added. "It's all so profoundly boring."

Being measured by what his grandfather accomplished is of no interest to him either: "I always wanted to do something that was purely mine and I never wanted my life to be one where I lived in the shadow of . . . my grandfather. He did a lot of extraordinary things, but that was him and it wasn't me."

At Wormsley, Mark put his stamp on things. In addition to *Vandalized Phone Box,* a collection of other modern sculptures, including pieces by Jeff Koons and Keith Sonnier, appeared on the landscape. And in the spring of 2011, a gleaming steel and glass structure rose, the six-hundred-seat Opera Pavilion. It was built as a home for the Garsington Opera, one of England's summer companies, which had recently lost its longtime home on an aristocratic estate in Oxfordshire.

"I love opera . . . and, when I heard that they were looking for a new home through a friend of mine, I thought it would be a terrific thing to happen here," he told a reporter from the *Telegraph* before Garsington's debut at Wormsley.

How did such a private person feel about thousands of strangers entering his gates? "Well, it's a big place, and the idea that one person should occupy it all, all the time, alone, is kind of absurd," he said with a laugh. (According to a family friend, the estate's level of security is high: "It's like getting into Fort Knox.")

When he spoke, the reporter detected "a touch of loneliness." That year, he and Domitilla divorced. Now a ceramicist and glassmaker, she lives full-time in Orgia, which has continued to be a magnet for Gettys from far and wide every summer, thanks to her as well as to Gail, still the matriarch of her branch of the clan.

Alexander, tall and dark-haired, moved to California for several years. Settling first in Los Angeles, he volunteered at Gettlove, his aunt Aileen's homeless shelter, while he pursued his interest in photography. He had been taking pictures since he was ten, when his father launched Getty Images. But it was his mother who gave him a camera and taught him how to use it. "He's the normal one in the family," says a friend. "Very down-to-earth. Spartan."

While photographing landscapes and architectural subjects, he worked for Airbnb, shooting homes for its website. He also met Tatum Yount, a bright MBA candidate at USC. The pair married in 2012 and moved to San Francisco. As their children, Jasper and Olivia, were born, she worked as a brand consultant for the health and wellness industry and he continued his fine-art photography. An exhibition of his landscapes, *Human/Nature*, appeared in 2013 at the Gauntlet Gallery, in the Tenderloin. Its opening night was full of Getty cousins, aunts, and uncles.

Joseph, Mark and Domitilla's second son, moved to Rhode Island for college, as a member of Brown University's Class of 2013, with a major in history. A clever teddy bear with perfect manners and an easygoing disposition, he is the bridge builder in his generation of the Getty tribe—fitting, for a middle child. In Providence one day, he discovered a stockpile of old red-and-orange Getty Oil signs at an abandoned gas station. (A drop of oil fills in the *G*.) The next day he had them picked up and shipped around the world to his various relatives, in whose houses and offices they now proudly hang.

At a dinner party one weekend in New York, he met Sabine Ghanem. Born in Geneva to a Lebanese father and an Egyptian mother, she was enrolled at the Gemological Institute of America in New York. Long-limbed, brown-eyed, with a bob of flaxen hair, she has a commanding personality and a cosmopolitan air. "I'm certain we'll be happy together, so you should be my girlfriend," he told her right off.

After earning their diplomas, they moved into a flat in London's Pimlico. He pursued a career in finance (later opening his own hedge fund, Getty Capital) and she launched her line of fine jewelry, Sabine G. Her fanciful pieces were soon adorning the likes of Celine Dion, Rihanna, Nicole Kidman, and Catherine Deneuve. Given her own extravagant style and outsize personality, glossy magazines began to avidly cover her. She also gained a large following on Instagram, where she showcased her jewelry and also provided peeks inside the Getty world.

On a trip to Harbour Island in the Bahamas in spring 2014, Joseph popped the question. It wasn't such a surprise—she had told him she should design her engagement ring because "you're going to mess this up." But she was thrilled with the 1920s emerald mounted with diamonds that he picked out for her at S.J. Phillips, the venerable Mayfair jeweler. Reportedly, when he previewed the ring to his mother, she told him it was beautiful, but wondered, "Isn't it a bit grand?" Which confirmed for him that he'd made the right choice for his bride-to-be.

For Sabine's thirtieth birthday that August, Joseph threw her a fabulous two-day party aboard the *Talitha*, the family superyacht (her name now trimmed of its initial *G*). She chose the theme: *The Party*, the 1960s Peter Sellers classic. She wore a vintage hot-pink dress by Azzaro, and the plunge pool was filled with bubble bath, which naturally she ended up in, as the *Talitha* floated off Porto Ercole on the Tuscan coast.

Sabine likes a theme party. For a Halloween dinner, she picked *Auntie Mame*, for which she wore a purple 1960s Pierre Cardin haute couture gown. Fashion-mad, she has described her style as Bob Mackie meets Catherine Deneuve. "I find clothes are very empowering. You have to live up to the magnificence of the piece you are wearing," she told *British Vogue*.

On a brilliant morning in late May 2015, a pack of paparazzi swarmed outside of Basilica dei Santi XII Apostoli in Rome. Thirty-three years after Mark and Domitilla were wed inside the sixth-century basilica, Joseph and Sabine chose to exchange their vows there.

A parade of young royals and *jeunesse dorée* arrived for the ceremony: Princess Beatrice, in pink pastels from her fanciful hat on down; Monaco's dashing Pierre Casiraghi with his fiancée, Beatrice Borromeo; and others with such names as Thurn und Taxis, Niarchos, Agnelli, Santo Domingo, and Brandolini.

But where was the bride, and where was her hooded cape? Since the latter stretched twenty-three feet and featured 500,000 sequins (hand-embroidered by Maison Lesage) shaped into an image of a radiating sun, it required its own minder and car, which threaded its way through Rome's tortuous traffic. At last the garment arrived and was fastened to the bride, who was already clad in a figure-hugging, long-sleeved duchess-silk dress—the handiwork, like the cape, of Schiaparelli Haute Couture.

Some 375 of the guests had barely recovered from the costume ball the night before—the theme being *Liaisons Dangereuses*—at the seventeenth-century Palazzo Taverna. Immediately following the ceremony, waiters in liveried tailcoats served lunch at that most hallowed hall, the Circolo della Caccia, where Joseph's great-grandfather, despite being the richest man in the world, had been denied membership. That night, on the seaside west of the city, there was another ball, at Castello Orsini-Odescalchi, where a *Spiegeltent*—a 1900s circus tent—was erected for a wild circus-meets-cabaret-themed celebration. Looming a stone's throw away was La Posta Vecchia, J. Paul Getty's former villa, now a luxury hotel.

That August, in Siena's Piazza del Campo, Mark Getty's losing streak finally ended. Polonski, his seven-year-old Sardinian Anglo-Arabian, ridden by a jockey named Giovanni "Tittia" Atzeni, got an early lead and veritably flew to the finish line, setting a new Palio speed record (1 minute, 12 seconds) and making Mark the first foreigner ever to run a winning horse. It only took eight centuries. "I lost all of my Anglo-Saxon reserve," he later said of his euphoria.

Capping this momentous year, in December Her Majesty the Queen awarded Mark (an Irish passport holder) an honorary knighthood, in recognition of his services to the arts and philanthropy.

Around this time, he began a new relationship with Caterina Nahberg, a Spanish-born beauty who resided in Rome, where she had been married to the scion of an ancient Italian noble family, Prince Filippo del Drago.

On the business front, in January 2016, Getty Images declared victory over their Seattle rival when the company acquired the distribution rights to Corbis's vast library of images, though in a roundabout way. When a Beijing-based company, Visual China Group (VCG), bought Corbis, Getty Images struck a deal with VCG to license those images around the world, except in China. "Almost twenty-one years but we got it. Lovely to get the milk, the cream, cheese, yogurt, and the meat without buying the cow," Jonathan Klein crowed.

In 2018, the Getty family acquired Carlyle's 51 percent equity stake for around $250 million (and rolled over the company's roughly $2.35 billion debt), taking back control. Three years later, in December 2021, the company came full circle when it announced plans to list itself again on the New York Stock Exchange, following a merger with CC Neuberger Principal Holdings II, a deal valued at $4.8 billion. As a public company, Getty Images would be able to "aggressively invest in more product," announced Mark, who remains the chairman. With annual revenues of nearly $900 million, the company's 300 million "assets," in addition to photos, included videos and music, as well as a stable of assignment photographers such as Getty Images' royal photographer Chris Jackson. A shot of Kate Middleton can move from his lens to news-media sites around the world almost instantly.

Arguably, Mark Getty had cornered the world photography market. "He's the Amazon of images," as one photographer put it. But not everybody is a fan of Getty Images, of course. It prospered as it undercut the prices for pictures, which reduced and, in some cases, wiped out the livelihoods of many photo stock agencies and photographers.

A year after the release of *All the Money in the World*, a documentary called *Gettys: The World's Richest Art Dynasty* was broadcast on the BBC. Featuring interviews with Mark and Gordon, as well as with a few intimates such as Christopher Gibbs, it seemed to be a united Getty family rejoinder to the movie. It burnished J. Paul Getty's legacy as a philanthropist and art collector, but Mark briefly addressed Ridley Scott's film. It "turned it into a story where he's the bad guy," he said, referring to his grandfather. "The kidnappers were the bad guys."

"I do lose a lot of sleep thinking about what the experience was like for my brother," he also said.

But happiness prevailed in 2018. Mark and Caterina, parents of an infant daughter, Sol, were married in the Walled Garden at Wormsley. Two acres of enchantment, the garden was begun in the 1700s but fell into disrepair for much of the twentieth century, before celebrated garden designer Penelope Hobhouse brought it back to life for Mark's father. It is divided into four distinct spaces, enabling visitors to move from "room to room."

Mark and Caterina began to spend much of the year in Rome, in a palazzo that he rented near the Borghese Gardens. He also published his first book, *Like Wildfire Blazing*, a fable-like novel about a group of beings at the beginning of the world, a tale of the elemental struggle between darkness and light. "I always wanted to write and found the process incredibly liberating. . . . I thought by writing about some of the issues people might face when they're creating a society, I would get closer to understanding what makes good and evil. Even in the current climate, I'm an optimist and believe that good will always triumph," Mark told the London *Sunday Times* about the book, which was published by Adelphi, a small press. Getty oversaw all aspects of the book's production, including its dark-blue cloth spine and endpapers, which he designed himself.

The younger generation were now deepening their roots at

Wormsley, and multiplying. Alexander, Tatum, and their children moved from San Francisco to the property, where he became the estate manager. There's a lot to manage: in addition to the opera, cricket, garden, and library, the property sometimes opens its grounds for weddings and events, as other aristocratic English country houses often do. While overseeing all that, Alexander and Tatum keep a low profile. "They lead a very simple life," says a friend. "No excesses of any kind. He hates anything showy."

Sabine and Joseph are a different story. "She's the most Getty of them all!" says a longtime Getty watcher, alluding to Sabine's dramatic style. Indeed, *Tatler*, the English society bible, ranked the couple number three in its 2019 "Social Power Index," behind the Duke and Duchess of Cambridge and just ahead of Harper Beckham, the in-demand, then seven-year-old daughter of David and Victoria. "She's easily the best-dressed at any event," the magazine commented of Sabine. A case in point: the pink Emilia Wickstead skirt suit, paired with a matching turban-like hat, that she wore to Princess Eugenie's wedding at Windsor Castle. In another issue of the same publication, Sabine poked good fun at the notion of dynasties when she and hotel heiress Nicky Hilton Rothschild posed for a lavish fashion spread and accompanying video wearing ball gowns and vamping it up à la Alexis and Krystle, in the style of the iconic 1980s TV soap *Dynasty*.

The couple, with their daughter Gene, born in 2017, and son Jupiter, born in 2019, weekend at Wormsley. In London, they moved to a capacious duplex facing Green Park, which previously belonged to Joseph's grandfather; Sir Paul acquired it in 1986, when he vacated his melancholy Cheyne Walk townhouse. Gibbs and David Mlinaric decorated it for him; the Tudor-era paneling that they installed (salvaged from Raby Castle in County Durham) set a baronial tone. For their young family, Sabine and Joseph refreshed it themselves— brightening it up with coats of tangerine, yellow, and other brightly hued paints, as well as with contemporary art and photography.

Hanging prominently in the drawing room is a large red Getty Oil sign. For furnishings, in addition to their own bold 1960s and '70s items, they were able to pick out antiques—including a number of pieces that once graced Paul and Talitha's Moroccan palace—from the Getty family's storage facilities. ("They never sell anything. They have warehouses around the world," said one family associate.)

And Julius, the youngest brother, emerged into the spotlight. The sensitive, cool one in the family, he sometimes sports floppy dark hair and sometimes a peroxide-blond buzz cut. Fond of art and books, he opened a pop-up art gallery in London's Fitzrovia, where the inaugural group show of groovy young artists was entitled *Dangerous Stuff*. Plans for a clothing and jewelry line, to be called Jetty, are on his drawing board. When *Tatler* compiled its list of 2020's "It Boys" ("today's crop of society studs"), he was included. His category: "Dynastic Dudes."

Appealing and colorful as members of the young generation are, they nonetheless seem tame compared to their really wild antecedents. "I know all the old-school gos [gossip]," one old hand reminisced. "But the young ones aren't very gossipy. They're just happily married."

7

Aileen

On a chilly afternoon in December 2019 in Washington, DC, Aileen Getty, then sixty, and Jane Fonda—just hours shy of her eighty-second birthday—had their hands zip-tied by the Capitol Police. They were arrested while attempting to occupy the Hart Senate Office Building.

It was another raucous Fire Drill Friday—a weekly protest against congressional inaction on climate change, which Fonda had started a few months previously, with major funding from Aileen Getty. (FDF arrestees that season also included Gloria Steinem, Sally Field, Lily Tomlin, and Viva Vadim, Jane's teenage granddaughter.)

As cops hauled off Fonda and Getty, both were defiant, and looking considerably younger than their years. Jane was in a long, operatic, crimson-colored cloth coat, while Aileen wore a student-like nylon anorak, with jeans, sneakers, and a knit cap.

It had been a productive year for Paul Jr.'s second-born child. Over the course of many weeks, her efforts had helped bring rush-hour traffic in parts of central London, Washington, and other major cities to a standstill. The blockages were orchestrated for a good cause: to call people's attention to the climate emergency. With the situation as dire as it is, the more measured, gradualist approaches tradition-

ally employed by mainstream environmental groups didn't cut it anymore, she decided. Among her initiatives, she became the lead donor
behind Extinction Rebellion, an international organization that uses
extreme, disruptive tactics and civil disobedience to spark change.

Stopping traffic in Piccadilly Circus and Dupont Circle: pretty
impressive, especially for a five-foot-four wisp who long ago had been
described in the media as a "junkie." Twenty-eight years earlier,
she'd even been declared to be all but dead.

"Elizabeth Taylor's former daughter-in-law is dying of AIDS, *A
Current Affair* will report Friday," *USA Today* wrote in 1991. "Doctors
now tell her she has from six months to a year to live."

Growing up in Rome and Tuscany, Aileen was the delicate child. A
few terms at Hatchlands, a posh girls' finishing school in England,
turned her into a rebel, and an avid consumer of alcohol. She kept
a stash of hard liquor in her room. Weekend visits with her grandfather at Sutton Place provided a measure of stability. "He was one of
the more nurturing members of the family," she recalled. And when
Teresa, his pet lion, gave birth, Aileen was accorded a special treat—
the cubs would be brought up to her room, one by one.

Leaving Hatchlands before graduation (lessons in contract bridge
and how to curtsy to the Queen didn't interest her), Getty moved to
Los Angeles. In 1981, at age twenty-two, she married into Hollywood royalty when she eloped with Christopher Wilding, the second son born to Elizabeth Taylor and her second husband, Michael
Wilding. Aileen and Christopher, who had been dating for a few
years, said "I do" in a chapel on the Sunset Strip. Beforehand, Gail
hosted a star-studded engagement party for the couple at her house in
Brentwood. Carol Burnett, Roddy McDowall, Sissy Spacek, Dudley
Moore, and Timothy Leary were among the guests. Miss Taylor—
then Mrs. John Warner—shimmered in pearls, while Aileen flashed
an engagement ring of imperial jade encircled by diamonds. Christo-

pher, a photographer and film editor, wore a gold hoop and diamond studs in his left ear.

Several pregnancies ended in miscarriages, and Aileen battled depression. The couple adopted their son Caleb in 1983, when he was twenty-two hours old; a year later, Christopher and his mother accompanied Aileen to the delivery room when she gave birth to Andrew. Then she descended deeper into depression.

To lift Aileen's spirits, her mother-in-law invited her to come along with her to Paris, where she was fund-raising for the American Foundation for AIDS Research (amfAR), which she had helped found earlier in 1985. In her hotel room, Aileen woke one morning drenched in sweat. "I got it," she thought with dread. A test soon confirmed that she was HIV-positive. She'd contracted it while having unprotected sex during an extramarital affair.

Six years went by before she publicly acknowledged her diagnosis, but she soon broke the news to her relatives. Her own kin initially had a difficult time expressing their emotions; they were still overwhelmed by their own multiple tragedies. With her mother-in-law, who was reeling from the death of her friend Rock Hudson, emotions poured out when Aileen and Chris went to her house in Bel-Air to tell her. "We all cried and cried," Aileen recalled. She later moved in with "Mom," as she called Taylor, who cradled a sobbing Aileen in her arms for many a night.

Panicked nonetheless, Aileen bolted with her young sons to New York, where she binged on coke. She lost custody of the boys, and the couple ultimately divorced in 1989. Taylor remained steadfast throughout. "I will always love Aileen as if she were my own child," she said.

Over the next several years, Aileen was in and out of clinics, hospitals, and psych wards (where she endured twelve shock treatments), as she battled her addictions, nervous breakdowns, and other issues, including anorexia and self-mutilation. By November 1991, she was in pretty good shape—she regained partial custody of the boys, along with a good relationship with Wilding. Even so, she was not quite ready to reveal her HIV status to the world. But producers of *A Current Affair*, the scandalmongering TV news show, outed her in an episode that was broadcast a week after basketball star Magic Johnson announced that he was positive.

Aileen found herself splashed on the covers of the *National Enquirer* and other tabloids. Not surprisingly, they didn't report her story the way she would have liked, which led her to sit down with writer Kevin Sessums. "The worst symptom of AIDS is denial," she said in the profile he wrote for the March 1992 issue of *Vanity Fair*.

She unloaded on the tabloids: "They totally trashed me. They bring all the rubbish in. So . . . I thought, Well, shit, just a second. Fuck that. I'm alive. I'm a fucking living miracle, man. What am I ashamed about?"

A few weeks later, she spoke at a press conference sponsored by the National Community on AIDS Partnership, the start of her new career as activist, in which she worked closely with her former mother-in-law. The first celebrity AIDS ally, Taylor spoke up forcefully, to presidents and everyone on down, to raise funds for research as well as to dispel the stigma and prejudice that carriers of the disease were contending with. (Aileen could attest to this personally. In spite of her being a Getty, a hospital in Los Angeles where she sought treatment had turned her away.)

Despite her own still-fragile state, Aileen gained a sense of purpose and self-worth through her work as a public advocate. "My grandfather probably would have been proud that I did something," she told *People* in April 1992. "He had a real hard time with people not using what they had. And I didn't use what I had for years and years."

In August 1993, Aileen and Elizabeth appeared on the cover of *Hello!* magazine with the cover line "How the Woman Who Has Fought Most for the AIDS Cause Faces the Illness in Her Own Family: Elizabeth Taylor at Home with Aileen Getty Who Has AIDS."

"I still feel like she's my daughter," Taylor told the magazine. "I think we are both survivors . . . very much so."

Still, before Aileen achieved lasting sobriety, there were relapses. Cocaine was her primary drug. She also did heroin, at one point reportedly with her nephew Balthazar. After one overdose, she went into a coma for twenty-four hours. In 1994, after the Northridge earthquake damaged her house, she and her sons moved in with Timothy Leary, the guru of psychedelic drugs. She accompanied him cross-country on a string of speaking engagements, as he promoted his VHS video *How to Operate Your Brain*. They also made some short films together.

In 2005, Aileen founded her first nonprofit, Gettlove, to provide meals for the homeless of Los Angeles. It grew into a full-service organization dedicated to meeting the spectrum of needs faced by homeless people, with a focus on housing.

"I would see her in the parking lot, distributing meals," recalls a Gettlove volunteer. "She knew every homeless person there by name. She would offer each one a choice of sandwiches—different ones on different days, with funny names, like the Elvis sandwich. It was such a respectful, sweet way to feed people."

About the same time, Aileen renewed some old family ties. In 2001, she began a relationship with Prince Bartolomeo Ruspoli, the third-born child of the celebrated Dado—her father's partying partner in Rome and elsewhere during the sixties.

"Maybe you've seen the following couple tooling around Los Angeles in their Rolls-Royce convertible," gossip columnist Liz Smith wrote about the pair shortly after their marriage in 2004. "He looks like a Botticelli angel and, when he's shirtless, shows his nipple ring and a tattoo across his chest reading 'Notorious.' She's a middle-aged hippie who comes from one of the richest families in America, and she is 'crazee' about her young bridegroom. He's 27; she's 46."

Bartolomeo's mother, Debra Berger, a California-born beauty, arrived in Rome at age seventeen and met Dado, forty-nine, at the home of Roman Polanski. In addition to "Meo," the couple produced another son, Tao, during their ten-year relationship. After it ended,

Debra moved back to California, giving her boys, scions of this charismatic, cultured, and decadent thousand-year-old Italian dynasty, a perch on the Pacific.

Tao studied philosophy at Berkeley, lived for a couple of years on a parking lot in Venice Beach in an old school bus, and was married for nine years to actress Olivia Wilde. A filmmaker, he produced and directed in 2002 a very personal and unflinching documentary, *Just Say Know*, about his parents and his brother. In it, each of them discussed their history of addiction.

"Heroin takes you by the hand, like it's your best life friend, so warm and trusting, and it leads you into the darkness," said Debra, who disclosed that she began using drugs at age twelve.

"When I was young, I shot heroin in my veins, then I realized there was no culture in the needle, so I learned the ritual of opium smoking. . . . Opium is like a beautiful woman," said Dado, describing his forty-five-year relationship with the substance.

Debra had become clean; with Dado, it was somewhat unclear. Meo, on the other hand, was in the throes of withdrawal during his interviews. He spoke as he tossed around in bed.

"I'd rather quit at home than in jail—it's hell laying your ass on a concrete floor," he said, revealing that he had started drinking at age seven and smoking weed at thirteen, before going on to mushrooms, acid, coke, speed, and crack.

Bartolomeo and Aileen, both the products of wealthy, complex, substance-using dynasties, certainly had much in common. Their marriage ended in 2006, but the two remain close (other Getty family members also maintain warm relations with him). "The Gangster Prince," as he called himself on his Instagram profile, enjoys the martial arts, horses, tattoos, cats, and muscle cars. Settled in Los Angeles, he has been sober since August 2017.

Aileen was able to conquer her addictions when she faced up to her underlying issues. "Drugs are about control over fear . . . and when you have AIDS, your lack of control is that much more evident. I tried to make up for that lack of being in control with a lot of cocaine," she said.

"She transformed her life completely. She went from darkness to light," said Princess Claudia Ruspoli, a cousin of Bartolomeo's. "She did it all by herself. She is amazingly strong. She has been completely clean for more than ten years now. And Bartolomeo has been clean more than three years now. They are survivors."

Over the years, Aileen has also suffered a number of the opportunistic infections that AIDS patients commonly face, including fungus and multi-drug-resistant tuberculosis. To overcome them, she went all-in on an organic, vegan diet. "She swapped bad addictions for good ones," according to an old friend in California. "Last time I saw her, she looked better than ever. Not only has she survived, she is fucking thriving."

That feat is all the more impressive considering her family background, as this friend, who is also familiar with other members of the Getty clan, observes: "When you have that kind of money and even a slightly addictive personality, when there is no end to the amount of drugs or sex you can get, and everyone is kissing your ass, nobody is telling you the truth—how do you survive? I am shocked any of them survived. *That's* when money is a burden."

Aileen's sons, now in their midthirties, are sturdy as well as kindly fellows. Caleb Wilding restores and rebuilds cars and motorcycles, in the West. Andrew Wilding, a Los Angeleno, is a filmmaker and musician. *Piano Man*, a black comedy he wrote, shot, and directed—which was produced by his London-based cousin Joseph—was released in 2010. In May 2020, he began releasing singles from an upcoming album, *Come Over*, under the stage name Kowloon (he has avoided any mention of being a Getty or Taylor descendant in promoting his work). Wilding wrote, performed, recorded, and mixed all the tracks in his home studio, blending vintage synthesizer, drum machines, and bass lines with eighties-inspired vocals. "Danceable love songs— albeit love songs set in a time of digital malaise and looming ecological catastrophe, with anxious, dread-filled lyrics that are as timely as they are postapocalyptic," according to Spotify.

Yet it's challenging to feel too angst-ridden when peering into Andrew's luminous, piercing blue eyes, which were well-displayed in a video made for his smooth single "Walk with Me" ("Walk with me, we can make it / Talk with me and let me answer your heart").

In 2012, Aileen established the Aileen Getty Foundation. While continuing to address homelessness, the organization expanded to support multiple causes, including the arts, meditation in schools, and peace-building in the Middle East, as well as HIV/AIDS research, for which it has collaborated with the Elizabeth Taylor AIDS Foundation, amfAR, and the Elton John AIDS Foundation (all of which have showered Aileen with accolades and thanks). Among her recent initiatives is a program to prevent the spread of HIV and AIDS in the American South, zeroing in on disadvantaged youths.

She has chaired some of amfAR's most successful fund-raising events. Her relatives have been supportive. In San Francisco, her aunt and uncle, Ann and Gordon, allowed their palatial mansion to be transformed into a very glamorous casino for an annual Charity Poker Tournament and Game Night. The 2019 edition, which raked in $400,000, was attended by the Bay Area elite, movie stars including Gwyneth Paltrow and Jon Hamm, and Gettys of all generations.

By 2019, Aileen came to the conclusion that one cause has unequivocally become more pressing than any other: the climate crisis. She shifted the bulk of her resources and time to address this existential threat. With her friends Rory Kennedy, the youngest child of the late Robert F. Kennedy, and Trevor Neilson, a well-connected advisor and investor, she cofounded the Climate Emergency Fund (CEF). Getty provided the group with a cornerstone grant of $600,000; it has subsequently raised about $3.5 million more in funding.

This is an all-hands-on-deck moment, they announced on their website: "We believe that only a peaceful planet-wide mobilization on the scale of World War II will give us a chance to avoid the worst-case scenarios and restore a safe climate."

And no more dawdling. "The world's philanthropists need to wake up to the reality that a gradualist approach to the climate emergency is doomed to fail," Trevor wrote in a post on the Medium platform in which he outlined CEF's goals, which include cutting emissions to net zero by 2025, establishing a citizens' assembly that would set climate policy, and urging governments and media to tell the truth about climate change.

While CEF provides grants to grassroots activists who are taking a disruptive approach and using aggressive tactics, such as Extinction Rebellion and Fire Drill Fridays, they draw the line at anything violent. Yet civil disobedience usually involves some degree of law-breaking. Extinction Rebellion was started by two British activists in October 2018. Causing traffic mayhem and gridlock is the best way to get people's attention, they reasoned. Irksome as that can be, it is "necessary because it is evident the public is still not sufficiently engaged," said Aileen. "We can't sugarcoat it anymore." Moreover, if people think *this* is disruptive, it's nothing compared to "the real disruption and the incomprehensible suffering of those that we love" that would result from climate change.

"Even if this approach isn't going to deliver the outcome we're hopeful it will, it's better than doing what we've been doing that hasn't amounted to any change," Aileen added. "However imperfect the actions will be . . . at least they are actions."

Kennedy, a filmmaker, shares Aileen's sense of urgency. "We're very much running out of time here," she said. The two can also relate on family matters. In an interview with the *New York Times*, Kennedy resisted efforts to lump members of her clan together. "There are a lot of us," she said—so best not to speak of them "as a unit." But there are shared values: "As a family, we have appreciated, over the years, the importance of protest," she said.

Early in 2020, it was announced that Aileen would serve as a host—along with Bill Clinton, Elton John, Barbra Streisand, the designer Valentino, Tom Hanks, and others—for what promised to be the most high-wattage charity benefit Los Angeles had seen in a while, the Elizabeth Taylor Ball to End AIDS. The first-ever Los Angeles fund raiser for the Elizabeth Taylor AIDS Foundation, it was to be held on the back lot of Fox, the studio that released *Cleopatra*, Taylor's most epic vehicle—which, naturally, would be the theme of the party. Aileen was two when filming on this colossal picture—the most costly yet made—commenced in Rome in 1961. The sixteen-month-long shoot riveted the Italian capital. Hollywood set designers built a twelve-acre reproduction of the Roman Forum (larger than the real thing), which may well have inspired J. Paul Getty, besotted with ancient Rome, to imagine what he could one day erect in Malibu. Perhaps the toddler Aileen even crossed paths with her future mother-in-law, or, for that matter, her future stepmother (Talitha was an extra). Sixty years later, the invitation to the Elizabeth Taylor Ball to End AIDS sort of encapsulated the sweep of the Gettys' Californian-Italian cross-pollination. Like everything else in 2020, the event went virtual. For her part, Aileen introduced President Clinton.

When Covid hit, Getty, Kennedy, and Neilson realized they could not support sending people to the streets to protest. CEF helped found and fund (with an initial grant of $100,000) the bipartisan Coalition for Sustainable Jobs (CSJ), a sort of rainbow coalition for the climate change community. It includes Republicans from many corners—including evangelicals, hunters, fishers, and young conservatives—all of whom agreed to push for moderate clean-energy and climate change policies.

Late in 2021, Aileen resassumed a more combative stance, coauthoring an opinion piece for the *Guardian* with Rebecca Rockefeller Lambert. "Fossil Fuels made our families rich. Now we want this industry to end" ran the headline. "We can't build back better unless we build back fossil-free," the women wrote.

Over the years, some journalists and commentators reporting on Aileen's philanthropy have predictably harped on the fossil-fuel origins of her fortune, and her not exactly modest lifestyle ("New Face on Climate Activism Scene Is Multimillionaire Who Owns Several Mansions" read a headline on Western Wire, a website funded by an association of oil and gas producers).

"I'm aware that the optics are what they are. I want to do what's correct and what's right," she told the *Chronicle of Philanthropy*. "It's not necessarily restitution, it's what I get to do as a human being. I happen to have resources that I get to bring into the mix."

At the end of the day, we all simply have to do "what's right," Aileen says. "There's legacy, and there's personal responsibility."

8

Ariadne

Ariadne—Gail and J. Paul Getty Jr.'s youngest child—was the shy one. She successfully dodged the public eye for most of her life, while her siblings became the subjects of headlines, though generally not by choice.

When eventually she did appear in the spotlight, she chose a venue as high-powered as it gets: the World Economic Forum in Davos, Switzerland.

On a frosty morning in January 2018, this diminutive fifty-five-year-old blonde, clad in dark blazer, slacks, and shiny Giuseppe Zanotti sneakers, joined the heads of state, captains of industry, and other potentates who gathered for the annual alpine summit.

WEF is where global leaders go to "move the needle" (a Davos catchphrase) on humanity's pressing issues: climate change, income inequality, Mideast peace. LGBTQ rights had never been on the main menu. In recent years, there had been a few "off-piste" events to address the subject, but it remained a fairly taboo topic, not tackled in the official panels.

Acceptance for LGBTQ people became a personal priority for Ari Getty (as she is generally called by friends and family) as soon as her children, Natalia (known as Nats) and August had each come out as gay, loudly and proudly, around 2010. (In 2021, Nats adopted the male pronoun, when he announced his gender transition.) When they advanced into their twenties, both launched careers as fashion designers, and Nats began to date Gigi Gorgeous, a Canadian-born transgender icon. Ariadne rejoiced in their identities. Then Donald Trump got elected. Ariadne grew fearful as his rhetoric and policies generated increasing discrimination and violence against LGBTQ people.

She journeyed to Davos to announce her response: a $15 million gift to GLAAD, the world's foremost LGBTQ media-monitoring organization. (It was founded in 1985, when a group of journalists gathered to protest defamatory, sensationalized AIDS coverage in the *New York Post*; two years later, it persuaded the *New York Times* to begin using the word *gay* in place of *homosexual* or other words that were pejoratives.)

Ariadne's donation—made through her Ariadne Getty Foundation (AGF)—was earmarked to establish the GLAAD Media Institute, which will train an army of ten thousand activists and leaders around the world to communicate accurately the stories of gay, lesbian, and transgender people.

When it was time to announce the new institute, Ariadne, previously a quiet philanthropist, realized she had to show up, and only one location would do. "We need to go to Davos, we need to be on center stage to do this, with the world's biggest companies," she said.

Leveraging the Getty fortune and name, she cosponsored, with GLAAD, a panel entitled "How Business, Philanthropy, and Media Can Lead to Achieving 100 Percent Acceptance for LGBTQ People." The corporate heavyweights who participated included Brad Smith, president of Microsoft; Serge Dumont, then vice chairman of Omnicom; and Jim Fitterling of Dow Chemical, the only openly gay CEO of a large industrial company. After the discussion, moderator Richard Quest, the CNN anchor, announced Ariadne's gift. As claps erupted, she remained in her seat in the audience, still a bit shy. But,

in an impassioned voice, she made a declaration: "Take a cause—
make it your one cause, make it stand out, make it shout out."

Born in Rome in 1962, Ariadne spent much of her childhood in the
Tuscan countryside around La Fuserna, the simple farmhouse that
her mother bought after her divorce from Paul and her remarriage,
to actor Lang Jeffries. Ariadne's chores included picking out toma-
toes, zucchini, and other bounty from the vegetable patch for family
meals, and starting the primitive electrical generator that was the
farmhouse's only source of power. In her free time, she would walk
the two miles to the tiny village of Orgia and go from house to house,
helping out the predominantly elderly population with their household tasks. In return, the matriarchs of the community doted on her.
"I literally was raised by a village," said Ariadne.

In the mid-1970s, following the kidnapping, Gail and the children
moved to England, where Ariadne attended boarding school in Sussex. On weekends and school breaks, she often came to stay at Sutton
Place with her grandfather, who was also her godfather. "I think I
got lucky, being the youngest," she recalled, over tea in Paris in 2019
before one of August's fashion shows. Initially Ariadne appeared shy,
but her natural warmth and effervescence soon surfaced.

Being the baby of the family, she was allowed to sit in her grandfather's study, while he was surrounded by piles of papers, books, and
visitors. His work ethic was "bananas," she said. Yet he was great fun.
She would tie his shoelaces together, making him giggle, until she
finally got too much in the way. Then he would say "Scat!" and send
her off to Bullimore and Parkes. She would "help" them polish the
silver, efforts that doubtless entailed more work for them.

"He wasn't such a talkative man, but you knew that you were
loved and taken care of," she said of her grandfather. "It was horri-
ble for me when my Nonno Getty died." (She was thirteen when he
passed away in 1976.)

When it was time for college, she came to America, enrolling at Bennington, the artsy and intense Vermont school, where her contemporaries included future literary stars Bret Easton Ellis, Donna Tartt, and Jonathan Lethem.

Academia wasn't for her. She dropped out and traveled, then lived between New York and Los Angeles. Using an old Pentax camera, she became a photographer, focusing on architectural subjects. Exhibitions of her hand-colored prints, held in galleries in both cities, were well-received. But around that time, the mid-1980s, she drew more notoriety from her choice of roommate—Cher.

Ariadne was Cher's long-term houseguest. She moved into one of the spare rooms in the star's Los Angeles mansion, and stayed about three years. ("Cher said to her, 'Make yourself at home.' So she did," August explained.)

In 1988, Ariadne married Justin Williams, an actor she'd been seeing for a couple years, and the pair moved into a small house in Brentwood. They had Nats in 1992 and August two years later. In his babyhood, August designed his first gowns by draping napkins over forks. Before long, he was repurposing his mother's silk Louboutin shoe bags to make new looks for his Barbie dolls. "Fashion was my first language," he later explained. Nats, on the other hand, was a tomboy, usually skateboarding or climbing trees.

Shy though Ariadne might have been, that didn't mean she wasn't tough and fiercely protective when it came to looking out for her children. They were brought up using their father's surname, Williams; until around the time Nats turned eight, they had no idea they were Gettys, much less what that meant.

In Los Angeles, the Getty name looms large, sometimes literally. When they passed signs for Getty Drive or Getty Circle on the freeways, for example, Ariadne would steer straight ahead without saying a word. Even on school field trips to the J. Paul Getty Museum, the children were unaware they had any connection to it. In retrospect, Nats says he should have had a clue: his mother always chaperoned those class trips.

"I wanted them to grow up without the weight of the name," Ariadne explained.

The Getty name, of course, comes with burdens as well as blessings. Ariadne was ten when her brother was kidnapped. Her young adult years—the early 1990s, when her sister, Aileen, battled AIDS—were also a frightening time. Little was known then about how the disease was spread. Before she went to the hospital to visit Aileen, Ariadne worried about possible transmission to baby Nats. But her pediatrician assured her it was safe for her to go. "Those were really scary days," she recalled.

Around 2000, the Williamses left Hollywood for Buckinghamshire in England, motivated in part by her wish to be close to her father. That's when Ariadne told her children about their Getty blood. She couldn't keep it from them any longer, as they would be going to schools with their cousins. (As adults, Nats and August chose to use the Getty surname.)

During the decade the family lived in England, where they resided in a house very close to Wormsley, Nats and August attended elite boarding schools, including St. Edward's and Dragon. Nats did well academically, but school was never for August. He did, however, find inspiration at Wormsley, in the Walled Garden.

Roaming alone through the mazes of flowers, inspired by beauty and decay, August (who described himself at the time as "a chubby, ginger, American gay kid") created imaginary scenarios and characters—including one he calls the Getty Girl, a sort of phantasm and muse. The bowered sanctuary was formative. "I like to live my life somewhere between fantasy and reality at all times," he said.

In 2004, around which time Ariadne and Justin divorced, she began to establish herself as a philanthropist when she started the Fuserna Foundation (she later renamed it the Ariadne Getty Foundation). Its mission statement was two words long: "Unpopular causes." She distributed money to worthy but underfunded initiatives, including a reading program for prisoners. Inmates were given books and offered £5 to finish them, with the funds going to a charity of their choice. Later she traveled to refugee camps in Uganda to supply generators known as "solar suitcases," which medical personnel used in areas without electricity.

She was also able to enjoy a good relationship with her father. After having been incapacitated by depression and illnesses for decades, he had finally overcome many of his problems. "It was wonderful . . . to watch him emerge. I feel we got very lucky," she said. "He found a much more expansive life. . . . For a family that was initially fragmented, we became a much closer family."

Around 2010, Ariadne and the kids moved back to Los Angeles. Nats flew to California a few months ahead of his mother and brother. Academically he was doing fine, but he needed to escape the boarding-school social scene, where he'd fallen into trouble. He was drinking and struggling with body-image issues, which would challenge him for years to come.

During those months in LA, his aunt Aileen looked after him. After her own battles with drugs and HIV, Aileen was now in a good place and running Gettlove, her nonprofit to aid the homeless. When Nats arrived, he and Aileen lived in a building attached to a men's sober-living center. "We would wake up at five every morning, make three hundred lunch bags, do the breakfast line, then we would drive around LA handing out bags with blankets and toothbrushes to homeless people," Nats recalled.

"It was hard-core, but one of the most meaningful and important things I've ever done, and it really set the tone for my life back in LA. It turned me into a mini version of my mom and my aunt."

Around the same time, 2,500 miles away in Mississauga, Ontario, Gregory Lazzarato was a high school athlete (a nationally ranked diver) with a secret. Lazzarato—who was born the same year as Nats and who later became Gigi Gorgeous—had discovered makeup.

Lazzarato began making videos in which she offered makeup tutorials, posting them on YouTube. They quickly gained viewers; in the process, she earned self-esteem. "I never felt beautiful earlier in my life. Makeup was a confidence tool for me, and it helped me identify with my femininity," she said.

But she was still embarrassed enough to hide her posts from her family. Eventually a relative saw them, and informed Gigi's mother, Judy. "She confronted me," recalled Gigi. "I thought she would be mad. Instead, she said, 'I'm your biggest fan. But we should probably keep this from your father for now.'" Soon enough, David, her dad, found out. His reaction: "Just be safe." Before long, Gigi began to receive checks from advertisers on her YouTube channel, and later from brands she partnered with. Her two brothers, one older, one younger, were supportive too.

In Los Angeles, Nats enrolled at Mount Saint Mary's University, where he double-majored in political science and business; August entered New Roads School. After he was asked to repeat freshman year, he dropped out. He began homeschooling, while teaching himself how to be a fashion designer. "I decided to take a whack at what I'd been doing since I was three," he said. "I was kind of the oddball in the family. I have a fascination with an absurd amount of glam. No one knows where it came from. I'm from a family of tomboys."

As the trio settled into a 6,000-square-foot penthouse atop the Montage Hotel in Beverly Hills, the kids were finding their identities. August's coming-out story, at age fifteen, involved a room service waiter at the Sunset Tower Hotel, as he later told the *New York Times*. Nats began to date girls. When they both told their mother about their orientations, it was no surprise, as Nats recollected: "When I told her I was gay, she looked at me and said, 'Nats, I gave birth to you. I knew the minute you came out of me.' I was like, 'Thanks, but, dude, Mom, you could have given me a heads-up!'" Said Ariadne, "I kept waiting for them to tell me, because I didn't want to tell them."

As her children explored gay life in Los Angeles, Ariadne welcomed their friends and lovers. She became a den mother to much of the city's queer community, members of which took to warmly calling her Mama G. One typical night, August stepped out of his bedroom around midnight and found six drag queens in the kitchen with Ariadne, who was making them bowls of pasta. "They were like, 'We're here to see your mom. Go back to bed,'" he recalled.

Even while rolling out hospitality, Ariadne was fretting about the darkening political climate and the threats it presented to Nats and August and people like them. Their coming out encouraged her to come out, as an activist. "That's when she got super involved in the LGBT Center and GLAAD. I think that's when she found her inner fire," said Nats. "It lit a fire under her ass. I'm so proud of her."

In 2012, August—eighteen, lean, tanned, and liberally tattooed—officially launched his career. He opened August Getty Atelier, in a spacious building his mother acquired in Culver City. Two years later, he debuted at New York Fashion Week, becoming one of the youngest designers ever to show there, with a collection of sculpted minidresses and chiffon gowns.

While at Mount Saint Mary's, Nats—gamine, with porcelain-pale skin, sometimes-platinum short hair, and his share of tattoos—began modeling, represented by Next Management. In November 2015, when August staged his next big show—an extravaganza on the Universal Studios lot, in collaboration with photographer David LaChapelle—Nats was cast to walk in it. So was Gigi Gorgeous; two years earlier, when Gregory announced her transgender status on social media, she'd adopted the name (legally, she changed it to Gigi Loren Lazzarato). About the same time she moved to LA, where, through mutual acquaintances, she met August. Self-described as "boy crazy," Gigi was dating men and identified as gay.

Already a tall, striking blonde with full breasts, she was still in her transition process, which had started quietly a few years before. Her path began when she met a transgender girl for the first time. "It clicked for me," Gigi said. "From that day on, in my mind I started living as a trans woman. It just took everyone else a little longer to find out." It also involved years of hormone treatments and surgeries, in locations ranging from Los Angeles to Bangkok. Every step of the way she documented her transition on social media. In the process, she gained some eight million followers across YouTube and other platforms, and a reputation as a trans role model.

Even though Gigi and Nats were both part of August's Universal Studios show, they didn't meet there. There were sixty models, and it was a huge, immersive production. (The Old West lot was transformed into "Heaven" and "Hell." Among the props in the latter were televisions rolling Fox News footage of presidential candidate Trump.)

They met a few months later, when they flew to Paris to walk in a show for August there.

At Charles de Gaulle Airport, Nats fell for Gigi. "I pretty much knew the second I saw her. She radiated an infectious amount of positive energy and happiness. She is this amazing bright light. I pretty much laid it on the table to her. I said, 'We're not going to be just friends. I'm obsessed with you. Can we go out on a date?'"

"Then, sooner rather than later, we both said, 'I love you,'" said Gigi. She came out as lesbian.

Gigi got an immediate stamp of approval from Ariadne. "I liked her straightaway. She's so full of life, you can't resist her," she said.

As the couple was finding happiness together, August Getty Atelier, with about twenty employees, was taking off. Rachel McAdams wore a slinky emerald-green satin halter-neck gown August designed for her to the 2016 Academy Awards, where her film *Spotlight* won Best Picture. His ever more extravagant custom creations were also being worn by Lady Gaga, Katy Perry, Miley Cyrus, and others.

"I just want to make the world a shinier place—one sequin at a time," said August, summing up his philosophy.

More accomplishments came in 2017. A feature-length documentary, *This Is Everything: Gigi Gorgeous*, directed by two-time Oscar winner Barbara Kopple, premiered at the Sundance Film Festival. For the occasion, Gigi wore an especially dazzling August Getty Atelier creation, which came to be known as the "Million Dollar Dress." Constructed from metal mesh, it was embroidered with 500,000 Swarovski crystals. Six artisans spent three months making it. A couple months later, Paris Hilton wore it to the Hollywood Beauty Awards. (Its name notwithstanding, it was estimated to be worth some $270,000.)

That September, August showed his Spring 2018 collection at the Four Seasons Hotel in Milan. "His vision translated well: models wore glamorous looks with red carpet appeal such as a silver and gold beaded white strapless gown," wrote *WWD*.

Next, it was Nats's turn to take the wraps off his fashion line. He began it in secret, as he completed his studies at Mount Saint Mary's. His grades were perfect, and he planned to become a lawyer. "But there was another side of me, and I didn't know how to express it," he said. His aha moment came via an Yves Saint Laurent jacket. "It was white leather. I had wanted it forever, and finally treated myself to it. I was so stoked."

But the joy was short-lived. "I went out with it on, and there were, like, five other people wearing it. I thought, *You've got to be kidding.* I had spent so much on it and now it didn't feel special." He remedied that by taking paint pens and Sharpies to it. His customized jacket was soon drawing praise from friends, who asked him to perform similar interventions on garments for them. Following some Instagram posts and word of mouth, his pieces—hoodies, trucker hats, and other staples of streetwear to which he gave an arty, luxe spin—became "a thing," as he recalled.

In the beginning, he financed it from his allowance and kept it a secret from his mother. "I was super insecure about it. It took a lot for me to say, 'Look at this' . . . because it's a representation of me." He needn't have worried. Actress Bella Thorne and singer Halsey were among the first customers who began snapping up the merch online.

The business, Strike Oil, launched officially in 2018 out of the Culver City building where August operates. Its large, stark-white rooms feature contemporary art, as well as a sizable vintage Getty Oil sign, a gift from cousin Joseph in London. Ariadne serves as CEO of both companies. The name Nats chose for his is a tribute to his great-grandfather and his famous statement that the key to success was "Rise early, work hard, and strike oil."

"It's one of my favorite rules to live by. I have it tattooed on my right ankle," he said. "So, when it came time to name my empire, if you will, I chose it as an homage to the family I have now and the ones that came before. It's my DNA.

"I always looked at leather as the black gold of fashion," he added, borrowing the term for oil. "When I start painting on a leather jacket, it feels like I am painting on oil, like I am striking oil."

(Great-grandfatherly inspiration and pride also run deep for his brother. "Whenever I am feeling sad or uninspired, I go to his grave. I sit and ponder, surrounded by nature, and think, *WWJPGD—what would J. Paul Getty do?*" said August. Recently, when he Instagrammed an image of the Getty Center's hilltop campus, he captioned it simply, "Feeling prideful AF.")

Many of the sketches Nats prints on his pieces are inspired by artists he was exposed to as a child—a number of whom Ariadne collects, including Keith Haring, Andy Warhol, Jean-Michel Basquiat, Jeff Koons, and Raymond Pettibon. The extended family, abounding with collectors, also provides inspiration. "Everybody kind of has their own vibe and taste," he explained. "Being surrounded by that even without knowing I was being exposed to it really shaped my love and appreciation of art."

At the same time, he had some harrowing experiences. In his social media posts, he has talked forthrightly about his battles. During the Covid lockdown in 2020, he reflected: "I never realized how ill I truly was. Between drugs, eating disorders, and mental health issues I honestly was knocking on deaths door. . . . After multiple over doses, a near coma, broken bones, and a body weight of under 80lbs I still returned to a life of drugs, darkness and self hate. . . . It has taken me years to recover and it is still a daily struggle."

Gigi helped him find the light. She was the first person he had dated "who saw me for me," he said. In March 2018, Nats proposed. The pair flew to Paris, where they boarded a helicopter. They hovered above the forests of the Île-de-France and landed at Château de Vaux-le-Vicomte, which Nats had rented for the occasion. Designed in the seventeenth century by Louis Le Vau, architect of Versailles, it is widely considered the most ideal château in France. (J. Paul Getty admired it too: he contemplated buying it, as he wrote in his diary.)

WILL YOU MARRY ME? appeared in large lights on the building's façade as the couple descended. Ariadne, August, and other family and friends were awaiting them inside with champagne. Cue the fireworks.

The jubilant scene inside was captured in a video that Gigi posted on YouTube. "I'm going to have a daughter-in-law!" said Ariadne, who was accompanied by her partner of more than a decade, Louie Rubio, a music producer. (His credits include soundtracks for numerous movies and TV shows, including *Baywatch* and *Brothers and Sisters*.)

Soon after, Gigi met most of the Getty clan when she traveled with Nats to Wormsley, to attend uncle Mark's wedding to Caterina Nahberg in the Walled Garden. On a podcast with Gigi, Nats later spoke of how well everybody got on, which he likened to "the icing on the cake" of their engagement: "When you met my entire extended family, it was like, 'Damn, if you can keep up with *this*—getting into it with them, and being able to hang—I am so down.'"

In June 2018, Ariadne, along with Nats and August, gave a pretty remarkable interview to Brooks Barnes, LA correspondent of the *New York Times*, for the profile entitled "Growing Up Getty."

Ariadne was nervous at the start. "I'm a super-shy introvert—this is not my comfort zone," she said, over sips of chicken soup in her apartment at the Montage, where she was also flanked by Bandit, her brown chihuahua, and a pair of Jeff Koons balloon dogs.

Talking about why she gave $15 million to GLAAD, which had been announced in Davos a few months earlier, she decried the Trump administration's assaults on gay rights—they were affronts to her family and others like theirs. At the same time, her family was dealing with a unique onslaught, from the new movie *All the Money in the World* and the TV series *Trust*, both of which plumbed the grisly details of her brother's kidnapping. "Our family has been under attack," she said. August and Nats, for their parts, called the films "demonizing" and "disgusting."

The Ridley Scott–directed movie, starring Christopher Plummer and Michelle Williams, had been released six months earlier. Danny Boyle's series, starring Donald Sutherland and Hilary Swank, was currently on FX—the ten episodes of Season One. Two more seasons had been envisioned by the producers. For Ariadne, a single season was more than enough. She not only vocalized her unhappiness (while the rest of her extended family largely opted not to comment), she hired Martin Singer, one of Hollywood's toughest and most powerful attorneys. A letter he sent to FX and Boyle stated that the series "falsified the dreadful story of Ariadne's brother's kidnapping to turn it into a cruel and mean-spirited depiction of the Getty family, maliciously and recklessly portraying them as greedily cooperating in and/or facilitating a kidnapping that left a family member mutilated." Seasons Two and Three did not go into production.

That September, the Los Angeles LGBT Center presented her with its Distinguished Achievement Award—her first-ever award for philanthropy. (A $4.5 million gift from Getty enabled construction of the organization's new Ariadne Getty Foundation Youth Academy and the forthcoming Ariadne Getty Foundation Senior Housing.) "I'm shaking like a leaf," she said when she got to the stage in the ballroom of the Beverly Hilton, even though her children had warmed up the 1,500 guests with a humorous introduction. In August's part, he offered details of his coming-out story: "I never came out. I just said one day, 'Mom, I'm going on a date with the room service guy.' All she said was, 'Which one?'" (Ari did go out later that night in search of one of the health-service vans that operate around West Hollywood; she loaded up on information packets and condoms, which she gave to her son.)

"I have recently stepped out of the shadows of my donating and my philanthropic work, which hasn't been that easy," said Ariadne in her remarks. "I've done it to encourage others to step forward and understand the impact of what it means to give . . . and to participate on a larger platform, to have things resonate. I encourage everybody to get connected, start being active, and don't be shy like me for all the years that I have been."

She also thanked one of August's ex-boyfriends for introducing her to the LGBT Center. "My office is filled with all of August's exes," she said.

In January 2019, August vaulted to fashion's stratosphere when he showed a collection he entitled "Confetti" alongside the haute couture collections during Paris Fashion Week. Inside the Salon d'Été, a glass-conservatory-like space at the Ritz Hotel, models in white silk, satin, and lace lounged around a grand piano. "Bridging the Old Hollywood glamour of his hometown with Parisian Grace," *WWD* wrote.

Showing his work during the Paris season at such a tender age wasn't stressful for him. "It was a natural progression. I don't get nervous. This is what I do," he said.

As soon as the presentation was over, August flew to Davos to join his sibling, Gigi, and Ariadne. Returning to the World Economic Forum, AGF and GLAAD sponsored another panel with top corporate executives, "Making Equality Equal: The Next Move Forward for LGBT Rights." The emphasis on corporate social responsibility reflects Ariadne's view that while governments—in the US and around the world—are lagging behind on human rights and moral leadership, big businesses can be more responsive and effective agents to advance social equity issues (something that became more fully apparent to others a couple years later, in the wake of battles over election laws and Black Lives Matter). "So, basically, we're here to strong-arm the corporate world, to make sure they do the right thing. Shame them, if necessary," she said.

A particularly moving moment came when Dr. Corinna Lathan, CEO of AnthroTronix, a robotics and biotech firm, spoke. AGF/GLAAD is helping to foster "a culture of LGBTQ acceptance" at Davos, she said; its panels were having unexpected impact. The previous year at Davos, she recounted, her main purpose had been to moderate a panel on the Earth BioGenome Project. Yet "the most powerful conversation that I had was with pop culture icon Gigi Gorgeous." Gigi, as it happens, is "the idol" of Lathan's own eleven-year-old transgender daughter, Eliza. A letter that Gigi subsequently wrote to Eliza was enormously inspirational to her. "The professional became personal," Lathan said.

When spring 2019 arrived, the spotlight was on Gigi. Harmony Books published her memoir, *He Said, She Said: Lessons, Stories, and Mistakes from My Transgender Journey.* In it, she disclosed that she had not yet proceeded with gender reassignment surgery. She was conflicted about having the procedure to remove her penis and construct a vagina. "Part of me wonders if I'm holding onto my anatomy so that Nats and I can have children," she wrote.

Shortly after the book appeared, she divulged in a YouTube video that she had flown to Bangkok for the operation but canceled it the day before, due to fears that the operation might not be totally successful: "I have had lots of friends who have gotten the surgery. I've seen a lot of vaginas—post-vaginas—and some are gorge and functioning and some are not so gorge. Obviously, it goes without saying, I want a gorge, functioning vagina." She and Nats, she added, were actively trying to conceive a child together.

July was a blockbuster month for the whole family. August returned to the Paris Ritz to present his next couture collection. With "Enigma," his theme was darkness. A gorgeous, gothic spectacle, it unfolded as models slowly began to materialize through an allée of pleached linden trees, planted in Versailles boxes, in the hotel's Grand Jardin. The procession of extravagant if macabre looks ranged from an armor-plated minidress molded from resin to look like a tombstone, to a boat-sized pannier skirt and bodice of black lace. Clad in a black sleeveless T-shirt, black jeans, studded belt, and boots, August beckoned the models forth as waiters served champagne to guests, classical music played, and a breeze rustled through the trees.

"I like to tell stories," he later explained. "With 'Enigma,' I wrote about tragedy and morbid love."

Nonetheless, the atmosphere was lively, in part thanks to more than a dozen friends who August flew to Paris to see the show. The multicultural group, most of whom live in West Hollywood and had not been to Paris before, included drag queens and transgender persons. It was definitely some fresh air at the Ritz.

At the same time, seasoned couture aficionados in the audiences were impressed. "Extraordinary. I've seen something today I've never seen before," said Houston doyenne Becca Cason Thrash, who has seen quite a bit in her time.

For August, there were just two opinions that really counted: his mom's and the French. "Both are a little scary because they are both hard-hitters," he said. He held his breath, then, when he saw Ari in the Grand Jardin: "I get nervous for my mom. She means the world to me."

Before the month was out, Ariadne celebrated her fifty-seventh birthday, *Variety* honored her as Philanthropist of the Year in a dinner at the Montage Hotel back in Beverly Hills, and Nats and Gigi were married.

The ceremony, July 12, had all the pomp one would expect for the marriage of a great-grandchild of J. Paul Getty. Two hundred twenty formally clad guests gathered on the lawn of the Rosewood Miramar Beach Hotel in Montecito, California, overlooking the Santa Barbara Channel. Pink and white rose petals were strewn everywhere as a violinist drew her bow and commenced the ceremony with the notes of Celine Dion's "Because You Loved Me."

Nats, wearing a white suit with a tailcoat that he had designed, waited by the altar with Ariadne and Louie. Gigi, in a white flowing gown by Michael Costello, walked down the white velvet carpet bordered with white cherry blossom trees, accompanied by her father.

After the couple was pronounced Gigi and Nats Getty, the guests (including Caitlyn Jenner) dined on pan-roasted filet mignon and chicken piccata. Video toasts to the newlyweds came from, among others, Katy Perry and Orlando Bloom ("Show us how it's done!") and Gavin Newsom, California's governor and Nats's godfather ("I'm proud of you and I'm proud of Gigi").

When 2020 began, the family returned to Davos, this time with one more Getty. Ariadne's brother Mark announced that his company, Getty Images, was partnering with GLAAD to build a new digital glossary and set of guidelines that prioritize intersectionality, allowing LGBTQ-related images shot by Getty's 250,000 photographers to be more easily found. "There's a huge opportunity here to break stereotypes, tell stories that haven't been told before," he said. The Ariadne Getty Foundation later posted photos of the brother and sister captioned: "We moved the needle in Davos. . . . Siblings changing the world."

As Covid-19 took hold, the Gettys, like most of the population, went relatively quiet. Nats took the opportunity to examine his life and reflect. In January 2021, he posted a photo of himself bare-chested on Instagram. His breasts had been removed. "I am transgender, nonbinary," he announced.

All his life, he explained, he had felt "not in sync with the body I was born with. . . . So I decided to start my physical transformation and get top surgery."

He also acknowledged the advantages he enjoys, which others might not. "While I feel so blessed to be able to start my transition surrounded by love and support, it's not lost on me the many people who are having to navigate this alone and in silence."

"I didn't fall in love with Nats because of his gender, I fell in love with the person that he is," said Gigi shortly afterward when, at the same time, she announced her new status as pansexual.

As the pandemic began to wane, the family got back to business. With its new "Oil Spill Tee," Strike Oil continued to attract buzz (Machine Gun Kelly was spotted wearing one). At the same time, the fledgling company recognized the ills of fossil-fuel extraction (15 percent of the sales proceeds went to the Marine Conservation Institute). And Ariadne awaited the opening of the Los Angeles LGBT Center's Ariadne Getty Foundation Senior Housing, a 70,000-square-foot, five-story tower adjacent to the two-year-old Ariadne Getty Foundation Youth Academy. Fostering a community where young and old cohabitate—where each can support and learn from the other—reminded her of her childhood in Orgia, she told *Los Angeles Blade.* "That's definitely the thing that makes me the happiest," she said of this coming together. "There's no room for loneliness."

Paul III

The Janiculum is the second-tallest hill in Rome. From its heights, the ancient capital stretches out below. The splendor and wonder of it all only increases when you gaze down from the Fontana dell'Acqua Paola, the monumental marble fountain atop the Janiculum, built in 1612 by Pope Paul V. Viewers of Paolo Sorrentino's masterful film *The Great Beauty* will recognize it from the opening scene.

Late one warm summer night in 1972, two teenagers jumped into the fountain's semicircular pool.

"We sat in it for hours. We were gazing down at the city, waiting for the light," remembered one of the boys, Pietro Cicognani. "When the sun came up, it was so glorious—the whole city was at our feet."

Cicognani would eventually move to New York and become a successful architect whose work was widely publicized. The last name of his companion that night was already world-famous, but few people outside Rome knew anything yet about red-haired, freckle-faced Paul himself.

Cicognani had been introduced to J. Paul Getty III by a cousin. "We hit it right off. He was a sweetheart—very gentle, sensitive," he recalled. "He wouldn't talk about his family. He just wanted to live life. He had a desire to feel the moment."

While his younger siblings seemed to flourish more in the Tuscan countryside, Paul was thoroughly at home in Rome. Over six feet tall and lithe, he loved speeding through every neighborhood and corner of the city on his motorbikes. Schools were seemingly the only places he didn't take well to. Creative but rebellious, he cycled through seven or eight educational institutions before, at sixteen, he convinced his mother, Gail, to let him leave school and focus on painting. (Paul III's father kept in sporadic contact with him from England or Morocco.)

Rome had changed a great deal since the days when his parents arrived, when the city was in its elegant *Dolce Vita* heyday. By the early 1970s, it had become a countercultural melting pot, filled with students from Latin America who had fled fascist regimes and hippies from around the world who were seeking some combination of enlightenment and escape.

Among them were a pair of beautiful German twins, Gisela and Jutta. After arriving in Rome in 1972, they spent a night on the beach at nearby Sperlonga where they dropped acid, a consciousness-altering experience that also served to introduce them to members of Rome's creative community.

As soon as Paul met them—both paled-skinned and dark-haired—the trio became inseparable; they moved into a basement apartment in Trastevere. Seven years Paul's senior, the young women were budding actresses, filmmakers, artists, and activists. Gisela—who for a time went by the name Martine—had recently given birth to a daughter, Anna, with her second husband, a German actor, from whom she soon parted. Anna was being cared for by the twins' family in Germany.

One of Paul's good friends was Carlo Scimone. The son of a proper Roman family, he was pursuing his interest in photography—often using Paul as a model. Among the portraits he took of Paul were artistic nudes, some of which appeared, rather scandalously, in *Playmen*, a fashionable Italian magazine. In their youth, Paul and his siblings would come to his house for meals and to hang out, and vice versa.

In the spring of 1973, Paul visited Cinecittà, where Paul Morrissey was shooting *Flesh for Frankenstein*. On the set, Paul met Andy Warhol, a friend of his father's. Andy had recently been in Milan, where he was transfixed by Leonardo da Vinci's mural *The Last Supper*. It would make a great movie, he told the young Getty.

Excited, Paul proposed the idea to Carlo. Filming soon began in the Trastevere basement. Carlo shot it with a Super 8 camera. With frizzy red hair, red lipstick, and mascara, Paul played an androgynous Jesus Christ, while a group of their friends served as the apostles. Instead of being crucified, Jesus was electrocuted.

The film was never shown. It was lost in the chaos that began to unfold a few weeks later when Paul was abducted, in the early-morning hours of July 10, 1973. He was walking home from Piazza Navona, where he'd been with friends, when three men jumped out and pulled him into a white car. Pistol-whipped, blindfolded, and chloroformed, he was driven 240 miles south, into the desolate reaches of Calabria.

Two days later, the kidnappers, members of the Calabrian mafia, phoned Gail and told her they had her son, and she should await their ransom demands. The Italian police and the press initially dismissed the story as a hoax. After the kidnappers demanded $17 million, J. Paul Getty issued his statement from Sutton Place: "If I pay a penny of ransom, I'll have fourteen kidnapped grandchildren."

Over the next five months, Paul III endured horrors, as he was dragged between a series of huts, caves, and bunkers. Much of the time he was chained like an animal, and plied with cheap whiskey, cognac, and other liquor to keep him docile (the beginning of his addiction to alcohol). In October, his captors brutally sliced off his right ear and sent it to a newspaper in Rome. Due to a postal strike, it took five weeks to arrive. After negotiations with the kidnappers, the Gettys agreed to a payment of $3.2 million, which was flown from California to Italy by Bill Newsom. After it was delivered to the kidnappers, Paul was released on a remote roadside in a snowstorm the night of December 15, 1973, and later found by police.

Afterward, Gail took Paul and his siblings away to the Austrian Alps for two months to help them all recover. But life was changed forever, for all the Gettys. Their "story" would be told and retold so many times, but rarely, if ever, by the people who were there.

Scimone, who went on to have a distinguished career in the Italian Foreign Ministry and make a family with his wife, Margherita Rostworowski, never spoke publicly about his childhood friend for more than forty years. But after seeing the portrayal of Paul in *All the Money in the World*—as an idle boy, at the mercy of events—Scimone agreed to talk to me.

"Paul was intelligent, vital, full of life," he recalled. "He would have done a lot, if he could have had a normal kid's life. I'm speaking now, giving the memory I have of Paul, because I want to give him back his dignity."

Paul "was not allowed to have a normal life," he continued. His siblings faced similar challenges: "They were burdened and overwhelmed by the weight of their last name. They wanted to be normal, simple—in jeans and T-shirts. But the minute people found out who they were, attitudes toward them changed. I remember being at a dinner with Paul and Mark. The whole atmosphere at the table suddenly changed when people found out their last name.

"They were golden kids. They had an aura around them. They were very empathetic. You wanted to be with them. Aileen . . . *cara ragazza* [dear girl]! . . . Gail was tender and sweet."

A few years ago, Scimone ran into Mark on a street in Rome. "I'd last seen him when he was a boy, in the country," he recalled. "I hugged him. I was glad to see a boy who was saved."

After his release, Paul didn't issue a statement. But several months later he gave an interview to Joe Eszterhas, which was published in the May 9, 1974, issue of *Rolling Stone*. A close-up portrait of a brooding Paul, shot by Annie Leibovitz, made the cover.

In an almost matter-of-fact fashion, Paul recalled many details of his ordeal. Just before the abduction, he remembered, he bought some newspapers and a Mickey Mouse comic book.

He described the pandemonium the night of his release, at the police station in Rome, where hordes of screaming reporters and photographers jostled. "It was madness," he said. And in the months following, he had no calm: "Everytime I went somewhere in Rome, I had a police escort. Motorcycles, sirens. I really couldn't go anywhere."

He became numb: "I felt it very difficult to talk, even to my family. . . . I said only essential things—'Pass the salt, pass the bread.'

"My mother and I talked a few times, but didn't say very much. . . . She keeps telling me that we have to sit down and talk about it, but— Oh, what in the world for? We should cry on each other's shoulders?

"I find I don't like speed anymore. It scares me. The other day I was in a taxi and the guy drove like a madman and I had to tell him to slow down."

In September 1974—nine months after the end of the kidnapping ordeal—J. Paul Getty III married Gisela at the town hall in Sovicille, near his mother's house in Tuscany. The bride was four months pregnant. At eighteen, the groom was four years below the age at which Gettys were permitted to marry, according to the terms of the trust that Paul Jr. and Gail, upon their divorce, set up for their children. The clause was meant to protect the girls from fortune hunters, but Paul III was nonetheless cut off financially.

His grandfather did agree to give him a small allowance. It was also decided that California would be a safer place for the newlyweds.

Weeks after the couple landed in Los Angeles, carrying hopes of putting hell behind them, their child, Paul Balthazar, was born at Tarzana Medical Center in January 1975. Soon after, Jutta arrived from Germany with three-year-old Anna. Paul legally adopted Anna several years later.

There was never going to be anything remotely conventional about Balthazar's and Anna's childhoods. The family set up housekeeping at the Chateau Marmont. The faux-Gothic hostelry, perched above Sunset Boulevard, had long been a favorite of Hollywood stars. ("If you must get into trouble, do it at the Chateau Marmont," Columbia Pictures boss Harry Cohn advised.) But in the mid-seventies, the establishment had fallen into disrepair; its threadbare rooms could be had for as little as $14 a night.

When the Gettys moved to a small house in Laurel Canyon, the electricity was sometimes turned off due to unpaid bills. The kids mingled with their parents' crowd, which included Warhol, Keith Richards, Leonard Cohen, Allen Ginsberg, William Burroughs, and Bob Dylan. Their babysitters included a teenage Sean Penn and Timothy Leary, the godfather of LSD.

Despite Paul's track record at school, his grandfather insisted he go to college. At Pepperdine University, where he studied Chinese history, he lasted one semester.

The trauma of his kidnapping overwhelmed him. Emotionally unable to talk about it, he turned to heroin, cocaine, and alcohol. His marriage suffered too. He had affairs, with musician Patti Smith among others, while Gisela became involved with actor Dennis Hopper.

In the late 1970s, Gisela relocated with the kids to the San Francisco Bay Area. Their dwellings there included a teepee at the Green Gulch Center in Marin County, one of the first Zen communities in America, where meditation began at dawn and the monks lovingly farmed organic fruits and vegetables. When the trio moved to a simple apartment in San Francisco, they slept on futons and Gisela made meals using lentils, whole wheat pasta, nutritional yeast flakes, and other organic ingredients then almost unheard of in most American households.

An artist, Gisela also engaged in a multitude of creative endeavors, from dervish dancing to esoteric Japanese drumming based on Zen thought.

In the apartment, there was no television. Instead, the kids put on plays, for which they wrote the scripts and made the costumes.

Everything was handmade, following the precepts of the Austrian philosopher and educator Rudolf Steiner, who believed that children should develop their intellectual, artistic, and practical skills in a holistic manner, a philosophy that spawned an independent school system known as Waldorf schools.

Even by the liberal standards of the Waldorf school that Balthazar and Anna attended, Gisela sometimes stood out. There was the day she came to pick up her kids with her head freshly shaven, and a spiked punk-rock collar around her neck.

Troubled as Paul was, friends recall him as someone with a lively, intelligent mind and great charm. "He was *truly* bright, curious, full of ideas and game for adventure," said photographer Jonathan Becker, who saw Paul often in Los Angeles in the late 1970s, after they met in 1976 in New York at Elaine's.

"He was very present in the here and now, he enjoyed life, he could focus on things, he was highly intuitive," Becker remembered.

"And naughty. He was sadly druggy—on and off the hard stuff and whatever. Around him were a lot of people with the same habits. In those days, people tended to do whatever the hell they wanted, and it was funny. Until you saw the consequences.

"There were days when Paul seemed checked out, but for the most part he enjoyed life, with a tremendous sense of humor about people. He got it."

Getty was also brave, Becker adds, recounting the story of a near-fatal sailing trip from Los Angeles to Catalina Island in 1977. Along with a few of Paul's friends, they rented a thirty-six-foot sloop for the voyage. Halfway back to the city, they encountered heavy seas: "A real squall, with thirty-knot winds growling, huge waves, the troughs as deep as the mast," said Becker, who was skippering. "We had to haul in and head up the face of every wave, otherwise the wave can roll you. It was eight hours like that. I was beyond exhaustion.

Paul was below barfing endlessly in the cabin with his friends. Stoned, useless, spoiled brats, I kept thinking. Finally, Paul came up alone and took the mainsheet—and we got there. Paul saved the day."

In 1981, Paul was working as a director's assistant and an actor (he appeared in Wim Wenders's *The State of Things*, which was released the following year). Trying to get himself together, he gave up drinking. To help him cope, doctors prescribed a variety of medications. After his years of drug and alcohol abuse, his liver shut down and he collapsed into a coma for six weeks. When he awoke, he was paralyzed from the neck down, and had lost much of his sight and ability to speak. Whole words were beyond him, but he could get out syllables, in a grunting fashion, which those close to him learned to decipher. Yet his brain and his emotions continued to function well. "He lives the life of the mind. He's a good poet. He loves music," said Bill Newsom, his godfather. "He's a great, great fellow."

He required round-the-clock care. At Gail's house in Brentwood, where he lived for a time, state-of-the-art medical and therapeutic facilities were installed. When he did go out, it was an elaborate production. "He was accompanied by two or three male nurses, and he was wheeled around the galleries in a sort of hospital trolley," a staff member at the J. Paul Getty Museum recalled of his occasional visits.

In 1986, Paul and Gisela officially separated. Around that time, Gail made some decisions for her grandchildren. "Enough of this hippie shit," she is said to have declared. At her instigation, Balthazar transferred to a school that was Waldorf's polar opposite—Gordonstoun, in Scotland. Famously severe and cold, it has educated generations of British aristocrats and royals, many of whom have testified to how miserable they were there. Prince Charles described it as "hell" and a "prison."

Balthazar fared surprisingly well. "You had to learn how to survive in the woods. I enjoyed it very much," he said.

Anna, meanwhile, continued her education in San Francisco at the Hamlin School for Girls, a prestigious academy in Pacific

Heights, then at the Sorbonne in Paris, where she studied for three years. "She had beautiful, long brown hair—her style was earthy and bohemian. She always seemed effortlessly glamorous," recalled a Hamlin classmate.

By the late eighties, Balthazar was back in California, enrolled at Bel Air Prep. One afternoon in 1988, a casting agent spotted the thirteen-year-old in detention (something about throwing a desk at a teacher).

English director Harry Hook was searching for the leads for his upcoming film adaptation of *Lord of the Flies*, William Golding's 1954 novel about a group of schoolboys stranded on an island. Hook didn't want to use professional actors. "I wanted fresh faces. I wanted to find kids who were real," the director said. Out of hundreds of candidates they interviewed, he felt Balthazar was the only one right for the part of Ralph, the voice of order and civilization. "With Balthazar, I felt there was an intensity and sense of morality to him, and that he was a very likable child."

Returning to LA later in 1988 from the intense four-month, hurricane-beset shoot in Jamaica, Balthazar had money in his pocket and an agent who was lining up new roles for him, beginning with *Young Guns II*. By the time both films were released in 1990, he was living the high life. He was unabashed about enjoying the bling. In interviews, he explained that *this* Getty wasn't born with a silver spoon. "I grew up scrappy. . . . The money wasn't there," he later reminisced on a podcast with actor Dean Delray.

At fifteen, he moved in with a twenty-year-old girlfriend, then dated Drew Barrymore; he went clubbing all night with friends including the Beastie Boys. Yet even with continued success—in such films as Oliver Stone's *Natural Born Killers* (1994) and David Lynch's *Lost Highway* (1997)—family sorrows took their toll. His father's misfortune wasn't just a private family matter; it was yet another manifestation of "the Getty curse," as the press repeated time and again. "That's a lot to cope with when you're growing up and I didn't handle it well," Balthazar said. "I got angry."

He became a third-generation heroin addict.

"For me the drugs were never about getting high, they were about adventure . . . the search for higher consciousness," he said.

"Without Mom's guidance, I'd be dead. In fact, I did die, several times. I was just lucky," he later told the London *Times* ("Member of a Troubled Dynasty" read the headline). "Normally these things don't have a happy ending, but my family are together and they made me want to be a better person."

Gisela and Paul divorced in 1993 and she moved to Europe. Living between a cottage in the Austrian Alps and an apartment in Munich, she has pursued fine art photography, writing, and documentary filmmaking. But she returned regularly to California to visit her children and Paul, with whom she remained close.

After finishing at the Sorbonne, Anna relocated to Los Angeles, where she pursued an acting career. She landed parts in a few independent films as well as in some of the 1990s' buzziest TV series, including *ER* and *Malibu, CA*.

On the eve of the new millennium, Balthazar met Rosetta Millington, with whom he found mutual understanding. The second of three children born to two hippie-artists, she grew up in an itinerant commune her family belonged to in Southern California. While it was a loving environment, "there weren't any boundaries," she recalled.

At fourteen, she began an international modeling career, which included campaigns for Azzedine Alaïa and shoots with Bruce Weber. Then she launched herself as a fashion designer and entrepreneur, with a children's wear line that had grown into a success by the time she met Balthazar.

"It was love at first sight, but it was also perfect in that all of our friends were the same and he was raised in a similar way," she said.

Their circle included the Arquette siblings. One of his closest friends is David; she has been best friends with Patricia since early childhood. At age eight, the girls had predicted their respective career paths, in fashion design and acting. "We were ambitious even then," said Rosetta, an elegant brunette with a precise manner.

She and Balthazar married at Los Angeles City Hall in 2000. Cassius (named after Muhammad Ali, a hero of Balthazar's) was born to the couple that year. Grace, Violet, and June came in 2001, 2003, and 2007, respectively.

They moved into a sprawling six-bedroom 1920s Spanish-style house with a lush garden, above Sunset Boulevard not far from the Chateau Marmont. On her visits from Germany, Gisela continued to drop into the old stamping ground, photos of which she sometimes posted on her Instagram page. ("And always the Chateau M," she captioned one picture.)

After her own wandering childhood, Rosetta prioritized providing a sense of stability for her children—a lively brood. Family dinners are served every night at six thirty. Fridays, the family observes Shabbat; Balthazar has studied the Kabbalah since 2009. The previous year had been tumultuous; a brief affair he had with the actress Sienna Miller was widely reported.

The Gettys' residence became a new nexus of hipster Hollywood. "Anyone who is anyone has been at the house," said Balthazar. (Jack Nicholson and Al Pacino are among the many who have attended the couple's parties and gatherings.)

Cassius once expressed to his mother a wish for his family to be "regular."

"I don't quite know what regular means," she said.

Meanwhile, husband and wife were succeeding in their creative endeavors. In 2006, Balthazar joined the cast of *Brothers and Sisters*, the hit series that ran for five tear-inducing seasons, in which he played Tommy Walker, scion of a wealthy California family.

After the birth of June, her youngest, Rosetta turned their guesthouse into an atelier and began producing a small collection of gowns and cocktail dresses under the label Riser Goodwyn. It was meant to be a line for just friends, but when you have friends like Demi Moore and Kirsten Dunst, word travels, and orders came in.

Between her film jobs, Anna was supporting herself as a caterer. She became an assistant to Akasha Richmond, organic chef to the stars (Michael Jackson and Barbra Streisand among them). The work reconnected Anna to her childhood cuisine. As a teenager, she had fallen off the organic wagon, rebelling against yeast flakes and the like.

Anna's August 2003 wedding in Tuscany, to screenwriter Gregory Pruss, brought together much of the Getty family, and spanned East and West. Some three hundred guests gathered for the hilltop ceremony. Balthazar walked Anna—resplendent in an antique diamond choker lent to her by her aunt Ariadne—down the aisle. She stopped to give a kiss to her wheelchair-bound father, Paul III, before she and Pruss were pronounced husband and wife by Gurmukh Kaur Khalsa, yoga guru to the stars (including Madonna and Courtney Love). She chanted "Sat Nam" ("I am truth") three times.

In Los Angeles, where the couple raised their children, India and Dante, born in 2004 and 2009, Anna forged a career as an advocate of holistic healthy living. Certified as an instructor in kundalini and prenatal yoga, she produced a DVD collection: *Anna Getty's Pre and Post Natal Yoga Workout*. But organic food became her primary focus. In 2010, Chronicle Books published *Anna Getty's Easy Green Organic: Cook Well—Eat Well—Live Well*.

In addition to recipes, it contained recollections of her mother's cooking as well as memories of the monks at Green Gulch tending their fruits and vegetables. "That's where my food education began," she wrote.

A healthy diet is the key to life, she stressed: "Reconnect to food and its power to nourish your mind, body, and spirit. Empower yourself through your kitchen and the food you prepare."

In the early 2010s, she crossed paths again with Scott Oster. They had met twenty-five years before at a West Hollywood nightclub, when he was beginning his career as a pro skateboarder and was about to be married. Now they were both recently divorced. They began dating, as he pursued his new career as an interior designer and she delved further into organic cooking. In 2014, they had a son, Roman. Later that year on a trip to Paris, when they were cycling by the Eiffel Tower, Scott proposed. Attendants at their 2015 ocean-side wedding in Big Sur included India, eleven, the maid of honor, and Dante, six, the ringbearer. This time, Anna walked herself down the aisle. The following year the family, including newborn Bodhi, settled in the idyllic valley town of Ojai, where Anna's aunt Aileen lived at the time. (When the *New York Times* Styles section published a somewhat snarky piece on the scene there in 2015, it described the two Getty women as "offbeat heiresses.")

Anna explained in another article, in *Greener Living Today*. "We've always worked," she said, speaking at least for herself and her brother. "People have passed on in my family and things have changed a bit, but not drastically. Even though my aunts and uncles live a very wonderful lifestyle, most of them drive Priuses and they're putting in solar panels at their properties.

"One thing that I constantly have to remind people of is that when you are an heir, you get money when people die," she added.

In 2011, J. Paul Getty III died at the age of fifty-four. He had been living with his mother in Ireland, at Gurthalougha House on a 100-acre lakefront estate in County Tipperary, but he passed away at Wormsley, with Gail and Gisela by his side.

Balthazar issued a statement: "[He] taught us how to live our lives and overcome obstacles and extreme adversity and we shall miss him dearly."

Even with Paul's physical limitations, he and Balthazar had found ways to open up to each other emotionally. "He would tell me he loved me. We had regular father-son moments," Balthazar recalled. "He would worry and he would cry. . . . To the day he died I would hop in bed next to him and tell stories or watch a film."

Thanks to his own earnings, as well as the Sarah C. Getty Trust, Balthazar's "scrappy" days were long gone. A weekend beach house in Malibu, a whopping gold Rolex, private jets, and a fleet of fancy cars became part of the lifestyle. His ground transport included a Lamborghini and a Porsche Turbo ("My first 'fuck you' car. I haven't normally done that. And that's part of being okay with 'it,'" he said in 2016—"it" meaning, presumably, being a Getty).

Music became his focus now. He made beats for a rock band, Ringside, and he formed a rap duo, the Wow, with South African rapper K.O. Using Pro Tools, a digital audio workstation (a birthday gift from Rosetta and their friend Joaquin Phoenix), he turned the guesthouse into his music studio, where he produced an album, *Solardrive*. Under his rap name, Balt Getty, he began DJing around the country—sometimes spinning several nights a week.

A turning point for Rosetta came in 2015. Patricia Arquette appeared at the Academy Awards wearing an elegant black and white column dress Rosetta had designed for her. Nominated as Best Supporting Actress for her role in Richard Linklater's *Boyhood*, Patricia took home the statue, and Rosetta garnered considerable buzz.

With June now in kindergarten, Rosetta took her work as a fashion designer to the next level and launched her eponymous line out of the pool house. Reflecting her minimalist sensibility, she created understated but beautifully cut pieces, made of superlative-quality silk, cashmere, and other materials. Devotees of the Rosetta Getty label soon included the likes of Margot Robbie, Tracee Ellis Ross, Dakota Johnson, Claire Foy, and Rihanna, while *Vogue* and *WWD* gave glowing coverage.

Each season she produces a limited number of wardrobe fundamentals—an assortment as rigorously curated as a museum collection. When she begins a collection, she usually chooses an artist or an architect to study and draw inspiration from (Louise Bourgeois and Louis Kahn are favorites), or she picks a young contemporary artist to collaborate with (such as Kayode Ojo or Anna-Sophie Berger).

Looming ahead in 2016 was the fortieth anniversary of the death of Balthazar's great-grandfather. By now, many of the millions who visited the J. Paul Getty Museum's sites in Brentwood and Pacific Palisades had no idea who J. Paul Getty was. Among the general public, the Getty name had come to be better associated with drugs, decadence, and tragedy. At the same time, to the youngest Gettys, their patriarch had become a fairly remote historical figure.

As the anniversary approached, both the museum and the Getty family delved into their history. At the Getty Center, curators prepared a permanent, interactive installation, *J. Paul Getty: Life and Legacy*, to tell the story of their patron's life as a businessman and an art collector; at the Getty family meetings in Italy, Balthazar and his uncle Mark put together lessons for the youngsters. Starting with their Scots-Irish roots and the pioneering days in Bartlesville, the tutorials explored the work ethic and unconventional thinking that enabled Getty to become the richest man of his time, and to create one of the world's greatest cultural assets. In addition to the museum, which has never charged an admission fee to any visitor, the J. Paul Getty Trust operates the Getty Conservation Institute and the Getty Research Institute, preeminent centers of scholarship and preservation.

As the museum put the finishing touches on its installation, the curators asked Balthazar to come and test the beta version of the interactive touch screens. In September 2016, just before it opened to the public, director Timothy Potts welcomed twenty-three Gettys to a private preview. Five generations, they ranged from age 8 (Veronica, Billy and Vanessa's youngest child) to 103 (Teddy, J. Paul Getty's last wife).

Aileen thanked Potts and his staff for "unearthing and shedding a more natural light on my grandfather" and for "making it possible to strip away some of the myth that was setting like stone."

As Balthazar said in an interview with *The Iris*, the blog of the J. Paul Getty Trust, it was an opportunity to reconnect with a legacy he had once shunned, and for his family as a whole to bolster its pride: "I think you rebel against these sorts of things because you want to create your identity and nobody wants to be seen as the great-grandson, or grandson, or son of anybody. You want to be your own man and create your own legacy . . . but the older I get the more pride I'm able to have in my family's history. As a family we feel incredibly proud. It's not about showing off. It's not about gloating. It's really just having pride in what Nonno was able to do. I do feel an incredible connection."

"Stand back—it's about to get wack!"

"Single droppin' in a couple hours. Wack—Balt Getty—wack."

Behind a turntable set up in the parking lot of a strip mall on Fairfax Avenue in Los Angeles, on an evening in June 2019, Paul Balthazar Getty was whipping up the crowd. At his invitation, a couple hundred hipsters and local characters—including Tommy the Clown, the freestyle-dancing LA legend—had gathered for a block party. Getty had multiple reasons to celebrate: Monk Punk, his luxe streetwear line, was debuting; his retail store (housed in a former RadioShack outlet) was opening; and his latest hip-hop track—which was entitled "Wack," if you hadn't guessed—was about to drop.

As the night progressed, the exuberant forty-four-year-old father of four also shared news of a significant milestone reached by his eldest, Cassius Paul: "What up, everybody, I'm Balt Getty. My son just graduated fucking high school. Man, I was cryin' like a baby, it was crazy."

Balthazar was now one of Hollywood's most multi-multi-hyphenates: actor–producer–director–DJ–musician–artist–fashion designer–shopkeeper.

His trajectory into fashion began when he started customizing items of clothing with his own sketches as well as with variations of the old Getty Oil logo. Not unlike what happened when his cousin Nats began her business, requests from friends came in. He began producing a line of affordable streetwear under a label he called Purplehaus (it's his favorite color). Then he took his designs to the next level, with a luxury range of accessories and clothing, including "the Paul," a long, collarless shirt inspired by his grandfather Paul Jr.'s Moroccan djellabas. He christened this line Monk Punk.

"It came to me one night," he explained to me inside the store, as friends such as actor David Arquette (in a bright-orange track suit and huge gold chain) milled about. "It makes you think of spirituality, being in touch with your emotional side, let's say. But then, you're still a punk. So—I'm not a pussy, you're not going to push me around. It's about embodying both sides, both of which I think are important."

Balthazar proceeded to point out images from Monk Punk's new look book. The models were not the usual fashion types, but former members of the Rollin 60's Neighborhood Crips, the fearsome street gang; they were photographed around Crenshaw and Sixtieth, epicenter of gang conflict in LA. "Instead of models, I said, 'Let's do something authentic. No styling.' I just said, 'You guys, just rock it how you would rock it,'" said Getty, who was clad in an oversized white Monk Punk T-shirt, a large gold chain, and a pink knit cap. (Before the photo shoot, he made a donation to Crenshaw Rams, a program that helps neighborhood youth, "because I believe in community and starting again," he told the *Hollywood Reporter.* "Not to mention how fly they looked in season one of my line Monk Punk.")

As she prepares her fashion collections, Rosetta often does research at the Getty Center. Her 2019 collaboration with the Getty Research Institute (GRI), was particularly resonant. That spring she immersed herself with the curators there as they prepared a landmark exhibition, *Bauhaus Beginnings*, a reexamination of the founding principles of that influential German art school, which had been established a century before.

While the show featured items by Bauhaus stars such as Wassily Kandinsky and Walter Gropius, Rosetta was captivated particularly with work produced by some of the school's lesser-known female students, such as a curtain fabric with interlocking red, black, and white lines. Rosetta alchemized that into a plaid she used in a double-breasted peak-lapel jacket.

Just before the opening of the exhibition, which Rosetta sponsored, she photographed her look book at the Getty Center. Models posed throughout the stark Richard Meier–designed campus, even in the hushed stacks of the GRI library. Coincidentally, just as she was shooting in this cerebral environment, her husband was shooting *his* look book at Sixtieth and Crenshaw, with a very different mood and cast.

About the same time, Anna launched her new project, Amalgam Kitchen, a website and Instagram account focused on mainly plant-based, low-sugar recipes that she creates. As its name suggests, Amalgam presents a blend of her knowledge of many different diets and ways of healthy eating.

Under the umbrella of his multimedia platform Purplehaus, Balthazar continued to expand his horizons. He launched collaborations with the fashion brands Moncler and Chrome Hearts. He produced a cycle of three-minute-long videos for a series he entitled *A Day in the Life*, which he described as "a reality show for people with ADD." In one, Balt, Rosetta, and the kids touch down in San Francisco and attend one of his great-uncle Gordon's lavish birthday parties; in another, they all descend on the Piazza del Campo in Siena for a running of the Palio. (Typically, the family spends six weeks each summer in Tuscany, communing with nature and their fellow Gettys.)

On the music front, Balthazar released a series of tracks. On some of them, he playfully grappled with the subject of wealth. One of the songs he wrote was entitled "Money."

To print some cash
Fuck that I think we'll pass . . .
Gettin' in for free
Even though I got my money
We wear the wreckage like a crown don't give a fuck can't take us down
Running through the streets livin' off monopoly money

"I like to poke fun at myself and the irony of it all . . . this material world we live in. . . . It's like warning people about a drug, but doing it too," Balthazar commented about the track. Yet he sees his output being in line with family tradition. "I think I'm a chip off the old block, in the sense—my grandfather, my great-grandfather—we're workers. I don't want to rest on my laurels. We all want to make our own names."

When the long period of Covid-induced home confinement ended, a member of the youngest generation of the family made the first splash. Seventeen-year-old Violet Getty, photographed by Collier Schorr, appeared on the cover of the Spring/Summer 2021 issue of *Self Service*, the extremely cool Paris-based fashion and culture biannual publication. Wearing a boyish brown silk jacket by YSL over a T-shirt of her own, she had an androgynous look, with her short brown hair and brown eyes.

Since she was small, Violet has opted to wear primarily boys' clothes. In her high school years, she identified as gay and introduced girlfriends to her supportive family. "She's so confident—such a doll with so much charisma," said a family friend. "She is going to become a big model."

Another chip off the old block, as Balthazar would say.

10

Tara

Tara Gabriel Galaxy Gramophone Getty—Paul Jr.'s fifth child, whom he had with Talitha, his second wife—is sometimes described as the "normal" Getty. In this family, of course, "normal" is relative. But considering the tumultuous circumstances of his childhood, his equilibrium is striking. He was three when his mother died tragically in Rome in 1971. In the aftermath, his father fled to London and spiraled downward into drug addiction and depression, while Gail took care of Tara, along with his four half siblings, in their apartment in Rome. Two years later, amidst the turmoil of Paul III's kidnapping, Tara's kindly maternal grandparents, Willem and Poppet Pol, became his surrogate parents.

They raised him in Ramatuelle, an idyllic French village in the hills above Saint-Tropez, where he went to a local school and took up sailing. There he got his hands on the tillers of Mirrors, Lasers, and other dinghies, before he graduated to more substantial boats. The sea, after all, was in his genes, his father having been born aboard ship off the coast of Liguria.

At fifteen, when Tara was in boarding school in England, more turbulence hit, with the eruption of the titanic legal battles between

Getty Oil and Gordon as well as between some extended family members and Gordon, the sole trustee. Unwittingly, Tara was thrust into the middle of these conflicts. In their campaign to avoid a sale of Getty Oil, the company's board members, executives, and lawyers in California concocted a complex scheme to dilute Gordon's voting power. This plan required a family member to petition the Superior Court for Los Angeles County to name a cotrustee. The lawyers decided a minor child would make the best plaintiff in this suit, and they chose Tara. Unlike some of his elder cousins, he didn't have a relationship with Gordon, or a strong parent like Gail, who, being fond of Gordon, was not likely to permit any of her children to sue their uncle. But Paul Jr., still in a weakened state, signed off on Tara's participation, after which a Getty Oil–aligned lawyer, appointed as his guardian ad litem, pressed the case in court. Tara was told that his interests were being looked after and he should not be concerned if his name began to appear in the newspapers. Even after Getty Oil was sold, this suit was at the crux of the legal squabbles that persisted for several years among some family members over Gordon's management of the Sarah C. Getty Trust, which ultimately led to its being partitioned into four separate trusts.

Per the Getty way, family relations continued amicably for Tara. Shortly after the trust litigation was resolved in 1986, he went to stay with his paternal grandmother, Ann Light (Gordon and Paul Jr.'s mother), in Palm Beach. "It is his first visit to the island," the *Palm Beach Daily News* reported.

Tara was nineteen when he stood in for his father at the Arts Benefactor of the Year gala dinner at the Savoy Hotel, accepting an award from Prince Charles on his father's behalf after Paul got cold feet. "My father has got [an] extremely bad toothache," Tara told the audience.

He had recently returned from Kenya, where he spent most of his gap year between boarding school and university working at a rhinoceros sanctuary. The African continent captivated him. "I did feel like Africa was going to be in my future from then on," he reminisced many years later.

Even as Tara began his studies at the Royal Agricultural University in bucolic Gloucestershire, a meeting in a London boardroom one day around 1990 ultimately brought him back to Africa.

At Hambros Bank, David Varty, a South African, was trying to raise funds to expand his fledgling company, Conservation Corporation Africa (CC Africa), one of the earliest exponents of ecotourism. Tara's half brother Mark (eight years his elder), a member of Hambros's corporate finance department, sat in on Varty's pitch meeting. Mark recognized the company's potential to be profitable as well as environmentally and socially beneficial (apartheid was coming to an end). He knew, too, that his younger brother could contribute to it.

Mark brought the proposition to his extended family. As they considered investing in it, Varty was run through the gauntlet of Getty financial advisors (including Judge Newsom) in New York and San Francisco. After he passed muster, a family delegation headed by Gordon flew to South Africa to make the final decision. Their large entourage descended on Varty's nascent game reserve, which was called Phinda (the Zulu word for "the return"). Close to the Indian Ocean in KwaZulu-Natal, it was located on 32,000 acres that had been devastated by decades of overfarming and hunting; the idea was to restore the land, repopulate it with animals, and help the local community in the process.

"There is one thing you should know," Mark told Varty as they set off on their inspection tour. "My uncle has arachnophobia. . . . If he sees a spider he'll leave."

"There's spiders everywhere you look," said a panicked Varty.

Indeed, their convoy of Land Rovers halted when the lead car came upon an impressive web strung across the road by a golden orb spider. Just then, as fate would have it, a spider-hunting wasp flew in and stung the arachnid to death in front of Gordon's eyes. Overjoyed by this good omen, he was now well-inclined to make the investment.

The deal was sealed a short time later when, with everyone sitting on overturned beer crates outside a staff hut, a local teacher articulated how the investment could contribute to the emerging democracy in South Africa led by Nelson Mandela. Newsom leaned in to his old school pal. "Gordon, we've got to support this," he said. The Getty family became CC Africa's majority shareholders.

In the years to come, various Gettys would intern there and contribute in different ways, but Tara moved there and put down roots. He began pitching in just after he finished his studies. "I was a dogsbody, just doing anything and everything that was around for me to do," he recalled. "I was like a stand-in ranger, but I was mainly a porter, carrying people's bags to their rooms."

Even as he settled into the bush, Tara—tanned, sandy-haired, and easygoing—was still captivated by the sea. And for a sailor, there was little that could be more exciting than the launch, in 1993, of his father's new superyacht.

A 262-foot art deco gem, she was commissioned in the 1920s by the chairman of the Packard Motor Car Company, who christened her *Reveler*. Later owners included Charles McCann—a lawyer and son-in-law of dime-store magnate F. W. Woolworth—who renamed her *Chalena*, and movie producer Robert Stigwood, for whom she was *Jezebel*. After Paul Getty Jr. acquired her in 1988, he entrusted a stern-to-bow refit to the preeminent naval architect Jon Bannenberg, whose celebrated commissions have included Saudi billionaire Adnan Khashoggi's *Nabila*, Malcolm Forbes's *Highlander*, and Microsoft cofounder Paul Allen's *Rising Sun* (now owned by music and movie mogul David Geffen). The five-year-long restoration of Getty's boat was so painstaking that steelworkers had to learn welding techniques that hadn't been used since World War II. Its saloons and six staterooms feature Lalique glass doors, skylights salvaged from a 1920s City of London bank, and open fireplaces, along with period art and furnishings sourced by Christopher Gibbs. "It's like being in a Noël Coward play or an Agatha Christie novel," according to one delighted passenger.

A twin-funneled, clipper-bowed beauty with a crew of eighteen, the *Talitha G*, as Paul renamed her, quickly set a new gold standard in superyacht design and service; she became a floating emblem of Getty glamour. In the eyes of many who care about these things, she remains peerless. The mere mention of her name can send pulses racing. "Utterly incomparable. . . . There is no other yacht in the world that can match the magnificence of this extraordinary vessel," said the late taste arbiter David Tang, a family friend. "Every detail of this yacht is unswitchable. Every detail balances into harmony. . . . To float and glide on *Talitha G* is like being on Solomon's carpet over water, breakfasting at Damascus and supping at Medina."

With Paul still in delicate health, however, getting him aboard was a challenge. He and Tara talked about crossing the Atlantic, but that voyage never happened. There were holidays on the Mediterranean and the Caribbean, though.

It was on a skiing holiday of his own, in Verbier, Switzerland, that Tara met Jessica Kelly. The daughter of a Sussex farmer, she was soft-spoken and down-to-earth, with brilliant blue eyes and blond hair. Tara gave Jessica her first look at the Phinda Private Game Reserve in 1995, when he invited her for a vacation. The next year, she joined him there full-time.

The whole operation was then still quite rough, which didn't bother her. "Africa seduced me, and I defected for good," recalled Jessica, who took a job as a bush-camp cook. "It was a real baptism-by-fire. Kind of sink or swim. My farm-girl background probably helped a bit. Tara and I, between us, are both very connected to the natural world."

As CC Africa acquired other properties and grew, Tara took on increasing responsibilities, managing the development of new lodges and serving as a nonexecutive director. (Eventually, when the company expanded its footprint outside Africa, it was renamed &Beyond;

the Enthoven family of South Africa became partners with the Gettys.) Together, Tara and Jessica began to steer the Africa Foundation, the business's nonprofit arm.

In 1998, the couple tied the knot—first in London, at the Chelsea Register Office off King's Road. Their church wedding took place soon afterward, in Ramatuelle. Upon their return to South Africa, they resided in a series of four thatched-roof cottages at Phinda, as well as a house in Cape Town. Two years later, their life expanded significantly. Their first child, born in August of 2001, was christened Orlando Willem Pol. "It's unusual without being crazy," Tara explained at the time, given the inevitable comparisons to the string of names his parents had chosen for him, prompting that memorable headline in San Francisco. Two months later, they added about 3,400 acres to their property portfolio when, with the backing of the Getty family trust, they acquired a property adjacent to Phinda called Zuka.

There, on the slope of a 200-million-year-old volcano crater, they built a 5,400-square-foot lodge using 200-year-old sandstone, its floor-to-ceiling windows affording spectacular views of the vast grassland and bushveld populated with elephants, zebras, giraffes, wildebeests, white rhinos, black rhinos, lions, leopards, and cheetahs, among other creatures. By the time they settled in, Orlando could tell a black rhino from a white one (the latter have square mouths), and "cheetah" was one of the first words that his baby brother, Caspar, learned to pronounce.

The Zuka Private Game Reserve—which within a few years expanded to encompass more than 25,000 acres—joined forces with Phinda and with another neighborhing property to form an immense protected nature reserve, the Mun-Ya-Wana Conservancy, named after the river that bisects the territory. Now a Big Five game reserve, it comprises some 70,000 acres.

Over the decades, Tara's relatives in California have been supportive of his Africa Foundation. Uncle Gordon and his wife, Ann, hosted fund-raising dinners and auctions at their mansion (Gavin

Newsom sometimes did the gaveling, and Gordon often bid). The senior member of the Getty clan has also paid return visits to Phinda, leading intergenerational family posses that have included his grand-nephew Balthazar and his granddaughter Ivy, who have assisted in conservation drives. For a number of years, Tara's sister Aileen has been a generous donor to the Africa Foundation.

Tara and Jessica remain the driving forces behind the Africa Foundation, which has funded hundreds of rural development projects in Botswana, Kenya, Mozambique, Namibia, South Africa, Tanzania, and Zanzibar. Bringing a new model of philanthropy to the continent, the organization has sought to work from the ground up, consulting and collaborating with local stakeholders, empowering them to develop their own communities on a sustainable scale.

&Beyond, led by CEO Joss Kent, has continued to expand. In 2020, it owned and operated twenty-nine deluxe lodges and camps in thirteen countries in Africa and Asia, which enables the company to positively impact more than 9 million acres of wildlife land and 2,000 kilometers of coastlines.

Together, the business and its nonprofit arm have provided a model in Africa for how to restore abused lands, and how to run wildlife and community projects side by side.

"If you want to take care of the wildlife, you have to take care of the people," said Tara. "There's no point in preserving rhinos if you don't care for the people who surround them. There'll be poaching and all sorts of problems. But if there's harmony and employment, and people can see the benefit of game to them, they'll protect it."

The Phinda Private Game Reserve—&Beyond's flagship property—employs some eighty full-time field rangers, as well as an arsenal of advanced technology, including artificial intelligence and big data. It's a smart camp: drones conduct twenty-four-hour surveillance over the reserve's acreage, picking up signals from ultrahigh-frequency ear tags that have been attached to the creatures. By tracking them in real time, the reserve hopes to keep them safe from poachers.

Protecting the reserve's crashes of extremely rare black rhinos is particularly challenging. Thanks to a seemingly insatiable black market for rhino horn, poaching of these animals has risen exponentially. The species is nearly decimated. But at Phinda, their numbers have actually been on the increase. A program to dehorn the animals has largely stopped the poaching. Dehorning a black rhino is a major production, involving helicopters and an array of vets, experts, rangers, and immobilizing drugs. The horns grow back every two to two and a half years, so these missions operate frequently.

Since ancient times, the bluebird has been a symbol of happiness, a reminder that joy is often just under our noses—but it can flutter away when one tries to grasp it.

One day in March 2004, Tara received a phone call letting him know that a bluebird of sorts was available, though half the world away. From the bushveld of KwaZulu-Natal, he scrambled to get on a plane. After landing in Amsterdam, he drove straight to a small Dutch port, where the object of his quest came into view.

"*Blue Bird* was in a very bad way and it was apparent that she was near the end of her days, but underneath the rust and ungainly add-ons one could make out the unmistakably sweet lines of a true classic. Clearly, she needed someone to rescue her," Tara recalled afterward in a book he commissioned, *Blue Bird: Seven Decades at Sea*.

This once-magnificent one-hundred-foot motor yacht had been launched in 1938 by Sir Malcolm Campbell, a British racing hero known as "the fastest man on earth." He had it built for a specific purpose—a voyage to Cocos, a remote, minuscule Pacific Island, where he hoped to dig up a legendary hoard of gold stolen in 1820 by pirates in Peru, which was the template for Robert Louis Stevenson's *Treasure Island*. War thwarted Campbell's plans. Requisitioned by the Admiralty, *Blue Bird* instead performed valiant service for king and country, most notably as one of the Little Ships that chugged from Southeast England in 1940 to evacuate soldiers trapped in Dunkirk—the "miracle of deliverance" without which Hitler would have surely prevailed.

She was considerably worse for wear when Campbell, himself in failing health, got her back after the war. He died in 1948, before he could undertake his intended voyage. Over the next decades, *Blue Bird* passed between various owners, under new names—*Sterope, Janick*, and then *Rescator*. In the 1980s, dilapidation set in, along with unpaid bills. By court order, she was chained to a quay on the Riviera, leading to a fire sale. When the US consul in Nice sealed the transfer of ownership to an American purchaser, a California trucking executive, perhaps titleship of the vessel seemed murky; in any event, the consul's document stated that the vessel "is henceforth to be known as *Blue Bird*."

By the time she ended up in the Dutch boatyard, she was on the verge of being sold for scrap. Tara Getty bought her on the spot. "I always liked older things. I quite like restoring things versus building from scratch," he explained. "That probably comes from my father, who was a great collector and also a restorer in his own way." ("It's a big driver for Tara," said Jessica of his urge to restore. "It's a strong thread in our lives, whether it's boats, houses, or land.")

When Tara bought *Blue Bird*, he was not lacking for nautical equipment. Getty had a collection of smaller motor- and sailboats, in addition to *Talitha*, which he and Mark, along with their siblings, inherited (when they did, they streamlined her name—dropping the *G*). Their sisters later opted to allocate their shares in the vessel to their brothers. But members of the entire family continue to pile aboard *Talitha* as she plies the seas—the Mediterranean and Caribbean, most commonly.

Gorgeous as the superyacht is, sometimes big is not better. Making it into some of the family's favorite bays was often a struggle. Tara wanted something that would suit his young family. *Blue Bird* was just right: a pocket superyacht.

The dream team that he assembled to restore her included the storied Scottish firm that built her, G. L. Watson, which was still in possession of the *Blue Bird*'s original plans. For the interiors, he went to Dickie Bannenberg, who'd taken over the family firm when his father died in 2002, a year before Sir Paul Getty. (In September 2003, Tara read the lesson at the bravura memorial mass for his father at Westminster Cathedral.)

Another Getty-Bannenberg collaboration was gratifying for both sons. "I'm sure this was in the back of Tara's mind when he came to us as a continuation," Dickie commented.

Bannenberg Senior had often been asked to name his favorite boat. His stock answer was always "the next one." His true favorite was *Talitha G*: "She was the benchmark in the family for a classic yacht," said Dickie.

Yet with *Blue Bird*, there were "different vibes," the designer added. "She carried a 1930s DNA . . . but it was all underpinned by a contemporary level of detailing. . . . It's a combination of things . . . for a young family with three kids, in that barefoot, easy-living way, but at the same time looking tailored, crisp, and rich in detail. It's a magnetic combination."

The saloon is outfitted with walnut paneling that reflects the ship's original interiors, while white-painted paneling strikes a modern note. On a table, there is a framed print of Lichfield's seminal 1969 portrait of Tara's parents in Marrakech. "It's a beautiful picture, and it sort of represents the wild sixties," Tara said of it.

The décor, however, was a breeze compared to the challenges of giving her a totally new superstructure from the main deck up, incorporating the latest engineering and technology into a 1930s vessel of this size, and, furthermore, meeting the exacting standards required for class certification by Lloyd's. Nobody had managed a similar feat before; *Blue Bird* pulled it off.

After more than three years of painstaking labor, Tara's new boat was christened amid much fanfare from family and friends in Saint-Tropez on May 30, 2007, his thirty-ninth birthday.

Tara and Jessica, whose third child, Talitha Leonora Pol, was born in 2008, spend some of the warm months in Ramatuelle in Tara's childhood house. "I consider myself very lucky that I came from here. . . . It's an amazing place to be brought up," he said.

They also pass time in England, where Tara, an Irish passport holder (as are several of his cousins), owns an estate adjacent to Wormsley. Their schedule is often dictated by the yachting calendar. In May 2010, *Blue Bird* joined some fifty of the other surviving Little Ships for the crossing from Ramsgate to Dunkirk, in commemoration of the seventieth anniversary of Operation Dynamo. Prince Michael of Kent, who was a passenger aboard *Blue Bird* with Tara and a group of friends, reflected on this unique flotilla in the foreword he wrote for *Blue Bird*: "Enemy action, obscurity, and even the relentless march of time have failed to dim their light. They all have stories to tell, but not many bring us such a varied and dramatic tale as *Blue Bird*." His Royal Highness also commended the quality of the boat's restoration: "Tara Getty and his team have brooked no compromise."

In 2011, Getty, now with a short, sea captain–worthy beard, took possession, following an eight-year-long restoration, of *Skylark*, a deliriously beautiful fifty-three-foot inboard yawl designed in 1937 by the storied Newport, Rhode Island, naval architects Sparkman & Stephens and built in Wiscasset, Maine.

He takes part in about eight regattas a year, including the two most elegant: the Corsica Classic and Les Voiles de Saint-Tropez. "The best part is when you're out at sea racing a steady ten knots on a beam reach with all sails set," he said.

When the magnificently restored *Skylark* made her debut in Mediterranean waters, at the 2011 Les Voiles, Getty hatched the idea to sponsor a new perpetual cup on the Thursday, a day that had traditionally been without an official race. Filling the void, he announced a challenge between *Skylark* and any one boat brave enough to race her. "Let's call it the Blue Bird Cup," he said. "Let's just have a fun day with a race and lunch."

Tara got his lunch handed to him that inaugural matchup. While *Skylark* led most of the way around the course, actor Griff Rhys Jones, in his Sparkman & Stephens yacht *Argyll*, picked his shifts well as breezes turned fickle. Overtaking Getty, Jones thus took possession of the silver Blue Bird Cup (made by Garrard of London in 1937 and presented to Malcolm Campbell).

The following year, Tara triumphed. After getting off to a commanding lead, *Skylark* sailed well ahead for the entire race, even with seven-year-old Caspar helming for a time. With every passing year (except for becalmed 2020), the Blue Bird Cup has gained momentum and cachet. "It's supercompetitive. Dog-eat-dog. Brutal. And everybody wants to be in it," said Jessica.

Tara also belongs to Pugs, self-described (by its founder, Taki Theodoracopulos) as "the most exclusive club in the world." There is no clubhouse or rulebook per se, just the proviso that no more than twenty-one gentlemen can belong. Owning a big boat seems to be prerequisite too.

Tara was elected to its ranks in 2014, joining Mark Getty; the maharaja of Jodhpur; Heinrich, Prince of Fürstenberg; Greek shipowner George Livanos; Sir Bob Geldof; Roger Taylor (the drummer of Queen); Crown Prince Pavlos of Greece; and Pavlos's father-in-law, tycoon Robert Miller, among others.

Each year the Pugs hold their own regatta, the location of which rotates between the Med's salubrious coasts. The *Talitha* and *Blue Bird* often serve as their "committee" boats. "These are by far the two best boats around. They have nothing to do with that modern shit—those refrigerators on steroids out there," Taki told me. "The Getty boats have all the modern things, but they've kept their original lines and classic style."

He added, speaking about the Gettys themselves: "They're quiet—they don't show off. A good-looking family. Nice. They don't bother anybody."

In 2015, *Blue Bird* fulfilled its destiny. That March, Tara and Jessica set off from Antigua on a three-month odyssey with Talitha, Caspar, and Orlando, who had just graduated from high school in South Africa and was about to move to England to attend Wellington College. The family's ultimate destination was Cocos. The five-mile-long island remains uninhabited and arduous to reach, owing to fierce seas and limited shelter. Even for an experienced sailor like Tara, it was a daunting voyage. He admits to having been "a bit concerned" about the eighty-year-old ship's prospects. "A hundred feet sounds big, but it's not really, when you are out so far in the Pacific."

When at last they reached Cocos, they found majestic waterfalls and mountains and primeval jungle—a scene straight out of *Jurassic Park*, they thought. Alas, no gold was unearthed. But the Gettys got their reward. "We pulled it off," said Tara. "It kind of closed the circle. The circle that hadn't been closed because the war came along."

"I have an adventurous and unconventional husband," commented Jessica.

Blue Bird had barely steamed back into its home port when Tara embarked on another major project. This time it was in a Los Angeles boatyard that he spotted his next rescue: the seventy-two-foot *Baruna*, another Sparkman & Stephens–designed yawl. "She was just languishing," said Getty morosely. "She had won all sorts of races, she was a part of American history. Somebody needed to restore this boat."

Five years later, in July 2021, he offered a progress report: "It's a really tricky one. It's going to be incredible when she launches— which was supposed to be two years ago."

Tara was speaking over Zoom, with Jessica alongside him. Both appeared relaxed, tanned, and a bit wet, which was to be expected, as they were aboard *Talitha*, cruising through the Dodecanese in the southeastern Aegean.

Jessica's holiday was particularly well-earned. She had just finished writing a detailed history of the family's endeavors in Africa and designing a new website, Zuka.earth, on which it can be read.

"Zuka is twenty years old this year," she said. "I decided it was time to tell the story."

Inspired by the anniversary, the couple also founded a new study center and reseach laboratory on the property, the Getty Asterism. They repurposed a collection of thatched-roof and stone cabins to serve as a hub for scientists and conservationists investigating ecology, geology, and marine biology. Even as these scientists plumb the depths of the seas and the earth, the name of the center (an asterism is a prominent pattern or group of stars) hearkened back to the galactic dimensions envisioned by Tara's parents when they christened him.

Over Zoom, he graciously fielded questions pertaining to conservation and sailing. And one of a personal nature: Is he, in fact, the "normal" Getty?

"I don't know whether there is such a thing as a normal one," he deadpanned.

"Am I normal?" he repeated the question, with a trace of a grin. "Possibly I haven't gone off the rails as much as some members of the family have.

"It's a pretty eclectic family. It's got all sorts of branches to it. I would say I'm more on the English side.

"There's not a lot of in-house fighting in any form. I have a very good relationship with my siblings. The whole family tries to get together once a year. A lot of families don't get together for years."

Summing up the state of the Getty clan, he concluded, "It's pretty strong. I don't think it's as dysfunctional as everyone makes out!"

As Tara reflected on his father's life, he touched on an uncanny ability possessed by some Gettys—the ones who've survived—to restore themselves: "After having had that gap, the bad years, he had a great last fifteen years. He managed to put the sad part of his life behind him. He got closer to all his children. It all ended up being really good."

IV.

THE GORDONS

11

Pacific Heights

Gordon Peter Getty's absent-minded, floppy-haired head, hovering well above six feet, often seemed to be lost in the clouds. At the University of San Francisco, a twenty-minute walk from his mother's house on Clay Street where he had grown up with his older brother, Paul Jr., he studied philosophy and literature. Emily Dickinson was his favorite poet. On visits overseas to see his father at Sutton Place, he could be found sitting at one of the two grand pianos in the Long Gallery, playing Schubert or one of his own compositions.

In 1956, with diploma in hand, Gordon entered the real world. J. Paul Getty got his fourth-born son started in the oil business, at the bottom. Gordon pumped gas and changed oil at a Tidewater station near his house. A few months later, thanks to President Eisenhower's Reserve Forces Act, he reported for active duty at Fort Lee, Virginia.

Gordon's next post, once again under his father's orders, was on more punishing ground: the Neutral Zone, the wasteland between Saudi Arabia and Kuwait, where the family fortune was being extracted from the earth. In 1959, after several months, it became apparent that Gordon wasn't cut out to be a line officer—somebody responsible for running things day-to-day. After one blunder—principally, a failure to understand the nuances of the Middle East's culture of *baksheesh* (bribery)—Gordon had to take the fall for a Getty Oil underling who had accidentally rammed a pipeline with his truck. The local emir sentenced Gordon to two weeks' house arrest, during which he read Shakespeare and Keats.

Upon his return to San Francisco, Gordon dared to pursue his real passion, music. In 1961, he enrolled at the San Francisco Conservatory of Music, where he studied harmony and counterpoint. According to Robina Lund, his father was "understandably disappointed" when Gordon left the family business, but he was nonetheless happy for him to aspire to a musical career. "Paul was immensely proud of Gordon's ability as a pianist and composer. . . . When Gordon came to stay, Paul would look forward all day to hearing him play."

During his time at the conservatory, Gordon succeeded in composing and publishing five short piano pieces. Just after, writer's block halted his creativity for nearly twenty years.

Despite San Francisco's small-town nature, it took a few years for him to meet Ann Gilbert, a striking five-foot-ten redhead who had arrived in 1958 at the age of seventeen. A native of California's Central Valley, she had picked peaches, packed walnuts, and driven tractors alongside her two brothers on their father's ranch; after graduating from East Nicolaus High School, she moved from her hometown of Wheatland to the Bay Area, where she studied anthropology and biology at UC Berkeley and worked at the cosmetics counter of Joseph Magnin, the fashionable department store near Union Square.

Gordon's and Ann's paths crossed one evening in 1964 at La Rocca's Corner, a popular North Beach tavern. She matched him in a blind beer-tasting game. A few months later, on Christmas Day 1964, they eloped to Las Vegas.

Ann's combination of practicality and charm helped propel the Getty fortune. In 1971, as Gordon's lawsuit over the terms of the Sarah C. Getty Trust dragged into its seventh year, Ann played an instrumental role in brokering a settlement. "See here, Mr. Getty, let's have an end to this," she said to her father-in-law, in a tone that was at once beguiling and assertive.

Even as she became one of the most extravagant women of her time, Ann kept her feet planted on the ground. Notwithstanding the couture wardrobe, private jets, and other accoutrements of wealth that she acquired, she liked to say she was still at heart a farmer.

Following J. Paul Getty's death in 1976, Gordon's income from the trust rose dramatically. Unlike most other Gettys, Ann wasn't shy about spending it. The couple purchased a magnificent five-story neoclassical mansion, designed by architect Willis Polk shortly after the 1906 earthquake. Perched atop Pacific Heights, with stunning views of San Francisco Bay, it sits on a two-and-a-half-block stretch of Outer Broadway, the bastion of San Francisco's gold rush and old money families.

To help her decorate it, Ann hired the blue-chip firm of Parish-Hadley, a partnership between the indomitable WASP grande dame Mrs. Henry "Sister" Parish II and Tennessee-born Albert Hadley, the nice one. Their client roster, a who's who of American aristocracy, included Jackie and John F. Kennedy, Babe and Bill Paley, and Betsey and Jock Whitney.

After many months and shopping trips to England—Ann became a top customer at London's auction houses and antiquaries—the Broadway mansion was transformed into one of the loveliest English-style houses in America. Sister was in charge, but Ann deployed the expertise and taste she'd sharpened from all her stays at Sutton Place. She also benefited from the guidance of Gillian Wilson, the decorative arts curator at the J. Paul Getty Museum (where Gordon was on the acquisitions committee). At the same time, Ann made sure Wilson was properly outfitted for her job. During one meeting, Ann clocked Wilson's cloth coat; she went upstairs to her closet and returned with a fur. "If you are going to these dealers in London and Paris, you need a good coat," she said as she handed the garment to Wilson, who wore it proudly for years to come and referred to it as "the curatorial mink." (Until her retirement in 2003, Wilson remained one of the museum's last living links to its founder.)

Ann and Gordon's mansion was fully operational by December 1979, when a feature story, "Christmas with the Gettys," appeared in *Town & Country*, with photographs by Slim Aarons. Nine-year-old William Paul—"Billy"—the baby of the family, was pictured valiantly hoisting a pole twice as tall as he was to light the candles on the eighteenth-century Russian crystal and gilded bronze chandelier in the unelectrified dining room, which was lined with eighteenth-century Chinese wallpaper. Meanwhile, his brothers—John Gilbert, eleven, Andrew Rork, twelve, and Gordon Peter Jr., fourteen (who is called Peter)—performed tree-trimming tasks.

According to the article's author, the men of the house knew who was boss: "She is in absolute control. Nothing daunts her and nine times out of ten, her way is the only way."

But she didn't do it all alone. Her seven-person staff included a French-Basque chef, Alphonse, as well as a couple familiar faces: Bullimore and Parkes had crossed over from Sutton Place. With them came a sense of continuity and family history—plus they could handle four rambunctious young boys.

In San Francisco, Bullimore ran the house with his customary dry wit, exacting standards, and field marshal manner. He was "imposing and impervious," one visitor observed. Dressed in a waistcoat, he appraised all visitors before they entered. He became a local notable himself, a figure quoted by Herb Caen, dean of San Francisco's columnists (who popularized the word *hippie*, during 1967's Summer of Love). Bullimore was underwhelmed by San Francisco society, Caen reported. "Not much going on, eh?" the butler said to him on a few occasions. In 1970s America, however, there was no more tolerant place for a gay man than San Francisco, which must have been a welcome change from England, where homosexuality was decriminalized only in 1967. According to Christopher Getty, Bullimore had been caught by police in London's Hyde Park while engaging in some amorous activity with another man. "Grandfather took care of it, as one does," he said.

Around 1970, Ann and Gordon attended a small gathering in San Francisco. Dr. Louis Leakey, the pioneering paleoanthropologist and archeologist, had come from Kenya to share with Americans news of his progress searching for evidence of the origins of man. (Drumming up funds to continue his research was certainly on his agenda too.)

Gordon had read of Leakey's work in newspaper articles and was eager to learn more. So, too, were friends Ron and Belinda "Barbara" Pelosi, as well as Ron's brother, Paul, and his wife, Nancy.

Since moving with her husband to the Pelosis' hometown in 1969, Baltimore-born Nancy, née D'Alesandro, had her hands full taking care of their four children; the fifth was born in 1970. (Though she'd grown up in a political household, the idea of herself taking office was still nearly two decades off.)

At the time, Ron and Barbara had the highest political profiles of any in the gang. Ron served on the San Francisco Board of Supervisors; Barbara, a third-generation San Franciscan, grew up steeped in Irish-Democratic politics, being one of six children born to William A. Newsom II, a real estate developer who was a close confidant and campaign manager for Edmund G. "Pat" Brown, who served as governor of California from 1959 to 1967; his son Jerry subsequently reclaimed the office in 1974 for the first of his four terms.

Barbara was born in 1935, a year before her brother William A. Newsom III—Bill, the St. Ignatius classmate of Gordon and his brother Paul. The Getty boys often hung out at Bill's lively Jefferson Street house. With their own father absent, the Getty brothers found a surrogate dad in the genial Newsom *père*. Their affection for him endured. (After Paul Jr. died in 2003, Bill found a framed photograph of his own father in Paul's bedroom at Wormsley.)

The three young couples became ardent supporters of the L. S. B. Leakey Foundation, which had been founded in 1968 to support the anthropologist's groundbreaking fieldwork and research. In that capacity, they honed their skills as they organized large public symposia, reviewed applications for grants the foundation dispensed to researchers, and performed sundry other tasks. Gordon, who became chairman, wrote and edited the brochures, then lugged them to the Central Post Office to make sure they got out on time. He made substantial financial contributions as well. (Dr. Leakey died in October 1972, but his legacy was carried on by his formidable, cigar-smoking widow, Mary.)

A two-day symposium they organized at the Palace of Fine Arts in December 1973 was a triumph. Australian anthropologist Raymond Dart recounted his seminal discovery of *Australopithecus africanus* at a cave in Taung, South Africa, in 1924; Mary Leakey brought the latest news of the digs at Olduvai Gorge in Tanzania; Dian Fossey discussed her study of the mountain gorillas of Rwanda; and Jane Goodall talked about her work with wild chimpanzees at Gombe Stream Research Center in Tanzania.

In the spring of 1975, a Leakey Fellows Day was convened at the Getty Museum in Malibu (attendees included Gloria Getty, George's first wife), where the star attraction was Dr. Donald C. Johanson, fresh from his sensational discovery in Ethiopia of *Australopithecus afarensis*, a 3.5-million-year-old hominoid female who became known as Lucy.

That fall, their conference in Washington, DC, assembled eleven of the world's foremost authorities in the field. Harvard professor Irven DeVore's talk on evolutionary biology and Hamilton's rule— a mathematical formula that provides a basis to explain "survival of the fittest"—captivated Gordon particularly. He developed a keen interest in bioeconomics—the field of social science that uses biology to explain economic events.

In 2013, the Leakey Foundation celebrated Gordon's forty years of service with a four-day celebration in the Bay Area, with toasts from attendees including life trustee Nancy Pelosi and her husband, Paul. According to a citation from Don Dana, president of the foundation, "No person has contributed more to the science of human origins than Gordon Getty."

In the decades after these families met and became intertwined, as they rose to the peaks of wealth and power, there have been inevitable accusations of cronyism. But they bonded over old bones. They were all fascinated by the science—though doubtless learning about survival of the fittest surely came in handy as they tangled with the modern hunter-gatherers of Pacific Heights, Capitol Hill, and beyond.

(Barbara and Ron divorced in 1977, after which she reverted to her maiden name of Newsom and served as the US representative to the United Nations. She remained a staunch supporter of her former sister-in-law and her nephew Gavin until her death from cancer in 2008, at age seventy-three.)

At age nine, Peter Getty, Gordon and Ann's eldest, left for boarding school. He was enrolled at Heatherdown in Berkshire, England. Here, once again, Britain's royals and future ruling class were educated in harsh, peculiar circumstances. His classmates included both Prince Edward and future prime minister David Cameron. "At bath time we had to line up naked in front of a row of Victorian metal baths and wait for the headmaster to blow a whistle before we got in," Cameron reminisced in his memoir, *For the Record*. "Another whistle would indicate that it was time to get out. In between we would have to cope with clouds of smoke from the omnipresent foul-smelling pipe clenched between his teeth."

The decision to send Peter to Heatherdown was no doubt made less out of an urge for him to rub shoulders with royals than a need for security. His cousin in Rome had only recently been released by his abductors; in the Bay Area, the Patricia Hearst drama was still playing out. (Hearst and her four sisters were about a decade older than the Getty boys and raised primarily down the Peninsula in Hillsborough, so the families didn't socialize.)

A few years later, when Billy began school, he stayed in the Bay Area, but for protection he traveled via a limousine driven by a former marine. "He was a sensitive, sweet kid, a gentle boy," recalls a classmate. When it came time for prep school, Billy went to Groton in Massachusetts. Peter and John went east too, to Phillips Exeter Academy in New Hampshire. Andrew stayed in California, attending the Dunn School, near Santa Barbara.

The Getty boys were sometimes portrayed in the media as spoiled brats. ("Peter Getty: Costumed Layabout Scion," read the headline of a *Gawker* piece.) One Exeter classmate of Peter's I spoke to had a different view. "Our classes were very small and discussion-based, so you really got a sense of who a person was. Peter was blazing smart, really well-read and well-rounded, with a lovely dry wit," she said. "He was also a kind person—one of the white hats. Those discussions could get pretty heated. If there was someone struggling, he would be the person to speak up and come to their rescue."

Having a father who was one of the richest men in the country wasn't anything Peter trumpeted. "That kind of thing didn't get you anywhere at Exeter," this classmate added, noting that Firestone and Coors were among their classmates' name-brand last names. "He never made anything of it. He kind of flew under the radar."

"But you knew when his mom was on campus," said a classmate of John Getty, who still vividly recalls the sight of Ann as she dropped John off the first day of school. She was not like the other moms. "She was wearing this short pink raincoat, with a short skirt and very high heels. It was a lot—definitely a bold look for parents' day." John was "popular and very attractive," he adds.

On breaks, the family took adventurous expeditions to Alaska, Nepal, the Galapagos Islands, and other far-flung spots. Billy's close friend Gavin Newsom sometimes went along. Other times, Gavin's father, Bill, took all the boys camping and rafting in the California wilderness. In the early 1970s, after his separation from Gavin's mother, Tessa, Bill moved to the Sierra Nevada foothills, where he opened a law office that specialized in environmental protection, a novelty then. In 1978, Governor Jerry Brown appointed him to the state's superior court bench in Placer County; later Judge Newsom was appointed to the California Courts of Appeal. (After retiring from the judiciary in 1995, he helped Gordon manage his affairs, including his ever-growing fortune.)

In the summer of 1980, Gordon had a breakthrough in Paris, where he was traveling with Ann and the boys. His writer's block lifted when he found a copy of the variorum edition of Emily Dickinson's poems—all 1,775 of them—in the WH Smith English-language bookstore.

When Gordon had studied Dickinson in college in the early fifties, only about a dozen of her poems had been widely published, and they had been bowdlerized. Squabbles among her heirs prevented publication of the bulk of her work until Harvard University Press published the variorum edition in 1955. For Getty, the poems were revelations. He rushed to his hotel suite and began making compositions in his head. Back in San Francisco, he set thirty-two of her poems to music, in a chronology that told the story of the poet's life. It coalesced into a song cycle for piano and female voice that he titled *The White Election*. (One of Dickinson's poems begins, "Mine—by the Right of the White Election! . . .")

Ann began spending an increasing amount of time in New York in the early 1980s, when the family purchased the spectacular seventh-floor apartment at 820 Fifth Avenue, a stately twelve-story limestone building constructed in 1916. Among the handful of cooperative apartment buildings in Manhattan ranked at the very top, 820 Fifth is considered number one by many arbiters. Part of its allure stemmed from Jayne Wrightsman, wife of J. Paul Getty's fellow oilman Charles Wrightsman, who occupied the third floor from 1956 until her death in 2019, at age ninety-nine. (As a collector and connoisseur of eighteenth-century French decorative arts, she had no peer.)

For the Gettys at 820, Parish-Hadley once again went all out on a years-long and costly renovation. A rumor circulated that the curtains alone were running $1 million. In fairness, the windows in the library stretched ten feet high, and the "curtains" in this room were actually made of wood. Inspired by the pelmets that Thomas Chippendale carved in the eighteenth century for the 1st Baron Harewood at Harewood House in Yorkshire, England, Parish-Hadley designers sketched out elaborate, baroque designs, with swags like muttonchops caught and tied with fringed and tasseled cords. The design was then painstakingly carved in wood, which, finally, was gilded and painted. "She wanted the unusual and she could afford it," says a friend of Albert Hadley's. Notwithstanding such opulence, he considered Ann quite down-to-earth: "She's very real. She's the kind of girl who can fix the engine on the tractor."

Yet, as the 1980s progressed, she was a fixture at the Paris couture shows and glittering social functions worldwide. In the *New York Times*, society reporter Charlotte Curtis declared that Ann "is rapidly becoming a superstar." Gordon, who had an aversion to parties, generally stayed home. When they traveled together, it was usually to a music festival—Salzburg, Bayreuth, St. Petersburg; Ann shared his passion for music, opera in particular.

Anywhere she went, Alecko Papamarkou was usually at her side. Now a senior VP at E. F. Hutton in New York, he "walked" Ann. In the parlance of gossip purveyors like *WWD*, "walkers" were always "longtime bachelors"—gays, by inference. Yet in addition to providing Ann with wise business advice, Alecko had a spiritual influence. In 1978, Ann was christened into the Greek Orthodox Church, Papamarkou's faith. Archbishop Iakovos, primate of the Greek

Orthodox Archdiocese of North and South America, performed the service in the chapel of his residence in New York; King Constantine of Greece stood as her godfather.

Papamarkou also kept ties to the inner circle of Ann's late father-in-law, including Paul's closest friend, Heini Thyssen-Bornemisza. In September 1982, Papamarkou cohosted a dinner in his honor, with Gordon and Ann, at the Getty home in San Francisco. Heini stood as he proposed his toast to "a misunderstood man and a great patron of the arts, the late J. Paul Getty."

That fall, Alecko, fifty-two, opened his own firm in New York, A. P. Papamarkou & Co., and the Gettys were among his first investors. Shortly before he hung out his shingle, he treated thirty-six friends to a lavish weeklong stay at the Golden Door, the very fashionable Southern California health spa. In addition to Ann, guests included broadcaster Barbara Walters; Teresa Heinz, wife of the Pennsylvania senator and condiments heir; Infanta Pilar, sister of the king of Spain; and Jonas Salk, the polio vaccine developer, with his wife, Françoise Gilot, Picasso's onetime muse. The Viennese-born British publisher Lord George Weidenfeld, portly and ebullient, was also there. His authors ranged from Vladimir Nabokov to Pope John Paul II; an acquaintance of J. Paul Getty, he had also published the first major catalog of the Getty Museum's collection. Recently he'd launched the literary career of another Golden Door guest, Arianna Stassinopoulos, when he published her biography of Maria Callas. All in all, it was quite a mix that Alecko gathered that week; from it, some substantial ventures would emerge before long.

In the glossy press, 1983 was a banner year for the Gettys. In April, Ann landed on the cover of *Town & Country*, clad in an Emanuel Ungaro couture gown and dripping with David Webb jewels, photographed by Norman Parkinson. On twelve pages inside, she modeled more finery in a succession of fanciful Bavarian castles built by "Mad" King Ludwig II.

In October, Gordon topped *Forbes*'s list of the wealthiest 400 Americans, with a net worth, according to the magazine, of $2.2 billion. At this point his annual income from the trust was reportedly $110 million, on top of which he drew a $20 million fee as the sole trustee. Once again, a Getty was "the richest American." The ranking didn't seem to please him. Gordon locked himself in his soundproof music room and refused to take calls from the Associated Press.

Overnight, there was palpable change in the atmosphere surrounding the Gettys, particularly in the drawing rooms of the Upper East Side. "Mercedes Kellogg [now Bass] used to give these killer Friday lunches in her apartment," recalls a Manhattan gentleman. "They were great fun, everyone came. Right after *Forbes* came out, we were all there one afternoon, whooping it up, when Ann and Gordon appeared at the door. Everybody went dead quiet. You would have thought Moses had come in, that way the room parted for them, like the Red Sea."

As 1983 drew to a close, the simmering tensions between the board of Getty Oil and Gordon exploded. The trigger had been pulled on November 14, when the lawsuit in his nephew Tara Getty's name was filed in Superior Court of Los Angeles County. This action also compelled Harold Williams, the president of the J. Paul Getty Trust, to go into high gear: he had to protect the value of the 12 percent of the stock that the museum owned.

Gordon and Ann flew to New York to meet with new, high-powered members of the Getty Oil board who had been nominated by Gordon but recruited by Ann—including Laurence A. Tisch, chairman of the Loews Corporation, and A. Alfred Taubman, the Detroit real estate developer who had recently acquired Sotheby's auction house.

With the apartment at 820 not yet ready, Ann and Gordon ensconced themselves in a suite at the Pierre Hotel, formerly owned by his father. The fate of Getty Oil hung in the balance. The stakes couldn't have been higher. Just then, Ann gave the most fabulous party New York had seen in ages.

The evening of November 30, a Wednesday, she put on a white satin Dior gown embroidered with gold and welcomed two hundred guests to a dinner in the Temple of Dendur at the Metropolitan Museum of Art, to celebrate Gordon's fiftieth birthday. In addition to a squadron of Gettys, including Gloria, Aileen, Ariadne, and Mark, there was a contingent of forty leading San Franciscans, including the indomitable Denise Hale, all of whom Ann had flown in. Among the notable New Yorkers and Europeans were Brooke Astor, Vicomtesse Jacqueline de Ribes, Lynn Wyatt, Nan Kempner, Bianca Jagger, Ahmet and Mica Ertegun, Carolina and Reinaldo Herrera, Robin Hambro, Pat Buckley, and, of course, Alecko Papamarkou.

After a performance by violinist Isaac Stern, Luciano Pavarotti rushed over from the Metropolitan Opera as soon as the curtain fell on his performance of *Ernani*, and surprised everyone with his rendition of "Happy Birthday."

"It was one of the best parties ever," proclaimed Mrs. Buckley. Five nights later, Buckley presided over the other most glamorous party of the season, under the same roof—the opening of the Yves Saint Laurent retrospective at the Met's Costume Institute, where Gordon's late sister-in-law, Talitha, was extolled.

The very next night, many of the same guests, and about a thousand others, filled Alice Tully Hall at Lincoln Center, to hear soprano Mignon Dunn of the Metropolitan Opera give a recital featuring eighteen songs from *The White Election*.

The drama was only beginning. A couple weeks later, J. Hugh Liedtke, chairman of Houston-based Pennzoil, announced a tender offer for 20 percent of Getty Oil's outstanding stock. The company was officially in play.

In San Francisco, Ann and Gordon had barely unpacked; they rushed back to New York, checking into the Pierre again. An enormous cast of characters representing all sides of the deal took up their positions in the suites and conference rooms of every leading hotel, law firm, and investment bank in town. Following frantic negotiations, Pennzoil raised its offer—it was now a $110 per share leveraged buyout. Considering that GET had been trading at around $50 a year before, it was, in many eyes, a great deal for shareholders— Gettys and non-Gettys alike.

Then things hit an impasse. Liedtke was frustrated because he had been able to deal only with Gordon's battery of bankers, lawyers, and advisors. He announced he would pull out if he couldn't meet with the man himself. "I don't want them telling Mr. Getty what I think or what I'm offering. I want to sit right across the table from him and tell him myself so there won't be any question," said the tough Texan, according to *The Taking of Getty Oil* by Steve Coll.

No way, Gordon's people responded.

Liedtke pondered how to get a message directly to Gordon. On December 30, seeking advice, he phoned fellow Houstonian Fayez Sarofim, a stock fund manager and investment advisor who also owned a big block of Getty Oil. Though he was now a well-established Texan, the Cairo-born Sarofim descended from Egyptian nobility. His ancestry, combined with his tight-lipped inscrutability, had earned him the nickname "the Sphinx" in financial circles.

Sarofim told Liedtke he knew how to handle it: he would call Papamarkou, who could in turn call Ann to ask her to pass Liedtke's meeting request to Gordon.

It worked. Close to midnight on New Year's Eve, the chairman boarded the Pennzoil corporate jet in Houston, bound for New York. His meeting with Gordon was set for New Year's Day.

Liedtke turned his Texan charm on Getty, recalling his wildcatting days in Oklahoma and his acquaintance with J. Paul Getty. His son agreed to a $112.50 a share offer from Pennzoil.

In essence, Ann and Alecko had gotten the biggest corporate acquisition in history back on track.

Then the whole thing jumped to a different track. Gordon's niece Claire got a judge to temporarily block the deal, so she and other family members could evaluate it. During the two-day pause, Texaco chairman John K. McKinley swooped in and offered $125 a share. After wild, round-the-clock negotiations (and after Claire dropped her opposition), Texaco officially won the prize when the papers for the $10 billion deal were signed around 3 a.m. in Gordon's suite at the Pierre.

Pennzoil promptly sued Texaco, claiming it had a deal with Getty Oil even if the contracts weren't signed. Thanks to a clause that Gordon had requested in the negotiations—in which Texaco indemnified the Getty Trust and the J. Paul Getty Museum against any lawsuits that might arise from the sale—the Getty family was not a party to this suit; they banked their billions. After a jury in Houston decided there had been a binding agreement, Texaco was ordered to pay Pennzoil $10.5 billion in damages, the largest jury verdict in history. The two oil companies battled for four more years in court over the judgment. Eventually, Texaco paid a $3 billion settlement to Pennzoil, and went bankrupt.

Getty Oil ceased to exist; twenty thousand employees lost their jobs.

Oil prices plunged. Having cashed out at the top of the market, the Getty family's $4 billion fortune was secure.

That's capitalism—as Gordon explained to an auditorium of University of San Francisco students a couple of years after the sale. "I'm in favor of takeovers, the more hostile the better," he declared. "I like to look at takeovers, and hostile takeovers in particular, as efficiency and economic evolution in action."

Whatever the explanation for their good fortune, the Gettys were, once again, on top.

12

The Richest American, Once Again

In January 1985, one year after the contracts for the largest corporate acquisition in history were signed, Ann and Alecko embarked on a two-week voyage down the Nile. According to some reports, it was about the most fabulous cruise since Cleopatra's golden barge. *Vanity Fair* called it "the most-talked-about sociocultural schlepp of the year."

Aboard the *Nile President* were eighty-three guests Ann and Alecko had flown to Egypt, an eclectic mix that included US ambassador to the United Nations Jeane Kirkpatrick, NYU president John Brademas, Peter Rockefeller (a grandson of Nelson's), King Simeon II of Bulgaria, Prince Alexander Romanov, Evangeline Bruce, Betsy Bloomingdale, Nan Kempner, Jerry Zipkin, George Weidenfeld, Greek shipping magnates galore, and Norna "Miki" Sarofim (Fayez's sister). Before they weighed anchor, Miki treated everyone to a gala dinner in Cairo, at which she informed guests about such ancient wonders as the great palace and temple of Akhenaten, located on land owned by her family. (Though the Sarofim heritage stretches back seemingly to the pharaohs, the family name today is perhaps most widely known thanks to Fayez's live-wire daughter, Allison, who throws New York's most extravagant and exclusive annual Halloween party in her West Village townhouse; Billy Getty's wife, Vanessa, is a regular guest.)

After trooping through innumerable tombs, temples, and pyramids, the party was flown across the desert to Saint Catherine's Monastery in the Sinai to see its icons—one of the greatest collections in Christendom—as well as the burning bush through which God spoke to Moses. "That's strange—I have one just like this in my garden in California," Bloomingdale said to the Greek Orthodox archbishop, their guide. Before the party departed the Nile, they returned to their barge to celebrate Alecko's fifty-fifth birthday, in Egyptian costumes.

A month after bestriding the colossi of ancient Egypt, Ann took on the titans of the New York publishing world. In March 1985, she paid $2 million for Grove Press, the esteemed, boundary-breaking independent house that had brought Samuel Beckett, Jean Genet, D. H. Lawrence, Henry Miller, and Bertolt Brecht to American readers, often after bruising courtroom battles over obscenity laws.

Since her Berkeley days, Ann had been a reader and admirer of Grove books, and *Evergreen Review*, its literary quarterly, which published William Burroughs, Jack Kerouac, and Allen Ginsberg. Over the years, there had been suitors for Grove—conglomerates such as Random House tried to buy it, as did Hugh Hefner. Its iconoclastic president, Barney Rosset, who bought the fledgling publishing house in 1951, fended them off, even though he had been losing money for years, as everyone knew.

In her endeavor, Ann partnered with Lord Weidenfeld. Perhaps the seeds of their alliance were planted that week at the Golden Door (they were seen departing in the same limousine, headed for a well-earned lunch in San Diego). He had long wished to enter the US publishing market; she loved books (and she had the cash). "I'm a publisher because it's a cover for my indulgence," she told the *New York Times* in 1989. "I love to read all day. But I come from nice Puritan stock, and I grew up believing that you have to work all day, so I made reading my work."

After convincing Rosset to sell, they gave him a five-year contract to stay on. Weidenfeld said they hoped to expand the roster of writers, yet "keep the character of a very literary house." From their offices in the Harper & Row Building on East 53rd Street, they also set up Weidenfeld & Nicolson New York, an American arm of the firm he'd founded in London in 1949. Top talent was hired away from other houses, and contracts for about a hundred books were signed in the first five months, many of them accompanied by big checks, such as the reported $1 million paid to Milan Kundera for his next novel. Meanwhile, Ann launched an ambitious nonprofit, the Wheatland Foundation, which organized dazzling conferences on literature and music, in locations around the world. Ann took her new business seriously. "She was always off to the Frankfurt Book Fair, or someplace like that," a New York friend recalled.

While Grove and Weidenfeld & Nicolson published a number of excellent books, including Arthur Miller's memoir, *Timebends: A Life*, and Harold Pinter's only novel, *The Dwarfs*, the ventures did not flourish. After editorial disagreements, Rosset was pushed out within a year. In 1989, Weidenfeld & Nicolson New York and Grove merged into Grove New York; two years later, after the ventures lost a reported $30 million, Getty family financial advisors pressed Ann to pull out. Grove later merged with Atlantic Monthly Press.

"The Gettys are surrounded by financial advisors who they listen to. Rich as they are, Gettys don't like to lose money," said the New York friend. In his memoir, *Remembering My Good Friends*, Weidenfeld explained that the undertaking foundered in part because neither he (who remained anchored in London) nor the San Francisco–based Ann could focus on it fully. He also apportioned some blame to the Getty advisors, who were "already laden with work for the Getty family." But there were no hard feelings, Weidenfeld wrote. After the plug was pulled, Ann and Gordon took him and his new bride, Annabelle, on a cruise along the Anatolian coast of Turkey.

Because she eloped, Ann Getty never had one of those storybook weddings. Perhaps the many extravagant nuptials she hosted for family members and friends over the years were her way of compensating. In any event, no one could throw a wedding like Ann Getty.

When it came time for her new best friend Arianna Stassinopoulos to march down the aisle, she pulled out all the stops.

Ann had, what's more, introduced Arianna to the man she was to marry: Roy Michael Huffington Jr., a quiet, handsome Texas oil heir. Ann had sat down with Arianna and made a list of prospective grooms on a legal pad. Huffington wasn't on it—but then Ann met him on a trip to Japan. *Bingo*, she thought, and phoned Arianna from Tokyo: "I've found him!" She invited both to be her guests at the San Francisco Symphony's opening-night gala in September 1985.

Seven months later, their wedding took place at the Episcopal St. Bartholomew's Church in New York, in a spectacular candlelit ceremony before some four hundred guests (from Shirley MacLaine to Henry Kissinger), followed by a dinner at the Metropolitan Club, all said to be underwritten by Ann to the tune of about $100,000, not counting the bride's gown by James Galanos, which cost $35,000. "In a year of big weddings, including Caroline Kennedy's and Prince Andrew's, the one people are *still* talking about is [Arianna's]," Bob Colacello reported in *Vanity Fair*.

(In 1994, Arianna encouraged Michael, a conservative Republican, to run against incumbent Dianne Feinstein—another close Getty family friend—for one of California's two US Senate seats. Gordon was in a quandary. He made up his mind after Huffington, then a congressman, voted for the Hyde Amendment, which bans federal Medicaid funding to cover almost all abortions. "The Bible-thumping worried me a little," Getty said, explaining his choice of Feinstein. In 1998, a year after Huffington and Arianna were divorced, Huffington revealed that he is gay.)

Having overcome his writer's block, Gordon threw himself into music composition. He set to work on an opera inspired by Sir John Falstaff, Shakespeare's comical yet poignant character from *Henry IV.* Titled *Plump Jack*, it had a lengthy development. Scene I premiered at the San Francisco Symphony in March 1985, Scene II at the Aspen Festival the next year, and Scene III at the University of New Mexico in March 1987. Three months later, the whole thing returned to San Francisco, in a gala concert performance by a 100-piece orchestra and a 60-member chorus. Getty later said the opera was not complete, and he continued to tinker with it.

Gordon faced criticism from the music press that sometimes seemed inordinately hostile. When you are "the world's wealthiest composer," as many articles about him underscored, can your work be judged on its merits?

"It doesn't take much daring to perform an hour of painless, faceless, unabashedly eclectic, pleasantly decorative, sporadically engaging music by a quasi-amateurish but ultra-supportive patron of the arts whom *Forbes* recently labeled the wealthiest man in America," wrote the *Los Angeles Times*'s critic in his review of the 1987 performance. He did offer some faint praise: "Getty, 53, is not without talent."

Gordon maintained a thick skin and a sense of humor about the reviews, and assertions by some that his music was only performed because of his last name: "The disproof of that claim is basically the kind of reviews I get," he commented.

A generational shift occurred on January 23, 1988. Ann Light, née Rork, the much-married matriarch of this branch of the family and the only wife of J. Paul Getty (his fourth) who produced a pair of full siblings—Paul Jr. and Gordon—died at age seventy-nine of emphysema.

In the end, she had equalled J. Paul Getty in trips to the altar. In 1960 she took her fifth march down the aisle, with Dr. Rudolph A. Light, a professor of neurosurgery and an Upjohn Company heir. Following his death ten years later, Ann, with a $25 million inheritance, continued to enjoy a vigorous life between Nashville, San Francisco, and Palm Beach.

At her funeral in St. Edward Catholic Church in Palm Beach, her grandson Mark and her son Gordon both spoke.

"Yes, she was difficult, and I loved her for it," said Mark.

Gordon recounted his mother's final days when she could hardly open her eyes or speak, but she brightened when she heard the voices of her children or grandchildren. "Family," he concluded, "lasts forever."

At a dinner party at home in San Francisco, Gordon later recalled to guests how his mother had taken him to his first opera, at the Hollywood Bowl, when he was seven: "*Madame Butterfly*, and it was so beautiful I wept through it all."

A few months after Ann's funeral, Peter graduated from college. An English major, he received his BA from Harvard (after taking a year off to work as a copy editor at Grove in New York). Within a few years, Andrew and Billy got their diplomas from NYU and Brown, respectively; John studied at Brown too. At six feet six, Billy was the tallest, eclipsing his father; but they all reached at least six feet. "They were unbelievably good-looking guys—smoking," recalled a schoolmate.

Even as Gordon's operatic treatment of Sir John Falstaff continued to gestate, images of the rotund, comical knight began appearing across the Bay Area.

First came PlumpJack Wine & Spirits, a storefront that opened in 1992 on Fillmore Street in Cow Hollow. It was the brainchild of Gavin Newsom and Billy Getty, along with his brothers. They'd all developed an appreciation for good wine thanks to their fathers, both passionate oenophiles. On summer trips to the Palio in Siena, teenage Gavin, for one, had perked his ears as the elders waxed rhapsodic about the new Super Tuscans, whose names tripped off the tongue—Sassicaia, Tignanello, Solaia. Now he and the boys decided to shake up the conservative wine world with a new type of shop—with whimsical design elements, a youthful but informed vibe, and cut-rate prices. PlumpJack was an immediate hit.

A total of $174,000 in seed money had been cobbled together from a dozen or so friends and relatives, including Matthew Pelosi (Ron and Barbara's son) and several Gettys: Gordon (who kicked in $15,000); cousins Christopher, Ariadne, and Mark; and brother Andrew, then twenty-four. It was Andrew who asked Gordon if they could name the venture after his opera. The title character's conviviality embodied the spirit they wanted for their business, and of course it was a nice tribute to Gordon. "Boys, I won't sue you," he said.

After his prep school days, John became obsessed with rock music. Living primarily between Los Angeles and London, he taught himself to play the guitar and styled himself like a rock star, complete with long hair and tattoos. Drugs were also part of his lifestyle. According to family friends, he became an addict.

In 1994 he fathered a daughter, Ivy Love Getty, with Alyssa Boothby, a woman with whom he had a short relationship in Los Angeles. Ann and Gordon were ecstatic over the arrival of their first grandchild. She had been born on December 20, Gordon's birthday—surely a good omen; Ann, who never had a daughter, was thrilled to help raise a girl. So Ivy grew up under their watchful eyes in the Getty mansion. "Ann made Ivy central to her life. The relationship meant a great deal to her," says a friend.

At two and a half, Ivy was already mixing with high society. "This is a great bunch—everyone from the chief justice of the California

Supreme Court to Ivy Getty," Denise Hale observed as she surveyed the group of twenty-four who had sat down to a lunch she was hosting in honor of couturier Gianfranco Ferré at her 8,000-acre ranch in Sonoma. (Ivy was wearing a lavender tutu.)

When Ivy was three, Ann founded a Montessori-based school in her capacious basement. It became known as the Playgroup. About two dozen neighborhood children were invited to attend, with never a fee or an application (it was said around town that kids were "tapped," rather like the Skull and Bones secret society at Yale). Seven full-time teachers were on staff, as well as a chef trained at Chez Panisse, who prepared organic lunches.

Peter, with his curly hair and professorial manner, bears the strongest resemblance to his father. He's musical as well. Gordon taught him to play piano at the age of two. With a college classmate, Peter formed a band called the Virgin-Whore Complex. Under the stage name Spats Ransom (a reference to his cousin's kidnapping), he was guitarist and vocalist, as well as the writer of many of the songs on the two albums they produced, *Stay Away from My Mother* and *Succumb*. He also founded a boutique record label, Emperor Norton, named after the eccentric nineteenth-century San Franciscan who proclaimed himself "Emperor of these United States."

By the mid-nineties Peter was living in Los Angeles and dating model and actress Lauren Hutton. Then he met Jacqueline "Jacqui" de la Fontaine, a stylish bohemian with wide brown eyes. She had a young daughter, Gia, from her relationship with Gian-Carlo Coppola, son of director Francis Ford Coppola. In 1986, when Jacqui was pregnant with her, twenty-two-year-old Gian-Carlo was killed in a speedboat accident. Peter moved into Jacqui's Spanish-style bungalow at the top of the Hollywood Hills, where he helped raise Gia.

Andrew, who was described by friends as "jolly," made an attempt at acting. In 1991 he starred in *Rex Justice*, a twenty-five-minute parody of the criminal justice system directed by his best friend, Chris Vietor, an heir to the Jell-O fortune (some of their pals, including

Gavin Newsom, had bit parts). Despite his sturdy six-foot-three build and fair-haired good looks, the consensus was that Andrew was no thespian. "I never want to act again," he said. Nonetheless, his parents hosted a lavish Academy Awards–themed premiere party, complete with red carpet, at Bimbo's, a hot nightclub. Most of the 450 guests were in their early twenties, but the Pelosis came, as did the *Hollywood Reporter*'s George Christy. Andrew subsequently moved to Los Angeles, where he enrolled at USC film school, with aspirations to write screenplays and direct. He moved into an eight-bedroom house in the Hollywood Hills.

Billy, the only son left in San Francisco, began dating Vanessa Jarman, a tall blonde with flawless looks and keen determination. They had known each other since sixth grade. A UCLA graduate, she was working as an artists' representative. At the time, Billy was on the midst of a three-year project to design what would be San Francisco's ultimate bachelor pad, a twenty-fifth-floor penthouse in Russian Hill with breathtaking views. Working with Modesto-based Leavitt/Weaver—the firm that had designed the PlumpJack store—he gutted the 5,500-square-foot space, installing hand-tinted concrete-slab floors and floor-to-ceiling windows that opened onto a wraparound terrace. The central elevator bank was encased in rough rock, which was then covered in 24K gold leaf—resembling a golden cave. The rest of the apartment was virtually transparent, aside from the movable fiberglass shoji screens. Along with kinetic furniture and black-and-white photography, there was ancient Hellenistic statuary in marble and bronze. When Ann saw it, she approved. It was "radical," she declared.

Simultaneously, Billy was busy expanding the business. In the city, he and Gavin opened a PlumpJack Cafe and acquired the venerable Balboa Cafe. In Napa Valley, they purchased a vineyard, where a Cabernet Sauvignon and other varieties of wine would be produced. Near Lake Tahoe, they opened the PlumpJack Squaw Valley Inn.

More would come, but that was the portfolio in the spring of 1996, when Billy, twenty-five, and Gavin, twenty-eight, sat down for an interview with a young journalist (me). With his long hair in a pony-tail, lanky Billy exuded a laid-back coolness. Gavin, six feet three, had already perfected his slick mane and smooth swagger.

"We wanted to develop a younger generation of wine enthusiasts and avoid the snobbery that is wine," said Newsom. Added Billy, "We went to every wine store in the Bay Area. We walked in in our baseball caps and jeans. Everyone told us, 'We don't sell beer, that's the corner store, boys.' We were disrespected."

They were just cocky enough to still be likable. And who could quibble with their mission to demystify the wine-buying process and offer terrific bottles at affordable prices? At the time, the shop sold two hundred wines with price tags $10 or under.

Gordon also spoke to me. "I offered no more input than any other daddy," he explained. "I said, 'I'll lend you money as long as you work hard. Because even if you lose, you'll learn something.'

"It's a lot of fun to see the entrepreneurial spirit bubbling up in the Getty clan again," he added with glee.

As it happened, a political spirit gurgled up from the same premises—from a mop sink, to be exact. When the young men were applying for their permits, city inspectors put the brakes on things because the space did not have all the requisite plumbing fixtures. "I was like, 'The whole store is carpeted. Why the hell do we need a mop sink?'" recalled Newsom. He became one of those "mad as hell and not going to take it anymore guys" as he attempted to take on city hall. Mayor Willie Brown, as lore has it, said, "I'm sick of this guy complaining." Thinking it would be better if Newsom were working for the city rather than against it, he appointed him to his first political position, on the Parking and Traffic Commission in 1996.

According to Billy, Ann was "very enthusiastic" about their new business. "But she's all over me for everything else," he added.

Ann herself was not available for comment then because she was in Ethiopia, where she was probably on her hands and knees with a shovel.

The Gettys had left New York behind. They sold the apartment at 820 Fifth Avenue to Warner Bros. boss Terry Semel in 1996, but in the previous few years they'd hardly turned on the lights. "I think they slept in it but five nights," said another resident. After all that, New York just wasn't for them.

Ann now preferred the Middle Awash paleoanthropological research area, deep inside the Afar Depression of Ethiopia, where fossil and artifact discoveries were producing the longest single record of human ancestors on earth.

She earned a place on the Middle Awash team after taking paleo-anthropology courses at Berkeley from Professor Tim White, a leading fossil finder. She could offer some team members a lift, too. In 1986, Gordon and Ann had acquired a Boeing 727, which was put to such frequent use, like a family station wagon, it became known around San Francisco as the Jetty. In the early 1990s it underwent a complete overhaul, and emerged as one of the most luxurious private rides in the skies.

The floor was made to resemble the stones in a temple near Bang-kok, inlays of forty exotic woods were used throughout, and the gold-leaf passageway that separates the two bedrooms was hung with six maps of the heavens created by Andreas Cellarius in the seventeenth century.

"We saw some excellent reproductions of these plates and we suggested to the client that they might be used here," project designer Craig Leavitt of Leavitt/Weaver told *Architectural Digest* when the jet was featured anonymously. "They're beautiful, we'll get the real ones," responded the client, who was identified only as "a student of paleoanthropology."

Gordon, also still fascinated with the origins of man, was providing generous financial backing to the Institute of Human Origins (IHO), a Berkeley-based organization led by Donald Johanson, the charismatic fossil hunter (and former mentor of White) who in 1974 had discovered the 3.2 million–year-old Lucy. She reigned as the oldest known human ancestor until 1992, when White and his team found *Ardipithecus ramidus*, a 4.4 million–year-old.

Then Gordon and Ann fell out with Johanson. They felt he was busier promoting himself than the science. Gordon, who had been underwriting half of the IHO's $2 million annual budget, withdrew his support, and the Gettys threw their backing behind the Berkeley Geochronology Center, a new group. Within the fossil world, it became a fracas of considerable proportion, the subject of much chatter. Paleoanthropology sounds not so different from politics or high society.

At Christmastime 1998, Billy and Vanessa announced their engagement. Naturally, Ann went into high gear planning the festivities for the first wedding in her family, which was scheduled for June. She also took a considerable interest in the bride's gown. She picked up the phone and called her friend Oscar de la Renta in New York. "I want you to dress Vanessa," she told him, according to Boaz Mazor, a longtime de la Renta executive. "I want her to be the most beautiful bride ever, I want her to look unbelievable."

"Oscar dropped everything. He called in all his assistants, the office was turned upside down," Mazor continued. "Then we got a call to cancel everything."

Vanessa decided to go with Narciso Rodriguez. For her, the new young star designer agreed to make his first wedding dress since the one that had launched him to stardom—Carolyn Bessette's, for her wedding to John Kennedy Jr. in 1996.

"Ann was livid! Furious!" says Mazor.

Yet when Vanessa made her entrance to the Renaissance-themed ceremony at a ranch in Napa Valley, riding sidesaddle on a speckled horse at sunset, pretty much everyone had to agree that she chose right. Her form-fitting matte satin gown with crystal-embroidered layers glistened.

The June 1999 ceremony was officiated by Judge Newsom. Gavin was best man and Gordon sang a Welsh song for the 165 guests. Among them were Gettys from far and wide, as well as a new assistant district attorney in town, a thirty-four-year-old up-and-comer named Kamala Harris—Vanessa's new friend. Two years later, Harris threw the shower before the birth of Vanessa and Billy's first child, Nicholas. Brother Alexander arrived in 2003. When Veronica Louise was born in 2008, Kamala was asked to be her godmother.

Vanessa and Kamala's friendship had been fostered by Denise Hale—Nicholas's godmother. Habitually bejeweled and chinchilla-draped, the Serbian-born social lioness is San Francisco's ultimate power broker, some say. "When I was ten years old in Belgrade, my grandmother sat me down and explained life," Hale once told me, in her Slavic accent. "She said, 'Don't waste your energy fighting your enemies. Just go to river and wait for the body of your enemy to pass by. And, my child, they always will.'"

Two months after the wedding in Napa, the Gettys were guests of their friend Kenneth Rainin, a medical products magnate, aboard his two-hundred-foot motor yacht *Rasselas*, named after Samuel Johnson's character, an "Abissinian" prince who traveled throughout ancient Arabia in search of bliss. (A pattern emerges: rich men, the names of their boats, and the search for happiness.)

Ann had certainly earned a holiday; that spring, she had staged yet another elaborate wedding at the Getty Mansion, for actor Don Johnson and Kelley Phleger, whose Chanel couture gown was a gift from Ann on a Jetty-propelled trip to Paris.

While floating somewhere on the Mediterranean, Gordon received a call from his lawyer, a call he knew would come one day. At some point, the media was bound to expose the existence of his other family, in Los Angeles. For years, a very small circle of San Franciscans, including Ann and his sons, had been aware of the situation, but it had so far remained a secret.

"It was the *San Jose* paper that broke the story," one society stalwart said to me, his voice dripping with derision. "The San Francisco papers would have never dared."

On August 20, 1999, the *San Jose Mercury News* went there:

BILLIONAIRE GORDON GETTY'S SECRET FAMILY OF 4 REVEALED

S.F. SOCIALITE HAS THREE DAUGHTERS, INHERITANCE BEING NEGOTIATED

According to a family friend, Gordon asked Ann if she wanted to debark from the *Rasselas* and fly home. "No, we're going on with the trip," she said.

Anticipating this day, Gordon's lawyer had a prepared statement from him. Now it was released: "Nicolette, Kendalle, and Alexandra are my children. Their mother, Cynthia Beck, and I, love them very much. The most important concern is that the children's needs be addressed with a minimum of disruption, and this will be our first priority. The Getty family has been fully supportive throughout this situation, and for that, I am very grateful."

Nicolette, then fourteen, Kendalle, age ten, and Alexandra, who was eight, had been brought up with the surname Beck. (Doing the math, Nicolette was presumably born in 1985, the year that began with Ann setting sail down the Nile.) In April 1999, a lawyer working on their behalf had filed documents in Los Angeles Superior Court requesting that their names be changed to Getty, which was what tipped off a *San Jose Mercury News* reporter.

"She is a nice lady and lives in the LA area," was all Gordon's attorney divulged about Cynthia after the story broke. The press, as well as the Sherlock Holmeses of high society, endeavored to learn details of Getty's other family, but few real facts ever emerged, in the papers or on the cocktail-party circuit. "No one we know knows her," a Beverly Hills doyenne declared to me, which was a common refrain.

According to another close Getty family friend, Gordon had revealed his secret first to his third-born son: "Gordon drove over to see John in Berkeley. 'You know, I have three daughters,' he said."

Understandably stunned, John kept the news to himself initially. Until one day when Gordon, Ann, and the four boys were all aloft on the Jetty. As a family discussion grew heated, John blurted it out: *"Dad has another family."* According to this family friend, Ann sat in her seat "stone-faced."

"She was upset when she found out, but they came to an understanding, and she was permissive about letting Gordon visit the girls," said another friend.

According to most accounts from the Getty social circle, Gordon ended the affair when the news of it exploded, though one of their intimates claims it continued. In any event, Gordon did introduce his Los Angeles family to his San Francisco family, in hopes of establishing cordial relations, which by and large happened. But not overnight. "There was a hiccup," says a childhood friend of the boys. Money was an issue. Gordon made it clear that his daughters and sons would be inheriting equal shares of his estate. "The boys weren't liking it—that everything suddenly had been diluted by about half," this source says. But in time everyone became amicable. And even with the addition of the three heirs, Gordon's children will, by most estimates, eventually receive hundreds of millions each.

Nonetheless, the revelation was society's equivalent of the San Francisco earthquake. This time, many awaited the aftershocks with glee. But exactly two months after the deluge of headlines around the world following the *Mercury News* scoop, here was the report in the *Chronicle*'s Social Scene column: "Dinner, anyone? Ann and Gordon Getty have been giving some simply MAHvelous dinner parties lately, such as the one they and Jo Schuman gave Sunday for author Dominick Dunne." The same week, the article reported, the Gettys also hosted suppers for pianists Katia and Marielle Labèque and for the writers in town for the National Kidney Foundation's Authors' Lunch.

The next month, much of San Francisco society assembled inside the Getty mansion, when Ann hosted a reception after the funeral of Pat Steger, who for twenty-five years had written the thrice-weekly Social Scene column for the *Chronicle*. In a town where "Society" still really mattered, Steger ranked high. A graduate of the Hamlin School for Girls, she reported diligently (usually clad in a mink coat) on the comings and goings of the Bay Area elite—Ann above all. Around town, it was believed that Steger was aware of Gordon's other family, but that this was one scoop she chose not to break.

Nor did anyone else in San Francisco's press corps. (Dan Reed, the *San Jose Mercury News*'s award-winning investigative reporter who did break the story, was, according to a colleague, a "Falstaffian" figure, with a "six foot four, 330-pound frame, uncombed beard, and untucked shirts.") After Steger's funeral mass at St. Ignatius, which was filled with 13,200 Ecuadorian white roses, Ann welcomed everybody to the house for vodka and cheese puffs, Pat's staples. "I always enjoyed her columns, but she was also a great personal friend," Ann commented to the *Chronicle*. "She came many times for dinners which were private. . . . She respected that and didn't write about it. I thought she was a wonderful person."

With her highly trained staff—and the near-constant services of Stanlee R. Gatti, the Bay Area's premiere event designer—it was nothing for Ann to throw a dinner for sixty, and sometimes many more. The Getty mansion functioned like an embassy, and a concert hall (Placido Domingo, Anna Netrebko, Jessye Norman, and other greats sang in the music room or the courtyard, usually after a dinner). When an important dignitary, cultural luminary, or royal came to town, more often than not Ann would host a formal event in their honor.

But sometimes she was absent. Upon arrival, guests would be informed that Mrs. Getty was indisposed or traveling; they would be hosted instead by Charlotte Mailliard Shultz, the state of California's chief of protocol and wife of former secretary of state George Shultz. On occasion, however, Ann just didn't feel like attending these formal functions. Shortly before sixty guests were due to arrive in black tie for a dinner in honor of celebrated art historian Rosamond Bernier, for example, Ann had her secretary call her friend Boaz Mazor; he was instructed to use a side door to the house that night, and meet his hostess upstairs. "We had the most marvelous, cozy dinner in Ann's bedroom while everyone was downstairs. She was wearing gray flannel pants and a brown sweater," he recalled. "*'I can't stand those dinners,'* Ann said."

On Sundays around this time, Ann took to hosting informal suppers in the kitchen for her family and their close friends, many of whom happened to be heavyweights in their fields, such as conductor Michael Tilson Thomas, Senator Feinstein, Mayor Brown, and Berkeley professor Alex Pines. When Kamala Harris was added to the list for Sunday Supper, she had really arrived.

Nearly every Sunday Supper (it became such a thing, it was uppercased) included Ann's best friend, Jo Schuman Silver. Around 2005, when Ann was redecorating Silver's apartment, she and Gordon installed her in one of their guest rooms, which features eighteenth-century Syro-Turkish paneling—hand-painted, gilded, and ornamented with semiprecious stones; Ann bought it at auction in London. The opulent mother-of-pearl and wood-inlaid bed is decorated with rare Qajar *verre églomisé.*

A five-foot, platinum-haired, Chanel-clad bundle of energy, the Brooklyn-born Jo arrived in San Francisco in 1977 with her second husband, a garment business owner. He died in 1985, by which time she had become soul mates with Steve Silver, who in 1974 had created *Beach Blanket Babylon,* a camp musical review, at the Savoy Tivoli theater. With a parade of performers in gaudy costumes and wigs, it spoofed celebrities and political culture and became a San Francisco institution.

In the early nineties, Steve contracted HIV. He and Jo married in 1994; he died the following year, and she took the reins of *BBB.* Having grown up in a show business–oriented family (music producer Clive Davis is a cousin), she took to producing naturally, and became a San Francisco icon herself—as well as the godmother of Ivy Getty. Whether or not it was a factor of being busy with the show, Schuman Silver stayed on in the sumptuous Turkish room. "Why would I ever leave?" she once asked rhetorically.

Ann and Gordon's marriage continued to sail. "They were made for each other," an old friend of theirs observed. "It has a lot to do with them loving the same things—music, wine, beautiful things. They're each eccentrics—they both have a certain madness."

13

New Vintages

In October 2000, Peter and Jacqui were married at the Coppola winery in Napa Valley. (Francis Ford Coppola walked her down the aisle.) Beforehand, Ann took Jacqui on the Jetty to Paris for fittings at the haute couture houses, at which the free-spirited Jacqui wore sneakers and a down jacket. Ann picked up the reported $600,000 tab for Jacqui's new wardrobe, including her Balmain wedding dress, which alone cost $100,000.

Jacqui's own natural style was embraced in Hollywood, where she became a stylist and costume designer. Her clients (who were often friends too) ranged from the Beastie Boys to Demi Moore. "I really trust her taste," Moore told *Harper's Bazaar.*

A year after Peter and Jacqui's nuptials, Ann orchestrated a wedding for the ages, when Gavin Newsom married Kimberly Guilfoyle, a prosecutor in the San Francisco District Attorney's Office (and a onetime girlfriend of Billy's). The couple met at a Democratic state fund raiser held at PlumpJack. Nearly every inch of the Italianate St. Ignatius Church was covered in garlands of gardenias for the evening service. The veil of her crystal-encrusted Vera Wang gown was anchored by an Edwardian diamond *trembleuse* (trembling) tiara lent by Ann. A lavish banquet followed at the Getty mansion for some five hundred guests, ranging from writer Danielle Steel to Mark Getty, a groomsman. But one couple was conspicuously absent: Billy and Vanessa.

Billy and Gavin's friendship had ruptured shortly after his wedding in Napa. Around town, there was speculation about the cause of the rift, but neither man has ever publicly commented. In the aftermath of the falling-out, Billy stepped away from PlumpJack. Gordon bought out his stake in the business. He and Ann remained devoted to Gavin; Gordon has said he considers him like a son. "Gavin is Fortinbras to the Hamlet of Billy," one San Franciscan wryly observed.

(Over the years, Newsom's political opponents have tried to weaponize his connections to the Gettys, portraying him as a child of privilege. But while the Gettys have contributed generously to his campaigns, other San Francisco families have given as much, if not more. In 2018, the *Los Angeles Times* reported that eighteen Gettys had contributed $516,925 to his nine campaigns, including his gubernatorial run that year; during the same span, members of the Pritzker dynasty had given him $608,000, while several other leading Bay Area families had given hundreds of thousands as well.)

In California government, a major changing of the guard was at hand. On January 8, 2004, Newsom was sworn in as San Francisco's youngest mayor in more than a century; Harris became the state's first Black district attorney. (Vanessa served on the finance committee of Harris's campaign.)

The politicians came up together, but Gavin's rise was meteoric. After issuing marriage licenses to same-sex couples, the charismatic thirty-six-year-old leaped onto the national stage as his approval ratings soared to an unheard-of 78 percent. One day he would make a strong run for the White House, it was commonly assumed around San Francisco, and certainly inside the Gettys' house.

For decades, Gordon and Ann had been intimate friends with senators and governors; but who would emerge in the family closest to the highest powers in the land? Those who knew Vanessa only from her appearances at society galas—her statuesque figure clad in glamorous gowns—might end up surprised.

In January 2005, Newsom and Guilfoyle (who had a frosty relationship with Harris when the two women worked together in the DA's office) announced their separation. "It was a bad match, but happily there were no children involved," Judge Newsom said after their divorce became official in 2006, when Guilfoyle joined Fox News in New York. Two years later, Gavin's wedding to actress and Stanford graduate Jennifer Siebel, on a meadow at her parents' ranch in Montana, was a down-home affair—even if many of the two hundred guests were movers and shakers of California politics and business who arrived by private plane. Within eight years, the couple had four children—Montana, Hunter, Brooklynn, and Dutch.

In Hollywood, Peter and Jacqui's house became one the coolest spots in town. The likes of Leonardo DiCaprio, the Olsen twins, Nicolas Ghesquière, Ashton Kutcher, and Demi Moore could be found hanging out in the couple's living room. And that was just a Tuesday. Her celebrity-packed parties—particularly her annual Halloween bash held amidst the tombstones of Hollywood Forever Cemetery—were major events.

Three years after their wedding, Ann paid $7 million for a landmark mansion in Cow Hollow for the couple, though they were not looking for a San Francisco residence at the time. "She really wanted Peter back in San Francisco, and she would not stop," says a friend. Ann embarked on a massive renovation of the Italianate Victorian mansion, built in 1876 by a music impresario named Leander Sherman. When she acquired it, it was a luxury hotel, Sherman House.

Before it ultimately became a home for Peter, Sherman House was a good project for Ann's fledgling career. After all those years of absorbing lessons from her father-in-law, Sister Parish, and various curators, she launched herself as a design professional. In the mid-1990s, she had quietly opened Ann Getty & Associates, an interior decorating firm, but the work didn't really come to the public's attention until 2003 when, simultaneously, she launched Ann Getty Home, a collection of custom furniture and reproductions of important historical pieces, and unveiled the renovation of one of the most extravagant homes in America—her own.

She and Gordon had bought the mansion next door. By dint of considerable engineering, it was eventually seamlessly joined to the Gettys' original house. Utilizing all her know-how, Ann completely reimagined her home of thirty years. Even as it was "completed," work continued: the Gettys bought the next house over. By the time the three properties were joined—which gave the couple some 30,000 square feet—she had created one of the most palatial private residences in America. "We're building all the way to Oakland, at this rate," a friend of Gordon's recalls him saying in jest.

"We joked that now that the children are gone, we needed a bigger house," Ann quipped.

In the fall of 2003, I visited the house to interview Ann about her burgeoning design career. We chatted in the dining room, which was lined with chinoiserie panels made in 1720 for the Elector of Saxony, as a butler served a lunch of chicken salad. (Alas, Francis Bullimore was no longer on duty. The revered majordomo died of a heart ailment in 1996 at age eighty-two, at the Getty residence. The Gettys had looked after him at home well after he reached retirement age, as they did with other staff members, including the boys' nanny. According to his obituary in the *San Francisco Examiner*, Bullimore was survived by a sister in Norfolk, England, "and his cherished schnauzer, Nietzsche.")

Gordon was occupied that morning composing music in his study downstairs, but he popped into the dining room for a moment. Looking very much the absent-minded professor, he offered an optimistic prediction of his wife's professional prospects. "New businesses usually fail, especially the fun ones, but I think this one has a definite chance of succeeding," he said as he took the opportunity to engage in some good-natured self-promotion, presenting me with a copy of his new CD, a recording of *Joan and the Bells*, a cantata portraying the trial and execution of Joan of Arc.

Ann, dressed in her daytime uniform of jeans and an immaculate white shirt, cut a commanding figure, standing at five feet ten with flowing red hair.

Stately as the Getty mansion was, there were unexpected touches, like the trampoline set up in the vast marble-lined interior court-yard, and coloring books strewn about the walnut-paneled library: although their classrooms were belowstairs, the schoolchildren had the run of the house.

Paintings by Canaletto, Degas, Matisse, Bonnard, and Mary Cassatt adorned the walls, and museum-quality furniture abounded, including true showstoppers such as a pair of *coffres de mariage* signed by master cabinetmaker André-Charles Boulle. Many items were made originally for England's stateliest homes, such as Badminton, Houghton Hall, and Spencer House, by such masters as Thomas Chippendale, Giles Grendey, and James Linnell.

"There's stuff in there any museum would kill for," an eminent antiques dealer later told me. An auction house expert said, "Ann took the cake for extravagance. She always went for the rarest, the most important things. But then she would hang things in a won-derfully irreverent way. She put a Degas in her bathroom. Well, I'd do it if I could. Though I don't know if I approve of her sawing up Coromandel screens."

With chinoiserie as her theme, Getty transformed her newly enlarged residence into a spectacular Aladdin's cave of treasures, exotic and layered.

"I like things on things," she said, explaining her design philoso-phy as well as the evolution of her house.

Since her formative years with Mrs. Parish, Ann's taste had grown bolder. She reached a point where she was ready to replace Parish-Hadley's signature yellow walls and chintzes with her own vision—though she still remembered Sister fondly: "She scared me, of course. She would march you through things and watch to see if you got it. . . . I couldn't make my mind up about anything. Finally she told me I had to make decisions—and I did."

When she began her own decorating business, Ann faced inevitable skepticism. "There may be the perception that I'm spoiled, have no sense of the price of things, that I just wouldn't understand a budget. . . . I can clear that up very easily," she said. "I can convince them that I work hard, have a good team, and can listen."

In addition to her originality, Ann had access to rare sources. (The Jetty helped.) In Myanmar, she discovered a textile made from hairs of the lotus flower, harvested after the rainy season. Monks traditionally stitched together their robes from the cloth, which is woven only in small pieces. "I thought it was just fabulous, because it is always cool to the touch," she said.

In a cavernous former army barrack in San Francisco's Presidio, Getty opened her atelier, stocked with acres of rare textiles, passementerie, porcelains, objets d'art, carpets, and antiques. Her staff included three full-time upholsterers/seamstresses. "[It's] like Santa's workshop," said one of Getty's clients, frozen-food heiress Alexis Swanson Traina. "There's nothing she can't do."

For Alexis and her husband, tech entrepreneur (and later US ambassador to Austria) Trevor Traina, Getty brought exoticism and fantasy to a sedate brick 1905 mansion the couple purchased. The walls of the library, for example, were covered with thousands of peacock feathers. "It's magic," Trevor said.

While Ann Getty also completed jobs for other prominent San Franciscans, including socialite Adrianna Pope Sullivan and philanthropist Terry Gross, her client roster included many family names. For Peter, she did succeed in bringing Sherman House back to its nineteenth-century glory days, and then some—even if he might initially have been reluctant to move in. In 2003, just after it was acquired, she had her work cut out for her. Peter was flying up from

Los Angeles that afternoon for a design meeting. "He should be here any minute, or he's a dead man," she remarked to me during our interview.

For John, she refurbished another historic house in Berkeley—Temple of the Wings, a stunning villa in the Aesthetic movement style that was designed in 1914 by architect Bernard Maybeck. John didn't seem to occupy it very much, however; he was mostly in London or Los Angeles.

She also gave Andrew some help with his house in the Hollywood Hills. But Billy and Vanessa went their own way, décor-wise. She "has her own ideas," Ann explained. After his wedding, Billy sold his Russian Hill penthouse (for $15 million, a new record price for an SF co-op), and the couple bought a five-story stucco mansion in Pacific Heights built in 1912.

Ann made attempts to decorate for Gavin too. But, just weeks before he was elected mayor, she was having little success. "He doesn't want furniture. His idea is just a park bench in the middle of the living room," she complained.

One Getty friend told me that Ann also helped decorate a house for Gordon's former mistress. "Cynthia liked Ann's taste. She asked for her help."

In Los Angeles, as the aughts progressed, Peter and Jacqui were veering apart. Invitations to her fabulous, movie star–filled parties were coveted by everyone except her introverted husband, it seemed. "Peter would hang out in the garage, smoke weed, and knit. He didn't want anything to do with the parties," recalled a friend. An avid knitter, Peter enjoyed creating brightly colored and quite lengthy scarves. "They were incredibly gorgeous—works of art."

By 2009, Peter had repatriated to San Francisco, where he settled into Sherman House. That summer, he and Billy wrote a blog on SFGate, the *Chronicle*'s website, entitled "What the Butler Didn't

See." In it, as they wrote in their inaugural post, they planned to explain "what's it like being rich."

They recalled the disconnect they felt as children when they visited friends' homes, where the furniture was comfortable, could be horsed around on, and "looked like it had been built within our lifetimes."

"Our furniture, on the other hand, looked like people had died in it, and half of it you couldn't even touch. . . . When it was finally impressed upon us that we came from a wealthy family, one of our thoughts was that perhaps we could now finally afford some proper furniture." And while their friends got to put up posters of rock bands and Farrah Fawcett, they had to stare at "scary" oil paintings.

The backlash was swift, and went viral. "Shut the fuck up. Shut the fuck up with your idle life," wrote *Gawker*, in the first of several online screeds.

Peter had to contend with more press the following year, when his divorce battle became public. As Jacqui sought a financial settlement, she made allegations in court involving Peter and drugs, abusive behavior, and pornography. Those allegations soon surfaced on the internet, including, of course, on *Gawker* ("You may remember Peter Getty as the obnoxious and self-consciously privileged San Francisco columnist. . . .").

Peter and Jacqui, who had no children together, eventually came to an agreement. Reportedly, he no longer keeps in touch with Jacqui or Gia. Jacqui remains close with Peter's relatives in Los Angeles.

"Gettys don't go for bitterness—not after everything they've been through," observed a family friend.

I returned to the Getty mansion for another interview in 2012, by which time Ann had completed an impressive body of design work. A selection of residences she had decorated appeared that October in a lavishly illustrated book, *Ann Getty Interior Style*, written by Diane Dorrans Saeks and published by Rizzoli.

When Saeks approached her with the idea of doing a book, Getty was reluctant. "I didn't feel right promoting myself," she told me. Fortuitously, just before our interview, an advance copy had arrived, which was resting on a George II carved parcel-gilt and ebonized stool in front of us. "I'm pleased with it," she announced as she paged through it. "I'm glad I did it. Because I think it's a nice record." (*Ann Getty Interior Style*, which went into a second printing, has become a collector's item; some rare-book dealers have charged as much as $2,000 for a copy.)

In our conversations, Ann also spoke fondly of her late father-in-law. "It's not fair!" she said about his misanthropic reputation. "He was funny and fun to be with."

Most people have a "very inaccurate impression" of him, she added. "He was sensitive and very intelligent. . . . He was careful with money, and not self-indulgent at all. His parents were very strict, and he continued to live as he had lived when he was a boy, quite simply, like a monk."

He suggested she start collecting fine French furniture. "My means were not so great" at the time, she recalled. "So, I started with English lacquer. When I bought my first piece, he said it looked like a soap box. . . . He was really quite expert."

The first of the next generation of Gettys made her debut in July 2013. In front of six hundred guests at the St. Francis Hotel, Gordon, in white tie, presented Ivy Love Getty at the 49th San Francisco Debutante Ball. That fall, she enrolled at Loyola Marymount University, where she studied studio arts and graphic design.

As always, the Gettys' December gala holiday party provided a grand finale to the year. Though it primarily fetes Gordon's birthday, it also celebrates Ivy's. In 2013, she turned nineteen, and it was his eightieth, which called for a particularly splendid affair.

For days before the event, their block ("Billionaires Row") was closed to traffic so an elaborate tent could be erected. Large as the Getty residence is, they needed extra room for the six hundred guests, all in long gowns, furs, jewels, and black tie. Lavish decorations abounded—"it was so opulent, you couldn't believe it," said one attendee—but the installation in the marble courtyard was poignant: an homage to Emily Dickinson and her poem "The White Election," the inspiration for Gordon's breakthrough composition. A portrait of Dickinson painted by Ann was on display.

In addition to the reigning powers of California politics and society, the guest list included many of Gordon's old cohorts from St. Ignatius, the Leakey Foundation, and the music world.

Foremost, it was a stunning gathering of Gettys—nearly every one of them, from every branch of the family, from around the world. After being depicted for so long as such a fragmented and fractious clan, here was a very different picture. All three of the Georgettes, for example, as well as their cousin Tara—now long free of his guardian ad litem—warmly embraced the uncle they had long ago sued.

Various ex-wives and widows—still in the bosom of the clan—mingled too, including Lady Victoria, Sir Paul's widow; Gloria, George's first wife; and Karin, Ronald's widow. Front and center was Teddy, looking fabulous at age one hundred. She held court on an antique silk-moiré divan, accompanied by her daughter, Gigi Gaston. ("He was the most amazing man I ever met in my life," Teddy said of her first husband shortly before she died in 2017 at 103, in Los Angeles.)

Gordon's daughters, the cause of so much shock when their existence was revealed, chatted genially with Ann—stunning in a yellow Carolina Herrera ball gown—and with their half brothers.

"We're a genuinely close family," Balthazar told *Chronicle* correspondent Catherine Bigelow (Pat Steger's former assistant, and successor on the society beat). "We're here to honor Gordon, who's such a wonderful uncle to all of us. And definitely one of the great characters of all time."

"In a freaky way, they really *are* tight-knit," another attendee at the party observed later. "No one else in the world knows what it's like to be them except them—that's part of their bond."

It was certainly a family that embraced many different personalities and styles. With her dark hair in dreadlocks, Nicolette, Gordon's eldest daughter, wore a beige woolen dress, black tights, and biker-style boots; Kendalle, in a black satin cocktail dress, topped her platinum hair with a small 1930s-style hat. Alexandra wasn't spotted (she spent a number of years in Japan), but at other Getty family parties she has appeared wearing elegant gowns, with long straight red hair and red lipstick highlighting her fair complexion.

Vanessa chose a stunning red satin strapless gown, one of the looks that doubtless led *Vanity Fair* to name her to the International Best-Dressed List in 2014. The only Bay Area resident chosen, she was in company with the Duchess of Cambridge and Cate Blanchett, among others. By this time, Ann had pulled back from the social scene, making her daughter-in-law her natural successor—especially when boosted by Denise Hale, who frequently announced that Vanessa was the next queen of San Francisco.

While Vanessa enjoyed socializing, her husband preferred golfing or staying home, much like his father and his brothers. "They all have a reclusive bent," said a childhood friend about the Getty men. "They are all quite happy to be alone at home."

In Los Angeles, John settled down somewhat, and created a couple of striking homes for himself. In the 2010s he bought two houses that had been designed in the 1920s by A. F. Leicht, an admired architect known for his eccentric style. One of them, dubbed the Castle, combined art deco, Spanish, and Assyrian styles. (Its previous residents included Bob Dylan and later Flea of the Red Hot Chili Peppers.)

Deploying a sharp eye for design that pleased his mother, he became a connoisseur of the Aesthetic movement, neo-Gothic, and Victorian periods. Among the important pieces that he acquired was the "Industry and Idleness" cabinet, designed circa 1860 by revered English architect William Burges. Massive yet delicately detailed, the polychrome and giltwood cabinet features fancifully decorated paneled doors and enameled tiles. In the 1960s, Christopher Gibbs acquired it for the Cheyne Walk house of John's uncle Paul. In 2004, after his death, it was among a small group of Sir Paul's furnishings auctioned at Christie's in London. According to a news report, it was purchased by an anonymous telephone buyer for £274,050. Lord Andrew Lloyd Webber was the underbidder.

John also amassed an outstanding collection of rare guitars—including a '63 Fender Jazz Bass, a '64 Gibson Hummingbird, a '69 Zemaitis twelve-string, and a '72 Fender Telecaster with a rosewood fingerboard—reflecting his passion for music, a source of pride for Gordon.

John's circle of friends included many musicians, some of whom he also jammed with, such as Tom Petty and Led Zeppelin's Jimmy Page; in Los Angeles, he was also close to his cousins and to his former sister-in-law, Jacqui. Yet he remained under the radar. Never photographed at parties, he was not a boldface name, unlike his relatives in San Francisco.

In his forties, he finally embraced parenthood. Ivy, then a teenager, enjoyed stays with him in Los Angeles and London. "We became extremely close and he jumped at finally playing the role of the father he always wanted to be and became this almost strict protective father," she later wrote. "He loved being my father and he was always so proud."

Though Ivy was primarily raised by Ann and Gordon, with a big assist from Jo Schuman Silver, Ivy's mother was involved too; Alyssa (who became a jewelry designer) and John stayed in touch and on good terms.

One of Ivy's happiest visits with her father was on his birthday in Los Angeles. They had dinner at Nobu Malibu, and then paid a visit to the grave site of his grandfather and uncles George and Timothy at the Getty Villa. "We had a beautiful and sentimental time. He was surrounded by his best friends and me," she recalled.

He was a cool dad. A dandy, his wardrobe included suits custom-made for him by Glen Palmer, an Englishman who moved to LA in 1975 and became the tailor to rock gods such as Rod Stewart, Tom Petty, Ronnie Wood, and the members of Fleetwood Mac (Palmer created the Renaissance-style garments they wore on the cover of *Rumours*).

Andrew Getty, also in Los Angeles, became increasingly secluded inside his house in the Hollywood Hills. He labored, in fits and starts, over one movie, as producer, director, and screenwriter. Purportedly, it was inspired by nightmares he had as a child.

In the film, *The Evil Within*, a young man named Dennis suffers from debilitating nightmares. A demon haunts Dennis through his own reflection in an antique, full-length mirror, and convinces him that committing murder is the only way to free himself.

Andrew reportedly invested about $6 million of his own money in the film. While his income from the family trust was ample, it could only stretch so far. To make ends meet, there were weeks when he ate only cereal, according to a staffer on the film. A good deal of his budget went into animatronic robots for the film, which Andrew built himself. (He studied engineering at NYU.)

But, said a friend, "He had been struggling with addictions." On March 31, 2015, Andrew, age forty-seven, was found dead on the floor of his bathroom. While there was a toxic level of meth in his system, the coroner determined that his death was caused by gastro-intestinal hemorrhage.

"It was heartbreaking," said the friend. "He was not a bad person but something bad happened to him."

Two years after Andrew's death, *The Evil Within* was released on

VOD and DVD. "A passion project built on a foundation of uncommon artistic commitment . . . [it stands] today as a testament to its creator's singular mad ambition," a critic wrote in the *Guardian*.

The afternoon of December 15, 2016, in the faux-marbled, three-story music room of Sherman House, Peter married Shannon Bavaro, a technology advisor. They had been dating a few years, and had a year-old daughter, Ava. Newly elected US senator Kamala Harris officiated. Before the ceremony, she offered advice to the bride. "She said to be in the moment, remember why I was there, and to embrace the love and the joy. She is so wise," Bavaro recalled afterward. Their son, Dexter, was born about a year later.

That evening, Gordon and Ann hosted a dinner dance at home for two hundred friends, ranging from Peter's old Virgin-Whore Complex bandmates to the Pelosis. The bride wore Vera Wang. "That's it. That's the one," Ann had said as soon as they saw the gown in Wang's New York showroom.

At long last, Gordon's musical compositions were receiving good reviews, particularly for two one-act operas he'd written. *Usher House*, based on Edgar Allan Poe's horror story, premiered in Cardiff with the Welsh National Opera in 2014, before going to San Francisco. *The Canterville Ghost*, based on the humorous Oscar Wilde story, premiered at Germany's Leipzig Opera in 2015. In 2018, both gothic tales were united under a bill dubbed *Scare Pair*, and staged at venues in LA and New York. *Los Angeles Times* critic Richard S. Ginell called *Canterville* "engaging" and "unexpectedly delightful."

As written by Wilde in 1887, "Canterville" begins as a rich American family, the Otises, move into Canterville Chase, an English country house, despite warnings that it is haunted. Indeed, its resident ghost, Sir Simon de Canterville, rises up to terrorize. But he is no match for these pragmatic Americans, particularly the couple's rather obnoxious twin boys, who torment the ghost. Getty added some contemporary satirical elements, such as the family using consumer products and litigation to solve their problems. Where does Gordon get these ideas?

He answered some questions in an hourlong documentary directed by Peter Rosen, *Gordon Getty: There Will Be Music*, which PBS stations broadcast in 2017. "If you are a composer, melodies are going on in your noggin all the time," he explained about his creative process. He also discussed his two-decade-long writer's block and how he overcame it: "I felt I couldn't be taken seriously, maybe even by myself, unless I could write something a little grander and more complicated . . . and then finally it dawned on me, that it isn't true—I could become even less complicated."

On an afternoon in November 2018, I was invited to lunch at Balboa Cafe with Gordon Peter Getty, to talk about wine.

The sky above Cow Hollow, like the entire city, had an alarming orange cast, the result of the devastating Camp Fire burning to the north. Before Gordon arrived, there was a commotion on Fillmore Street: a car halted suddenly, and the driver honked and gawked at California's new governor-elect crossing the street. "You'd be a good Bruce Wayne!" she yelled. Gavin Newsom did look pretty movie star–like as he strolled into the restaurant.

His inauguration as California's fortieth governor was just weeks away, but the opportunity to have a taste of the PlumpJack 2016 Cabernet Sauvignon Reserve, which would not be released until the following autumn, had apparently drawn him to Balboa today.

Then Getty arrived. With unruly hair, he was clad in a plaid shirt, rumpled khakis, and a maroon parka shell, which he never took off. A few weeks shy of his eighty-fifth birthday, he had strikingly luminous blue eyes. His father was known for his blue eyes.

Gordon and Gavin exchanged a warm hug. But they quickly got down to business.

"I've only tasted this in the barrel," said Newsom, eyeing the 2016.

"This is a helluva wine," commented Gordon as soon as he took a sip, after which the two of them exchanged comments on the structure and expressiveness of the vintage.

(Wine authority Robert Parker awarded the Cab a rare "100" score. "Hits the ground running with the most stunning perfume of crushed black cherries . . . ," he wrote in his rave, in which he also gushed over how the "rich, decadent palate is beautifully lifted with fantastic freshness." His conclusion: "If 'PlumpJack awesome' isn't a phrase to the describe the ultimate in deliciousness, it should be.")

Getty's lunch was a hamburger, served rare, with no bun. For about seventeen years, he has followed a strict paleo-style diet, abstaining from starches and sugar. "It's not a diet, it's a religion," he said.

The octogenarian did seem full of beans. When another guest at the table, PlumpJack's general manager John Conover, noted that the PlumpJack 2016 Cabernet Sauvignon Reserve was still five years away from its optimal drinking time, Gordon scoffed. "I'm the Roy Moore of wines—I like 'em young," he said boisterously.

His spriteliness somehow brought to mind all those Gettys who are in line for massive windfalls when he leaves this earth. Per the terms set in 1934, the Getty family trusts terminate at the end of the last "measuring" life of J. Paul Getty's sons. Gordon's surviving children and their cousins will presumably each be collecting hundreds of millions.

"Gordon has tried to be as nice and as generous as possible to everyone in the family, because he doesn't want them rooting for him to die," someone once involved in managing Getty family finances said.

Getty's enthusiasm for the wine business certainly remained robust. As PlumpJack's wines developed a cult-like following, the

PlumpJack Group continued to grow. Along with more shops, restaurants, and hotels, two other Napa vineyards were acquired— Odette and Cade. When Newsom became mayor, he sold his shares in PlumpJack's San Francisco enterprises to Gordon Getty; he bought them back when he became lieutenant governor. Then, when he was elected governor, Newsom placed his stake in the companies in a blind trust run by a family friend. Since 2009, operations have been overseen by the group's president, Hilary Newsom Callan, Gavin's sister. (She and her husband, Jeff, have two daughters, Talitha and Siena.)

Gordon, the majority owner, ultimately calls the shots. "My idea is to make the best wine I can make . . . to see if I can make as good a wine as anyone in the world," he said.

A fine glass of wine is also literally a distillation of his belief that biology and economics are intertwined. "Believe it!" he said. "Natural selection and market selection are the same thing."

A few years ago, Getty roiled the wine world when he became the first owner of a luxury brand to seal some of his bottles with screw caps—that type of enclosure known to consumers of Boone's Farm Apple Wine and jugs of the ilk.

While cork has been the material of choice to seal wines since the early seventeenth century, about one in ten bottles suffers from cork taint and oxygen seepage. Even so, high-end winemakers always scoffed at the idea of screw caps.

"I thought it would be better for quality, but everybody was afraid to do it," said Gordon. "I said, 'I'm not.' I thought, it's a no-brainer— under the right circumstances. I said, 'Just make sure UC Davis [with its respected Department of Viticulture and Enology] is guiding us through every step of the process, and that we only do it with our very best, most expensive wine.' And never more than fifty percent, so you could compare to cork over time."

News of his initiative flummoxed the trade. "There was a lot of harrumphing that we had no respect for tradition," Getty recalled. "Wine is a very conservative business."

Brisk sales and more rave reviews vindicated him. The 2012 Odette Reserve Cab and the 2013 PlumpJack Reserve Cabernet Sauvignon were the first screw-tops ever to get perfect scores from Parker. And other prestigious winemakers have followed Getty's lead.

"Even if we failed, we would have gotten bragging rights as innovators, for doing something everybody else was afraid to do," he said. "I'm a risk taker . . . so was my father. It worked out pretty good for him.

"It's all true about him being a tightwad," he added. "But he was a dear. I was the apple of his eye."

Nonetheless, after eight decades, it appeared that Gordon had finally escaped his father's shadow: "Critics used to write about me as 'the son of.' Not anymore. Now my work is taken more on its own merits," he said, bringing the conversation around to music.

His considerable body of compositions, including operas, choral and orchestral works, piano pieces, and songs, has been performed worldwide, at such venues as New York's Carnegie Hall, London's Royal Festival Hall, Vienna's Brahms-Saal, Moscow's Bolshoi Theatre, and Beijing's National Centre for the Performing Arts. The Pentatone label has released about a dozen recordings of his works, which are published by his company, Rork Music.

In the end, music provided his escape from "the curse."

"You can gag on that silver spoon," he said. "Having too much money is dangerous, especially for children. More than you need is a curse. . . . [but] if you have ideals, and that ideal is something bigger than you—music is something bigger than me, it's a mountain I'm trying to climb—then you might escape the curse. There are other Gettys who have dodged it, others have been clobbered."

14

Passing the Baton

Less than a month after that lunch, on December 12, 2018, Bill Newsom died at home, of unspecified causes at age eighty-four.

The same day, Kendalle posted on her Instagram account a portrait she had painted in oil of Gordon eight years earlier. "Today, my father, depicted here as The Emperor tarot card, lost his very best friend in the world," she wrote. (In the tarot deck, the Emperor is the father figure.) "They'd known each other since they were about 12. . . . I loved Bill, and I still do. Today hurts so badly and I'm so tired of having feelings."

She didn't use the Getty surname on any of her social media accounts. She was "Kendalle Aubra" on Twitter and Instagram, where her account was called "Freudian.slit." When she was photographed in 2010 at a charity benefit in San Francisco, she was identified as "Kendalle Fiasco." Like her sisters, she grew up in Los Angeles with their mother. After living in Brooklyn for several years in the mid-2010s, she returned to LA, where she lives with her boyfriend, Johnny Latu, a musician.

She has close relationships with her father and other Getty relatives. In March 2019, she flew with Gordon, Ivy, Balthazar, and his family to Africa, where she assisted Phinda staff on their missions dehorning black rhinos. On Instagram, she posted photos and detailed the laborious procedure, which involves tranquilizing an animal with a dart, blindfolding it, and inserting plugs in its ears, prior to the cutting. Kendalle took a particular shine to one rhino. "They sprayed her horn nubs with a purple antibacterial spray that I got excited about, and they let me spray her toenails with it and add a heart to her side! I named her Fiona. She's six years old," she wrote.

One post drew a snarky comment, accusing Kendalle (who serves on the advisory board of the Africa Foundation, along with her sister Nicolette and Alexander, Mark's eldest son) of wasting jet fuel. Kendalle wrote an informed reply. She rattled off a long list of facts and statistics detailing the foundation's efforts on behalf of wildlife conservation and human rights before concluding, "How about you ask questions before you judge and stop wasting so much hate?"

While many San Franciscans have greeted Kendalle and her sisters at the Gettys' large parties, few saw them outside of those events or knew much about the young women or their creative and political endeavors.

An activist since the age of thirteen, Kendalle founded the Angry Feminist Pin-Up Calendar in 2018 to aid survivors of abuse and violence. Net proceeds are donated to organizations including Planned Parenthood and the Battered Women's Justice Project.

In the calendar, she upends traditional pin-up tropes "to empower femme-identified people of all shapes, colors, sizes, and backgrounds," as she wrote. For her own turn as Miss March, her theme was inspired by some strong characters, she explained, though she didn't mention that she was related to one of them: "We paid homage to one of my all-time favorite films, #Barbarella (of course) from that fierce scene where #TalithaGetty, uncredited, offers Barbarella a hit of 'Essence of Man.' Thank you, 1968, for so many incredible films," she wrote.

Kendalle's most prominent tattoo, running down her right arm, is a depiction of Barbarella. A nose ring and frequently changing hair coloring (green, oftentimes) are among her other features.

In 2020, after long being intrigued by talk of the so-called gay agenda, she published The Gay Agenda—a weekly planner meant to be, in her words, "fabulous" as well as "radical and fierce . . . something to reinforce and reunite the LGBTQi+ with my kind of feminism—intersectional feminism, of course—to join our political avant-gardes together in the battle for cultural progressivism."

Kendalle is also an active member of the Poetry Brothel, a roving, risqué literary burlesque whose patron saint is Oscar Wilde, where she recites her poetry under the stage name Ophelia Up. Inspired by turn-of-the-century brothels in New Orleans, Paris, and Buenos Aires, the Poetry Brothel, according to its site, "strives to promote empowered sexuality practices and radically open artistic expression."

On Twitter, Kendalle described herself as "Artist, Activist, Cotton Candy Barbarella." On other platforms, she called herself "a contemporary flapper, a pre-apocalyptic Tank Girl," and "a retro-futurist weened on riot grrrl and Edgar Allan Poe." According to the introduction she wrote for a blog, "I'm a bit of a cultural bastard, which has enabled me to look at pop culture in a disentangled, disengaged way. For this I am incredibly thankful."

Her elder sister, Nicolette Beck, has lived in San Francisco's Mission District for the past decade with her husband, Michael Hays, a musician and performance artist. In recent years, they became distressed watching the fabric of the neighborhood change as gentrification made the area unaffordable to many longtime residents and businesses. In 2020 they founded a nonprofit, Bigote de Gato, which will function as a theater, a school, an arts incubator, and a community center. Class subjects will include mime, improv, clown theater, and puppetry. They intend to form a bilingual theater troupe from their student body—creating a path for anyone to become a performer. "We believe that by facilitating creative expression in more people, we can help heal our city and perhaps our world," Nicolette explained.

Alexandra, the youngest, lived in Japan for some years, where she studied art and modeled. Her bio: "Freethinking person. Vegan. I paint and box for fun." Working in watercolors, pen and ink, and digital, she is producing figurative portraits, anatomical studies, and manga art. She is the youngest of J. Paul Getty's nineteen grandchildren—born some thirty-nine years after Anne G. Earhart, the eldest. On social media she identifies herself as Alice Sarah Beck, but she generally goes by her middle name, Sarah, making her the namesake of the family matriarch.

Considering how their existences became widely known—with their petition in court to change their surname to Getty—it is notable that none of Gordon's daughters, by this point, chose to use the name.

While the young women came into view in public forums, their mother remained virtually unknown. Even after one of the most bizarre police raids in Los Angeles history.

On May 8, 2019, the LAPD swarmed an eight-thousand-square-foot mansion in Bel-Air. They seized about a thousand firearms—a shocking arsenal that included AR15-style rifles and submachine guns—and arrested a resident of the house, Girard Damian Saenz, age fifty-seven.

"I had never seen so many weapons in my career of thirty-one years," one of the LAPD officers commented.

After pleading not guilty to sixty-four felony counts—for which he could face forty-eight years in prison—Saenz was released from custody after posting a $100,000 bond. At a preliminary hearing in February 2020 three of the charges were dropped. More than eighteen months later there had been no further action in the case, according to the website of the Superior Court of California, County of Los Angeles.

The most shocking part: Cynthia Beck was identified as the owner of the home, and, according to some reports, the "longtime companion" of Saenz as well as the former mistress of Gordon. She was not present in the house at the time of the raid, nor charged with any crimes. No other information about her has appeared in the media.

Notwithstanding that Beverly Hills doyenne's pronouncement that "no one we know knows her," Cynthia's father was wealthy and accomplished. He was also one of Gordon's fellow board members at the Leakey Foundation.

Born in 1926, Robert M. Beck was brought up by a single mother in Dust Bowl–era Nebraska. He served as a navy radarman in the Pacific during World War II, then studied physics on a GI Bill scholarship at UCLA, before he emerged as one of the pioneers of computing. After working for Northrop and Packard Bell, he joined the founding group of Scientific Data Systems. In 1967, having earned a fortune, he retired from the business. He and his wife, Helene, Cynthia's mother, raised cattle on their ranch in Montana; on their farm in Southern California, they grew persimmons, kumquats, and other exotic fruits, following Rudolf Steiner's strict biodynamic precepts. Beck also provided significant support to the search for the origins of man. A $1 million challenge gift that he made to the two-year-old Leakey Foundation in 1970 was instrumental in getting the organization off the ground. He died in 2014 after a long struggle with Parkinson's.

Three weeks after the drama of the police raid in Bel-Air, Ann and Gordon hosted a $28,000-a-couple fund raiser for Kamala Harris's presidential bid at home in San Francisco. An enjoyable summer followed. The couple took the Jetty to Croatia for the annual family meeting (a change of pace: the event is traditionally held in Italy). From there, they flew with Billy, Vanessa, and their three children to Argentina, to watch the total solar eclipse.

Ivy was particularly active. Having obtained her BFA from Loyola Marymount, she was drawing and painting, as well as walking red carpets, clad in extravagant looks by Alexander McQueen, Gucci, and other designers. At the star-studded amfAR Gala Cannes at the Hôtel du Cap, she wowed in a dramatic floral creation by Australian designer Toni Maticevski; with her soft blond tresses, she conjured Bardot. After the Côte d'Azur, she ventured through the Season in London and the couture shows in Paris (where she saw her cousin August's show at the Ritz), before flying back to California for the wedding of August's sibling, Nats, to Gigi Gorgeous. "Welcome to the family @gigigorgeous," Ivy declared in an IG post from "#nigiwedding" in Montecito.

For the Gettys, as well as for legions of San Franciscans, there was a bittersweet finale to 2019. It was the end of the line for *Beach Blanket Babylon*. Forty-five years on, it claimed to be the world's longest-running musical revue; with its seemingly never-ending parade of over-the-top costumes, wigs, and laughs, it had become one of the town's most beloved institutions, part of the fabric of the city.

While Jo Schuman Silver, at seventy-four, was still crackling with energy—and still ensconced in one of Ann and Gordon's guest rooms—she felt it was time to end the show. At its farewell performance on New Year's Eve, Club Fugazi (to which it had transferred in 1974) was packed with the powers that be, including Speaker Pelosi, Senator Dianne Feinstein, and Governor Newsom (who said he was first taken to the show by his grandfather). There was a palpable feeling that a chapter in the life of the city was closing. But a new one seemed to be beginning. When the curtain rose, Ivy Love Getty, resplendent in a red and gold sequined gown and a red sequined top hat, shimmied confidently to center stage.

Two weeks later, at the San Francisco Ballet's opening-night gala, she descended the long marble staircase under the rotunda of the ornate Beaux Arts–style City Hall wearing an ice-blue satin ball gown that Oscar de la Renta had made for her grandmother thirty years before, paired with gold opera-length gloves and a shimmering headband holding her hair in an elevated ballet bun updo. She was accompanied by her boyfriend of two years, Tobias "Toby" Engel, a twenty-eight-year-old English/Austrian photographer whose dark floppy hair recalled Timothée Chalamet.

"A full-on Cinderella moment," gulped one onlooker (although this Cinderella skipped the cinders part).

"The feeling was, the baton was being passed," observed Tony Bravo, the *Chronicle*'s young arts and culture columnist.

A month later, the Gettys, like everyone, had their future plans upended by Covid-19. The much-anticipated world premiere of Gordon's new opera, *Goodbye, Mr. Chips*, slated to open the Festival Napa Valley in the summer, was postponed. Going virtual, Billy (by now a fervent health and fitness enthusiast) and Vanessa helped the Biden/Harris ticket rake in over $8 million on one Zoom fund raiser alone, along with high-powered cohosts from Hollywood such as Jeffrey Katzenberg, Ryan Murphy, and J. J. Abrams. Ivy took to Instagram, clad in skimpy leopard-print spandex, to implore her growing following to elect Joe and Kamala, by showing off a voter-themed handbag and mask (courtesy of Hilary Newsom). Meanwhile, Gordon donated $1 million to the Lincoln Project, reportedly making him the largest contributor to the organization.

In the most bizarre election cycle in memory, some airtime was devoted to pondering Kimberly Guilfoyle's path from Gavin Newsom to recent beau Donald Trump Jr. "I think I got it right this time," she told Breitbart. "Life's interesting," Newsom said diplomatically, when BuzzFeed brought up the topic with him.

At the Democratic National Convention, when Harris accepted her historic nomination for vice president, she acknowledged people she considers family: "Family is my best friend, my nieces, and my godchildren."

Not everything in 2020 was political or virtual. Ivy (now represented as a digital influencer by the Ford Models agency) and Toby managed to slip onto Capri, where he proposed in the Italian moonlight on September 1. "A very magical evening," she captioned a shot she posted of her ring finger sparkling with her sapphire engagement ring, which prompted an avalanche of comments. "Congrats duuude welcome to the wifey club ♥♥♥" read the one from cousin Nats.

From Capri, Ivy FaceTimed her adored grandmother to share the news. "Monga," as Ivy called her, naturally commenced planning for the wedding, scheduled for November 2021.

But joy was soon replaced by grief and shock. On September 13 Ann Gilbert Getty, by all appearances still vigorous at seventy-nine, suffered a heart attack after she sat down for Sunday Supper at home, with her husband and Jo. She was rushed to the hospital, where she died the following morning.

"Devastated," "unmoored," "shut-down" were words that a friend used to describe Gordon several weeks later.

Ivy, also shattered by the loss, posted a stream of tributes to her grandmother, as did many family members, including Gordon's daughters. "She was an inspirational, spunky, strong, beautiful woman. The world grieves her loss," remarked Sarah.

"R.I.P. goddess," Kendalle wrote.

Had it not been for the pandemic, there would doubtless have been an epic funeral and other public events to mourn Ann's death and celebrate her life. San Francisco was shaken by the passing of this woman who had loomed so large for half a century. "The whole city is quite saddened. People saw a world disappear. So many looked up to her," said Martin Chapman, curator of European decorative arts at the Fine Arts Museums of San Francisco.

Of the San Francisco–reared Gettys, John Gilbert Getty was the least well known. He succeeded in evading the public eye. To most Getty-watchers, he was an absent, enigmatic figure.

When his body was found in San Antonio, Texas, on Friday, November 20, 2020, his family was plunged into mourning again. Even as the circumstances of his death were initially unknown and mysterious, a picture of his life began to develop. He had battled addictions and troubles, but he had also been able to lead, by many measures, quite a rewarding life before he died at fifty-two.

Information began to filter out the next day, as John's relatives and friends shared their disbelief and grief on social media. Among the first was John's childhood friend Chris Vietor, who posted photos from a Getty family trip to Africa in 1984. Gisela Getty wrote a remembrance of John from the days when she was married to his elder cousin, Paul III: "I still see you, as this beautiful boy sitting in my kitchen in S.F. with great curiosity about life. You always came to see your cousins Anna, Balthazar in a time that was difficult for me. I will always hold you very dear in my heart. Highest Namaskar."

"I will miss laughing with you and talking to you for hours and hours about everything and nothing. . . . We had such a colorful life and you often helped me to remember moments I had forgotten," wrote his cousin Aileen.

Jacqui posted a photo of John in a white three-piece Glen Palmer suit. "I am saddened by the loss of my once upon a time brother in law," she wrote.

It took seventy-two hours for word of his death to drop on a media site: TMZ reported on Monday that his body had been discovered unresponsive in a hotel room and that no foul play was suspected, while the cause of death was pending an autopsy. A family spokesman provided a statement: "With a heavy heart, Gordon Getty announces the death of his son, John Gilbert Getty. . . . John was a talented musician who loved rock and roll. He will be deeply missed."

Around the world, the predictable deluge of "Tragic Dynasty" headlines rolled. The reports beneath them carried very little information; they largely rehashed previous drug-related deaths of other Gettys, perpetuating the image of the entire family as messed up and dysfunctional.

A week later, London's *Daily Mail* revealed that John's body had been found in his room at the Hotel Emma, a luxury property. The room was neat; John was sitting upright on the bed, propped by pillows, with his legs crossed—the lotus position used in meditation. His eyes were open, his glasses were in his left hand, and his laptop was open in front of him. Ultimately, the Bexar County Medical Examiner's Office reported that Getty died of "cardiomyopathy and chronic obstructive pulmonary disease [COPD, an inflammatory lung disease] complicated by fentanyl toxicity." The manner of the death was accidental, the office determined.

Getty was in San Antonio because he was preparing to move there. He had become enamored of the city.

Two weeks before his death, he had phoned an old friend in Los Angeles. "He sounded in really good spirits. He said he wanted to have dinner soon," she told me.

"He was magical . . . so handsome, so charismatic, with a heart of gold," she added. "He was incredibly smart. *People* smart. He could see through any situation that was bullshit. He had a really pure soul. He was unbelievably empathetic."

In a stream of posts in the days after his death, Ivy illuminated aspects of her father's character: "He never tried to ignore me he called me all the time as a kid—it was me that was always hesitant because I was so used to female figures running my life, but I instantly let that all go when I became a teenager and felt like we related so much. . . ."

She also expressed pride in being "the only consistent woman in my father's life." He never married, perhaps because she was "a complete bitch" to all of his girlfriends. "I was scared if he found someone else he would stop being a father to me," Ivy recounted. He "lived and breathed music" and "understood fashion like no other. He used to keep a whole walk-in closet of vintage Pucci women's clothing just because he liked it."

In her post, Kendalle reflected on her late sibling, and her own situation: "Two days ago, for the second time in my life, one of my brothers died. John, we were never close but I find myself very affected by this loss anyway. You were hard on me. I guess you felt that it was your duty. It's been scary being the bastard daughter of our father and his mistress in a family that is so notorious. I hid my truth, but never because I hated you guys. I'm sorry. I promise to take care of your daughter from here on out. . . ."

The next day, she changed her name on her IG bio. She was now Kendalle Getty.

Under the brilliant sunshine of Labor Day 2021, as the pandemic appeared to be finally in retreat, Kendalle kicked off a season of new beginnings and closure for the Gordon Gettys. On vacation in Greece with her boyfriend Johnny Latu, she climbed to the Acropolis, where on bended knee, he proposed.

The following week, the grandees of San Francisco emerged from isolation and assembled at the Conservatory of Music to memorialize Ann on the first anniversary of her death. It was what was left of San Francisco society, anyway. *"Old, old,"* said one attendee of the crowd. But there was one bright face among them. On the day that only weeks earlier some prognosticators predicted might be *his* political funeral—the California gubernatorial recall election—Gavin Newsom was beaming. At 11 a.m. that morning, as the service began, he was clearly confident of the resounding victory he would have that night, which renewed talk of a presidential run, and an old rivalry ("Are Newsom and Harris on a Collision Course?" asked a *Los Angeles Times* headline).

That fall, other momentous events unfolded. Capping three days of celebrations that began with a ball at the Palace of Fine Arts, where Earth, Wind & Fire performed, Ivy Love Getty and Tobias Alexander Engel were joined in holy matrimony under the stately dome of San Francisco City Hall. When the ceremony began at 6 p.m. on Saturday, November 6, Nancy Pelosi, the officiant, was resplendent in a gold Giorgio Armani pantsuit. Just before midnight the previous evening, the Speaker of the House, under the rotunda of the US Capitol, had signed the historic $1.8 trillion Bipartisan Infrastructure Framework. "I hightailed it out of there for Ivy, who I've known since she was a baby," Pelosi told the crowd. Ivy's spectacular gown, rumored to have cost $500,000, featured four layers— the outermost one resembling fragments of a mirror—behind which trailed a sixteen-foot embroidered veil. It was the handiwork of one of her grandmother's favorite designers, John Galliano, who also dressed the bridal party, including maid of honor Anya Taylor-Joy, the bright new star. At the gala dinner that followed at the Getty mansion, Pelosi stayed past midnight, mixing with hundreds of Ivy's and Tobias's young friends and relatives. (The Los Angeles contingent included August, Nats, Gigi, and Kendalle, as well as Balthazar, with his daughter Violet and her girlfriend.) "It was all so inclusive— you could let your freak flag fly," commented one guest. The baton had officially been passed to the new generation.

But the senior most member of the dynasty wasn't done. Days later, *Goodbye, Mr. Chips*, Gordon Getty's fourth opera, received its world premiere. While Covid had indeed derailed plans for the fully staged live performances that had been scheduled for Festival Napa Valley, the eighty-seven-year-old composer took the opportunity to reimagine his opera for film. Over the course of the pandemic, a large cast, orchestra, and chorus were recorded separately, then filmed on sets in San Francisco and New York. As critic A.A. Cristi observed in BroadwayWorld, the new medium allowed for "seamless storytelling," giving Gordon the opportunity to more fluidly present his musical adaptation of the beloved 1934 novella of the same name, the tale of an emotionally repressed and disheveled English schoolmaster who blossoms over the course of his long career, in the face of some profound losses along the way.

If Gordon Getty were ever to write an opera based on his own family, it would be loaded with extraordinary characters, and require many acts.

Conclusion

From Los Angeles, San Francisco, Baja California, and Kodiak Island to London, Rome, Cape Town, and Bangkok, Gettys have left their marks on fields including art, music, marine and wildlife conservation, climate change, media, intellectual property, politics, LGBTQ rights, gender transitioning, fashion, interior design, high society, film, wine, books, yachting, horse racing, holistic living, and finance.

Yet in the public imagination, they are often still thought of as "the tragic dynasty."

While misfortune has continued to befall some Gettys—sometimes in cinematic fashion—the family has proven remarkably durable. Of the seventy-six individuals who appeared in *Fortune*'s inaugural 1957 rich list, direct descendants of just three of them made it onto the 2020 Forbes 400: Ray Lee Hunt, youngest son of Texas wildcatter H. L. Hunt; Bennett Dorrance and Mary Alice Dorrance Malone, grandchildren of John T. Dorrance, inventor of the Campbell Soup formula; and Gordon Getty.

Other than suggesting that oil and soup have been the most lucrative commodities over the last six decades, this statistic serves as evidence that fortunes are fleeting. And it demonstrates that, while some people born to privilege compound their good fortune, others squander their assets.

In addition to mere wealth, a dynasty has to be judged by what the founder and his heirs have contributed to society. The cohesiveness of the family—or lack thereof—is also a yardstick. Compared to their peers, the Gettys stack up well. H. L. Hunt used his fortune to support and fuse together far-right political extremism and Christian evangelism—begetting movements that spawned the Tea Party, Trumpism, and other toxins—while his descendants have not made particularly significant charitable or cultural contributions. John T. Dorrance's progeny—who, in contrast to the Gettys, never sold their company—lead decorous but dull lives of leisure. "You would never describe *any* of them as cosmopolitan," said one of their Philadelphia neighbors.

In an interview conducted shortly before her death in 2020, an heiress to the Anglo-Irish Guinness brewing fortune offered her opinion that the public doesn't want to know about a dynastic family's positive contributions—which is why such families remain press-shy. "If you are a member of any of these families, you really don't want to talk—because the press always uses the wrong bit . . . they are not interested in the goody-goody bits. Because the public is not interested in the goody-goody bits. That's the problem, always," said Lindy, the Marchioness of Dufferin and Ava—a daughter of Loel Guinness and a niece of Lady Ursula d'Abo, J. Paul Getty's last mistress.

"What the public wants to read about is the dramas . . . the money. . . . ," she scoffed. "When you talk about these things, you're compounding the sadnesses of the families. That's the snag."

Americans, on the whole, venerate wealth, and are voracious viewers of ostentatious displays of it; but picturing a person who is rich and happy is less appealing. "The idea that people who are reputedly wealthy must be miserable seems to gladden countless hearts," J. Paul Getty himself observed in his final memoir. "After a time, a person who is wealthy grows a tough impervious skin. It is a protective carapace essential for survival."

As his son Gordon noted, some Gettys have been "clobbered."

Given the unlimited opportunities for indulgence that their fortune afforded them, it's perhaps surprising that more of them didn't meet a tragic fate. ("I am shocked that any of them have survived," as one of their friends said.)

Why did some founder and some flourish?

In the interviews William Newsom gave in 2008 and 2009 to the Regional Oral History Office at UC Berkeley's Bancroft Library, he made these observations:

"I have learned that simply giving a person a lot of money and saying, 'Here, have a good time,' is a mistake.

"The only people I've ever seen who are satisfied with life are people who achieve something beyond mere wealth.

"Paul's children are doing well, but it wasn't money that made them do well. It was something else they had inside them. Aileen has become a very passionate worker in the AIDS field. Tara, the youngest, is in Africa now running a business. Mark Getty has done remarkably well with Getty Images."

In addition to being unconventional, the Gettys have been, and continue to be, curious and progressive people—in their thinking, in their politics, even in their consideration of gender.

"Pretty much since we came out of the womb, we've been who we are," as Nats Getty explained. "And no one was going to tell us otherwise."

Acknowledgments

My *Growing Up Getty* journey commenced when I visited the Getty Research Institute, in Los Angeles, where I became absorbed in J. Paul Getty's diaries and correspondence. My acknowledgments begin, then, with sincere thanks to the dedicated and learned GRI staff who helped me access and navigate through this wealth of material.

I didn't realize it at the time, but my research for this book had begun decades before. In my magazine career—at *Vanity Fair* and *W,* and as a contributor to *Town & Country* and *Sotheby's* magazine— my travels sometimes took me to such extraordinary places as Outer Broadway in San Francisco and Wormsley Manor in Buckingham- shire. I had the very good fortune to interview a number of Gettys and learn about some of their endeavors and passions. Then there were the many fascinating people in the orbit of this dynasty who I profiled and stayed in touch with (Christopher Gibbs and Gillian Wil- son, to name just a couple favorites). Among them, the gravitational pull toward this charismatic and often elusive clan was palpable.

On a visit to Rome, Carlo Scimone and Margherita Rostworowski so graciously welcomed me into their home, where he shared his extraordinary memories and photographs with me.

In the course of my reporting for this book, many of the people I spoke to preferred to remain anonymous. Public as some Gettys are, most of them remain resolutely private. I am especially indebted to the family members who did speak to me and engage with me in various ways for this book.

At Gallery Books, my heartfelt thanks to the miraculous, meticulous, and always supportive editorial director, Aimee Bell. In her office, associate editor Max Meltzer was a tireless force for good sense. Under the same roof (virtual though it was during the making of this book) my gratitude extends from Simon & Schuster president Jonathan Karp to the entire Gallery Books team, including publisher Jennifer Bergstrom, deputy publisher Jennifer Long, director of publicity and marketing Sally Marvin, executive publicist Jennifer Robinson, managing editor Caroline Pallotta, and senior production editor Samantha Hoback.

At Aevitas Creative Management, my sincere thanks go to David Kuhn and Nate Muscato and their team.

In my research, I benefited hugely from the heroic work of Abby Field Gerry. Thanks also to Dale Brauner. When it was time to search for photos, Mark Jacobson and Cole Giordano sorted through myriad Getty images.

Many of the twentieth century's most celebrated photographers including Slim Aarons and Horst focused their lenses on Gettys; some of their iconic portraits are reproduced in this volume. I am extremely grateful to be able to also publish superb photographs by Jonathan Becker, Simon Watson, Dafydd Jones, and Firooz Zahedi.

While writing in Covid-era Manhattan, communications from far-flung sources enlivened the solitary days. An especially helpful and generous email arrived one morning from Robina Lund, who wrote from her home in Aberdeenshire (after Jenny Morrison, features writer for the Scottish *Sunday Mail* and *Daily Record*, graciously helped me locate her). Robina succinctly explained how some of the key myths surrounding the Gettys had been created and perpetuated—payphone included.

Bibliography

GENERAL REFERENCES

Argyll, Margaret Campbell. *Forget Not: The Autobiography of Margaret, Duchess of Argyll.* London: W. H. Allen, 1975.

Bedford, Nicole Russell. *Nicole Nobody: The Autobiography of the Duchess of Bedford.* Garden City, NY: Doubleday, 1975.

d'Abo, Lady Ursula. *The Girl with the Widow's Peak: The Memoirs.* Dorset, England: Dorset Press, 2014.

de Chair, Somerset. *Getty on Getty: A Man in a Billion.* London: Cassel, 1989.

Fredericksen, Burton B. *The Burdens of Wealth: Paul Getty and His Museum.* Bloomington, IN: Archway, 2015.

Gaston, Theodora Getty. *Alone Together: My Life with J. Paul Getty.* New York: Ecco/HarperCollins, 2013.

Getty, Gordon. *Logic and Economics: Free Growth and Other Surprises.* Gold River, CA: Authority Publishing, 2018.

Getty, J. Paul. *As I See It: The Autobiography of J. Paul Getty.* New York: Prentice-Hall, 1976.

———. Diaries 1938–1976. Getty Research Institute, Los Angeles.

———. *How to Be Rich.* New York: Playboy Press, 1965.

———. *The Joys of Collecting.* New York: Hawthorn Books, 1965.

———. *My Life and Fortunes: The Autobiography of One of the World's Wealthiest Men.* New York: Duell, Sloan and Pearce, 1963.

Hewins, Ralph. *The Richest American: J. Paul Getty.* New York: E. P. Dutton, 1960.

Lund, Robina. *The Getty I Knew: An Intimate Biography.* Kansas City, MO: Sheed Andrews and McMeel, 1977.

Newsom, William. "Politics, Law, and Human Rights." Interviewed by Martin Meeker, 2008–2009. Regional Oral History Office, Bancroft Library, University of California, Berkeley, 2009.

Pearson, John. *All the Money in the World: The Outrageous Fortune and Misfortunes of the Heirs of J. Paul Getty.* London: William Collins, 2017. (Originally published as *Painfully Rich.*)

Reginato, James. "Boulle Fighter: The Getty's Decorative Arts Curator Unveils Her Spectacular Galleries." *W*, October 1997.

———. *Great Houses, Modern Aristocrats*. New York: Rizzoli, 2016.

Rosen, Peter, dir. *Gordon Getty: There Will Be Music*. New York: Peter Rosen Productions, 2015.

Shulman, David, dir. *Gettys: The World's Richest Art Dynasty*. London: BBC Studios Documentary Unit, 2018.

Smith, Richard Austin. "The Fifty-Million-Dollar Man." *Fortune*, November 1957.

Spence, Lyndsy. *The Grit in the Pearl: The Scandalous Life of Margaret, Duchess of Argyll*. Stroud, Gloucestershire: History Press, 2019.

CHAPTER ONE: SUTTON PLACE

Billington, Joy. "What Does All That Money Buy." *Cincinnati Enquirer*, October 26, 1975.

Cooney, Kevin. "The Seven Sisters." *New York Times*, October 19, 1975.

Dupre, John. "Mrs. Paul Getty the Sixth?" *Australian Women's Weekly*, November 5, 1975.

Eakin, Hugh. "Self-Portrait of the Oilman as Collector." *New York Times*, December 24, 2010.

Evan, Peter. "Jean Paul Getty (the Richest Man in the World) Talks about Women." *Cosmopolitan*, September 1968.

Farnsworth, Clyde H. "Surrey Estate of Getty Empire: 'Richest Man' Label Irks Getty." *New York Times*, July 30, 1964.

Fontevecchia, Augustino. "The Getty Family: A Cautionary Tale of Oil, Adultery, and Death." *Forbes*, April 23, 2015.

Getty Family Papers. Getty Research Institute, Los Angeles (1987.1A.09-01).

Gold, Jack, prod. *The Solitary Billionaire: J. Paul Getty*. Interview by Alan Whicker. London: BBC, aired February 24, 1963.

Jackson, Debbie. "Throwback Tulsa: Billionaire J. Paul Getty Got His Start in Tulsa." *Tulsa World*, December 10, 2017.

Lenzner, Robert. *The Great Getty: The Life and Loves of J. Paul Getty—Richest Man in the World*. New York: Crown, 1985.

Long, Ralph W. "Buys Pierre Leasehold." *New York Times*, December 19, 1939.

Lubac, Robert. "The Odd Mr. Getty." *Fortune*, March 17, 1986.

Mallory, Carole. "*Alone Together*." The Wrap (website), September 24, 2013.

———. "Theodora (Teddy) Lynch Getty Gaston Talks about the Gettys, Oil, Plastic Surgery and Elephants." *HuffPost* (blog), February 16, 2011.

Marble, Steve. "Teddy Getty Gaston, Who Wrote an Unflinching Memoir about Her Marriage to J. Paul Getty, Dies at 103." *Los Angeles Times*, March 12, 2017.

Marlowe, Lisa. "Chez Getty: Staying in Luxury at Billionaire's Rome Home Turned into a Treasure-Filled Hotel." *New York Times*, December 14, 1997.

Martin-Robinson, John. "From Edwardian Idyll to Meetings with Nehru: The Life of Lady Ursula d'Abo." *Spectator*, July 5, 2014.

Miller, Mike. "Louise Dudley 'Teddy' Lynch, J. Paul Getty's Fifth and Final Wife, Has Died at 103." *People*, March 10, 2017.

Miller, Russell. *The House of Getty*. London: Bloomsbury, 1985.

Newman, Judith. "His Favorite Wife." *New York Times*, August 30, 2013.

Newsweek. "Incredible Billionaire." March 7, 1960.

New York Times. "76 in U.S. Found to Have Fortunes above $75,000,000." October 28, 1957.

Nicholas, Sadie. "Lady Ursula d'Abo—the Beautiful Girl Who Outshone the Queen." *Express* (London), November 8, 2017.

O'Reilly, Jane. "Isn't It Funny What Money Can Do?" *New York Times*, March 30, 1986.

Rork, Ann. Letters. Getty Research Institute, Los Angeles (1987.1A.48-06).

Rozhon, Tracie. "A Rooftop Palazzo with a Split Personality." *New York Times*, January 15, 1998.

Shuster, Alvin. "Getty, 80, Feted on Birthday." *New York Times*, December 16, 1972.

Suzy. "J. Paul Getty: The Absolute Billionaire." *Town & Country*, July 1964.

Telegraph. "Lady Ursula d'Abo, Train Bearer at the 1937 Coronation." November 6, 2017.

Time. "Real Estate: Hate Those Hotels." October 26, 1959.

Vincent, Alice. "'Penny Pincher? I Don't Even Know the Girl': The Surprisingly Prodigious Sexual Appetite of J. Paul Getty." *Telegraph* (UK), September 13, 2018.

Weinraub, Judith. "She Was 'the Top': A Duchess's Memoirs of a Lively Lifetime." *New York Times*, December 7, 1975.

Wilson, Gillian. *Baroque & Régence: Catalogue of the J. Paul Getty Museum Collection*. Los Angeles: J. Paul Getty Museum, 2008.

Chapter Two: The Tragic Years

Coll, Steve. *The Taking of Getty Oil*. New York: Atheneum, 1987.

Didion, Joan. *The White Album*. New York: Simon & Schuster, 1979.

Gebhard, David. "Getty Museum: Is It 'Disgusting' and 'Downright Outrageous'?" *Architecture Plus*, September 1974.

Jones, David. "Call Girl Who Nearly Toppled a Government Reveals All." *Daily Mail*, January 26, 2007.

Kotkin, Joel. "The Problems of Having $720 Million." *Washington Post*, February 6, 1977.

MacIntyre, Ben. "The Dirty Duchess of Argyll Was Ahead of Her Time." *Times* (London), February 2, 2019.

Mega, Marcello. "I Was the Secret Lover of the World's Richest Man." *Scottish Mail on Sunday*, September 9, 2017.

Morrison, Jenny. "Oil Tycoon Paul Getty's Lover Says New TV Drama Based on His Life Is Full of Lies." *Daily Record* (Glasgow), September 9, 2018.

Muchnic, Suzanne. "A Getty Chronicle: The Malibu Years." *Los Angeles Times*, July 6, 1997.

New York Times. "Roman Villa Is Recreated on Coast to House Getty Art Collection." January 17, 1974.

O'Neill, Anne-Marie. "Can't Buy Me Love." *People*, April 13, 1998.

People. "For a Dozen Lucky Ladies in J. Paul Getty's Life, the Party Isn't Over Yet." July 19, 1976.

Bibliography

————. "World's Richest Man." March 18, 1974.

Petzinger, Thomas, Jr. *Oil and Honor: The Texaco-Pennzoil Wars*. New York: G. P. Putnam's Sons, 1987.

Potts, Timothy. "20 Years at the Getty Center: A Getty Museum Perspective." *The Iris* (blog), May 31, 2018. http://blogs.getty.edu.

Reginato, James. "The Luck of the Lambtons." *Vanity Fair*, November 2012.

Roberts, Glenda D. "Interview with Robina Lund, Lawyer and Personal Advisor to Jean Paul Getty 1st." *Emotional Wellbeing* (podcast), Abderdeen: 2018. https://www.mixcloud.com/uxwbob/glenda-d-roberts-interview-with-robina-lund-lawyer-and-personal-adviser-to-jean-paul-getty-1st/.

Warhol, Andy. *The Andy Warhol Diaries*. Edited by Pat Hackett. New York: Warner Books, 1991.

Whitman, Alden. "Paul Getty Dead at 83; Amassed Billions from Oil." *New York Times*, June 6, 1976.

Wilson, Andrew. "Who Framed Margaret of Argyll?" *Tatler*, March 2014.

Wilson, William. "A Preview of Pompeii-on-the-Pacific." *Los Angeles Times*, January 6, 1974.

Wong, Amelia. "The Never-Boring Life of J. Paul Getty, World's Richest Man." *The Iris* (blog), October 18, 2016. http://blogs.getty.edu.

Chapter Three: The Georgettes

Adams, John H. *A Force for Nature: The Story of NRDC and Its Fight to Save Our Planet*. San Francisco: Chronicle Books, 2010.

Associated Press. "FPPC Seeks Getty Fine." *Sacramento Bee*, October 17, 2003.

————. "Getty Heiress Settles Campaign Finance Suit." *Los Angeles Times*, March 31, 2004.

————. "Getty Son Sued for Divorce on Cruelty Grounds." *San Bernardino County Sun*, August 2, 1967.

————. "Nature Conservancy's Mystery Donor Is Southern California Oil Heiress." *Napa Valley Register*, May 11, 2002.

Astre, K. "Highland: Thailand's Marijuana Awakening." *Cannabis Now*, June 8, 2017. cannabisnow.com.

Batti, Renee. "The Art of Change: Noel Perry's Art and Education Efforts Are Aimed at Creating a Better Future." *Almanac News* (San Mateo County), May 25, 2005.

Bennett, Laurie. "Getty Oil Heir Quietly Supports Democrats." *Forbes*, July 30, 2012.

Blair, James. "Conservation and Community in Laguna San Ignacio." *ICFND.org*, May 3, 2018.

Bluth, Alexa A. "Oil Heiress Settles Case on Ballot Donations." *Sacramento Bee*, March 31, 2004.

Boots, Michelle Therialt. "Alaska's Biggest Ever Commercial Seaweed Harvest Is Happening Right Now." *Anchorage Daily News*, May 19, 2019.

Brazil, Ben. "Orange County Philanthropist Helped Save Crucial Mexican Lagoon Used by Gray Whales for Breeding." *Los Angeles Times*, October 11, 2019.

Carnegie Medal of Philanthropy. "Announcing the 2019 Carnegie Medal of

Philanthropy Recipients" (press release). http://www.Medalofphilanthropy
.org/anne-g-earhart.

Cecco, Leyland. "Meet the 'Star Ingredient' Changing Fortunes in Alaska's
Waters: Seaweed." *Guardian,* June 11, 2019.

Christine, Bill. "Dame Fortune Continues to Smile on Riordan." *Los Angeles Times,*
March 27, 1986.

Clinton, Mary Jane. Talk of the Times. *Times* (San Mateo, CA), September 9, 1969.

———. Talk of the Times. *Times* (San Mateo, CA), January 26, 1972.

Conroy, Sarah Booth. "The Founding Force of Wilhelmina Holladay." *Washington
Post,* February 15, 1987.

Corkery, P. J. "Cube Me." *San Francisco Examiner,* July 8, 2002.

Daly, Kate. "Water World: Woodside Resident Curates 'California: The Art of
Water' at the Cantor." *Almanac News* (San Mateo County), November 2016.

Darling, Juanita. "Ecologists Fear Baja Salt Mine Would Threaten Gray Whales."
Los Angeles Times, March 6, 1995.

Dedina, Serge. "In Memory of Don Pachico." Wildcoast (website), undated post.

———. *Saving the Gray Whale.* Tuscon: University of Arizona Press, 2000.

de Waal-Montgomery, Michael. "Coconuts Is a Local News Startup Fast Becoming the Patch of Southeast Asia." *Venture Beat,* January 4, 2016.

Dillow, Gordon. "Getting Close Up and Personal with Whales." *Los Angeles Times,*
April 3, 1994.

Earhart, Nico. "Coming to Fruition." *The Wind-Blown Golfer* (blog), April 24, 2019.
https://www.thewind-blowngolfer.com.

Encyclopedia.com. "Mitsubishi Oil Co., Ltd." March 13, 2020.

Evey, Stuart. *ESPN: Creating an Empire.* Chicago: Triumph Books, 2004.

Farmed Seafood. "Healthy, Sustainable, and All-Around Virtuous: Blue Evolution
Seaweed." May 7, 2018. https://farmed-seafood.com.

Fatsis, Stefan. "At $5.2 Billion, Metromedia's Kluge Tops Forbes' Richest Ameri-
can List." *Salinas Californian,* October 11, 1989.

Fox, Christy. "Gettys on Their Honeymoon." *Los Angeles Times,* May 21, 1971.

Frater, Patrick. "Netflix Buys 'Highland' Thai Marijuana Documentary." *Variety,*
May 24, 2017.

Ganguly, Shicani. "Olazul: Small Aquaculture Is Beautiful." Triple Pundit (website), December 27, 2012. https://TriplePundit.com.

Gates, Bob. "Jackie Getty: Turf Globetrotter." *Los Angeles Times,* September 7,
1975.

Gorlick, Adam. "Stanford Historian, Venture Capitalist Energizes Votes over
Political Reform." *Stanford Report,* May 24, 2010.

Halper, Evan. "Political Donors Shielded by Loophole." *Los Angeles Times,* September 30, 2002.

Hicks, Cordell. "Just Wed Gettys Will Take Europe Cruise." *Los Angeles Times,*
June 30, 1951.

Hicks, Robin. "Q&A with Coconuts Media Founder Byron Perry." Mumbrella
(website), July 2015.

Holladay, Wilhelmina Cole. *A Museum of Their Own.* New York: Abbeville Press, 2008.

Bibliography

———. "Oral History Interview with Wilhelmina Holladay." Interviewed by Krystyna Wasserman. Archives of American Art, Smithsonian Institution, Washington, DC, 2005.

Jacobs, Jody. "The Next Best Thing to Walking on Water." *Los Angeles Times*, October 16, 1974.

———. "A Tribute to Jimmy Durante." *Los Angeles Times*, November 15, 1976.

Jones, Jack. "J. Paul Getty Eulogized at Services." *Los Angeles Times*, June 11, 1976.

Kennedy, Robert F., Jr. "Poisoning a Sanctuary for the Sake of Salt." *Los Angeles Times*, August 5, 1998.

Knoerle, Jane. "California Dreaming: Woodside Woman Stages Major Exhibit of California Images at Stanford Art Museum." *Almanac News* (San Mateo County), May 19, 1999.

Lawrence, Steve. "State Watchdog Asks Court to Fine Heiress." *Napa Valley Register*, October 17, 2003.

Lenzner, Robert. "Splitting Up Getty's $4 Billion." *Boston Globe*, October 21, 1984.

Los Angeles Times. "Gloria Alice Gordon Betrothal Announced." March 13, 1951.

———. "Mexico Deep-Sixes Plan for Baja Lagoon Saltworks." March 3, 2000.

MacNiven, Jamis. "Beau Perry's Premium Oceanic." *Buck's Stories* (blog), September 7, 2014.

Moran, Dan. "Fair Political Practices Panel Accuses Getty Heiress of 'Campaign Money Laundering.'" *Los Angeles Times*, October 17, 2003.

Moran, Sheila. "Getty Heir Part of Racing Scene." *Los Angeles Times*, March 17, 1977.

Multiplier (website). "An Interview with Beau Perry, Founder and Former Director, Olazul." September 7, 2013. https://multiplier.org.

New York Times. "George F. Getty 2nd, Oldest Son of Oil Billionaire, Dies on Coast." June 7, 1973.

———. "Japan Fighting Her Biggest Oil Spill." December 25, 1974.

Palmer, Barbara. "Children in 19th-Century Art Reflect Nation's Fears." *Stanford Report*, March 1, 2006.

Perlman, Jeffrey A. "Tollway Foes Find Ally in Foundation." *Los Angeles Times*, December 27, 1992.

Perry, Claire. *The Great American Hall of Wonders: Art, Science, and Invention in the Nineteenth Century*. London: D. Giles Ltd., with the Smithsonian American Art Museum, 2011.

———. *Pacific Arcadia: Images of California, 1600–1915*. New York: Oxford University Press, 1999.

———. *Young America: Childhood in 19th-Century Art and Culture*. New Haven: Yale University Press, 2006.

Princeton Alumni Weekly. "Class of '46 Notes." May 9, 1952.

Rao, Amrita. "Claire Perry: Art as an American Wonder." *Stanford Daily*, October 24, 2011.

Rogers, Patrick. "The Man Behind the Mission." NRDC (website), April 19, 2016. https://www.NRDC.org.

———. "Saving the Breeding Grounds of the Pacific Gray Whale." NRDC (website), May 12, 2016. https://www.NRDC.org.

Roosevelt, Margot. "Prop 23 Battle Marks New Era in Environmental Politics." *Los Angeles Times*, November 4, 2010.

Rubenstein, Steve. "Getty Campaign Gifts Questioned: Water, Park Bond Measures Allegedly Favored by Heiress." *San Francisco Chronicle*, October 17, 2003.

Sandomir, Richard. "Stuart Evey, a Founding Force at ESPN, Is Dead at 84." *New York Times*, December 12, 2017.

San Francisco Chronicle. "Getty Heir Agrees to Pay $135,000 Fine." March 31, 2004.

Schiller, Ben. "Farming Gets a New Crop—Seaweed." *Fast Company*, October 23, 2014.

Schreibman, Jack. "Elite Meet to Weep over Last Trader Vic's Lunch." *Napa Valley Register*, March 24, 1990.

Shamdasani, Pavan. "Local Content Delivered Fast Is the Secret of Success for Byron Perry's Coconuts Websites." *South China Morning Post*, December 13, 2014.

Shiver, Jube, Jr. "Gettys Resolve Dispute over Trust: Agreement Reached on Provision for Unborn Heirs." *New York Times*, May 31, 1985.

Silva, Horacio. "Family Ties." *New York Times*, September 25, 2001.

Smith, James F. "Activists Break New Ground to Help Shake Off Saltworks Project." *Los Angeles Times*, April 23, 2000.

Solina, Samie. "Seaweed Farming Could Make Waves in the Future." KTUU (Alaska), July 2, 2019. https://www. KTUU.com.

Soon, Alan. "Coconuts, a Fast-Growing, Cities-Focused Network of Sites in Asia, Takes a Hard Right into Paid Memberships." Nieman Lab (website), April 2018. https://www.niemanlab.org.

Suh, Rhea. "Laguna San Ignacio: A Living Testament to NRDC's Work." NRDC (website), March 2018. https://www.NRDC.org.

Suzy. "Charles—Prince of a Host for World Colleges." *New York Daily News*, June 13, 1984.

United Press International. "Getty's Son Dies; Wounds Are Found." *Sacramento Bee*, June 7, 1973.

———. "Rites Today for J. Paul Getty's Eldest Son." *San Francisco Examiner*, June 9, 1973.

Welch, Laine. "Dutch Harbor Stays in Top among U.S. Fishing Ports." *Anchorage Daily News*, Februrary 25, 2020.

———. "Fish Factor: Alaskan Interest in Growing Keeps Growing." *Cordova Times*, June 5, 2021.

Williams, Tate. "A Growing Pool-Funding Effort to Support Environmental Defenders." *Inside Philanthropy*, July 17, 2018.

———. "The Oil Company Heiress Devoting Her Wealth to Oceans." *Inside Philanthropy*, May 23, 2014.

———. "Three Things to Know about Marisla's Beto Bedolfe." *Inside Philanthropy*, May 29, 2014.

Woody, Todd. "Koch Brothers Jump into Prop 23 Fight." Grist (website), September 2, 2010. https://grist.org.

———. "No on Prop 23 Campaign Rakes in Cash as Enviro Justice Advocates Join the Fight." Grist (website), September 28, 2010. https://grist.org.

CHAPTER FOUR: THE RONALD LINE

Associated Press. "Getty Son Bankruptcy." *New York Times*, December 18, 1992.
———. "Getty's Son, J. Ronald, Turns Interest to Movies." *San Antonio Express*, February 4, 1971.
Barraclough, Leo. "Johnny Kenton, Debs Paterson Receive Pia Pressure Awards." *Variety*, April 3, 2016.
Charleston, Libby-Jane. "Meet the Miller Sisters." 9Honey (website), April 2021. https://honey.nine.com.au.
Colacello, Bob. "A Royal Family Affair." *Vanity Fair*, February 2008.
Croffey, Amy. "Stars and Socialites Swoop on Zimmermann's Miami Launch." *Sun-Herald* (Sydney), July 30, 2017.
Gao, Alice Longyu. "22-Year-Old Isabel Getty on Working with Dolce & Gabbana and Overcoming Tradition: New Face, Fresh Style." *Billboard*, March 28, 2017.
Harrison, Annabel. "Isabel Getty, Sabrina Percy & Amber Le Bon's Artworks for Royal Ascot." Luxury London (website), June 19, 2019. https://luxurylondon.co.uk.
Hello!. "Christina Getty Weds Arin Maercks in a Picture Perfect Florida Ceremony." January 21, 2002.
Holden, Adam. "A Moment with Constantia Glen's Alexander Waibel." *Berry Bros. & Rudd Wine Blog*, February 12, 2021. https://blog.bbr.com.
Lawrence, James. "Grape Expectations: A Tour of South Africa's Vineyards." Luxury London (website), May 7, 2019. https://luxurylondon.co.uk.
Lawrence, Vanessa. "High Note." *W*, November 2017.
Madrid, Graham Keeley. "Euro Royals Go Wild in the Cotswolds." *Times* (London), July 5, 2017.
Maule, Henry. "The Billionaire Who Got Blackballed." *Daily News* (New York), May 22, 1966.
Money-Coutts, Sophia. "Meet Isabel Getty!" *Tatler*, September 28, 2016.
New York Post. "Thanking Lenny." February 8, 2016.
Norwich, William. "Sister Act." *Vogue*, July 1995.
O'Donaghue, Clare. *Constantia Glen: A Timeless History*. Rondebosch, South Africa: Quivertree, 2018.
Page, Bruce. "The Spoils of Sutton Place: Will Getty's Will Be Done?" *New York*, December 18, 1976.
Peres, Daniel. "Sister Act." *W*, May 1997.
Powell, Rosalind. "Princess Olympia of Greece Puts on a Stylish Show to Toast Two Landmark Royal Birthdays." *Hello!*, July 2017.
Salvat, Maryanne. "Getty's Fabulous Getty." *Miami Socialholic*, August 30, 2012.
Shakespeare, Sebastian. "The New Marie-Antoinette!" *Daily Mail*, July 6, 2017.
Steuer, Joseph. "The Marvelous Miller Girls." *W*, December 1992.
Suzy. "Inside the Glamorous Royal Wedding and All the Glittering Parties." *W*, August 1995.
Tatler. "High Summer." September 2019.
Thomas, Kevin. "Getty Son Rigging for a Movie Gusher." *Los Angeles Times*, June 11, 1970.

Thorpe, Sophie. "The Power of Restraint." *Berry Bros. & Rudd Wine Blog*, November 8, 2014. https://blog.bbr.com.

United Press International. "Billionaire's Son Weds in German Church Service." *Green Bay Press-Gazette*, October 25, 1964.

———. "Jean-Ronald Getty Weds German Girl." *New York Times*, October 24, 1964.

Wallace, Lisa. "Constantia Views: Two Families Share a Winemaker, a Winery and a Love of Bordeaux Wines." *House & Garden*, September 29, 2016.

CHAPTER FIVE: PAUL JR.

Barber, Lynn. "J. Paul Getty: Money Talks." *Sydney Morning Herald*, August 29, 1987.

BBC News. "Profile: Sir John Paul Getty II." June 13, 2001.

Beaton, Cecil. *Beaton in the Sixties: The Cecil Beaton Diaries as They Were Written*. London: Weidenfeld & Nicolson, 2003.

Bosworth, Patricia. *Jane Fonda: The Private Life of a Public Woman*. Houghton Mifflin Harcourt, 2011.

Cash, William. "The New Gettys." *Evening Standard* (London), October 10, 2003.

Drake, Alicia. *The Beautiful Fall: Fashion, Genius, and Glorious Excess in 1970s Paris*. New York: Little, Brown, 2006.

Dunne, Dominick. "Fatal Charm Part Two." *Vanity Fair*, September 1985.

Edmonds, Frances. "Cricket: A Love as Boundless as His Wealth." *Independent* (London), May 16, 1993.

Faithfull, Marianne. *Faithfull*. New York: Little, Brown, 1994.

Fitzgerald, Olda. "England's Getty Center." *Architectural Digest*, March 1998.

Fletcher, H. George, ed. *The Wormsley Library: A Personal Selection by Sir Paul Getty, K.B.E.* London: Maggs Bros. with the Pierpont Morgan Library, 1999.

Gaignault, Fabrice. *Égéries Sixties*. Paris: Fayard, 2006.

Gale, Laurence. "Wormsley Cricket Ground—a Lasting Legacy." Pitchcare (website), July 31, 2015. https://www.pitchare.com.

Haden-Guest, Anthony. "Light Shines on a Dark Star." *Financial Times*, May 25, 2020.

Hambly, Vivienne. "Beautiful Music." *The English Garden*, May 2019.

Hamilton, Alan. "Getty: Proud to Be British." *Times* (London), March 11, 1998.

Hicks, India. "Victoria Getty." India Hicks (website), February 15, 2015.

Hopkins, John. *The Tangier Diaries 1962–1979*. New York: Cadmus Editions, 1997.

Howard, Paul. *I Read the News Today, Oh Boy: The Short and Gilded Life of Tara Browne, the Man Who Inspired the Beatles' Greatest Song*. London: Picador, 2016.

Hughes, Simon. "Simon Hughes Meets John Paul Getty." ESPN, September 12, 1998. https://www.espn.com.

Johns, Glyn. *Sound Man: A Life of Recording Hits with the Rolling Stones*. New York: Plume, 2015.

Kavanagh, Julie. *Nureyev: The Life*. New York: Pantheon Books, 2007.

Levy, Shawn. *Dolce Vita Confidential: Fellini, Loren, Pucci, Paparazzi, and the Swinging High Life of 1950s Rome*. New York: W. W. Norton, 2016.

———. *Ready, Steady, Go!: Swinging London and the Invention of Cool*. New York: HarperCollins, 2002.

McEvoy, Marian. *Bill Willis*. Marrakech: Jardin Majorelle, 2011.

Medford, Sarah. "Palais Intrigue." *Wall Street Journal*, September 12, 2017.

New York Times. "Talitha Pol, Wife of Paul Getty Jr." July 14, 1971.

Petkanas, Christopher. "Fabulous Dead People: Decorator Bill Willis." *New York Times*, May 14, 2010.

Reginato, James. "The Prince of Pimlico: In Matters of Art and Décor, London Antiques Dealer Christopher Gibbs Rules Britannia." *W*, November 1998.

Richards, Keith. *Life*. New York: Little, Brown, 2010.

Rocca, Fiammetta. "Paul Getty's New Life." *Vanity Fair*, August 1994.

Runtagh, Jordan. "Beatles' 'Sgt. Pepper' at 50: The Doomed Socialite Behind 'A Day in the Life.'" *Rolling Stone*, May 31, 2017.

Saxon, Wolfgang. "J. Paul Getty Jr., Philanthropist, Dies at 70." *New York Times*, April 18, 2003.

Smith, Roberta. "Library Treasures, Bound for Eternity." *New York Times*, January 29, 1999.

Telegraph (UK). "Prince Dado Ruspoli." January 15, 2015.

———. "Sir Paul Getty." March 4, 2003.

Times (London). "Sir Paul Getty." September 10, 2003.

Tuohy, William. "Bestowing a Look at Britain's Benefactor." *Los Angeles Times*, August 19, 1994.

———. "Court Deals a Blow to Getty Quest for 'Graces.'" *Los Angeles Times*, October 28, 1994.

Vogue. "Moroccan Wake-Up: Mr. and Mrs. Paul Getty Junior Have Shaken to Life a Deserted House in Marrakech, Made It Imaginative, Rare—with a Little Mystery." January 1970.

Vreeland, Diana, ed. *Yves Saint Laurent*. New York: Metropolitan Museum of Art, 1983.

Vyner, Harriet. *Groovy Bob: The Life and Times of Robert Fraser*. London: Faber and Faber, 1999.

Wallace, William. "John Paul Getty Jr., 70; Oil Heir Evolved from Excess, Tragedy into Patron of British Culture." *Los Angeles Times*, April 18, 2003.

Yaeger, Lynn. "The Mysterious Allure of Talitha Getty's Bohemian Marrakech Style." *Vogue*, August 2015.

CHAPTER SIX: MARK

Ashworth, Jon. "Gettys Focus Cash on UK Prospects." *Times* (London), April 4, 1994.

Asome, Carolyn. "Home! Bright Young Things." *Times* (London), June 23, 2018.

Bagley, Christopher. "Jewelry Designer Sabine Getty Rocks the Boat." *W*, May 2016.

BBC News. "Artist's Cold Call Cuts Off Phone." April 7, 2006.

———. "Mass Honours Sir Paul Getty's Life." September 9, 2003.

Beckerman, Josh. "Getty Family to Regain Majority Stake of Getty Images." *Wall Street Journal*, September 4, 2018.

Bigelow, Catherine. "Getty-a-Go-Go." SFGate (website), August 16, 2013. https://www.sfgate.com.

Blackhurst, Chris. "The MT Interview: Mark Getty." *Management Today*, August 31, 2010.

Caracciolo, Marella. "Up at the Villa." *W*, April 2005.

Carleton, Will. "Mark Getty's Son Photographer Alexander Getty Features Work in New Exhibition." *Photo Archive News*, December 23, 2014.

Carlson, Erin. "The Wardrobe on Tatum Getty." *Nob Hill Gazette*, June 5, 2018.

Chaffin, Joshua. "Getty Images in $2.4bn Buy Out." *Financial Times*, February 25, 2008.

Cook, John. "Getty Images Moving from Nasdaq to NYSE." *Seattle Post-Intelligencer*, October 29, 2009.

Corcoran, Jason. "How I Made It: Mark Getty, Chairman of Getty Images." *Sunday Times* (London), February 2, 2003.

di Robilant, Andrea. "The Most Dangerous Horse Race in the World." *Town & Country*, June 2016.

Economist. "Blood and Oil." March 2, 2000.

Ellsworth-Jones, Will. *Banksy: The Man Behind the Wall*. New York: St. Martin's Press, 2012.

Elwick-Bates, Emma. "Memphis Beat." *Vogue*, December 2016.

Evening Standard. "Banksy and Bono Dial £20m for Aids." February 15, 2008.

Feitelberg, Rosemary. "Nats Getty Talks 'Strike Oil' Fashion, Activism, Ridley Scott, Artistic Escapades." *WWD*, October 17, 2018.

Forbes. "Looking for a Gusher in . . . File Photos?" October 13, 1997.

Garrahan, Matthew. "Getty Chief Jonathan Klein to Refocus on Chairman's Role." *Financial Times*, March 13, 2015.

———. "Getty Images Back in the Family as Carlyle Group Sells Out." *Financial Times*, September 4, 2018.

Getty, Mark. *Like Wildfire Blazing*. London: Adelphi, 2018.

Getty, Sabine. "Original G." *Tatler*, September 2019.

Gillman, Ollie. "Princess Beatrice Attends Joseph Getty and Sabine Ghanem's Rome Wedding." *Daily Mail*, May 30, 2015.

Henderson, Violet. "Diamond Life." *Vogue UK*, March 2015.

Hurley, James. ". . . And the Award for Best Picture Goes to Getty Images (More Often than Not)." *Times* (London), March 29, 2019.

Kennedy, Maev. "Getty Heir's £10M Gift to National Gallery." *Guardian*, July 12, 2001.

Khan, Nura. "Inside Sabine and Joseph Getty's Rehearsal Dinner." *Vogue UK*, December 30, 2016.

Lerman, Rachel. "Corbis Sale to Chinese Company May Be Boon to Getty." *Seattle Times*, January 22, 2016.

Lewis, Jane. "Mark Getty: 'I'm One of Those People Everyone Hates.'" *Money Week*, April 8, 2019.

Macon, Alexandra. "Ivy Getty Wears John Galliano for Maison Margiela to Walk Down the Aisle at City Hall in San Francisco." Vogue.com, November 7, 2021.

Magnaghi, Brooke. "Fashion It-Girl Sabine Ghanem Dishes on Her Personal Style and Impossibly Chic Wardrobe." *HuffPost*, November 4, 2015.

Masters, Sam. "How Mark Getty Grew from the Child Seen in *All the Money in the World* to Be One of Britain's Richest Men." *Independent* (London), January 3, 2018.

Murphy, David. "Seven Gettys Sign Up for Irish Passports." *Independent* (London), September 30, 1999.

Nikkhah, Roya. "Garsington Opera: Behind the Getty Gates." *Telegraph* (UK), May 29, 2011.

Nisse, Jason. "Getty Family Takes Stake in UK Acquisition Venture." *Independent* (London), January 9, 1994.

Peretz, Evgenia. "Postcards from Paradise." *Vanity Fair*, December 2003.

Pithers, Ellie. "Life in Full Color." *Vogue UK*, March 2018.

Reguly, Eric. "Getty Snaps Up Supplier of Images in £100m Deal." *Times* (London), September 17, 1997.

Roberts, Paul. "It's Crunch Time for Seattle-Based Photo Giant Getty Images, and for Photographers." *Seattle Times*, December 1, 2019.

Studeman, Kristin Tice. "Getty's Images." *W*, December 18, 2014.

Tatler. "How to Win at the Social Season." May 21, 2019.

———. "The Social Power Index." August 2019.

Tharp, Paul. "Fund Grabs Getty." *New York Post*, February 26, 2008.

Tregaskes, Chandler. "They've Got It: The Evolution of the It Boy." *Tatler*, October 2020.

von Thurn und Taxis, Elisabeth. "Sabine Ghanem's Fairy-Tale Wedding to Joseph Getty at a Castle in Rome." *Vogue*, July 29, 2015.

Wintle, Angela. "Businessman and Author Mark Getty on His Passion for Italy and His Family's English Country Estates." *Sunday Times* (London), July 1, 2018.

Zhang, Michael. "Getty Images to be Fully Controlled by the Getty Family Once Again." PetaPixel (website), September 5, 2018. https://petapixel.com.

Chapter Seven: Aileen

Arnold, Amanda. "Jane Fonda's 82nd Birthday Party Was Wild." *The Cut* (*New York Magazine* blog), December 23, 2019. https://www.thecut.com.

Beck, Marilyn. "New—Naughty—Nicole in the Works." *Province* (Vancouver), August 18, 1994.

Bigelow, Catherine. "Gettys Gamble Big at Annual AIDS Research Fundraiser." *San Francisco Chronicle*, November 26, 2019.

Brolley, Brittany. "Elizabeth Taylor's Grandchildren Grew Up to Be Gorgeous." The List (website), July 13, 2018. https://www.thelist.com.

Collins, Nancy. "Liz's AIDS Odyssey." *Vanity Fair*, November 1992.

Economist. "How the Anarchists of Extinction Rebellion Got So Well Organized." October 10, 2019.

Firozi, Paulina. "Cash, Banners and Bullhorns: Big Philanthropists Throw Weight behind Disruptive Climate Activists." *Washington Post*, July 12, 2019.

Gardner, Chris. "Elizabeth Taylor's AIDS Foundation to Host Inaugural Fundraising Gala on Fox Lot." *Hollywood Reporter*, February 12, 2020.

Gliatto, Tom. "Hanging In." *People*, April 6, 1992.

Greenfield, Robert. *Timothy Leary: A Biography.* New York: Harcourt, 2006.

Harder, Amy. "Climate-Change Funders Shift Focus amid Pandemic and Election." Axios (website), May 14, 2020.

Hello!. "Elizabeth Taylor and Her Beloved Former Daughter-in-Law Aileen Getty." August 14, 1993.

Hook, Leslie. "Donations Pour In as Extinction Rebellion Goes Global." *Financial Times*, October 11, 2019.

Jenkins, David. "Meet the Man behind the World's Coolest Festival." *Tatler*, November 2016.

Jewell, Bryony. "Getty Oil Heiress Donates £500,000 to Fund Backing Protesters Extinction Rebellion." *Daily Mail*, September 6, 2019.

Knight, Sam. "Does Extinction Rebellion Have the Solution to the Climate Crisis?" *New Yorker*, July 21, 2018.

Lewis, Judith. "Aileen Getty Comes Clean." *Poz*, May 1996.

Matthews, Damion. "Gwyneth Paltrow Cochaired a Black-Tie Poker Party for amfAR at the Getty Mansion in San Francisco." *Vogue* online, November 18, 2019.

Needle, Chad. "Positive Connection." *A&U*, December 2015.

Neilson, Trevor. "Introducing the Climate Emergency Fund." Medium (website), July 11, 2019.

Ochs, Alyssa. "A Newcomer with a Famous Name Steps Up for HIV/AIDS Funding in the American South." *Inside Philanthropy*, March 4, 2018.

Oumano, Elana. "Dark Victory." *San Francisco Examiner*, January 10, 1993.

Patchen, Tyler. "Alabama AIDS Initiatives Earn Grants from Elton John AIDS Foundation and Others." *Birmingham Business Journal*, April 27, 2018.

People. "Heiress Aileen Getty Becomes Elizabeth Taylor's Almost Daughter-in-Law." March 17, 1980.

"Q&A Piano Man—Director," undated. ispirazzjoni.com.

Reginato, James. "The Elton John AIDS Foundation Pulled Out All the Stops at Its Fall Gala." *Vanity Fair* online, November 8, 2017, https://www.vanityfair .com/style/2017/11/elton-john-aids-foundation-gala.

Reynolds, Daniel. "Project Angel Food Honors Aileen Getty with Elizabeth Taylor Leadership Award." HIVPlusMag (website), September 10, 2014. https:// www.hivplusmag.com.

Ruspoli, Tao, dir. *Just Say Know.* Los Angeles: LAFCO, 2002.

Schwartz, John. "Meet the Millionaires Helping to Pay for Climate Protests." *New York Times*, September 29, 2019.

Sessums, Kevin. "The Gettys' Painful Legacy." *Vanity Fair*, March 1992.

Snow, Shauna. "A Getty against Establishment." *Los Angeles Times*, May 29, 1990.

South China Morning Post. "Drug Addict Getty Heiress Has AIDS." January 13, 1988.

SubmitHub. "Kowloon," undated. https://www.submithub.com.

Weaver, Hilary. "Jane Fonda Was Arrested for a Fifth Time at a Climate Change Protest the Day before Her Birthday." *Elle*, December 21, 2019.

Webster, Ben. "Getty's Oil Cash Goes to Extinction Rebellion." *Times* (London), September 7, 2019.

———. "Philanthropist Aileen Getty Has a Long History of Giving Cash to Good Causes." *Times* (London), September 6, 2019.

West, Kevin. "Celluloid Prince." *W*, April 2009.

Williams, Jeanne. "AIDS Grips Liz's Ex-Daughter-in-Law." *USA Today*, November 14, 1991.

Williams, Paige. "A Journal of Reclamation Reaches a Peak in Spain." *New York Times*, August 10, 2006.

Williamson, Elizabeth. "Fonda Brings Hollywood to Capital for Protests." *New York Times*, December 21, 2019.

Wyllie, Julie. "Aileen Getty and Rory Kennedy Lead New Climate Fund to Support Activists and Protestors." *Chronicle of Philanthropy*, July 12, 2019.

Yarbrough, Jeff. "The Passion of Elizabeth Taylor." *Advocate*, October 15, 1996.

CHAPTER EIGHT: ARIADNE

Abramian, Alexandria. "Heir Time." *LA Confidential*, February 2015.

Allende, Mayte. "August Getty RTW Spring 2018." *WWD*, September 2017.

Bala, Divya. "From American Dynasty to Parisian Couture: *Vogue* Speaks to Designer August Getty." *Vogue Australia*, July 2, 2019. vogue.com.au.

Barnes, Brooks. "GLAAD's Bold New Campaign: An L.G.B.T. Constitutional Amendment." *New York Times*, June 29, 2019.

———. "Growing Up Getty." *New York Times*, June 23, 2018.

Carter, Lee. "August Start." *W*, October 2014.

Channel Q (internet radio). "Let's Go There: August Getty." April 15, 2019. https://www.google.com/url?sa=t&rct=j&q=&esrc=s&source=web&cd=&ved=2ahUKEwiZqfP6vZDxAhWtFlkFHds0AREQFjABegQIBhAD&url=https%3A%2F%2Fwww.audacy.com%2Fwearechannelq%2Fblogs%2Flets-go-there-w-shira-ryan%2Faugust-getty&usg=AOvVaw3v0xAurA2bSc4tji7OzWR3.

Chikhoune, Ryma. "Gigi Gorgeous Releases Own Cosmetics Line with Ipsy." *WWD*, October 2019.

Cox, Rich. "The Gayest Davos in History Still Isn't Gay Enough." Reuters, January 20, 2020.

Deeny, Godfrey. "August Getty Plans to Bring Glamour Back to the Paris Couture." Fashion Network (website), November 12, 2018. https://us.fashionnetwork.com.

Diaz, Gil. "Ariadne Getty: A Visionary With a Heart of Gold." LGBT News Now (website), November 2, 2021.

Directo-Meston, Danielle. "Inside Rising Designer August Getty's Surrealist Show at Universal Studios." Racked Los Angeles (website), November 12, 2015. https://la.racked.com.

Eytan, Declan. "Meet the 24-Year-Old Heir to the Getty Family Fortune, Who Is Banking on Ball Gowns as Big Business." *Forbes*, July 27, 2018.

Ferraro, Rich. "GLAAD and Ariadne Getty Foundation Host LGBTQ Panel during the World Economic Forum Annual Meeting in Davos and Call for Action." GLAAD blog, January 24, 2019. https://www.glaad.org/blog.

Foreman, Katya. "August Getty Atelier Spring Couture 2019." *WWD*, January 24, 2019.

Garcia, Michelle. "Buying Art in the Age of Instagram." *Out*, April 25, 2019.

Ginsberg, Steve. "Ready Getty Go." *WWD*, December 1, 1987.

GLAAD (website). "The Ariadne Getty Foundation Pledges $15 million to GLAAD." February 1, 2018. https://www.google.com/url?sa=t&rct=j&q=&esrc=s&source =video&cd=&ved=2ahUKEwih36H8vJDxAhUPbc0KHWGsCwgQtwIw AXoECAkQAw&url=https%3A%2F%2Fwww.glaad.org%2Fblog%2Fariadne -getty-foundation-pledges-15m-glaad-and-brings-lgbtq-inclusion-world-stage -world&usg=AOvVaw0fzVKcu-9WwnZtCfThZwip.

Goldsmith, Belinda. "How Gigi Gorgeous and the Gettys Are Pushing LGBT+ at Davos." Reuters, January 25, 2020.

Gorgeous, Gigi. *He Said, She Said: Lessons, Stories, and Mistakes from My Transgender Journey.* New York: Harmony Books, 2019.

———. "The Proposal: Nats & Gigi." YouTube video, March 8, 2018. https:// www.google.com/url?sa=t&rct=j&q=&esrc=s&source=web&cd=&ved =2ahUKEwjl6YbugJHxAhUvGFkFHeIiBS0QwqsBMAB6BAgUEAE &url=https%3A%2F%2Fwww.youtube.com%2Fwatch%3Fv%3DVxTyFSNe JBQ&usg=AOvVawl2EWlurKZUK9G5WnTzfIbs.

Gorgeous, Gigi, and Mimi. "All the Money in the World with Nats Getty." *Queer-ified with Gigi Gorgeous and Mimi* (podcast). June 2021. https://podcasts.apple .com/us/podcast/queerified-with-gigi-gorgeous-mimi/id1568356118?i= 1000525701562.

Guerrero, Desirée. "Gorgeous & Getty." *Advocate*, April/May 2019.

Hallemann, Caroline. "Ariadne Getty Gives $1 Million to GLAAD." *Town & Country*, December 20, 2017.

———. "A Member of the Getty Family Speaks Out about *All the Money in the World*." *Town & Country*, December 20, 2017.

Heath, Ryan. "Queer Davos Peeks Through." Politico (website), January 25, 2019.

Howard, Justin. "Framing a Getty." *Black Chalk*, December 2015.

Jackson, Corinn. "David LaChapelle and August Getty Created a Dystopian Model Wasteland at Universal Studios." Fashionista (website), November 12, 2015.

Janklow, Angela. "Getty Goil." *Vanity Fair*, March 1988.

Johns, Merryn. "Rainbow Rebel." *Curve*, Spring 2019.

Journal News (White Plains, New York). "Cher Shares Home with Getty Heiress." February 19, 1988.

Keveney, Bill. "Getty Lawyer Says FX's 'Trust' Portrays Family in 'Defamatory, Wildly Sensationalized' Way." *USA Today*, March 16, 2018.

Kopple, Barbara, dir. *This Is Everything: Gigi Gorgeous.* New York: Sander/Moses Productions, 2017.

Lathan, Corinna. "What Davos Taught Me about Supporting My Transgender Child." World Economic Forum (website), February 16, 2018.

Lawson, Richard. "Introducing Gigi Gorgeous, Who Needs No Introduction." *Vanity Fair* online, February 9, 2017, https://www.vanityfair.com/hollywood /2017/02/gigi-gorgeous-this-is-everything-sundance-interview.

London, Lela. "Oil Heir Nats Getty Debuts Lifestyle Fashion Brand with the Help of YouTuber Gigi Gorgeous." *Forbes*, February 6, 2019.

Lopez, Julyssa. "Gigi Gorgeous Had a Stunning Beach-Front Wedding." *Brides*, September 24, 2019.

Los Angeles LGBT Center. "Honoree Ariadne Getty—49th Anniversary Gala Vanguard Awards." YouTube video. Los Angeles: September 24, 2018. https://www.google.com/url?sa=t&rct=j&q=&esrc=s&source=web&cd=&ved=2ahUKEwiYmfmpu5DxAhV0FVkFHdMaBDAQtwIwBHoECAUQAw&url=https%3A%2F%2Fwww.youtube.com%2Fwatch%3Fv%3DXP6PcWDzQQk&usg=AOvVaw1ZrCDYQxKAhM45LZMbwmzC.

Magsaysay, Melissa. "Fashioning New Perspectives: August Getty, Gigi Gorgeous & Nats Getty." *LALA*, Summer 2019.

Malkin, Mark. "Ariadne Getty Honored as *Variety*'s Philanthropist of the Year." *Variety*, July 31, 2019.

McKenzie, Lesley. "Artist & Activist Nats Getty Debuts Lifestyle Brand Strike Oil." *Hollywood Reporter*, January 15, 2019.

Megarry, Daniel. "August Getty." *Gay Times*, February 2019.

Moore, Booth. "Ariadne Getty, August Getty, Nats Getty and Gigi Gorgeous Celebrate LGBTQ Advocacy." *WWD*, July 31, 2019.

Musto, Michael. "August Getty Wears His Colors Out, Loud and Proud." *Los Angeles Blade*, June 23, 2020.

Ocamb, Karen. "Ari Getty and a Camelot of Her Own Creation." *Los Angeles Blade*, January 29, 2021.

———. "Nats Getty Unmasked." *Los Angeles Blade*, June 25, 2020.

Ohland, Gloria. "Photo Finish." *LA Weekly*, June 25, 1987.

Politico (website). "Rainbow Wave." January 21, 2020.

Preston, Devon. "The Skin I'm In." *Inked*, June 2021.

Quinn, Dave. "Get a First Look at the Cover of Gigi Gorgeous' Memoir as She Reveals 'Emotional' Writing Process." *People*, October 16, 2018.

Reginato, James. "Outrageous Fortune: This Is Not Your Mother's Getty Family." *Town & Country*, February 2020.

Salessy, Heloise. "A Look at the 500,000-Swarovski-Encrusted 'Million Dollar Dress.'" *Vogue France*, November 2018.

Sessums, Kevin. "'Define Yourself': Ariadne Getty on Family, Philanthropy and Queer Activism." *Washington Blade*, October 20, 2019.

Sheeler, Jason. "How August Getty Navigated the Fashion Industry as a Member of One of America's Wealthiest Families." *Telegraph* (UK), February 14, 2020.

Sloan, Elizabeth. "Gigi Gorgeous & Nats Getty: 5 Fast Facts." Heavy (website), July 13, 2019. https://heavy.com.

Stratis, Niko. "Nats Getty on Becoming His Authentic Self." *Paper*, June 16, 2021.

Tempesta, Erica. "Transgender YouTube Star Gigi Gorgeous Reveals She Backed Out of Sex Reassignment Surgery." *Daily Mail*, March 3, 2019.

Tran, Khanh. "David LaChapelle and August Getty Meld Art and Fashion in Hollywood." *WWD*, November 12, 2015.

United Press International. "Getty Heir Converts Snap into Art Form." *Scrantonian Tribune*, February 21, 1988.

Varian, Ethan. "Fixture in Her YouTube Videos, and Now in Her Life." *New York Times,* July 28, 2019.

Wagmeister, Elizabeth. "Gigi Gorgeous and Nats Getty on Meeting, Marrying and the Importance of Representation." *Variety,* June 4, 2020.

West, Melanie Grayer. "A Gift for City Tourists." *Wall Street Journal,* May 24, 2011.

WWD. "August Getty RTW Spring 2015." September 2014.

Wynne, Alex. "August Getty Atelier Couture Fall 2019." *WWD,* July 8, 2019.

———. "August Getty Atelier Couture Spring 2020." *WWD,* January 22, 2020.

———. "August Getty Atelier Sets Paris Presentation during Couture." *WWD,* October 1, 2018.

CHAPTER NINE: PAUL III

Abramovitch, Seth. "Balthazar Getty on Growing Up Getty." *Hollywood Reporter,* February 9, 2021.

Brunner, Jeryl. "Talking Money with a Getty." *Forbes,* December 14, 2018.

Creeden, Molly. "A Clothes Collection Inspired by the Bauhaus." *T* (*New York Times*), August 9, 2019.

Croft, Claudia. "Design: Rosetta Getty." *Sunday Times* (London), May 3, 2015.

Delray, Dean. "Balthazar Getty, Actor/Musician, Artist." *Let There Be Talk.* (podcast), May 4, 2020. https://www.google.com/url?sa=t&rct=j&q=&esrc=s&source=web&cd=&ved=2ahUKEwjV48eFzZDxAhWiUt8KHc3vAI0QtwIwBXoECAcQAw&url=https%3A%2F%2Fwww.youtube.com%2Fwatch%3Fv%3DbcFrSvspT64&usg=AOvVawlJmrQCvrh9wgpUs-G2uk-J.

Directo-Meston, Danielle. "Balthazar Getty on His New L.A. Store, Monk Punk Fashion Line and Music." *Hollywood Reporter,* June 13, 2019.

Edwardes, Charlotte. "Balthazar Getty: I'm Finally OK with Being a Getty." *Evening Standard,* July 18, 2016.

Egan, Maura. "Dynasty's Child." *New York Times,* September 23, 2001.

Fleetwood, Amelia. "Breath of Fresh Air." *Santa Barbara,* March 2019.

Gerstein, Josh. "Anna Getty May Have Renounced U.S. Citizenship." Politico (website), February 2, 2012.

Getty, Anna. *Anna Getty's Easy Green Organic: Cook Well—Eat Well—Live Well.* San Francisco: Chronicle Books, 2010.

Goldstein, Melissa. "Higher Ground." *C,* January 2016.

Greener Living Today. "Anna Getty Interview with *Greener Living Today.*" May 2009.

Haldeman, Peter. "Ojai's Golden Hour." *New York Times,* July 11, 2015.

Hilton, Perez. "Balthazar Getty Turns to Kabbalah to Save Marriage." December 14, 2009. https://perezhilton.com (blog).

KTLA 5. "Balt Getty on New Single 'Money.'" *KTLA LA Morning News,* December 14, 2018. https://www.google.com/url?sa=t&rct=j&q=&esrc=s&source=web&cd=&ved=2ahUKEwiQ5NqUzpDxAhWmY98KHdDICbkQwqsBMAF6BAgIEAE&url=https%3A%2F%2Fwww.youtube.com%2Fwatch%3Fv%3DT44vh6E493w&usg=AOvVawllPC5wCvyt5fQ35t4swyl8.

Lawler, Danielle. "Head over Hills." *Tatler,* April 2020.

Lennon, Christine. "A Fashionable Life: Rosetta and Balthazar Getty." *Harper's Bazaar*, September 2010.

Macalister-Smith, Tilly. "Free-Style." *Telegraph* (UK), August 1, 2015.

McCully, Martha. "Fashion House." *California*, May 2018.

Moore, Booth. "Rosetta Getty RTW Spring 2020." *WWD*, September 8, 2019.

O'Sullivan, Eleanor. "Mutual Admiration Abounds off the Set." *Asbury Park Press*, March 19, 1990.

Price, Jason. "Solardrive: Balthazar Getty and His Collaborators Discuss His New Project." Icon vs. Icon (website), May 8, 2013. https://www.iconvsicon.com.

Ruffer, Zoe. "Rosetta Getty Takes Spring Break on a South African Safari." *Vogue* online, May 9, 2019.

Scott, Danny. "A Life in the Day of Balthazar Getty, Member of a Troubled Dynasty." *Times* (London), August 28, 2016.

Singer, Maya. "A Weekend under the Tuscan Sun with Rosetta Getty." *Vogue*, July 3, 2018.

Spargo, Chris. "All the Money in the World: Billionaire Heirs Rosetta and Balthazar Getty Treat Guests to Horse Races, Dinner under the Stars, and Fireworks at Their Fourth of July Party in Tuscany." *Daily Mail*, July 5, 2018.

Sykes, Plum. "The Power of a Name: Dynasty." *Vogue*, March 2001.

Turro, Alessandra. "Rosetta Getty, Farfetch Celebrate Fourth of July in Tuscany." *WWD*, July 6, 2015.

Warner, Kara. "How Balthazar Getty 'Struggled' with Billionaire Family's Dark Legacy—and Survived Scandal." *People*, January 4, 2018.

Wong, Amelia. "Not-Your-Average Visitor's Take on the Getty." *The Iris* (blog), December 15, 2016. http://blogs.getty.edu.

WWD. "Very Marry." August 14, 2003.

CHAPTER TEN: TARA

Arden, Isabella. "Bits & People." *Palm Beach Daily News*, November 23, 1986.

Ashton, Paul. "SuperYacht World Hall of Fame: *Talitha*." *SuperYacht World*, July 1, 2016.

Bigelow, Catherine. "Getty Hosts the Africa Foundation." SFGate (website), November 24, 2015. https://www.sfgate.com.

Brooks, Phillip. "Sails Now On." Sail the World (website), January 12, 2017. https://sailtheworld.info.

Campbell, Stewart. "Treasure Hunter: Yacht Owner Tara Getty on His Epic Round-the-World Adventure." *Boat International*, May 5, 2016.

Carroll, Jerry. "Getty's Rocky Marriage." *San Francisco Chronicle*, February 24, 1986.

Cunliffe, Tom. *Blue Bird: Seven Decades at Sea*. West Sussex, UK: Kos Picture Source, 2010.

Departures. "Tara Getty: Africa Foundation." September 2013.

Eden, Richard. "Talitha Getty Lives On." *Telegraph* (UK), August 9, 2008.

Elkann, Alain. "Gisela Getty." Interview, August 19, 2018. https://www.alainelkanninterviews.com.

Eszterhas, Joe. "Exclusive Interview with Paul Getty." *Rolling Stone*, May 9, 1974.

Fortescue, Sam. "Second Wind." *Boat International*, September 2020.

Getty, Tara. "Life on a South African Game Reserve." *Evening Standard*, September 11, 2009.

Haldeman, Peter. "Phinda Getty House." *Architectural Digest*, February 2008.

Hossenally, Rooksana. "The Corsica Classic Regatta Celebrates Its 10th Anniversary This August Despite the Coronavirus." *Forbes*, August 15, 2020.

Houston, Dan. "Griff's First Win." *Classic Boat*, October 2012.

Johnson, Laurie. "2 Getty Kidnappers Sentenced in Italy." *New York Times*, July 30, 1976.

Kellett, Francisca. "Safari School." *Financial Times*, February 19, 2019.

Lyons, Madeleine. "John Paul Getty's Home Sells for Close to €2.45m." *Irish Times*, October 20, 2012.

Manners, Dorothy. "Gossips Keep Eye on 'Pool.'" *San Francisco Examiner*, August 22, 1968.

McNeil, Donald G. "Company Draws Rich Eco-Tourists to Africa." *New York Times*, June 25, 1997.

Miami Herald. "J. Paul Getty III Marries Ex-Model." September 14, 1974.

Orlando Sentinel. "Court Names Protector for Getty's Grandson." March 26, 1975.

Parker, Jennifer Leigh. "Want to Stop Poaching? Build a Smart Park." *Forbes*, December 2019.

Ross, Rory. "Jon Bannenberg, the Godfather of Modern Yacht Design." *Vanity Fair*, August 2018.

Rozzo, Mark. "The Virtually Unknown Saga of Gisela Getty and Jutta Winkelmann, It Girls on a Bumpy Ride." *Vanity Fair*, April 2018.

San Francisco Examiner. "Reclusive Getty." June 5, 1987.

———. "Rich Kid with a Silly Name." September 22, 1968.

Seal, Mark. "The Good Life Aquatic." *Vanity Fair*, May 2005.

———. "Too Big to Sail?" *Vanity Fair*, November 2010.

Taki. "Coming Soon: My Engagement to Kristin Scott Thomas." *Spectator*, June 21, 2014.

———. "A Very Exclusive Club." *Quest*, September 2014.

———. "High Life." *Spectator*, June 15, 2013.

Tang, David. "Take a Bow." *Financial Times*, August 16, 2017.

Telegraph (UK). "Bush Barons." March 25, 2006.

———. "A Grandson Makes Getty Even Richer." August 31, 2001.

Time. "Catching the Kidnappers." January 28, 1974.

Tisdall, Nigel. "The Corsica Classic." *Telegraph* (UK), March 20, 2017.

United Press International. "Getty Set to Meet Demands." July 16, 1973.

Varty, Dave. *The Full Circle: To Londolozi and Back Again*. Johannesburg: Penguin, 2008.

Weber, Bruce. "J. Paul Getty III, 54, Dies; Had Ear Cut Off by Captors." *New York Times*, February 7, 2011.

Woo, Elaine. "J. Paul Getty III Dies at 54; Scion of Oil Dynasty." *Los Angeles Times*, March 13, 2014.

WWD. "Getty Up." June 22, 2006.

CHAPTER ELEVEN: PACIFIC HEIGHTS

Anderson, Susan Heller. "Only the Flight Is Economy Class." *New York Times*, November 30, 1983.

Associated Press. "Nation's Richest Man Upset by Forbes List." October 1, 1983.

Bernheimer, Martin. "In San Francisco: Premiere of Getty's 'Plump Jack.'" *Los Angeles Times*, June 29, 1987.

Caen, Herb. "Ramblin' Man." *San Francisco Chronicle*, August 1, 1995.

Castro, Janet. "Texaco's Star Falls." *Time*, June 24, 2001.

Cocks, Anna Somers. "The Getty Museum Curator Who Hired the Rolling Stones for 15 Shillings a Head." *Art Newspaper*, January 10, 2020.

Cole, Robert J. "Father Thought He Screwed Up. His Judgement Is Again in Question." *New York Times*, April 24, 1984.

Coll, Steve. "Gettys at Center of Historic Fight." *Washington Post*, April 12, 1987.

Commanday, Robert. "Getty's 'Plump Jack' in Its Gala Debut." *San Francisco Chronicle*, June 29, 1987.

Curtis, Charlotte. "A Dance at the Met." *New York Times*, May 22, 1984.

———. "The Gregarious Ann Getty." *New York Times*, October 8, 1985.

———. "The Reserved Gettys." *New York Times*, May 8, 1984.

———. "Society's New Order Takes Over." *New York Times*, March 18, 1986.

———. "Wall Street's Mystery Man." *New York Times*, March 6, 1984.

Dana, Don. "Dear Friends of the Leakey Foundation." *AnthroQuest, the Newsletter of the Leakey Foundation*, Fall/Winter 2013.

Goodman, Peter. "Gordon P. Getty Emerges as a Composer." *Newsday*, April 18, 1986.

Hayes, Thomas. "Bitter Flareup at Getty over Control of Trust." *New York Times*, November 25, 1983.

———. "Gordon Getty's Goal Realized." *New York Times*, January 10, 1984.

Henken, John. "Gordon Getty Bringing His 'Plump Jack' to L.A." *Los Angeles Times*, March 19, 1988.

Holland, Bernard. "Recital: Mignon Dunn." *New York Times*, December 4, 1983.

Jacobs, Jody. "Leakey Fellows to Host Day," *Los Angeles Times*, May 9, 1975.

Jepson, Barbara. "The World's Wealthiest Composer." *Wall Street Journal*, March 21, 1985.

Lenzner, Robert. "Splitting Up J. Paul Getty's $4 Billion." *Boston Globe*, October 21, 1984.

Loomis, Carol J. "The War between the Gettys." *Fortune*, January 21, 1985.

L. S. B. Foundation News. "D.C. Symposium to Bring Together Famed Scientists 'In Search of Man.'" Fall 1975.

———. "Fourth Annual Leakey Memorial Symposium Scheduled for Nov. 1–2." Summer 1975.

———. "Johanson Reports on Afar at Caltech Lecture Series." Spring 1975.

McCarthy, Brian, and Bunny Williams. *Parish-Hadley: Tree of Life*. New York: Stewart, Tabori & Chang, 2015.

Meenan, Monica. "Christmas with the Gettys." *Town & Country*, December 1979.

Montandon, Pat. "The Big Apple." *San Francisco Examiner*, September 30, 1982.

Morch, Albert. "Man and Fox Set the Tone." *San Francisco Examiner*, December 3, 1973.

Pelosi, Barbara. "Profile: Gordon P. Getty." *L. S. B. Leakey Foundation News*, Spring 1980.

Pelosi, Nancy. *Know Your Power: A Message to America's Daughters.* New York: Random House, 2008.

Pender, Kathleen. "Gordon Getty Gets Down to Business." *San Francisco Chronicle*, February 5, 1987.

———. "S.F. Billionaire under Siege." *San Francisco Chronicle*, March 16, 1987.

San Francisco Examiner. "Dr. Leakey's Spell." May 5, 1972.

———. "Francis Bullimore." April 5, 1996.

Sansweet, Stephen J. "Scion's Struggle." *Wall Street Journal*, January 13, 1984.

Schonberg, Harold C. "The Wealthiest Composer of Our Time." *New York Times*, July 27, 1986.

Shiver, Jube. "Court Rules against Getty Heirs." *Los Angeles Times*, March 19, 1985.

———. "Gettys Resolve Dispute over Trust." *Los Angeles Times*, May 31, 1985.

Suzy. "How a King Made a Convert." *Daily News* (New York), May 11, 1978.

———. "An Ordinary Billionaire's Birthday Bash." *Daily News* (New York), December 4, 1983.

Town & Country. "Dreams of Beauty." April 1983.

Vogue. "House with Heart." October 1977.

Whitefield, Debra. "The Deal: How Getty Ended Up with Texaco." *Los Angeles Times*, January 9, 1986.

CHAPTER TWELVE: THE RICHEST AMERICAN, ONCE AGAIN

Andrews, Susanna. "Arianna Calling." *Vanity Fair*, December 2005.

Begley, Adam. "Ann Getty: Publish or Perish." *New York Times*, October 22, 1989.

Behbehaal, Mandy. "Red Carpet Premiere for Andrew Getty Movie." *San Francisco Examiner*, September 29, 1991.

Borger, Julian. "Getty's Double Life Stuns California High Society." *Guardian*, August 22, 1999.

Brown, Tina. *The Vanity Fair Diaries 1983–1992.* New York: Henry Holt, 2017.

Canedy, Dana. "Alexander Papamarkou, 68, an International Financier." *New York Times*, April 26, 1998.

Cohen, Edie. "Getty's Center." *Interior Design*, June 1998.

Colacello, Bob. "The Rise of Insight." *Vanity Fair*, September 1986.

Corkery, P. J. "Border-Line." *San Francisco Chronicle*, May 8, 2001.

Duka, John. "Alecko Papamarkou: Why the Rich Are Different." *Institutional Investor*, July 1985.

Finz, Stacy. "Getty's Secret Double Life/Second Family in L.A.—3 Daughters." SFGate (website), August 21, 1999. https://www.sfgate.com.

Gibbons, Ann. *The First Human: The Race to Discover Our Earliest Ancestor.* New York: Anchor Books, 2007.

Goodman, Wendy. "Billy Getty's Rise to the Top." *Harper's Bazaar*, March 1998.

Haberman, Douglas. "Billionaire Getty's Double Life." *Daily News* (New York), August 21, 1999.

Hamlin, Jesse. "Publisher Getty Calls It Quits." *San Francisco Chronicle*, March 1, 1990.

Hartlaub, Peter. "Getty's Secret Kids Demand Rights." *San Francisco Examiner*, August 21, 1999.

———. "Getty's Shocking Secret Family: Legal Papers Hint They Want His Name." *San Francisco Examiner*, August 20, 1999.

Hochman, Steve. "A Getty Getting into the Music Business." *San Francisco Chronicle*, October 15, 2000.

Kalb, Jon. *Adventures in the Bone Trade: The Race to Discover Human Ancestors in Ethiopia's Afar Depression.* New York: Copernicus Books, 2000.

Kjaergaard, Peter C. "The Fossil Trade: Paying a Price for Human Origins." *Isis* 103, no. 2 (June 2015).

La Ganga, Maria L. "Gordon Getty's Second Family Was an Open Secret." *Los Angeles Times*, August 30, 1999.

Los Angeles Times. "Engagements: Jarman–Getty." February 7, 1999.

Love, Iris. "Iris Love's Nile Diary." *Vanity Fair*, June 1985.

Mahon, Gigi. "Lord on the Fly." *New York*, February 24, 1986.

Mansfield, Stephanie. "In the Jetstream with Arianna." *Washington Post*, February 1987.

McGlynchey, Kevin. "Philanthropist Ann Light Dies at 79." *Palm Beach Daily News*, January 25, 1988.

McLeod, Beth. "'Frank and Outspoken,' Ann Light Remembered by Relatives, Friends." *Palm Beach Post*, January 31, 1988.

Nolte, Carl. "Kenneth Rainin—Entrepreneur, Donor." SFGate (website), May 6, 2007. https://www.sfgate.com.

Oney, Steve. "The Many Faces of Arianna." *Los Angeles*, October 2004.

Perlez, Jane. "Grove Sold to Ann Getty and British Publisher." *New York Times*, March 5, 1985.

Petit, Charles. "Battle over Old Bones Cools Off." *San Francisco Chronicle*, October 22, 1996.

———. "Berkeley Institute in Battle over Fossils." *San Francisco Chronicle*, April 26, 1995.

———. "Getty Withdraws Backing for 'Origins' Institute in Berkeley." *San Francisco Chronicle*, May 25, 1994.

Reed, Dan. "Billionaire Gordon Getty's Secret Family of 4 Revealed." *San Jose Mercury News*, August 20, 1999.

Reginato, James. "Getty's New Vintage." *W*, March 1996.

———. "Hale Storm." *W*, February 1998.

Reid, Calvin. "Barney Rosset Remembered." *Publishers Weekly*, February 24, 2012.

Reuters. "Getty Name Adopted by His 'Second Family.'" *San Francisco Examiner*, January 29, 2000.

Robins, Cynthia. "Witty Mix of People at Hale Ranch." *San Francisco Examiner*, September 8, 1987.

Rowlands, Penelope. "The Getty Gang." *WWD,* July 11, 1991.

Rubenstein, Steve. "San Francisco Says Goodbye to Pat Steger." *San Francisco Chronicle,* November 19, 1999.

Saeks, Diane Dorran. "On Top of the World: Billy Getty Turns Two Russian Hill Apartments into a Spectacular Penthouse." *San Francisco Chronicle,* March 4, 1999.

San Francisco Chronicle. "A Wealth of Talent." March 1, 1998.

Smith, Randall. "Friendship and Favors Win Wealthy Clients for a New York Broker." *Wall Street Journal,* July 16, 1985.

Steger, Pat. "Billy Getty Pops the Question." *San Francisco Chronicle,* December 29, 1998.

———. "Birthday Bashes and a Getty Blast." *San Francisco Chronicle,* October 14, 1996.

———. "Block Party by the Bay." *WWD,* March 12, 1990.

———. "Dinner Music." *WWD,* July 26, 1990.

———. "Don and Kelly Get Married at the Gettys'." *San Francisco Chronicle,* April 30, 1999.

———. "An Engaging Party Purely for Love. Vanessa and Billy Celebrate at Mom's." *San Francisco Chronicle,* February 17, 1999.

———. "Fairy-Tale Wedding for Getty-Jarman in Napa Valley." *San Francisco Chronicle,* June 21, 1999.

———. "Gavin Bids Bye-Bye to His Roaring 20s: Getty Boys Toss Him a Super Bash for His 30th." *San Francisco Chronicle,* October 13, 1997.

———. "Gettys' Party a Blockbuster." *San Francisco Chronicle,* March 12, 1990.

———. "High-Flying Getty Joins Used-Jet Set." *San Francisco Chronicle,* May 2, 1986.

———. "A Literati Soiree/Dominick Dunne Dines and Signs." *San Francisco Chronicle,* October 1999.

———. "A New Face in Cosmetics Shopping/Sephora Opens with Glitz and a Getty." *San Francisco Chronicle,* December 2, 1998.

———. "PlumpJack's Delicious Anniversary Dinner Was Fine, So Were the Cats." *San Francisco Chronicle,* April 14, 1999.

———. "Uganda and East Bay Highland Flings/It's a Real Social Jungle Out There." *San Francisco Chronicle,* September 9, 1996.

———. "Wedding of Year Is Perfect Match of Oil and Ink." *Palm Beach Daily News,* April 17, 1986.

University of California, Berkeley. "Project History." Middle Awash Project Ethiopia (website), undated. https://middleawash.berkeley.edu.

Varney, Carleton. "Donna Long." *International Opulence,* undated.

Weaver, William. "Flying First Class." *Architectural Digest,* March 1995.

Weidenfeld, George. *Remembering My Good Friends.* New York: HarperCollins, 1994.

Whiting, Sam. "Money Talks." *San Francisco Chronicle,* January 8, 1995.

WWD. "Gettys Are Redecorating 'The Jetty.'" March 2, 1993.

———. "The New Getty." June 24, 1999.

Chapter Thirteen: New Vintages

American Luxury. "Marlon Brando's Home in Hollywood Hills West Purchased by John Gilbert Getty, for $3.9M." November 29, 2018.

Beale, Lauren. "John Gilbert Getty Sells Los Feliz Home for $8.3 Million." *Los Angeles Times*, October 3, 2014.

Bennett, Will. "A Return to True Victorian Values." *Telegraph* (UK), November 29, 2004.

Bernstein, Jacob. "Getty Divorce: Details on Hollywood's Billionaire Scandal." Daily Beast (website), May 25, 2010.

Bigelow, Catherine. "Celebration of Note for Composer Getty's 80th." SFGate (website), December 15, 2013. https://www.sfgate.com.

———. "Design by Getty: Arts Patron Ann Getty Spins Antique Collecting into a Full-Blown Business." *San Francisco Chronicle*, October 26, 2003.

———. "Getty-a-Go-Go." SFGate (website), December 18, 2005. https://www.sfgate.com.

———. "Getty's Intuitive Style." *San Francisco Chronicle*, October 7, 2012.

———. "Gordon Getty's 85th Birthday Soiree, Shared with Granddaughter, a Fairy Tale Come True." SFGate (website), December 22, 2018. https://www.sfgate.com.

———. "Guests of Gettys Aglow." *San Francisco Chronicle*, December 16, 2009.

———. "Peter Getty Seals the Deal on a Long-Ago First Date." SFGate (website), February 16, 2017. https://www.sfgate.com.

———. "S.F. Arts Medallion Awarded to Swig." SFGate (website), October 29, 2012. https://www.sfgate.com.

———. "S.F. Debs Step into a New Era." SFGate (website), July 5, 2013. https://www.sfgate.com.

———. "Swells." SFGate (website), April 18, 2004. https://www.sfgate.com.

———. "Swells." SFGate (website), August 8, 2004. https://www.sfgate.com.

Bing, Jonathan. "Showbiz Has a New Party Line." *Variety*, November 25, 2002.

Bramesco, Charles. "A Millionaire, His Meth Addiction and the Horror Movie 15 Years in the Making." *Guardian*, March 14, 2017.

Butter, Susannah. "His Life Was a Struggle. I Wish I Could Have Protected Him." *Evening Standard*, March 2, 2015.

Byrne, Peter. "How William Newsom's Pipeline into the Getty Fortune Has Put Money—Lots of It—in His Politically Ambitious Son's Pocket." *SF Weekly*, April 2, 2003.

Christiansen, Robert. "Gordon Getty: 'My Dad Thought Music Was Something I Could Do on the Side.'" *Telegraph* (UK), June 2014.

Clark, Andrew. "Yes, We're Doing the Getty Opera." *Financial Times*, October 12, 2012.

Coffey, Brendan. "Tips from Billionaire Gordon Getty." *Bloomberg Markets*, May 2015.

Comiskey, Patrick. "A Wine Guy at City Hall." *Los Angeles Times*, August 3, 2005.

Corkery, P. J. "At the Peak." *San Francisco Examiner*, December 10, 2001.

Feinblatt, Scott. "Gordon Getty's Scare Pair Delivers Shivers and Laughs at Broad Stage." *LA Weekly*, June 26, 2018.

Finnie, Chuck. "Newsom's Portfolio." *San Francisco Chronicle*, February 23, 2003.

Flemming, Jack. "John Gilbert Getty Picks Up a Dramatic Dwelling Designed by A. F. Leicht." *Los Angeles Times*, November 21, 2016.

Friedman, Emily. "Oil Heir Peter Getty Embroiled in Nasty Divorce." ABC News, May 28, 2010. https://abcnews.go.com.

Friend, Tad. "Going Places." *New Yorker*, October 4, 2004.

Getty, Peter, and Billy Getty. *What the Butler Didn't See*, blog on SFGate, June 15, 2009. https://www.sfgate.com.

Ginell, Richard S. "L.A. Opera's 'Scare Pair' at the Broad Stage." *Los Angeles Times*, June 25, 2018.

Gonzales, Sandra. "Former *Mercury News* Reporter Dan Reed Dead at 50." *San Jose Mercury News*, January 8, 2009.

Graff, Amy. "San Francisco's Getty Preschool under Scrutiny." SFGate (website), March 14, 2011. https://www.sfgate.com.

Guthrie, Julian. "Belinda Barbara Newsom Dies at 73." SFGate (website), November 24, 2008. https://www.sfgate.com.

Hamilton, Matt. "Coroner: Getty Heir Had Ulcers, Methamphetamine, Heart Disease." *Los Angeles Times*, June 16, 2015.

Isle, Ray. "California's Governor Blends Politics and Napa." *Food & Wine*, October 2015.

Johnson, Betty. "Niche Fruit Grower Is Also Marketing Director." *San Diego Union-Tribune*, July 20, 2005.

Keeling, Brock. "Reading This Post Will Make You Want to Kill a Getty (Except Vanessa, That Is)." SFist (website), June 16, 2009. https://sfist.com.

Kruse, Michael. "How San Francisco's Wealthiest Families Launched Kamala Harris." Politico (website), August 9, 2019.

Lawrence, Ann. "See and Be Scene." *San Francisco Examiner*, December 11, 2001.

Leitereg, Neal. "John Gilbert Getty of the J. Paul Getty Oil Family Has Sold His Home in Hollywood Hills West for $1.575 Million." *Los Angeles Times*, April 15, 2016.

Macon, Alexandra. "Shannon Bavaro and Peter Getty's Wedding Celebration at the Getty Mansion—the Groom's Parents' Home." *Vogue*, January 30, 2017.

Martin, J. J. "A Fashionable Life: Jacqui Getty." *Harper's Bazaar*, May 1, 2007.

Mather, Kate. "Getty Oil Heir Had Serious Medical Condition, Court Documents Say." *Los Angeles Times*, March 31, 2015.

Matier, Phillip. "Society Pals' Falling Out Affects Newsom, Getty Families." *San Francisco Chronicle*, August 11, 2000.

McNeil, Liz. "How Music Helped Gordon Getty Escape His Family's Famous Curse." *People*, February 9, 2016.

Moffat, Frances. "The Gold Coasters." *Nob Hill Gazette*, September 2010.

Moyer, Justin Wm. "Andrew Getty, 47, Dead in Latest Getty Family Tragedy." *Washington Post*, April 1, 2015.

Naff, Lycia. "Hard-Partying Getty Scion Was on Meth When He Died in His Bathroom of Massive Gastrointestinal Hemorrhage." *Daily Mail,* June 16, 2015.

Nolan, Hamilton. "Rich Getty Heir Wants Blog Fight!" *Gawker* (blog), June 19, 2009. https://www.gawker.com.

———. "Rich Guys Blog, to Make You Mad." *Gawker* (blog), June 16, 2009. https://www.gawker.com.

NRM Streamcast (online network). "*The Evil Within*—Andrew Getty's Original Nightmare." Undated. https://www.nrmstreamcast.com.

Nugget. "Peter Getty's War." *The Daily Nugget* (blog), June 19, 2009.

Reginato, James. "Ann Getty's Exotic Interiors." *Sotheby's,* 2012.

———. "Getty Fabulous." *W,* October 2003.

Reuters. "Andrew Getty Died of Haemorrhage, Ulcer, Bad Heart and Meth—Coroner." *Guardian,* June 17, 2015.

Rich, Nathaniel. "The Fashionable and Philanthropic Force That Is Vanessa Getty." *Vanity Fair,* August 23, 2018.

Ritman, Alex. "Late Getty Heir's Directorial Debut 'The Evil Within' Lands after 15 Years." *Hollywood Reporter,* March 6, 2017.

Rosenblum, Joshua. "Getty: *Plump Jack.*" *Opera News,* September 2013.

Saeks, Diane Dorrans. "Ann Getty Believes Rooms Should Be Witty, Not Fussy." 1stdibs (website), March 3, 2010.

———. *Ann Getty Interior Style.* New York: Rizzoli International, 2012.

———. "Getty Glamour." *Harper's Bazaar,* October 2012.

———. "Gordon Getty Celebrates His 85th Birthday with a Bash at Home." *WWD,* December 17, 2018.

Sernoffsky, Evan. "No Foul Play Suspected in Death of Getty Heir." *San Francisco Chronicle,* April 2, 2015.

7x7. "The Gettys' Blog: Burning Up the Internet." June 16, 2009.

Shadowproof (website). "Sex, Drugs and Violence: Getty Divorce Court Date Today." May 7, 2010. https://shadowproof.com.

Spotswood, Beth. "My Grandmother Would Be Appalled . . ." SFGate (website), June 17, 2009. https://www.sfgate.com.

Stevens, Elizabeth Lesly. "In Gettys' Exclusive Preschool, It's Tough to Fly from Gilded Cage." *New York Times,* March 12, 2011.

Tate, Ryan. "Getty Heir's Humiliating Battle with the Godfather Family." *Gawker* (blog), May 10, 2010.

———. "Nasty Divorce Splits the Coppolas and the Gettys." *Gawker* (blog), March 31, 2010.

———. "Peter Getty: Costumed Layabout Scion." *Gawker* (blog), June 19, 2009.

Thurman, Judith. "A Tale of Two Houses." *Architectural Digest,* March 2003.

Vanity Fair. "The 2014 International Best-Dressed List." September 2014.

Walters, Dan. "Gavin Newsom's Keeping It All in the Family." *Los Angeles Times,* January 6, 2019.

West, Kevin. "In Her Court." *W,* November 2004.

———. "Pacific Heights." *W,* January 2007.

Williams, Kate. "Son of Gordon, Ann Getty Found Dead in L.A. Home." *Los Angeles Times*, April 1, 2015.

WWD. "Freaky Chic," November 4, 2002.

———. "The Price Is Right: Jacqui Getty's Monthly Allowance Request." March 30, 2010.

Yeomans, Jeannine. "Coppolas, Gettys Toast Happy Union." *San Francisco Chronicle*, October 6, 2000.

Zinko, Carolyne. "A Wedding to Remember: Newsom-Guilfoyle Nuptials Talk of the Town." *San Francisco Chronicle*, December 16, 2001.

CHAPTER FOURTEEN: PASSING THE BATON

AnthroQuest. "In Memoriam: Robert M. Beck." Fall/Winter 2014.

Ardehali, Rod. "Man, 58, Who Was Arrested at Bel Air Mansion Where the Feds Found a Huge Cache of Guns Faces 64 Felony Counts and 48 Years in Prison if Found Guilty." *Daily Mail*, July 16, 2019.

Associated Press. "Suspect out of Jail after 1000 Guns Seized from an LA Mansion." May 10, 2019.

Barabak, Mark Z. "Are Newsom and Harris on Collision Course?" *Los Angeles Times*, September 21, 2021.

Beck, Helene. *Jewels from My Grove: Persimmons Kumquats & Blood Oranges—Reflections & Recipes*. San Diego: Chefs Press, 2015.

Beyer, Rebecca. "Judge and Getty Family Advisor." *Stanford*, July 2019.

Bigelow, Catherine. "Miss Bigelow's Babble On by the Bay." Nob Hill Gazette (website), February 18, 2021.

Bravo, Tony. "5 Standout Looks from the 2020 San Francisco Ballet Gala." *San Francisco Chronicle*, January 17, 2020.

———. "Jo Schuman Silver Wants 'Beach Blanket Babylon' Vision to Live On after Show Closes." *San Francisco Chronicle*, December 12, 2019.

Cadelago, Christopher. "This Millionaire Might Be California's Next Governor." *Sacramento Bee*, July 31, 2017.

Criscitiello, Alexa. "Opera by Gordon Getty Out Now from Pentatone." BroadwayWorld (website), September 9, 2020. https://www.broadwayworld.com.

Cristi, A. A. "Goodbye Mr. Chips By Gordon Getty: An Opera Reimagined For Film to Receive World Premiere." BroadwayWorld (website), October 1, 2021.

Diaz, Alexa. "Man Charged with 64 Felony Counts after 1,000 Guns Seized at Bel-Air Mansion." *Los Angeles Times*, July 16, 2019.

Elinson, Zusha. "Suspect Who Stockpiled More than 1,000 Firearms in Mansion May Face Federal Charges." *Wall Street Journal*, May 14, 2019.

Friend, Tad. "Gavin Newsom, the Next Head of the California Resistance." *New Yorker*, November 5, 2018.

Fry, Hannah. "A Run-Down Mansion, a Getty Connection: The Tale of the Weapons Cache at an L.A. Home." *Los Angeles Times*, May 10, 2019.

Grimes, Kamala. "'Kamala Harris for the People' Holds Fundraiser at Getty Home on 'Billionaires Row' in SF." *California Globe*, June 1, 2019.

Janiak, Lily. "'Beach Blanket Babylon' Says Goodbye with the Performance of a Lifetime." *San Francisco Chronicle,* January 1, 2020.

Justice William Newsom Fund. "Hon. William A. Newsom III Obituary." Undated. https://www.justicewilliamnewsomfund.org.

Kennedy, Dana. "Will Getty Family Curse Claim the Next Generation after the Latest Death?" *New York Post*, November 28, 2020.

Lawrence, Allie. "The Angry Feminist Pin-Up Calendar Is What We Need to Start 2019 Off Right." *Bust* online, December 18, 2018.

Lenthang, Marlene. "Revealed: John Gilbert Getty, 52, Died of a Fentanyl Overdose Coupled with Heart Complications." *Daily Mail,* January 27, 2021.

Levin, Sam. "A Thousand Guns Were Found in an LA Mansion. Then the Mystery Deepened." *Guardian*, May 11, 2019.

L. S. B. Leakey Foundation News. "Robert M. Beck: Rancher, Real Estate Investor, Philanthropist, Vice President, Board of Trustees." Spring/Summer 1977.

Mehta, Seema. "How Eight Elite San Francisco Families Funded Gavin Newsom's Political Ascent." *Los Angeles Times*, September 7, 2018.

Parry, Ryan. "Cops Found John Gilbert Getty Dead with His Eyes and Mouth Open in an 'Indian Style Sitting Pose' in His $500-a-Night San Antonio Hotel Suite." *Daily Mail*, November 30, 2020.

Patten, Dominic. "Kamala Harris' Big Hollywood Virtual Fundraiser Rakes in Big Big Bucks." Deadline (website), September 4, 2020. https://deadline.com.

Ramzi, Lilah. "How the Pandemic Changed Weddings." *Vogue* (website), May 24, 2021, https://www.vogue.com/article/how-the-pandemic-changed-weddings.

Roberts, Sam. "Ann Getty, 79, a Publisher and a Bicoastal Arts Patron." *New York Times*, September 19, 2020.

Ronayne, Kathleen. "William A. Newsom III, California Judge and Environmental Advocate, Dies at 84." *Washington Post*, December 18, 2018.

Ross, Martha. "From Gavin Newsom to Donald Trump Jr." *San Jose Mercury News*, July 16, 2018.

———. "Gavin Newsom Muses on Kimberly Guilfoyle Dating Donald Trump Jr." *San Jose Mercury News*, March 8, 2019.

SFGate (website). "John Gilbert Getty." November 30, 2020. https://www.sfgate.com.

TMZ. "John Gilbert Getty, Heir to Getty Fortune, Dead at 52." November 23, 2020.

Tweedie, James. "Multi-Million Dollar Bel Air Mansion Where the Feds Found Huge Cache of Guns Belongs to Billionaire Getty Scion's Former Mistress with Whom He Had a Secret Family." *Daily Mail*, May 9, 2019.

Wick, Julie. "Essential California: The Ballad of Gavin and Kimberly (and Kamala)." *Los Angeles Times*, August 26, 2020.

CONCLUSION

Bivens, Terry. "The Dorrance Dynasty Battles Itself." *Philadelphia Enquirer*, March 17, 1991.

Bibliography

Dolan, Kerry A., ed. "The Forbes 400." *Forbes*, October 2020.
Kovach, Gretel C. "Hunt vs. Hunt: The Fight Inside Dallas' Wealthiest Family." *D*, March 2008.
Lombardo, Cara. "A Family Feud Threatens Campbell's Dynasty." *Wall Street Journal*, November 23, 2018.

Index